CONDENSED BOOKS

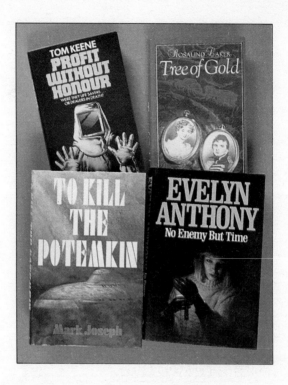

THE READER'S DIGEST ASSOCIATION LIMITED
25 Berkeley Square, London W1X 6AB

THE READER'S DIGEST ASSOCIATION
SOUTH AFRICA (PTY) LTD
Reader's Digest House, 130 Strand Street, Cape Town

Printed by Petty & Sons Ltd, Leeds
Bound by Hazell, Watson & Viney Ltd, Aylesbury

Original cover design by Jeffery Matthews FSIAD

For information as to ownership
of copyright in the material in this book see last page

CONDENSED BOOKS

PROFIT WITHOUT HONOUR

by Tom Keene

A research chemist disappears without trace; an elderly woman suffers a nearly fatal attack of high blood pressure; a fisherman collapses whilst at sea . . . When young Jenny Macrae, a speech therapist in the Scottish town of Gleninver, suspects there may be a link between these events, her inquiries lead her to Highland Pharmaceuticals Limited, a local firm about to launch a new wonder drug. Jenny finds that part of HPL's research is shrouded in secrecy. Risking all, she ventures into the very heart of the company's operations—where she makes a horrifying discovery . . .

A compelling thriller about a high-level cover-up of chilling proportions.

NO ENEMY BUT TIME

by Evelyn Anthony

Claire Fraser has come home to County Kildare because Frank, the half-brother whom she adores, is in desperate trouble. On the run. Kidnapped, possibly. Or maybe even murdered. By the very people whose cause he has embraced—the IRA. But whilst there is still a glimmer of hope for his survival, Claire is determined to find him. Alone and vulnerable, she heads for the one place she thinks he may have gone to: a special hiding place known only to the two of them, which they discovered years earlier . . .

With *No Enemy but Time*, Evelyn Anthony has created her most powerful and ambitious novel to date: a marvellously haunting story of loyalty, courage and betrayal.

TO KILL THE *POTEMKIN*
by Mark Joseph

Potemkin is the most dangerous submarine in the Soviet nuclear fleet: fast, deep-running, and so technologically advanced that her existence has been kept top secret. Until now. For while *Potemkin* has been quietly stalking American warships in the Mediterranean, a talented sonarman aboard a US sub has picked up her distinctive sound. And the Americans are not going to let *Potemkin* slip away before they have learned as much as possible about her. The chase is on—and the stage is set for a tense under-sea contest which could, at any moment, escalate into nuclear war.

This suspense-filled novel, inspired by actual events in recent submarine history, builds up to a shocking climax.

TREE OF GOLD
by Rosalind Laker

In the glittering world of the silk-makers of nineteenth-century France, the feud between Maison Roche and Maison Devaux is legendary. For generations the two families have fought bitterly for the best commissions. But in the hands of the beautiful, fiery Gabrielle Roche and the dashing Nicolas Devaux, the competition takes a new twist. Dedicated rivals in business, the two come to share a forbidden, secret love that threatens to destroy them both.

Set against the backdrop of Napoleon's turbulent reign, this rich historical drama is the latest triumph for the much-loved author of *This Shining Land*, a recent, very popular, Condensed Books selection.

PROFIT WITHOUT HONOUR

A CONDENSATION OF THE BOOK BY

TOM KEENE

ILLUSTRATED BY JOHN RAYNES

At Highland Pharmaceuticals, in the remote Scottish countryside, the launch of a miraculous new heart drug is only days away. Maurice Jackman, Project Development Manager for the firm, is determined that *nothing* shall interfere with the success of the publicity campaign.

But even as Jackman attends a PR reception in HPL's main building, disaster strikes. Nearby, in a laboratory area known only as RD7, a scientist lies dying in a pool of yellow liquid.

Jackman is informed, and immediately begins a swift and ruthless cover-up operation. For the research carried out in RD7 must be kept secret at any cost . . .

CHAPTER 1

Three men in a boat. Four if you counted the corpse.

"A bit further," Jackman ordered quietly from the stern, and the dark shadows that were Steevenson and Parsons hunched forward over their oars. There was no moon. Only the faint swirl of phosphorescence marked their passage as they slid silently out over the deep waters of Loch Linnhe.

They had taken the rowing boat from the old wooden jetty near the laboratories of Highland Pharmaceuticals Limited, where Professor Highcroft had died. The shrouded body of the professor lay wedged across the thwarts, a dark mound sensed rather than seen as the men pulled on their oars to the accompaniment of just three sounds: the faint murmur of water beneath their bows, the dry squeal of the oars in their rowlocks, and the harsh, steady exhalation of the men's breath through the filters of their respirators.

Yet the evening had begun innocently enough . . .

THE PRESENTATION CEREMONY at Highland Pharmaceuticals had been well into its stride as Bob Harris, the overweight editor of the weekly *Gleninver Times*, helped himself to another free Scotch and slipped a creased notebook out of his pocket.

Harris was one of sixty visitors enjoying the company's hospitality in the staff canteen. Jostling at his shoulder were a number of local councillors and their wives, with perhaps twenty business colleagues from smaller concerns elsewhere in the valley. Among them all circulated HPL executives, and the focus of all this hospitable attention stood beside the dais at the far end of the canteen, looking ill at ease. Sandy Tulloch was more at home running marathons than collecting pledges from his sponsors in best suit and tie. He had come a creditable sixty-third in the recent London Marathon—but he had first run the four hundred and eighty-five miles south from Gleninver to the capital. That, together with the fact that he was fifty-five years old, made him news. Highland Pharmaceuticals had offered to sponsor him at two pounds a mile, every step of the way. Which made them news too.

The motive for such open-handed generosity was both complex and covert. Complex because, although HPL was held in high regard by the local community, no pharmaceutical company seriously engaged in the manufacture of more than four and a half million pills, tablets and preparations a year could afford to ignore the smallest opportunity to enhance its reputation with a notoriously fickle public. Covert because, in the calculating opinion of a small inner coterie of HPL directors, such *bonhomie* provided the best possible camouflage.

Beside Bob Harris stood Hamish Owen. Tall and thin and just twenty-one years old, Hamish Owen had been in the job of junior reporter for eleven weeks. Before that he had been at university. Now, he fumbled for his notebook and pencil as the chatter of voices and the chink of glasses fell away and a spare-framed man in his late fifties strode briskly to the centre of the dais. "Ladies and gentlemen, good evening. I don't intend to hold up the celebrations for more than a moment, I assure you. I just want to thank you all for coming here tonight to join us in paying tribute to a gallant gentleman who's done so much over the last few weeks to raise money for local charities . . ."

The relaxed voice ran on, and Hamish Owen's pencil kept pace. He wrote in shorthand, a skill that endeared him little to an editor who disapproved of trainee reporters in general, and smart-aleck, graduate shorthand writers in particular. As the man on the dais paused, Hamish glanced up. "Who's the speaker?" he whispered.

Harris shot Hamish a withering glance. "Have you learned nothing in the weeks you've been here? The man's name, laddie, is Harold Engel."

"What's his position?"

"Chairman, Chief Executive, Lord God Almighty. You can take your pick," Harris muttered. "It's his company, laddie." Wrong, of course, but Harris wasn't to know that. Not then.

"Ah, Mr. Harris—everything all right?" asked a voice.

Harris swung round. "Oh, aye, Mr. Jackman, thank you very much. We'll get this one on the front page for you, no worry."

"Excellent. What I believe you people call a good human-interest story, is that not so?" A flicker of a smile touched Jackman's lips. He was in his early forties, with pale, straight hair receding from a high, domed

10

forehead and he wore light-reactive spectacles that added to an air of clinical detachment.

"Right enough, Mr. Jackman, right enough. Oh, by the way"—Harris waved his notebook towards Hamish Owen—"this is the new junior I was telling you about. What head office calls a trainee." Harris laid disparaging emphasis on the last two syllables. He turned to Hamish. "Mr. Jackman here is HPL's Project Development Manager."

Jackman gave a formal little nod. "Welcome to Highland Pharmaceuticals, Mr. Owen. I hope you'll visit us for a look round one of these days. We have a number of exciting new projects coming up soon that should provide good copy."

ONE OF THOSE PROJECTS was housed on the second and third floors of the three-storey Research and Development block, three quarters of a mile from the canteen and the administrative buildings where Jackman, Harris and Hamish Owen stood talking. The OMAHA project, however, would never be included in any report on commercial activities. Nor would its laboratories be part of any guided tour, although what was happening in them at that moment would undoubtedly have made extremely good copy. And very chilling, very frightening, reading.

Douglas Parsons was Duty Shift Manager in an area known simply as RD7. He sat alone now in front of the monitors, his eyes moving with mounting alarm across the display in front of him as orange CONTAM panels flashed into life. Parsons glanced up at the television monitor above his head. Whatever had gone wrong in section nine, two floors above, had done so with terrifying swiftness. And for one man at least, it was already too late. Professor Malcolm Highcroft lay on his back on the floor next to the laboratory workbench, his arms flung wide, his white coat torn askew as his body twitched spasmodically in a widening pool of yellow liquid on the tiles.

Parsons looked away hurriedly. Beyond the glass partition, on the far side of his control console, Steevenson was already struggling into protective clothing, with thick boots and rubber gloves, hood and full-face respirator. Then he moved to the lift that would take him up to the third floor and, through two airlocks, into section nine itself.

At the console, Parsons breathed a sigh of relief. Two of the orange CONTAM panels had flickered and turned green. That told him the air filtration plant was already extracting, purifying and recycling the contaminated air within. Parsons reached for the telephone.

"Page Mr. Jackman, please. Quick as you can."

"DO ALL YOUR PRODUCTS come in pill form, then?" asked Hamish Owen, the new reporter, notebook poised.

Jackman shook his head. "Oh no. I should estimate no more than sixty per cent leave our warehouse as tablets, Mr. Owen. The rest go out as capsules, drops, sachets, skin preparations. In all, we market seventy-nine different medical—" He broke off as a pocket pager began to bleep from his breast pocket. "You'll have to excuse me." He smiled briefly and turned on his heel to move smoothly through the press of guests. He plucked a telephone off the wall. "This is Jackman. You paged me."

"Oh, yes, Mr. Jackman. Would you please call extension 645 right away?"

Jackman replaced the receiver. 645. That placed the summons inside RD7. He moved quietly out of the canteen and down the corridor to a vacant office. He shut the door behind him and sat down in front of a bare desk. His call was answered immediately.

"We've gone to Condition Orange on the third floor, Mr. Jackman," stated Parsons.

"You've *what?*"

"Condition Orange, Mr. Jackman. Sections seven, eight and nine. There's at least one casualty."

"Right, I'm on my way over," snapped Jackman. "No one is to enter or leave the compound until I arrive, is that clearly understood?"

"What about an ambulance, Mr. Jackman? Shouldn't I—"

"No! No ambulance! Wait until I get there!" Jackman slammed down the receiver and sat back, breathing deeply. Call an ambulance? With half the council and all the local press knocking back free drinks as it went screaming past the window with its siren going? Good God.

Jackman went out into the corridor. Engel ought to be told, but the first priority was secrecy. The second, to assess and contain the damage. He hurried outside, slipped behind the wheel of his company Rover and drove out of the crowded car park.

HPL's Research and Development wing, three quarters of a mile from the company's main administrative buildings, was screened from sight by a thick plantation of fir, rowan and beech. The three-storey building where the accident had happened, standing out now like a lighthouse, with lights blazing from all three floors, was the heart of the company's endeavour, the key to its very existence here in western Scotland. Locked behind its own chain-link fence, access to it was by special pass through a gate guarded night and day by the company's own security specialists. In an industry where the theft of a single chemical formula could invalidate a decade of expensive research, such precautions against trespass, theft and the industrial curiosity of a rival company had long ceased to excite comment.

The guard opened the gate and Jackman brought the Rover to a smooth halt outside the building. He took a plastic card from his wallet and presented this, face downwards, across the scanner eye set into a metal plate beside the heavy doors. They opened. Seconds later the lift doors sighed back on the first floor. Parsons was standing there to meet him, looking pale and anxious in his white lab coat.

"He's . . . he's dead, Mr. Jackman. Professor Highcroft. Steevenson injected atropine into his thigh as soon as he reached him, but he'd . . . he'd already gone."

Professor Highcroft had been one of their senior microbiologists and would be hard to replace. He was also a married man with three children.

"All right—what else?"

"All three sections—that's seven, eight and nine, on the third floor— have downgraded to Condition Green."

"Good."

Both men turned and watched through a glass partition as the lift doors at the far end of the sterile area opened. Steevenson, still wearing protective clothing and respirator, emerged wheeling a stretcher. Professor Highcroft's body was enclosed in a grey plastic body-bag and strapped tightly onto the stretcher cradle.

Jackman moved swiftly to the control desk and pressed the microphone switch. "Hold it there. I'll come to you." He opened a cupboard, took down two vacuum-sealed packs of protective clothing and started dressing rapidly in loose-fitting smock and overtrousers. As he bent to tie the last of the tapes, the telephone rang on the control desk. Parsons, who was nearest, reached for the call.

"Research and Development." He listened. "Er . . . one moment, please." He covered the mouthpiece. "It's Mrs. Highcroft," he whispered, visibly shaken.

There was a moment of frozen silence. Then Jackman took the receiver. "Good evening, Mrs. Highcroft," he began easily. "It's Maurice Jackman. What can I do for you?"

"Oh. I . . . I was hoping to speak to Malcolm," began a woman's voice brightly.

"Your husband?" Jackman queried, with just the right amount of puzzled surprise in his voice. "I was under the impression he left some hours ago. One moment and I'll check." Jackman lowered the receiver slowly, gazed at Parsons with blank, cold eyes for several seconds and then raised the receiver once more. "No, I'm sorry, Mrs. Highcroft. Your husband left here at the usual time."

"Oh, that's strange." Mrs. Highcroft gave an apologetic little laugh. "He promised he'd be home by half past eight at the latest. Oh, well. Sorry I troubled you."

"Not at all, Mrs. Highcroft. Goodnight." Jackman replaced the receiver slowly.

Parsons gazed at him with a mixture of disbelief and horror. "That . . . that was his *wife*," he managed. Jackman nodded. "You gave her the impression everything was all right. That her husband was still alive . . .

You can't seriously expect to keep his death a secret, for God's sake! There'll have to be an inquest!"

"There will only be a Fatal Accident Inquiry, Mr. Parsons, if there is a body. And there will only be a body"—Jackman glanced through the partition at the shrouded corpse lying on the stretcher—"if Professor Highcroft is allowed to die."

THREE MILES AWAY, in a detached modern house on the outskirts of the town, Helen Highcroft closed the oven door and went through into the sitting room where Sarah, Mark and Simon were sprawled in front of the television. "Right, kids: who wants to eat?" she asked brightly, unease pushed to the back of her mind. He'd probably forgotten, that was all. In nineteen years of marriage she had become accustomed to the irregularities of her brilliant, absent-minded husband.

Sarah twisted round. "Aren't we going to wait for Dad?"

Her mother shook her head. "No, he'll be back later on. I've put his in the oven. Come on, it's on the table."

They went through to the kitchen, sat down and began to eat, an empty place at the head of the table.

IT WAS COLD ON THE LOCH. The nearest lights were more than a mile away. There was complete silence.

Jackman crouched down beside the corpse and dragged the body-bag open. He looked over his shoulder towards Parsons and Steevenson. "Come on—what are you waiting for?" he hissed, the words muffled by his respirator. Steevenson picked up the first of the heavy stones they had loaded into the boat and passed it across to him. Jackman stuffed it inside the body-bag and gestured impatiently for another. A dozen heavy stones were pressed down tight against the corpse. Finally, Jackman was satisfied. "That'll do," he said, and tugged the zipper closed. "Help me," he ordered, dragging the body sideways towards the gunwale.

They hauled the weighted body to the side, grunting with the effort, then, with a final heave, slid it over and watched it disappear into the dark loch with a silent ripple and a trail of tiny silver bubbles.

CHAPTER 2

Jenny Macrae came up the narrow lane above the town, swung her Citroën Dyane between imposing granite gateposts and braked to a halt beside the weathered granite mansion overlooking Loch Linnhe.

She sat for a moment behind the wheel, gathering strength from the silence after the telephones, tensions and unceasing demands of another long day at the clinic. Then she sighed and glanced briefly at her

14

reflection in the driving mirror, frowning in irritation as she raked slim fingers through thick, unruly brown hair. Jenny was twenty-four, with a natural, glowing complexion that testified to a childhood spent sailing, climbing and walking this same rugged, gale-swept coastline. The grey-green eyes that gazed back at her from the mirror held a directness that spoke of character and stubborn determination. In view of her errand, perhaps that was just as well. She scooped up her shoulder bag, walked briskly across the gravel to the front door, and rang the bell. A light snapped on above her head, and the door opened.

"I'm sorry to disturb you at this hour, Mrs. Ennis," Jenny apologized carefully. "But I've been working late at the clinic, and since I was passing I thought I'd just drop in to see if you'd changed your mind." She smiled with more confidence than she felt, a Scottish lilt softening her voice.

Although there was less than a decade between them, the two women were a study in contrasts. Mrs. Ennis, the company executive wife, with not a lacquered hair out of place, impeccably dressed; and Jenny, the working girl, standing in the porch in skirt and sweater, thick brown hair ruffled into disarray by the wind.

Mrs. Ennis glanced up at the first floor. "He's asleep. I don't want to wake him."

"It's you I want to see, Mrs. Ennis, not Jamie." Jenny paused. "Is your husband in just now?"

The older woman shook her head. "He's out on council business, I'm afraid. Some civic presentation up at Highland Pharmaceuticals."

Highland Pharmaceuticals: the biggest employer in Gleninver and the company whose sudden arrival in the valley four years ago had set the declining fishing town back on the long road from the brink of financial extinction. Jenny remembered now that, apart from his various business interests in the town, John Ennis was also a local councillor.

"May I step inside just one moment?" Jenny asked.

Mrs. Ennis sighed. "Yes—yes, of course. Do come in." She led the way into the hall and through to a spacious drawing room. She gestured Jenny to an armchair and sat down opposite her. "Before we go any further, Miss Macrae," she began, twisting her fingers together nervously, "I owe you an apology for ending our conversation so abruptly on the telephone this morning. I'm not usually so rude to people who, after all, are only trying to help."

Yes, you are, thought Jenny. You're also patronizing and over-protective. You're half Jamie's problem. But she said none of these things. Instead, she smiled. "There's no need to apologize, Mrs. Ennis, really." Jenny noticed the framed photograph of Jamie on the table at his mother's elbow. The boy was smiling into the camera, a shock of fair hair falling across his forehead. He looked almost normal. It was only when you studied the eyes that you noticed the vacant look that told of some deep, inner isolation.

"Nevertheless," persisted Mrs. Ennis, "the answer is still no."

Jenny leaned forward. "But why, for goodness' sake? It would only be for a few hours. I could pick him up midmorning and . . ."

"Because I do not consider it necessary," retorted Mrs. Ennis primly. "Jamie is not like other children, Miss Macrae. He needs special care, special attention. Left on his own . . ."

"But he *won't* be on his own, don't you see?" Jenny insisted with quiet intensity. "He'll be with me. Away from all this." She swept a hand round the immaculate drawing room.

Mrs. Ennis sat a little straighter in her chair. "The 'this' you refer to is Jamie's home, Miss Macrae. He is happy here. Secure. It's all he knows."

"That's exactly my point, Mrs. Ennis. It's *all* he knows. Tell me: when was the last time Jamie went out to play with other children? When did you last take him to a . . . to a fairground? When did he last play football with children his own age who—"

"He's not ready yet," Mrs. Ennis interrupted, with a note of protective desperation creeping into her voice. "I know you mean well, but I really must be permitted to know what is best for my child—"

"Your son is deaf, Mrs. Ennis," Jenny interrupted bluntly. "And because he is deaf he has no natural comprehension of speech, of words—*but that is all.* In every other respect, Jamie is perfectly normal." She paused. "Visual stimulation is everything to your son. Every single thing he understands, everything he learns, arrives at his brain by the same route: through his eyes. Yes, he is making progress; yes, his vocabulary is growing all the time. But it is growing much, much too slowly. Jamie is eight, Mrs. Ennis. He isn't a baby any more."

"What are you trying to tell me?" demanded Mrs. Ennis.

"I am trying to tell you that we are running out of time. Jamie isn't my only concern. The department has forty, fifty other children with speech delay and communication difficulties, between here and Fort William. Anywhere else in Britain you'd have an audiologist *and* a speech therapist. Here, I'm doing both jobs at the same time and, frankly, there isn't enough of me to go round. Another year, eighteen months at the outside, and Jamie will have to go away for special schooling—unless, between now and then, he shows signs of major improvement." She paused, watching the words sink in.

There was a silence that lasted several seconds. "You really believe that this . . . this outing you propose could stimulate a breakthrough?"

Jenny held up a hand. "It would be a start. Let go a little, that's all," she urged. "Let him spread his wings a bit."

Still Mrs. Ennis hesitated. "Tell me," she stalled, "what does Mrs. Ross think of this idea of yours?" Pamela Ross was Jenny's nominal superior at the health clinic.

"I don't know," Jenny replied simply. "I haven't told her. Officially, tomorrow is my half day."

Mrs. Ennis looked embarrassed. "You mean you're giving up your afternoon off? To take my son to the seaside?"

"It's no trouble. I'd probably have gone to the beach anyway . . ."

There was silence. Then Mrs. Ennis sighed. "All right. What do you want me to do?" she asked in a subdued voice.

Jenny rose to her feet. "I'll be round for Jamie at about eleven fifteen. I've got one or two appointments first, but that should leave us plenty of time to catch the bus from the square at half past."

"A *bus?*" Mrs. Ennis echoed, faintly alarmed. "Jamie's never been on a bus before. I'm not sure that—" Then she caught the look in Jenny's eye and laughed at last at the irrationality of her fears. "I can't help it. If anything ever happened to him . . ." Mrs. Ennis couldn't finish, the prospect too awful to contemplate. "You will look after him tomorrow, won't you, Miss Macrae? See that he doesn't come to any harm?"

Jenny patted her hand soothingly. "I'll take care of him, Mrs. Ennis, I promise you."

IT WAS AFTER ELEVEN that same evening when Jackman emerged alone from the Research and Development block where Professor Highcroft had died. By then his plans were as foolproof as cold premeditation could make them.

He had found the keys to Professor Highcroft's car in the pocket of a jacket hanging behind the door in his office in section nine—an office that, like its late occupant, had suddenly ceased to exist. Jackman now carried a large cardboard box to the professor's estate car, parked at the rear of the building, and placed it in the boot. Then he slid behind the wheel and drove round the perimeter road, back towards the administrative centre of Highland Pharmaceuticals.

The public reception for the local marathon runner had ended more than an hour earlier, and the building was deserted. Clutching the cardboard box, Jackman let himself in through a side door and walked down the corridor to the empty office he had used earlier that evening. He closed the door, drew the curtains, turned on the desk lamp and began arranging the items of personal and professional identification he had taken from Professor Highcroft's office. On top of the desk he left Highcroft's leather-bound engagement diary, a random batch of innocent lab reports and a framed photograph of three smiling children playing together on a climbing frame. Everything else he had collected went into the drawers of the desk.

If Jackman felt any emotion, any pricking of conscience, as he sat there confronted by the photograph of Highcroft's three children, he did not show it. He linked his hands behind his head and began rocking backwards and forwards in his chair as he studied the effect he had created with slow, critical eyes that missed nothing.

Then he turned off the light and, using the fire-escape stairs at the far end of the building, made his way to the personnel department on the second floor. It took him two minutes to find the particular file he wanted. As he had assumed, there were dozens of applications for work at Highland Pharmaceuticals, many of which enclosed a photograph of the applicant. He soon found exactly what he was looking for.

Back downstairs, in Professor Highcroft's new office once more, Jackman laid the postcard-sized photograph on the desk and studied it. It showed a girl of twenty-three or twenty-four smiling up into the camera, her hair blown back from her face by the wind. She looked vivacious and attractive. According to the file her name was Susan Sanders. Five months ago she had been short-listed for a job as secretary to one of the directors, but then discarded in the final selection process.

Jackman took out his fountain pen and wrote across the back of the picture, "To my darling Malcolm—with all my love, until we can be together. Your adoring Monica." Then he slipped the photograph inside Professor Highcroft's diary and reached for the telephone. He would make two calls, one local and one to London.

AS JENNY MACRAE FINISHED cutting the sandwiches she and Jamie would take with them to Ardtornish the next afternoon, she was humming happily to herself. The weather man had forecast another beautiful day.

There was a sudden tapping on the ceiling. Jenny put down her kitchen knife and groaned. "Damn!" she muttered under her breath. "All right, Mrs. Proctor. All right, I'm coming!" she called.

Jenny rented a self-contained flat on the ground floor of what had once been a substantial detached family house on the eastern outskirts of the town. Her landlady, Mrs. Proctor, lived on the first floor. Widowed many years earlier, Mrs. Proctor had a heart condition and was a hypochondriac who saw herself as a bed-bound invalid, hovering for ever in Doctor Death's waiting room. She looked about ninety, but was nearer seventy. And, thought Jenny bleakly as she went up the stairs, chances are she'll outlive us all. She knocked on the door. "Hello? Mrs. Proctor? It's Jenny—Jenny Macrae." She tried the handle. The door was locked. Pushing back the flap of the letterbox, she reached inside for the key dangling on a length of ribbon. She let herself in. The hall was in darkness. "Hello? Mrs. Proctor?"

"Jen? Is that you, dearie?" wavered a thin, frail voice. Jenny hurried into the bedroom. Mrs. Proctor lay in her nightdress between the bed and the washbasin, a walking stick clenched in one thin hand. Somehow in falling she had managed to drag the lamp off the bedside table, scattering pills, bottles and tablets in all directions.

"Whatever happened?" Jenny demanded anxiously, dropping to one knee beside the old woman. Mrs. Proctor coughed a dry, tight little cough.

"I . . . I don't remember . . . I must have passed out. I . . . I remember getting up to get a drink of water and . . . that's all."

"Can you move your arms? Your legs?" There was a cautious moment of experimentation. "Good . . . good. Now—d'you want me to call Dr. Erskine?"

Mrs. Proctor shook her head. "If you could just help me back to my bed . . ."

They managed it between them, eventually. Jenny replaced the lamp and began picking up the pills and tablets scattered on the carpet.

Some of the pills came in a little, green tinfoil strip.

"YOU CAN'T BE SERIOUS," muttered Harold Engel, ashen with shock, as he listened to Jackman's remorseless disclosures. "You mean to tell me the three of you dumped his body in the loch?"

Jackman sipped his Scotch and nodded. "There wasn't any choice."

"Choice?" Engel whirled round angrily from the drinks cabinet in one corner of his study, and set his glass down with a crack. "Choice? Of course you had a choice! You could have moved him out of section nine at the same time as you called the ambulance! OMAHA would never have been compromised, and the professor might still be alive!"

"It would not have made the slightest difference," corrected Jackman quietly. "Professor Highcroft was a doomed man the moment he placed his hands inside the glove box and saw that the rubber seal had perished. Better than anyone else, he knew what that meant. Calling an ambulance would have ensured only one thing, Mr. Engel: a public inquest. By the time section nine went to Condition Orange, Professor Highcroft was already dead. Faced with that fact . . ." Jackman shrugged. "I did what had to be done, that's all."

"But to throw his body in the loch like that . . . it's, well, it's . . . inhuman," Engel protested. A new thought struck him. "And his wife, Helen? What will you tell her?"

"Yes, I have thought about that," Jackman admitted. He told Engel about the photograph he had taken from the personnel department and what he expected Engel to do in support of his actions. When he had finished, Engel stared at him. "You'd do that?" he whispered. "You'd put the man's family through that sort of hell?"

Jackman shrugged. "They will be shocked at first, naturally. But they will adjust. Come to terms with the new reality."

"*Come to terms with the new reality?*" echoed Harold Engel, aghast. "This may come as a surprise to you, Mr. Jackman, but the man you and your cronies disposed of so efficiently out there was a friend of mine. Someone I liked, trusted! And you . . . you have the nerve, the sheer cold-blooded effrontery to sit here . . ." Shaking his head as though unable to believe the evidence of his own ears, he crossed to his desk and picked up the telephone. "This madness has gone far enough." He began tapping out a number.

Jackman rose and placed his forefinger across the arm of the receiver. "Tell me something," he invited quietly, his eyes hard and cold as round black pebbles. "You really believe in this company of yours, don't you? In your handpicked bunch of scientists? In that pretty little helicopter of yours?" Engel piloted the company's executive four-seater helicopter. It was one of the few perks he permitted himself.

"It's my life, you know that," Engel replied shortly.

"And this new drug of yours?" persisted Jackman. "You believe in that too, don't you?"

"Cardocol? Of course!"

The launch date for Cardocol, HPL's new heart drug, was now less than one week away. "Indeed, Mr. Engel! It's your chance of vindication, isn't it? A second chance. Remember that, Mr. Engel. All right—so, very properly, you alert the authorities to the fate of the unfortunate professor. Excellent. Duty done." He paused. "What happens? I shall tell you exactly what happens. This dream of yours, this second chance— all over. No Cardocol. No life-giving new heart drug for the needy thousands whose lives you are about to transform. And why? Because your company, HPL, will cease to exist. You'll be finished, along with that breakthrough drug of yours. Or do you seriously imagine you could build up again from scratch, for the *third* time? Forget it. Without government support, government backing, government *permission?* And all those people, all those thousands of people you so desperately want to help, will just have to go on suffering—all because you put the death of one man before them. One man!" Jackman gestured at the telephone. "However, if you want to make that call, go right ahead." He waited a moment, then he took his glass over to Harold Engel's drinks cabinet and poured himself another Scotch.

As a gesture of moral domination, its timing was perfect.

CHAPTER 3

Jenny rose to her feet, smoothed down her white coat and turned to the boy's mother. "That's fine, Mrs. Frazer. If you'd like to bring Angus back at the same time next week, we'll have another go. And Angus"—she waited for the ginger-haired little boy to join them by the door—"see if you can't bring me a few Ws, all right?" He nodded. "See you next week then." Mother and son left and the door closed quietly behind them.

Alone in her office, Jenny sighed and walked slowly back to her desk. She sat down, her shoulders slumped, and stared vacantly for a moment at the far wall. Then she reached into her coat pocket and took out Danny's letter. It had arrived that morning.

> . . . I've given it a great deal of thought, Jen, believe me. I know in my heart it could never really have worked. The easy thing would be just to go on pretending that one day you'll come down to work in Newcastle or I'll come back up to Gleninver, but that kind of compromise wouldn't be fair to either of us.
>
> I haven't met anyone else, Jen, and I'll never forget the last five months, not as long as I live, but I just don't see how we can go on, not at this distance, seeing each other for perhaps one weekend in eight . . . I know it's corny to say I hope we can remain friends, Jen, but I really do. You're a wonderful girl and, from the bottom of my heart, I wish you every happiness in the world.
>
> With my love, always,
> Danny

Jenny folded the letter slowly. Bastard, she thought. Oh, you bastard, Danny. But the words lacked conviction and she sat back numbly, remembering the laughter and the meals together and the long walks over the hills that had started earlier in the year, when Danny had begun his mandatory six months as junior houseman at County Royal Hospital. Now it was over, finished.

There was a tap on the door. Jenny thrust Danny's letter into her coat pocket, wiped her eyes and pretended to be looking for something in her desk as Pam Ross bustled in. Short, grey-haired, married with three teenage children, Pam was more than just Jenny's superior at the clinic. She was also both a friend and a confidante. "Sorry to trouble you, love," she said, "but I wonder if you'd mind—what's the matter?" Jenny had glanced round with a sudden, forced smile.

"Nothing. Why?"

Pam studied her for a moment. "Have you heard from him?"

Jenny started to shake her head, then found herself nodding. "He thinks it's best if we just . . . call it a day." Her eyes were brimming with tears as she opened out the letter and let Pam read it.

Pam folded the letter and handed it back. "D'you want to go down there?" she asked. "Take a few days off and go and sort things out?"

"I can't just go running after him."

"Why ever not?" challenged Pam. "'Course you can—if you feel enough for the man. Do you?"

Jenny sighed. "God knows. I used to think I did. Now . . ." She shook her head. "No, I'm not going down there after him, there's no point. Besides, I'm supposed to be taking Jamie Ennis to the beach."

"That's just an excuse," Pam interrupted firmly. "I can look after him, if that's all that's stopping you."

"After the trouble I had persuading his mother to let him out of her sight in the first place? Not on your life!" retorted Jenny with a flash of her former self, as she glanced at her watch and rose to her feet. "I'd better go, Pam. I promised I'd pick him up at eleven fifteen." She made for the door and then paused. "You're right," she admitted. "It *is* just an excuse. Danny doesn't want to put down roots in a little picture-postcard town like this, and I don't want to dig up my roots for precisely the opposite reasons. This is my home, Pam—I've known Gleninver all my life! I couldn't give it all up for somewhere like Newcastle." She sighed. "Men, Pam—bloody men: who needs them?"

"AND WHEN DID YOU LAST SEE your husband, Mrs. Highcroft?" asked the police sergeant, as he leaned across the station counter.

Helen Highcroft looked pale and dishevelled. She had spent half the night on the telephone and the rest of the time dozing fitfully in an armchair. She had telephoned the hospital three times, the police station twice. Now she was here to make the report official. She sighed heavily. "Breakfast. Breakfast time yesterday." It seemed much longer.

Sergeant McInnes made a careful note in his ledger. "Tell me, Mrs. Highcroft—your husband works as a scientist up at Highland Pharmaceuticals, is that right?"

"That's right, yes."

"What sort of work would that be?"

She looked blank. "I've really no idea. I mean, I know he's engaged in pharmaceutical research, of course. I just don't happen to know what he's working on specifically."

"Would you say your husband was under particular stress just now, Mrs. Highcroft? There's been a lot of talk about this new wonder drug that's on its way. I'd have thought that if perhaps your husband—"

"No, not particularly. He's always busy, of course, but then that's only natural. They all are."

Sergeant McInnes made another careful entry in the incident book and looked up. "Tell me, Mrs. Highcroft . . ." He cleared his throat. "Everything was quite all right when he left yesterday morning? Between the two of you, I mean?" Mrs. Highcroft frowned.

"I mean, you hadn't had a row with your husband? An argument, say, just before he left?"

She shook her head emphatically. "No, nothing like that."

"Would you say that the pair of you were happily married?"

Helen Highcroft found the spirit to bridle at that. "Yes, if you must know, Sergeant. Yes, I would say we are very happily married, strange as that may seem." She was irritated that he should force her to scrutinize a relationship that had been the unquestioned touchstone of her happiness, of her life, for the last nineteen years. That, she was discovering, was the most unsettling thing of all.

"THERE NOW, MRS. HAMILTON. If you'd just like to take this along to the chemist, he'll be able to fix you up in no time at all." In his cluttered little surgery behind Gleninver's Market Hall Square, Stanley Erskine blotted the prescription carefully and handed it across his rolltop desk with the same reassuring smile that had been comforting patients for years. Dr. Erskine was a craggy, fifty-nine-year-old Scot with salt-and-pepper hair, who had worked in Gleninver all his life.

Mrs. Hamilton took the proffered slip of paper, folded it carefully into her purse and rose to her feet. "Thank you, Doctor."

The door closed behind her and the doctor made a routine entry in her case notes before he pressed the buzzer on his desk. "Send in the next patient, please."

"That's the last just now, Doctor. But there's a Mr. Ransome waiting outside to see you." Roger Ransome, one of the clinical trials' team from Highland Pharmaceuticals. Dr. Erskine brightened.

"Send him in, lassie, send him in." Presently there was a knock on the door. "Come along in," Erskine called. The door, surprisingly, did not open. Frowning, he rose and opened it himself.

Roger Ransome was standing outside smiling and gripping the handles of a metal trolley on which there was a large parcel. The doctor looked from Ransome to the parcel. "They've arrived?"

Ransome nodded. "Came up from London this morning. Thought I'd better bring them over right away."

Dr. Erskine rubbed his hands together. "Come along in, come along in. I feel just like a child at Christmastime, Mr. Ransome. Oh, but it's very generous, you know—very generous indeed. All I did—"

Ransome held up a hand good-naturedly. "Now, don't start that again, please. Go on, Doctor—they're your books."

Two minutes later the carpet was strewn with brown paper, string and corrugated cardboard. On Erskine's desk, stacked almost two feet high, stood all nine volumes of Albert Groesner's medical classic, *The Wisdom of Healing*. Individually, each leather-bound and lavishly illustrated volume retailed at £49.50. Dr. Erskine picked up the top copy, his face that of a man who has seen his dreams come true. "I've been promising myself a set of Groesners for almost as long as I can remember."

Ransome smiled. "We're delighted to have been able to help."

That "we" brought the doctor back to earth with a bump. He replaced the book on the pile, opened one of the drawers and took out a pair of pale green cards.

"I almost forgot—here are a couple more stage threes for those analysts of yours. I'll be sending on the paperwork in a day or so." Ransome slipped the medical data cards into a pocket as Dr. Erskine turned back to his books, still stunned by the generosity of the gift.

"You've been very good to us over the last few months with this Cardocol business, Dr. Erskine," said the man from HPL. "It's just our way of showing our appreciation, that's all."

The doctor made a small gesture of self-depreciation. "One does what one can, you know." It never occurred to him that he was being bribed.

JENNY LEANED BACK against the breakwater, closed her eyes and tilted her face towards the sun. She felt drained by the emotional hammer-blow of Danny's letter but was pleased that the outing to Ardtornish was working, at least. She could sense it every time Jamie turned to point out something new, his eyes sparkling with an animation she had never seen in him before. Her hunch was paying off.

When Jenny called at the house at eleven fifteen, Jamie's mother had announced that she would accompany them as far as the bus stop. Through gritted teeth, Jenny had agreed: the bus stop, but no further.

There, eight-year-old Jamie had waited quietly at Jenny's side, and only the thin little fingers tightly clutching her hand had told of the excitement bubbling away beneath the surface, as his mother smoothed a hand over his shock of fair hair and fussed with the nylon straps of the phonic ear he always wore strapped across his chest. Jenny had almost to prise their beach bag away from Mrs. Ennis's grasp as the bus came to a halt. The bag was a vital part of her strategy for, apart from their sandwiches, it contained sketchbooks and crayons. Give Jamie a sheet of paper and a coloured crayon, Jenny had discovered, and you unlocked a small door to his silent world.

Now there came a sudden shout from below, and Jenny stirred and looked down.

"How am I looking, then?" asked an elderly, silver-haired fisherman in baggy grey sweater and old, paint-flecked trousers, tending his lobster pots in the stern of a twenty-five-foot fishing boat moored just inside Ardtornish harbour. Jenny crossed to Jamie's side. The boy was sitting with his back against a bollard, his bare toes dangling over the edge of the breakwater, his drawing book open on his knees and a box of coloured crayons at his side. Jenny glanced down at the picture and then back at the old man working in the stern of his boat.

"A vast improvement, Robbie," she called. "A vast improvement on the original!" Robbie gave a wave and bent to his lobster pots as Jenny crouched down beside Jamie and studied the picture in more detail. For a boy of eight, the drawing was remarkably adult. There was no mistaking which boat he was drawing, nor the figure standing in the stern, pipe clenched between his teeth.

"Good, Jamie—very good," she encouraged. Jamie looked up into her face and smiled. "Can you tell me what it is?" she asked.

He couldn't say, "It's a man in a fishing boat, stupid!" but he came close. Jenny pointed down at Robbie. "Go on—show him what you've done. Show Robbie the picture." The boy reversed the drawing and held it out. Robbie nodded approvingly.

"Aye, that's very good, laddie—very good indeed, although I didn't know I looked quite like that!" Jamie couldn't hear. He shook his head angrily, bending over the controls on his chest set and straining to break through, to understand. The old man saw him struggle. He hauled on a line and deftly drew the stern in towards an iron ladder running up the side of the breakwater. He pulled himself heavily up the rungs to the top, walked over and bent down to study the sketch.

"Aye, you've got something there, laddie—no doubt about it." Jamie looked up into the man's face and smiled happily. Then the fisherman turned to Jenny. "Another of your stray lambs, Jen?" They'd known one another for years. Some of Jenny's happiest memories had been built around this harbour, these boats, this old man who seemed as unchanging as the weathered granite of the breakwater.

"He needed a change—outside stimulation. A chance to get out from under his mum's feet."

Robbie nodded. "I was wondering, watching the lad just then . . ." He paused, puffing gently on his pipe. "I'm away out to check the lobster pots in a wee while. Just out round the island there." He pointed to a whalebacked hump of land sticking out of the sparkling sea a mile or so offshore. "I thought if the lad there had a mind to come along, I could maybe show him a lobster or two—what d'you say?"

Jenny hesitated, a natural professional reluctance to entrust her charge to the care of another vying with the knowledge that just such an experience—away from both mother *and* speech therapist—was exactly what the child needed to bolster up his self-confidence.

"We wouldn't be gone more than an hour."

Jenny shook her head. "It's very kind of you, Robbie, but I really think I'd better say no. Thanks all the same."

"Oh, well, it was only a suggestion." The hurt was plain to see in the old man's eyes as he turned and pointed out to sea. "If it's the weather you're worried about, there's no need." He began coughing—a dry, rasping cough that went on for several seconds.

"It isn't the weather, Robbie, it's—"

"You can trust me, you know, Jen. I'm not about to go running off with the lad. You're welcome to come too, if you like."

The suggestion that she didn't trust him, that after all the years of friendship between them she might harbour some private reservation, tipped the balance. Besides, hadn't she brought Jamie here for just such an experience, to soak up and enjoy whatever opportunity placed before him? She was getting as bad as his mother . . . "You'd best go and ask Jamie," she said.

The battered old face creased into a sudden smile. "Aye. Grand." Jenny watched him bend down as he laid a hand on Jamie's shoulder and began to talk, pointing first at the boat, then out into the bay. It was as though someone had touched a switch. Jamie scrambled to his feet, sketchbook and crayons forgotten as he rushed up to Jenny, eyes on fire, head bobbing as he wrestled to control his excitement and marshal his scattered, kaleidoscopic vocabulary, all at the same time. With a gigantic effort he said, "Jen, pl-pl-please can I g-g-go? In the . . . in the boat?"

After that there was, of course, only one possible answer.

Ten minutes later, Jenny stood on the breakwater as the little fishing boat headed bravely out between the steep harbour walls. Robbie waved, one hand on the tiller. In the bows, Jamie Ennis leaned forward into the breeze, Robbie's binoculars slung importantly round his neck.

The boat moved out into deep water.

"HERE HE COMES . . . here he comes. Ready, laddie?" Robbie Roberts hauled in wet line as Jamie Ennis stared over the side of the boat into the clear, cold depths. The lobster pot broke surface. Robbie reached over and swept pot, line and lobster into the bottom of the boat in a cascade of seawater that had Jamie laughing delightedly. There were already two lobsters in the crate beneath the for'ard bench, scratching at the walls of their prison as they blew out bubbles of salt water. "Now then, me beauty, let's have a look at you." Reaching inside the trap to pin the lobster deftly behind the creases of its thick carapace, Robbie lifted it, snapping and flapping, into the sunlight, its antennae waving indignantly.

He shook his head. It was too small, it would have to go back. "OK, then, Jamie—this one's got to go back—understand what I'm saying?" He pointed at the sea. "It's too small for the table. We'll come back for it next year maybe, eh?" He lowered the lobster gently over the side, and they both watched as it slid away into the depths.

Robbie straightened up. "Right then, Cap'n, find us the next one," he ordered. Jamie scrambled into the bows and began searching the sea for the next orange marker float. They were perhaps a mile and a half from the mainland, working their way round the western side of the island.

"There!" Jamie pointed excitedly. Robbie pressed the starter button and they began curving away over the sunlit sea towards the next lobster pot. Jamie picked up the boat hook and pointed it at their target as they swung in. Then he turned and grinned at the old fisherman, his teeth white in the sunlight. He'd never had so much fun, never in all his life. Pipe clenched contentedly between his teeth, Robbie nodded.

And then, suddenly, the engine spluttered and died, and they fell away off course, to wallow on the easy swell. Robbie stabbed impatiently at the starter button. Nothing happened. Crouching down, he unfastened the casing hatches at his feet, lifted back the engine cover and looked inside. Nothing was obviously wrong. He unscrewed the fuel tap and peered inside the tank. Plenty of juice, too. Perhaps it was a blocked fuel line. He took a torch from his toolbox and played its beam along the fuel feed to the carburettor. Ah! The thing was dry—blocked! Muttering, Robbie uncoupled the jubilee clip, tugged the plastic tubing free, and began sucking vigorously. The stoppage freed itself. Robbie jammed his thumb over the end, scrambled to his feet, spat hard over the side and raised a hand to Jamie in the bows. "It's all right now, laddie, I've—" He got no further. Dark clouds of pain and dizziness seemed to press down suddenly upon the centre of his skull—his vision blurred and the world was reduced to a narrow band of agony.

He sagged weakly against the tiller, the fuel pipe dropping from his fingers. Petrol pumped out across the floorboards. Robbie clawed at the side of the boat and then slumped sideways, cracking his head as he crumpled in the stern of the boat. His pipe fell from his mouth, and a plug of smouldering tobacco rolled across the floorboards towards that widening pool of petrol. Then the boat rolled to a gentle wave and petrol washed quietly across the decking.

With a sudden *whoomph!* of flame, Robbie's boat began to burn.

In the bows, Jamie cried out in fear as that first blast of fire blew gouts of blazing fuel half the length of the boat. He looked round wildly for help, but there was no boat in sight and the island was two hundred metres away. Robbie lay motionless amid the flames.

Jamie scrambled aft, coughing in the smoke. He grabbed one of Robbie's feet and began pulling, shouting, begging him in his strange, private language to get up, to make the flames, the smoke and the fear go away. Then the wind shifted suddenly, fanning the flames towards him. He backed off. His heel caught in the lobster crate and he fell against a thwart, the lobsters spilling out across the deck to slither towards him as the boat wallowed in the water. Jamie started to cry. Alone in a sea of roaring flames, he was very, very frightened.

CHAPTER 4

"Hey, Steve—what's that smoke, then?"
"Smoke? Where?"
"You blind or something? There, out by the island."

"Oh. Oh, yeah . . ."

The words drifted into Jenny's consciousness as she lay back against the warm stone of the breakwater, her eyes closed. For a moment they were without significance. Then they clicked together with terrible clarity and she was scrambling to her feet, heart pounding.

Smoke. As in fire.

There were two teenagers in jeans and T-shirts standing by a slot-machine telescope fixed onto the breakwater. One of the boys was peering out to sea through the eyepiece. The other glanced at Jenny speculatively as she hurried up. "Please—can I have a look? It's very urgent," asked Jenny. She could see the smoke herself now as it rose in a thin, oily cloud towards the rim of the island.

The boy grinned. "'Ere, Steve, bird 'ere wants to get 'er 'ands on your telescope."

Jenny groaned. "Look, please, I—"

The boy called Steve straightened up with a grin. Jenny brushed him impatiently aside. "All right, all right, take it easy," complained the boy. But Jenny wasn't listening. The smoke filled the telescope: a ragged banner of black that vanished behind a low hillock of island. Had to be a boat, thought Jenny with awful certainty: had to be. She panned the telescope quickly across the empty bay and prayed: please, God, let them be somewhere else—*please*. But the sea was deserted. When she picked up the smoke again it had drifted slightly and she saw something low in the water at the base of the smoke column. Something that might once, at a pinch, have been a twenty-five-foot fishing boat . . .

"God, no!" Jenny turned towards the people on the breakwater. "*Fire!*" She pointed dramatically. "There's a boat on fire!" They stared at her stupidly. "She's on *fire,* don't you understand?"

People glanced at one another uneasily. She turned suddenly as she felt a tap on her shoulder. "You're sure?" It was Steve, the teenager. "You're not muckin' about?"

Jenny shook her head vehemently. "No. No, I'm not." She swallowed. "There's an old man and . . . and a boy. Only he's deaf and he can't—"

"I'll call the coastguard, right?" Steve broke into a run, and Jenny set off after him. They ran along the quay, dodged across the road and pulled up panting outside a call box. Steve didn't hesitate. He banged the receiver rest up and down and then dialled three nines. Jenny watched from the door in an agony of impatience.

"Emergency. Which service do you require?"

"Coastguard. And get your skates on. We've got a boat on fire."

EVEN AS JENNY LISTENED, the emergency operator was connecting the call to the Marine Rescue Sub-Centre at Oban, thirty miles down the coast. The MRSC controls the use and deployment of the four RNLI lifeboats stationed at Islay, Oban, Mallaig and Barra. They also have direct radio access to the RAF helicopter rescue flights at RAF Leuchars, RAF Lossiemouth and RAF Glenhaddon. Now, as the call was patched through to the main desk controller in Oban, and Steve began blurting out details of the emergency, the controller spun round in his chair and ran his eyes down the availability board. It would be fifty minutes, perhaps even longer, before the nearest RNLI lifeboat could hope to reach Ardtornish. But they didn't have an hour. What they did have, however, was a Royal Air Force Search and Rescue Wessex helicopter at fifteen minutes' readiness on the ground at RAF Glenhaddon. And Glenhaddon was eighteen minutes' flying time from Ardtornish.

The controller flipped a switch . . . "Glenhaddon Rescue, this is Oban. Immediate."

The crew of RESCUE 44 were lounging in the crewroom in their dark green flying overalls, drinking coffee. They were coming towards the end of their fourth consecutive twenty-four-hour duty shift and it had been quiet. Then they heard the message from Oban relayed over the tannoy. Before the corporal in Operations at the end of the corridor had even acknowledged Oban's preamble, the crew were on their feet.

They burst through into Operations with the pilot, Flight Lieutenant Dave Bourne, in the lead. Hard on his heels came navigator Pete Sleaman and Flight Sergeant Tony Lockhart, their winchman. The alarm bells rang out all over Search and Rescue Flight, bringing ground-crew mechanics sprinting towards the yellow Wessex helicopter in the centre of the landing circle. As the mechanics began dragging off the orange covers, wheeling up the fire cart and switching external power through to the aircraft for start-up, Dave Bourne glanced up at the control desk. "What have we got?" he demanded, fingers fastening the buttons of his Mae West lifevest. There was a squawk-box on the desk that relayed his question directly to the Oban controller.

"Glenhaddon, this is Oban. Fishing boat on fire approximately two nautical miles west of Ardtornish. Two on board. One's a child."

Bourne swept up helmet and gloves and made for the door. His priority was to get out to the aircraft and start pre-takeoff checks.

Behind him, navigator and winch operator Pete Sleaman paused at the door to study the 1:50,000 scale map of the Western Highlands, picked up his navbag containing charts, maps and aerial photographs of every town and hospital approach in a two-hundred-mile radius, and turned to see how Tony was doing. "Come on, Winchie—pull your finger out." He grinned.

As the winchman, Tony Lockhart was the one member of the crew required to leave the aircraft, to go down on the wire if necessary to rescue survivors. Because of this, he was struggling into a one-piece total-immersion suit of bright orange with integral boots and rubber seals at wrists and neck and a single diagonal zip that slashed from right shoulder to left buttock. It was this heavy-duty zip Tony was struggling with now. Then he too grabbed a yellow helmet and dirty, chamois-leather gloves, and followed Pete out to the aircraft.

They ran forward, Pete to climb into the left-hand seat beside the pilot, Tony to scramble into the open cabin and plug himself in to the aircraft's internal communications system.

Instantly, his ears filled with the sudden hiss of static, overlaid with the murmur of the pilot's patter as he completed his list of cockpit checks: start starboard engine, start port engine, auto-stabilizer, rotor start . . . Within moments Dave was calling up Air Traffic Control, who confirmed that they were clear for takeoff.

"Roger." The brakes were released, the collective lever at Dave's left hand was raised to increase the thrust of the main rotor, and the ground began to drop away. They were airborne.

"Come left on two four zero degrees, Boss," said Pete, the navigator.

"Left on two four zero degrees," acknowledged Dave Bourne, as the aircraft banked sharply onto heading.

"Oban Coastguard, Oban Coastguard, this is RESCUE 44 airborne this time with three souls on board. ETA Ardtornish harbour eighteen repeat one eighter minutes. Listening out two five two eighter, over."

"RESCUE 44, this is Oban Coastguard. All copied. Listening out."

Tony hauled the door closed against the blasting wind and moved to the rear of the aircraft. On a canvas bench seat was stacked the winchman's emergency medical equipment. Tony pulled a canvas bag towards him and lifted out a heavy oxygen cylinder and face mask. Then he reached for the next medical satchel. He was preparing for the worst. Time and again, reality had justified such prudent planning.

THE WIND GUSTED SUDDENLY, and Jamie threw up a hand with a cry of pain as he tried to ward off the flames that licked towards him. He scrambled up onto the scrap of decking in the bows. Robbie had gone, lost somewhere behind the wall of fire as it ate its way forward. Already the boat was awash and sinking slowly beneath him. A few more seconds, and he would be forced into the sea.

Swimming was something else his mother had omitted to teach him.

"RESCUE 44, THIS IS OBAN COASTGUARD. Advise ETA Ardtornish harbour, over."

Pete Sleaman made a rapid calculation. "Six minutes, Boss."

Dave Bourne nodded. "Oban Coastguard, Oban Coastguard—this is RESCUE 44, ETA six minutes. Any update, over?"

There was a brief pause, then: "RESCUE 44, this is Oban Coastguard. Be advised the child is deaf, repeat deaf, over."

Pete and Dave exchanged glances. Behind, in the cabin, Tony muttered, "That's all we need: rescue by Braille." A deaf survivor wouldn't hear them coming, wouldn't hear vital, shouted instructions.

"Oban Coastguard, Oban Coastguard, this is RESCUE 44. All noted. ETA now five minutes, over."

Tony stood up, took a webbing harness and bosun's chair from a bag behind him and stepped into it. He moved to the door and pulled it back. Light flooded into the cabin. They were now at six hundred feet. Leaning out, he could see the flat gleam of the sea stretching ahead and the outskirts of a small town coming up directly on track: Ardtornish. The aircraft banked steeply and began to lose height.

Reaching up, Tony pressed the winch switch and the hook directly above the door began to unwind towards him.

They carried three hundred feet of cable on the winch and another one hundred and twenty feet of tape. Tony drew the cable into the cabin and stopped the winch. Then he snapped the hook through the eye of the strap attached to the bosun's harness and pushed home the pin.

"OK, Boss—I'm off downstairs," said Pete, who was about to change from navigator to winch operator, with Tony's life at the tip of his finger. He achieved this by folding back his seat and wriggling backwards and down through a space little bigger than the door of a washing machine. He slithered down beside Tony, plugged himself into the intercom, strapped himself into a monkey-harness and crouched beside the door.

"All set?"

Tony gave him a thumbs-up, unbuckled his safety belt and wriggled forward until he was sitting on the edge of the door, boots dangling into space. "All set downstairs, Boss."

"Roger, Pete."

"RESCUE 44, this is Coastguard Mobile at Ardtornish harbour. Casualty positioned two nautical miles due west this location and drifting north. Watch for my orange smoke, over."

"Wilco, out."

They banked sharply over the sea and turned back along a north-westerly bearing. Almost immediately, "Orange smoke, Boss. Your two o'clock," reported Tony. At the same moment Pete spotted a thin column of black smoke rising from the sea. Now Dave saw it too and spun the helicopter towards it. He put the burning hulk slightly ahead and to his right and the helicopter swooped down.

The boat was empty. It wallowed in the swell, almost awash, the flames confined now to a flickering glow at the bows.

RESCUE 44 came to the hover sixty feet overhead. Three pairs of eyes hunted for survivors. Nothing. No one clinging to the wreckage, no one floundering in the water nearby. One circuit, another, and then Dave began crabbing the aircraft gently sideways, following tidal drift. Perhaps thirty seconds passed in silence as they moved slowly out across open water, then—

"Something in the sea, Dave. One hundred metres at four o'clock."

"Roger." RESCUE 44 swung round. "Got him." Arms spread out in the position of crucifixion, a bubble of air trapped under his shirt high above his shoulders, Jamie Ennis floated face down in the gentle swell.

"Preparing to winch out," warned Pete over the intercom, as Tony clipped an orange lifting strap onto his harness, took off his helmet and signalled that he was ready. "Winching out." There was a sharp tug as Pete flicked up the switch and Tony was pulled off the sill and swung out of the door into space.

"Tony is clear of the door. Winching out . . . Ten feet of cable . . . twenty . . . thirty . . . Holding it there." Tony hung suspended below the aircraft, head buffeted by the down-draught as he swung in his harness, kicking his legs violently to swing himself round so that he faced the casualty. Pete leaned out of the door, one eye on the position of the casualty, the other on Tony, swinging below him. "Forward thirty." Obediently, the helicopter moved forward as Tony began walking his legs through the air to keep directional stability. He was six feet above the sea and thirty yards from the body floating in the water. A hand signal from Tony and Peter lowered him slowly until little feathers of spray told him that Tony's boots were just breaking through the crests of the swell and he had begun trawling towards the casualty. "Forward twenty . . . forward fifteen . . . ten . . . height is good . . . eight . . . six . . . five . . . four . . . three . . . two . . . one . . . and steady. Steady." Pete flicked out another three feet of cable and Tony sank down into the sea. "Tony is in the water. He's moving to the casualty."

Tony grasped the boy by the shoulder and hauled him over onto his back. His eyes were closed and a mop of fair hair fell forward across the pale forehead, above lips that were already tinged with blue. Lifting Jamie's chin clear of the sea, Tony forced the boy's jaws apart, pushed a gloved finger inside his mouth and swept it round to clear away any debris. Then, still treading water, and with the boy clutched to his chest, Tony blew several quick, short breaths into his lungs. There was no response. Nothing.

He looped the orange strap over Jamie's head and arms and waved urgently upwards. Instantly the cable started to winch in and they were hauled clear of the water, Tony's legs wrapped tightly round the boy's slim body. Even as they swung upwards, Tony was forcing air into those congested lungs, looking for signs of life.

"Winching in . . . Twenty feet of cable to come . . . ten feet of cable to come . . . They're by the sill." Tony drew his feet suddenly together and swung them both neatly inside the cabin. Pete moved back from the door. "They're inside. Inside and off the cable."

Dave acknowledged, as Pete helped Tony drag off the strap and haul Jamie to the rear of the cabin. Within seconds Pete had the sucker out and forced between Jamie's lips, running it quickly backwards and forwards as it cleared away the last of the detritus.

Unclipped from the winch cable, water streaming off his immersion suit, panting harshly from exertion, Tony pulled on his helmet and jammed his intercom lead into the jack-plug. Then he tore off his sodden gloves and pressed flat fingers against the boy's jugular. Pete glanced up, oxygen bottle ready to slide into place. "Pulse?"

Tony shook his head briefly. "Can't find it."

At that moment, Jamie Ennis was clinically dead.

Tony and Pete bent over him, trying desperately to revive him. Pete was at the head giving mouth-to-mouth resuscitation. Tony was working on the chest, giving cardiac compression: five compressions of the chest—one inflation; five—and then one; five—and then one. He pressed again, harder this time but with great care. Still nothing.

"He isn't—" began Pete, and then stopped. For, quite suddenly, he had seen the chest rise of its own accord. There it was again.

Pete thumped Tony on the shoulder. Beneath the visor of his helmet, Tony's face creased into a sudden smile. The sixty-four-thousand dollar moment. They were bringing him back.

With winchman and navigator both busy in the cabin, it was up to pilot Dave Bourne to quarter the sea ahead as they crabbed slowly northwest across the sky, searching for the second casualty. They had drifted perhaps five hundred metres when Dave spotted the body of a man, floating just below the surface.

"There's the other one," he reported tersely over the intercom. "Fifty metres at three o'clock."

Bending over the unconscious boy, Pete and Tony exchanged a look that spoke volumes. Experience told them it would take between three and five minutes to winch Tony down, pick up the second casualty and get back aboard. And in that time . . . the child would have to take his chances, that was all. They had wrapped him in a blanket, inserted a plastic airway into his mouth and settled the oxygen mask over mouth and nose. As long as he remained unconscious, the airway would prevent him suffocating; as long as his heart kept beating, oxygen should keep him breathing and his condition stable. That, at least, was the theory. But for five minutes, perhaps longer? If they were lucky.

Forty-five seconds later, Tony was splashing down into the water and grasping the shoulder of the second casualty. He hauled him over onto his back and saw with sudden revulsion that most of the right side of his face, head and neck had been burned away. His eyes were already glazed and cold. Tony made one or two quick checks to confirm the man was dead, and gave the signal to hoist.

Pete read all he needed to know in the way Tony swung his burden forward onto the cabin floor. "Wasting our time on this one, Pete," he said. "How's the boy?" They crouched their way aft as Dave banked RESCUE 44 steeply to starboard and sent them racing towards the shore at less than one hundred feet, the water flashing past the open door.

The boy was still alive—a pale shape lost in a swathe of thick white blanket, clinging to life on the floor of the noisy, vibrating helicopter.

"One bagged and ready to go, Dave," reported Tony with the affected cynicism they adopted to shield one another from involvement, from caring too much. "But the kid's still hanging on by his fingernails."

"Roger. Pete, you'd better get up here. Tony, better get on the blower to Coastguard Mobile. Get them to warn Casualty at County Royal."

"Roger." Tony could take over radio communications from a duplicated set of controls mounted on a panel to the left of the door. Switching to the coastguard frequency he said, "Coastguard Mobile, this is RESCUE 44. Mission completed with five passengers on board. One male adult, Code Purple. One male child, unconscious, hypothermic. Condition critical. Will fly direct County Royal. Alert Casualty. Our ETA that location . . . zero niner minutes, over."

RESCUE 44 raced towards the harbour wall, twisted away to starboard and began to climb as Pete took them on a course over the town and south towards Gleninver.

CHAPTER 5

On shore, Jenny glanced round with tears coursing down her cheeks, her eyes shining with excitement and relief. "Did you see?" She pointed, not caring if anyone saw her tears, her hair torn back from her face by the wind. "They've got them! Thank God . . . Jamie's going to be all right!"

But with the fire quenched, the boat sunk, the helicopter gone and the excitement over, the crowds had dispersed. Even the ambulance and the coastguard Land-Rover had melted back into the brickwork. The only sign of officialdom was an elderly traffic warden strolling along beside the parked cars on the quay. Jenny hurried up to him. "Excuse me," she began. "Where would they have taken them? The . . . the helicopter, I mean?"

He peered at her. "The helicopter?"

Jenny pointed impatiently out to sea. "The yellow helicopter. The one that was here just a few minutes ago. Where would they take the people they've rescued, d'you know?"

"Well now . . . I daresay you could try the County Royal, away down in Gleninver."

"The County Royal, of course. Thank you," interrupted Jenny hastily. She saw a rank of taxis waiting over by the bus station and hurried across the road. "County Royal Hospital in Gleninver, please. It's very urgent."

IN THE SHABBY OFFICES of the *Gleninver Times*, Hamish Owen pushed away the wedding report he had been typing and craned his head out of the window as the yellow helicopter flashed overhead. He thought for a moment, flicked open a contact book and dialled coastguard head-quarters at Oban. A minute later he was slamming down the telephone and scrabbling around for notebook and pencil.

The editor's door was closed. When Hamish entered he was confronted by Bob Harris in his shirtsleeves poring over a page layout. He frowned at the interruption. "*Now* what is it, laddie?"

"The helicopter that—"

"You finished that wedding I gave you?"

Hamish shook his head. "Almost. I—"

Harris stabbed a thick finger towards his junior. "Aye, I thought not. Get it finished, laddie—get it finished before you come blathering to me about any helicopter. You're holding up an early page."

"I called the coastguard. There's been a fire at sea off Ardtornish. They're taking two casualties to the County Royal. One of them's Code Purple, he said."

That stopped Harris. "Purple, did you say?"

"That's what the controller told me, yes."

Harris waved him away. "Well, what are you waiting for, laddie, a starter's gun up your backside? Get on up there, get on up there."

JENNY'S TAXI ENTERED the grounds of County Royal Hospital and followed the white and red arrows towards the Casualty Department. Upon a wide expanse of open grass stood the yellow rescue helicopter, its door open, its rotors silent.

Jenny felt suddenly afraid. Apprehensive for Jamie, desperately worried about his safety, certainly—but scared, too, for herself. For what these people might think of her. She was to blame for putting them at risk, to so much trouble. She pressed a fiver into the taxi driver's hand and hurried towards Casualty.

Beyond the receptionist, Jenny saw two of the crewmen from the rescue helicopter, sitting hunched over paper cups of coffee. One wore an orange rubber suit, his dark hair pushed up into rough spikes by the sweat and exertion of the rescue. Both men looked drawn.

"Yes? Can I help you?" It was the receptionist. Jenny walked up to the desk. "Oh, yes—good morning. I . . . er . . . I understand a young boy was brought in here just now by those . . . those gentlemen." She gestured down the corridor and the men glanced up. "I was wondering . . .

could you tell me how he is, please? His name is Jamie. Jamie Ennis."

"Yes . . . we identified him from the serial number on his phonic ear.
You're his mother, I presume?"

"No. No, I'm not. I'm . . . I'm his speech therapist. I was looking after
him when . . . when the accident happened."

"I see." A first faint hint of disapproval. "I'm sorry, but we are not
permitted to release information to anyone other than next of kin.
However, he has been admitted, yes. He's in Intensive Care."

Jenny absorbed this in shocked silence. She walked slowly down the
corridor, dazed. Intensive Care. That meant it was serious. That Jamie
could die. And she, Jenny Macrae, she was to blame. The two crewmen

looked up as she came towards them. "How is he?" she asked quietly. "The boy, I mean. The boy you picked out of the water."

Tony Lockhart shrugged. "He'd been in the water a while when we got to him. He was unconscious."

"But he's alive? He is going to be all right, isn't he?"

"When we brought him into Casualty? Yes, he was still alive."

"And Robbie? The old man with him in the boat?"

Tony paused. "I'm sorry. He didn't make it. He'd drowned before we could reach him." Jenny sat down slowly, thinking of that craggy, earnest face as he asked if he could take Jamie out to the lobster pots. All that warmth and kindness down through the years, just suddenly . . . gone.

37

"I . . . I watched you. From the shore," Jenny said. "You . . . you were marvellous. You all were," she said simply. Tony stared into the bottom of his coffee cup. Marvellous? 'Course they were. Regular Action Men, the lot of them. Especially when someone got away, slipped through their hands, like now. Like this man Roberts. Tony looked up suddenly as the double doors at the end of the corridor were pushed open and a policeman led the way into Casualty, followed by Mr. and Mrs. Ennis. Jenny hurried forward. "Mrs. Ennis, I'm terribly, terribly sorry."

"Who're you?" demanded John Ennis, a heavy-faced businessman.

"I'm Jenny Macrae," Jenny explained. "Jamie's speech therapist."

"Just tell me how he is," began Mrs. Ennis. Her husband stepped forward. "I'll deal with this now, love, if you don't mind," he interrupted sternly. "Now then, Miss . . . as I understand it, you were supposed to be looking after my son, correct?"

Jenny swallowed. "That is correct, yes, Mr. Ennis. A fisherman offered to take Jamie with him when he went to look at his lobster pots. I . . . I thought it would be good experience for him," she admitted quietly.

"Good experience for him?" echoed John Ennis incredulously. "The boy's stone deaf—you do know that, I suppose?"

"I should never have agreed to it," interrupted his wife dully.

"Mr. and Mrs. Ennis?" asked a quiet voice behind them. They all turned. "Might I have a word, please? In private." No one had noticed the doctor walk quietly down the corridor towards them. "I'm Dr. Dorman. Would you both like to come this way, please?" Jenny, the policeman and the two helicopter crewmen watched in silence.

Tony crushed his coffee carton in his fist and tossed it into the wastebasket. "Oh, God," he groaned, "I thought we'd got him." He stood up, and Jenny looked from one crewman to the other, puzzled. Like the police, Pete and Tony knew what lay behind that casual invitation to accompany the doctor to the far end of the corridor.

Jenny watched the doctor pause on the far side of a glass screen, turn to Jamie's parents and begin to talk. Gradually, very gradually, a terrible suspicion took root in her mind, blossoming into a certainty that was confirmed by the sudden slump of Mrs. Ennis's shoulders, by the crash of her husband's palm against the glass screen, by the sad final shake of the doctor's head.

"No . . ." whispered Jenny. "Oh, please . . . no."

CHAPTER 6

Jackman pushed through the glass doors into the main concourse at Glasgow Airport and melted into the crowd at the northwestern corner of the building, where a cluster of newsmen were grouped around the familiar, portly figure of the Right Honourable James Belcher MP, Secretary of State for Industry. Jackman moved unobtrusively round the outer ring of reporters, his eyes not upon the minister but upon one of the officials from Whitehall who had come up with him on the shuttle from London.

Ewan Baxter was in his early fifties, with short, iron-grey hair and pale, piercing blue eyes. A former officer in the Royal Engineers, Baxter had been moved discreetly sideways into the shadows of SIS five years earlier, for what were still euphemistically referred to as "additional duties". Now, as Jackman watched and waited, Baxter glanced up, saw him and glanced away without a flicker of recognition. Jackman turned and walked casually towards a kiosk where he bought a newspaper. He was standing there reading when Baxter stepped quietly to his side a few minutes later.

"How's Engel taking it?" Baxter asked without preamble.

"Predictably, I'm afraid. Wanted to wash his hands of the whole business to begin with. Even threatened to call the police, until I reminded him of certain . . . commitments. Professor Highcroft was a personal friend of the family. That hardly helped."

"Oh dear, I see. And now?"

"Now?" Jackman shrugged. "Now I suppose you could say he's going through an equally predictable period of self-loathing. Don't worry, he'll get over it. He's too far in for second thoughts at this stage."

Baxter nodded. "Right, let's get on then, shall we? Porton want all the sordid details, I'm afraid. They're hopping mad." Porton Down, the government chemical and biological research establishment on the edge of Salisbury Plain.

"I'm not surprised," agreed Jackman candidly. He glanced round. "You've time for a coffee, I take it? We can talk over there." He gestured towards the cafeteria. Baxter glanced at his watch and smiled. "Belcher's just launched into his 'You have my solemn word' routine. On past showing, I can give you exactly twenty minutes."

Ten of those minutes had gone before Ewan Baxter had the salient events of the previous night fixed firmly in his neat, military mind. By then, Jackman had told him about the sudden emergency summons to RD7, the disposal of Professor Highcroft's body, and the steps he had taken to hide the fact of his death from the professor's wife and family.

"Those two men you mentioned," Baxter mused, glancing at the names he had written on a small memo pad. "Parsons and Steevenson. You're sure they're the only ones who saw what happened to Highcroft?"

Jackman nodded. "Quite sure."

"And they can be trusted, these men?"

"I assume so, otherwise they'd never have been cleared by your people to work on OMAHA. Steevenson has been with us a long time. He was positively vetted long before he came up from Porton. Anyway, by now both men will have received an additional incentive to erase the matter completely from their minds."

"Incentive?" Baxter asked. "What sort of incentive?"

"Two thousand. Each. In cash."

Baxter nodded slowly. "That seems fair enough." He sat back in his chair in speculative silence for several moments. "All right," he said finally, "my report will show that there was nothing more you could reasonably have done, given the time and facilities at your disposal. However"—he made a little note on his pad—"there are still too many mouths. I think we should put someone in on the ground, don't you? Someone to keep an eye on things. Just for a few days. Just in case."

"Anyone particular in mind?" Jackman asked.

"There's a chap I sometimes use," Baxter replied.

BACK AT RAF GLENHADDON, Tony stepped out of the shower in the washroom and began dressing. Although he was coming off duty with the other two members of the crew after a total of twenty-five hours on call, he would still be officially on second standby until dusk. Because of this he was required to travel home in uniform. Adjusting his tie in the mirror, he slipped into the tunic blouse with the small golden eagle above the sergeant's chevrons, the symbol of operational aircrew status, and crammed his dirty clothes into a holdall.

Hefting the bag, he went out across the tarmac and slid behind the wheel of his Ford Escort, parked on the other side of the hangar. He had just begun to swing the car towards the perimeter road when Pete Sleaman came sprinting across the grass towards him. Tony stopped and Pete bent down to the car window.

"Dave and I reckon we'll sink a few down at the Dolphin a bit later on. Why don't you come along too?"

After four days as first crew and four evenings tethered to the station on the end of a telephone as second standby, tonight would be their first opportunity for serious drinking for almost a week. As bachelors living in the officers' mess with minimal domestic overheads to worry about, both men intended to make the most of it. But Tony shook his head. "No thanks, Pete."

"Why not? Do you the power of good, mate. You can't just sit around on your own for ever."

"Yeah, I know. Thanks, Pete."

"See you there?"

"Definitely maybe, OK?" Tony reached down for the ignition and then paused. "Know who I feel sorry for?"

"Who?"

"That girl. The one with the brown hair, waiting at the hospital."

"It was her fault, wasn't it? He'd still be alive if she hadn't let him out of her sight."

"Did you see her face?" asked Tony thoughtfully. "The look in her eyes when she realized the doc was telling them their son had snuffed it. She knows what hell's like."

JENNY PUSHED THE FRONT DOOR closed and walked slowly down the narrow hall of her flat towards the sitting room, her mind a blur of grief and bitter self-recrimination. She had no recollection of talking to the police, of answering their questions and making a statement before leaving the hospital; no memory of driving home; no awareness of pain in her shoulder as the rope handles of the beach bag sawed through the thin cotton of her blouse. Just numbness. In a trance she moved through to the sitting room, where she spilled the contents of the beach bag across the floor. She went down on hands and knees to pick up the pathetic debris of their trip: Jamie's blue sweater and bag of crayons; a plastic box of leftover cheese sandwiches; a packet of seashells bought at a stall. And, at the bottom of the pile, Jamie's sketchbook. Jenny opened it at the last picture, the sketch of Robbie. She stared at it, then sank back to weep anguished, silent tears, her face screwed into a mask of pain. She was sitting there still, with the tears coursing down her cheeks, when the doorbell rang.

She got to her feet and, crossing to the mirror, looked with dismay at her red-rimmed eyes and tear-blotched cheeks. The bell rang again as she went to the door. "Who is it?" she called dully.

"Miss Macrae?" A man's voice. "It's . . . er . . . it's Hamish Owen, Miss Macrae. May I speak to you for a moment, please?"

Jenny never imagined for one minute that the caller had something to do with Jamie's death. She pulled the door open.

A tall young man was standing outside, a notebook in one hand. "Hamish Owen, Miss Macrae. *Gleninver Times.* I wonder if I might just—"

Jenny shook her head. "I'm not . . . I don't want to talk to the press."

"Please, Miss Macrae—it won't take a moment." Hamish Owen suddenly saw himself returning to the office empty-handed. "If you could just confirm a few details, that's all. The police gave me your address." Not strictly true, for he had lifted it out of the incident book when the desk sergeant's back had been turned, but it gave his questions a certain superficial legitimacy.

Jenny wavered, a hand on the doorknob. "Well, I . . . ."

"Please, Miss Macrae—just two minutes. Just to set the record straight," he pleaded. Jenny sighed. "All right—you'd better come in."

If she had been able to foresee the newspaper headlines the next morning, however, she would never have opened the door.

FLIGHT SERGEANT TONY LOCKHART turned his Ford Escort into Bruneval Close and drove down between the rows of identical semidetached houses towards his own married quarter at the bottom of the cul-de-sac. He drove onto the concrete drive in front of the garage. Hauling a bag of groceries off the passenger seat and pushing the door closed with his hip, he let himself in at the side door.

The silence of the place still hit him every time he came through the door, even though it was already several months since Maureen had left him.

Ordinary, less stressed, marriages might be torn apart by infidelity, by boredom even, but Maureen Lockhart's "other woman" had been a Royal Air Force Wessex Search and Rescue helicopter. To Maureen, the procession of SAR incidents had seemed endless: danger upon danger, risks without end. With Tony always, always, putting his work before his family. Before her.

Finally, after a bitter row, she had decided she could take no more of it. Tony had stormed out of the house and back to work, slamming the door behind him. When he returned at the end of the shift she had gone to her parents in the south. Taking Paul with her.

Now Tony looked slowly round the domestic shambles of his kitchen, at the stack of dirty dishes piled in the sink and the mountains of creased clothes waiting for him on the ironing board. He turned away abruptly and began unpacking his groceries.

It was only later when he went through into the hall that he noticed the brown envelope lying on the doormat. It was from RAF Glenhaddon's housing officer, and it advised him crisply that married quarters were allocated on a "need" basis to married members of HM Forces and, regretfully, not to separated aircrew flight sergeants who lived alone. Under the circumstances, they would be grateful if Flight Sergeant Lockhart A.J. could make alternative arrangements and vacate the quarter within six months.

TWO HOURS LATER, in his airless little office on the first floor of the *Gleninver Times*, editor Bob Harris was subbing Hamish Owen's story about the fire at sea and the deaths of Jamie Ennis and Robbie Roberts. Tragedy at sea always made good copy, but this one was magic. It had everything: a child who was deaf, *and* the son of a prominent local councillor; a heroic helicopter winchman; even a scapegoat, someone to blame for the tragedy, this speech therapist woman, Jennifer Macrae. He had rejigged most of the front page.

Harris ran an approving eye over the new layout. The sea story, with its dramatic central picture, would run across six columns.

It quite swamped the other human-interest story tucked away in a single column and headlined simply HUSBAND MISSING.

CHAPTER 7

"This is Radio Firth. The time is just coming up to fourteen minutes after four, and that was Neil Diamond with a track from his *Diamonds* album called 'Mr. Bojangles'. This is Mike Mitchell, ready to take the next call on Mike's Open Line. Hello, who's that?"

"Hello. My . . . my name is Helen. Helen Highcroft," began a hesitant voice.

"Yes, Helen, my darling, what can I do for you?"

"I'm not . . . not sure. I've . . . I've never even thought of calling a radio station before. I—"

"Where are you calling from, sweetheart?"

"From . . . from Gleninver. I'm in a call box."

"Gleninver. I see. Smashing part of the world down there. Well now, Helen, what can I do for you?"

"I'm trying to find my . . . my husband," explained Helen Highcroft. In the studio on the outskirts of Glasgow, the DJ glanced up with a frown at his producer, who was listening through headphones on the other side of the soundproof screen.

"Trying to find your husband?" rattled on the DJ. "Lot of people I know are trying to lose theirs, Helen!" He laughed easily.

"Please, Mr. Mitchell. This isn't a . . . a joke. My husband has just . . . vanished. Disappeared. I thought perhaps if he was listening to your programme somewhere . . . or if I told you a little bit about him, gave a description, then perhaps one of your listeners might—"

"What about the police, love? We're not really able to—"

"I've already been to the police. I've tried all our friends, all our relatives. I . . . I was driving around just now with the radio on and I just thought . . . please, I'm desperate. I don't know what else to try," she begged, her voice beginning to break up. At the radio station, people had stopped work and were staring up at the speakers on the walls. In strictly commercial terms, of course, it was riveting stuff. In the studio, the DJ glanced at his producer, who gave a cautious thumbs-up.

"OK, Helen, why not? Helping people solve their problems is what it's all about, right? So let's give it a whirl—and all you Radio Firth listeners out there, why don't you stop what you're doing for a minute and just listen, OK? Helen, the floor's yours."

"Thank you." They all heard her give a long sigh. "My . . . my husband's name is Malcolm—Malcolm Highcroft. We've . . . we've been together almost twenty years. He's . . . forty-nine years old, about five foot ten inches tall, with brown hair although there's not . . . not a lot of that left." She tried a nervous little laugh. "We . . . we all had breakfast together at the usual time yesterday and then . . . ."

DOUGLAS PARSONS, THE MAN RESPONSIBLE for isolating section nine when the third floor of RD7 had gone to Condition Orange, was off duty and at home in the garden, mending the lawnmower. His wife was weeding a flowerbed and Laura, his thirteen-year-old daughter, was lying on an airbed, sunbathing, a transistor radio beside her. It was tuned to Radio Firth. Now, as she heard HPL mentioned, she propped herself up on one elbow. "Dad? Did you hear that? It's someone from the company."

Her father nodded impatiently, sucking on a knuckle. At the first mention of Helen Highcroft's name he had started violently, the spanner had slipped, and he had skinned his hand on the bolt he was trying to loosen.

". . . if you're listening somewhere, darling, if we've upset you in some way . . . I don't know what you're thinking about but, please, come back to us soon. We love you very much . . ."

Douglas Parsons crossed over to the radio and turned it off violently. "That's quite enough of that, thank you very much!"

His wife twisted round. "Doug? What's the matter?"

"Nothing!" he snapped. He turned and strode quickly towards the house. Mrs. Parsons set off after him. She found him holding his hand under the cold tap in the kitchen, a tin of plasters on the draining board beside him. "Doug? What is it? What's the matter? It's not like you . . ."

"Nothing. I told you."

"Ever since you got in you've been het up about something or other. Now that thing on the radio . . . Here, let me do that." She took the plaster from his hand and stuck if deftly over the raw knuckle. "There." Her husband flexed his hand experimentally. "Do you know him? This Professor whatshisname?"

"Highcroft?" Douglas Parsons nodded. "Yes. Yes, I do, as a matter of fact." He turned. "I've got to go out." He smiled a brief, automatic smile and reached for his jacket.

A minute later he slipped into the garden shed, moved over to the workbench and looked cautiously out of the window. Laura was still sunbathing. His wife had returned to her weeding. Parsons unlocked his tool cupboard, lifted down several heavy jam jars full of nuts, nails and screws and reached to the very back of the shelf. He took down an old Oxo tin and placed it carefully on his workbench as though it contained something rather dangerous, his breathing unusually loud in the warm shed. He prised off the lid. A thick brown envelope lay in the bottom. He tipped the contents out onto the palm of his hand. Two thousand pounds. Enough for a new car or a holiday abroad for the whole family.

Seeing the money in his hand crystallized all the worry and uncertainty that had been gnawing at him. Blood money, that's what it is, he told himself: nothing more, nothing less. A bribe for keeping quiet, for saying nothing, so that Helen Highcroft would go on believing her husband was still alive somewhere, that he had just run off and left her. Parsons thrust the money angrily into his pocket. Well, he'd had enough. He would go and see Jackman and return the money. Now.

THE ANGUISH WITH WHICH HELEN HIGHCROFT had talked on the radio had spurred Douglas Parsons into action. It acted upon Joyce Engel, wife of Highland Pharmaceuticals' founder and managing director, in much the same way. She was in the kitchen with the radio on as Helen Highcroft described the last time she had seen her husband, and begged for the slightest scrap of information from anyone. When she had finished, Joyce was almost in tears. She crossed to the telephone to dial through to her husband's office at Highland Pharmaceuticals. There was no reply.

SHE HAD MISSED HER HUSBAND by two minutes. Until then he had been sitting at his desk surrounded by reports, expenditure estimates and promotional schedules, all needing his urgent consideration. But he had been unable to concentrate, his mind dwelling instead upon the nightmarish events surrounding Professor Highcroft's death.

He groaned, sat back in his chair and gazed across the office at a photograph on the far wall. It showed a younger Harold Engel shaking hands with the then Secretary of State for Health at Engel Laboratories in Bookham, Surrey. The photograph had been taken during the boom years of the early sixties, when Engel was beginning to carve a reputation for himself as an independent pharmaceutical manufacturer by undercutting the overpriced branded products of the big drug companies with his own non-branded substitutes. For almost two years things had gone splendidly, and then one morning his secretary had brought him a confidential letter from something calling itself the Defence Procurement Secretariat. That had been his first step down the slippery path of professional compromise that, month by month, had robbed him of his integrity and made him what he was today: a rich, outwardly successful entrepreneur, trapped in a cage.

Engel pushed suddenly to his feet, slipped into a white coat and clapped one of the mandatory white nylon hats on his head. He left the office and went down the back stairs to the ground floor, to stand where he always stood when he needed to get away from the telephone and think: watching the production line.

If RD7 was the penalty for cooperation with the Defence Procurement Secretariat, then the smoothly efficient production line running in front of him now was undoubtedly one of the prizes. Gleaming, silent, totally efficient, it occupied almost two hundred and fifty feet, punctuated every few paces by a worker in white coat and hat monitoring the production of thousands of white, oval tablets vibrating their way down shining steel ramps, to be fed, in green tinfoil blister strips, fourteen at a time, into bright, emerald green cartons that were labelled and passed to the finished-goods compound ready for dispatch.

Engel felt the old familiar stirring of excitement. He was responsible for all this. A few more days and thousands of *his* pills would be dispersed in warehouses across the length and breadth of Britain, poised to meet the demand created by HPL's skilful promotion campaign and by a series of carefully orchestrated leaks to a number of influential medical journals—leaks that hinted at the arrival of a new miracle drug. With Cardocol, Engel fervently believed HPL's team of research chemists had broken through one of the last great pharmacological barriers. Cardocol would be more than just another new heart drug. It would be the first adrenergic neurone-blocker on the market whose medical data sheet would *not* carry black-edged warnings about the risk of an adverse effect among the elderly known as postural hypotension, or severe and sudden fall in blood pressure upon standing.

Cardocol was about to make HPL a very great deal of money. And with that money, Engel knew, would come prestige and a newfound, hard-won degree of autonomy. A chance to dictate terms from a position of strength rather than having to agree to "cooperation" with people like the Defence Procurement Secretariat. People like Jackman.

Harold Engel turned and pushed through the heavy rubber doors leading to the other love of his life, the company helicopter. The flying bug had bitten deep during his National Service and had stayed with him into civilian life. Now he flew whenever he felt able to justify it. He walked across the concrete towards the landing circle and felt that customary lift to his spirits as the helicopter came into view. The five-seater Aerospatiale Squirrel 350 had a range of just over four hundred miles and a top speed of 150 mph. It had come to symbolize freedom—freedom from interference, from Whitehall, from Jackman. Harold Engel moved to the pilot's door, saw the headset lying there waiting for him on the seat, and glanced instinctively at his watch. A minute from now, two at the most and he could be—

"Mr. Engel?" He turned, suddenly wrenched back to reality. Martin Lear, one of his managers, was hurrying towards him across the concrete. "Call for you, Mr. Engel. It's your wife."

"Ask her to give me another couple of minutes, will you? I'll take it upstairs in my office."

When she rang back, he was waiting for her call.

"Sorry to disturb you, darling," she began, "I know how busy you must be, but Helen Highcroft was on the radio asking if anyone had seen Malcolm. The poor woman was almost in tears."

Harold Engel sat forward abruptly. "She was *what?*"

"She was on the radio. Some phone-in programme. Just called in out of the blue and asked for help. There's no news, I suppose?"

"News?"

"About Malcolm!"

Harold dragged a hand over his hair. "Look, Joyce. I . . . I can't talk now—someone's just come in. I'll . . . I'll get back to you later."

"Then will you at least promise me you'll—" But she was talking to herself. She replaced the receiver slowly and frowned. She frowned not at the sudden termination of their conversation—that had been fairly typical in recent weeks, as the pre-launch pressure had mounted—but at the sudden realization that there had been an edginess, an unfathomed tension between them ever since Malcolm Highcroft had disappeared.

ENGEL SAT LOOKING at the telephone for a moment, then stabbed at the intercom. "Ask Mr. Jackman to step into my office, will you?"

Two minutes later Jackman entered, coming in with that brief smile of urbane self-assurance that never ceased to remind Engel of his own impotence.

"Well?" Engel snapped. "You saw your Mr. Baxter at the airport, I assume?"

"Yes, I did. We agreed upon certain . . . precautions."

"But you're not prepared to tell me what those precautions are, is that it?"

Jackman shrugged. "We feel it best if you are not involved."

"You told me last night, Mr. Jackman," Engel said slowly, "that all this Highcroft business would just 'blow over'—you remember? Would it interest you to know that the widow of the man you . . . you disposed of so efficiently, has been on the radio, asking total strangers to keep an eye open for her husband?" He paused to let that sink in. "I hardly think London would call that 'blowing over', do you?"

"DOUGLAS PARSONS IS WAITING OUTSIDE to see you, Mr. Jackman." Jackman was sitting at his desk back in the administration building, penning his name to a clutch of letters and internal memos. Now, as his secretary mentioned Parsons's name, he paused fractionally.

"Show him in, please, Frances." He sat back in his chair, a smile of welcome already in place. Parsons entered. He appeared ill at ease. Jackman beckoned him forward. "So—what can I do for you?"

Parsons took the money out of his pocket and laid it on Jackman's desk. "You can take this back, for a start," he said.

"Oh? And why is that?"

Parsons shrugged uncomfortably. "Because it's a buy-off, isn't it?"

"Nonsense!" snorted Jackman. "It's nothing of the sort! Your duties last night involved you in a certain . . . unpleasantness. You came under considerable pressure and performed very creditably. Look upon it as an efficiency bonus if you like; that's all."

"My duties?" challenged Parsons bitterly. "Is that what they were? Carrying him down to the loch. And Mrs. Highcroft? Did she 'perform' well, too? How much does she get?"

Jackman frowned. "I'm afraid I don't follow."

"She was on the radio this afternoon, begging her husband to come home! She thinks he's just . . . gone off, left them in the lurch. I can tell you, listening to that and knowing all the time that . . . that . . ." The words trailed away. Then he recovered and stepped up to Jackman's desk, his face tight and determined. "Look, Mr. Jackman. Before we agreed to accept your . . . efficiency bonus, as you call it, you promised she would be told. I'd never have gone along with your crackpot scheme if I'd known you were going to keep her deliberately in the dark like this. She's going quietly out of her mind with worry—surely you can see that? Or does the question of 'security' blot out everything else?"

"In this case, yes, I'm rather afraid that it does," Jackman admitted, as he quietly evaluated the man opposite him. He had been wrong, guilty of a serious error of judgment: Parsons *was* a threat. "Tell me. What about Steevenson. Does he share your views?"

Parsons shrugged. "I've no idea. I'm just speaking for myself."

"And your wife? Does she share this"—Jackman gestured at the pile of money on his desk—"this crisis of conscience?"

"Of course not! She doesn't even know the money exists."

Jackman nodded, thankful for small mercies. "So what do you expect me to do—apart, that is, from resuscitate the dead?"

"You can give me your word that Mrs. Highcroft will be told. Put out of her misery. Told that he won't be coming home."

"I see. As simple as that. And when she asks about his body for burial, or an inquest? What do you suggest I tell her then?"

"That's your lookout, Mr. Jackman—not mine." Parsons stepped back. "Well, I've said what I came here to say. Thank you for seeing me, Mr. Jackman." The door closed behind him.

Jackman sat for several moments, then he locked Parsons's money in his own briefcase and lifted the telephone. He dialled an unlisted London number. His call was answered almost immediately.

"Baxter."

"This is Jackman." He stared out at the waters of the loch that glittered flat and smooth in the late summer sunshine. "We have a problem."

HELEN HIGHCROFT DROVE INTO THE GARAGE, turned off the engine and doused the lights. It had been a wasted day with nothing achieved, despite the radio interview.

She walked back to the house and had just begun to reach for the front-door keys when the telephone rang in the hall. Fumbling in her haste, she rushed in. "Yes?" she panted breathlessly. "Yes? Malcolm?"

"Mrs. Highcroft?" It was a man's voice, but it wasn't her husband's.

"Yes?"

"I . . . I heard you on the radio today. Asking about your husband."

"Have you seen him? *Please*—do you know where he is?"

There was a pause. "He won't be coming home, Mrs. Highcroft. I was there. I saw it happen."

"Saw what happen? Look, who is this?"

"Your husband is dead, Mrs. Highcroft." There was a click, as the caller replaced the receiver.

CHAPTER 8

"Then we . . . we saw the smoke. Through one of those beach telescope things." Jenny gazed sightlessly into her cup of tea as she relived once more that awful moment on the quayside. "We . . . we called the coastguard, and they sent a helicopter, but it was too late. When it arrived, Jamie was already . . . already dead." Eyes swimming with tears, Jenny looked up at Pam Ross, sitting silent in an armchair across the sitting room. "If only I'd gone with him, Pam!" she cried.

Pam leaned forward. "Suppose, just for the sake of argument, Jamie had come back. Would you have told his parents about the trip?"

"Of course I would have done—yes."

"And you wouldn't have felt guilty?"

Jenny frowned. "What about?"

"About letting Jamie go off in the boat? Without you beside him to hold his hand."

There was silence while Jenny examined that question. Then she looked up. "No. I don't believe I would have felt guilty."

A gleam appeared in Pam's eye. "Why not?"

Jenny shrugged. "Because . . . I don't know . . . because it was an adventure—something Jamie had set out to accomplish on his own without that mother of his hanging on to his shirttails."

Pam nodded triumphantly. "Exactly! That was the whole point about letting him go out with that friend of yours, wasn't it? You almost went with them. But you didn't because you wanted the boy to be able to think Me! I did that, all on my own!"

"That's . . . that's right," Jenny whispered, the tears once again very near the surface. "That's *exactly* what I thought! How did you—?"

"How did I know? Because I've read Jamie's case notes too, remember?" Pam rose, crossed the room and crouched down beside Jenny to take both her hands in hers. "If it makes you feel any better, I'd

49

have done exactly the same thing, all right?" she said softly. "I'd have let him go. Alone with Robbie."

Jenny looked up slowly. "You're just saying that."

Pam shook her head. "I'm not, I promise you, Jenny. That's exactly what I would have done. Now then—" She stood up and went back to her seat, suddenly all brisk efficiency. "The boat just burst into flames, isn't that what you said?"

"That's right, yes."

"Why?"

Jenny looked blank. "I've no idea. It doesn't matter."

"Of course it matters," corrected Pam stoutly. "It matters very much! Fishing boats don't just burst into flames without a reason. Wouldn't you like to know *why* that boat caught fire?"

Jenny shrugged. "Well, yes. But I don't see . . ."

"What about these helicopter people? That man, the one who rescued the bodies from the sea—he was near the boat when it was on fire, wasn't he?"

"Yes, but I can't just—"

"—phone up and ask? Why not? What have you got to lose?" She broke off as the telephone began to ring.

Jenny picked up the receiver. It was Danny.

"I . . . I was just watching the news," he began, the shock still fresh in his mind. "Jen—what happened? That . . . that was you they were talking about, wasn't it?"

She gripped the telephone a little tighter. "Yes. That was me."

"God, what a stupid thing to say. What I mean is: if there's anything I can do? You know . . . if you need someone to . . ."

"It's all right. Really." She paused. "And I . . . I got your letter."

"Oh. That was really why I was calling, Jen. That and the . . . the accident. It was really good timing, wasn't it?" he said. "The letter, I mean."

"It could have been better," Jenny replied, with a lightness she did not feel.

"Would you like me to come up for a few days? So we could talk things over?" Jenny closed her eyes for a moment. Yes, if he hadn't posted that letter. No, because he had.

"No, really. I'll . . . drop you a line about it, OK? In a day or so."

"You're *sure* there's nothing I can do?"

"Quite sure," she managed huskily. There was a dragging silence as Danny racked his brain for some way to bring things to a painless end. He didn't find it.

"Be . . . be in touch, OK? I . . . goodbye, Jenny."

"See you," she whispered. "Take care." She felt as though her heart would break.

CHAPTER 9

In the spare bedroom at the top of his terraced house in Chiswick, Dennis Ridley sat in silence at a worktable illuminated by a single pool of hard, white light. A spare, fit-looking man in his late thirties, with short brown hair, he sat hunched forward, peering intently through a magnifying glass at a white lead model of a soldier. Now he dipped his paintbrush into a tin of enamel and began painting the white piping that denoted infantry onto the soldier's dark grey shoulder straps.

When the model was completed, the soldier, with his 9 mm Schmeisser submachine gun, would take his place with the others of his regiment in the diorama that took up three quarters of the rear of the bedroom.

A timid knock on the door. Ridley didn't hear it at first, so absorbed was he in his hobby, his obsessive interest in the battles and campaigns of recent history. The knock came again, a little louder this time, and Ridley frowned. "Come," he ordered.

His wife hovered in the doorway. "It's that man again, Dennis . . . Downstairs in the hall. Would you like me to—?"

"Show him up? Yes, why don't you?" suggested Ridley quietly. He smiled to himself. So—he had come back.

There was another soft tap on the door. "Mr. Ridley? Might I come in?" Ewan Baxter waited politely in the doorway.

"Ah, Mr. Baxter. I thought it must be about time for another of your little visits. Please, take a chair."

Baxter stepped into the bedroom and sat down. He noticed the German soldier lying on the table.

"Still at it, I see." He smiled. "I've . . . er . . . brought you a little present." He took an oblong box out of his pocket and laid it on the worktable. "Please open it." He watched as Ridley lifted the lid, then sat back with a sudden sigh. Inside, lying on its side in its original wrapping, lay a model of a German army vehicle, a VW Kübelwagen with every spring, panel and bolt reproduced in the most faithful detail. Ridley lifted it out of the box as though it were the Turin shroud.

"I didn't think there were more than half a dozen left in Europe," he murmured, turning the box over and pointing at a yellowed label gummed to its base. "Nineteen fifty-two. One of the originals." He replaced the model carefully and looked up. "I assume this is just a beckoner? That there is something you would like done? Outside the . . . usual channels?"

Baxter inclined his head slightly. "Perhaps. If you're interested."

"Where?"

"UK this time, I'm afraid. Scotland. Little hole-in-the-wall sort of place called Gleninver. Ever been there?"

Ridley shook his head. "Gleninver? Never even heard of it."

"Good. Excellent. Then we can start with a clear pool, can't we?"

Ridley looked momentarily puzzled. He was a hunter, not a fisherman.

JENNY DROVE HER CITROËN into the crowded car park and pulled to a halt. The sound of music and laughter drifted towards her from the pub's open windows. She got out, locked the car door, took a deep breath and walked firmly across the gravelled forecourt towards the pub.

The Dolphin was crowded with holidaymakers. It was a comfortable, low-beamed free house, less than three miles from RAF Glenhaddon. For that reason alone, it was a popular watering hole for off-duty aircrew from Rescue Flight. Jenny edged her way towards the bar.

Dave, Pete and Tony were sitting together over their pints at a table in the corner. Now Dave drained his glass, set it down with a smack and exhaled gustily. "Not a bad drop of wallop, that. Right then—same again, lads?" He was about to push to his feet when one of the regulars eased his way through, and began solemnly distributing brimming pint glasses among the three members of RESCUE 44. "There you go, boys."

Dave twisted round. "George? You feeling all right? Won the pools or something?"

The old man clapped a hand on the pilot's shoulder.

"You did all right," he offered, with the slow deliberation of a drinker already well on his way. "No worry, boys. It wasn't your fault, out there in the bay." He leaned closer, and a gust of beery breath fanned across Tony's face as he added, "I seen you, man. On the telly. It was that lassie's fault—she's the one to blame, if you ask me." He lifted his glass and drank deeply. "Good health to you . . ."

The barman edged towards Jenny at last. "Yes, love, what can I do you for?" No recognition. Thank God.

"Oh. A . . . an orange juice, please. I'm looking for Flight Sergeant Tony Lockhart," she said. "I was told I might find him here."

The barman poured deftly. "Forty-five pence." He looked up. "One of the RAF Glenhaddon lot, is he?"

Jenny nodded. "That's right, yes. The crewroom said he might be here."

The barman gestured towards the far window. "There's three of 'em over there, love. Just past Space Invaders."

"Thanks." Jenny picked up her glass and moved slowly across the crowded bar. She recognized them straight away, despite the fact that they were in civilian clothes. She stood watching them uncertainly. Dave grinned, not recognizing her.

"Hello, darling. Looking for somewhere to sit?" he asked.

Jenny gave a quick shake of the head. "No. I was looking for Flight Sergeant Lockhart."

52

Tony swung round. His hair had been combed so that it lay flat instead of sticking up in dark spikes, and he wore a jacket and open-necked shirt instead of the orange rubber suit, yet Jenny recognized him instantly, every image pin-sharp from that nightmare moment of realization in the hospital corridor.

"Hello. I'm . . . I'm sorry to trouble you when you're off duty. We . . . we met briefly this afternoon . . ."

Tony nodded. "I remember. At the hospital, wasn't it?"

Jenny swallowed. "That's right, yes." She held out her hand and Tony shook it. "I'm Jenny—Jenny Macrae." Her fingers felt small, frail and very cold engulfed in his own.

He gestured briefly round the table. "Pete Sleaman—Dave Bourne. Please, take a seat."

"No, really. I . . . I can't stay long. I just wanted to thank you, all of you. For what you did. What you—tried to do." She took a nervous sip of her orange juice.

"I'm sorry we couldn't have done more," replied Tony, the banal words of sympathy hiding the true depth of his feelings.

"I would also like to . . . to apologize," Jenny offered quietly, determined to see it through. "For putting you all to so much trouble and at so much risk."

Tony shrugged. "No bother. It's what we're here for."

"I suppose . . . I suppose you think it was all my fault, do you?" Jenny asked, the words out before she could stop them. "I wouldn't blame you if you did. Everyone else seems to."

"We're not in the business of allocating blame, Miss Macrae. We—" He broke off suddenly as a hand landed heavily on his shoulder.

"That's her, isn't it?" demanded George indignantly, peering at Jenny as though she was Quasimodo, down from the belfry. "It's that bloody woman, cool as you please!" Jenny felt the colour drain from her cheeks as people stopped talking. "It's her! The woman on the telly!" insisted George, his voice ringing out across the crowded bar.

"Now, George, take it easy," placated Tony.

"Me? An' . . . an' what about that poor wee lad drowned out there in the bay, eh? An' . . . an' here she is, bold as brass, without so much as—"

"I shouldn't have come." Jenny began to back away. "Thank you . . . thank you for . . ." She turned and pushed blindly through the crowd of people, reached the door, and broke into a run across the car park.

"You idiot, George," Tony muttered, making for the door. There had surely been enough pain, enough suffering . . .

He hurried outside and looked around for signs of the girl. Nothing. Not a thing. A little Citroën reversed jerkily out of the car park and disappeared down the lane into the night.

CHAPTER 10

Ridley parked in a side road and darted across Chiswick's Southfield Road into the post office on the opposite corner. They always used post offices; post offices were easy, safe, anonymous. He smiled at the old lady sitting surrounded by ledgers of stamps and postal orders. "Good morning. You have a parcel for me, I believe—poste restante. The name is Spackman."

The old lady vanished into the rear of the shop and returned with a brown package. "Here you are, Mr. Spackman. It arrived only this morning."

Ridley took possession of the parcel and returned to his car. Making sure he was not being watched, he slit it open. The two packets of ten-pound notes went into an inner pocket without a second glance. He studied the air ticket briefly, looked at the map Baxter had thoughtfully included, and placed them both in an attaché case. Then he opened an envelope and tipped a black-and-white photograph into his hand. He studied it for several seconds and glanced at the back where a name had been written in pencil: Douglas Parsons.

IT WAS MIDMORNING when the swing doors of the health clinic banged shut and Jenny hurried down the steps to her car, bag slung over her shoulder, a bundle of newspapers jammed under one arm. She tossed papers and bag angrily onto the passenger seat and slid behind the wheel. She sat there for a moment, staring at the place where she had worked, seeing once again Corbett's bureaucratic little face and the tight, pursed line of his mouth as he read her report. Corbett was the district administrator for the Social Services Department. Jenny started the engine and was about to reverse out of the car park when Pam came hurrying towards her. "I just heard," she said. "Jen, what can I say? I'm so sorry: if there's anything I can do to—"

"Suspended!" said Jenny bitterly. "He had made up his mind before he even came through the door!"

"It's only temporary, you know. Suspended doesn't mean guilty, Jen. *Or* innocent. It means exactly what it says: suspended. In limbo."

Jenny shook her head impatiently. "You know what he said—Corbett? He said 'a gesture' was needed. The department needed to be seen to be reacting to public concern. What do they think I am? Some sort of . . . of child molester! Just look at these!" Jenny gestured at the newspapers strewn on the seat beside her where half a dozen front-page paragraphs had been ringed in red. "Corbett marked all those—see what I mean? Not one of them refers to Jamie, or to me, or to his parents—they all refer to Corbett or to the department. It makes you sick."

"All right—what would you have done in his place?"

Jenny shrugged. "About me, you mean? I don't know . . . I've lived here all my life, Pam! Yet already it's as though I'm a non-person. People pretend not to see me, they look away, they won't talk to me—"

"I'm still talking to you."

There was a flicker of a smile. "You know what I mean."

Pam nodded. "'Course I do. But it'll blow over, given time. These things always do."

"With John Ennis on the council, and Corbett disowning me every time the telephone rings from County Hall? You really think so?" Jenny banged a hand against the steering wheel. "I feel sorry about what happened. Terribly, terribly sorry. But I don't feel *guilty*, not any more. I know I did yesterday, I didn't have room for anything else. But today . . ." She shrugged. "I don't know—I must have used up all those guilt feelings or something, can you understand that?"

Pam nodded. "Yes, I can understand. It sounds to me as if you're beginning to come to terms with what happened; with yourself." She paused. "So what are you going to do? Now, I mean."

Jenny reached down for the handbrake. "Me? Haven't a clue."

"Well, don't forget. If you want to talk or just have a good cry on someone's shoulder, give me a call, all right?"

Jenny nodded and backed slowly out of the car park. She'd lied to Pam, for she knew exactly what she was going to do next. She was going to talk to Amy Roberts, Robbie Roberts's widow. Her name and address appeared in most of the papers the punctilious Mr. Corbett had brought with him from Glasgow.

IN THE FIRST-FLOOR ADMINISTRATIVE OFFICES of Highland Pharmaceuticals, the promotions manager was drawing to a close yet another pre-launch presentation with managing director Harold Engel, when a telephone sounded on his desk. He held out the receiver to Engel. "For you, sir."

Engel took the call. "This is reception. I have Mrs. Helen Highcroft in reception, Mr. Engel. She has asked to speak to you."

Harold Engel did some rapid thinking. "Yes, yes of course. I'll be down in just a minute." He put the telephone down. "You'll have to continue without me for a minute or so, I'm afraid, David," he said, forcing a smile. "But from what I've heard so far—excellent, really excellent. Please continue."

Engel stepped out into the corridor. With the door closed behind him, he wiped a shaking hand over his forehead and tried to think clearly. He couldn't go down and see her himself, that was out of the question. Think! This was Jackman's doing, Jackman's . . . mess: let him clear it up. He hurried into Jackman's office.

"She's here," he said tersely. "Now. Downstairs in reception."

Jackman sat back in his chair, took off his spectacles and began polishing them. "By 'she', I take it you mean Mrs. Highcroft?"

Engel nodded. "She's downstairs. Waiting for me. I can't." He swallowed nervously. "I . . . I won't . . . if you want to pull the wool over that woman's eyes, you'll have to do it without my help."

"All right." Jackman replaced his spectacles and glanced up. "I'll go and see her. I'll let you know when she's gone."

Jackman went quietly down the back stairs and along the corridor that led towards both the reception area and the empty office he had selected the night Professor Highcroft had died in RD7. He paused outside the office, took a name-card from his wallet and slipped it into the metal card-holder on the door. He then continued along the corridor towards the reception hall.

Helen Highcroft was sitting on one of the sofas set just inside the main doors. She looked tense, drawn and exhausted.

"Maurice Jackman, Mrs. Highcroft," he introduced himself, sitting down beside her. "Mr. Engel asked me to see if there was anything I could do."

"Have you . . . have you heard anything? From my husband?"

Jackman shook his head sadly. "I'm afraid not, Mrs. Highcroft—not a thing. We've made our own inquiries, naturally, but . . . nothing."

"I had a phone call last night. The caller wouldn't say who he was, just that Malcolm was . . . was dead. That he wouldn't be coming home."

"This caller told you he was *dead?*" Parsons, thought Jackman darkly, Douglas Parsons—got to be.

She nodded. "That's right, yes. He said he was with my husband when he . . . when he was killed."

"Good God!" said Jackman, genuinely shocked. "What a monstrous thing to say! Did you recognize his voice?" Helen Highcroft shook her head and he breathed a sigh of relief.

"What can I say, Mrs. Highcroft? Did you report this to the police?"

"No. No, I didn't." She shrugged apologetically. "I thought I'd better sleep on it first. Then, this morning . . . I thought I'd do better coming here instead."

"I'm glad you did, although I'm not sure how we—"

"I . . . I was wondering if you would mind showing me Malcolm's office, let me look at his diaries, things like that? There might be something there . . . some clue . . ." Jackman managed to look a little doubtful. Helen Highcroft touched his arm. "I know it isn't company policy to let people into the working area, Mr. Jackman, but perhaps . . ."

Jackman rose to his feet. "Of course." He smiled reassuringly. "If you'd like to come with me, Mrs. Highcroft?"

Jackman was not only ruthless, he was also a superb chess player who

56

had planned and plotted Mrs. Highcroft's various moves with almost mathematical precision. He led her down the corridor and paused outside the office just long enough to ensure that she saw her husband's name on the door. "Here you are." He switched on the light, ushered her in, and crossed to the windows to draw back the curtains. Helen Highcroft gazed slowly round. It was not quite how she had imagined it. It was . . . smaller.

Jackman pushed Professor Highcroft's engagement diary casually across the desk towards her. She picked it up and began leafing through the pages as Jackman watched her carefully out of the corner of his eye. Any moment now . . .

She gave a sudden little, strangled cry. "What is it?" Jackman demanded sharply.

She sat down, frozen with shock, holding out a photograph of an attractive young girl with the wind blowing her hair away from her face. Jackman didn't have to ask about the inscription written on the back: "To my darling Malcolm. With all my love until we can be together. Your adoring Monica."

SEAVIEW ROAD TURNED OUT to be a narrow ribbon of terraced fishermen's cottages clinging to the hills overlooking Ardtornish harbour. It took Jenny half an hour to drive back along the coast from Gleninver, and another ten minutes before she had parked and climbed up the steep, cobbled lane to Mrs. Roberts's home.

She rang the bell. The door was opened by an elderly woman with untidy grey hair, wearing a shapeless mauve cardigan. Jenny hesitated. "Mrs. Roberts?"

The woman shook her head. "She's in the sitting room. I'm her neighbour, Mrs. Leity. You'd best step inside." Jenny followed Mrs. Leity into the sitting room.

Amy Roberts was sitting in an armchair beside the unlit fire. A frail, bird-like woman in her seventies, whose white hair was scraped back from her forehead in a severe bun, she looked up inquiringly with eyes red from weeping. Jenny stepped forward hesitantly.

"Mrs. Roberts? I . . . I'm sorry to trouble you just now. I was with your husband on the breakwater yesterday afternoon just before the accident. My name's Jenny . . . Jenny Macrae."

Mrs. Roberts nodded slowly. "The wee boy," she said. "The one who was deaf. He was in your care, wasn't he? It's him I keep thinking of as I sit here. Him with all of his life in front of him . . ." Her voice trailed away and Jenny followed her gaze to a photograph of Robbie on top of an old upright piano in the corner. "We never managed any children of our own, you see, Miss Macrae. But Robbie . . . oh, he loved them. Always . . . always being friendly like that. Taking them out for little

58

trips and such." She turned away so that Jenny wouldn't see her tears.

Mrs. Leity cleared her throat. "I'll be next door if you need me," she offered. There was a fragile silence as the door closed, leaving Jenny and Mrs. Roberts alone together. Jenny sat down.

"Please, Mrs. Roberts—no one's blaming Robbie for what happened."

Mrs. Roberts smiled a sad, slow smile. "No, lass—they're blaming you, aren't they?"

Jenny nodded. "The newspapers are, yes."

"And are they right? To blame you for what happened?"

Jenny spread her hands in a gesture of helplessness. "Jamie was my responsibility, certainly, but it's not as simple as that. At least, it isn't to me."

She told Mrs. Roberts about Jamie, and about his over-protective mother, and about her conversation with Robbie down on the break-water, and then she said, "Can you tell me anything about Robbie's boat, Mrs. Roberts? Anything at all that might explain why it suddenly caught fire like that?"

Mrs. Roberts shook her head. "I can't think of anything, no . . . Robbie kept everything in very good order. The boat took up most of his time after he retired—that and the lobsters and such, when the weather was kind and the wind didn't start him up coughing. Too much of his time, maybe."

"Too much? Why do you say that?"

Mrs. Roberts shrugged. "Och, just that the doctor told him to take it easy. Not to go overdoing things the first few weeks."

Jenny leaned a little closer. "You mean Robbie had been ill?"

"Ill? Robbie? Och, no, he never had a day's illness in his life. Just a wee bit of blood pressure, that's all, Dr. Erskine said. He gave him some pills, told him to take it easy, and said he'd soon be as right as rain. Robbie took that to mean spend all the time he could down in the harbour, tinkering about with that boat of his." She sighed. "Well—you haven't come all this way to listen to an old woman blathering away, have you now? Will you join me in a cup of tea?"

"Thank you, I'd like that," Jenny replied warmly. "Here, let me help you."

They went together into the small kitchen where Mrs. Roberts boiled a kettle and guided Jenny towards the cups and saucers.

It was when Jenny was looking round for the sugar that she saw the bottle of cough mixture and the packet of pills standing together on the table. The pills were in an emerald green packet.

Mrs. Roberts glanced over her shoulder. "Aye, they're the ones," she said. "Made all the difference to Robbie, they did."

Jenny turned the pills in her hands, trying to remember where she had seen them before.

CHAPTER 11

Jenny drove home feeling depressed, lonely. She was just about to open the door of her flat when she heard a movement upstairs. Looking up from the hallway she saw that Mrs. Proctor's door was ajar. "Hello?" she called. "Hello? Who's there?" Then the door at the top of the stairs opened and Jenny sighed with relief. "Mrs. Elliot—you gave me quite a shock. Today's not Tuesday." Mrs. Elliott came in once a week to tidy up and collect Mrs. Proctor's laundry. A dour, dumpy package of a woman, she studied Jenny sternly.

"They've taken her. It's a fortunate thing I came by to drop off the laundry, that's all I can say. There she was, just lying beside the bed. Gave me a proper fright, I can tell you."

"*Who's* taken her?" Jenny asked.

"The ambulance people, of course. Not twenty minutes ago."

They both turned at a sudden tap on the glass panelling in the door downstairs.

"Good afternoon," called a well-dressed man in his late thirties. He stepped into the hall. He was carrying a black briefcase.

"Where might I find Miss Jennifer Macrae?"

"You're speaking to her."

He held out his hand. "My name is Smithson, Miss Macrae. From the sheriff clerk's office. I'm the fiscal." The procurator fiscal, that rank peculiar to the Scottish legal profession. "I wonder if I could have a few words?"

"Yes. Yes, of course." Jenny opened the front door of her flat and ushered Smithson into the sitting room and to a chair.

"How can I help you?" she asked, sitting down opposite him.

"Well," Smithson began carefully, "as you may already be aware, whenever there is a . . . an incident, such as there was the other afternoon, it is my job to collect eyewitness accounts of what took place, to bring all relevant facts out into the open."

"I'd have thought they were publicized enough. The accident was all over the television. And the newspapers."

"Indeed. So it was. However, it is my task to try and formalize those statements, so to speak; to enter them upon the public record. It will then be up to the sheriff to decide whether or not the public interest would be best served by the institution of criminal proceedings against any particular party."

Jenny felt herself go suddenly cold. "Against me. That's what you really mean, isn't it?" she challenged.

The fiscal shrugged. "That is a possibility that cannot be excluded, yes, Miss Macrae."

HELEN HIGHCROFT ARRIVED HOME from HPL in a daze, the photograph she had discovered in Malcolm's diary on the front seat beside her.

The front door was wrenched open almost as soon as she reached out to press the buzzer. It was opened by Sarah. Mark and Simon pressed tightly against her shoulders as they all waited for news of their father. "What did they say?" Sarah asked immediately.

"There's still no news, I'm afraid," Helen managed. She closed the door behind her and turned to watch the three faces crumple dejectedly. Then she looked up to see her friend and neighbour Elizabeth Chalice coming down the hall. "Have they been good?" Helen asked over her children's heads.

"Good as gold," said Elizabeth, noticing what it cost her friend to maintain that outward air of composure in the presence of her children. She clapped her hands together smartly. "Right—out into the garden, now!" she ordered, propelling the children gently on their way. When the last of them was out of earshot, "Nothing?" she demanded quietly. "Not a word?"

The mask cracked. Helen's shoulders slumped as she fumbled with the clasp of her handbag. Elizabeth guided her into the lounge and shut the door behind them. Helen took out the photograph of the girl and held it out without a word. Elizabeth took the picture slowly and read the inscription. "Oh no," she breathed. "Oh, Helen . . ."

"It was in his diary. Malcolm had left it in his diary."

"Do you know who she is?"

Helen shook her head. "I've never seen her before."

"What about the name—Monica? Did you . . . what I mean is . . . did you suspect that perhaps Malcolm might be . . . you know. . . ?"

Helen looked up, the tears running down her cheeks. "Be having an affair? No . . . no, never. We were . . . so *happy*." She groaned. "Not for one moment. After last night I just . . . I just don't know what to think any more . . ."

The sudden ringing of the telephone rescued Elizabeth Chalice from a lengthening silence. Helen crossed the room and picked up the receiver. "Yes?"

"Mrs. Highcroft? Sorry to trouble you. It's Maurice Jackman here, from Highland Pharmaceuticals."

"Yes? Have you heard anything?"

"I'm afraid it's looking pretty definite, Mrs. Highcroft. The police have just called. They've found your husband's car in the station forecourt."

THE PROCURATOR FISCAL slipped Jenny's four-page handwritten statement into his briefcase. "Right then, Miss Macrae—that all seems straightforward enough." He rose to leave. "Thank you for answering my questions so candidly. You're . . . ah . . . not planning to go away anywhere in the next few days, I take it? I'd just like to know where I can reach you if I have any further questions."

Jenny shook her head. "No, I'm not planning to go anywhere."

"Good. Fine. Excellent, Then I'll bid you good day.."

Jenny got up too. "Do you have any idea when you will decide? Whether or not there are to be criminal proceedings against . . . anyone?"

Smithson gave a shrug. "I'm sorry, Miss Macrae, that would be quite impossible to say. After the Fatal Accident Inquiry, anyway." They walked down the hall together, shook hands, and Jenny watched as Smithson crossed the road and disappeared briskly from sight.

She turned back indoors and glanced up at the landing. Mrs. Proctor's door was shut and there was now no sign of Mrs. Elliott. On a sudden impulse, she went upstairs, fished the key out of the letterbox on its length of ribbon, and let herself into Mrs. Proctor's flat. She had suddenly remembered where she had seen Robbie's pills before.

Mrs. Elliott had given the bedroom her usual perfunctory tidy. It seemed strange without Mrs. Proctor propped up there on her pillows with her walking stick beside her.

Jenny went over to Mrs. Proctor's bedside table and looked at the old lady's private pharmacy of pills, tablets and potions. The pills she was looking for were beside a bottle of cough mixture. She sat down on the edge of the bed and tried to marshal the thoughts milling around in her head: Mrs. Proctor had collapsed beside her bed with an emerald green packet of Cardocol pills on the floor beside her; those same pills had been lying on Robbie Roberts's kitchen table. Coincidence?

Jenny picked up one or two bottles of tablets and looked at the chemist's label gummed to the front. All the medicines had been supplied by Archie Hooper, the chemist opposite the post office.

GLENINVER'S ONLY CHEMIST was busy, with a little queue of sufferers waiting patiently for Archie Hooper to dispense their prescriptions.

"Can I help you?" asked the young assistant as Jenny stepped up to the counter.

"May I speak to Mr. Hooper, please? It's . . . it's a private matter." The girl disappeared behind a screen, and Jenny heard the low murmur of voices. Then a tall, bearded man in his mid-forties came round the screen. It was a small town and Jenny knew him by sight.

"It's Jenny Macrae, isn't it?" he asked pleasantly.

"That's right, yes."

"Thought so. What can I do for you?"

In answer, Jenny took out the emerald green packet of Cardocol pills. "D'you think you could tell me what these are for?"

Archie Hooper picked up the packet of pills and turned it over. He frowned. "No, I can't. Not offhand. They look like some sort of anti-hypertensive. Why?"

"You mean you don't prescribe them?"

"Doctors do the prescribing, Miss Macrae."

"But if a doctor prescribes this Cardocol . . . you mean to say you don't stock it?"

The chemist shook his head. "No."

"Oh," Jenny said, nonplussed. "I assumed you did. This . . . this person I know gets all her pills and things from here. Regularly."

"Well, she didn't get these, I can promise you. Officially, I've never even seen them before."

"But if she—wait a minute. What d'you mean, 'officially'?"

The chemist shrugged.

"Cardocol. They're the new heart drug HPL's been burning the midnight oil over, these last few months. I'm almost sure they're not yet listed. Hang on a second." He went back behind the screen, returned with the current issue of MIMS, the Monthly Index of Medical Specialties, and began leafing through the pages. Presently he closed the book with a snap. "Nothing. Cardocol's not listed."

"Could my friend have bought them in some other chemist's?"

An emphatic shake of the head. "No. We all carry the same drugs, order from the same stock lists. Perhaps you'd better tell me who's taking them, eh?"

. "I'd . . . er . . . I'd rather not, if you don't mind," Jenny replied, without really knowing why, knowing only that she needed time to think. "Not just now, anyway. Thanks for your help." And she picked up Mrs. Proctor's pills and turned for the door, her mind whirling.

HELEN HIGHCROFT WAS ON HER WAY home again. A little earlier she had taken a taxi to the police station, where she had signed for her husband's car keys. Then she had gone to the railway station, to find their Volvo neatly parked at the end of the station forecourt. She had approached the car almost with caution, as though there might even now be some note or letter propped against the dashboard to tell her where she had failed as a wife and companion. Instead there was nothing, and she had slipped behind the wheel to weep bitter tears, for that, in a way, had wounded deepest of all.

Now Helen was about to drive past their local garage on the way home. She glanced down automatically at the fuel gauge and saw that the needle was hovering around empty. She waited for a break in the traffic and turned in across the forecourt. She waited until the garage hand had filled the tank and then went over to the office to sign for the petrol on their monthly account. As she did so, a blue-overalled mechanic hurried from the workshops.

"Afternoon, Mrs. Highcroft—almost given you up. If you've the key handy I'll drive it round myself."

She looked up, puzzled. "I'm sorry?"

"The keys, Mrs. Highcroft, the keys to the Volvo. I'll drive it round myself. To the service bay. Save you the trouble."

She shook her head. "I'm sorry, Billy—I haven't the faintest idea what you're talking about."

"The service, Mrs. Highcroft," explained Billy patiently. "The twenty-thousand service." He took a clipboard from a hook behind the counter and ran a dirty thumbnail down the list of vehicle registration numbers. "There you are: XOD 62X. Mind you, you've cut it pretty fine. Any later and I couldn't promise we'd have the job finished today."

"But I didn't book the car in for a service."

"Didn't he tell you? Och, he's always doing that. Your husband—the professor. Came in the day before yesterday on his way to work."

Helen gripped him by the arm. "You're *sure?*"

The mechanic nodded. "Aye, I'm sure, right enough. I wrote it down myself." For the first time he noticed her pale face. "Is there anything wrong, Mrs. Highcroft?"

Why would Malcolm bother to book the Volvo in for a service if he knew he was going to abandon the car at the station less than twelve hours later? *Why?*

"Mrs. Highcroft. . . ?"

She didn't hear him.

JENNY TOOK HER MUG OF COFFEE through from the kitchen and sat down. With nothing else to do, no appointments to keep, she had taken the phone off the hook and sat back to try to piece together the fragments of fact that skated elusively around her mind. There was something there, she was sure of it: something that might link Jamie's death, the pills she had found on Robbie Roberts's kitchen table and Mrs. Proctor's collapse upstairs. Those pills somehow were the key. Pills that had been manufactured by Highland Pharmaceuticals Limited, but which had yet to be released to the local chemist.

The doorbell rang.

Jenny went down the hall. "Who is it?" she called warily.

"Miss Macrae?" A man's voice, vaguely familiar. "It's Flight Sergeant Tony Lockhart. From RAF Glenhaddon. We met last night."

The winchman. The man who had tried to save Jamie, done his best to put her at ease before all those hostile faces started staring in the pub. She took the chain off the door and slipped up the catch.

"Sorry. I don't usually shout at people through the door like that. It's just that I've been a bit . . . you know . . . pestered."

Tony nodded and held up a copy of a morning paper.

"They got the address right, at least. I . . . ah . . . I was just passing, so I thought I'd call in and apologize. For what happened in the pub, I mean. You don't want to pay any attention to old George back there. Nobody else does. Especially when he's had a skinful."

"That's very kind of you, Flight Sergeant, but I'm sorry I made such a fool of myself, running off like that. Thank you for calling." She began to close the door.

"Whoa! Wait a minute, will you? What's the matter?"

"Nothing. It's just that I don't need your pity. I made a mistake, the boy died, and I'm going to pay for it, all right? The fiscal came round this afternoon and took a statement."

"Look, I didn't come here to offer pity. I . . . I just thought you got a raw deal, that's all. If you want me to leave—fine. I'm on my way. Sorry I troubled you." Tony turned on his heel.

Jenny watched his retreating back. "Flight Sergeant!" He stopped. "I'm sorry. I didn't mean to bite your head off."

"That's OK," he said gruffly.

"Look . . . would you like to come in? I've just made some coffee. Peace offering?"

Tony hesitated. "Fresh or instant?"

"Instant."

He smiled. "You're on." He came back up the garden path. "Oh, the name's Tony, all right?"

RIDLEY PULLED IN TO THE SIDE of the road and turned off the engine. He had just driven slowly past Douglas Parsons's neat home. One quick glance had confirmed what the estate agents' map had told him: there was no garage adjacent to the property itself. It would be found, he suspected, behind the row of identical semidetached properties, in a special service area.

He followed the slip road round to the back. It was as he had imagined: twelve identical, neatly numbered steel-doored garages. The area appeared to be deserted. Very quiet and deserted. Which made his task that much easier.

Two minutes more and Ridley was driving away as anonymously as he had arrived, his reconnaissance completed. All that remained now was the final phase of the operation: the execution.

CHAPTER **12**

Jenny glanced up at the clock on the mantelpiece and saw with surprise that almost fifty minutes had slipped by since Tony Lockhart had accepted her invitation to coffee. He was sitting opposite her, both hands cupped round his mug, describing how he had tried to revive Jamie as they were winched up into the helicopter. Jenny closed her eyes for a moment, seeing it all so vividly. When she looked up she saw that Tony too had a faraway look in his eyes. "I'm sorry," she apologized. "I shouldn't have asked you to relive it. I just . . . needed to know. Do you mind talking about it? When it's all over, I mean?"

The question took Tony by surprise. With Maureen, his wife, he had minded intensely—it had been a major source of friction between them. But here, now, talking to this woman . . .

"No, I don't mind," he admitted.

"I suppose you just get used to it?"

Tony shook his head slowly. "Used to it? Can't say I do, no."

"Why do you do it? Search and rescue work, I mean?"

"Because I love it. Because it's my life," Tony admitted simply. "Show me any other sort of work with half the same job satisfaction and I'll jack this lot in tomorrow." There was a brief silence.

"When you went out to Robbie's boat, did you see anything that might have caused the fire?"

Tony shrugged. "Could have been anything. The boat was almost awash when we got there."

"And Robbie? You said at the hospital that he'd died before you got to him? What happened to him?"

Tony looked at her doubtfully. "Well, he wasn't a very pretty sight. He'd been badly burned. Face and neck, mostly. It looked as though he'd fallen into the flames."

"But how would anyone do that? Fall into the flames?"

"God knows. Perhaps the boat rolled and he slipped."

Jenny shook her head. "Robbie had been working with that boat of his for years. Besides, there wasn't any swell. It was a flat calm. Just . . . just a minute!" She hunched forward excitedly. "The burns would have to come *before* he drowned, yes? Otherwise the water would have quenched the flames." Tony nodded. "And for Robbie to be badly burned," continued Jenny slowly, feeling her way, "he'd . . . he'd have to be lying there, wouldn't he? In the bottom of the boat."

"I suppose so, yes."

"Could he . . . What I mean is: if for some reason he had been unconscious first, and had *then* fallen into the flames, that would account for those burns, wouldn't it?"

Tony thought for a moment. "Yes . . . yes, that would have done it."

Jenny picked up the packet of Cardocol pills from a side table and held it out. "Ever seen these before?" she asked.

Twenty minutes later, she was on her way to see Mrs. Proctor in hospital. And by then it seemed perfectly natural that Tony should go with her.

THE NURSE PAUSED OUTSIDE the door of one of the smaller wards. "She's in here," she said. "But she's still very weak, so please keep your visit brief. And preferably, if only one of you . . ."

Tony nodded. "It's OK. I'll wait here."

Jenny opened the door and slipped inside. Mrs. Proctor was lying back against her pillows. She looked shrunken and frail.

Jenny bent forward. "Mrs. Proctor, can you hear me? It's Jenny—Jenny Macrae." The eyelids fluttered open, a ghost of a smile touched the dry lips, and a hand moved slowly across the sheets towards her. Jenny pressed it tightly and lifted the flowers she had brought. "I've brought you these." There was a tiny nod. Jenny sat down beside her. "How're you feeling?"

"T . . . tired," the old woman whispered.

"You're going to be all right, understand? You're in good hands. I've just spoken to the nurse." Jenny paused, and then squeezed the old lady's hand once more. "You had another of your falls, didn't you? Do you remember what happened? Do you remember getting out of bed?" A slow shake of the head. Jenny took out the Cardocol pills and held them up. "Did you take one of these this morning?"

"After . . . breakfast."

"Where did you get them, Mrs. Proctor? Who gave them to you?"

The eyelids fluttered open again. "Doctor . . . gave them to me," she whispered.

"No, no, Mrs. Proctor—which *chemist*? Can you remember?"

"Doctor . . . Doctor Erskine," she insisted weakly.

"GOODNIGHT, DARLINGS. And try not to worry." Helen Highcroft stood at the door of Mark's and Simon's bedroom, her hand on the light switch, and looked back at the two dark shapes beneath the covers.

"Goodnight," answered Mark, a small, drowsy voice from the corner. A pause, then, "Mummy? He will be coming home, won't he?"

"I . . . I expect so, darling. We'll just have to wait and see, won't we?" she tried, with as much lightness as she could muster. "Now then, off to sleep, the pair of you." She pulled the door closed and went downstairs to pour herself a stiff drink and sit down heavily in an armchair.

A little later her glass was empty. She helped herself to another. Then she took down the pile of photograph albums from the shelf by the window, returned to her chair and began leafing through them. As though by flicking through that testimony to past happiness she might find some clue to what had gone wrong with the present.

The photographs had all been taken quite recently: there was Mark at Cubs' camp, and Sarah proudly holding up the drama cup she had won at the end of spring term, and a Polaroid of Malcolm at the office Christmas party, sitting at his desk surrounded by a cluster of colleagues. Helen gazed sightlessly at the photograph as she felt all the tiredness and unhappiness well up inside her. One minute everything was fine and there didn't appear to be a cloud on the horizon, the next, it was as if— she sat up suddenly and picked up the Polaroid again. The window, the window in Malcolm's office. It had a blind, not curtains.

A blind, not curtains.

Malcolm hadn't changed offices in the past year, she was sure. Yet the office Jackman had taken her to earlier that morning had curtains, she was certain. He'd drawn them as they went in. Hadn't he?

Helen leaned back in the armchair and closed her eyes, conscious of a sudden inner stillness that seemed to cut away some of the fog of confusion and despair that had swirled about her for so long. Then she remembered Billy, the mechanic at the garage, insisting that Malcolm had booked the car in for a service less than twelve hours before he disappeared—and suddenly she wasn't sure of anything any more. Nothing beyond a tiny, gnawing suspicion.

ON THE SECOND FLOOR of the Seaview Hotel, on the hilly outskirts of Gleninver, Ridley finished his solitary meal and looked at his watch. Parsons would be coming off duty soon. It was time to get ready.

He rose, lifted his suitcase from beneath the bed, unlocked it, took out a plastic bag and reached inside. Slowly, one by one, he placed the items he would need in a straight line on the bedspread. Harmless in themselves, they were, collectively, the tools of the trade.

DOUGLAS PARSONS PUSHED through the double glass doors and stepped gratefully into the cool night air. It always took him a few minutes to rejoin the human race after leaving the laboratory, to brush all thoughts of work from his mind before starting the drive home. He recalled his ultimatum to Jackman. He sighed and slid behind the wheel. Well, he had done all he could and now he felt better for it. He drove home looking forward to bed, to sleep. It was a clear, dry night and there was little traffic on the road back into Gleninver. Shortly after eleven twenty, Parsons halted outside his garage. He got out, sent the garage door rolling up and back, and then drove forward, to stop the car and sit back for a moment, savouring the silence. Suddenly, the driver's door was wrenched open. "Mr. Douglas Parsons?" asked a quiet voice.

"Yes? Who are you? What do you want?"

"I wonder if I might have a word?" The interior light had gone on as the door opened: Parsons could see the gleam of the blade quite clearly.

"PLEASE, JUST TELL ME. Where are we going?" Douglas Parsons begged again, with a tremor of fear in his voice. Ridley smiled grimly to himself in the darkness of the moving car. "Nearly there," he soothed, the knife a dull gleam on his lap as they drove away from Gleninver towards the seclusion of the open countryside.

"Look—whoever you are. If it's . . . if it's money you want . . ." Parsons fumbled in his jacket and took out his wallet. "Here, take it. That's all I have on me."

Ridley plucked the wallet from his hand, glanced briefly at its contents and slipped it into his own pocket. Parsons seemed to take that as some sort of agreement. He sighed with relief. "Now, please put that knife away and let me turn this car round."

Ridley laughed quietly. It was a chilling, unnerving sound, devoid of humour or feeling of any kind.

"Why . . . why are you laughing?" asked Parsons tremulously, the fear drying his mouth so that he was unable to swallow. This nightmare wasn't real; it wasn't happening to him, it couldn't be . . .

Ridley didn't bother to answer. Another minute passed in silence, then, "Slow down," he ordered. "There's a turning coming up on your left. A track. There! Turn down there."

"Where are you—?"

"Do it!"

The words lashed out, and Parsons braked and turned off the road. They bumped slowly along an overgrown track, their headlights carving a swathe of brilliance through the thick summer woodland. Ridley had chosen the track with care: the nearest cottage was half a mile away and, once past the bend in the track, they would be invisible from the road.

"Right—this'll do. Stop here." Parsons obeyed. "Turn off the engine. Lights too." The only sound was Parsons's frightened breathing in the darkness. Ridley turned on the interior light.

"What are you going to do?" Parsons managed fearfully. "Why have you brought me here?" More silence. And with it, a chilling glimmer of realization. "It's not . . . not just the money, is it?"

Ridley slowly shook his head. "Jackman has hired me to kill you."

The words didn't register, not at first. When they did, Parsons sagged sideways against the door, his face putty-grey. "To *kill* me? But that's . . . that's ridiculous! Jackman would never get away with . . . with murder! There must be some mistake!"

"No mistake." Ridley moved closer.

"Wait! Please! Listen to me!" beseeched Parsons. "It's because of Highcroft, isn't it? Because I saw Highcroft die?"

"You tried to apply pressure." Ridley leaned suddenly closer, knife raised. "Listen to me. You don't have to die. Do what I tell you, instantly and without question, and you will live. Do you understand?"

Parsons found his voice at last. "I . . . I understand."

Ridley nodded. "You are to stay exactly where you are. Do not move. Try to get out, and I will kill you. Do you understand that?"

"Yes," Parsons whispered, the word almost a croak.

"Hands on the steering wheel. Keep them there."

Parsons hurried to do what he was told as Ridley reached across and removed the keys from the ignition. Getting out, he moved to the rear door, reached inside the plastic carrier bag lying on the back seat and took out a pair of motorcycle gauntlets and a roll of thick carpet tape. He moved round to the driver's door, pulled it open and held the gauntlets out. "Put them on!" he ordered. "Hands together."

Parsons did as he was told, hypnotized by the man's menace. Ridley gripped both of Parsons's wrists with one lean hand and began binding the carpet tape around them until they were trussed tightly together. Then he passed the roll of tape through the centre of the steering wheel and round the steering column, forcing Parsons forward. He worked on swiftly, then moved back to the rear of the car, reached inside his plastic bag and returned with a towel, which he wrapped round Parsons's ankles. He bound more tape over the towel until ankles too were bound securely, both to one another and to the steering column above.

"Please . . ." Parsons begged with a terrible earnestness, as he sensed, through a rising tide of panic, that somehow he had been fatally duped. "Please. I . . . I beg you. You promised you'd let me live if—" He got no further, for Ridley jammed a napkin into his mouth. Then he stepped back and studied his victim with cold, flat eyes. "I know," he said softly. "I lied."

Parsons began to scream—a weird, subhuman sound of terror from somewhere deep down in his throat. Ridley watched him a moment longer and then hurried round to the rear of the car.

He took a length of garden hosepipe and another large towel from the back seat, jammed one end of the hosepipe into the exhaust and trailed the rest round to the front of the car. Opening the nearside front passenger window, he draped the hosepipe inside, closed the door carefully and got into the back of the car. Reaching forward, he wound up the front window until the hosepipe was trapped against the top of the door, and then pushed the towel into the gap that was left, forming an airtight seal round the pipe.

Ridley checked each of the other windows in turn and then returned to the driver's door. He took the ignition key out of his pocket, slipped it into the ignition and turned it. The engine fired and the first fumes of carbon monoxide began to fill the car.

Ridley smoothed Parsons's hair over his forehead, patted his cheek in farewell, closed the door firmly and moved away. He sat quietly on a flat stone, listening to the hoot of an owl in the distance and the soft, ominous bubbling of the exhaust closer to hand.

At last the engine of Parsons's car faltered and cut out.

Ridley rose to his feet and walked slowly forward. He tugged open the driver's door and stepped back as the gas swirled out into the air.

Parsons was slumped sideways across the wheel. No movement. Nothing.

When he was quite satisfied that Parsons was dead, Ridley tugged the napkin out of his mouth and sliced through the bands of carpet tape binding his wrists and ankles together. Taking the motorcycle gauntlets off the hands, he inspected the wrists carefully and saw that, as he had intended, the thick leather padding on the deep cuffs had prevented the tape sawing into raw flesh as Parsons had struggled desperately to free himself. Ridley looked at the ankles and then rose to his feet, well satisfied: there was not the slightest mark anywhere that might cause a coroner familiar with suicide by carbon-monoxide poisoning to raise so much as an eyebrow.

Thrusting tape, gauntlets, napkin and towel into his plastic bag, Ridley arranged Parsons's body carefully behind the wheel, started the engine again and closed the door. As the car began to fill once more with carbon monoxide, he painstakingly erased every trace of his presence in the lane and then set off westwards through the woods. With luck, he would be back in his motel bedroom well before dawn.

CHAPTER 13

"Miss Macrae?" Jenny glanced up from the dog-eared copy of *Country Life* she had been reading. It was the next morning and she was sitting in Dr. Erskine's old-fashioned surgery behind Gleninver's Market Hall Square. "Dr. Erskine will see you now, Miss Macrae," said the receptionist.

Jenny walked down the corridor and knocked on the doctor's door.

"Come along in!" Dr. Erskine was sitting behind his rolltop desk, writing something. Now he looked up and laid his pen aside, and a genial smile creased his craggy face. "Ah, if it isn't Jenny, my very favourite patient. Sit you down, lassie, sit you down."

Jenny smiled. "Bet you say that to all the girls, you old rogue."

His eyes twinkled merrily. "Only to those under eighty-five. So, Jenny lass: how're you keeping? I was sorry to see the back of that doctor friend of yours, Danny . . . what was the man's name, now?"

"Kindersley—Danny Kindersley. Yes, I was too," Jenny admitted. Dr. Erskine nodded, watching her shrewdly.

"I read about what happened in the papers," he said. "Oh, I'm not going to go on about it"—he held up a hand—"but I'm very, very sorry for you, Jenny—and I'd just maybe add this: not all of us here are as ready as some to attribute blame. You've still got a lot of friends here, lass—" He cleared his throat. "Now then, that receptionist of mine tells me you wanted to see me about a personal matter. Am I right in thinking it's got something to do with what happened out in the bay?"

"It's about that, yes. It's also about a couple of your patients."

"My patients? Well now . . . what passes between a doctor and those who come to see him is strictly confidential. But you must have a reason for asking. Who are they, anyway?"

"One's Mrs. Proctor—you know, my landlady. She went into hospital yesterday. The other is a man called Roberts. Robbie Roberts."

Dr. Erskine sighed. "The man in the boat with the wee boy?"

Jenny nodded, took out Mrs. Proctor's Cardocol pills and leaned forward. "Both Robbie and Mrs. Proctor were taking these," she said. "I went down to Archie Hooper's, here in the town, but he's never filled a prescription for Cardocol. In fact, he's never even *seen* pills like these before." She paused. "Then, when I saw Mrs. Proctor in hospital yesterday she told me she got the pills from you. Is that right?"

There was a silence while Dr. Erskine studied the green packet carefully, as though he too was seeing it for the first time. "She . . . she must have been mistaken," he muttered, his eyes sliding away.

HAMISH OWEN WAS IN THE FRONT OFFICE at Gleninver police station, doing his routine morning call. There had been one or two incidents during the night, but nothing worth more than a paragraph or two on the front page. "Anything else?" he asked, leaning across the counter and twisting round to get a better look at the incident book.

Sergeant McInnes shook his head. "That's your lot for today, Hamish."

"What about that man who went missing? The one who worked at Highland Pharmaceuticals? Anything more on that?"

The sergeant scratched a bare arm and shook his head again. "Professor Highcroft, you mean? He hasn't turned up. But you're wasting your time there. It's a domestic—between him"—he jerked a thumb to one side—"and her."

"You mean he just walked out on his wife?" Hamish asked.

"Aye, that's right. Just like that." He leaned forward. "And when that happens, we stay right out of it. You'd be well advised to do the same."

"Thanks for the advice." Hamish shut his notebook. "Right then. See you tomorrow."

"I'll be looking forward to it," replied Sergeant McInnes drily.

Hamish was about to push through the swing doors into the street when a young PC in shirtsleeves came through into the main office and reached for the incident book. Something about his air of urgent preoccupation made Hamish pause and turn back. "Morning," he tried, conversationally. "Anything interesting?"

The policeman glanced up.

"Press. *Gleninver Times.*" Like it was *Newsweek* or the *Sunday Times.*

Surprisingly, the policeman nodded. "Might have something for you, as it happens. Bloke's gone and gassed himself in a car a few miles outside town. Couple of campers found him an hour or so back."

Hamish had his notebook out in a flash. "Can you . . . can you tell me the man's name?" he asked eagerly, pencil poised.

"Don't see why not," shrugged the policeman. He traced a finger across the form. "Parsons. Douglas Walter Parsons."

IN THE MAIN RECEPTION AREA at Highland Pharmaceuticals, Helen Highcroft was sitting alone, glancing at her watch impatiently.

She had lain awake most of the night. What with the photograph she had found at the back of the family album, and the business of the service for the Volvo . . . Her frustration had crystallized into a decision to confront Jackman with her suspicions, stupid and groundless though they might prove to be. Something was wrong, deeply wrong, she was sure of it. Something was going on—here, in the company. Something that linked her husband's disappearance to that office not fifty yards from where she was waiting. An office that had curtains, not blinds.

She had been waiting for Jackman for almost forty minutes. I'll give him just five more minutes, she told herself angrily, and not a moment longer. She twisted round as the glass doors behind her sighed back and a young woman entered the building and walked up to the reception desk.

Helen looked round her casually. Apart from two painters working over in a corner, the reception area was empty. A quick glance at the receptionist and she rose to her feet and moved swiftly towards the swing doors leading to the corridor Jackman had showed her earlier. The corridor and the office that was supposed to be Malcolm's . . .

"And your name?" asked the receptionist politely, cradling the phone against an immaculate shoulder as she dialled a number.

"Jenny Macrae."

The receptionist nodded. "Oh, Richard? Carole here, in reception. I wonder if you could help me? There's a Miss Jenny Macrae down here who'd very much like to talk to someone about one of our products. No, no, I don't think so. Hang on a moment and I'll just ask." She covered the mouthpiece with her hand. "You're not with any particular firm are you?" Jenny shook her head, and the girl spoke into the telephone once more. "No, she's not. She says she'd just like some advice, that's all. Yes. Yes . . . yes, that's what I thought. No . . . about Cardocol." She listened a moment longer and then replaced the receiver. "Someone will be down to see you in a moment. Oh—" She looked round and frowned. Where had that other woman disappeared to, that Mrs. Highcroft?

Helen turned down the empty corridor. This was the door. She hesitated, for the card-holder which had displayed Malcolm's name was now empty. She tried the handle, the door opened, and she slipped inside and looked round. Yes, this was it, quite definitely—and she had been right. This office did have curtains.

The desk was bare now and there was no sign of either her husband's diary or the framed photograph that had been there before. She opened each drawer of the desk. Empty. Not a letter, not a file nor a paperclip in sight. Nothing. She looked around the walls. They too were bare. The place looked as if it had never been used.

She sat down on the edge of the desk and tried to work out what it all meant. Surely they wouldn't have cleared out Malcolm's desk already? He was too senior to be just . . . written off, wasn't he? Helen twisted the telephone idly towards her, and then she froze. The extension number was different. If she wanted to call Malcolm at work she asked for extension 644. This was extension 476.

Helen felt the walls of the little office begin to close in around her and suddenly she felt very frightened. Something terrible had happened to Malcolm, she knew it.

She eased the door open a few inches, stepped out into the corridor and closed the door softly behind her. As she walked back towards the main entrance, the receptionist came hurrying towards her. "Mrs. Highcroft, please!" she called. "I've been looking everywhere for you! This area is out of bounds to visitors. Didn't you see the signs? Please come with me." They went back through the swing doors. "Oh, by the way, Mr. Jackman phoned down. He sends his apologies but he's been called to a meeting."

Helen sighed. "All right, then, I'll wait."

"He . . . er . . . he told me to tell you he'll be tied up most of the day. He won't be able to see you at all. I'm sorry."

"What, not at all? Not even for five minutes?" Helen demanded incredulously, her raised voice drawing the attention of both the painters and the young woman sitting waiting nearby.

"I'm afraid not. But if you'd care to make an appointment . . ."

"Where is Mr. Jackman's office?" Helen demanded.

The girl looked up, startled. "On the . . . on the first floor. But you can't go up there, Mrs. Highcroft! Visitors are not permitted onto the working levels! Now I'm sure if you—"

"A visitor? Is that all I am now? Well, let me tell you something. For the last three and a half years, my husband has worked all the hours God sent to get Cardocol onto the market on schedule, and now, just before the launch, he's disappeared—vanished! Something terrible's happened to him, only I . . . I can't find out what it is." The words broke off into a choking sob and Helen reached for her handkerchief.

"Now then, what's all this?"

The receptionist turned with relief towards the comforting bulk of the

74

security guard, summoned by the buzz of the alarm under her desk.

"Oh, George—perhaps you'd help Mrs. Highcroft. She's . . . very distressed. She's had to wait almost an hour to see Mr. Jackman. Unfortunately he's been called away, and although he's sent his apologies she's really become . . . well, as you can see . . ."

The security guard put a well-meaning arm around Helen's shoulders. "There now, Mrs. Highcroft—don't fret. You just come along with me."

With a great effort of will, Helen stopped the tears. She saw that it was hopeless. Nothing she could say or do would achieve anything. It was bad enough that she was making a spectacle of herself in the foyer of Highland Pharmaceuticals. Unprotesting, she allowed herself to be guided out into the sunshine, to her car. She felt beaten, exhausted, as she bent down to unlock the door.

"Mrs. Highcroft?" She turned suddenly, for she had not heard the footsteps running lightly up behind her. It was the young woman who had been sitting alone in HPL's reception area a few minutes earlier.

"Yes?" she acknowledged warily.

"I'm sorry to trouble you, but I couldn't help hearing what you were saying just now about your husband and his work with Cardocol. I . . . I wonder if I could talk to you somewhere for a few minutes?" She held out a slim hand. "My name's Jenny. Jenny Macrae."

IN HIS OFFICE on the first floor of the administrative building, Jackman was standing by the window, waiting for Ridley to finish talking on the phone to Baxter in London. He had thus been able to watch from above as Helen Highcroft was escorted from the building by the security guard. Then he frowned, as another woman suddenly hurried after her. They spoke for a few minutes and then separated. The younger of the two walked across to a yellow Citroën Dyane and reversed quickly out of her parking space, and the two cars followed one another slowly down the approach road.

Ridley was still on the phone to London. Jackman crossed the room to another telephone. "Who was that who just left the building after Mrs. Highcroft, Carole? Young woman, twenty-five, thirty, dark hair?"

"Miss Jennifer Macrae, Mr. Jackman," the receptionist answered promptly. "She came in about ten minutes ago, asking to speak to somebody about Cardocol. Richard Connor was coming down to see her, then she . . . well . . . she just left."

Jackman rang off, dialled again, and asked the security guard for the registration number of the yellow Citroën that was just leaving. The number had been logged on entry as a matter of company policy. He replaced the receiver and sat forward over his notepad, joining the name "Jenny Macrae" to her car number inside a pencilled box. He drummed his pencil absently against the notepad. Perhaps it was nothing. But just possibly it might be trouble. He was still worrying when Ridley put down the phone.

"I take it London is satisfied?" Jackman asked.

"About Parsons? Oh yes, I think so." Ridley picked up a sheet of paper and glanced at the notes he had made. "I understand it was you who vouched for Steevenson? To Baxter?"

"That's right, yes. I did."

"You told Baxter he could be trusted. You told Baxter he would be discreet." It was almost an accusation.

"What the hell are you driving at?"

Ridley smiled. "I did a little investigating of my own this morning, before coming here." He glanced down at his notes. "Your Mr. Steevenson's just put a fifteen hundred pound cash deposit on a BMW." He looked up reproachfully with those cold, dead eyes. "Now, Mr. Jackman, I ask you: you'd hardly call that discreet, would you?"

"I'll have a word with him."

Ridley shook his head slowly. "Not to worry, Mr. Jackman. Baxter wants *me* to take care of it."

CHAPTER 14

"More tea?"

"Mmm, thanks."

Jenny was in Helen Highcroft's kitchen. It was a large, cheerful room; a room at odds with the haunted, careworn face of the woman who pushed the teacup across the table towards her.

They had been sitting talking quietly together for perhaps forty minutes. Slowly, an initial wariness had given way to mutual liking and trust as they began to exchange confidences. On the drive home from Highland Pharmaceuticals, Helen had told herself that she would give away nothing to the woman who had approached her so unexpectedly in the car park. For all she knew Jenny might have been planted by Jackman to sound out her suspicions, find out what she knew.

And yet, once they had begun to talk, such caution had become unnecessary. For Jenny Macrae wasn't a plant, she couldn't be. There was too much honesty, too much pain and fresh suffering in her face as she told Helen about the fire and what had followed. Soon Helen found herself telling Jenny about the photograph of Malcolm at the office party, about the Volvo, about the anonymous, late-night telephone call telling her that Malcolm was dead, and about the empty office with the wrong extension number and the curtains.

"What did your husband actually *do* at HPL?" Jenny asked, as she tried to decide whether to tell Helen about the pills Robbie and Mrs.

Proctor had taken, and about her own suspicions concerning Cardocol. "I heard you say to that girl in reception that your husband spent the last three years working on Cardocol, is that right?"

Helen nodded. "That's right, yes. We . . . we moved here when Sarah was ten. That's three and a half years ago. Malcolm was involved in the project right from the start."

Jenny opened her handbag, took out Mrs. Proctor's pills and placed them on the table. "With these, you mean?"

Helen picked up the emerald green packet, saw the name and nodded abstractedly. "Yes."

Jenny leaned forward. "What exactly is Cardocol?"

"It's some kind of heart drug. For people with high blood pressure. It's very new. It's not even on the market yet." Helen smiled. "Where have you been living these last few weeks? That's what all the fuss is about up at HPL. Those painters and gardeners all over the place." She traced the shape of a sign in the air. "The Grand Launching." She picked up Mrs. Proctor's pills and studied them. "So where did you get these?" she asked. "If you don't mind me asking."

Jenny paused. "It's a little complicated," she said finally, and launched into her story, telling Helen about the pills Mrs. Roberts had shown her after Robbie's death, and then about Mrs. Proctor's collapse. She told about her visit to the hospital, and about Dr. Erskine's denial that he had ever given Cardocol to the old lady. "But he *must* have given her the pills, don't you see? Mrs. Proctor would never have invented something like that, not in her condition." She leaned forward. "Could something have gone wrong—with the drug, I mean? What if . . . what if your husband found out something? What if he . . . I don't know . . . How important is Cardocol? To the company?"

"It's vital," Helen replied immediately. "It's their flagship." She shook her head impatiently. "But that doesn't mean they'd get rid of Malcolm to cover up a mistake! If something was wrong, better to find out about it now, invent some excuse for postponing the launch and put things right, rather than risk a scandal of that magnitude. Think of the publicity—they'd go out of business overnight!"

Jenny nodded. She had felt that all along. "You're right. Of course they wouldn't do that." She paused, and then added slowly, "But what other possible explanation is there? Why else would this man Jackman go to such lengths to mislead you, if there wasn't something to hide?"

"I don't know," Helen answered, suddenly close to tears.

There was an awkward silence. Then Jenny glanced round. "D'you think I could use your telephone for a minute, please?"

Helen nodded.

"I thought I'd try Dr. Erskine again," Jenny explained. "I've just had an idea." She dialled the surgery number and waited. "Dr. Erskine,

77

please. It's Jenny Macrae. I came to see him earlier this morning." She listened for several seconds, then: "Oh. Oh, I see. Well, not to worry. D'you have any idea when he'll be back? He will? Grand. I'll call again then." She replaced the receiver as Helen twisted round.

"No luck?"

Jenny returned to the table and sat down. "He's at the hospital."

IT WAS VERY QUIET in the medical ward, but even so, Dr. Erskine had to lean down to catch what she was saying.

"I'm not . . . not going to die, am I, Doctor?" Mrs. Proctor whispered.

Dr. Erskine smiled that craggy smile of his and patted the thin hand reassuringly.

"No, no, Mrs. Proctor, you're not going to die. You'll be out of here in no time, no time at all, so don't you worry. A fall, a faint, a wee bang on the head—it's all been a bit of a shock to the system. But don't you worry: you'll soon be as right as rain." He rose from her bedside and patted her hand again. "Now then—you're to get plenty of sleep, d'you hear? I'll look in on you again just as soon as you get home. Goodbye for now, Mrs. Proctor." He turned towards the door.

"Doctor?" she called faintly. "Thank you. For everything." Dr. Erskine nodded and slipped out into the corridor. He closed the door softly, his smile of professional reassurance replaced now by a frown of concern. He asked where he could find the duty houseman, for by now he was a very worried man.

STEEVENSON WAS SITTING in Jackman's office. An Ordnance Survey map of the area was unfolded across the desk between them, and Jackman was leaning forward, tapping a pencil against the little village of Dalrean, eleven miles away along the coast. "He'll be waiting for you there," said Jackman.

"Seems a helluva long way to go just for a chat," Steevenson observed doubtfully. "Why couldn't I meet him here?"

"With Professor Highcroft's disappearance still fresh in everyone's minds, Mr. Baxter thought it would be politic if he steered clear of the plant for a few weeks. Just in case someone did put two and two together."

"Did he say what it was about?" queried Steevenson.

Jackman smiled a confident smile.

"You acquitted yourself well the other night," he confided. "I said as much in my report to London. When Baxter read it he felt you might be suitable for involvement in another similar project further south. There could well be a substantial salary increase." Jackman tapped the map again with the tip of his pencil. "The sooner you meet him, the sooner you'll hear what he has in mind, from the horse's mouth, so to speak."

Steevenson glanced at his watch. "Half past eleven, did you say?"

Jackman nodded. "That's right, yes. He'll be in a white Rover, in the car park behind a pub called 'The Clansman'. Oh—" He opened a drawer and took out a set of car keys. "You can take one of the reps' cars parked outside." He tossed the keys across to Steevenson and nodded pleasantly, signalling that the meeting was over.

Steevenson made for the door. "Just one more thing." Steevenson turned. "You haven't spoken to Douglas Parsons recently, have you?"

"Parsons? No," shrugged Steevenson, a hand on the doorknob. "Not since the night of the accident."

Jackman looked satisfied. "Right, then. That will be all." He leaned forward over the papers that littered his desk.

"Oh—Mr. Jackman?"

Jackman glanced up. "Yes?"

"Thank you . . . you know . . . for putting in the word."

Jackman smiled. "Not at all."

Later, from his window, Jackman watched Steevenson drive out of sight down the approach road. He dialled an outside number. The call was answered immediately. "He's just left," Jackman reported. "Travelling in a dark blue Vauxhall Cavalier, registration number DRX 652Y. Should be on the coast road in about twenty minutes."

The line went dead and Jackman replaced the receiver slowly. It should never have got as far as this, he thought, with the first faint stirrings of panic. Never.

FIFTEEN MINUTES LATER, the dark blue Vauxhall Cavalier began winding up the coast road that twisted along the sheer cliffs towards Dalrean. Steevenson made good time as he negotiated the sharp bends and climbed slowly higher, the waters of Loch Linnhe's eastern shoreline, a glittering mosaic of blues, greens and greys, lapping against the tumbled rocks in the sunshine sixty feet below his nearside wheels.

He changed down for another bend, swung tightly into the corner, and had just begun to straighten up when he saw a man running down the middle of the road towards him, jacket flapping in the wind. Steevenson brought the car to a halt and wound down the window.

"What's up?" he called pleasantly, as Ridley drew level.

JENNY BANGED THE DOOR of her flat shut behind her and walked through to her sitting room, deep in thought. She had gone to Helen expecting, if not actual answers, then at least some measure of illumination. Instead, she had driven home more baffled, more confused than ever. She sighed. If only Danny were here; he'd know what to do. At the very least he'd be able to put a fellow doctor's denials into some sort of context.

The thought had no sooner entered her mind than Jenny crossed to the telephone. She remembered what he'd said the night he phoned. *If you want help, all you have to do is call.*

She dialled his number. "Dr. Kindersley, please. It's a personal call."

"Oh. One moment, please."

"Dr. Kindersley."

"Danny? It's . . . it's me."

"Jen! How are you, kid?"

"I'm . . . I'm fine," she managed. "Bearing up under the strain, as they say. Am I calling at a bad time?"

"No. No, of course not."

Jenny hesitated. "I . . . I called because I wanted to ask you something. As a doctor, I mean . . ."

"Private or National Health?" Danny replied, jokingly.

"I . . . it's about a drug. I know it'll probably sound crazy, but have you heard of a new heart drug called Cardocol? It's manufactured up here by Highland Pharmaceuticals."

Danny laughed. "Yes, I've heard of Cardocol. So has every other GP by now, I shouldn't wonder, if he isn't deaf or blind."

"Why's that?"

"The post's been full of the stuff for days—pamphlets, handouts, promotional gimmicks, that sort of thing. There's even a supplement in this week's *British Medical Journal*, now I come to think of it . . . Yes, here we go"—Jenny heard pages being flicked over in the background— " 'Cardocol—A Heartbeat Closer. HPL pushes back the frontiers of preventive medication'. D'you want me to go on?"

Jenny had cradled the telephone against her shoulder and was writing furiously. "What was that? After 'Heartbeat Closer'?"

" 'HPL pushes back the frontiers of preventive medication.' It's just a way of saying they think they've found something new."

"And haven't they?"

Danny thought for a moment. "No. At least, it's unlikely. They're just not big enough. As a useful rule of thumb, the more a medium-sized company like HPL spends on promotion, the less they've got to back it up. Real drug breakthroughs are usually left to the big boys like ICI, Glaxo or Geigy. Without having read the promotional material in any detail, I'd say this looks like just another 'Me-tooer'."

"What on earth's that?"

"A 'Me-tooer'? A variation on a pharmacological theme that's just different enough to skirt round the original patent." Danny paused. "Jen, why your sudden interest in Cardocol?"

Jenny hesitated. "I'm not sure," she admitted finally. "It's just that there's something funny going on up at HPL that involves a missing scientist—" She paused. "Cardocol's not available yet, is it?"

"To GPs, you mean? No, not officially."

"What would you say if I told you I know of two people who were both given Cardocol by the same doctor more than a week ago—and that one of them is now dead and the other is in hospital?"

There was silence for a moment. "Which doctor?"

"Dr. Erskine."

"Down by Market Hall Square?"

"The very same."

"I'd have to say you'd probably got your facts wrong," Danny replied carefully. "Erskine wouldn't prescribe a drug before date of licence. No doctor would."

"That's just my point, Danny—he didn't even bother with a prescription! He just gave them the pills in his surgery!"

"You sure?"

"Pretty sure, yes. Remember Mrs. Proctor? The old woman upstairs? Well, she collapsed yesterday morning and had to be rushed into hospital. When I went to take her some flowers, she insisted she'd been given the pills by Erskine himself. Personally."

"All right. What does Dr. Erskine say?"

"He practically threw me out on my ear and denied giving the pills to anyone. But he was lying, I know he was."

"Why should he do that?"

"Well, wouldn't you? If you'd been caught giving pills to patients before you were supposed to?"

"I might be a bit embarrassed, but I certainly don't think I'd deliberately lie about it," Danny replied. "Who's the other one? This person who's supposed to have died?"

"Robbie Roberts. He'd been given Cardocol too. That's what started me off. His wife told me he'd got the pills from Dr. Erskine."

"Roberts? The old man in the boat?"

"Yes, that's the one."

"But just because this man Roberts may have been given Cardocol doesn't necessarily mean that—"

"But it might, don't you see, Danny? It might! Why else would he suddenly collapse like that? If I could only prove those pills contributed in some way to Robbie's accident, then I . . . then I wouldn't be to blame for Jamie's death, would I? Not entirely."

"No, you wouldn't," Danny agreed cautiously. "Not if you could prove it."

"Well, it's possible, isn't it? For there to be something wrong with the drug?"

"I'd have thought the chances were remote, quite frankly. It's too late in the day, Jenny! All the tests have been done—the surveys, the clinical trials, the—"

"But it's still *possible*, isn't it?" insisted Jenny doggedly. "I mean—look at what happened to Opren, and that other one, Debendox. Everyone thought they were OK, too, until things started to go wrong."

"Yes, that's true," Danny admitted reluctantly. "But . . ."

"But what? Go on."

"I just don't think you should pin your hopes on a miracle, that's all. It's an outside chance, Jen. The odds must be . . . oh . . . a thousand, ten thousand to one."

CHAPTER 15

Tony Lockhart, Dave Bourne and Pete Sleaman were in RESCUE 44 on a training flight across the bay, flying low over the sea. Dave brought them down to thirty feet. "OK, Winchie. Anywhere round here."

Tony reached behind him for a battered metal drum and tossed it out of the door. "Drums" was part of any SAR aircrew's monthly training programme. Toss a metal canister into the sea and try to recover same in the shortest possible time, using a special grappling hook on the end of the cable. The exercise was designed to sharpen pilot/winch-operator cooperation as they ran down onto an object in the sea. Sometimes it went like clockwork. And at other times . . .

Tony leaned out of the door and watched the drum slide past the hook thirty feet below. "Give that man a coconut," he grinned.

"Come right . . . right . . . steady. Height is good. Ten . . . eight . . . six . . ."

"RESCUE 44, RESCUE 44, this is Oban. Immediate." Pete and Tony tensed as, above them, Dave acknowledged, then: "RESCUE 44, this is Oban. We have a report of a vehicle over the cliffs two miles south of Dalrean. Can you respond, over?"

Down in the cabin, Pete was already unfastening his monkey-harness prior to wriggling back to the navigator's seat as Tony began bringing in the winch cable, the drum forgotten.

"Oban, this is RESCUE 44. Responding, over."

"RESCUE 44, this is Oban. Many thanks. That location: two miles south of Dalrean. Picnickers reported seeing something down on the rocks twenty minutes ago. Coastguard mobile at the scene has just confirmed the sighting; it's definitely a car . . ."

"All copied, Oban. We shall be closing from the southwest, over."

Tony hauled the door shut and struggled into bosun's harness even as they flew towards the cliffs and the coast road. He unclipped the first aid backpack from the cabin wall and began adjusting the straps.

"There we are, Boss! See it? Your two o'clock," said Pete.

Tony thrust the Pye pocket phone down the front of his lifevest and hauled back the door. Pete wriggled down into the cabin. The aircraft banked steeply to port and began flying up the coast at two hundred feet as Tony studied the cliffs. Forty yards from the cliff face . . . thirty . . . twenty . . . ten . . . Tony clipped himself onto the winch cable and sat forward into the door. Now they could see the coastguard Land-Rover. Four people stood near the edge of the cliff, pointing downwards and waving.

"There!" Pete pointed suddenly. "See it? God . . ." Tony followed his pointing finger down one hundred and thirty feet of sloping, crumbling rock face and nodded, his mouth suddenly dry.

A dark blue Vauxhall Cavalier lay crumpled at the base of a narrow ledge of sloping scree, its front wheels and bonnet hanging over empty space. Right side up, precariously balanced, the car looked as if it was waiting for no more than a sudden gust of wind before starting a final death plunge to the rocks that waited eighty feet below like a row of rotten, hungry teeth.

Hands and feet feather-light on the controls, Dave manoeuvred RESCUE 44 away from the cliffs, lost height and brought them in to hover exactly opposite the damaged car, about sixty feet away from the cliffs. Tony focused his binoculars on the vehicle. It looked like something out of a wrecker's yard. There was no sign of life. He focused upon the rocks above, trying to plan the best approach as Dave brought RESCUE 44 round in an easy, climbing curve until they were thirty feet above the clifftop and the coastguard Land-Rover, which was surrounded now by a cluster of upturned faces.

"Ready to winch out," Pete intoned, as Tony disconnected his headset and nodded. "Winching out." A slight tug and Tony was swinging gently down from the aircraft, head and shoulders buffeted by the down-draught, conscious of the weight of the first-aid pack between his shoulders. He kicked round to the left as he spun slowly clockwise and the clifftop came up to meet him. Down . . . down . . . A few more feet and Tony had touched. Leaning into his harness, he began walking down the cliff, back towards the sea, his boots bouncing off the slabs of sun-warmed slate as the helicopter dwindled away to a small yellow square in the sky and the world became quieter around him.

He dropped into a shallow gully and paused, aware of the sweat running down the inside of his sealed rubber suit and of the sharpness of the slate beneath his hands. He reached for the pocket phone. "Dave, this is Tony. Do you read, over?"

"Loud and clear, Tony. How's it looking?"

"OK, so far. Another thirty feet or so and I'll have to go off the wire, OK? I don't want it chafing against that overhang, over."

Leaning back onto the cable, Tony gestured downwards. He was out on more than one hundred and fifty feet of wire, and at that distance from the cabin his hand signals were little more than specks of orange movement against the greys and whites of the rocks below. Feeling for a toehold in his soft rubber boots, he edged slowly backwards, working his way across and down towards the overhang. Presently he pressed the transmit button on the radio. "OK, Boss. Coming off . . . now." He twisted the quick-release box and waved upwards. The cable snaked away, and Tony was left alone on the cliff face. The easy part was over.

RESCUE 44 swung out to sea and stood off like some benevolent guardian angel. "Tony, this is Pete. You're now about thirty feet above and slightly left of the car, over."

Body pressed tightly against the cliff face, fingers locked into every offered crevice, Tony slowly inched his way round the overhang. One step, then another, and the rear of the car slid into view.

He began walking warily down the sloping shelf of scree towards the car, each step a cold-blooded gamble that he was not about to start a rock slide. Ten feet to the boot of the car. Five . . . there! He'd made it. Tony reached out automatically for support, and then pulled back as the car began to sway and groan alarmingly on the metal belly that was its centre of balance.

Edging slowly round to the back window, Tony looked inside. No one in the back. Thank God. Another careful foot forward and Tony peered over the front of the driver's seat and froze. A man was slumped sideways across the passenger seat with both legs twisted under the mangled remains of the steering column. Oh, God . . . Tony moved back a few paces and reached for the radio. "Dave? Found one. Driver's side and fallen left across the front passenger seat."

"Alive?"

"Don't know. Shouldn't have thought so. He—wait a second." Tony broke off suddenly and cocked his head. There it was again: a low moan of pain from the car. Tony leaned as far forward as he dared, and was rewarded by the slightest movement of a bloody hand as the car began to rock once again.

"It's all right, mate, don't worry," he called. "Soon have you out of there, OK? Only don't try to move." Tony stepped back and crouched down. "Dave, the guy's alive! I just saw him move."

"Can you reach him?"

"Negative. He's in the front of the car. If I start clambering in there after him, the extra weight'll topple us over the cliff."

There was a pause. "Want to wait for the Cliff Rescue team?"

"The way this thing's balanced? It may not be here by the time they arrive. No, thanks, Boss. There isn't time. I've . . . er . . . I've had an idea." He shared it with them and there was a brief, stunned silence.

"You're raving mad," observed Pete.

"Anyone got a better idea?" Dave asked briskly. Another silence. "Right then, we'll give it a whirl. Let him have all the cable you can."

Tony watched as the helicopter came in high and then began crabbing gingerly along the cliff face towards him, the winch hook trailing below at the full extent of the cable as Dave jockeyed it within reach. It was pilot-winchman cooperation of a very high order indeed. The hook swung closer, and Tony grabbed it. He pressed the transmit button. "OK, Boss. Hold it there. Moving forward now."

"Roger," came the reply.

Tony gripped the cable hook firmly, inched his way along the body of the car, and paused. He had hoped to be able to loop the cable through the broken windscreen and round the steering column, but he discovered now that he couldn't reach. Instead, he had to settle for the offside door pillar. He looped the cable round, snapped the hook back upon itself and edged away. He pressed the transmit button. "It's fixed, Dave. You're anchored to the offside front pillar support."

"Understood," Dave acknowledged tersely, all his concentration focused now upon holding six tons of helicopter motionless in the sky.

"Up one foot," ordered Tony.

"Up one foot, roger," Dave repeated.

Eyes locked on the winch cable, Tony watched as the aircraft's downward thrust moved the car's point of balance back a precious couple of feet.

"Steady . . . Steady . . . Hold it there," Tony ordered, as the helicopter took the strain, the winch cable became bar-taut, and the bonnet of the car lifted level. Moving round to the rear door, Tony took hold of one of the handles and pulled. Nothing happened. Once, twice, three times he tugged. Finally, just as he thought it was hopeless, the door burst open. He stood back, panting with effort, and began struggling out of his bosun's harness and lifevest. Then, ducking down, he reached forward for the seat-tilt lever and raked the driver's seat back towards him until it was almost horizontal. He did the same with the passenger seat, and then began worming gently forwards into the car, the radio held in one hand. As he reached for the shoulder of the unconscious driver, the car suddenly began to rock and sway. He froze. "Up six inches, Dave! Quick as you can! Up six inches!"

"Will do," Dave's voice came back calmly. The bonnet rose fractionally, the swaying ceased, and Tony allowed himself to breathe again. He shook the casualty urgently. "Oi! Can you hear me?" No response, no movement. Tony didn't waste any more time. The priority now was to get them both out of the wreck before the rear wheels slipped, the car toppled forward, and they ended up on the rocks eighty feet below.

Gripping the man under the armpits, Tony pulled him backwards. The heavy body slid towards him and then the legs snagged in the tangle of wreckage where the pedals ought to have been, and refused to move any further. "Come on . . ." Tony muttered under his breath as he grunted and strained. It was no use. Cursing steadily, he wriggled forward. Again the car began to sway, and again he held his breath, the sweat running into his eyes. Slowly, slowly, it stopped. There. Good. Stay there. Please. Just a few more minutes.

Hooking his hands under the sole of one shoe, Tony eased the twisted foot sideways, ignoring the gleam of white shinbone protruding from blood-soaked trousers. And again. There! It was free. Panting loudly, Tony wriggled slowly back across the driver's seat. Hauling the man after him out of the car, he dragged him away from the edge of the slope and lowered him onto the rocks. Out came the radio. "This one's still alive, Boss," he panted.

"Stretcher's on its way down," Dave acknowledged.

"Nice one, Winchie," Pete called, the words failing to conceal his relief.

Tony crouched beside the man he had saved. A brief examination told him the casualty was critically injured, probably dying; a special pass in his bloodstained wallet told him Thomas Steevenson was cleared by Internal Security to work at Highland Pharmaceuticals, in a restricted area described simply as RD7.

JONATHAN TOMALIN WAS A NEAT, dapper little man, responsible for coordinating the press reception at the Cardocol launch in just two days' time. He ran a hand over a carefully groomed head of silver grey hair, stepped up to the display board at the far end of HPL's boardroom, and glanced towards Harold Engel. Sitting at the head of the table, with Maurice Jackman seated on his right, Engel nodded for him to continue, vaguely irritated by the man's obsequious efficiency.

"If I may press on," Tomalin resumed, tapping the tip of his pointer briskly against a large white letter H on the diagram in front of him, "the first helicopter from Glasgow Airport is scheduled to arrive at eleven thirty precisely. The company has sent out a total of one hundred and forty-six double invitations. So far, one hundred and nine have replied saying they wish to attend. Discounting our local guests—press, GPs and so forth—seventy-seven have indicated that they wish to travel here from Glasgow Airport by helicopter. Most of those, of course—" He broke off as the boardroom door opened and one of the senior secretaries appeared in the doorway.

"I'm sorry to interrupt, Mr. Engel," she said, "but I wonder if I might speak to you for a moment, please?"

Engel rose to his feet, sensing trouble. "Gentlemen? If you will excuse me for one moment?" He stepped outside.

"I'm sorry to burst in like that, Mr. Engel," the girl began. "There's been a terrible accident. Mr. Steevenson's car went over the cliffs! He's been taken to hospital! They say he may die . . ."

Steevenson had worked in RD7 with Douglas Parsons, the man who had committed suicide the previous night. Or so Engel had been led to believe. Unless . . . A sudden chill shiver of suspicion, almost of certainty. *Three* deaths in so short a time—all from the same department?

"Mr. Engel? Sir? Are you all right?"

Harold Engel forced himself to concentrate, to pay attention. As far as the rest of HPL's staff were concerned, RD7 was engaged solely in secret commercial research into the next generation of heart drugs . . .

"What? Yes, yes, perfectly all right, thank you." He closed his eyes briefly. "Was anyone else involved? Any other vehicle?"

She shook her head. "No, no, the police didn't think so."

No, there wouldn't be, Engel thought grimly: not if that bastard Jackman was up to his usual standard of chilling, cold-blooded efficiency. A sudden sense of outrage welled up inside him. All this was Jackman's fault, and London's; all this subterfuge, all these sudden accidents . . . He forced himself to smile. "Ask Mr. Jackman to come to my office, would you? Oh—and don't worry. Everything's going to be all right."

She gave HPL's chairman and chief executive a puzzled glance and then nodded. "Yes, Mr. Engel."

Harold Engel's final, strange words of reassurance had been directed not at her, but at himself. Despite Jackman, despite London and Baxter, and all that RD7 had come to represent over the years since he had first allowed himself to be lured into such a partnership through a mixture of flattery, greed and sophisticated blackmail, Highland Pharmaceuticals Limited was still his company, his creation. Cardocol was *his* triumph, these people *his* employees. It would be all right. He would make it be.

Eight minutes later there was a soft tap on his door and Jackman entered his office. Engel waved him to a chair without looking up, for he was still on the telephone to the police station. "Yes . . . yes, I see. No, no, I don't suppose there is. Thanks very much." He replaced the receiver slowly and looked up. "You told me this morning that Douglas Parsons, one of the men in RD7, had committed suicide. 'Pressure of work' I believe was the phrase you used."

Jackman nodded warily. "Yes, that's right. He'd been under a lot of pressure." A casual shrug. "Always did push himself too hard, in my view. Took Highcroft's accident particularly badly, so I was told—felt he was partly to blame."

Engel studied Jackman across his desk. "And Steevenson—what about him?" he asked softly.

"I'm sorry? I'm afraid I don't know what you mean."

"Don't you?" challenged Engel. "Steevenson is in hospital, critically injured. His car—one of our cars—went over the cliff on the road to Dalrean some time after ten this morning."

88

"Oh."

There was silence. Engel stared at him, hunched forward. "I want, Mr. Jackman, to hear you tell me this 'accident' has nothing whatever to do with you, nothing to do with London."

There was a long, stretching silence, then, "Tricky bit of road, that," Jackman observed quietly.

CHAPTER **16**

Ridley stepped through from the bathroom adjoining his bedroom on the second floor of the Seaview Motel. Apart from a towel wrapped round his waist he was naked, the clothes he had worn for the cliff job lying in a plastic bag at the foot of the bed, never to be worn again. In front of the mirror, comb in hand, he paused to stare through his own unsmiling reflection at the memory of that moment when he pushed the Vauxhall Cavalier towards the edge of the cliff road, the passenger lolling unconscious in his seat as the car gathered speed and plunged headlong over the edge.

Ridley began combing his hair slowly. Another scene, this time more than an hour later, as the yellow helicopter raised a stretcher with the winchman in his orange suit hanging on to the side of the cradle. Ridley had moved nearer to the coastguard Land-Rover, within earshot of the coastguard radio relaying the helicopter's messages. His worst suspicions had been confirmed: the man was still alive. Still alive. Ridley brushed his hair carefully, finished dressing, then sat down on the bed and lifted the telephone. "Would you put me through to the local hospital, please?"

The call went through and Ridley asked for the casualty department. "Good afternoon," he began politely. "I understand a Mr. Steevenson was admitted to your department this afternoon."

"One moment, please. Who is calling?"

"A friend. I just wanted to know how he is."

"Well, Mr. . . . er . . ."

"Henderson."

"Mr. Henderson. We don't usually disclose information of that nature over the telephone. When he arrived here, you see, he was very severely injured. If—"

"But he is still alive?"

"Och, yes, Mr. Henderson, he's still alive. He—"

"I see. Thank you." He replaced the receiver slowly.

JENNY SAT IN THE WINDOW SEAT of Helen Highcroft's kitchen, and watched the cluster of children playing in the garden, her thoughts not on them but upon Danny and the *BMJ* Cardocol supplement she had just read in the library. Behind her Helen Highcroft sighed, and Jenny turned back into the room. They were sitting at the kitchen table, cups of tea in front of them. They had been drinking a lot of tea recently. Helen tapped the five photocopied pages of the Cardocol supplement into a neat pile and slid it back across the table. "Well . . ." she began, "it all sounds very thorough, doesn't it? Very responsible."

"You mean you could actually understand it?" A fleeting smile.

"About one word in four, if you want the honest truth. The technical stuff just went over my head."

Jenny nodded. "Me too."

The telephone rang and Helen spun round and lifted the receiver. "Hello? Yes?" she said, her whole body tensed, expectant. Then, as Jenny watched, the shoulders slumped dejectedly. "Oh. Yes. Yes, she is." She turned. "For you," she said simply. "A Dr. Kindersley."

Jenny squeezed round the end of the table to take the call. "I'm sorry, that was thoughtless of me," she apologized. "I knew I was coming here so I gave him your number. He's . . . a friend of mine. I thought he might be able to interpret for us." Jenny took the outstretched receiver. "Danny?"

Defeated by the Cardocol supplement, she had called Danny in desperation the moment she returned home from the library, requesting an "idiot's guide".

"Have you read the supplement?" she asked.

"I have, yes, ma'am. From cover to cover, as per your instructions," Danny replied. "And I found it rather impressive actually. Now I've really studied the promotional material I can see what they're getting at. It's certainly an intriguing possibility."

"Why? What makes it so intriguing?"

"Well, they're billing it as an anti-hypertensive adrenergic neurone-blocker. That means it—"

"Whoa, Danny," Jenny interrupted in alarm, "this is me you're talking to, remember? Just put all that into English, will you?"

"Sorry. Right, let's see. It's a heart drug, OK? A drug aimed at reducing high blood pressure, particularly among the elderly. No one really knows for sure what causes high blood pressure. What is known, however, is that blood pressure goes up when you get old because the arteries narrow, and it therefore takes more effort—more pressure—to force blood along the arteries from the heart. OK so far?"

"OK so far," echoed Jenny faithfully.

"Good. Now then, the narrowing of those arteries is controlled by the release of certain chemicals which in turn are controlled by nervous impulses from the brain. We haven't yet learned how to control those nervous impulses, but we have learned to block that signal on its way down from the brain and so stop the release of those chemicals at the end of the nerve fibres. Further up the chain of command, as it were, are things called ganglia, sort of impulse-transmitters, fuelled by another chemical. We've learned to block them, too. Still with me?"

"By the skin of my teeth," Jenny muttered.

"Basically, Cardocol's what is known as a blocker. Blockers are drugs that block either the impulse-transmitter—that's the ganglion; the nerve ending—known as the neurone; or the receptor site at the end of the adrenergic nerve—the alpha or beta receptor. Stimulate those alpha receptors and you trigger constriction of the blood vessels. *Block* that stimulation—"

"By stopping the release of those chemicals—"

"Correct—"

"And blood pressure does not rise, yes?"

"You've got it, kid."

Jenny sighed with relief. "Thank God for that." She paused, suddenly puzzled. "And all that's *new?* I mean, that's what HPL have discovered, all on their own in little old Gleninver?"

Danny laughed. "No, no, there's nothing new about neurone-blockers—or alpha- or beta-blockers either, for that matter. Guanethidine's been in use for . . . oh . . . must be all of fifteen, twenty years by now."

"Then you've lost me," Jenny announced. "I don't see why—"

"Because there's always a problem, Jen, a price to be paid. With any drug you're interfering not just with the body mechanism you're aiming at, but with everything else as well. It's . . . it's like firing a shotgun at one particular flower in a crowded flowerbed—everything else gets hit as well. So, with drugs, you have to try and balance the benefit you hope to achieve against the side effects you'd much rather do without. Anyway, guanethidine's a thing of the past now, by and large, because of its basic crudeness, its lack of discrimination. It was cumulative, too. It took a long time to build up adequate control levels . . . Is this helping at all, Jen, or am I getting off course?"

"No, it's fascinating," Jenny replied. "I never realized it was all so . . . so complex. Where do HPL and Cardocol fit into all this?"

"Ah! Now, they've been very crafty. When everyone else wrote off guanethidine as a dead end and went haring off after vasodilators and beta-blockers, HPL looked round, saw the field well nigh empty of competition, and put their maximum research effort into overcoming guanethidine's side effects and bringing high blood pressure under immediate control. It's called creating a gap in the market."

"How did they manage it? A company the size of HPL, I mean? Compared to the big boys it hardly rates, does it?"

"God knows how they managed it. An industrial secret like that must be worth an absolute fortune. All they're giving away in the brochure is that it's tied in somehow with a special delay-release formulation in the

91

pill's outer coating that makes it dissolve evenly over a twenty-four-hour cycle, giving—and I quote . . . hang on a second . . . 'consistently low systolic and diastolic pressure readings over a statistically significant range of hypertensive conditions' unquote. And there's virtually no risk of postural hypotension. Or so they say."

"Postural hypotension? What on earth's that?"

"One of the unwanted side effects I was telling you about—the major side effect, in fact. Guanethidine was so effective at preventing constriction that if a patient stood up suddenly and actually *needed* the blood vessels to constrict, to pump blood up to the brain, it took a fair old while for the message to get through. By which time they'd blacked out."

Jenny began to listen very hard. "Blacked out, did you say?"

"That's right. All the blood's still down in the trunk and feet, you see. The brain's starved of oxygen, it needs more blood, but the blood can't get up there fast enough. Result? They fall to the ground like a felled oak. Quite spectacular to watch, actually."

"Or to the bottom of a boat," Jenny said quietly.

"Sorry?"

"I was thinking of Robbie Roberts," admitted Jenny. "He had high blood pressure, I know he had. His wife told me."

"So now you think he collapsed because of postural hypotension, is that it?" demanded Danny. "Maybe with guanethidine he might have done, Jen, but not with this new drug, Cardocol. That's the very problem HPL claim they've overcome!"

"I know it is," Jenny said quietly. "But what if they're wrong, Danny? Just suppose—what if they're wrong?"

IN THE EDITOR'S OFFICE of the *Gleninver Times*, Bob Harris was sitting at his desk in his shirtsleeves, working on the layout for the first early pages of the next week's edition, his heavy face flushed from the warmth of the stuffy little office. In exchange for the promise of extensive news coverage of the Cardocol launch in two days' time, Harris had been able to generate four more pages of local advertising, two of them whole-page advertisements taken out by Highland Pharmaceuticals itself, where the company thanked the local work force for their efficiency and predicted even greater prosperity in the future.

There was a sudden tap on the frosted glass door. It opened and Hamish Owen stood in the doorway, notebook in hand. "I've been thinking . . ." he began.

Harris sighed. "God, laddie, not again. I don't think I can bear it. Have you got that picture for me yet?"

Hamish Owen shook his head. Harris had sent him round to Douglas Parsons's home, to borrow a photograph to go with the story. Hamish had got no further than the front step and he had been forced to return to the office empty-handed. Harris had pounced upon his failure with relish and hailed it as yet another example of the futility of academic training.

"About that suicide," Hamish persisted doggedly, "and the man in the car that went over the cliff this morning—Steevenson."

"What about them?" asked Harris shortly.

"They came from the same company, HPL."

Harris nodded. "Aye, laddie, so they did. What about it?"

Hamish made a helpless gesture with his notebook. "Well, don't you think that's a bit of a coincidence? And that other man who disappeared: the professor. Put him in with the others and that's three, all from the same company!"

Harris slammed a hand down angrily on his desk. "You've been a reporter how long?"

"Twelve weeks."

"Aye. Twelve weeks. And in that time, have you learned to hand in a decent Women's Institute report? No. Can you write up the results of a flower show without spelling half the names wrong? No. Can you do a simple thing like borrowing a photograph from the next of kin without having the door slammed in your face? You cannot. But give yourself half a bloody chance and you'll find murder under every stone!"

"But three people dead—or disappeared—in the last week! From the same company! The statistical chances of that happening—"

"I don't give a damn about your 'statistical chances'!" Harris stormed, pushing angrily to his feet. "Professor Whatshisname didn't disappear, he went off with a younger bit of stuff, OK? It happens all the time, although you wouldn't know that, would you, you with your head stuffed full of all that university rubbish!" He turned and flung out a hand towards the grimy windows. "Look out there!" he ordered. "Go on, laddie—look out there and tell me what you see."

Hamish moved to the window. "Well . . . I can see the town. The streets . . . the harbour. The—"

Harris shook his head impatiently. "You see *people*, laddie—people and jobs! At least half the jobs in this town revolve round HPL, either directly up at the plant or by providing some of the service industries that support it. Half! You and your pet theories about murder," he scoffed. "Gleninver *is* Highland Pharmaceuticals. It's about time a man as brainy as you're supposed to be sorted that out. D'you hear what I'm saying?"

CHAPTER **17**

It was dusk as Jenny locked the Citroën and walked towards her flat, feeling in her bag for her door key. As she rummaged around, a figure loomed suddenly out of the darkness and she spun round, startled.

A man in uniform. She caught the gleam of his cap visor, recognized the face beneath, and let out a sigh of relief.

"Phew—Tony! You made me jump."

"Sorry. How're you?"

"Fine."

"Can I have a word? It's about that drug you were telling me about."

Jenny looked up sharply. "Cardocol?"

"That's the one."

"You'd better come in. Mind the step."

In the sitting room she turned on the lights and drew the curtains. "Like a drink? Sherry? It's all I've got, I'm afraid."

Tony shook his head, and sat down on the sofa.

"We had a job today," he began quietly. "Car went over the cliffs at a place called Dalrean, about ten miles or so down the coast."

Jenny nodded. "I heard something about that on the car radio."

"A man was critically injured: Steevenson. He worked for HPL."

"I see," Jenny said slowly, not seeing anything at all. What did this have to do with her? Tony got up and walked restlessly towards the window. He turned.

"I probably shouldn't be telling you this, but this man carried a special pass, issued by Internal Security. I found it in his wallet when I had to look for identification."

"HPL's internal security? I don't see what—"

"No. Not HPL's internal security. It was issued by MoD. In London."

"The Ministry of Defence? But that's . . . that's crazy! I thought—"

"Internal Security's part of MI5. It deals with the screening and security clearance of civilians who work in sensitive government areas— GCHQ, the Ministry of Defence—places like that."

Jenny hunched forward. "HPL's not a . . . a military installation, for goodness' sake! But that man with the pass. He was working there—you said so yourself, just now!"

Tony nodded. "That's right, I did. In somewhere called RD7. Have a think about it . . . Anyway, time I was going." He turned towards the door.

"Tony? Tell me something—why are you bothering? With all this, I mean? With me? Coming here yesterday. And again this evening."

Tony shrugged, suddenly awkward. "I think you got a rough deal, from the press and that—even your own people here in the town could have been a bit more understanding, couldn't they?"

"A bit," agreed Jenny, smiling slightly.

"I suppose too . . . because the boy reminded me of Paul."

"Paul?"

"My son," Tony explained briefly.

"I didn't know you had a son."

"Didn't I tell you?" Tony asked, knowing full well he hadn't and surprised that he had now.

"You didn't tell me very much at all," smiled Jenny. "You just listened, mostly. I want you to know I appreciate it."

He gave another awkward little shrug. "There's not much to tell. Maureen—that's my wife—she packed her bags at the start of the summer. I came home off shift one day and found a note," he admitted, the bitterness in his voice unmistakable. "She took Paul with her, back to her parents in the south." He paused. "She's got custody, of course. I tried to fight it at first, but with my job? No chance." He forced a smile. "Still, it could be worse. I'll be able to see him every four months, once the papers have gone through."

"I'm sorry," she said inadequately.

"So am I," agreed Tony. "It's what we call an occupational hazard." He looked up. "So I suppose what I'm saying is: when you ask me why I'm bothering, let's just say I know a little bit about loneliness too."

"I'M SORRY, MR. HENDERSON, but your friend Mr. Steevenson died forty minutes ago." In his room in the Seaview Motel, Ridley's face blossomed slowly into a smile. He replaced the receiver and sat back. Presently, he lifted the receiver once more. "I'd like to place a call to London, please," he said, giving Baxter's private number. It was time to report in.

". . . and that ties up all the loose ends, I think you'll find. As per our agreement," Ridley concluded.

In faraway London, Ewan Baxter drew a jotting pad towards the telephone. Earlier that same evening he had been talking to somebody else in Gleninver: Maurice Jackman.

"No . . . not quite all," he mused. "I'd like you to stay on a few more days, if you wouldn't mind. Just a watching brief at this stage, I think. Who they're seeing, what they're up to, the usual sort of thing. Our mutual friend seems to think they have the capacity to cause a certain amount of embarrassment." Baxter glanced down at the notepad. "The names are Helen Highcroft and Jennifer Macrae—have you got that?"

"Got it," Ridley confirmed quietly.

AS TONY'S CAR DISAPPEARED down the road, Jenny hurried over to her desk and began jotting down what he had told her. What was it? "Internal Security is part of MI5 and deals with the screening and security clearance of civilians who work in particularly sensitive government areas?" That was it, Jenny thought, her mind racing. So what about Helen's husband? Had he also been working in a "particularly sensitive government area?" And what was RD7?

On impulse, Jenny looked up a number in the phone book. She hurried to the telephone and began dialling.

"Good evening. Highland Pharmaceuticals—may I help you?"

"RD7, please." There was a moment's silence. Jenny wasn't to know that those who knew of RD7's existence were required to refer to it only by an innocuous-sounding series of extension numbers.

"I'm sorry?"

"Put me through to RD7, please," tried Jenny, trying to bluster her way past the telephonist.

"I'm sorry, caller, but we have no department listed by that designation. Who is it you are trying to contact, please?"

"No. It doesn't matter."

"Who is this calling?"

Jenny hung up hurriedly, worrying in case the girl had recognized her voice from her visit to the firm earlier that morning. She made herself calm down before dialling again. This time it was Helen's number.

"Hello?" A girl's voice. Her daughter, perhaps.

"Hello, Sarah, it's Jenny Macrae, you remember? I was round at your house talking to your mother earlier on. Is she there?"

"She's just gone out. She's gone round to see Mrs. Engel."

The name rang a bell. "Would that be Harold Engel's wife, d'you know? The man who owns Highland Pharmaceuticals?"

"That's right," Sarah agreed readily. "Dad's boss."

HELEN HIGHCROFT STOOD under the porch light of Harold Engel's expensive home and waited nervously. It was now a quarter to eleven, and she wondered belatedly if she should have waited until morning. But it was Harold she wanted to see and that would have meant getting past the receptionist again, at the plant. Now she heard heels tapping through the hall towards her and the door opened.

"Helen! Come in!" greeted Joyce. Helen hesitated.

"It's not too late? You're not just off to bed or anything?" she asked.

"Of course not. Please—do come in. Any news? Has he rung?"

Helen shook her head. "No. Not a word. I—"

Harold Engel came into the hallway, a glass in his hand.

"It's Helen. Helen Highcroft," Joyce called over her shoulder.

"So I . . . so I see." He raised his glass and took a quick swallow. "What can . . . what can we do for you, hmm?" he asked, with the slightest slur in his voice.

"I tried to see you yesterday. At the office," Helen began.

"About Malcolm. Yes, yes, I know. I was . . . tied up," he apologized, with a generous wave of his glass. "All this . . . all this damn launch business, I'm afraid."

"I understand."

Joyce steered her firmly towards the drawing room. "Come and sit down, Helen. Can I get you something? Tea or coffee? A drink, perhaps?"

96

Helen shook her head. She sensed that Malcolm's disappearance, and Harold Engel's sudden, uncharacteristic transformation from cool-headed executive to domestic drunk, might somehow be connected.

"No, really. Would you mind if I asked a few questions now, Harold? About Malcolm?"

"Not . . . not at all." He followed them into the drawing room and helped himself to a fresh drink from the cabinet. There was the chink of glass against bottles carelessly handled, and Joyce forced an apologetic little smile.

"When did you last see Malcolm?" Helen asked.

"Well now, let me see. Must have been . . . yes . . . Monday morning."

"And did he seem . . . normal, then? He didn't seem upset? Moody, or distracted about something?"

Engel shrugged. "No. He seemed perfectly normal."

Helen thought for a moment, studying her hands. Then she looked up. "Harold, tell me honestly, as a friend. Did Malcolm ever say anything to you about a woman called Monica?"

"No. No, he didn't." Engel paused, remembering he was supposed to have first heard about the photograph from Jackman when he returned upstairs to the boardroom. "I'm sorry, Helen. About the photograph and everything. Mr. Jackman told me, of course. After you left."

"That's very kind of you," Helen replied. "But anyway, I don't believe it. I simply don't believe Malcolm did have a mistress tucked away somewhere."

"You . . . don't believe it?" echoed Harold Engel, sobering up fast. "But the . . . the photograph in Malcolm's diary? Surely that—"

"Yes, I know about the photograph," Helen replied calmly. "But I also know my husband. I don't believe he's just run off with some woman half his age. What did Malcolm actually *do* at HPL? He was working on Cardocol, wasn't he?"

Engel hesitated. "Well, yes. Indirectly. He . . . he was involved in research. Much of his work was very secret, naturally."

"Where did he work?" Helen asked innocently.

"I'm sorry?"

"Where did he work? Where was Malcolm's office?"

Harold Engel relaxed. "Oh, I see. In the administration building."

"Was that where you last saw him?"

"That's right. He was just coming out of his office, and we travelled down in the lift together."

"You travelled down together in the lift?" asked Helen as casually as she could.

"Yes, that's right." He paused. "Why? What's the matter?"

"I'm not sure," Helen replied slowly. "It's just that when Mr. Jackman showed me Malcolm's office, it was on the ground floor."

LIGHTS WERE STILL BURNING in a downstairs office at the *Gleninver Times*. Hamish Owen was in the library, leafing through large, dust-covered volumes of back copies. He was working his way through the year before Highland Pharmaceuticals arrived in Gleninver. He was looking for background; digging into the past.

A quarter of an hour later, Hamish found what he was looking for: a brief piece on the man heading the company that was coming to Gleninver. Hamish made notes and then hurried upstairs. A flick through Willing's *Press Guide* and he was dialling a number in Surrey, calling up the local weekly newspaper in Leatherhead.

For Leatherhead, he had discovered, took in a place called Bookham. And Bookham, according to the files, had once been home to a company called Engel Laboratories.

CHAPTER 18

The shrill ringing of the telephone downstairs woke Tony from the depths of sleep. He padded down to the hall and reached drowsily for the receiver.

"Tony? John Murdoch. Sorry to haul you out of your pit." John Murdoch, another winchie on SAR Flight. Tony squinted at his watch. Eight o'clock. He groaned.

"Boss wants you in here right away."

"What? I'm off duty, for God's sake! Get him to look at the flying roster, will you, John? Tell him to take a look at my hours!"

"I'm not talking about flying, chum. There's a couple of blokes from S5 who'd like a word with you."

"S5? What the hell do they want from me?" S5 was a division of Military Security.

"Don't ask me, mate. I haven't a clue. I'm just passing the message, OK? Only I wouldn't keep 'em waiting too long, if I were you. They look a mean couple of bastards to me."

JOHN MURDOCH WAS RIGHT. They *were* a mean couple of bastards. Warrant Officer Metcalf and Sergeant Eason were sitting waiting for Tony in the flight commander's office—two lean, hard-looking men in their late thirties, with civilian suits with sharp creases, highly polished shoes, and watchful eyes. Tony's commanding officer, Flight Lieutenant Churchill, was waiting for him too, standing with his back to the room, looking out across the airfield with his arms folded. Tony could sense the mutual dislike between those who flew and those who investigated service betrayal and breaches of national security, the moment he stepped into the office. S5 was universally detested throughout the Royal

Air Force, a fact that bothered Metcalf, Eason and their colleagues not at all. Tony closed the door firmly behind him and turned, his hat under his arm. "I'm Lockhart," he said warily.

Warrant Officer Metcalf looked up. "You are Anthony Peter Lockhart, service number 2542844, and you are currently serving as a Winchman Flight Sergeant with 'A' Flight, 29 Squadron, engaged on Search and Rescue duties and stationed at RAF Glenhaddon?"

"That's right, yes."

"You were on a job yesterday afternoon. Flight Lieutenant Bourne, Flight Lieutenant Sleaman and yourself—correct?"

"Correct," Tony acknowledged.

Warrant Officer Metcalf closed the file in front of him and leaned forward. "Tell me about it," he encouraged. "From the moment you were diverted from routine training."

Tony glanced across at Churchill, who nodded.

He complied. In brief sentences, Tony told the two men about the walk down the cliff face on the wire, about the position of the car, and about the casualty, Steevenson.

"How did you know his name, Flight Sergeant?"

Tony sighed. "You've seen my report—it's all in there. When I got Steevenson out of the car, I went through his pockets for identification—that's standard procedure. I found a pass in his wallet with his name on it."

"What sort of pass?" Metcalf asked quietly.

"A security pass, issued by the Ministry of Defence."

"Go on."

"Authorizing the holder to enter somewhere called RD7 at Highland Pharmaceuticals. That's a big drug firm in Gleninver."

"So we understand," Metcalf nodded drily. "Go on."

Tony shrugged. "That's it. Then the stretcher came down and up we went—look, what is all this? You've got all that information already. If you—"

"What happened to that pass, Flight Sergeant?"

"It went back in the wallet. I assume the police or the hospital staff took care of it when they were looking for personal effects."

Metcalf studied Tony for several seconds, then reached down to a briefcase and took out a clear plastic envelope. "Is this the pass you saw?"

Tony studied it briefly. "That's it."

Metcalf looked up. "You told a PC Ayres about the pass."

Tony nodded. "Yes. He was the incident officer on the clifftop."

"Who else have you told?"

Tony decided to lie, to shield Jenny. "No one."

"You're sure?"

Tony stared him straight in the eyes. "Yes, sir."

Metcalf closed the file. "I will remind you, Flight Sergeant, that as a serving noncommissioned officer in Her Majesty's Royal Air Force, you have signed the Official Secrets Act, and that any unauthorized disclosure which may be considered a breach of national security—"

"Look—what the hell's going on?" Tony exploded. "All I did was follow SOPs, all right? What's all this about 'national security'?"

Metcalf looked up with calm, cold eyes. "Forget what you saw down there on those cliffs, Flight Sergeant, is that clear? Forget about Steevenson, and forget about that pass, understand?"

GLENINVER TIMES'S EDITOR, Bob Harris, was on the telephone to photographic, finalizing details of the next day's coverage of the official launch at HPL. "I don't give a monkey's about the sea-angling competition," he was saying. "I want Mike on the job, covering the helipad arrivals, by eleven at the latest. Angus should be in the main building by then too, got it? Yes . . . yes, I know. Well, he'll just have to bloody well unfix it, won't he?" Harris slammed down the telephone with a crash, pushed to his feet and went through to editorial.

Hamish Owen was sitting at his desk making notes from a newspaper spread open in front of him. "Before I forget, laddie, when you get to Highland Pharmaceuticals in the morning—" Harris broke off, frowning. "What the hell are you doing with that?"

Hamish looked up. "It's the *Leatherhead Advertiser*. I ordered it."

"You *ordered* it?"

"That's right, yes," Hamish admitted, confident that Harris would applaud such initiative. "They stuck it on the train last night. I was checking back in the files about HPL. We only reported the fact that HPL was coming to the valley—there was nothing about Engel's previous company down in Surrey. Then I remembered that the paper down there would have covered the closure of Engel Laboratories just as closely as we're going to cover this launch tomorrow, so I gave them a call. They remembered it well—it was a big story at the time, see?" He turned the paper round so Harris could see the headline: ENGEL LABS— SHOCK CLOSURE AS GOVT STEPS IN.

Harris brushed the paper aside. "Who the hell told you to start ordering copy, eh? The only person authorized to order copy on behalf of this newspaper is the editor, got it, laddie? That's me, understand?"

"I'm sorry. I just assumed—"

"You just 'assumed', did you? And who do you think's going to pay for this ordered copy of yours, eh?"

"I thought petty cash would—"

"Petty cash? Petty cash? Over my dead body, it will. I'll tell you who's going to pay for it, laddie—you are!"

Hamish felt his patience run out. He rose recklessly to his feet. "All right—I'll pay! But doesn't it strike you as a bit strange that the same man who's forced to shut down Engel Laboratories because of certain"— he snatched up his notebook—" 'unspecified but serious irregularities', should turn up here, in Gleninver, less than three years later, with apparently limitless funding and a product licence issued by the same government department that put out the press release I just quoted?"

It was the first time he had hit back like that, and the outburst took them both by surprise. In the silence that ensued, Harris stepped up menacingly to Hamish and stabbed out a short, blunt finger. "You ever pull another stunt like that, laddie," he said, "and you'll find yourself on the next train back to that university of yours, I bloody well promise you, d'you hear?" Harris reached down to the *Leatherhead Advertiser*, mashed it into a large, untidy ball, and tossed it towards the wastepaper basket. Then he stormed back to his office.

Hamish stared at the closed door for a moment. Then he rose, retrieved the crumpled pages of the *Leatherhead Advertiser* and carefully cut out the feature on the sudden, unexpected collapse of Engel Laboratories.

JENNY WAS UNLOADING SHOPPING onto the kitchen table, and the sealed envelope containing the photographs was at the bottom of her basket. When everything else was stored away, she picked up the packet of prints and went into the sitting room. To Jenny, at that moment, they were unique, irreplaceable. They were her one link with the past. With Danny, and with the child whose trust she believed she had betrayed.

She sat down and opened the wallet. The first photographs were of Pam, sitting smiling on the steps outside the clinic, and of Danny, clowning around in the stern of a dinghy they had hired. There were more photographs of Danny, a couple of general views taken in the hills, and then one or two of her, all taken that same sunny weekend. The last photograph was of Jamie Ennis.

He was sitting on the breakwater at Ardtornish harbour on the last day of his life, bare feet dangling over the edge as he twisted round with that lopsided grin of his and looked up into the camera. Jenny studied that photograph and then the tears began to slide down her cheeks. She wept for him. She wept for Robbie and Mrs. Roberts and for Mr. and Mrs. Ennis. She wept for them all.

At length, she pushed the photographs back into their wallet, all except the picture of Jamie, which she took through into her kitchen and pinned carefully onto her noticeboard.

The picture of Jamie was there as a private pledge to a victim, to a small boy no longer able to fight for himself. Standing alone in her narrow kitchen, Jenny tried to marshal her thoughts.

She remembered the look on Dr. Erskine's face when she asked him about Cardocol, and heard again Tony Lockhart's warning about something called RD7 at Highland Pharmaceuticals; heard again the fears and suspicions of her new friend and ally Helen Highcroft as she searched for something that might explain her husband's disappearance. No, the questions weren't over yet, and nor were the obligations.

Jenny dialled Directory Enquiries. "London, please, Central London," she said in a firm voice. "The Committee on the Safety of Medicines."

HELEN HIGHCROFT WAS UPSTAIRS making the children's beds, with the sounds of Radio Two washing through from the bedside radio next door. The children were out again with friends. She found now that she needed the radio to blot out the silence, to fill the brooding emptiness that told her Malcolm was never coming home.

The last bed was finished. Helen went through into her own bedroom and turned off the radio. There it was again, that silence. She was alone, that was the hardest thing: alone with no one to turn to.

But not quite alone, she remembered, thinking suddenly of Jenny—Jenny Macrae. Yes, that was it: she'd go and see her. Right now.

Helen hurried downstairs, swept up her car keys and handbag, scrawled a note for the children and slammed the front door behind her.

Ridley watched her leave.

He waited until the Volvo had swung into the main road and then set off quietly in pursuit. Nobody noticed the hired Ford Capri tuck itself neatly into the traffic and follow the Volvo all the way across the town until it braked to a halt outside Jenny's ground-floor flat in Elgin Terrace.

CHAPTER 19

Jenny was still on the telephone to the Committee on the Safety of Medicines. "Yes, I can see that," she was saying. "But you mean to tell me no one actually *checks* the submissions made to the committee? No one bothers to go through them line by line?"

The man on the other end of the telephone sighed. "Of course we bother, Miss Macrae. Each submission is examined most carefully. But we're hardly in a position to *test* each and every application individually. It's a question of time. Of money."

"But you're the people who issue the licences! We're . . . we're talking here about drugs that affect people's lives!" protested Jenny.

"Do you have any idea just how many submissions the committee receives each year, Miss Macrae? Between six and seven hundred."

"Each year?" Jenny echoed incredulously.

"Each year. Not only do we have to process an increasing number of

product licence applications," the clerk continued remorselessly, "but we also have a statutory obligation to monitor the safety of some sixteen thousand products already on the market." He paused. "I tell you this, Miss Macrae, to give you some idea of scale."

Just then the doorbell rang. Jenny glanced over her shoulder. "Could you hold on one second?" She put down the telephone and hurried down the hall, pulled the door open cautiously, and smiled with relief when she saw who it was. "Oh, Helen, hello—come along in. I'm on the phone. Won't be a moment. Come through." Jenny hurried back and picked up the telephone again. "Hello? You . . . you were saying it was impossible to inspect every application individually. Are you saying that you have to rely heavily upon the integrity of the drug firms themselves? Upon what they choose to tell you?"

"There has to be a certain measure of trust. An application for licensing only reaches us after a great deal of time and money has been spent on research—in the case of one of the larger companies about to launch a major new product, we could be talking about forty million pounds, and perhaps ten years' research and development. And after all, a flawed product is in no one's interest. Word would soon get back if a new drug started piling up yellow cards."

"Yellow cards?"

"We send prepaid yellow cards to every GP and hospital doctor in the country. If they use a drug that throws up some unexpected adverse reaction in the patient, then we ask them to send the card back to us with all the relevant details. If enough yellow cards come in, registering the same adverse reaction to the same drug . . . well, then the alarm bells start to ring."

Jenny frowned. "You *ask* them to send the card back—that's all? There's no legal obligation on them to do so? And this yellow card business: it's only done *after* a drug has been put on the market?"

"Yes. We want to monitor a significant number of adverse reactions—and we are only likely to get that sort of quantitative feedback after the drug has been exposed to a large number of patients."

"But isn't that all a bit late in the day?" Jenny persisted. "The damage could have been done by then, surely?"

"Miss Macrae, forgive me, but I really cannot afford to go on discussing a purely hypothetical situation that—"

"One last question, please. If I . . . if I wanted to look at the results of those clinical trials you mentioned earlier—the ones on Cardocol—where would I have to go?"

"Nowhere, I'm afraid. Clinical trials are part of the company's product licence application."

"All right, then. Where can I see HPL's product licence application?"

"You can't, Miss Macrae. All PLAs are dealt with in the strictest confidence. Whatever transpires between ourselves and the various drug companies is never disclosed to a third party. Apart from our own records here, the only place you'd find a copy of that application would be at Highland Pharmaceuticals itself."

"Highland Pharmaceuticals itself," Jenny mused. "Thank you . . . thank you very much indeed. You've been very helpful." Jenny replaced the telephone and looked up slowly. He had just given her an idea.

RIDLEY SAT PATIENTLY outside Jenny's flat for more than half an hour. There was a book on his lap to suggest his presence there was wholly innocent: a salesman perhaps, killing time before his next appointment.

But Ridley's eyes were not on the printed page. They were fixed on the bay window of the ground-floor flat opposite; he was able to see both women clearly against the light as Jenny replaced the telephone and turned to Helen. He watched as Helen listened and then shook her head emphatically, and took to pacing the room. Ridley had seen enough. Enough, that is, to realize that the two women were more than chance acquaintances. They were partners in something, he decided. Conspirators. It was time Jackman was told.

Ridley drove round onto the main road. As he did so, he turned on the car radio, for the news. At the end of the local bulletin came an announcement that the man injured in the car-over-the-cliff drama had died in hospital. Ridley smiled. Two hours ago the same story had been higher up in the running order. Another hour, another bad accident or traffic jam, and the story would be forgotten.

BUT THERE RIDLEY WAS WRONG. In the offices of the *Gleninver Times*, Hamish Owen was on the telephone to HPL, asking for the usual biographical details to go with the story of the fatal car crash. And this time, just for once, he was acting on the editor's instructions.

"And can you tell me something about his work with the company, Mr. Jackman?"

"He was engaged as laboratory technician as part of our Forward Planning Development team. You . . . ah . . . appreciate, Mr. Owen, that I'd rather not be drawn on specific details. For obvious reasons."

Hamish presumed that Jackman was referring to commercial rivalry.

"Yes, of course. I understand."

"What I feel I can say is that Tom will be sadly missed. His death will be felt as a personal loss by us all." He might have been reading the eulogy.

"Yes. Yes, of course," Hamish Owen agreed, dutifully recording every word in his notebook. "You've . . . er . . . you've had a tragic time recently, haven't you?"

"I'm sorry?"

"What with Douglas Parsons committing suicide . . ."

"Oh, I see what you mean. Yes, indeed we have."

". . . and Professor Highcroft just disappearing like that."

"Professor Highcroft? Oh." Jackman tried a little offhand laugh. "I'd hardly lump that in with the others, Mr. Owen."

"Yes. Yes, of course," Hamish agreed, his mind already elsewhere. "Going back to the accident, Mr. Jackman, I . . . I was just wondering—d'you happen to know how old he was?"

"Yes, I can tell you that straight away. Thomas Steevenson was thirty-five, and single. Was there anything else, Mr. Owen?" Jackman asked, with just the politest hint of impatience.

"No. You've been very helpful, Mr. Jackman, thanks very much."

"Not at all." Jackman rang off.

Hamish Owen sat back in his chair, a pencil tapping thoughtfully against his teeth as he checked over his notes. Harris was going to want to know why he hadn't tracked down the next of kin, why he hadn't found out where Steevenson worked before joining HPL . . . He flicked open his contact book, and a moment later was dialling the London number of ASTMS, the white-collar, scientific trades union. He asked to be put through to records.

"Steevenson . . . What was his date of birth?" asked a young clerk.

"It would have been . . . 1950."

"Half a mo." Hamish waited.

"I've got a T. W. Steevenson, that any good?"

"That sounds like him, yes. D'you have an address?"

"Well . . . I'm not sure it'll be much use," the girl replied doubtfully. "It's eight years old. After that it's NLN."

"It's a start, anyway," Hamish replied. "What's NLN?"

"NLN? It means he's taken himself off the register, hasn't he? No Longer Notified."

"No longer notified of what?"

"Jobs, pension rights, arbitration decisions, local area meetings—all that sort of thing."

"Why would he do that—go off the register, I mean?"

The girl paused. "I dunno, really. Quite a lot of 'em do that when they move into more sensitive areas—defence contracts, stuff like that. They like to cover their tracks a bit. Stops rival companies picking up on the competition. Headhunting they call it."

"Can you give me that address, anyway?"

"Don't see why not. It's ten, Springfield Lane, Pitton, Wiltshire."

Hamish wrote it down. "Thanks a lot. Could you try one more?"

The girl sighed. "Go on, then."

"Thanks. The bloke's name is Parsons. OK? Douglas Parsons. I don't know his date of birth."

"Hang about." He waited once again. "He's the same as the other one, NLN. An' guess where he lived . . . ?"

"Wiltshire?"

"Yeah, Wiltshire. Place called Allington." She hesitated, curiosity aroused. "What have these blokes bin up to, then?"

"I'm not sure," Hamish replied slowly, and rang off. He rose to his feet, took down the office atlas and looked up the first of the two Wiltshire villages in the index. Pitton, he discovered, lay a few miles east of Salisbury. Allington was just south of Bulford. Hamish felt a sudden shiver of excitement. For there, within easy commuting distance of Pitton and Allington, lay the village of Porton. Porton as in Porton Down, the government's chemical warfare establishment.

CHAPTER 20

Dr. Stanley Erskine was sitting in a doctor's surgery, waiting. It was a novel experience.

He had spent most of the morning driving northwards along the eastern bank of Loch Linnhe, to see Dr. Hastings, the duty GP at this, one of several doctors' surgeries in Fort William.

Glancing down at the worn leather briefcase at his feet, Erskine wondered just why he had felt compelled to drive all this way along the coast instead of simply using the telephone. He was not at all sure that he knew. What he did know was that his presence here in Fort William had to do with Jenny Macrae, and a new heart drug called Cardocol; with two of his patients, one of whom was already dead; and with a sense of shame that he had, however briefly, traded the traditional scepticism of his calling for the suspension of disbelief and a handsome set of leather-bound medical reference books. And had therefore broken faith with those he was pledged to serve.

"Dr. Erskine?" He looked up at the receptionist. "Dr. Hastings will see you now." He picked up his briefcase and walked down a short corridor to Dr. Hastings's consulting room.

Twenty years his junior, Dr. Hastings rose from behind his desk and stretched out a hand. Florid, fair-haired and with a firm, crisp hand-shake, he exuded an air of overworked, likable efficiency.

"Well now, Dr. Erskine—" he began. "What brings you to our neck of the woods?"

Dr. Erskine opened his briefcase and took out a sheaf of notes. "It's about Highland Pharmaceuticals. I understand one of their representa-tive chappies calls here fairly regularly? I take it he's been . . . ah . . . extolling the virtues of this new drug of theirs just recently?"

"The neurone-blocker? Cardocol? Naturally."

Erskine rummaged around in the pockets of his baggy sports coat and pulled out a packet of Cardocol pills. "You've received a few of these already, have you not?"

The younger man nodded. "A few, yes. As promotional samples."

"Aye, that would be it: promotional samples. Would I be right in saying you've maybe given one or two of these 'promotional samples' to a couple of your patients already, Doctor?"

"Yes. As a matter of fact, I have," Hastings admitted stiffly. "Three. Possibly more. I couldn't be certain, not without checking my case notes."

Dr. Erskine nodded. "But three, anyway. Tell me this: were there any adverse reactions? Postural hypotension, for example?"

"No, of course not!" Hastings objected impatiently. "The whole point of Cardocol is that they've eliminated the risk of an inconsistent blood-pressure reading and postural hypotension!"

"You mean that's what they're *claiming* they've done," Erskine corrected gently. "The two don't necessarily add up to the same thing in my experience—not the same thing at all." He picked up the notes he had compiled after talking to the houseman at County Royal Hospital and examining Mrs. Proctor's blood samples. "Read these. They refer to one of my patients who was admitted to Intensive Care with all the initial symptoms of postural hypotension, and later developed a blood pressure of 230/130! She's lucky to be alive."

Dr. Hastings looked blank. "I'm sorry. I don't see the connection."

"She's been on two hundred milligrams of Cardocol for the last six days," Erskine explained quietly. "What happened to her was supposed to be statistically impossible."

Dr. Hastings finished reading Dr. Erskine's notes, and rocked back in his chair, frowning with a mixture of worry and concentration. Dr. Erskine watched him in silence, aware that at the very least he had managed to breach the younger doctor's wall of professional scepticism.

Now Dr. Hastings rose to his feet and crossed to a metal filing cabinet in the corner. He extracted four files, and returned to his desk. Then he pulled the telephone towards him.

"Who are you going to call?" Dr. Erskine asked.

"My partners," Hastings said. "They ought to see these right away."

RIDLEY MADE A CAREFUL ENTRY in his notebook and glanced up from behind the wheel of the Capri. The Volvo hadn't moved. The two women were still sitting inside, talking.

Ten minutes earlier, Helen Highcroft and Jenny Macrae had left the flat in Elgin Terrace and driven to this lay-by, halfway along the country road that led past Highland Pharmaceuticals. Ridley had tucked himself away behind a caravanette to watch.

He was puzzled. They were up to something, definitely. The two women had spent most of the afternoon in Macrae's flat, drinking tea, talking and looking frequently at their watches. As though they were waiting for something to happen or someone to arrive.

"I STILL THINK YOU'RE MAD!" Helen was saying, twisting round to face Jenny in the Volvo beside her. "You'll never get away with it!"

Jenny sighed impatiently. They'd been over all this in her flat. "Why not? I'll use the office you did, the one that was supposed to be Malcolm's."

"Yes, but . . ."

"Well, there you are then—nothing could be simpler. I'll just wait there and then, when everyone else has gone home, I'll slip out."

Helen grasped her arm. "Look, Jenny. I . . . I appreciate what you're trying to do, really I do. But it's madness! You can't go creeping around someone else's property. It's . . . well . . . it's illegal, for one thing."

"So? So it's illegal—so what? So's giving out pills before you're supposed to; so's swapping people's offices round and then lying to their wives, you know? Or it should be." Jenny paused and then added, "Or don't you really want to find out what happened to Malcolm?"

"Of course I do, you know that. That's not the point."

"Yes, it is! That's exactly the point! There's no other way—you told me yourself your questions get you nowhere. Look, Helen. Something *has* to be going on up there, agreed? Why else would Jackman lie? Why else would Harold Engel make such a crass mistake about the lift?"

"What if you're caught?"

Jenny shrugged. "I'd have to tell the truth then, wouldn't I? At worst I'd get a fine. HPL wouldn't dare prosecute, anyway. They'd never risk it all coming out in the open."

"Then at least let me come with you," Helen offered impulsively.

"Wonderful. And whose car's going to be left there in the car park, sticking out like a sore thumb when everyone else has gone home?"

"Oh. I hadn't thought of that."

"I had. Just help me to get inside, OK? I'll manage the rest. Now"— she glanced at the clock on the Volvo's dashboard—"are you with me or against me, as they say? If we sit around here chatting much longer we'll miss the five-thirty rush."

Helen nodded. "I'm with you."

Jenny reached over and kissed her impulsively.

"You're sure you've got everything?" Helen persisted.

Jenny patted her large handbag. "Yep. Torch. Sandwiches. Thermos. Notebook and pencil. Gloves. A book to read—oh, and a clean handkerchief." They both laughed, a welcome release of tension.

"As we agreed," Helen said, "tomorrow morning at nine thirty, from reception, I'll ask for extension 476. I'll let it ring four times, then hang, up. That's your signal. When it stops ringing, I'll go straight up to the desk and start talking to that girl again." Helen smiled grimly. "When she sees me coming at her for the third time, she'll be distracted all right, I guarantee it. You shouldn't have any trouble slipping back into reception. Just go straight out to the car and wait for me there. I'll be in the same car park where we met. Tomorrow's launch day, so nobody's going to be paying you much attention."

Jenny got out, opened the back door and slid across the rear seat. She glanced quickly through the rear window, and totally failed to notice Ridley's Capri a little further back in the lay-by. "All clear," she called. Pulling the travel rug over herself, she dropped onto hands and knees on the floor of the car.

Helen glanced over her shoulder and drove out of the lay-by. "We're on the road," she reported. Behind her Jenny crouched in the warm darkness, and behind them both came Ridley, eyes narrowing with suspicion as the Volvo headed towards Highland Pharmaceuticals.

A few minutes later, "Gate coming up," Helen said, her hands suddenly damp on the steering wheel as she brought the car to a halt for the man on the gate, and wound down the window. She forced a smile. "Mrs. Highcroft to see . . . er . . . Mr. Engel. Harold Engel," she hurried, rattling off the first name that came into her head. The security man nodded as he made a careful note of the car's registration number on his clipboard. It seemed to take an age. Then, at last, he handed a visitor's pass in through the window. Helen slipped the car into gear and drove forward. "We're through, Jenny!" she announced.

Jenny tossed the rug aside and sat up as Helen slowed down for the car-park turning. A minute later they were getting out, tension mounting as they walked towards the main entrance and the stream of people emerging, homeward-bound, from HPL's administration building. Jenny looked at her watch: 5:27. As they paused outside the main doors, she felt Helen's hand rest lightly on her shoulder. "Good luck, Jenny. See you in the morning."

Once through the revolving doors, the two women separated, Helen to make for the reception desk, Jenny to walk casually towards the sofa nearest the door leading to the ground-floor corridor. She sat down and waited for her cue.

The reception area was busy. Apart from HPL employees emptying out of the lifts and hurrying outside, there were half a dozen workmen putting the finishing touches to a Cardocol promotional display.

Jenny glanced towards the door leading to the corridor. Before they had left the flat, she had made Helen draw her a diagram, a ground plan showing exactly where she had to go. Now she waited, poised, her bag over her shoulder.

"Excuse me . . ." Helen pushed forward into the cluster of people waiting at the reception desk. "I said, excuse me . . ." Jenny didn't wait. She went straight through the door and down the corridor. Past one door, and another. There! The third. A quick look round: no one in sight. She turned the handle, stepped inside. One bare desk, one chair and a filing cabinet. Jenny whipped the door shut, and froze, listening for a sudden voice saying, Oi! Where d'you think you're going?

Nothing. Not a sound. She relaxed and moved away from the door. She'd done it. Presently she opened her bag, took out her sandwiches, torch, notebook and thermos and arranged them all neatly round her. It wouldn't be dark much before nine. She picked up her novel and settled down to wait.

AS THE VOLVO TURNED back along the road towards Gleninver, Ridley noted: *17:38, Volvo leaves HPL. Direction Gleninver. One occupant.* Stowing away his notebook, he started the Capri and set off after the Volvo. So that was their little game. It was enough to make you weep. He'd better check in, let Jackman know what the Macrae woman was up to. Then he had a better idea. If Macrae was still inside HPL then her flat would be empty, wouldn't it? And Ridley really enjoyed searching people's flats.

CHAPTER **21**

Helen Highcroft turned into her own driveway and braked sharply to a halt. An ancient Morris Minor was blocking the entrance to her garage, and there was a tall, thin young man she had never seen before standing outside her front door. He came towards her.

"Mrs. Highcroft?"

"That's right. What d'you want?"

"Hamish Owen, Mrs. Highcroft—*Gleninver Times*," he said. "I'd like to ask you one or two questions."

Helen shook her head emphatically. "Sorry—no."

"It's not just about your husband, Mrs. Highcroft. Not just about his disappearance, anyway. I'm not interested in private details about your marriage. About why he left you," he hurried on.

Helen got out of the car and slammed the driver's door, angrily. "My husband didn't 'leave' me, as you put it," she snapped. "My husband has disappeared! Vanished! There's a difference. Now, if you don't mind—"

"Please, Mrs. Highcroft—could you just tell me, have you and your husband ever lived in Wiltshire?"

Helen looked at the young reporter for a moment. "How on earth did you know that?" she asked.

RIDLEY RANG JENNY'S DOORBELL and waited with a plausible story ready on his lips. He knew she wasn't in there, of course, but he had not been watching the flat long enough to be absolutely sure that there wasn't a boyfriend, a bed-bound granny or a yapping poodle waiting for him. So he rang the doorbell and waited. Silence.

A careful glance round, an expert squint at the lock, and he was inside with the door pushed closed behind him in the time it took ordinary people to find the front-door key.

He moved down the hall and swiftly through to the kitchen to unlock the back door and open up an escape route, just in case. Then he was ready to start.

He began as he always did with women, in the bedroom. He found nothing. Nothing of any importance, anyway. Not there. He went through into Jenny's sitting room, and found Helen's diagram without the slightest difficulty, crumpled into a ball and thrown away. Ridley smoothed it out. "HPL" had been doodled across the top of the paper, and the word "Reception". And a child of five could have followed the pencilled arrow through the door and down the corridor to the office marked "X" on the plan. Just like Cluedo, thought Ridley scornfully—and froze. A man was coming up the path.

Tony rang the bell to Jenny's flat. Silence. He rang again. As he did so, he noticed that the door was slightly ajar and pushed it gently. It swung open and he took a cautious step forward. "Hello?" he called. "Jenny? It's me, Tony."

He walked slowly down the hall, looked into the sitting room and started suddenly. A man was sitting on Jenny's sofa, a newspaper open in his lap. "Who the hell are you?" he demanded.

"Could ask you the same question," the stranger countered calmly.

"Flight Sergeant Lockhart. A friend of Jenny's." Tony gestured over his shoulder. "The door was ajar. And you?"

"Just a friend."

"Where's Jenny?"

"She's gone out. Shopping." Ridley returned to his paper as Tony studied him in silence.

"Jenny gave you a key, did she?" he asked casually.

"That's right. Jenny gave me a key."

You're too cool, thought Tony suddenly, suspicion crystallizing into certainty as he remembered the two visitors to RAF Glenhaddon earlier that same morning. Men with the same polite, icy hardness, the same lurking cruelty beneath the sharp creases and the short haircuts.

"You're not a friend of hers at all, are you?" he accused suddenly. "You're another of those bastards from S5."

Ridley laid the paper aside and rose to his feet. "That's right," he admitted agreeably, "I'm just another of those bastards from S5." Whatever that was.

Tony nodded grimly and glanced round. "You've been searching here, haven't you? I can bloody well smell it!"

"Something like that," admitted Ridley softly, stepping closer.

Tony stopped him with an impatient click of his fingers. "Right, sunshine: let's see some ID."

"Sure." Ridley reached obligingly inside his jacket, took out his leather wallet and held it out. "Help yourself," he smiled easily. Tony took the wallet and looked down.

Jumbled impressions then: of several slender black tools in a case; of a rushing movement towards him and of a brief, sharp, agonizing pain between neck and collarbone. Then darkness. Oblivion.

Ridley watched his mark fall sideways without a flicker of satisfaction. Flight Sergeant Lockhart, lying there in a crumpled heap with his head against the sofa, represented an additional complication, that was all. Ridley retrieved his wallet of skeleton keys and crossed to the telephone. He dialled HPL and asked for Jackman's extension.

"Maurice Jackman."

"You know who this is, Mr. Jackman," Ridley said quietly.

"Where are you?"

"Gleninver. Inside Macrae's flat."

"You're *where?* Good God, man—is she with you?"

Ridley permitted himself a brief laugh. "No, squire, she's with you. In the main building."

"What!" Jackman hissed. "Where is she? If she's—"

"Where she's not doing any harm. It's all right, Mr. Jackman, just relax. She won't do anything until it gets dark. But she does plan a little snoop round, believe me."

"You sound very certain. What has she found out? What is she after?"

"I don't know, do I? That's why I'd better come and collect her. When everything is nice and quiet. When everyone's gone home."

"You're sure you know where she is?"

"Oh yes, Mr. Jackman," Ridley soothed, turning Helen's sketch slowly towards him. "I know where she is all right. To the inch."

DR. ERSKINE FOLDED HIS ARMS and regarded the group of doctors over the top of his spectacles. There were eight of them now, including himself, in Dr. Hastings's surgery in Fort William, and all of them had studied Mrs. Proctor's case notes and asked whatever supplementary questions they considered necessary. Now they all wore an air of attentive concern.

Except for one. Dr. Harrard was sitting back, arms folded, holding forth. "If we take the simple business of numbers, gentlemen," he was saying, "then we know that forty-seven patients in and around the Fort William area have already switched to Cardocol from one or other of the usual beta-blockers or vasodilators. Of these"—he glanced down at a notepad—"something in the region of ninety-four per cent have reported an immediate and significant reduction in blood pressure sustained over the full twenty-four-hour cycle without resort to additional drugs or medication and with almost negligible side effects. Not one of the patients—"

"If I can stop you a moment there, Doctor," Erskine interrupted. "Would you mind telling us what side effects you *have* seen?"

Dr. Harrard glanced down at his notes, scarcely bothering to conceal the fact that he considered it all a gross waste of his very valuable time. Dr. Erskine's patient showed worrying symptoms, certainly, but that was a problem for Gleninver, not Fort William. And certainly not for Cardocol. He found the entry he was looking for.

"A slight dry cough, that's all," he said shortly. "Which disappeared completely with the use of ordinary cough mixture. A small price to pay, I should have thought, for the relief of symptoms which—"

"I'm sorry to interrupt you," said Dr. Erskine, "but I wonder how many of us here are familiar with the fact that Cardocol causes a wee bit of bronchial inflammation?" There was a brief exchange of glances and then the hands began to go up. One . . . two . . . three . . .

Over the next few minutes they established that out of forty-seven patients, no fewer than seventeen had developed a dry, irritating cough soon after starting the new heart drug. Predictably, it was Harrard who chose to ignore the significance of the discovery.

"What exactly is the point you wish to make, Doctor? Even if one hundred per cent of Cardocol patients developed a slight dry cough, I am sure that they, like me—like most of us here—would consider it cheap at the price."

"I don't know," Dr. Erskine admitted thoughtfully. "I don't know that I am making a point at all. Except to say that if we are representative of the British Isles, then if twenty thousand people start taking Cardocol . . ." He spread his hands. "At the very least that's an awful lot of coughs, would you not agree, Dr. Harrard?"

HAMISH OWEN LEANED FORWARD slowly towards the coffee table in Helen Highcroft's sitting room as he waited for her to go on; she gazed sightlessly into her empty coffee cup. Into the past. "I . . . I thought all that was over, you see—finished. After we came back from America we . . . we never talked about his work any more. I suppose deep down I may have realized he was still involved, but I wanted to believe he'd kept his word. That he'd got out."

"Where were you living? In America?" Hamish asked carefully, aware that an insensitive, badly timed question could smash the fragile bond of trust he had built between them since he had told her about Steevenson and Parsons and their link with Porton Down. It was as though he had thrown a switch. Turned a key.

"Oh . . . near a place called Pine Bluff, Arkansas. It sounds rather nice, doesn't it?" She gave a nervous little shudder. "It wasn't nice at all. Malcolm worked at Fort Detrick, you see."

"Fort Detrick? I don't think I've ever heard of that."

"You're not supposed to have. That's where we . . . that's where the Pentagon put the Army Medical Research Institute of Infectious Diseases when America renounced germ warfare and handed the whole place over to the National Cancer Institute. Malcolm worked on there in secret for months as an exchange microbiologist."

"But we're not supposed to have any germ warfare capability, are we? No NATO countries are, including the United States."

"Oh, we do," sighed Helen cynically. "Only our work is always 'purely defensive'. We do research just to keep up with what the other side may use against us. They, of course, are doing exactly the same thing for exactly the same reason. It's madness. Malcolm was part of something called the 'Watchtower Capability'—peering into the scientific future and helping to devise better, more economical ways of killing other human beings. That's what he was doing at Porton, too, I suppose." She sighed.

"And here, Mrs. Highcroft? What about up here at Highland Pharmaceuticals?" Hamish asked.

"I don't know, Mr. Owen," she said quietly. "I . . . honestly don't know. I never had the courage to ask."

CHAPTER **22**

It was dark. Fifteen minutes ago, Jackman had pulled his Rover onto the soft shoulder of the perimeter track and doused the lights. He was about thirty yards from one of the locked chain-link gates set into the perimeter fencing that enclosed Highland Pharmaceuticals on three sides. The only light came from the car park and the main reception area, three hundred metres away. Taking a pair of binoculars from the glove compartment, he focused on the distant reception hall and watched as the elderly security guard yawned, stretched, and rose heavily to his feet.

"You won't find her there, Mr. Jackman," said a voice quietly. Jackman jumped. He hadn't heard Ridley come up. There had just been the faintest breeze on the left side of his face and then that quiet mocking voice as Ridley slid into the passenger seat beside him. "Any change?"

Jackman shook his head. "She must still be in there. I checked with security a while ago. Helen Highcroft went in and out on her own at around half past five. No one called Jennifer Macrae's been anywhere near the place."

"Not officially, anyway," corrected Ridley. "Right—time I was away. Give the gate the word, will you?"

Jackman reached for the car phone. "Security, this is Maurice Jackman. I'm doing a perimeter check out on the east side. Will you please isolate gate four until further notice."

"Right you are then, Mr. Jackman." Jackman waited. "Gate four is now isolated. Alarms registered as inert."

Jackman replaced the receiver.

"Thank you," nodded Ridley. He held out a gloved hand. "Keys?"

Jackman handed them across.

Then Ridley was off, running: a dark shadow heading soundlessly towards HPL, towards Jenny. A man unleashed.

THE LUMP OF SHADOW on the floor of the darkened flat in Elgin Terrace stirred, groaned and tried to sit up. Tony felt the room tilt and sway beneath him and closed his eyes again as he struggled to hang on to consciousness, fight the gnawing pain in his left shoulder and work out what the hell had happened to him.

It came back slowly, piece by piece, and he groaned again as he remembered. The bastard he'd thought was from S5 but who couldn't be:

S5 didn't need to go round breaking people's collarbones and knocking them unconscious.

Tony gritted his teeth, hauled himself up and edged his way gingerly towards the bathroom.

He tugged on the light, ran water into the handbasin and dunked his head in it. That helped, it helped a great deal. It cleared his head but it didn't do much for the throbbing agony in his shoulder. He jerked open the linen cupboard and searched for anything that would do as a makeshift sling. He improvised with a tea towel, gulped down a couple of paracetamol from a bottle he found in Jenny's medicine cupboard, and eased himself slowly through to the kitchen, grimacing with effort as he tried to remember something important, something to do with the man who had been waiting for him in Jenny's sitting room.

That was it, wasn't it? That was the whole point! He hadn't been waiting for him, had he? He'd been waiting for her—for Jenny. And if he wasn't from S5, then that meant . . . God! He had to warn her. So think: where would she be? He looked at his watch and saw that he had been out for hours. Jenny could be anywhere. The office? No, stupid! She's been suspended. What about that woman, Helen Highcroft? The woman who'd listened to all those wild, crackpot theories of Jenny's that suddenly didn't seem so farfetched after all?

Back in the sitting room, Tony took the telephone off the hook and dialled Enquiries. "Yes. I'd . . . I'd like the number of a Professor Highcroft—it's very urgent."

HELEN HIGHCROFT WAITED until the taillight of Hamish Owen's Morris had turned into the main road and then shut the front door.

Malcolm was dead. Somehow, somewhere, he had died. She knew that now, and the knowledge brought with it a sense of release from the uncertainty, the self-doubt and endless self-examination that had haunted her these last few days. Steevenson and Parsons—they had both worked at Porton, and both were dead. Malcolm had worked at Porton too. Now he was dead as well, she could feel it. Hamish Owen's questions had forced her to recognize the true nature of her husband's work, but they had also opened her eyes to the danger, not just to herself but to Jenny. Jenny, who was inside HPL right now. Helen snatched up the telephone and began dialling feverishly. If she could only reach her in time, warn her to get out.

TONY DIALLED THE HIGHCROFTS' NUMBER. Engaged. He slammed down the telephone impatiently. The operator had given him Helen Highcroft's address. It was only a few minutes across the town, if he could drive. He hurried down the hall, slammed the door, and clambered awkwardly behind the wheel of his car.

116

JENNY ROSE CAUTIOUSLY to her feet. It was time to move. Not daring yet to use her torch in case she was seen from outside, she stuffed her things into her bag and reached for the door handle, was actually just beginning to turn it when the telephone rang on the desk.

She whirled round, fluttering with panic. It might be Helen. Who else knew there was anyone inside this particular office long after everyone else had gone home? But what if it was a wrong number? What if even now someone was coming down the corridor to answer it? Someone from security, for example? That decided her. Jenny stepped out into the corridor, closing the door behind her.

No one was in sight. Not a sound apart from the muffled ringing of the telephone. A quick glance over her shoulder and Jenny was running lightly down the corridor towards the staircase that led up to the offices on the floor above. Leaving her thermos on the office floor behind her.

Helen slammed down the telephone and groaned. She was too late.

RIDLEY FLATTENED HIMSELF against the northeastern corner of HPL's main building and paused, his every sense alive to the sight, feel and sound of the night around him: the feel of the bricks coarse beneath his hands; the distant murmur of the traffic; the thin cry of some night bird hunting nearby. Another predator.

He moved silently along the wall towards the fire-escape door at the far side of HPL's main building. A moment's delay while he worked on the deadlock, and then he was inside.

JENNY GROPED HER WAY up the unfamiliar staircase to the first floor. Here, using the torch just to get her bearings, she walked cautiously forward, and entered what she hoped would prove to be Malcolm Highcroft's office. Another quick flash of the torch: desk, chairs, filing cabinet. Potted plants on the windowsill, medical posters and calendars. Jenny slipped behind the desk, pulled open the top drawer and switched on her torch again: an office diary. She flicked it open and looked in the flyleaf: Stuart Young.

Jenny frowned. So they had both been wrong: downstairs might not have been Malcolm's office, but this one wasn't either. She closed the diary and, putting it back in the drawer, saw that it had been lying on top of an internal HPL telephone directory. Jenny began turning over the pages under the shaded beam of her torch, looking for Malcolm's extension number. It wasn't hard to find in the alphabetical list: Highcroft, Prof. M....644. Helen had been right.

Jenny bent forward and looked at the face of the telephone in front of her. There, beneath the instruction DIAL 0 FOR OUTSIDE LINE, she read the extension number: 482.

Dial 0 for an outside line . . . Impulsively Jenny dialled 0, winced at the noise and took out her diary to look up Helen's home number. The call began to ring in.

"Hello?"

"Helen? It's me—Jenny," she whispered.

"Jenny! Thank God. I was trying to—"

"Sssh! Keep your voice down," Jenny hissed fiercely. "I'm in Malcolm's office on the first floor. At least, what we thought was Malcolm's office, next to the lifts. Only—"

"Jenny, listen to me," Helen urged desperately. "I . . . I want you out of there. Now. I mean it. There isn't time to explain now but there's . . . there's more going on than you think. More than just Cardocol."

Jenny frowned. "More than just Cardocol? What d'you mean?"

"You remember that reporter you told me about? Hamish Owen—the one from the local rag? He came here to see me. He'd been doing some digging, about Engel and the company. And about those . . . those other men who died, you remember?"

"Go on," Jenny whispered, hunching closer to the telephone.

"He thinks something . . . something happened to them. He found out they'd both been working at Porton, too."

"Too? Who else worked there? I'm sorry, I don't follow."

"Porton Down's some sort of secret chemical warfare establishment. Malcolm . . . Malcolm used to work there. A long time ago. Before we came up to Scotland."

There was silence while that sank in. Jenny forced herself to remain calm. "Let's just think. This . . . this Hamish Owen reckons they all worked together, is that it?"

"He doesn't know for certain yet. He—"

"Wait a second," Jenny pulled pencil, paper and internal directory towards her. "What were those names, can you remember?"

"Tony . . . no . . . Thomas Steevenson, and Douglas Parsons."

"Hang about." Jenny ran a finger rapidly down the page. Parsons, D:... 645. Then Steevenson, T, right at the back: 646. They *had* all been working together! She swept a finger down the right-hand column of numbers, searching for any other extension with a six-four prefix.

Heyer, Dr P 383
Highcroft, Prof. M......................644
Inger, J 866
Jackman, M 640/483

"Malcolm and Jackman, Helen," she said matter-of-factly. "They worked with them too, although Jackman appears—" She leaned forward suddenly, looking not at Jackman's six-four prefix but at the three-number digit that followed it. And then at the face of the telephone she was using herself: 482. "Jackman has two extension numbers, Helen," she said urgently, her voice pitched low with excitement. "640

118

and 483. 483 must be next door! I'll see if it's open, OK? Then I'll—"

"Jenny, please. Don't be a fool! If you—"

"Call you back." She rang off, pulled an anguished face at the *ting!* of the telephone as it went down on its cradle, put diary and internal directory back where she had found them and rose to her feet. One thing, she had the building to herself, and there was plenty of time.

HELEN GROANED WITH FRUSTRATION, and was just turning back to the kitchen when she heard a long ring on the doorbell. She went into the hallway. It was late for callers. She dropped the chain onto its catch, turned on the porch light and pulled the door cautiously towards her. There was a man outside with his arm in some sort of sling.

"Mrs. . . . Mrs. Highcroft?"

"Yes? What do you want?"

"Is Jenny with you? Jenny Macrae?"

"I don't—"

"Please, Mrs. Highcroft, just tell me. It's very important."

"Why do you want to know?"

"My name's Tony Lockhart. I'm a . . . a friend."

RIDLEY STROLLED DOWN THE CORRIDOR. He had spent twenty minutes in his motel bedroom studying the floor plan of the building and was now able to move around the labyrinth of unlit passages and empty offices with confidence.

Nothing to worry about from reception, he thought contemptuously. The security guard was leaning back in his chair, one fat hand groping at an open box of sandwiches, his eyes glued to a portable TV set.

Ridley paused outside the third door along, the one marked "X" on the diagram he had found in Jenny Macrae's flat. Then he slipped in, whipped the door shut behind him, turned the key and pressed back against the wall to listen intently in the darkness.

JACKMAN'S DOOR WAS UNLOCKED. Jenny moved carefully past his secretary's desk and tried the handle of the inner office. That opened, too. Another quick, surreptitious flash of the torch: same sort of office as before, only more spacious: wide desk, chair and a row of filing cabinets; modern sofa along one wall with, nearby, a computer terminal on a pine table. Nothing special in the top drawer of the desk this time apart from a plastic identity tag for Mr. Maurice Jackman, Project Development Manager.

But in the bottom drawer she found a jumble of miscellaneous personal possessions, among which was a bundle of internal laboratory analysis reports sent from somewhere called E11 to Professor M. Highcroft, RD7.

In the grey pencil tray that slid out of the top right-hand side of Jackman's desk, Jenny discovered a silver metal key. She took it over to the filing cabinets and found that it fitted the centre lock. The drawer rolled obediently towards her on smooth runners.

Whatever else Jackman might be, he was a tidy, methodical professional who kept his files in apple-pie order. There were several at the front marked simply: CARDOCOL. Jenny took them over to the desk and switched on her torch.

The first was a thick, green ring-binder marked CONFIDENTIAL. CARDOCOL CLINICAL TRIALS, SERIES 886/FGJ. Jenny opened it and with a little shiver of excitement began to read.

TONY HURRIED DOWN Helen Highcroft's front steps, and slid awkwardly behind the wheel of his car again. Helen watched anxiously. "What about the police?" she called suddenly. "If you went to them surely they'd—"

"The police?" Tony shook his head and started the car. "I'd just be wasting my time," he shouted over the noise of the engine. He put the car into gear and drove out onto the main road.

THE SILENCE OF JACKMAN'S OFFICE was broken by the slow turning of a page as Jenny leaned forward appalled, torch in hand, and read again that final, damning paragraph, just to be certain there was no mistake:

. . . while volunteers undergoing clinical trials at registered outpatient clinics and surgeries have shown an incidence of adverse reaction deemed to be commercially unacceptable, those in hospitals have not. It is therefore recommended that consideration be given to the selective amalgamation of both sets of statistics shown in 17/AEK (attached) before submission to CSM. It is anticipated that an adjustment of as little as between seven and eleven per cent overall would be sufficient to deflect an adverse decision by the licensing authority.

There was a small neat tick at the bottom of the paragraph with, beside it, one word and two initials: "Agreed. M.J." Maurice Jackman.

Jenny sat back in her chair, stunned. There it was, in black and white. HPL, with the endorsement of its own Project Development Manager, had cold-bloodedly decided to stack the deck, bend the rules: to cheat. Not by much, perhaps, but by enough to ensure that the granting of their application for a product licence was a foregone conclusion. Postural hypotension, the condition whose mastery was at the very core of Cardocol's appeal, had never been at issue with seven to eleven per cent of those volunteers who had taken part in HPL's clinical trials. Because they had been flat on their backs, bed-bound in some hospital ward.

Jenny closed the ring-binder, slid it into her bag and replaced the other files where she had found them, conscious of a raging fury at what she had discovered. There had been nothing there about people. Or illness. Or caring. Nothing about Robbie Roberts or Jamie Ennis. Just commercial considerations about profit. Profit without honour.

RIDLEY BENT DOWN and felt on the office floor for the object he had just brushed with his foot. He found it, identified Jenny's thermos and rose to his feet. She'd been here, definitely. He placed the thermos on the desk and slipped out into the corridor, turning right towards the staircase and the offices above.

JENNY PUSHED THE FILING CABINET closed, turned round—and froze as she thought she heard something. She listened carefully. Nothing. She must have imagined it. Picking up the piece of paper on which she had written the names Steevenson and Parsons, she went towards Jackman's computer, a plan forming in her mind. She switched on her torch for a moment and recognized the model immediately. They had an identical one in the clinic.

She sat down in front of it, glanced round nervously at the silent room watching her, and then back at the screen, wondering if she dared. She brought the machine to life, thought for a moment and then keyed in: PERSONNEL SEARCH. The words were displayed instantly in front of her eyes, white on green, and were followed by the instruction: INPUT LOAD. Jenny's fingers worked over the keys.

HIGHCROFT M. JACKMAN M. PARSONS D. STEEVENSON T. She paused then, while the cursor blinked at her patiently from the screen's top left-hand corner, as she tried to remember the language. SEARCH COMMONALITY she typed. Blink. Blink. Blink:

SECURITY CLEARANCE came the reply.

WRONG banged in Jenny, using lies to trick the machine into divulging more than it should.

CORRECT . . . CORRECT . . . insisted the computer, angry now. HIGHCROFT M JACKMAN M PARSONS D STEEVENSON T ALL CLEARED FOR ACCESS RD7.

DEFINE RD7 ACCESS tried Jenny. And blew it. The ploy was too obvious. The computer didn't buy it, not for a moment.

VERIFY OPERATOR CLEARANCE PROJECT OMAHA the computer demanded sternly.

Omaha? thought Jenny. What the hell was Omaha? There was a noise next door: the smallest, quietest click. Jenny froze, then reached out a stealthy hand and turned off the terminal. The screen cleared, the low hum sighed away to silence, and Jenny slid away from the chair, crossed the office and crouched down beside Jackman's desk. Worried, yes, but not terrified. Not yet, for she was still thinking in terms of detection and

embarrassment, not in terms of her own survival. It was probably just the security man doing his rounds.

It wasn't. It was Ridley, working methodically along the first floor from one empty office to another. He paused outside Jackman's outer office door, a gloved hand on the door jamb. She had been in here. He could smell it, quite literally. He moved on, past the secretary's desk, silent as the dark that enveloped him. He sank down to his haunches and waited. She was close now, very close . . .

HELEN STOOD ALONE and irresolute in her hallway, her fears for Jenny magnified tenfold by Tony's visit and his brief, terse description of the man he had found waiting in Jenny's flat. Finally, she could bear the waiting no longer. She picked up the telephone and began dialling the number Jenny had given her a few minutes earlier. The number of Jackman's office.

The telephone rang suddenly on Jackman's desk, inches from Jenny's head. She started violently and banged her head against the edge of the desk. Oh, Helen—no! In some half-thought-out attempt to repair the damage already done by that single strident ring of the bell, Jenny rose from behind the desk and reached for the telephone. Her hand encountered not the smooth plastic of the receiver, but the soft leather of a glove covering a human hand.

"Snap," said a voice softly.

CHAPTER 23

Jenny let out a stifled scream and pulled her hand away as though it had been scalded. Stumbling back towards the window, she fumbled with the torch and switched it on. The beam wavered, settled on a dark blue arm and moved up to the thin, drawn face of a man, weirdly streaked with camouflage cream. The telephone rang on.

"Well?" said the man softly. "Aren't you going to answer it?"

Jenny tried to speak but the words wouldn't come. She wondered wildly if she had gone suddenly mad. "Who . . . who are you?" she managed finally. "What are you doing here like . . . like that?"

"What am *I* doing here? I might . . . ah." The telephone stopped ringing and there was silence. Ridley sighed regretfully. "You should always answer the telephone, didn't they ever tell you that, Jennifer?"

"How do you know my name?" she whispered. Ridley said nothing. "If you're going to call the police, I—"

"Call the police, Jennifer? No. I don't think I'll do that I—*turn that off!*" Jenny had switched on Jackman's desk lamp. The man was clearer now. Jenny could see that he was wearing a two-piece, dark blue tracksuit with the hood folded down round his neck; and that he was holding a slender-bladed knife down against his right thigh. In that instant she knew that he had nothing to do with the police or with the company security men. This man meant death.

As Ridley reached for the lamp switch, Jenny darted forward, swept the lamp off the desk towards him and lunged at the door. A fleeting impression then of Ridley swerving aside as the lamp fell to the floor and the room was plunged into darkness. Through the far door and spinning right to hurtle down the corridor, with Ridley somewhere behind her. Terror lent her wings. Crashing through another door and flinging it back behind her, she ran blindly along the first-floor corridor, not caring if there were steps or walls or the deepest hole in the world waiting for her ahead. She wanted only to get away. One second, two, three—then *bang!* She heard Ridley flat-hand his way through the same swing door and come racing silently after her.

Round another corner, more darkness to her left, the lighter outline of a door and window to her right, the slightest delay as she hesitated, and it was too late. A hand grabbed her roughly by the hair. "Far enough, girlie."

Jenny screamed with fear and pain as Ridley jerked her viciously back and round against the wall. "Game over." There was a sudden glint of steel as he moved closer.

THE GATEHOUSE SLID INTO VIEW. Tony trod on the accelerator and surged past. Round the bend and on, the headlights swinging across the shadows.

The main building with its ground-floor lights loomed into view. Left arm and shoulder aching with the effort, Tony glanced to right and left, searching for a car, lights, anything that might give him a lead. Both car parks were empty. Then something caught his eye. He flicked his headlights on to full beam. Jenny!

A man was forcing Jenny forward in front of him across the grass, the pair turning now, frozen in the glare of his headlights. Tony slewed the car across the car park towards them, bumped up onto the lawn from the tarmac and accelerated across the grass. Jenny broke free and began to run to the right, away from Ridley. Tony didn't hesitate. Ridley was the threat, the danger. He swung the car towards him, aimed for the widening gap between Jenny and his target and kept going, eyes flinty-hard as he crouched behind the wheel and Ridley began to run. Tony swung the car after him—thirty yards . . . twenty . . . ten . . . A swerve, a slight thud and Ridley had gone, lost somewhere in the darkness behind him as he swung the car away in a wide, slithering turn and twisted round, looking for Jenny.

There she was! Over at the edge of the car park, one hand to her mouth. He bumped back onto the tarmac and screeched to a halt beside her. Reaching over, he flung open the passenger door. "Get in. Quickly. Before that bastard gets back." Breathlessly, Jenny scrambled in. Tony accelerated forward, throwing her back against the seat as the door slammed shut. "You OK?"

Jenny nodded, quivering with shock. "I . . . I think so."

They swerved out of the car park with a screech of rubber and sped down towards the main gate.

Ridley rose to his feet and watched as their taillights disappeared. He had leaped aside at the last moment, banged a hand against the side of Tony's car as it swept past. He hadn't been hurt at all.

It had suddenly become very personal.

DR. ERSKINE CLOSED THE COTTAGE DOOR behind him and began to walk down the steep cobbled lane towards his car. He paused by the sea wall to stare out across the bay, his mind heavy with a sense of personal guilt, of failure, that linked the bottle of cough mixture in his pocket to a new heart drug called Cardocol and to a patient who had died out there by that island less than a week ago, taking a small child with him.

Dr. Erskine had spent the last half hour talking to Robbie Roberts's widow. As always, she had received him with unfailing kindness. That only made him feel worse, for now he believed that he was personally to blame for her husband's death.

He walked heavily down the cobbled lane. As he got into his car, he felt the little bottle of cough mixture he had found on Mrs. Roberts's kitchen table digging into his hip. He took it out of his pocket and tossed it onto the seat beside him.

A few days ago—was it only then?—the presentation of that complete set of Groesners had seemed like a harmless perk, an innocent gesture of appreciation from a local manufacturer to a local doctor. Now he saw it as a reward for compliance and the suspension of scepticism. The books would be returned in the morning—that was easy enough. Meanwhile, however, there was something he still had to do before he could sleep. He would go and see Harold Engel, the managing director of Highland Pharmaceuticals. There was something he had to tell him.

JENNY SWUNG TOWARDS TONY as they jolted over another darkened pothole. "This isn't the way to the hospital."

"I know," he replied tersely, concentrating on keeping the car on the road. HPL was a couple of miles behind them now.

"Your shoulder, Tony! If we don't—"

"They'll be watching the hospital. Your place too."

"*My* place? But—"

"That's where I got this shoulder. That bastard back there was waiting inside. For you."

"But you got him, didn't you? Back there! It's over—finished! All we have to do now—what's the matter?"

"You still don't understand, do you? It isn't 'finished', as you put it, until 'they' say it is. They're not messing around, these people. They're serious, professional." He paused. "Have you got any idea what you've stumbled into? It's a damn sight more important than some minor scandal over a new heart drug, I'll tell you that."

Jenny gazed into the darkness as she remembered what Helen had told her on the telephone, and saw again those two words punched up on the computer display: PROJECT OMAHA.

"HPL's some sort of cover for something to do with chemical warfare—at least, I think it is," she said quietly. "Malcolm Highcroft

125

used to work at Porton Down. So did both Parsons and Steevenson."

The car swerved suddenly. "Chemical warfare!" Tony muttered. They drove on in silence for a moment or two.

"You still haven't told me where we're going," Jenny said.

Tony hesitated. He had been thinking: the local hospital, Gleninver police, even RAF Glenhaddon—all offered danger, for he knew now who "they" were. "They" were the state, the government, the authorities—and he and Jenny had suddenly become Very Undesirable People. Yet they couldn't just keep on driving, blundering aimlessly through the night until they ran out of petrol. He needed time. Time to think and rest, plan and recover.

"Home," he decided finally. "My house—all right? Just to get this shoulder of mine sorted out. Then . . . then we'll go east. A town. Somewhere nice and big."

"Like *Glasgow?*" Jenny asked incredulously.

"Glasgow," Tony confirmed definitely, as the idea took hold. "Glasgow hospital. Then Glasgow newspapers, Glasgow television. Lots and lots of lovely exposure." He paused. "Got any better ideas?"

"YOU ARE WORRYING UNNECESSARILY," said Jackman wearily. They were standing over a plan of HPL's site in Harold Engel's study, and running over the final details of the launch the next day. "Nothing will go wrong. Everything's been taken care of, right down to the last detail. No one will be permitted anywhere near RD7, so relax. Forget about it. Have a drink. Tomorrow's supposed to be your day, isn't it? God knows, you've worked hard enough for it." The words weren't getting through, he could sense it. "Look," he soothed, "I know we've had our differences over this Highcroft business—"

Engel's head snapped up. "Differences? *Differences?* Is that all you think they are? They're more than just 'differences', I assure you."

Jackman shrugged. "Very well, I accept that, for the sake of argument. But you can't bring him back. So—look to the future. Another month, two at the most, and Cardocol will be a household name. Yours will be too." He paused. "Well? That's what you want, isn't it?"

"Don't tell me what I want, Jackman. Don't you dare tell me what I want—ever," said Harold Engel with quiet, cold fury. "You don't begin to understand what I want. You and I are so far apart we might as well be on different planets."

Jackman smiled, not in the least put out. "Nonsense!" he said briskly. "We're after the same thing, you and I. We just travel to the same destination by different routes, that's all. I, at least, pride myself on being a realist. To achieve results I accept there must inevitably be compromise, sacrifice, decisions that are sometimes . . . unpleasant. But you? You?" he scoffed. "You choose to delude yourself that you can

126

somehow keep your hands clean. RD7 would not exist without HPL—true. But the converse is also true. HPL—Cardocol—would not exist without RD7. The ends, Harold, always justify the means. They always will. You choose to forget that if you hadn't been in such desperate financial straits in that factory of yours, and so desperate for another chance, our paths would never have crossed. We—"

"Let me make you a promise, Jackman," Engel interrupted with deadly seriousness. "If Cardocol's a success, I will never, *never* permit my company to be used by you and your people again, is that clear? I've done things for you that will be on my conscience for the rest of my days. Well, you can find someone else to blackmail into providing you with your . . . your facilities!" He almost spat the word out.

"Blackmail? Come now, Harold, it was hardly that—" They both turned at a knock on the door. Joyce Engel stood in the doorway.

"Sorry to interrupt. There's a Dr. Erskine to see you, Harold."

"What—at this time of night?"

"I suggested waiting until morning but he . . . he said it was urgent."

"Did he say what it was about?"

Joyce nodded. "About tomorrow. About Cardocol."

"Well, you'd better show him in."

Engel and Jackman waited. Presently, Erskine entered the study. He looked surprised. He had obviously been expecting to find only Engel in the room.

"Dr. Erskine? I am Harold Engel. This is Mr. Jackman, our Project Development Manager at HPL." Dr. Erskine nodded. "I understand that you want to see me urgently. Something about Cardocol?"

"I've some bad news for you, Mr. Engel," the doctor began simply. "You must cancel the launch of your new drug."

Harold Engel snorted in disbelief. "Cancel it? Now? After all the work that's gone into it? The tests, the clinical trials?"

"I'm perfectly serious, Mr. Engel," Dr. Erskine replied calmly, as he took a packet of Cardocol pills from his jacket pocket. "I'm what you might call one of your 'tame' doctors, Mr. Engel," he began. "At least, I was. Your people would come knocking on my door with their free samples, their offers of business lunches and their donations to 'surgery expenses', and I'd play along. Mutual support, you might say—the perks of the profession. I even put a couple of my patients on Cardocol for you. Just to keep everyone happy. A wee bit early, perhaps, but then that's no crime, is it? Not if it helps the patient. And, I must be fair—Cardocol did its stuff. To begin with, anyway."

"Would you kindly explain the point you wish—"

"The point? The *point*, Mr. Engel, is that six days after starting to take this wonder-drug of yours, my patient was rushed into hospital with a blood-pressure reading that had gone through the roof!" He paused and

127

then added, almost as an afterthought, "She also had a little cough, by the way, although that didn't register as significant, not at the time. A dry, ticklish little cough."

"EASY . . . EASY . . . GOD!" With a groan, Tony eased himself down onto the sofa in his sitting room, and Jenny stood back, panting after the struggle of helping him from the car. "Lock . . . lock the door and draw the curtains," he ordered, waving a hand weakly at the windows. Jenny did as she was bidden, and then returned to stand over Tony. He looked awful, clammy and pain-racked.

"A couple . . . couple of minutes' rest and I'll . . . I'll be as right as rain. God . . ." he groaned again. Jenny leaned down and peered closely at his shoulder.

"You can't drive another fifty yards with that, far less to Glasgow," she announced. "It's broken, you know that, don't you?" She waited in silence as he tried to gather his strength, with head thrown back and eyes closed. After several minutes he said, "Help me to get upstairs, will you? To the . . . the bathroom."

With Tony leaning heavily against her, they made it eventually. In the bathroom Jenny helped him ease off shirt and jacket. The skin around the collarbone was puffed and swollen, and there was an angular projection that told of broken bone.

"You *must* see a doctor," Jenny said. "You haven't any choice."

"In Glasgow, OK? In Glasgow."

"That's miles away! You'll never get there." Jenny took another glance at his broken collarbone and made up her mind. She made for the stairs, and the telephone.

Tony lurched awkwardly to the bathroom door. "Where are you going?"

"To call a doctor. Don't worry, this one's OK. It's the one I was telling you about—Dr. Erskine."

"Erskine? But he . . . he's the one who lied to you, for God's sake!"

At the bottom of the stairs Jenny opened her handbag and took out the report on the clinical trials which she had stolen from Jackman's office. "This'll change his mind, don't you think?" She went to the telephone in the hall and began dialling his home number.

"Yes?" A woman's voice. His wife, perhaps.

"May I speak to Dr. Erskine, please?"

"Dr. Erskine is away on a call just now, I'm sorry."

"Oh." Jenny thought for a moment. "Could you tell me where I could reach him, please? It's an emergency."

"One moment." There was a brief delay, then, "You could try to reach him on Gleninver 1455."

Jenny scribbled down the number. "Thanks." She rang off.

"THERE'S NOTHING PARTICULARLY UNUSUAL about a minor irritating cough, Dr. Erskine," said Harold Engel. "The medical data sheet we issue with each packet states quite clearly that there is some risk of bronchial inflammation—particularly among elderly patients. Somewhere in the region of four or five per cent."

"The medical data sheet? You mean this wee thing?" Contemptuously Erskine rummaged in another pocket and pulled out a crumpled piece of paper filled with long lines of tiny, close-set type. "Aye, I'll give you that much, Mr. Engel. You do warn people they may get a bit of a cough." He paused. "What you do not say, down there in the small print, is that it's near as dammit a cast-iron certainty. That would get in the way of 'commercial considerations', would it not?"

"What d'you mean, a cast-iron certainty? I told you, the incidence of bronchial irritation is no more than four or five per cent! If you mean to imply that—" They turned to another tap on the door, and Joyce Engel came into the room once more.

"Sorry to trouble you again," she said, turning to Dr. Erskine. "There's an emergency call for you, Doctor. A Miss Jenny Macrae."

CHAPTER **24**

As soon as Dr. Erskine had left, "I wonder if I might make a brief phone call?" Jackman asked politely.

"What? Oh, yes. The phone's in the hall." Harold Engel answered distractedly, for he was worrying about what the doctor had told him about Cardocol. A "cast-iron certainty"? The man must be unhinged.

Jackman closed the door softly behind him. Jennifer Macrae, making an emergency call to Dr. Erskine? What had gone wrong? He dialled the operator, his face a mask of stone. "Pagephone 3447," he ordered when she answered. "Subscriber is to call"—he glanced down—"Gleninver 1455, immediately."

"Gleninver 1455. One moment, caller." Jackman replaced the receiver and waited. The telephone rang. It was Ridley.

"What happened?" Jackman snapped.

"She had a friend, didn't she? A chum in a car. Once I've—"

"She is now at number seventeen, Bruneval Close, have you got that? Seventeen, Bruneval Close." He glanced over his shoulder at the empty hall. "And this time, I want it finished, understand? Finished."

TONY WAS BACK ON THE SOFA downstairs. Jenny watched as Dr. Erskine eased back his shirt, inspected his shoulder and broken collarbone briefly, and grunted. "You've been to the police, I take it? You've reported the homicidal maniac who did this?"

129

Tony and Jenny exchanged looks. "No police," Tony said, after a brief silence. "And no hospital, either. Not in Gleninver, anyway."

Dr. Erskine looked up sharply. "Don't be daft, man—this shoulder of yours needs proper hospital treatment. And an X-ray."

"Later, Doctor. Later."

Dr. Erskine shut his bag with an angry snap. "Would one of you mind telling me, please, just what the hell is going on?" There was silence for a moment, and then Jenny began to tell him. She told him, if not the whole truth, then at least the part of it that touched upon Robbie Roberts, Jamie Ennis, Mrs. Proctor and Cardocol.

"Would you read this, please?" she said finally, as she opened her bag and took out the report she had stolen from HPL.

Dr. Erskine glanced at the word CONFIDENTIAL, opened his mouth to make some comment, thought better of it and began to read, the frown on his face deepening as he turned back a page to compare some figures. "Where did you get this?" he demanded.

"From HPL," replied Jenny. Truthfully.

"They *gave* it to you? Lent you a copy?"

"Not exactly, no. I took it. It's . . . it's quite genuine."

"So I see." Dr. Erskine let the report drop onto his lap. "At least it supports what I was telling Harold Engel just now."

"Just now?" asked Tony, almost missing it.

"Yes," Dr. Erskine nodded. "He . . . he didn't believe me, of course— didn't *want* to believe me, I should say. Anyway . . . he invited me to return to his office with all the relevant facts and figures first thing in the morning." He leaned forward. "He simply denied that the incidence of bronchial inflammation was particularly high. I . . . I got the impression he really believed that! When I tried to tell him that my colleagues in Fort William and I—"

"Just now?" Tony repeated. "You saw Mr. Engel just now?"

Dr. Erskine nodded. "That's where I was when you called—with Mr. Engel. Oh, and that Project Development Manager of his, Maurice Jackman. Odd-looking fellow."

A cold, oily spectre of fear uncoiled in Tony's stomach. "Did you tell them you were coming here?" he asked.

"Well . . . yes. Yes, I did, as a matter of fact," Dr. Erskine admitted. He glanced uneasily at their faces. "Did I say anything wrong?"

RIDLEY PULLED THE CAR in to the side of the road, switched off the lights and reached across to the glove compartment. He took out a street map, turned on a torch and glanced down. Yes, that was right. Bruneval Close. The torch clicked off.

From beneath the driver's seat he eased out a flat, heavy package wrapped in chamois leather. Carefully he began unfolding the cloth. It was a disassembled Model II Ingram automatic pistol: the weapon itself, a filled thirty-round box magazine in .38 calibre, and an eight-inch-long black rubber suppressor.

Ridley smiled as he slipped the silencer over the end of the short barrel, picked up the box magazine, and slid it into the base of the weapon's handgrip. He tapped it home, wiped the assembled weapon carefully with the chamois leather and laid the gun on the passenger seat beside him. Then he wound down the window and taking a pair of miniature binoculars from the glove compartment, raised them to his eyes. He had parked outside numbers ten and twelve on the right-hand side of the road. Number seventeen, the target house, was the last on the opposite side. The binoculars panned across the front of the house. Lights. And a Ford Escort parked outside. Ridley picked up the silenced Ingram, tucked it inside the folds of his raincoat, opened the driver's door and stepped quietly into the shadows.

JENNY WAS STANDING in the sitting room with a hand to her mouth, looking towards the front door, as though she expected to see it burst open at any moment. After the departure of Dr. Erskine, Tony's house suddenly seemed very small and very still, as though it was waiting breathlessly for something terrible to happen. Jenny felt trapped, hemmed in, and very frightened. She turned towards Tony, still sitting on the sofa. "Perhaps if we just—"

"I'm trying to think," Tony muttered, aware even as he delayed that he was squandering moments that could save their lives.

"Look, Tony"—Jenny crouched beside him, wide, frightened eyes in a pale, frightened face—"we can't just . . . just sit here, for God's sake! You heard what Dr. Erskine said. They know where we are! You said yourself the only safe place left is Glasgow, a large town. We have to go now!" she urged. "It's our only chance."

"Turn off the light," Tony ordered quietly, coming to a decision and hoping he wasn't making the worst mistake of his life. He hauled himself painfully off the sofa, his left arm pinned across his chest by the sling Dr. Erskine had given him. He reached for the little screw of paper containing the painkillers. One, the doctor had said, one every four hours or when the pain was really bad. Tony took two, swallowed them down dry. When he looked up, Jenny still hadn't moved. "The light. Turn it off. Now."

"The *light?*"

"Don't argue, for God's sake, there isn't time." Looking at Tony as though he were mad, Jenny turned off the standard lamp behind the sofa. The room was lit now only by the light washing through from the hall. "Wait here." Jenny waited, totally baffled, as Tony hurried awkwardly through to the kitchen. Then he was back, with something in his hand. In the gloom, Jenny couldn't make out what it was, not at first. When she could, her stomach turned over.

"What . . . what are you going to do with that?"

"We're too late," Tony said simply, by way of explanation, as he held the claw hammer down at his side. It was the only thing he had been able to find without going outside to the garage. The only weapon.

"Too late? Too late for what?"

"For Glasgow. For running. Dr. Erskine was at Engel's home when? An hour ago?"

"About that, yes. Maybe a little longer."

"An hour ago," Tony agreed softly. "And once he'd left, what d'you think they did?" He paused. "They got on the blower to whoever it is they use on people like us, and passed on this address, right? And they did that . . . sixty minutes ago. At least."

"What are you saying?"

"I'm saying, they're out there already, waiting for us. One, maybe two—I don't know. What I do know is that the moment we open that door . . . well, it'll be all over."

"We'll be killed, you mean?"

"Something along those lines I should imagine, yes."

"But—"

"So we don't go through that door. We don't go through the windows, either. We stay here. We let them come to us." Jenny nodded calmly as though it all made perfect sense. "We've something else up our sleeve too, don't forget."

"What's that?"

"Surprise. We know they know we're here. But they don't *know* we know—get it? So in a moment we'll both go upstairs to bed. We're going to turn off all the lights down here and go upstairs, just as though everything's normal. Then we'll wait."

"We'll *wait?* Oh, terrific!" said Jenny, as all her fears exploded to the surface. "Oh, marvellous! We just lie here tucked up in bed and *wait* until that animal, or someone like him, decides to pay us a visit, is that it?"

"We're wasting time," Tony said shortly, moving towards the stairs.

Jenny hurried after him. "Isn't there . . . isn't there something else we could do?"

"Like what?"

Jenny thought, then suddenly snapped her fingers. "I know! You . . . you know all the people round here, yes? Your neighbours?" Tony nodded. "Well . . . what if you phoned them all? Now. Told them . . . told them their garages were being broken into. That would get them all outside, wouldn't it? It would turn the road into broad daylight! They'd never dare do anything then, would they?" Tony began going up the stairs. "Well? It's an idea, isn't it?" Jenny called after him.

"How're you going to contact them? By phone?" Tony pointed. He'd tried earlier, immediately after Dr. Erskine had left.

Jenny lifted the receiver. "It's dead," she said in a small voice.

"That's what I mean," Tony said. "We haven't any choice."

"RIGHT—THAT'LL HAVE TO DO," Tony whispered. They'd moved the hall mirror, swapped it with the watercolour at the head of the stairs beside the airing cupboard. Now he stepped back and inspected the mirror critically. Down the stairs stealthily, to draw back the narrow curtains at the bottom of the staircase, then up again, quickly, ears cocked for the slightest sound. He reached out for Jenny's hand. "Come on, in here," he whispered. He led her through into what had been Paul's bedroom and gestured at the narrow space between bed and floor. "Down there," he whispered. "Flat on your stomach and, whatever happens, stay there, understand?"

Jenny swallowed. "But you—"

"*Stay there.* I'll be OK. Promise?" She nodded.

"Right. See you in the morning, I hope." He turned to the door.

Jenny reached out impulsively and put a hand on his arm. The good one. "Tony? I'm sorry. For getting you into this mess. If I hadn't been such a fool in the first place . . . I just want you to know I'm sorry, OK? And very grateful. For everything." She reached up suddenly and kissed him. "Be careful," she whispered.

Tony's tired face creased into a smile. "I won't say 'you're welcome', but . . . you're welcome. Now, down there. And *don't move.*" He slipped out onto the landing, the door closed softly behind him, and Jenny lay down alongside the bed, her hands tucked under her body, her head flat on the carpet, twisted to one side as she listened to the wild thudding of her heart in the silence.

The waiting began.

"BUT WHY?" JOYCE ENGEL BEGGED, kneeling in front of her husband with both his hands gripped tightly in hers. "*Why*, Harold?"

"Because we were running into deep financial difficulties. I couldn't have built up again from scratch, not without help. Didn't you ever wonder where the money was coming from? The money for the move up to Scotland? All that plant and machinery?"

Joyce shrugged helplessly. "I presumed friends in the City—"

"Friends in the City?" Harold Engel threw back his head and laughed harshly, remembering as though it was yesterday the nightmare of collapse, the frantic telephone calls, the brisk empty smiles and averted gazes. The silence of defeat. Of failure.

"But why *you*, Harold? Why not—I don't know—Porton Down?"

"After all the attention places like Greenham Common and Molesworth have been getting? They stopped doing sensitive work in places like that months ago, for that very reason."

"But there must have been other companies just as suitable?"

Harold Engel shook his head. "Not really, no. They found out very early on that I was interested in blockers—anti-hypertensives. That meant that our own research chemists would be coming into contact with two specific chemicals: cholinesterase and acetylcholine. The first controls the muscles by breaking down the second, you see; the chemical which makes the muscles contract."

"But I don't understand. What's that got to do with this . . . this Project OMAHA thing that killed Malcolm?"

"Rather a lot," said Engel gently. "The chemical nerve agents they were working with in RD7 all block the release of cholinesterase. As a result, the level of acetylcholine builds up unchecked until ultimately the body poisons itself."

Joyce looked as if she was going to be sick. "And you . . . you've been working on this . . . this thing all this time? Without telling me? All these months, these years? How . . . how could you?"

"OMAHA was the price of commercial survival. It was either cooperate or go under. God help me, I decided to cooperate."

TONY THOUGHT HE HAD IMAGINED IT at first. The faintest crunching sound, as though someone was munching an apple downstairs. Or, just possibly, using something to muffle the sound of breaking glass. He crouched lower and changed his grip on the shaft of the hammer as he squinted through the crack in the door and stifled a groan of pain. He had been bent almost double now for hours. His watch said 3:15. The hour before dawn. Dawn attack.

Ridley dropped lightly into the kitchen.

He paused. Listening, looking. Not a sound. Not a light. He gently closed the window, twisting home the locking-catch beneath the broken pane of glass. Then he moved across the kitchen and listened again. Still nothing. One hand holding the Ingram across his body, he slipped off the safety catch, eased back the cocking handle and waited. Then slowly he moved down the hall and paused to look out through the little window at the foot of the stairs. The glow of the street light fell through onto the staircase. Ridley slowly pulled the curtain closed.

Tony watched him through the crack in the airing-cupboard door and cursed silently. He had hoped he would miss the window, would come on up the stairs and past the cupboard door with his every step back-lit against that small square of light reflected in the mirror at the top of the stairs. Now the stairs were in darkness. And all Tony knew for sure was that the man was there somewhere, coming steadily towards him with an automatic pistol in his hands. Oh, God!

He waited, mouth dry, heart pounding furiously. The slightest rustle of cloth in the darkness: Tony sensed rather than saw a movement in the reflection of the mirror and erupted from his hiding place, smashing the door of the cupboard back across the landing and swinging to his right with the hammer. It glanced off metal and found flesh. Ridley stumbled backwards. Tony hurled himself after him, using his body as a battering ram. He charged into Ridley and felt the hammer strike home again, this time against the side of the man's face, and he saw the gleam of teeth, an animal snarl of pain. The Ingram clattered to the landing as the dark figure lost its footing and toppled backwards. Tony didn't hesitate. Hurling the heavy hammer after the crumpling figure as it crashed down the narrow staircase, he groped feverishly for the automatic lying somewhere at his feet. He found it, pointed it blindly down the stairs into the darkness and pressed the trigger. The Ingram jumped and kicked in his hands. There was a soft thudding sound, the crash of breaking glass, and then silence. Tony took his finger off the trigger and crouched down by the banister rail. The bedroom door creaked open and he spun round, finger back on the trigger.

"Tony?" a terrified whisper out of the darkness.

"*Stay there! Get down!*" he shouted. Jenny dropped to her knees. Tony waited. No sound. Nothing. Just darkness and silence. He waited a few more moments, then, "Jenny," he whispered, "there's a torch in the drawer of the bedside table behind me. Get it. Only don't turn it on till I tell you." He heard her wriggle across the landing into the bedroom. Then she was back, crawling to his side. Still no sound from below.

He took the torch, pushed Jenny back towards Paul's bedroom. What if there was more than one? Someone else, waiting in the shadows at the bottom of the stairs? Tony crawled cautiously along the landing until he guessed he was roughly above the half landing where the stairs turned down into the hall. He rose cautiously to his feet, trained the Ingram downwards, held the torch away from his body and switched it on.

God! Ridley lay in a tangle of arms and legs at the bottom of the stairs, eyes staring emptily into space, mouth hanging open. The burst of .38 calibre shells had caught him in the stomach, blowing out most of his side before stitching a neat row of holes across the window and into the wall. Blood lay puddled on the carpet. The curtain stirred softly in the breeze, beside the shattered window.

"What . . . what are you going to do now?" Jenny whispered.

Tony clicked off the torch. "I wouldn't look too closely if I was you," he advised quietly, "it isn't very pretty." He had recognized the ruins of that face and he was gambling now that, as before, both at Jenny's flat and at HPL, the man was working on his own. Which might just give them their chance. He went into Paul's bedroom, twitched the bedspread off the bed and returned to the landing to let it fall down over the body.

Then he decided to take another chance and turned on the hall light. "Come on," he said.

Jenny shied back. "I . . . I can't," she managed.

Tony placed a hand on her shoulder. "Yes, you can," he said softly. "We're nearly there, Jenny—nearly out of this mess. For the moment, his boss"—he gestured down the stairs—"thinks *we're* the ones who're dead, right? And they'll go on thinking that for a few more hours at least. By the time they wake up to what's happened, we can be in Glasgow. And then it will be over. Finished."

Jenny closed her eyes and swallowed. "OK," she whispered.

Tony took her hand and led the way. Together they squeezed past the grotesque bundle at the bottom of the stairs, and minutes later they were on the road out of Gleninver.

Out of Gleninver, but not out of the wood.

Jenny was driving. They were on a quiet stretch of country road about sixteen miles east of Gleninver, when a sheep darted across the road. A sheep, that was all—but it could have been a man with a rifle, or Ridley himself, for the effect upon Jenny's raw nerves. She screamed and wrenched the wheel violently to the left. The Escort slewed across the road towards a stone humpbacked bridge at more than forty miles an hour. Jenny saw that coming, at least. Another wrench of the wheel. The car missed the bridge by inches, crashed through a flimsy wooden fence, bucketed down a steep earth bank and finally rammed its nose into the bed of a shallow stream, pitching Tony and Jenny forward into darkness.

CHAPTER **25**

Jackman should have been asleep in bed, dreaming fond thoughts about the morning. He wasn't. He was pacing his sitting room, still fully dressed, and looking constantly at his watch. He was still getting no reply on Pagephone 3447.

"Perhaps he's turned it off?" the operator suggested. "I mean, it is after four o'clock in the morning."

"I am perfectly aware what time it is," Jackman replied acidly.

Ridley was not permitted to turn it off. So why hadn't he reported in?

"Thank you, operator." Jackman replaced the receiver, then from a drawer of his desk took out a map of the town and began looking for Bruneval Close.

Twenty minutes later he was walking cautiously up to the front door of number seventeen. Broken glass crunched under his feet and he saw the shattered window and the curtains moving gently in the breeze. He pushed the front door experimentally. It swung open and he stepped furtively inside.

He smelt it first. Tasted the gagging sweetness of death on the roof of his mouth long before he turned on the torch.

A couple of minutes later he was stumbling out again with Ridley's Ingram stuffed under his coat. After finding Ridley in the hallway, he had forced himself upstairs, expecting to find at least one more body in one of the bedrooms, but he found nothing. Well, it wasn't just down to him any longer. They had contingency plans to deal with something like this. He stopped at the first phone-box he came to and dialled Cheltenham Control direct, without going through any of the usual safe-houses first. "This is Jackman," he reported. "Jackman for Baxter, reference OMAHA. Tell him . . . tell him we have a Code Yellow up here. Code Yellow with one of his soldiers down."

JENNY MOANED, STIRRED and tried to sit up. She put a drowsy hand to the pain above her eyes, and realized with a jolt of alarm that the wetness on her forehead was her own blood, dripping from a deep cut. That shocked her back to full consciousness and she became aware that it was now daylight.

It all came back to her then—the wild skidding across the road, the splintering crash as they tore through the fence, the—*Tony!*

Jenny forced herself to sit up and look round. The car was resting a dozen feet or so from where she had been lying, half in and half out of a narrow, boulder-strewn stream. The bridge was a few feet beyond that, with the road and the remains of the fence somewhere above her. Gritting her teeth she hauled herself unsteadily to her feet and stumbled towards the battered wreck of their car. Her door had burst open, but Tony's had stayed shut and he had been pitched forwards against the windscreen. Jenny could see him now, his head sagging down against the passenger window. He wasn't moving, his eyes were closed, and there was a thick smear of blood on the windscreen. Jenny scrambled round to the passenger door and wrenched it open. She lunged forward just in time to prevent Tony falling out sideways onto the rocks. She cradled his body in her arms and lowered him gently to the ground. He *must* be alive! He must! Please, please God . . . Then she heard the ragged rasp of his breathing, and sat back with a groan of relief. She watched him anxiously for a moment, then scrambled round to the back of the car, found an old RAF mackintosh in the boot and covered him with that, bitterly aware of the inadequacy of what she was doing. If they stayed where they were, they would be found. If she flagged someone down and called for an ambulance, she was just playing into "their" hands. What should she do? The wind tugged at her hair, the stream chuckled merrily beside her and there was no reply.

The farm! They'd passed a farm a few miles back, hadn't they? And farms had cars, vehicles, tractors! Jenny lurched painfully to her feet.

137

Somehow, she would find a car, a lorry, even a tractor, something that would carry them on. She must. She had lost Jamie Ennis. She was not going to lose Tony, too.

It was almost six in the morning when Jenny began hobbling towards the farm, but when she finally saw the old farmhouse with its cluster of untidy outbuildings, the sun had risen into a clear blue sky and it was a few minutes after seven, on the day that Highland Pharmaceuticals were launching a new heart drug called Cardocol upon the British public.

IN THE EDITOR'S OFFICE at the *Gleninver Times*, the two journalists were at work. Bob Harris turned over the last folio of copy and looked up, his face flushed with excitement. "Just where the hell did you get all this?" he demanded. He had been roused from his bed an hour earlier to come in and read a story which, if true, would make the lead with every national newspaper in the country. It had been presented to him, on a plate, by his young trainee reporter, who now expected him to run it across the front page of the *Gleninver Times*, circulation eleven thousand, six hundred and eighty-seven, excluding returns. The boy looked as though he'd been up half the night putting it all together.

"From Mrs. Highcroft and Mrs. Parsons," Hamish replied calmly.

"And you've checked these facts, laddie?" Hamish nodded, and there was a moment's silence as Harris thought giddily about the repercussions, the local fallout. "What about the company? You haven't got a quote here from the company about these allegations? That HPL had two men murdered . . . that the company's nothing but a . . . a front for some chemical warfare programme we're not supposed to know anything about, that—"

"No, I haven't spoken to them, not yet. I . . . I thought you might prefer to do that yourself," Hamish replied.

Harris studied his junior for a long moment. Then he chuckled. "Aye, Hamish," he said at last. "Aye, I might just do that. Let's you and I go and make this bastard Engel's day for him."

Hamish Owen smiled. You could forget about your national press awards, your investigative profiles and single-column photographs in the UK *Press Gazette*. Right now he would settle for something much simpler—the use of his own Christian name. Not laddie. Not ever again.

JENNY CROUCHED DOWN, PANTING, beside the corner of the old stone barn, and watched the farmyard. At last her luck had changed. A young labourer in a battered maroon Morris Traveller had driven into the farmyard, got out and sauntered into the dairy.

Jenny heard the crash of milk churns. Now. Crouching as low as she could, she hobbled forward, reached the car and looked inside. He had left the key in the ignition! A quick look round and Jenny had the door open and was easing herself gingerly inside amidst a clutter of baling twine, wisps of straw, and the pungent reminder of sheep. She twisted the key, an angry clashing of gears, and she was lurching out of the farmyard, foot hard down on the accelerator, as the labourer rushed out of the dairy and stared after her, hands on hips. At last something had gone right! They were going to make it, she knew they were.

She hadn't seen the farmhand running inside to the telephone.

Jenny was back at the granite bridge twelve minutes later, to find Tony, pale, but conscious now, where she had left him. Just the look on his face, and the smile of "welcome back" behind the pain in his eyes, sent her spirits soaring.

It took her almost five minutes to struggle back up the slope to the Morris with Tony leaning heavily on her shoulder. They made it, and Jenny staggered round to collapse in the driver's seat as Tony leaned back beside her, both too spent for words.

Jenny forced the car into gear, and they were off with a sudden lurch that made them both cry out with pain.

The police turned up at the farm with commendable promptness. Turning east after taking a statement from an angry farmhand, they followed the moorland road and found the break in the fence and the abandoned Escort at the bottom of the slope.

Jenny and Tony had less than forty minutes' start. In a clapped-out Morris Traveller that smelt of sheep and looked as if it was held together with baling wire.

As TOMALIN KEPT TELLING anyone with the time to listen, the weather was *heavenly*; just *exactly* what he had been praying for all week—hot, clear and blue with the merest *feather* of wind.

By seven forty-five, the subcontractors were rolling into Highland Pharmaceuticals in a steady stream. Workmen on tall stepladders were stringing bunting across the approach road, and a posse of locally recruited waitresses in frilly white blouses and black skirts were busy shaking out starched tablecloths and counting wineglasses.

Inside the main hall of the administrative complex, members of HPL's Press and Publicity Department were laying a glossy, emerald green Cardocol promotional wallet on every one of the three hundred seats that filled the hall, and on the raised stage men ran out wires from a cluster of microphones and made the early morning hideous with their "Testing, testing . . ."

Harold Engel stood alone, looking about him. He had dreamed of this moment, and yet now that it had arrived he felt detached from it all, isolated by his private knowledge of the tarnished reality. He had changed, he realized bleakly, his attitude. Not towards the drug itself, but towards the compromise that had made it all possible. He had never really questioned that before—not until last night with Joyce. There was no doubt in his mind now that he had bartered his very soul for this one last chance of success.

He saw Jackman talking to someone on the flagged terrace outside. He stepped out, and Jackman turned to greet him. So too did Baxter, up from London on the first available flight. Baxter, Engel's initial contact. The man who'd set things up. Anger flared suddenly.

"What are you doing here?" Engel demanded. "I thought we had an agreement?"

Baxter glanced at Jackman. "We've had . . . one or two problems. Mr. Jackman called me, and I thought I'd just pop up and get the lie of the land for myself."

"Problems?" Engel demanded sharply, swinging towards his Project Development Manager, the man with two hats but only one set of loyalties. "What sort of problems?"

Baxter held up a hand. "Oh, nothing for you to worry about, Harold. Just internal problems of . . . reorganization. Now then"—he rubbed his hands together briskly—"d'you think we might be able to rustle up some real coffee from somewhere? The stuff they give you on the plane . . ." He shuddered. Chitchat, thought Engel bleakly; social chitchat; observing the niceties while people choked and died in his laboratories.

"You're not welcome here, Baxter. I'd like you to leave."

Baxter looked mildly amused. "To leave?" He turned to lead them down the path so they could continue without being overheard. "But for my persuasive powers with certain government ministries, today would never have happened, you do appreciate that, I suppose?"

"You've turned my facility into a battleground with your . . . developments," Engel retorted. "I want our agreement terminated." He gestured at Jackman. "No doubt your minder here will fill you in on the details." He paused. "I won't compromise your little operation," he continued. "But RD7 is to close down. Within—what shall we say—four months? Yes, that seems reasonable."

"Otherwise?" Baxter inquired mildly.

Engel shrugged. "I don't deal in threats, Mr. Baxter, you know that."

Baxter nodded agreeably. "I see. I had no idea you'd taken this Highcroft business so personally, Harold. We shall have to take more account of that in future. In the meantime, might I suggest you—" They turned. A uniformed police inspector was coming towards them.

"Ah, Inspector," greeted Baxter. "You know Mr. Engel, I presume?" As though it was his company, his premises, his occasion.

The inspector nodded. "Yes, sir. We have met." He turned to Jackman. "Might I have a word, sir?" The two moved away.

"Inspector?"

"My men have been instructed to cooperate with your people over this roadblock business, and they've found the car you were asking about."

"They have? Where?"

The inspector took out a notebook and flipped it open. "Approximately fifteen miles along the road to Crianlarich. It appeared to have been involved in an accident."

"What about the occupants?"

The inspector shook his head. "No, sir. Nothing."

"Have you tried the hospitals?"

The inspector nodded, stone-faced. "A vehicle was reported stolen by a young woman, from a farm a few miles to the west of where this particular car was found, shortly after seven this morning. That could be them, I suppose. One of them, anyway."

Jackman nodded. "It could indeed. Get me a map, will you, Inspector? Then I shall need a police car and . . . no. On second thoughs, I think I'd better drive myself."

Four minutes later he was on the road and driving fast. With the Ingram under a coat on the seat beside him.

THE ANCIENT MORRIS laboured on the steep, heather-clad hill, with Jenny hunched over the wheel, willing the car onwards. Something was wrong—she could feel it in the way the engine was straining, and Tony appeared to have gone to sleep again, his head lolling against his chest in a way she didn't like at all. Only another seventy miles to Glasgow. That was all. Seventy.

JACKMAN IN HIS SPEEDING ROVER apart, events were already gathering momentum behind them.

A white delivery van stopped outside number seventeen, Bruneval Close, and three men got out of the driver's cab. They looked smart and efficient with their clipboards and their white coats with the words FREEZER DELIVERY SERVICE stitched in red across the top breast pocket. At a nod from their leader they moved round to the rear of the van, and carefully manhandled a large packing case with FRAGILE stamped across its side onto a porter's trolley, which they then wheeled down the drive of number seventeen.

By lunchtime the broken window would have been replaced, the bullet holes replastered, the wall repainted and new carpet laid on the stairs. Bundled like so much dirty washing into the packing case, Ridley would leave Bruneval Close exactly as he had arrived almost twelve hours earlier: with no one seeing a thing.

JACKMAN STEPPED BACK from the wrecked Escort and climbed up the slope to the waiting police car, the map he had found in the glove compartment in his hands. It had Tony's name on it. He tossed it into the back of the police car and nodded. "That's them all right," he confirmed. He opened out the map the inspector had given him and traced their probable route with a finger. If they were travelling west and had left here a little over an hour ago . . . He frowned. Either they'd gone to ground, turned off somewhere along the way, or—"You're sure they haven't gone through Winnoch?" he demanded.

The policeman nodded. "Not according to the next checkpoint, no, sir."

"Right then. Thanks for your help." That settled it. They had to be somewhere in front of him, somewhere between here and the village of Altrunn. Jackman walked briskly back to the Rover.

"You like us to come along with you, sir?" the policeman called after him.

Jackman shook his head. "No need, thank you, officer, no need. I'll take it from here."

He slid behind the wheel and drove quickly away.

"THIS WAY, DR. ERSKINE," gestured the secretary with a bright smile. "I think you'll find Mr. Engel through in the main hall."

"Thank you." He glanced round uneasily, clutching a copy of Jenny's stolen report under his arm, and hurried after the girl. She pushed open the swing doors at the end of the corridor, looked round the hall and pointed. "There he is—over there by the window looking at the helicopter." She laughed brightly. "Honestly, he's like a child with a new toy with that thing!"

Dr. Erskine walked slowly through the forest of empty chairs towards the chairman of Highland Pharmaceuticals.

Harold Engel turned to face him. "Dr. Erskine. Good morning."

"Mr. Engel. You remember you invited me to substantiate those allegations I made in your home last night?"

Harold Engel nodded and gestured the doctor to be seated. Dr. Erskine lifted his briefcase onto his knees, took out a thick bundle of notes and held them out. Harold Engel glanced briefly at them.

"Perhaps if you could just tell me what this has to do with Cardocol. As you've probably noticed, we're rather busy."

"Aye. Well, I'll be as brief as I can. You remember that old man, the one who died in the fire out in the bay with that wee boy?"

"Yes, of course. A tragic accident."

Dr. Erskine nodded. "Indeed. So it was. Last night, in your home, I told you I'd given Cardocol to a couple of my patients on an . . . experimental basis, you remember? Well, he was one of them: Robbie Roberts. The postmortem said he drowned." He shook his head. "No, Mr. Engel. Mr. Roberts died because he mixed Cardocol with cough mixture; cough mixture for a cough *caused* by your drug. It was the

142

combined side effects of the two that caused his collapse. He drowned because he collapsed, not because of the fire on the boat."

"What cough mixture?" Engel demanded.

"He mixed Cardocol with—" Dr. Erskine rummaged in a pocket and pulled out the bottle he had found on Robbie's kitchen table, the one identical to that in Mrs. Proctor's bedroom—"with this. Soothaway." He paused. "Soothaway's another new product but, unlike Cardocol, you don't need a doctor's prescription for this—you can buy it over the counter, easy as you please. A lot of people are doing just that, thanks to advertising, and in ninety-nine cases out of a hundred, it's perfectly harmless. Except when it's taken with—"

"Cardocol? Oh, don't be ridiculous! If—"

"With Cardocol, yes. Mix Soothaway with Cardocol's new delay-release mechanism and patients aren't taking pills any more, they're swallowing time bombs! High blood pressure doesn't *fall*, it goes through the roof! That's what made Robbie Roberts collapse, d'you see?"

"Poppycock! I've never heard such rubbish! The unfortunate death of one man, a patient under *your* supervision—look, Doctor, for this so-called interaction of yours to take place to any appreciable degree, a large number of elderly patients taking Cardocol would need to get a cough, yes?" Erskine nodded. Engel took a deep breath. "I told you last night and I'm telling you again now: the incidence of bronchial inflammation among elderly patients taking Cardocol on our clinical trials programme was well within permissible levels. Something in the region of four or five per cent, that's all! I know. I've checked! We've gone through the figures a hundred times! Your Mr. Roberts is an isolated case, that's all—an isolated case!"

"And if he wasn't?" Dr. Erskine asked quietly.

"What d'you mean?"

"What would the proven incidence of bronchial inflammation have to be before you would concede that it was too high—given that Soothaway and Cardocol were found to be incompatible?"

"Well, I . . ." Engel hesitated, sensing he might be walking into a trap. "Eleven. Eleven per cent. Anywhere between eleven and fifteen per cent."

"So if eleven people out of any hundred taking Cardocol developed a cough, you would consider that number to be unacceptably high?"

"I suppose so . . . But, as I say, our figures are much lower."

"I'd like you to study this for a moment." Dr. Erskine held out a copy of the HPL report Jenny had stolen from Jackman's office.

Harold Engel read it quickly. He looked up, his face ashen. "They've . . . they've distorted the figures," he whispered. "They told me four per cent, months ago! I didn't . . . I didn't know . . ."

Dr. Erskine nodded slowly. "I accept that. If you look at the front you

143

will see that the distribution list was very . . . restricted." Engel did so: Jackman; Baxter; half a dozen names he'd never heard before. Names in London. Names in the Defence Procurement Secretariat. His own was nowhere in sight.

"The true incidence of bronchial inflammation was higher by a factor of almost ten. If CSM had known that . . ." Dr. Erskine shrugged. "You'd never have got Cardocol anywhere near the committee. You'd never have got your licence." He glanced round the hall. At the chairs and the microphones, all waiting. CARDOCOL—A HEARTBEAT CLOSER. "You'll have to call it off," he said gently. "You do know that, don't you, Mr. Engel? You'll have to call it off."

"TONY?" JENNY REACHED OVER and shook Tony gently by the sleeve. "Tony? Are you all right?" He groaned. "Can you hear me? I'm going to stop, OK? Just for a moment." Jenny was terrified that he was about to die on her. She eased the car to a gentle stop on the verge. Sixty-two miles to Glasgow. With Jackman coming up fast, nine miles behind.

TEN MINUTES LATER, Dr. Erskine had left and Harold Engel was alone in his office. Alone with his shattered dreams, his realization that he had been tricked by the men he had once trusted because they had offered him a chance of survival. Men who wanted only a legitimate cover for their operations, for RD7.

He walked to the window, staring down onto the lawns, the tents and the people he employed, people who had trusted him. Then he saw Baxter, standing beside the company helicopter—his helicopter—talking to one of the prettier secretaries, making her laugh. An idea began to form in his mind. A way of getting back.

He sat down at his desk and began to write a confession. It did not take long. When he had finished, he propped it against the photograph frame on his desk and glanced up at the blue sky, conscious, suddenly, that there was little time. Soon the chartered helicopters would begin to arrive, bringing the doctors and the journalists to witness the launch of Cardocol. CARDOCOL—A HEARTBEAT CLOSER. Engel closed his eyes and shuddered, trying to shut out the pain.

"Mr. Engel? Mr. Engel, are you in there? There are two reporters in reception—from the *Gleninver Times*. They insist on talking to you about something called RD7. Hello, Mr. Engel . . . ?"

But he'd left already. Down the back stairs to search for one man: Baxter. He tried to appear calm, relaxed. Like a man who didn't know that his world had just ended. There was Baxter. Engel walked up and laid a hand on his sleeve. Baxter turned, and frowned with a flicker of irritation. "Harold." He smiled. "I was just telling . . . ah . . . Cindy here what a tremendous achievement all this is. For you, I mean."

144

Engel smiled back. "Thank you. I wonder if I might have a quick word?" They moved away. "What I said earlier," Engel began, "I . . . I was too hasty. I hope you'll overlook what I said."

"That's better, Harold. Just so we understand one another."

"I was hoping perhaps you'd let me show you something—by way of amends, if you like." Engel gestured across at the helicopter. "Just five minutes, that's all. The view should be terrific."

Baxter swallowed. He hated heights. "Oh, very well. Just five minutes."

Soon they were airborne, rising slowly into the sky, to hover above the site at four hundred feet. Baxter sat in the front beside Engel and began to relax. Engel was quite right, the view really was superb. And there was hardly any sensation of movement. The helicopter turned slowly through ninety degrees, rose up another three hundred feet, and set off due east away from HPL, away from Gleninver.

"Where are we going?" asked Baxter.

Harold Engel looked across and smiled.

Without warning, he flung the helicopter over onto its side and sent it swooping down in a wide spiral. "Where's Jackman?" he asked, pulling smoothly out of the dive and rolling the helicopter through one hundred and eighty degrees until Baxter was looking down at him, and the gasp of the man's fear filled his headphones.

"I . . . I don't know," Baxter answered weakly, pulling his tie away from his neck, his face white and clammy with sweat.

Harold Engel reached for an airsickness bag and threw it across. "Think about it," he advised shortly, and flicked up the switch that cut off further conversation. They began to loop—a steep climb up the side of the sky that rammed Baxter into the back of his seat, his eyes glazed with terror. Corkscrew port, corkscrew starboard . . .

Engel flicked the intercom switch. "I asked you a question," he repeated civilly. "I know you sent him off on one of your little errands, Baxter, so tell me, where's Jackman?"

"On . . . on the road to . . . oh God . . . to . . . Crianlarich," Baxter spluttered. "Now, please. Can . . . can we go down?"

Engel studied him without pity. "Well, we certainly can't stay up here for ever, can we?" he mused, in a quiet voice that Baxter found as terrifying as the next seven minutes of aerobatics.

JENNY DABBED AT TONY'S FACE with a wet handkerchief. "There—any better?"

He managed a weak smile. "Terrific. Makes me feel like a . . . a million dollars." He was sitting on the ground propped against the front wheel, with his legs sticking out in front of him. He looked terrible. And wonderful.

"Yes, I know—all green and wrinkled." She smiled, relieved beyond measure that he had regained consciousness. They were going to be all right now, she knew it. She could feel it in her bones.

THE WHITE ROVER breasted the last hill. There! By the stream. Jackman stopped the car, took out a pair of binoculars and focused on the battered Morris pulled in to the side of the road. He put away the glasses and reached across to the passenger seat. It was while he was checking the mechanism of the Ingram that he heard it: a faint buzzing in the sky.

A WHITE SPECK ON THE ROADSIDE: Jackman's car, stationary on an empty ribbon of twisting Highland road. Engel eased back on the stick as he estimated height and distance, angles of approach. Holding the aircraft steady with one hand, he reached into his breast pocket and removed a photograph of Joyce and the children. He studied it for a moment, and Baxter felt his skin crawl as a terrible suspicion took root in his mind. Engel switched on the intercom.

"What . . . what are you going to do?" Baxter whispered.

Engel brought them round in a slow, sweeping turn that steadied the Rover in the exact centre of the perspex nose and held them there, stationary in the sky, for a moment.

"I read Jackman's report," he said quietly, as they began to race forward, gathering speed. "Guess."

Baxter started to scream.

He was still screaming when they hit the Rover.

THE UNIFORMED SECURITY OFFICER in the foyer of the *Scottish Star* offices in Glasgow's Connaught Street placed his midmorning cup of tea carefully to one side and nudged his companion. "Aye, aye," he muttered, gesturing outside, "here comes trouble." He rose heavily to his feet. A battered maroon Morris Traveller had braked to an untidy halt in a parking space reserved for senior management. A young woman got out and hurried towards the newspaper's front office, her thick brown hair a windblown tangle, her coat flapping open, her shoes muddy. The girl pushed urgently into the revolving doors, and the security guard moved forward to intercept her. "Morning, miss," he began, and she swung, startled, towards him. "Can't park there, I'm afraid. That's reserved. You—"

"I . . . I have to see the editor. Please. It's very urgent." Jenny's eyes darted round the foyer as she took in the calm order and comfort of her surroundings. She shuddered involuntarily. It all reminded her of somewhere else. Somewhere evil. HPL.

"You'll have to ask at reception. Could you open your handbag, please? Just routine." Jenny surrendered her bag without protest, too distracted by the urgency of her mission to take offence. For his part, the guard was taking no chances. She didn't look like a nutter, but then they seldom did. He looked inside, saw a thick bundle of papers and then handed the bag back, satisfied. "Thank you, miss. Now, if you wouldn't mind just moving that car, I'm sure . . ." But he was talking to himself. Jenny had hurried past him to the receptionist. She repeated her request.

She was asked to wait, and the girl gestured at some leather armchairs. Jenny sat down, twisting her fingers together nervously as she suddenly became aware of the curious glances of well-dressed passersby, of her own untidy hair and torn, mudstained clothes. Out there, on the road heading north towards the hospital, with Tony slumped white-faced in pain beside her, all that had mattered was reaching the safety of Glasgow.

Now, for the first time, it dawned upon Jenny that just possibly they might not believe her. She tried to take a grip on her fears, to force herself to appear calm as she waited. But the sense of enveloping fear and rising panic persisted, for if they turned her away she was finished. There was nowhere else to go. Nowhere else to run. Jenny closed her eyes.

She need not have worried. For even as she was driving through the outskirts of Glasgow to the hospital, and weeping with relief as white-coated nurses and doctors hurried forward to assume responsibility for Tony's recovery, the HPL story had begun to crack wide open. Rumours that the helicopter carrying HPL's chairman was missing, and that burning wreckage had been sighted on a remote Scottish hillside, soon came flooding into the Glasgow newsroom, speculative stories fuelled by the shock and alarm of the HPL work force, who were still gathered in marquees on the green lawn leading down to the still, dark waters of Loch Linnhe.

As Jenny waited in reception, the editor of the *Star* was on the phone to Bob Harris of the *Gleninver Times*, who was insisting with rising impatience that he now had a letter signed by the missing chairman. Together with a raft of secret reports, it showed that HPL had been, and still was, a front for a secret government chemical warfare factory in the Scottish bloody Highlands, and if the editor of the *Scottish* bloody *Star* didn't run the story across seven columns, then this would be the only bloody newspaper in the country that wouldn't. It was at that moment that a senior reporter pushed into the editor's office, eyes gleaming with excitement. "Sorry to interrupt," he began, "it's this HPL story. There's a bird downstairs we've got to use. Her name's Macrae—Jenny Macrae. She's absolute dynamite."

The paper used Jenny's story, backing it up with pictures, the stolen report, and a bedside interview with Tony. And for once in its short tabloid life, the *Scottish Star* was not guilty of hyperbole.

148

AT FIVE THAT EVENING the government belatedly stepped in and attempted to slap a "D" notice on the story, to prevent publication. They might as well have tried to stop a moving train with a sheet of newspaper: the futility of such a ploy served merely to highlight the importance of a story that was by then being carried as a main item by every major news outlet. Denials were shown on ITV's *News At Ten* that same evening, together with damning secret correspondence between Harold Engel and the Defence Procurement Secretariat. By then, too, an enterprising photographer had managed somehow to penetrate into RD7, so ITN had pictures of the laboratories as well. By early morning the *Today* programme on BBC's Radio Four was carrying a hasty withdrawal of the government denial, and the press had begun asking pointed questions about something no-one appeared to have heard of before, called the Defence Procurement Secretariat. There were strident demands for a full Public Inquiry.

Meanwhile, it was left to the medical profession to police itself, through the offices of the British Medical Association and the Committee on the Safety of Medicines. Unusually, perhaps, for such organizations, they moved swiftly, decisively and in unison. A special committee was set up to examine the relationship between drug companies and local GPs. Those who had been too eager to assist HPL in their clinical trials programme found themselves being questioned at length, and a new set of guidelines was issued, to ensure that clinical trials could only be conducted on healthy human volunteers with the written, certifiable, permission of the Department of Health. It is now a criminal offence for patients to receive any drug that has not been properly licensed. The "yellow card" system still exists, but the evaluation of adverse reactions to specific drugs has been greatly improved with the advent of mainline computers.

TONY CAME OUT OF HOSPITAL to find that his shoulder injury had left him seriously weakened and no longer able to work as a winchman. Refusing the desk job that the RAF offered him, he decided that after the events of the last few months, particularly the breakdown of his marriage, it was time for a change. A vacancy came up for an Air-Sea Rescue instructor in one of the Gulf States, and when Tony was suggested for the post, he eagerly accepted.

For Jenny, too, much had changed. After the Fatal Accident Inquiry it was decided not to bring criminal proceedings against her, especially since Jamie Ennis's father no longer wished to press charges. By then Corbett, the district administrator, had been moved away to Stirling, and a letter arrived one sunny morning informing Jenny that she was free to resume work at the clinic whenever she wished. Surprisingly perhaps, she did just that, for there were still patients to consider, still a need for a speech therapist in Gleninver. She kept in touch with Tony, and the last that was heard of her, she was planning a trip to the Middle East . . .

RD7 never opened its doors again. The laboratories were sealed off, and the HPL buildings were shut down while their future was reviewed. Eighteen months later the offices were gutted and refitted as a government-sponsored Adventure Training Centre for the long-term unemployed. There were many of them by then, in Gleninver.

Two people who found friendship and a new sense of purpose in helping those with no prospect of work were Helen Highcroft and Joyce Engel, both widows, drawn together by common loss. On summer evenings Helen Highcroft can still sometimes be seen standing alone by the shore of Loch Linnhe, gazing out at the dark, still waters and thinking private thoughts about the husband she lost, and about the love that never died.

TOM KEENE

Tom Keene is a very happy man. He is among the very few of us who can truthfully say they have fulfilled a life's ambition. "From a very early age, my one goal was to have a novel published," he told us at a recent interview. At only thirty-eight years of age he can claim, as he does with disarming modesty but obvious pleasure, that he has no less than five best-sellers under his belt. What's more, his first novel, *Spyship*, was made into a highly-acclaimed BBC television series.

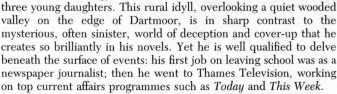

Recently, Tom took a breather from writing to renovate the old Devon farmhouse where he lives with his wife, Margy, and their three young daughters. This rural idyll, overlooking a quiet wooded valley on the edge of Dartmoor, is in sharp contrast to the mysterious, often sinister, world of deception and cover-up that he creates so brilliantly in his novels. Yet he is well qualified to delve beneath the surface of events: his first job on leaving school was as a newspaper journalist; then he went to Thames Television, working on top current affairs programmes such as *Today* and *This Week*.

He puts enormous enthusiasm into researching his books. When he was working on *Profit without Honour* he spent a week with the helicopter rescue crews at RAF Chivenor, near his home. Living and working with the teams twenty-four hours a day he gained a vivid idea of the tensions and rewards that a winchman like Tony Lockhart would experience. Once, he accompanied a team on a search for two young brothers whose empty dinghy had been found drifting out to sea. As they combed the area, news came through on Tom's headphones that both boys were safe and sound. The din in the aircraft was so great that the only way he could break the news to the anguished father sitting beside him was to write a note. He recalls the stirring of his own emotions as he watched relief and delight wash over the man's face when he read the message.

At the moment Tom is working on a new thriller called *Runner*, the story of a Russian airforce officer on the run in peacetime Britain.

No Enemy But Time

A CONDENSATION OF THE BOOK BY

EVELYN ANTHONY

ILLUSTRATED BY PAM MASCO

The innocent and the beautiful
Have no enemy but time.

Handsome Frank Arbuthnot and his attractive half-sister Claire share happy memories of an idyllic childhood full of fun and innocent adventure. They are close and devoted friends, and intend to remain so for the rest of their lives.

Time, however, is against them, for they have been born into a twentieth-century Anglo-Irish family torn apart by bitter conflict. While Frank's Irish blood has drawn him into collaboration with the IRA, his English blood still ties him to Claire—and Claire has married a British cabinet minister.

With heartbreaking intensity, Evelyn Anthony chronicles a poignant story of a divided family, with divided loyalties in a divided land.

CHAPTER 1

The dawn was breaking as the cars rolled off the ferry in Dublin; there was a sullen, red-streaked sky with banks of threatening clouds building up on the horizon. She opened the car window wide and gulped down the clean sea air, a welcome relief after enduring the stale fug of the tiny cabin. It was a hired car. If they were watching for her, they wouldn't expect her to travel on the night ferry from Liverpool, with the rough Irish Sea battering at the boat and the drunks and the seasick throwing up in the smelly lounges.

Even so, she had hidden herself in the claustrophobic cabin, afraid she might be recognized. She was difficult to disguise, being tall and strikingly blonde, with a face that had appeared too often in newspapers and smart magazines. The charming wife of the youngest member of the cabinet. Articles about her family life, their handsome Georgian house in Gloucestershire, *Vogue* profile material. All the prepackaged nonsense of a plastic person, she had said once, but that made her husband angry. "If you hate it all so much, why don't you go back to the bogs?" was his retort. The bogs—that was how he dismissed Ireland. He'd said it once too often, and this time she'd taken him at his word.

Slowly the line of cars inched towards the customs sheds. She had nothing to declare and was waved on. She didn't realize until she was bumping along the road away from the dock that she'd been shaking like a leaf. There had been no time for a cup of coffee, and she'd eaten nothing the night before, having gone straight to her cabin. Now she felt weak and her head ached. Early-open cafes tempted her as she drove through

Dublin on her way south, but she resisted. The Irish are the most inquisitive race in the world. She couldn't risk being spotted.

The roads were empty in the grey light, and she made smart time. As she turned onto the dual carriageway, which ended only a few miles beyond Naas, the rain began to spit against the windscreen. "That's Our Lady weeping for your sins, Miss Claire," their cook used to say when the heavens opened. So many tears, she thought, and so many sins to be washed away. And so much blood. Centuries of bloodletting.

It was so dark she switched on her headlights. She saw the signpost pointing to the turn-off, opposite Kill. How many times she had felt a lift of excitement when she saw that sign and knew that home was only ten minutes away. Coming back from school in England, being met at the airport by Frank, running to hug him without being in the least self-conscious. He was her brother, and she loved him best in the world. And next came Riverstown, the wonderful, handsome, shabby old house where they had grown up together. Less than a mile now. The storm had spent itself, and a thin sun was showing through the clouds. There at the end of the road was the turning to their gates. Opposite their driveway was a signpost saying "Clane" on one arm and "Naas" on the other. The local children loved to turn it round; visitors would travel miles in the wrong direction.

From the gates ahead she had left for her wedding in 1972, eight years ago, in the big Protestant church in Naas. Miss Claire Arbuthnot, shrouded in her English mother's family lace, with pearls shining like drops of new milk round her neck. Claire had heard the Irish maids talking in the kitchen: "Pearls are tears. . . . God love her, she shouldn't be wearin' those on her weddin' day." The girls' whispering had been right. She still had the pearls, but there had been many tears since she first wore them.

Claire didn't turn in at the gates of Riverstown, although they were open, which struck her as strange since she knew that her mother was not at home. Instead, she drove past, bearing left down a small side road.

Billy Cavanagh's cottage was set back off the road, behind a neat little hedge. He kept lurchers, and they were barking now. When she and Frank were children, Billy used to take Frank lamping for rabbits. She had been furious that he wouldn't take her too. It wasn't fit for a young girl to go scrambling over the fields at night with a powerful torch to light up the rabbits, he'd explained in his thick brogue, while her brother had grinned and mocked her behind his back.

The dogs continued to bark as she walked to Billy's front door and knocked. The door opened and he stood there, a squat little old man in shirtsleeves. For a moment he stared, and then his face broke into a smile. "Mercy, it's yerself! Will ye come in?"

Sitting in his kitchen with a cup of steaming tea, she didn't try to pretend when he said, "What's wrong wit' ye, Claire?" Billy had been there to pick her up when she fell off her first pony, he'd taught her to fish, and whatever mischief she and Frank had got up to, he never told a tale. Claire loved him, and he loved her as if she were his own.

"I've come to help Frankie," she said.

Fear shuttered his face. "Sure an' there's no helping him," he muttered. "Not God himself could do anything for him."

"Billy," she said quietly, "he's my brother."

"Only the half of him," the old man said. He poured more tea into her cup. "It's the other half that's been the death of him."

"Death!" she exclaimed. "You mean they've found him?"

"No, no, no ... not yet so, but they're lookin'. He's no time left at all. Have you been up to the house yet?"

"No, but I saw the gates were open, although mother is away."

He frowned. "She is. Went off to stay wit' auld missus Keys down in Cork. 'You're to bolt and bar the house up,' she says to me. 'Frank will not hide himself at Riverstown.' Open? I padlocked them gates after herself drove away."

Claire, knowing that the Irish police would have to come to Billy for the key, said, "They were open. Would it be the Gardai who opened them?"

He was frightened and irritated, for he'd not opened the gates. "What if it's the others in there, waitin' for him?"

"It's not them," she said. "They'd know Frankie wouldn't come home. But it could be the Special Branch waiting for me."

He let out a deep breath. "Ye? What have ye to do wit' this?"

"I told you, I've come to try and find Frankie," she answered. "I didn't tell anyone, not even my husband. I just got on the ferry. But my husband will guess I've come back, and why. He'll tell the authorities in Dublin. You're going to help me, Billy, aren't you?"

He shook his head vigorously. "No. Ye'll get yerself into trouble. Go home to England and yer husband and children."

She felt very tired suddenly. "You don't have to help me," she said. "I'll manage on my own."

He muttered a curse. "Ye'll stay where ye are." He heaved himself up from the kitchen chair. "I'll take the dogs for a walk and see what's to be seen."

Claire stood at the window and watched Billy move slowly towards the kennels where the lurchers lived. He was an old man, she thought, and frightened of the death squad of his countrymen, yet allegiance to them was in his blood—a deeper allegiance than his love for the children of the Anglo–Irish landlord he had worked for since he was a lad. Why should Billy put himself at risk for the sake of his hereditary enemies, whether he'd helped to bring them up or not? And she remembered then the old adage tossed around the dinner table by her parents and their friends: "The trouble is, you just can't trust them. All smiles to your face, and the minute your back's turned, they'll rob you blind." They were talking of servants, of course, but many Anglo–Irish truly believed that the taint was there, throughout the race of native Irish. You couldn't trust them. And you never intermarried. It wasn't just class, as Frank used to say when he raged against the system. It was race, and there would never be peace while the discrimination lasted.

Claire turned away from the window. She sat down in the one comfortable chair. The turf stove was alight, and she felt drowsy in the warmth. When they were on holiday from school, she and Frank used to come here and sit in Billy's kitchen drinking tea.

She knew that Billy wouldn't find Frank in the house. Nor, thank God, would the merciless executioners of the IRA.

He was being hunted; she was the only person in the world who knew where he would go to hide.

BILLY PASSED THE MAIN DRIVE and saw that the gates were indeed open. He then trudged up the long path to the kitchen garden and the back of the house, cursing his own folly in coming up here. But he couldn't turn back now. Whoever was inside the house could have seen him from the windows; better that they met him than Claire, he thought.

"Billy! I was just comin' down to the cottage to look for you." There, framed in the back doorway, was young Joe Burns, looking to Billy like a guardian angel in his blue Garda uniform.

Billy gasped with relief. "I thought ye was a burglar... I'll tie up the dogs." For a moment he was too relieved to ask what Joe was doing in Mrs. Arbuthnot's house, or how he'd managed to get in.

He didn't get time to ask, because as soon as he entered the kitchen the policeman said in his friendly way, "It's a careless man ye are, Billy, leavin' them gates and the kitchen door open." He was a pleasant boy, newly recruited into the local force at Clane. The Burnses had been part of the village for generations.

"I locked up everything meself," Billy insisted.

Joe Burns shook his head. "Ye thought ye did. We knew at the Garda station that Mrs. Arbuthnot was away; she always lets us know. I was passing when I saw the gates not shut properly."

"I'd swear I locked them," Billy muttered. I've been locking them gates for thirty years, he was thinking. I didn't forget. He looked into the smiling blue eyes of the policeman. There were three cigarette butts in a saucer on the kitchen table. He'd been in the kitchen for some time.

"Well, now," Burns said, "ye've saved me the trouble of comin' down to see you. When's Mrs. Arbuthnot comin' back?"

Billy said, "I don't know. She'll ring me up the day before."

"It must be terrible for her," Joe went on. "Her son gone missing and all this stuff about him on the radio and television."

"He's her stepson," Billy mumbled. "It's not the same."

"Ah, you're right." Joe Burns nodded. "It's the daughter she had . . . the one that married that fella in the English government. Ye've known them all, Billy," the easy voice went on. "Is it true what's said about them two?"

"What two?" he asked.

"The brother and sister. It's said they were so close she'd be after coming over when he disappeared. I don't think she'd take a risk like that meself."

"What risk would that be?" Billy gazed at him in innocence, but he could sense danger. The blue uniform didn't signify safety any longer. Billy didn't know what was wrong; he only knew that something was. Generations of subservience had taught the humble serving class not to answer any question that might get them into trouble.

Joe Burns lowered his voice. "She's married to this important politician," he said. "The IRA might do some harm to her. Listen, Billy, if ye hear she's come back, ye'll give me a call at the station. Ask for me, if there's any news of her."

"Sure an' I will. But I can't believe I forgot them gates and the kitchen door . . . Shouldn't we check through the house?"

"I've already done that, Billy. Don't worry yerself."

Billy nodded, and the two men went out together. Billy locked the kitchen door and gathered his dogs.

Joe waved cheerfully to him and walked back to the main entrance. "I'll see ye," he called.

Billy didn't hurry until Joe Burns was out of sight. The policeman was lying about checking the house. The door from the kitchen into the main hall was always locked, and the key to that was in Billy's pocket. Somehow Burns had managed to open the gates and the kitchen door and slip inside. Billy had caught him by surprise.

As he came back towards his cottage Billy knew the name of the danger in the kitchen at last. Fear flooded over him. He saw the car with its English licence plates parked in full view of the road. She'd left the key in it, and he didn't waste time. He had an old Renault, bought with a legacy from Philip Arbuthnot. He backed it out of the shed where it was parked and drove Claire's car in off the road. He shut the shed doors so her car was hidden. His dogs waited patiently outside the cottage door.

He didn't go inside at once, but sat on the doorstep and tried to think. Frank Arbuthnot had disappeared from his Dublin bank six days ago. LEADING MERCHANT BANKER VANISHES. FEAR FOR HIS SAFETY. That was the headline in the *Irish Independent*. There had been strong hints about his IRA sympathies, rumours that he'd been kidnapped or murdered as part of the split that was rending the Provisionals and the old Republican idealists. Billy had listened to the TV pundits and read the papers and said to himself it was sure to happen in the end. Frank

Arbuthnot had supped with the devil, and no spoon was long enough. And now the sister had come back, putting herself in danger for the sake of that brother. He sighed a deep, despairing sigh. She must go back to England. It wasn't just Frank they were looking for.

Claire got up when he came into the kitchen. "You found someone up there," she said, seeing his face.

He cleared his throat. "Only Joe Burns. He's in the Gardai now," he said. "I left the gate open and he went in to check the place."

Claire sat down again. "Don't lie to me, Billy. You've never forgotten to lock up in your life. I don't believe it was Joe Burns."

"It was so!" he insisted. "Asking questions about yerself. I'm to ring him if ye come here, says he."

"I've nothing to fear from the Gardai here," she said. "I've known them all my life. And Joe Burns's father used to work at Riverstown as a cattleman. You know that, Billy."

"Ye can't stay here," he muttered. "Claire, half the police in Ireland are lookin' for Frankie. If they can't find him, how can ye? Now I'll make us a bite to eat. Then I'll drive ye to the airport and ye'll catch a plane home."

"I am home," Claire said simply. "And I'm not going anywhere until I find Frank. Don't worry, Billy, I won't stay more than a few hours, and by that time I'll know one way or the other. Let's have the bite to eat, shall we? I'm starving."

After they'd eaten, she said, "Billy, I'll need to borrow your car. I can't drive a car with English plates. That's the first thing anyone would look at round here."

"The first thing they'd look at," Billy countered, "is a woman drivin' my auld rattlebones of a car! Have ye no sense at all? And where would ye be goin' then?"

"I can't tell you," Claire said. "You mustn't know, Billy. It's better not. I'll take the English car and be done with it."

He slapped his fist on his knee in exasperation. She had him and he knew it. "I'll change the plates from my car to the other one."

She followed him to the door of the shed; he got some tools out of a box and squatted down to unscrew the plates from his car.

Claire said, "Will it take long? I'd like to go up to the house. Give me the keys, will you, Billy? Just throw them over."

"Here ye are." He tossed the bunch to her. She caught them neatly. Frank had taught her how to catch. And how to shoot the rooks nesting high up in the trees. Vermin, he called them, when she protested at his killing a sitting bird. They slaughtered all the other fledglings and grabbed the space for themselves, he said. Just like the English in Ireland.

"Thank you," she said. "I'll be back in a little while." What Claire Fraser didn't give him was an indication of her precise destination—the gun room at Riverstown.

NEIL FRASER'S SECRETARY buzzed him on the intercom. "Mr. Brownlow is here, sir."

"Thanks, Jean. Show him in, please."

Mr. Brownlow came in and shook hands with the Minister for Trade and Industry, the Right Honourable Neil Fraser. "Good morning, sir," Brownlow said. "No news of your wife, I take it?"

Fraser's face was grey and drawn. "None, I'm afraid. Please sit down."

Brownlow looked like a senior civil servant, not a hard-nosed Special Branch officer. He said, "We've traced the taxi, and the garage where she hired a car. And she bought a ticket on the night ferry from Liverpool. So there's no doubt she's gone over."

Neil Fraser leaned back in his chair. "I never imagined she'd go."

"It's such a pity you didn't contact us yesterday evening, immediately after you found her gone. We might have got her at the ferry."

Brownlow was right, Neil knew. He had delayed until midnight, hoping against all hope that Claire hadn't snapped the last link between them and gone to look for that brother of hers.

Now Fraser said wearily. "Have you been on to Dublin?"

"No, sir. There are some things to be cleared up first. I'd like to ask you some questions. They may be a bit personal; I hope you don't mind. But it's your wife's life at stake. If they get their hands on her, they'll kill her."

"Ask anything you feel is necessary," Neil Fraser said.

"Was there a crisis that brought this to a head? A quarrel?"

Neil nodded. "Yes, on Sunday night. I came up to London early Monday and it wasn't made up. That's why I went back to the country last night; normally I stay in London during the week."

"What was the row about?" Brownlow asked.

"Ireland. And her half-brother. Frank Arbuthnot."

"The one that's gone missing in Dublin. He's been an IRA paymaster for years. Was your wife a sympathizer?"

"With the IRA? No! But she's devoted to her brother. She wouldn't hear a word against him."

"And is that why she's gone to Ireland?"

"Yes," Neil Fraser replied. "That's what we argued about. I'm afraid I lost my temper and said if he'd fallen foul of the IRA, it bloody well served him right for supporting them. She took this pretty badly. But I never thought she'd actually go ... I pointed out how dangerous it would be, and ... well, how damaging to my position if she went at a time like this."

"Quite so," Brownlow agreed. "Having Frank Arbuthnot for a brother-in-law must have been embarrassing at times."

"That's exactly what I told her. Her going to Ireland could ..." The minister paused and then said angrily, "It could ruin me."

Brownlow waited for a moment, made a note. "You rang her home in Ireland, and there was no reply?"

Fraser nodded. "That's all I could do, without alerting everyone in the neighbourhood. I tried at regular intervals through the night and first thing this morning. There's no one there. Won't you be getting through to Dublin?" he repeated.

"No," Brownlow answered. "Their people are very good, but we can't take a chance on this, sir. One careless word could set those IRA bastards on your wife. That country's like an echo chamber. One word and everyone gets to hear of it. The Provos have got contacts everywhere. So we can't ask the Irish Special Branch for help. We'll have to sort it out ourselves."

"How can you?" Fraser asked. "What can you possibly do?"

"Send in an expert. A specialist, used to working over there. Under cover. Find your wife and bring her out."

Fraser seemed suddenly positive. "If that's what you propose, I've got the man. He's a personal friend, and my wife likes him." He wrote a name down and handed Brownlow the slip of paper. "If anyone can persuade Claire to come home, and be a good man in case of trouble, it's him."

Brownlow read the name and the rank and put the slip in his wallet. There was no denying his qualifications if he belonged to *that* branch. He got up. "I'll get on to it right away. Say nothing to anyone about your wife's disappearance; say she's with friends. With a bit of luck she'll be home before you know it."

They shook hands again.

"Thank you for coming." Neil Fraser opened the door to the outer office himself.

Brownlow went down in the lift, found his car in the side street and got in. He told the driver to take him back to his office, where he called a conference among his senior colleagues. An hour later he put in a call to Major Michael Harvey in an army barracks in South Wales.

THE PATH FROM BILLY'S COTTAGE to the main house wound down towards the riverbank. The early morning rain had left little puddles in the dips along the way. When Claire and Frank were children, they used to skip the puddles, or sometimes land in the middle, spattering themselves and shouting with glee. The air here was fresh and sweet, and the shady ground was now a blue and white carpet of anemones. Later the daffodils would muster, blazing like an army of yellow heads the length of the bank, and right up to the steps leading to the old house. So many happy memories met Claire with every step she took. A childhood full of games and innocent adventures, the changing retinue of family dogs, ponies to ride and to hunt, with Frank taking the leading rein. Her parents were always up at the front, out hunting. Only her brother was willing to go home early, towing a child on a fat pony.

How often she and Frank had spent the day down by the river, fishing for trout or lazing in the damp grass talking. He was five years older than she, and her earliest memory was of him holding her tightly by the hand, when she was just a toddler, in case she strayed too near the rushing river. There had been a nurse, and her parents, but they were dim figures compared to Frank. He was tall and strong, and kept her safe. He shared his secrets with her, and from childhood on Claire would have given her life to please him. If she had a nightmare, he was first to comfort her and laugh the fears away. He told her about the fairies who lived in the holes on the riverbank, and how Billy Cavanagh was half leprechaun. They used to giggle when they saw the old man, thinking of him sitting on a toadstool in the moonlight. She learned about their ancestors from Frank, how they had come to Ireland and built Riverstown. She felt so close to him as she retraced the steps of her childhood and young adult life that for a moment she was overcome by pain.

There was a worn and weather-beaten seat hewn out of a fallen tree trunk. Claire sat down, as they had done so many times together, and the years fell away as if they had never been apart.

"I'm different from you, Clarry." Frank was fourteen then.

"You're a boy, that's what's different." She had resented his raising a barrier between them. She was nine, blonde as a daisy, with big blue eyes. Rather a tomboy, unaware of her own prettiness.

"I know that, you idiot," he retorted. "I mean really different. I'm half Irish."

Claire stared at him. "What's different then? We're all Irish."

"No. You're an Anglo. So's Dad. My mother was a Catholic from the bogs. Her family, the Ryans, are native Irish."

Still worried, Claire said crossly, "Everyone knows that. You're not different from me, Frankie. Mummy's *English*—"

He looked down, at that. "I know," he said. Claire's mother wasn't Frank's mother, who had died when he was born.

Claire pulled at his sleeve. "Don't be different from me, Frankie. I don't want you to be different." Tears filled her eyes. His were very dark; his hair was black. He was amazingly like Daddy.

Suddenly he hugged her, then as abruptly pushed her away and jumped up. "Don't be such a silly crybaby. Race you to the old seat!" he said, rushing away.

By the time she hurtled up to him, he was sitting and laughing at her. "It's not fair," she gasped, scarlet-faced and out of breath. "I can't run as fast as you."

"That's because you're an Anglo," he taunted, and was off, daring her to try to catch him.

A few drops of rain fell on Claire. Claire Fraser now, twenty-four years later, sitting on the log seat with tears in her eyes. The sun was slipping behind a bank of shower-filled clouds. She got up and quickened her walk

163

to the house. Out of so much love, so much misery had come. Out of closeness, such division. Was it true, what he had said that wretched day they said goodbye? "It's not anybody's fault, Claire. Not Dad's nor Claudia's or mine. If you want to know why things have turned out as they are, you've got to go back to the beginning."

She let herself into the kitchen of Riverstown and unlocked the door to the main part of the house. It was dark in the hall, and she flooded it with electric light. There was a whisper of dampness in the air. You couldn't close up an Irish house without the weather getting into the fabric. And there they were, the portraits of her ancestors, watching her from the walls. Nearly two hundred unbroken years at Riverstown. Births and marriages and deaths; the tombstones in Naas church a testimonial, her own father's the most recent. But his first wife, Eileen Ryan Arbuthnot, was not buried there. The division had begun with her.

CHAPTER 2

The first Arbuthnot, Judge Hugh Arbuthnot, came to Ireland in 1798 to try the rebels who had burned the English garrison alive in their barracks at Prosperous. An odd name for a poverty-stricken Irish village in County Kildare. Judge Arbuthnot, known as the Hanging Judge, had hanged the Irishmen of Prosperous like apples from the gallows tree.

He took time off from his duties to tour the countryside, and decided that apart from its inhabitants, Kildare was one of the most beautiful places on earth. The fields were green and lush with pasture, the River Liffey flowed through land that was as rich as his Scottish farm was bleak and poor. In Ireland, cattle grew fat and the rivers abounded with fish. The air was mild, and the rain didn't trouble a Scotsman. He applied for a land grant, which was sold to him for a nominal sum. He neither knew nor cared who had been evicted from it and left destitute. The site where Hugh Arbuthnot built his house was a rise in the ground overlooking the river. He brought his wife and children over from Scotland, and they settled into the fine house, which he named Riverstown.

His son built a wall high enough to keep the poachers out, with handsome wrought-iron gates. The stone pineapples on the two piers at his gateway signified that the owner was a justice. The judge was a shrewd man, not over kind-hearted, but when the misery of the famine brought people dying of hunger to his gates, they were not turned away. Over the generations the Arbuthnots prospered. They married with a view to inheritance and attended the local Protestant church. Their sons and daughters went to English boarding schools, then to Trinity College, Dublin, where Catholics were barred, or to English universities. Younger sons went into the British army or the Royal Navy. They would always describe themselves as Irish. Their excellent record as landlords and non-involvement in local politics saved Riverstown from being burned down by the IRA in 1922, when civil war broke out. Neighbours who were not so well thought of stood and watched at gunpoint while their homes went up in flames.

Claire's father, Philip Arbuthnot, inherited Riverstown and its eleven hundred acres in 1938, when he was twenty-seven and already married. He was the only surviving son; his eldest brother had been killed in the Great War, and the next son had died in infancy. Philip was tall, with curly black hair and a little moustache that made him look old-fashioned. He was a sportsman and a countryman, uncomplicated in his attitude to people and to life. When he met Eileen Ryan, she was sitting on a riverbank with a dazed look, her bicycle upended in a ditch. Her fine red hair glittered like gold in the sunlight. Philip stopped his car, got out, and asked her if she was all right.

"I don't know for sure. Where am I?" There was a sweet lilt of brogue in her voice.

At the moment Philip helped her into his car, he fell in love with her. It wasn't a long courtship. It wasn't a courtship at all, according to Eileen's outraged family. They didn't want a member of the Protestant gentry hanging round Eileen, who was too young yet to know what a fool she was making of herself.

Several weeks after they met, Philip and Eileen eloped to England and were married in London. The Protestant marriage didn't reconcile his father or mother, who flatly refused to receive a daughter-in-law who was no better than one of their own maids. The fact that the Ryans were wealthy farmers made no difference to them. The Ryans were bog Irish.

In 1938, eighteen months after Philip's marriage, his father died of lung cancer. He hadn't disinherited his son, as some of his more extreme friends advised, nor did he tell Philip's mother that he had met his daughter-in-law briefly in London. A pretty little wisp of a girl, she obviously adored Philip. She had a delicacy and charm about her that the old man recognized. He wished Philip and Eileen happiness, but he didn't ask them to come home.

When he died, his widow, Blanche, moved to a property in County Meath, and Philip brought his young Irish wife back to Ireland to live at Riverstown. Mrs. Gerard, the old housekeeper, had given notice. She was not, she told Mrs. Arbuthnot, prepared to work for the likes of *her*.

The young couple drove through the gates and up the avenue of ancient lime trees. It was a bright autumn day, and as they rounded the bend and came in sight of the river, Philip took her hand and said, "Look, darling, isn't that wonderful? Just look at the leaf colour all along the bank there."

She saw the excitement in his face and smiled, to please him. Surely the great blaze of reds and golden yellows was a marvellous sight, but it did nothing to ease the apprehension in her heart. "It's lovely, Phil," she said softly. "Like a picture painting."

He squeezed her hand. "A painting, sweetheart. Not a picture painting." He didn't see the faint blush of embarrassment, because she turned her head away.

The gardener was waiting for them at the front door. He opened the car door for Philip, who handed his wife out.

"This is Doyle," he said, introducing her.

"Welcome, ma'am."

Philip guided her by the arm into the hall, where a frightening array of maids in uniform, and the cook, whom Eileen had known since she was a child, came up one by one and greeted her. She could feel her cheeks burning as girls she'd been to the convent school with in Naas said, "Welcome, ma'am."

"We'd like tea in the library," Philip said. "And early dinner, please, Mary. We had a long journey." Eileen stood there while he chatted to the cook, Mary Donovan, who was a cousin on the Ryan side.

"It's wonderful to be back," he said when they were alone in the library. "Wonderful you're with me, darling. You're going to love Riverstown. How about a little smile then?"

He sat her down on his knee and kissed her, waking all the wicked senses she'd been taught to suppress all her life.

It was Eileen who heard the knock and leaped away from him before the door opened. The silver tray was set down by Lily, the senior parlour maid. She didn't look at Eileen. She addressed herself to Philip. "What time would you be wanting dinner, sir?"

Philip knew her well. She had been his mother's toady.

He said, "Ask Mrs. Arbuthnot."

Eileen panicked. What time? Philip didn't eat tea as they did at home. He ate dinner.

"Cook says, What time would you be wanting yer dinner, ma'am?" The gleam in Lily's eye was mocking as she repeated the question.

Eileen remembered their routine in London, where they had rented a flat. It had taken her months to get used to eating so late and so many times a day. "Eight o'clock, please."

"Very good, ma'am."

The door closed and Philip held out his arms. There was no desire left in her, and she shook her head.

"We can go upstairs early to bed," he suggested.

"Not here, Phil. Not with all of them watching and sniggering."

"Don't be ridiculous! Nobody's watching! It's bound to be a bit strange for you at first, but saying you won't make love to your own husband in your own house because of the servants . . ."

"They're servants to you," she said quietly. "But I went to school with them. Mary Donovan is a cousin of my father's! How am I going to manage this house and be a wife you can be proud of when I've been brought up a different way, and everybody in the place knows it?"

He could look quite hard, she thought suddenly. Quite the Arbuthnot, dealing with some nonsense from the Irish.

"If there's any difficulty, Eileen, because you used to know them, we'll sack the lot and get a completely new staff. By the way, I want you to change the furniture round, get new curtains, that sort of thing. It's your home now. Remember that."

Her eyes filled with tears. "I do love you," she said. "I'll do my best, I promise you. I'll love Riverstown because it's yours."

THERE WAS A CONFERENCE going on around the kitchen table. Tea had been made and a big cake like the one served in the library had been cut up in thick slices. Lily was holding forth, her pinched face sallow with indignation.

"And there she was, playing the high an' mighty madam. 'Eight o'clock, please.'" She mimicked Eileen's voice. "If ye'd seen the airs of her!"

Mary Donovan sat with her fat hands cradling the teacup. She decided that Lily needed putting in her place. "I'd mind yerself, Lily," she said. "It's himself we've got to please, not her. He'll not put up wit' yer nonsense any more than the major would." Philip's father had served in the Irish Guards in the Great War and was always referred to by his rank.

Upstairs, Eileen and Philip made love, and then she fell asleep. He woke her gently, smiling at her.

"We've got to change, darling, so you'd better get up."

He saw her bewilderment and said, "We always change for dinner at Riverstown. How about the blue we bought together?"

It was a tactful way of explaining that change meant evening dress for her and dinner jacket for him. Poor sweet, he thought. It was all very strange to her, but she'd soon get used to it.

He gave her a glass of champagne in the drawing room before dinner. She looked beautiful in the long, slim blue dress and the pearls he'd given her as a wedding present. He noticed that there was a little blue brooch pinned to the neck of her dress.

"Where did you get that, darling?" He touched it lightly.

"It's my granny's," she explained. "She give it to me on my eighteenth birthday."

"It's very pretty," Philip said. "Grandmother, darling, not granny. It makes you sound like a child. And she *gave* it to you."

"Sure an' I know she did." Suddenly, cheekily, she spun round in front of him, mocking his attempts to turn her into an Anglo-Irish lady. "Ye'll not make this particular sow's ear into a silk purse, young fella-me-lad!"

Lily, about to knock on the door to announce dinner, heard them laughing and paused, listening. She heard Philip say, "Quite right, sweetheart. You've married a pompous idiot!" She couldn't make out Eileen's answer, but she muttered, "Eejit, is right," before she knocked on the door. "Dinner is served, sir and mam."

THEY HAD BEEN LIVING at Riverstown for two months before the first invitation came. It was addressed to Mrs. Philip Arbuthnot, and a letter from Lady Hamilton was enclosed with the card. Eileen knew the name, of course. The family was not rich; much of their land had been sold to pay the debts of successive wastrel sons. The family had been relieved of the embarrassment of a huge unmanageable Georgian house by a convenient fire in the 1920s. Sir William Hamilton was said to have started it himself, rather than repair the roof, which let in torrents of water in one wing. The insurance company, refusing to accept the IRA as culprits, declined to pay. The family found themselves with a gutted ruin and one surviving wing. A local builder obliged by knocking down the remains in exchange for the materials he could salvage, and the place had been known as the Half House ever since. The present Lady Hamilton was English and had some private money. Eileen read her letter slowly.

Dear Mrs. Arbuthnot,
We hear that you and your husband are living at Riverstown since the poor major's death and would be so pleased if you could dine with us on December 19th. We are so looking forward to meeting you, and do hope you can come.

Sincerely,
Claudia Hamilton

Eileen passed the letter to Philip. "You'll like her," he said. "She's fun, marvellous horsewoman. He's a good chap too. I think we should go."

"All right," she said. "If you want to."

"Sooner or later you've got to mix with our neighbours, and this is a good way to start. Now, I've got to be off. See you at lunch."

He got up from the breakfast table, kissed her, and was gone. She had been surprised how hard he worked on the estate at Riverstown. She, on the contrary, had little to do.

When she left the dining room that November morning, she decided to walk down by the river. The weather was mild, with a wintry sunshine dappling the ground under the trees. Eileen loved the river. She didn't fish, of course. Sports were not considered fit for Irish girls.

Philip wanted her to accept the Hamiltons' invitation, that was clear. Marrying him had been one thing; loving him and defying her family had taken more courage and determination than she had imagined. Earning the obedience and respect of the servants, who saw her as no better than they were, had been another battle. Yet it was all but won. In these weeks they had realized that, although she was shy and lacking in confidence, she was also a woman of surprising strength, and gradually they had accepted her. Even the house, with its big, grand rooms and dark paintings of Arbuthnots, seemed less strange now that she had altered the bedroom and rearranged the study into a cosy sitting room.

But meeting the neighbours, who knew who she was and that her mother-in-law had moved to another county rather than come face to face with her—that really frightened her. She was native Irish. All her life she had been taught that Philip and his kind were aliens in possession of land they had stolen from its rightful owners. Oppressors of Ireland and its people, persecutors of the Catholic Church. The terrible wrongs of the past were stronger than the Christian commandment to forgive. Eileen knew what she had thought of the Arbuthnots and their kind until she fell in love with Philip. She knew what they in turn thought of her and her people. It had been made very plain over the centuries. And fundamentally nothing had changed.

There was a bench, fashioned out of a fallen tree trunk, and Eileen sat down on it to think. She remembered that terrible scene with her father, when he forbade her to marry Philip. "Marry in the Protestant Church! No daughter of mine'll set foot in it—I'd see ye dead first!" All he could see was the shame and disgrace such an alliance would bring.

She'd gone to her room and cried in misery. And there her mother came to add her warnings. She sat on the edge of the bed and reminded Eileen what was at stake. The damnation of her soul. None of her family or friends would speak to her; she'd be cut off from her own kind. And what about *his* friends? Did she imagine they'd accept her? "Bog trotters," Bridget Ryan reminded her, "that's what they call us. Paddy an' his pig. We're all right in our place, but that place is under their feet."

The next morning Eileen had left the farm. She was never to hear from her parents or her brothers again.

She took Claudia Hamilton's letter out of her pocket and reread it. Dinner on December 19th.

Philip was confident she'd be a success. He was always telling her how pretty she was, how well she ran Riverstown. He was a happy man, deeply in love with his wife. Twice he'd driven over to see his mother and come back optimistic that she'd reconcile herself to the marriage and visit them one day soon. Everything was wonderful, he said, and Eileen knew it was, for him. And if his mother came, she'd have to entertain her, instead of slamming the door in her face for the way she'd behaved. Philip had written a very conciliatory letter to Eileen's parents, hoping they'd accept him as a son-in-law. Eileen was amazed that he expected a reply.

She got up, suddenly chilled after sitting so long, and walked slowly back to the house.

"YOU LOOK LOVELY, sweetheart," Philip said. Eileen was dressed and ready for the Hamiltons' dinner party. "Now, get your wrap on. Claudia is English, and she doesn't like people to be late."

He squeezed her hand as they pulled in to the drive of the Half House. "You'll be a wild success," he murmured.

Claudia Hamilton was very tall and thin. She had fair hair that was done in a roll round her head, bright blue eyes and a loud English voice. She greeted Philip with a kiss; then she gave Eileen's hand a strong clasp that made her wince.

"How lovely to meet you. And what a divine dress. Come along in and let me introduce you."

Eileen didn't know any of the names; she smiled and shook hands and was passed from one to the other like a parcel. Being inspected, appraised. Philip's Irish wife. Everyone was very friendly. She was given a dry martini, which she hated and put down almost untouched on a table when nobody was looking. People made conversation with her, avoiding awkward topics like her marriage. Talking about London was safe, and she answered questions about their stay there and managed to smile and be animated. Claudia was talking to Philip. Eileen wished he was beside her, but after the first ten minutes he'd been taken to talk to someone else. When they went in to dinner, she glanced anxiously at Philip, who was on the other side of the table.

"You're here, next to James." Claudia guided her to the seat on the host's left.

Eileen picked at the first course and let James Hamilton carry the conversation. He chatted about the weather, the racing, the poor scent out hunting—did she hunt? Well, of course, she must take it up; his wife was mad on it. Terribly sad about her father-in-law's death. How was poor Blanche these days?

"I don't know," she said. "I've never met my mother-in-law."

Hamilton looked puzzled. His wife had explained the situation to him, but he never listened to what he called women's gossip.

"Haven't you? Why ever not?"

"She didn't want Philip to marry me." Eileen couldn't stop herself. They must know, she thought. I'm not ashamed. "That's why she went to Meath. To be out of the house before I came."

"Really?" He looked at her with interest. How very embarrassing to say all that in front of everybody. Philip must clue her in a bit about how to behave. "I'm sure she'll come round," he said.

"She may," Eileen answered, "but I won't."

She drank a little wine and noticed that the man on her other side was staring at her. "Tell me, Mrs. Arbuthnot," he said. "Do you think there'll be a war?"

"War?" She shook her head. "War with who?"

"Germany. You girls are all the same. Never read anything in the papers except the fashion articles. I'm afraid there will be."

"But we won't be in the war. It's nothing to do with us."

"Not for some people, I suppose," he said. "But I can't see Philip sitting back and doing nothing about it. Anyway"—he gave her a distant smile—"let's talk about something more cheerful. How do you like living at Riverstown?"

She muttered something noncommittal. What did he mean about Philip? If England went to war, why should he fight?

She knew that after the meal the women left the men to linger in the dining room. She was prepared for the move when it came and followed Claudia Hamilton and the other ladies upstairs. A girl called Maggie turned to Eileen and said, "How long have you been married?"

"Nearly a year," Eileen answered. "You're engaged, I see—when's the wedding?"

"Next spring," said Maggie. "Of course, if this beastly war breaks out we'll have to make it earlier. Maybe it won't; my father says it'll be over in six months anyway, so none of them will have to go."

"I don't see why anyone wants to fight for England," Eileen said. "Not now we're independent. I won't let my husband go joining up."

"My brother can't wait," was the answer. "But men are so silly, aren't they? But I don't think you'll keep the Paddies out of it, they love a fight."

The Paddies! Eileen had blushed scarlet at the contemptuous word, and the equally contemptuous way it was said. I'm a Paddy, she wanted to say. And proud of it.

But she said nothing and followed the women into the drawing room.

Soon the men joined them. Philip came over to her. He noticed that she looked very flushed. He bent and kissed her lightly on the forehead.

"Hello, darling. Sorry we were so long. Are you all right?"

She told the sort of feeble lie she would have despised in someone else. A little social lie, which one of those drawling females would have used. "I've got a bit of a headache," she murmured. "Don't lets stay too long."

"It wasn't too bad, was it?" he asked her when they got home.

She didn't want to disappoint his hopes that she would integrate and enjoy being with his friends. "It was nice," she said. "But what's this talk of war?"

"Don't bother your head about it," he said, dismissing it lightly.

Over at the Half House the party was still going strong. Brandies were poured, cigars pierced and lit. There was a lot of laughter. And naturally they gave their opinions on the new Mrs. Arbuthnot.

"I think she's a bit gauche, but quite sweet," Claudia said.

"Damned pretty girl," several of the men agreed.

"I don't think she's sweet at all," a woman named Maggie announced.

"She had the cheek to say no one should fight for England if there's a war. We all know she's a Paddy, but she'd better keep those remarks to herself. I love Philip, he's a dear, but I'm not having her in the house."

"Don't be silly, Maggie, you can't take that attitude," put in another guest. "The Arbuthnots have been here for generations. You can't refuse to have Philip's wife to parties."

"People with her attitude burned my grandmother's home to the ground in 'twenty-two," Maggie declared. "I'm not having someone like that near me. And David won't either, will you, darling?"

"We'll see," her fiancé said soothingly. "Don't get het up about it now." He didn't share his future wife's passionate feelings about the past. He loved his home in Ireland and got on with the people. But he was a newcomer from England, and it amused him to think how much Maggie and Eileen Arbuthnot had in common, with their rooted prejudices.

ANOTHER DAY DAWNED and the mists from the river swirled and eddied round the banks and crept up to the house the Hanging Judge had built. In the master bedroom Philip woke as the sun came up. He turned and looked at Eileen sleeping beside him. He did love her so much. She was the most girlish girl he'd ever known. Most of the well-bred girls he knew were coarse as cows beside her. He loved her courage and her loyalty. Once committed to him, she had withstood her family and, even more difficult, the power of her Church. He regretted her family's intractability because he felt it made her unhappy. His own mother was rather a stranger to him, so he didn't feel the loss of her so keenly. Nurses had brought him up, and by the age of seven he was away at private school in England. Blanche Arbuthnot was a busy woman, much occupied with her dogs and horses. But she'd call on them one day, he was confident of that. When there were grandchildren. She was old and a snob. He understood her and didn't blame her; he didn't really care enough to be hurt. He missed his father, though. He would have warmed to Eileen, had he lived long enough to get to know her.

If war broke out, he'd have to join his father's regiment, but he wasn't going to tell Eileen that. He wasn't going to let anything worry her. In his heart he sensed that she was lonely and ill at ease. The servants weren't a problem any more. It wasn't just fear of him that had made them change. They respected Eileen. No, what she wanted was a baby. He could leave her if there was a child; and he knew, as all his friends had agreed the night before, that if England went to war with Germany, Ireland might remain neutral, but they, the Anglo-Irish, could not.

It was two long years of disappointment before Eileen conceived. From the start it was a difficult pregnancy. She felt so sick in the mornings that it was often lunchtime before she could drag herself out of bed and come downstairs.

"She's fine," Dr. Baron reassured Philip. "She's a fine, healthy girl, and all she is is a bit queasy of a morning. That'll pass when the baby turns. Nothing to worry about at all."

After three months Eileen had not improved. She felt weak and seedy, and if she went for a walk her ankles puffed up. Mary Donovan made her special brews to take the swelling down.

"Poor soul," Mary said, as the servants drank their midmorning tea in the kitchen. "There's something wrong there, for sure."

"It's a sad state to be in," Lily agreed. "And not a move from her mother."

"What about her brothers?" asked Doyle, the gardener.

"Not a murmur out o' them," Mary answered. "Shamus sittin' there like a stuck pig, and Kevin lookin' at his teacup. I tell ye, I was sorry I'd taken the trouble to tell them."

Eileen's mother, Bridget Ryan, never came, nor was there an answer to the letter Philip sent her. But when Eileen was in her seventh month, Mrs. Blanche Arbuthnot came to Riverstown on her way to stay with friends in Limerick.

She drove in through the gates of her old home. Her Labrador retriever, Bunny, bounded onto the back seat, excited by familiar smells. Blanche quelled her with a brisk command.

The green lawns were bright and cut close; there were still white-painted stones along the edges of the drive. It all looked so familiar. Nothing had changed since she had come there as a bride more than forty years ago. She wouldn't admit that she felt nervous. She switched off the engine, glanced at herself in the driving mirror and got out, letting Bunny jump onto the drive. The front door opened before she had time to walk up to it, and there was Philip and, behind him, her daughter-in-law.

She received his kiss on one cheek without returning it.

"Hello, Phil, dear," she said. "I've brought Bunny. I hope you don't mind."

"Of course not," he said, and then came the moment she had been dreading. "Mother, this is Eileen."

She was smaller and slighter than Blanche had imagined. The baby overbalanced her; she moved awkwardly when she came up and held out her hand. "How do you do, Mrs. Arbuthnot," she said. Her mouth smiled, but the light-coloured eyes were full of hatred. Philip couldn't see, of course. He was standing beside her, smiling in his good-natured way.

"How do you do. It's so nice to meet you," said Blanche.

"Do come inside," the girl said, and stood back to let her mother-in-law go ahead of her.

"Where are we having tea, darling?" Philip asked, as if he didn't know.

"In the den," his wife replied.

"The den?" Blanche knew immediately she shouldn't have asked, but the word made no sense to her. Where would you find a "den" at Riverstown?

"Dad's old study. Eileen's made it very cosy."

"We use it a lot," the girl said, showing her into the room.

Blanche looked at the papered walls and the flounced pink curtains and said, "How nice. Such a pretty colour scheme."

She sat down and the Labrador flopped at her feet. This had been her husband's favourite room. There was no trace of him now. She was surprised how much it hurt. Philip looked very well and kept giving his wife reassuring looks that Blanche wasn't supposed to see. If he was happy, that was something; but for how long? How long before the difference in their backgrounds began to jar? This dreadful, vulgar room!

Lily brought in tea and one of Mary's marvellous sponge cakes.

Blanche smiled up at her. "How are you, Lily? It's so nice to see you. You're looking very well."

"Oh, I am, Mrs. Arbuthnot, ma'am."

"How do you like your tea?" Eileen asked.

For a moment their eyes met. "Not too strong. Just milk, no sugar. Thank you." There was silence. Blanche Arbuthnot had never felt so uncomfortable in her life. Her son was married, her daughter-in-law expecting their first baby, and she didn't know what to say next. They haven't mentioned the baby, she thought. I suppose it's up to me.

She cleared her throat. "Philip told me the splendid news, Eileen. When will the baby arrive?"

"Early August, Dr. Baron says," the girl answered.

"Baron?" Blanche was aghast. "Surely he's not looking after you? He's an absolute idiot. I wouldn't have him to whelp Bunny. My dear, you must get somebody from Dublin."

She knew that she had made a fatal mistake. The girl's pale face flushed an unbecoming red. "He's been our doctor since I was born," she replied. "He's good enough for me."

Blanche suddenly felt quite tired. There was no point of contact and there never would be. She pulled herself together and said, "Anyway, it's splendid news. One more cup of tea and then I really must be on my way. It's quite a drive."

Philip said, "Mother's going to stay with the Dornaways."

"Who are the Dornaways?" asked Eileen.

"The earl and countess ... Dornaway Castle is quite a place. I'll take you down there one day. They're awfully sweet," he added, trying to be jolly again.

"They've asked me for ten days," Blanche said. "It's such a lovely house. Your father and I always enjoyed going there. You must drive Eileen over to meet Bobby and Jilly. I'm sure you'd like them," she added.

The red flush had faded, leaving Eileen terribly pale. She said quietly, "I think they'd be a bit grand for me, Mrs. Arbuthnot."

Blanche put down her cup. "They're not at all grand. Bobby is my nephew. I'm sure they'd be delighted to meet you. It's so nice I can take Bunny. She moped so badly after your father died," she said to Philip. "I didn't know what to do. The local vet kept saying I should put her down. He's not a patch on old Pat Farrel—he was marvellous with dogs."

"Pat Farrel is a cousin of my father's," Eileen said. "He's a good man with cattle too."

"Yes, so he is. Such a nice man. I keep Bunny in the house now," Blanche hurried on. "She was so miserable in the kennel, poor old girl. So now she's a house dog." She bent down and patted the silky black head. "Aren't you, you silly old thing?"

"Will you excuse me a moment?" Eileen got up, glanced at Philip and her mother-in-law. He looked concerned.

"Are you all right, darling? Not feeling sick, are you?"

"No." She managed a smile. "No, I'm fine. I won't be long."

"Poor little thing," he said to Blanche after Eileen had left. "She's had such a rotten time. Been sick practically the whole seven months. By the way, you shouldn't have said that about Dr. Baron. He's always looked after the Ryans. Eileen insisted on having him."

"I'm sorry." Blanche wasn't used to being rebuked by her son. "But Baron's a butcher. She's not a very robust girl, I'd say. But it's not really my business. I only meant it for the best. Good Lord, Philip, look at the time. I must be getting on my way."

"I'll go and call Eileen." He got up and left her sitting alone.

Eileen was not sick. She had thought that the spasm of pain would be followed by vomiting, as it often was, but by the time she reached her bedroom it had passed. She crawled onto the bed and hugged herself like a child with no one there to bring comfort. That hateful, arrogant old woman, with her chilly snobbishness, talking about the child Eileen was carrying as "splendid news". So cold and unfeeling; Eileen couldn't have imagined anyone behaving in her own son's home as if she were a stranger, making small talk and occasionally bestowing a few words on her daughter-in-law. Dismissing the doctor who had brought her and her brothers into the world as someone she wouldn't have to whelp her mangy bitch. Patronizing Pat Farrel, knowing, surely, that he and the Ryans were related. Eileen didn't mean to cry, but she felt angry and degraded, and tears came so easily these days. She couldn't stop crying, and then the pain came back and nagged at her until she held her hands to her belly.

Philip came running down the stairs. Blanche was already in the hall, clutching Bunny's lead.

"Is she all right?" she asked, seeing him come down alone. Her son was white-faced, a sure sign of anger in the Arbuthnots.

176

"She's thoroughly upset," he snapped. "Why couldn't you have been nicer to her, Mother?"

They stood facing each other in the hall, mother and son who had never been close, locked in the eternal triangle.

"I did my best," Blanche Arbuthnot answered. "She wasn't exactly friendly to me."

Philip said, "She's having pains. If anything happens, I'll never forgive you." He turned and went back upstairs.

Coming out of the study with the tea tray, Lily saw Mrs. Arbuthnot open the front door and slam it after her. Then Lily hurried out to the kitchen to tell them all the news.

Blanche got into the car and settled the old dog on the seat beside her. She was trembling. It was too much, at sixty-three, too much to have lost her husband and two of her sons, and to be left with only this son and his dreadful marriage. She switched on the engine and swung out onto the Naas road. Three hours later she was safe in Dornaway Castle, where she seemed so shaken that they put her straight to bed.

"I DID EVERYTHING YOU TOLD ME," Eileen mumbled. "I did my best. She was so horrible ..." Tears were trickling down her cheeks. Philip wiped them away, murmuring to her to forget about it, not to worry.

"I hate her," she whispered. "She hates me and I hate her."

"Don't say that," Philip begged. "Please, sweetheart."

By nine o'clock that night Eileen's pains had become stronger. Philip telephoned Dr. Baron. He was out on a call.

When he came upstairs to the bedroom, he found Lily standing by the bed and Eileen clutching her hand and moaning.

"The missus rang for me," Lily whispered. "Sure, God love her, she's goin' to give birth."

"The doctor's out," Philip said. "Nobody knows where he is or when he'll be back! Lily, stay here with Mrs. Arbuthnot. I'm going to telephone Lady Hamilton to come over."

Claudia Hamilton drove the ten miles at reckless speed. She knew panic when she heard it, and sheer panic was in Philip's voice. She ran into the hall and up the stairs. She was in a dinner dress, with a coat thrown over it. She saw Mary Donovan, the cook, standing on one side of the bed with Lily, the senior parlour maid. Philip, hollow-eyed with fear, was holding Eileen's hand.

Claudia didn't waste a minute. "Philip, get the car out. Lily, pack some things for Mrs. Arbuthnot. Mary, you hold her hand. I'm going to phone the hospital and say we're bringing her in."

Claudia insisted on driving. Philip sat in the back, cradling his wife in his arms. When they reached the hospital, he carried her inside, where she was hurried into the labour ward. Philip stood by helplessly while Claudia exerted her considerable authority to get the doctor called immediately. Then she turned to Philip and took his arm.

"Come on, we'll go to the waiting room. They'll bring us tea."

It wasn't a long vigil. They sat in the dingy room, with its green-painted walls and picture of the Sacred Heart.

"She'll be all right," Claudia insisted. And then, because she had spoken to the ward sister, she thought it best to warn him. "It may be a bit difficult for the baby. It's very early, you see."

"I don't care about the baby," Philip said, and with those few words he doomed his unborn son. "I want Eileen safe. That's all I care about."

When the door opened and the sister beckoned, he sprang up and followed her out of the waiting room.

Eileen floated between dreams and fits of consciousness. She saw Philip leaning over her, and she thought someone said, "You've got a lovely little boy, thanks be to God," but it didn't seem real. Her mother-in-law was real. The anger wouldn't go away. "I hate her . . . I hate them all," she mumbled in delirium.

The doctor had left; there was no more he could do. The pain had stopped. So had the warm, gushing blood that streamed out of her body, taking her life with it.

The sister whispered, "Your wife said she was a Catholic. I've sent for the priest. Here's Father Cochran now." She was surprised and offended when Philip left the room.

He stood in the corridor while the priest prepared his wife for death. He couldn't cry, he couldn't feel; he didn't know how long he stood outside the door, leaning against the greasy wall. It was a boy, they told him. Very small, but breathing normally, thanks be to God. He must have closed his eyes, because the priest was suddenly in front of him.

"You can go in to her now," the priest said. "It was a beautiful death she made. She just smiled and went to heaven." He touched Philip on the arm. "God's given you a child," he said. "Try to be comforted."

There was nothing Philip could say. What was beautiful about the death of a young girl, leaving a motherless child? He turned his back on the priest and went in to say goodbye to his wife.

CLAUDIA HAMILTON MADE THE ARRANGEMENTS. Philip didn't want Eileen to lie in the gaudy Catholic cemetery in Naas, and the dignified place reserved for the Arbuthnots was forbidden to her. She was buried in Dublin. Her family was not invited to attend.

The baby was strong enough after six weeks to go home to Riverstown with a trained nurse, and he was duly baptized a Protestant in the church in Naas. Claudia was one of his godparents. He was christened Francis Alexander William, which were all Arbuthnot family names.

Philip was not allowed to be lonely. Friends rallied to him, and Claudia installed a housekeeper and a nanny. Frank, as the little boy had come to be called, flourished. Philip went to see him twice a day, encouraged by Claudia, who hoped the child would make up to him for Eileen. But Philip turned more and more to her. James Hamilton had joined the British army when war broke out. After he was killed in North Africa, Claudia and Philip became lovers. Then, just before Christmas 1942, Philip joined the regiment his father had fought in during the last war.

It was Mary Donovan who suggested that Eileen's younger brother might slip in to see his nephew before he left for America. Even though Kevin Ryan didn't say much, he had always been kind to Eileen and fond of her. Now, two days before he sailed for New York, Mary smuggled Kevin in through the back door and up the back stairs to the nursery.

Kevin Ryan had never seen a nursery before. A cot swathed in draperies and blue ribbon stood isolated in a corner. He approached and looked in at the boy.

The baby had a thatch of black hair and wide dark eyes. There was nothing to remind him of Eileen. Just a black Arbuthnot, like the rest of them. He turned away, and his eyes filled with tears.

"So that's all that's left of her," he said. "And he'll never know the Irish half of him. Arbuthnot had him baptized a Protestant."

"Yes," said Mary. "But the nurse who brought him home from the hospital said the ward sister baptized him herself the very night he was born. So, much good did it do them to take him up to that church in Naas. God's grace is in him, Kevin."

He leaned down and touched the child. The skin was soft and smelled sweet. "Good luck to him," he said. "Maybe one day he'll know the truth about himself." He turned away. He wanted to get out of this hated house and everything it represented. Many of his friends were joining the British army. It seemed a kind of treason. He had relatives in America on his mother's side. He would have shared the farm with his brother, Shamus, in the end, as was the Irish custom, but he didn't want that kind of life. He didn't want to end up an ignorant man like his father. There was no real future for the Irish in Ireland while people like the Arbuthnots held the land and the power.

He said goodbye to Mary and hurried away down the drive.

CHAPTER 3

Claire went into the gun room at Riverstown. Years ago it had held the family collection of sporting guns, encased in mahogany. It belonged to an age she could well remember, when there were big shooting parties at Riverstown and she followed on foot with her mother and joined the guests for lunch. Frank had been a superb shot. That, at least, he and his father had in common. When she and Frank were young there had been no need to lock the gun room. But for years now, since the trouble began in the North, all firearms had been kept under lock and key. Her father gave up shooting quite suddenly after Frank left home. Occasionally, when she came over from England with Neil, they'd go out and take a few pigeons on a Sunday morning, but his heart wasn't in it.

Now, in 1980, the cases were almost empty. The Purdey shotguns had been sold after her father's death. But hanging from a hook, in its holster, was his army revolver. She stood hesitating. Where had her father kept the ammunition for it? In one of the bottom drawers she found the clip with the cartridges. She put them in her pocket, found the right key and unlocked the cabinet and removed the revolver. It was heavy and clumsy, difficult to hide. She took off her jacket, wrapped it round the gun, and folded it awkwardly over one arm. She locked up after her. She knew where Frank was, and she knew that he would need a gun.

Her car was ready when she got back to the cottage. Clutching the jacket with its hidden weapon close to her side, she forced herself to smile at Billy.

"Changing the plates was a dirty old job," he complained. "Drive it out, and I'll put mine inside. Did ye lock up after ye?"

"Yes. It's fine; don't worry."

She opened the car door and dropped the jacket and the gun on the back seat. She reversed the car out and swung it round to give Billy room to put his in its place.

"Have ye far to go?" Billy asked.

She shook her head. "Not too far. Thanks, Billy. And don't worry about me. I'll be back before dark."

She waved at him out of the window and drove off towards the road. He waved back, and as the car disappeared from sight he let out a groan of frustration. Where was Frank Arbuthnot hiding that half the police in Ireland and the IRA couldn't find him and Claire thought she could? They'd always had secrets, those two. He watching over her, and she thinking he was the Lord himself. She'd grown up into a beautiful, fair young woman, and every lad in the county had his eye on her. But all Frank needed to do was speak against any of them, and that made an end. She had preferred to go riding or fishing with him than to a party or a dance. So she was packed off to England and came back with an Englishman. Billy spat in disgust and went into his cottage.

Claire didn't need to consult the signposts. She knew every mile of the back roads to Kells and Cloncarrig. How often they'd driven there in Frank's car, towing the horse trailer behind them, excited by the prospect of a day's hunting with the Meath.

For a moment her eyes blurred at the memories of happy days, before Kevin Ryan came back from America and bought the Half House from the last improvident Hamilton. That was when everything changed. Until then Frank had been safe, because they had each other, and the things that troubled him were half buried and might well have sunk past danger. But as if Eileen Arbuthnot cried for vengeance from the grave, her brother Kevin had come back and laid claim to her son.

It was midday and gloriously bright. Claire drove down the main street of Kells and made the final turn to Cloncarrig.

Frank's voice during that last telephone call, made only a few days before he disappeared, came back to her.

"Claire, I've got something to tell you. I'm finished with them."

"Oh, thank God. But can you break off just like that?"

"I can and I have," he said.

"Come over here," she begged him. "You can't stay in Ireland if you've fallen out with them."

She heard the mocking laugh, but it was bitter.

"I don't think Neil would be exactly overjoyed to see me. Don't you worry about me. I've friends who'll pull strings. Nobody will dare touch me. And anyway, I can always hole up in our secret place. Remember Reynard, and his folly?" And then he'd asked if she was well and happy, and she'd lied and said she was.

"God bless you then," was his goodbye.

She drove the car slowly, looking for the turning she remembered. It was still there, a gap where a gate should have been, leading onto a rutted farm track. She drove in and bumped along, stopped at a clump of beech trees, where the car would be hidden from the road. Broad green fields surrounded her, with distant woods bounding the horizon. She took the revolver and ammunition, and her jacket to wrap them in, and began to walk towards the woods. Beyond the woods lay a valley and in the valley a lake, in which, on a clear day, the ruins of a fine Georgian house were reflected. And beyond that, past a gentle rise, she would find her brother, if he were still alive.

THE ARMY HELICOPTER TOOK OFF from South Wales at ten thirty in the morning, an hour after Superintendent Brownlow of Special Branch had spoken to Major Michael Harvey on the phone. Before noon it landed at the heliport, and a car was waiting to speed its passenger to London.

Major Harvey, Wellington and Green Jackets, ex-Sandhurst, was not at all what Brownlow had expected. He was a slight man, a little above average height. He wore shabby corduroys and a jacket, and looked thoroughly nondescript. He could have been anything except an army officer in the most sensitive intelligence branch, renowned for undercover operations in Northern Ireland.

"You know the Frasers socially, I believe," Brownlow said as they shook hands.

"Yes. I've stayed with them several times. Had some days' shooting with them. They're a nice couple."

"How come he knows about you? I thought you people kept top security at all times."

"I was assigned to look after him for a while," Harvey answered. "We got on very well. He was a high risk at the time. We became friendly."

"The wife too? How did she take to you, Major? I gather she's pretty pro-Irish."

Harvey said, "I didn't think she was particularly pro anything. Besides she grew up there. So did I, as a matter of fact."

"Did you?" Brownlow felt he'd been rebuked. He sat up straight and became official. "The view is, she's gone over to look for her brother. The story goes that he's fallen out with his friends in the Provos, and he's either on the run or they've murdered him. The nasty part is that either way it could be a ploy to get Mrs. Fraser into the Republic where they can kidnap her."

"That seems highly likely," said Harvey.

Brownlow went on, "As I explained to Fraser, we can't risk saying a word to the Irish police. So it's got to be handled from our end, and with the utmost security and discretion. We want Mrs. Fraser brought home, but no shoot-outs. No repercussions."

"Is that the official instruction," Harvey asked him, "or just a general directive?"

"A general directive," Brownlow admitted. "Nobody can tell you how to do your job."

"Doesn't stop them from trying," was the retort. Michael Harvey looked at his watch and stood up. "I'll be in touch. With any luck I could be back this evening. If I'm not, assume that things have gone wrong. But I'm optimistic. She's not a fool, and she knows what she's dealing with." He shook hands and went out.

Fifty minutes later he was airborne, en route to Dublin. He leaned back in his seat and thought about Claire Fraser and the first time they met, at Brandon Manor, in Gloucestershire.

It was three and a half years ago, when her husband was a new cabinet minister, and informers had named him as a possible target for the IRA. Michael Harvey was assigned to look after him inside the house. He could mix unobtrusively with their friends and cause no comment. It was just after Christmas, when the January weather was at its worst. He remembered it all too well.

"Hello." Claire Fraser came to meet him at the door. She had a charming smile. "Come in and have a drink. Gin and tonic?"

"Whisky and soda, if that's all right. It's whisky weather."

"That's a very Irish way of putting it," she said.

He took the glass she offered him. "My home was in Galway."

"Really? We had some cousins there—the Grahams. Did you know them?"

"My family did. I spent holidays at home, but went to school over here, and then into the army. The place is sold now anyway." He sipped the drink.

There had been a big log fire, the inevitable Labrador stretched out in front of it, and nice, expensive furniture. Neil Fraser was a rich man. He was on his way from London at that very moment, suitably escorted. Harvey was staying at Brandon Manor for the weekend. Claire Fraser was a very good-looking woman, he decided, watching her pour a drink and sit down opposite him. Good figure, smart clothes, very blonde. But he was completely immune to women when he was on a job. After Belfast he knew what women could do and smile at the same time.

"I haven't been home since last Easter," Claire said. He noticed the word. Home. Keep your eyes open, he'd been told, she has a brother who's highly suspect. "Neil hates going to Ireland. And now, of course, we can't."

"No," Harvey agreed. "It wouldn't be very wise."

"I talk to my parents on the phone," she remarked. "But it's not the same thing. I do miss going over. Do you know Kildare at all?"

"Not well," he said, which wasn't true, but Claire seemed anxious to talk.

"My mother was married to James Hamilton," she went on. "They lived at a place called the Half House. He was killed in the war and the estate went to his nephew. Then she married my father. The property was sold about seven years ago. It was so Irish to call it the Half House," she said, sounding casual. "One of the Hamiltons burned it to get the insurance and made a mess of it. So the descendants lived in one wing and everybody called it that. It was even on the writing paper, if you can believe it." She laughed and Harvey joined in. "Kevin Ryan bought it."

"Isn't he an American politician?" he asked.

"Yes," she said. "And a very powerful businessman."

"Have you met him?" Harvey asked. There was something uneasy about her. She was asking something from him, the stranger whose job here was to shoot the IRA assassins if they came.

"No," Claire Fraser answered. "But my brother, my half-brother, is his nephew."

"Oh," he said.

She got up and poured herself another drink for something to do. With her back to him she said, "Ryan is one of the bosses of Noraid. He raises considerable funds for the IRA. He turned my brother, Frank. Completely. Major Harvey, can you imagine how guilty I feel, with Neil's life being threatened by them?"

"It's nothing to do with you," he said. "And don't worry. Nothing's going to happen to your husband. Actually, I think that's him coming in now. Excuse me." He put his glass down.

Dinner was strained. Neil Fraser looked tired and on edge; his wife was subdued and made an excuse to leave them early. When they were alone, Neil offered Harvey a brandy.

"No, thanks. I've got to keep my wits about me."

"I'm very grateful to you, Major," Neil said. "My wife and I feel much happier knowing you're in the house. How long will it be before they give me the all clear, do you think?"

Harvey shrugged. "My feeling is, if they haven't made an attempt by now, the scheme's been blown and they've called it off. As soon as the situation's normal, you can be rid of me."

Neil sipped rather too deeply at his brandy. "The trouble is, Claire feels as if this whole thing were her fault. She was quite upset tonight. Perhaps you noticed?"

"No, I didn't. We were chatting about Ireland before you arrived." Harvey wished Fraser would finish his drink and go to bed. The last thing he wanted was to be drawn into a personal discussion.

"It's her half-brother that's the problem." Fraser was going to get this off his chest, and nothing was going to stop him. Harvey kept quiet. "Claire's father married an Irish girl. The family wouldn't accept her at any price. Then she died having the boy. There was some story about her and Claire's grandmother having a set-to and she had the baby too early. Anyway, my father-in-law never spoke to his mother again. Typically Irish, I'm afraid. Seems to me they live on feuds." He finished his brandy.

Harvey eased his sleeve up and looked at his watch.

"The old boy married a second time, and she's a splendid woman. English-born, actually, and we get on like a house on fire." Neil looked gloomily at his empty glass. "Trouble is, Claire and that brother were inseparable. He was always jealous because she married me. And he's up to his neck in it."

"Gone over to the other side?" Harvey queried.

"Back and forth to the States, speaks at Noraid rallies. Nothing can be pinned on him, but it weighs on Claire. Wasn't too easy for me when I was standing for election."

Harvey moved out of his chair. "I can well understand," he said. "I think we should shut up shop, if you don't mind. The new night shift is coming on outside, and they'll expect the household to be in bed."

"Yes, it is late. Goodnight, Major. See you at breakfast."

As he got ready for bed Harvey could not help wondering what kind of brother Frank Arbuthnot was. Clearly, he was very much under both the Frasers' skins.

Harvey had been relieved from duty by the end of that week. Neil Fraser was no longer considered to be at risk.

"What are you going to do now?" Fraser asked him. "Or is that a tactless question?"

"I'm due for leave," he said.

"Oh? Then why not come down and have a day's shooting with us next Saturday?" Fraser suggested. "We'd really like to give you a good day. Wouldn't we, darling?"

"Yes, we certainly would." Claire was enthusiastic. "Do come down, Major. The shooting is marvellous!"

"Well, if you're sure you can stand the sight of me, I'd love to."

That had been the start of their friendship. It was irregular, because his duties took him out of touch for weeks at a time. But whenever he rang up, he was welcome to come for a night or to meet them in London and have dinner.

Now the plane was making its descent on Dublin. Inevitably, it was raining.

Frank Arbuthnot was missing. Michael Harvey agreed with Brownlow that he was either on the run or dead and buried. It was not his brief to find Arbuthnot. But Claire Fraser was out there, and he had undertaken to find her and persuade her to come home. He was quite prepared to use force if necessary. He had hesitated when asked to go; one mistake could blow his cover and ruin years of careful work in the North. Then he had remembered something, and knew he was duty bound to take that risk. A Sunday lunch in the Frasers' Gloucestershire garden, by the pool. The sun beating down on them and their son, Peter, and some other children splashing and laughing in the shallow end. The most unlikely moment for Claire to talk about a long-ago day when she and her brother had gone walking across the land of a man named Reynard, who believed he would come back from the dead as a fox.

Harvey disembarked. He went through customs and out into the main lounge. A man with a cardboard sign saying "Mr. Keogh" came up to him. He followed the man out to the hired car, took the keys from him, and drove off. Some distance from the airport he pulled up by the roadside and lifted the rear seat. Weapons and ammunition were underneath it. A bag with a change of clothes was in the boot. Jeans, a heavy sweater, an anorak, scuffed jodhpur boots. Kildare was racing country. If he dressed like that, no one would look at him twice. The first thing, he decided, was to check out Riverstown in case Claire had gone there.

IT WAS A LONG WALK. The woods were damp and overgrown; Claire stumbled through brambles and fallen branches. At the head of the valley she was forced to catch her breath. It was a marvellous site and, seen from so far away, the house didn't look a ruin. What parties they'd been to there, when they were young and Tom Reynard had held court for his friends and their children.

The Arbuthnots had hunted with the Meath, and Tom Reynard lived for the sport. He was reputed to be rich and was famous for his hospitality. He never married, but there was always a stream of people staying at his Cloncarrig estate. Life was joyful, and Tom, red-haired and ruddy-faced, presided over the dissipation of his fortune without giving it a thought.

"Why should I worry myself about money?" he would demand, glassful of whiskey in hand after a day's sport. "I've built my follies and made provision for all I'm ever going to need!" And he'd join in his guests' laughter.

"Does he really believe it, Daddy?" Claire had asked her father one evening in 1956, when they were back at Riverstown after a long, wet day of hunting and a huge tea at Reynard's.

"Believe what, darling?"

They were sitting in the study, toasting by the fire before going in to dinner. Frank was stretched out in an armchair, eyes closed, as if he were half asleep. Claudia was upstairs, resting. She'd led the field with Tom Reynard for a five-mile point at the end of the day.

"Believe he'll turn into a fox when he dies," Claire said.

Philip Arbuthnot smiled. He adored his daughter; he couldn't resist ruffling her bright blonde hair. She reminded him so much of Claudia. "I think he believes it," he answered. "He's spent enough money on the idea anyway. And if those follies make him happy, what's the harm?"

"Why are they called follies?" Claire asked.

"Folly comes from the French word *folie*, which means something foolish," Philip told her. "It is used to describe costly but generally useless buildings erected on the estates of rich eccentrics. Old Reynard certainly is one of those!"

"But when he dies, we'll never be able to hunt in Meath again, in case the fox we're after is *him*," Claire pointed out.

Philip laughed at the simple practicality. She was such a natural, uncomplicated child, so unlike his son. You never knew for sure what Frank was thinking. He'd loll in his chair, as he was doing now, then suddenly come out with a remark that made everyone uncomfortable. He was going to Rowden, a boarding school in England, after the Christmas holidays were over.

He was fourteen, and it was a late start because of the poor education he'd received at the local Protestant school. He should have gone away to school at nine, but Claudia hadn't wanted him to feel rejected, sent away while his half-sister stayed at home. So he'd remained in Ireland. A tutor and lots of hard studying had helped him catch up. Philip hoped he would take advantage of the chance and do his best.

"I don't want to go to England!" Frank had blurted out.

"I've explained it often enough to you, Frank," his father said. "An Irish education isn't good enough for someone in your position. None of our family went to school over here. Even Claire will go to England to a decent finishing school, and she's a girl."

Frank protested. "But I'm Irish," he said, and it sounded aggressive because he didn't want his voice to quiver.

Philip Arbuthnot's colour faded. "You're an Arbuthnot," he said. "And you're not going to grow up an Irish yob! You're going to Rowden, and that's an end of it!"

The boy got up. He was tall and thin. For months he had lived with the fear of this exile to England, separated from his home and his family for a reason he rejected. Fear of his father and fear of a strange environment fused into a passionate anger. At last his father had put into words what Frank had known instinctively lay between them. I'm not to grow up an Irish yob, he thought. I'm to forget that half of me is Irish. "If you say that about the Irish," he asked his father, "why did you marry my mother?"

Claire had burst into tears. Philip started out of his chair. He half raised his hand to strike his son; then he turned away. "Go to your room," he said. "Don't you ever dare speak about your mother like that to me. Get out!"

Claudia opened the door to find Claire sobbing uncontrollably. "What on earth—" she started to say, but Philip interrupted.

"Frank's not having dinner tonight. And I think Claire's had a long day. Go upstairs with Mummy, darling."

Frank brushed past his stepmother, went up and locked the door of his room. He didn't break down at once. He cursed his father and slammed his fist on the chest by the window, so that the photograph of his mother fell on its face. He turned it over. He couldn't flesh her out, however hard he studied the picture. She was just a girl with a sweet smile, a pretty face and fine red hair. She could have been any girl in any photograph.

Claudia was real. Claudia, with her made-up face and her bad language in the hunting field, had supplanted the frail Irish girl who hadn't survived his birth. He didn't like Claudia's energy and her enthusiasm; she made too much noise in his life. She had stopped trying to make him like her; that was a relief. The one good thing she'd done was to give him Claire as a sister. He slumped down on his bed and gave way to a fit of crying. When a knock came on his door, he thought it must be a maid with some food, sent up by Claudia. It was the sort of thing she'd do, thinking it wrong to punish a boy by making him go hungry.

"I don't want anything, thank you. I'm going to sleep."

"It's me," Claire said. "Let me in, Frankie, please." She was in her dressing gown, and her face was pink and puffed from crying.

"What are you doing?" he whispered. "You'll get into a terrible row being out of your bed. Go back, like a good girl."

Instead, she climbed on his bed. "What's the matter with your eyes? You've been howling!"

187

"No, I haven't," he cried. "You're the crybaby, not me."

"Daddy was going to hit you," she said. "Don't be cross with him. I'll ask him not to send you to England. But don't say anything more to make him cross!"

The big blue eyes were brimming over again. He put his arm round her. "I won't," he promised. "I'll go to his school, but they won't make an Englishman out of me."

Claire was feeling sleepy and reassured. She yawned. "All right. Kiss goodnight?" It was their ritual, ever since she'd been able to string words together.

"Kiss goodnight," he said, wanting her to go. He felt hurt and angry and older than he'd ever felt in his life before.

"I love you," Claire said. "You're my best brother."

"PHILIP, YOU'LL HAVE TO TALK TO HIM," Claudia had said. "You can't ignore it and have this thing festering about his mother." They'd finished dinner and were sitting in the study.

"There's nothing festering," he said irritably. "He's scared stiff of going away to school, and all this Irish nonsense is just an excuse to get out of it!"

"I expect he *is* scared," she said. "Weren't you, at his age?"

"I'd already been away since I was seven," Philip retorted. "We kept him at home and mollycoddled him, that's the trouble."

"It's not," she said, "and you know it. He feels alienated."

"Alienated, my foot!"

"You should talk to him about Eileen," she insisted. "He's looking for an identity, and he hasn't found it with you."

"I told him about his identity tonight," he snapped. "I told him he was an Arbuthnot."

Claudia didn't say anything for a moment. Philip didn't love the boy, that was the real trouble. And the boy knew it. It was the mixed blood Philip didn't like, the native Irish in Frank that lived uneasily with all that dour Scots ancestry. But Philip would never admit such a thing. Claudia loved him, and their life was happy in all respects. But he had hardened after Eileen died. He had broken the rules, and the punishment had warped him. For years Claudia had tried to reconcile him to his mother, Blanche. It was hopeless. He said flatly that she had upset Eileen and brought on premature labour. He had never seen or spoken to her since.

At last Claudia said, "Philip, have you ever talked to him about Eileen? It might help if he realized how much you loved her."

He reached to take her hand. "No, my darling. I haven't discussed Eileen with Frank, and I don't intend to. He's my son and I love him, just as I love Claire. I shall do my very best for him. Now stop worrying about the boy. He'll be fine in the morning."

The morning came, and they breakfasted together. Nothing was said.

Frank didn't apologize, and Philip behaved as if nothing had happened. At the beginning of January, Frank travelled to England to start his first term at Rowden.

"BLANCHE, ARE YOU QUITE SURE you want to do this?" Hugh Lorimer asked, not very long before the old lady died.

Blanche Arbuthnot finished pouring him a cup of tea. He noticed she needed two hands to lift the silver pot. She had grown very frail. Hugh Lorimer had been her lawyer for years; he was also a family friend.

Blanche said, "Of course I'm sure. You know I don't make up my mind in a hurry."

He took the teacup from her. "Quarrelling with Philip is one thing," he said, "but disinheriting him completely..."

"Blaming me for his wife's death and refusing to speak to me for fifteen years is hardly 'quarrelling'," she retorted. "It's no good, Hugh. My money's going to my grandson. And this place. Philip's very well off. He has Riverstown. And I'll see my jewellery goes to him. He won't suffer."

"Tell me, Blanche, does he know you're ill?"

She said casually, "I think the Dornaways wrote to him, but I haven't heard any more. He's very proud, it's too difficult for him to do anything about it now. And too late, as far as I'm concerned."

"It's never too late. Let me write to him."

"No, Hugh dear. Philip knows I've got cancer. I've got to put my affairs in order. I want you to draw up the will exactly as I've said."

"You've never seen the lad?"

"Not officially. I've seen him twice out hunting, when I was following by car. He's the image of Philip. Nice-looking boy. I think about him a lot, you know. Cake?"

Hugh Lorimer shook his head. If the son was proud, the mother was no less so. But she couldn't hide the pain. "It was so dreadful, his mother dying like that. I know Claudia's been a good stepmother—she's the kindest woman in the world—but I thought he looked a sad sort of a boy. And I want to make amends for the way I treated his mother. I wasn't at all kind, and that's been on my conscience ever since."

"It's no good blaming yourself," Lorimer countered. "Her death was a tragedy, but you can't hold yourself responsible."

"I don't," Blanche Arbuthnot said. "But, Hugh, I've heard rumours that Philip doesn't like his boy. The favourite is my granddaughter, Claire. I want to protect Francis in case he and his father fall out. I know the Arbuthnots." She smiled. "They're as hard as the Scots and as unforgiving as the Irish."

"All right," the lawyer said. "If you really want the will done this way, I'll get it drawn up and sent down for you to sign. You can always change your mind, my dear."

"Not unless I do it in the next three months," she told him.

He said, "I didn't know it was that soon. I'm so sorry."

"Don't be. I've had a very good life and quite a long one."

Blanche Arbuthnot was buried in the family plot at Naas. Claudia Arbuthnot attended, with a crowd of cousins and old friends. Frank was at school in England, and Claire was considered too young. It gave Hugh Lorimer some satisfaction to inform Philip that his son had inherited the estate in Meath and a personal fortune of a quarter of a million pounds.

CHAPTER 4

The TWA jet from Boston landed at Dublin Airport at just after ten o'clock in the morning. It was 1970, and Kevin Ryan hadn't been back to Ireland in twenty-eight years. He had slept during the flight and awoke refreshed, with a tremor of excitement niggling in his stomach. He wondered how much he would find changed. He was very different from the dour young man who'd set off all those years ago. Now he was thicker-set, with a suspicion of belly overhanging the crocodile belt; his sandy-grey hair had been fashionably cut, and he wore glasses.

He also wore a big gold bracelet watch and cuff links inset with tiny emerald shamrocks. He was rich and he liked to show it. His wife, Mary Rose, slipped into a mink coat as they prepared to disembark. They had been married nineteen years and had four strapping children. Kevin peered out of the window at the grey tarmac and the rain, and wondered what the family would say when they saw him and his wife. Photographs had winged their way across the Atlantic, and presents at Christmas and Easter, with Mammy's birthday a speciality.

The father was long dead. Kevin had been poor then, and unable to get home for the funeral. A visit to the grave was on his schedule. His eyes pricked at the thought. He had long forgotten how he had despised the old man for being mean and ignorant. That was one pilgrimage to make with Mary Rose.

The other he reserved for himself. Not that he hadn't told her the story of his sainted sister Eileen and how she died giving birth to her child. Hounded to her death by a cruel mother-in-law, neglected by her husband ... It was a grim tale and his children were brought up on it, along with Mary Rose, who ummed and aahed in horror every time she heard it.

It was part of the folklore among their friends, part of the legend which was growing up around Kevin Ryan, the man who'd married old Heraghty's daughter and made a small furniture manufacturing business into a multimillion-dollar corporation: Ryan, the Irish philanthropist and champion of Irish freedom. He had political ambitions, and knew how to make friends. He was generous with his money. He supported orphanages and schools, underprivileged children went on camping holidays at his expense. He was a financial and moral pillar of the Catholic Church, and Mary Rose devoted herself to committees and fundraising when he decided to run for the Senate.

He had been talking of going home for years, but excuses always came up for delaying till next year, and then the year after. Now the time was suddenly right. He had just been elected to the state Senate, and he was rich and confident enough to introduce Mary Rose to his terrible clod of a brother and his wife, and to Mammy, who was old and senile. He would be the big success come home, and the Ryan family and friends would be in awe of him.

He'd hired a smart car for their triumphant visit, and as they drove to the Ryan farm in Kildare, Mary expressed her delight with the quaint roads. And wasn't Dublin just beautiful, with all those darling old buildings? But she sighed over the poverty they had to pass through on their way out of the city.

"Over seven hundred years of British rule," Kevin declared, and she saw the tight line of his mouth. "You don't undo that in a hurry."

The drive up to the farm was muddy and unkempt. The old house with its dirty grey stone facade loomed up at them from a shelter of laurel bushes.

Kevin didn't pause to open the door for his wife. He sprang out of the car and banged on the front door. His brother opened it; the heavy figure of his wife, Norah, was in the hallway behind him.

"Hello there, Shamus!"

They grasped hands and pumped up and down, and Mary Rose picked her way through the mud and approached, her smile at the ready. The brothers weren't alike, except for the sandy hair. Shamus was thinner and looked quite a lot older. She noticed that his cardigan had a hole in the elbow.

"Come in, come in," he urged them. "There's tea in the kitchen, and a drink if ye'd rather."

Kevin detained him for a moment. "Is Mammy all right?"

"Ah, sure, she's not too bad at all," his brother said. "Norah minds her like a saint, don't ye?"

The plain, large woman in a flowered housedress said quietly, "I do me best. Come in, she's waitin' for ye. Not that she'll recognize ye; her sight's none too good."

It was very warm in the kitchen. Mary Rose took off her mink and handed it to a large redheaded girl, who stroked the fur before she hung it up on the back door among the anoraks.

Kevin caught Mary Rose's arm. "Come and say hello to Mammy."

The old woman sat in a corner, very upright, like a wizened doll. Her hair was snow white and brushed back into a neat bun. Kevin bent down and kissed her. She grasped his hand with a thin claw. "Kevin? Is it ye, Kevin?"

He held on to her, stroking the bony little hand. He swallowed and said, "Mammy, this is Mary Rose."

She peered past him. "Who? Who'd ye say?"

"My wife, Mary Rose," he repeated, guiding her hand for Mary Rose to take.

"'Tis a pretty name," Mrs. Ryan said gently.

Mary Rose bent and kissed her mother-in-law on the cheek. But it was Kevin the old woman wanted. Mary Rose moved to one side gracefully and sat down. She made conversation with Norah, who asked if she'd like to see the house.

It was a dark house, Mary Rose thought, climbing the stairs to the second floor. It needed fresh paint and bright curtains.

"Kevin's room," she said, standing in the open doorway. "It's just wonderful to think of him being a little boy." Three beds cluttered one wall. Kevin had shared the room with Shamus. Norah's three daughters used it now. It wasn't at all tidy. A large picture of the Sacred Heart gazed down at her; the blue-eyed Saviour with his smooth red hair and silky beard looked faintly sorrowful. A red devotional oil lamp burned on the table below.

"It's wonderful to see all this," Mary Rose murmured. Then she said, "Kevin's told me all about his sister, Eileen. What a sad thing to happen."

"She got what she deserved," Norah Ryan replied. "Deserting her family and her faith. She broke Mammy's heart!"

Mary Rose couldn't believe she'd heard her properly. Eileen was a saint to Kevin, but perhaps the folks at home knew more than he did. Deserted her faith? That was very shocking.

"Oh," she said. "Kevin didn't say anything about that."

Norah shrugged. "Kevin was the only one had time for her," she said. "She was no good. Her name is never spoken in this house. We'd best go down, and I'll show ye the sittin' room."

Kevin got up when they finished the tour and came back to the kitchen. "We're going out tonight, the four of us," he announced proudly. "I'm takin' us all out to the Cill Dara, and we'll have a fine dinner." Mary Rose noticed that his brogue had thickened and he'd lost his American accent. He had his jacket off and was standing in front of the fire with a glass in his hand. He looked different. Coarser.

He came towards her and threw his arm round her. "We'll be off to the hotel now," he said. "We'll meet ye all at the Curragh Bar for a few good old jars, and then we'll go on to the restaurant. Mind ye dress up, Norah."

They left, with Shamus and Norah waving goodbye.

192

"Ye'd best drive," Kevin told Mary Rose. "I don't want the Gardai pullin' me in for drunken drivin'."

They met at the Curragh Bar as arranged. It was a smoky place, the walls plastered with horseracing pictures.

Kevin kept on meeting old friends. The talk was loud and nostalgic, incomprehensible to Mary Rose. At one point she heard Kevin say, "I'd sure like to have a place of my own here in Ireland," and she felt quite shaken.

When they were about to leave for the restaurant, a man standing near the bar came up to Kevin and said, "If ye're wanting a place here, the Half House is on the market."

"We might look at it," Kevin suggested, the next day. "There'd be no harm."

The estate agent came down from Dublin to show them the Half House.

They drove up the short drive, past a lodge with a roof in need of mending, good grass fields, and post-and-rail fencing that looked like broken teeth after years of neglect. The Half House met them round a corner, and Mary Rose exclaimed, "Oh, isn't it just beautiful!"

Kevin had never been there before. They got out, and he stood looking at it for a moment or two before he walked to the door after Mary Rose. It was well named. The wing of a Georgian pile, with its handsome windows and fine mahogany front door. Three floors of it, and the ubiquitous Irish basement. Splendid trees and a glimpse of garden that had run down badly. The hunting, shooting Hamiltons, so grand in their heyday, were bankrupt and gone. Kevin walked into the hall and wandered slowly through the rooms. He didn't listen to the sales talk. It was a fine, big house, and the more he saw, the more it pleased him.

"It·needs a fortune spent on it," Kevin said to the agent. "The roof's bad, there's no central heating, there's damp, and the cellars are full of rot. I'm interested, but not at anything like the price." He wasn't putting any more money into the pockets of the Hamiltons than he could help.

"The land alone is worth the price," the man protested.

"Then why isn't it sold?" Kevin demanded, and named a ruthless sum.

The agent nodded and said, "I'll have a word with the solicitor looking after Captain Hamilton's affairs. He's in England."

Captain Hamilton, living in a modest flat in London, was only too relieved to get rid of the house and the whole burden of debt. Kevin Ryan got the property at half the asking price. He returned to America, and two months later the workmen moved in.

"I'M SO EXCITED, MUMMY," Claire said. "I can't believe he'll be here any minute. Do you realize I haven't seen Frank for two years?"

It was a glorious summer's day in 1970, and Claire was bobbing up and down, looking through the window and listening for the sound of the car.

Philip had gone to meet his son, who was coming home to settle in Ireland for good. Tactfully, and without Claire's realizing the true reason, Claudia had dissuaded her from going up to the airport with her father. "Daddy wants to be the first to congratulate Frank," she had explained. "It's good for them to have time alone together."

Claire was so easy to manipulate, she thought sadly. All anyone needed was to appeal to her kind heart. On the surface she was a beautiful and sophisticated young woman of twenty-three, who had gone to finishing school in London and had spent a year in Florence. Underneath, the excited child held sway, bubbling over because her brother was coming home. Claudia was disappointed. She had hoped that the long separation and new friends would have loosened the bond between them. Maybe he'd changed and Claire wouldn't find him such a hero now that they were both grown up.

"He's done so brilliantly," Claire said to her. "Daddy must be thrilled. I remember all those years ago when Frank begged not to go to Rowden and was way below all the other boys. Daddy must be so proud of him!"

A car turned into the gravel sweep. Claire hurried out to the hall and through the front door. Her mother followed slowly, stubbing out her cigarette on the way. Certainly, Philip should be proud of his son. He had distinguished himself academically at Rowden and left Oxford with a first. Two years at Harvard Business School had ended with equal success. He'd spent three years at the World Bank in Washington. Now he was coming back home. She didn't know why it made her so uneasy. Father and son had developed a cordial working relationship, but there was no human warmth between them when they were together.

Claudia came out onto the forecourt. Frank had matured. He was heavier, tanned, rather American in his blazer and button-down shirt. She kissed him. "Hello, my dear. Welcome home."

Standing there while Billy Cavanagh unloaded the bags from the car, Frank Arbuthnot saw the familiar scene of so many homecomings. Back for the school holidays. Met at the airport, either by Claudia or his father, with Claire rushing to meet him. Nothing had changed, except that his father looked older and Claudia seemed more made-up and horsy. But Claire was there, bright as the sunshine, blonde and lovely in her cotton dress. Suddenly happiness overflowed in him.

"Claire!" He stepped forward and they hugged each other, and both of them were laughing with the joy of the reunion.

Billy paused, a suitcase in each hand. He grinned at Philip Arbuthnot. "'Tis grand to see them two together, sir," he said.

Philip nodded. His son had an extra polish acquired during his time at the World Bank. He'd talked most impressively about banking during the drive home. Philip was proud of him. From now on, everything would go smoothly, he felt sure.

194

"You're looking very well, Claudia," said Frank. They exchanged a pleasant kiss. He'd met so many Claudias when he was up at university. Tweedy, lipsticked matrons, with "sporting type" branded on their foreheads like the mark of Cain. He'd hunted and shot with their sons at weekends and stayed in their houses; he understood a lot more about his stepmother as a result. It would be easier to accept her now.

"I'll put my bags in my room," Frank said. "Here, give me those, Billy. They're much too heavy for you to lug upstairs."

"I'm coming too," Claire insisted.

Upstairs, Frank heaved his suitcases onto the bed and sat beside them. "My, am I glad to be home!" he said.

Claire burst out laughing. "You've got an American accent."

"Don't worry, I'll soon lose it." Frank grinned. "I've got a present for you. I'll give it to you after tea."

"Why can't I have it now?" Claire demanded.

"It's buried at the bottom of the suitcase, that's why. And all good things are worth waiting for."

"I bet you didn't keep the girls in America waiting," she said. "And I bet you had a lot of girlfriends."

"A few," he said. "One very nice one. I was really sorry to say goodbye to her."

Claudia's voice carried up the stairwell. "Come on, you two. Tea's waiting."

Frank smiled. "Nothing changes," he said. "Come on."

THE OLD TRADITION of changing for dinner had been dropped at Riverstown. Claudia said it was pompous when the big staff had been reduced to a cook and a maid. But that night they celebrated Frank's return. Claudia and Philip drank champagne in the drawing room before the young people came down, and Philip looked relaxed and happy.

"It's nice to be all together again," Claudia said. "Frank seems delighted to be back."

"Yes, he is," Philip responded. "He's full of plans for opening a merchant bank in Dublin. I told him he'd have plenty to do running his grandmother's estate at Meath. Also, he's got to decide what to do with the house."

"He might want to live there," she suggested.

Philip frowned. "Why should he? He'll inherit Riverstown. I shall advise him to sell it. Ah, Frank, there you are. Help yourself to a glass of champagne. We've opened a nice bottle."

His father and stepmother had been standing together, arms linked, when he came through the door; he wondered where Claire was. She came in just as he was sipping the champagne. Claudia said it first.

"Darling, that's a stunning dress—haven't seen it before."

It was sapphire-blue taffeta, flounced impudently at the knee. Something blue sparkled in the light as she came towards them.

"Look," she said to her parents, "look what Frank's given me."

Philip stared at the little sapphire brooch that had belonged to Eileen, pinned at his daughter's breast.

Frank said quietly, "I wanted to give her something special, and I thought maybe mother's brooch would do."

"Isn't it lovely?" Claire demanded.

Philip turned to his son. "Where did you get that, Frank?"

"Old Mary Donovan gave it to me," Frank said. "She said it was Mother's. I supposed Mother must have given it to her."

"She didn't," he said.

Claudia said quickly, "Of course she did." She lowered her voice. "They were cousins, don't forget."

"Mary stole it," Philip said. "She must have taken it the night Eileen died." He spoke to his son. "You never mentioned it before. How long have you had this? Mary's been dead for years."

"Since before I left for Rowden," Frank answered. "She said it was Mother's and she'd been keeping it for me. Dad, if this has upset you, I'm very sorry. I didn't know it mattered. I wanted to give Clarry a present, something personal." He slipped into the old childhood nickname.

Philip sighed. "Everything your mother had belongs to you, Frank. I was keeping it all to give you one day. But never mind. You can't trust them. It was a nice idea, my boy, giving it to your sister. Very nice. Let's have some more champagne."

The chasm had opened at their feet and closed again. The dinner was excellent, the conversation animated.

"We could go over to Meath tomorrow if you like," Philip said to Frank. "Jim and Biddy Mahoney have been living in. They've kept everything in order for you while you were away."

Claudia added, "The trouble is, we've had a spate of burglaries, and the minute anyone knows a house is standing empty, they go in and strip it. The crime rate has doubled since this wretched business broke out in the North."

Frank leaned towards her. "It's an old problem, Claudia, and sooner or later it's got to be faced and solved."

"Solved in what way?" Philip asked. "You'll never get those in the North to see reason."

"They'd see it soon enough if Britain withdrew," Frank said.

Claire sat quietly, wishing they'd change the subject.

"If Britain got out," Philip said forcefully, "there'd be civil war and we'd be dragged into it. And that's what the reality is when people talk about a united Ireland."

"That's not the view in the States," said Frank.

196

"Maybe," his father said, "but they don't live here. The Irish–American element is only interested in being anti-British. I hope you put them straight if they talked this rubbish to you! Anyway, I'm free tomorrow, so why don't we go over to Meath?"

"Why not?" Frank agreed. "I'd like to look the place over. I remember I liked the house itself."

His father shook his head. "It's a barracks. Basement, attics, far too big for this day and age."

Claudia turned to her daughter. "Claire, why don't we go into Dublin tomorrow if your father and Frank are going off?"

Claire hesitated. "I'd rather go and see the house," she said.

"Another time," Philip said. "You go off to Dublin with your mother. And don't spend too much money!"

They all laughed at that.

Frank said, "I'll take you over to Meath next week."

"I'll take *you*," Claire said triumphantly. "I've got a car and I passed my test! First time."

"They must be crazy to let you near a car," her brother said, teasing. "I'm taking *you*, or we don't go."

They bantered like children, and Philip watched benevolently. His son had changed. The old aggressiveness had gone, leaving a reasonable young man who didn't contradict on principle. When he was at Oxford, a discussion on the North would have ended in a sullen row. Philip felt relieved and happy. Except for the anger burning in him over the brooch. Mary Donovan. What a treacherous creature, and after all the years she'd worked for them. What a people, he fumed inwardly. And there was the memory of Eileen, also wearing blue, with the cheap little brooch pinned to her dress, standing in the same room where Claire had stood earlier. Eileen going off to Claudia Hamilton's dinner party. It still hurt him to think of her. Poor little thing, so vulnerable and young.

They left the table, and Philip said, "Let's have coffee in the study." He didn't want to go back into the drawing room.

IT WAS SUCH A HAPPY SUMMER. There were tennis parties, a trip to the west of Ireland where Claudia had a fishing lodge, swimming in the sea, cold enough to take your breath away—and the joy of riding round the farm. Both farms, because Frank had thrown himself into improving his inheritance at Meath.

Claire went over the house with him and agreed with their father. It was too big and needed modernizing. Besides, she didn't want Frank to move out of Riverstown.

"I won't sell, Clarry," he insisted. "I like it. It's mine, she left it to me. I might want to live here one day."

"Then let it," she suggested. "That's sensible."

He hesitated, looking round the rooms, on one of their tours of the house. Claudia had undertaken to sort through the clothes and personal possessions of the old lady, and her solicitor, Hugh Lorimer, had gone over the land titles and estate papers with Frank. Part of the farm was tenanted. Frank had dismissed any suggestion that he might try to repossess. "Nobody gets turned out of their homes by me," he had said. "There's been enough of that in Ireland."

Lorimer had stared at him for a moment and then let the remark pass, feeling he might not be able to handle this young man's affairs with any sympathy.

"No. I'm not going to let it either," Frank said. "I'll keep the Mahoneys on, for now. I might spend a few weeks a year here—build up some shooting. And hunt a couple of days with the Meath. Whatever happened to old Reynard's house, by the way?"

Claire shrugged. "Nothing. The nephews sold off the land, and the local butcher bought it. He left the house to fall down; it's no good to him and nobody else wanted it. Dad said he sold all the lead off the roof and got a big price for it."

Frank said, "We'll go over one day and take a look. Maybe we can see the old devil come back as a fox, skulking under a hedge."

Claire laughed. "Oh, people swear they've seen him. Even Mummy said she saw a fox vanish in one of the hideaways."

"Claudia is just as superstitious as the rest," Frank said. "Who's the butcher?"

"Flanagan," Claire told him. "He's got a chain of shops in Dublin and he's gone into land. Dad says he's a millionaire. And a vandal," she added, quoting.

"I don't see what some big Anglo house means to Flanagan. Why should he care what happens to it?"

"But it's part of history," Claire protested.

"It's not part of Flanagan's history," Frank said. "If I were he, I wouldn't just strip the roof, I'd dynamite the house and everything it stands for."

"Frank!" She stared at him, horrified.

He shook his head. "Don't worry; I'm not going to say anything like that at home."

A frightening idea came to her. "Frank," she said, "you haven't joined anything, have you?"

"No, if you mean the IRA."

"Thank goodness for that!" she said, giving a sigh of relief.

"Come on, Clarry," he said. "We should go or we'll be late for dinner."

They drove home in silence, until she asked, "Are you going to the Butlers' dance? We've been asked to stay, Mummy says."

"I might," Frank said, "if you're going."

"They'll have that fat lump Olivia lined up for you," Claire said mischievously. "It's in honour of her twenty-first birthday."

"She's a very pretty girl," he retorted. "You're jealous."

"Jealous of her big fat bottom? Thunder Thighs, that's her nickname. The dance might be fun, though."

He smiled at her. "Do you really want to go?"

She nodded.

"Then we will," he said. "Look, there's poor old Donny, waiting to see the Dublin train come by."

"Let's stop," Claire suggested. "I haven't seen him for ages."

Donny and his obsession with trains had been a part of their childhood. When they rode down to Sallins on their bicycles, they would see him standing on the bridge over the railway line, gazing intently up the track, watching for the train. Frank pulled over and they got out.

Donny saw them and grinned. Simple-minded from birth, it was his passion for the trains that kept him rooted to the bridge in hopes of seeing one. As children, Frank and Claire had always given him sweets.

"Hello there, Donny," Frank said now. "How are you?"

He gabbled happily that he was well and then said, surprising them both, "Ye've been gone long away!"

"Yes, but we're home now, Donny," Frank answered. He found some change in his pocket. "Here, get yourself some cigarettes."

His eyes were bright with pleasure. "God bless ye. God bless ye." He watched them get back into the car and waved to them as they drove off. Through the rear window Claire saw him turn back to his vigil.

"Fancy him noticing we'd been away," she said.

"He's not that stupid," her brother answered. "Given special schooling, he mightn't have been so bad. But it's too late now. So long as he has his trains now and then, he'll be happy enough."

"That's the wonderful thing about Ireland," she said. "Nobody bothers him. He'd be taken into some mental hospital if this was England."

"Or America," Frank pointed out. "But the Irish aren't frightened or ashamed of handicapped people. To them they're as much children of God as anyone else, and they leave them alone."

"And so they should," she agreed. Children of God, she thought; she'd never heard Frank talk in that way before. Surely he wasn't becoming religious? She'd have to tease him to find out.

WHEN THEY GOT HOME, Philip and Claudia were out and Claire disappeared upstairs. Frank went into the study. He was glad to be alone, to have time to himself to think.

He shouldn't have spoken out to Claire. There was no way she would understand how America had affected him. It had been a curious liberation, a chance to expand beyond the confines of his class, education

199

and background. A challenge, because only achievement counted, and he had set out to achieve from the time he had gone to an English school with his father's dictate echoing through his mind: "You're not going to grow up an Irish yob!" Nobody could deny what he had done, but they wouldn't understand why he had done it. Not for himself, not for his father, but for the faded image in the photograph. For the whole half of him that had always been denied, as if it carried shame. For the first time in his life he was in a position to make his own judgments. The past was a lamentable record; nothing could excuse that. What was needed was a change in attitude, an expiation, if necessary, for the sins of all their forebears. The first goal must be to redress the wrongs of the Irish in the North.

He wasn't going to relinquish the house in Meath, however hard his family pressed him. It was his grandmother's restitution to his dead mother; Hugh Lorimer, the old woman's lawyer, had told him as much.

He thought of his sister, so worried that there might be conflict between the people she loved. Generous-hearted, open-natured, she combined all that was best in Claudia and in Philip. For her sake he would keep the peace at Riverstown.

At dinner he said, "Claire and I are going to the dance at Butlers Castle."

Claudia said, "Sylvia told me they've got English guests for the weekend. We won't be going, but you should enjoy yourselves."

The following week they drove down to Cork for the dance. And that was how Claire met Neil Fraser.

CHAPTER 5

Billy Cavanagh sat at the kitchen table and poured his tea. He felt miserable. He was frightened for himself and for Claire. How long would she be gone? Back before dark, she'd said. He took a sip of tea and felt it would choke him.

Suddenly he felt them in the room behind him, and he put his cup down and turned very slowly. There was young Joe Burns in his Garda uniform, and another man that Billy didn't know. He hadn't heard them knock, and his dogs hadn't given a warning.

Joe Burns said, "Havin' yer tea, Billy?"

"I am so," he said, and his voice sounded thick.

Joe Burns came closer. "We knew ye were in, Billy," he said, "because yer car's in the garage. What have ye done with the numberplates?"

Billy gave a moan of fear.

"We found the other plates," Joe said. "The English ones. She's been here, Billy, and ye never let me know like ye promised."

Billy started to say, "I was going to ..." and then stopped.

Joe Burns turned to his companion. "He has a bad heart."

"Let's see how bad it is," the other man replied.

THE GATES TO RIVERSTOWN were padlocked. Major Michael Harvey stopped the car and got out to make certain. He knew the Irish custom well. When the family was away, the main drive was always locked from the inside, the back drive was left open. He got back into the car and set off down the twisty road leading to the rear of the property. Claire Fraser had talked a lot about the old gardener, Billy Cavanagh. She was very fond of him, spoke as if he were a grandfather by adoption. It was not unlikely that Claire, finding that padlocked gate, would have gone to Billy for help. Harvey drove past the rear entrance and the little cottage and parked in a bend of the road. He got out, unlocked the boot of the car and slipped the automatic pistol into his anorak, just in case. Then he walked back along the roadside and turned into Billy's driveway. A garage with both doors shut. Kennels, but no dogs barking at his approach. Michael Harvey walked up to the kennels. Two big sandy lurchers lay shot dead behind the wire run. There was silence all around him. He recognized it. A very special silence that was stronger than birds or the breeze ruffling through the trees overhead. He leaped for the cottage door, his gun exposed in his right hand, and kicked once, sending it crashing open.

Billy Cavanagh was in the kitchen. He had been shot through the head at close range. And he'd been badly beaten first. Harvey didn't touch him. He backed out, pulling the door shut behind him. The garage. He opened it and saw what had doomed the poor devil. The car, the English plates lying on the ground. Claire Fraser had come to Billy for help, and he'd helped all right. How much had they beaten out of him, Michael Harvey wondered, before they murdered him? If Cavanagh knew where Claire was heading and told, the men who had killed him would be on the road to Kells by now.

Harvey got back into his car and set off. He knew where he was heading; if he found a car hidden anywhere near, he'd abandon caution and go in with the automatic rifle. Just because they'd shot Cavanagh it didn't prove he hadn't told them about Claire. The IRA didn't leave witnesses. The one chance was that Cavanagh hadn't known where Claire was going, and they had murdered him in frustration. The only chance. But they would have the number of Cavanagh's licence plates to go on, and a network that operated at extraordinary levels throughout the country. They would find the car Claire had hired soon enough.

THE HOUSING ESTATE at Santry was on the airport road. Twenty-five small houses, each with a square of garden back and front and a garage; architect-designed, it was claimed, although the fittings were cheap and much of the woodwork had warped. Joe Burns and his companions were sitting at a table in the back room of one of the houses. They were facing two men and a woman who sat round the table.

The man who had gone to Billy's cottage with Joe Burns was talking. His name was Willie and he had a strong Dublin accent. "He was havin' a heart attack," he said.

The younger of the two men sitting across the table looked at him. "Then why did you hit him so hard?" he asked.

"Ah, we didn't." It was shrugged off. "I smacked him a couple of times; Joe gave him a bump or two. Just enough to scare him a bit. Isn't that right, Joe?"

"It is," Joe confirmed. He looked at the three of them uneasily. He'd seen the girl only a few times. He didn't like the look of her at all. "Cavanagh said he didn't know where Claire Fraser'd gone," he insisted. "We did get rough, but not so's to kill him. I know my job, Sean. But he had a bad heart. I told ye so before we went."

"I'd swear he didn't know her whereabouts," Willie said. "We hurt him bad enough to get it out of him if he did know!"

"So you shot him," the girl said.

"We had to," Joe explained. "Sure he was taken bad, but there wasn't time to hang about till he died. We had to make sure."

"You made a mess of it, you fools!" she spat at them. "Cavanagh changed the plates for her. Of course he knew where she was going. You beat him up and got nothing out of him!"

The younger man touched her arm. "Quiet yourself, Marie. We know the number of the car she's driving. We'll find her. Joe, you get back to the station. Wait at home, Willie. You may be needed later."

When they had gone, the older man spoke up. He had a thick Ulster accent, and he was wanted for murders and bombings across the border. His name was Hugh Macbride. "Marie's right. They blew it. My lads would have done a proper job."

"This is my operation," the younger man replied. "When I need your lads, I'll let you know."

The two comrades-in-arms didn't like each other. Macbride was a hard man from the North—a seasoned, ruthless fighter. He thought his southern counterparts were soft. He particularly disliked the young man sitting at the table with him, the respected psychiatrist Dr. Sean Filey. He distrusted all comfortable middle-class revolutionaries. And most of all he resented having a woman like Marie Dempster sitting with the men and giving her opinions. The women of Ulster knew their place. They were never admitted to the higher councils of their men.

He said, "I'd watch that Garda. He might just decide to save his own skin if things get bad."

Sean Filey dismissed the idea. "He's a good man; he's true. And he's in too deep now. There's no going back on a murder."

Macbride only grunted. Plenty of men he knew had squealed to the security forces just because they *had* murdered, and wanted to get off. But you couldn't convince a man like Filey. He was an intellectual. A great one for plans and working out the details, but not strong enough to make them work. Two days ago they'd had Frank Arbuthnot tethered like a goat in this very house, the bait to catch an English cabinet minister's wife in a trap sprung by the Provisional IRA. The coup of the decade. Neil Fraser's wife held for ransom. He thought of the publicity and prestige the organization would have milked from the situation, and felt sick with fury at the way it had been bungled.

Now they had lost the bait, and Macbride had been sent down from the North to pull the operation together before it failed completely. To get Claire Fraser, even if her half-brother had escaped. But Macbride was only second-in-command. Filey was still in charge. The Provisionals in the South were touchy men, sensitive with their brothers in the North.

"How's about a wee whiskey?" Macbride addressed Marie. She was a dark-haired woman, with blue eyes. One side of her very pretty face was swollen and bruised.

"You know where it's kept," she said. "Help yourself."

He gave her a look of menace and left the room. When he had closed the door, she said, "He thinks I let Frank escape."

"I cleared you," Sean Filey countered. "I was the first one here after Arbuthnot escaped, and Macbride accepted what I said."

She shrugged. "He doesn't believe it. Or if he does, he doesn't care. Back home, he told me, they'd shoot me."

"This isn't the North," Sean said. "You're safe enough, because *I* believe you. You wouldn't have let Frank Arbuthnot escape. You want him dead and I know why. The same reason you want us to capture his sister. You want them both dead because your own jealousy is killing you."

"Leave me alone!" It was a cry of anguish. "Don't taunt me."

"I'm protecting you," he answered. "You've done great things for the cause, Marie. Your mistake was to love outside your own kind. We'll catch Frank, and we'll catch his sister. Then you'll be at peace. Now, why don't you make the telephone calls?"

She pushed past Macbride as he came back into the room with the whiskey bottle. "Some man should take his belt to her," he remarked to Sean. "Where's she going?"

"Down to the call box to make the contact calls," Filey answered. "If Fraser's wife is anywhere within fifty miles of here, we'll know it soon."

She made eight calls, giving the number of the car they were looking for. She stressed the urgency, repeated the telephone number of the house on the airport road for all reports, and hurried back there. She met Sean Filey in the hall.

"I'm going to my consulting rooms," he told her. "Contact me immediately if you hear any news."

She looked round. "Where's Macbride?" She didn't want to be in the house alone with him.

"Gone. He's left a number where you can reach him." He paused for a moment. "Do you have enough painkillers?"

"Plenty," she said.

"Don't take too many; they can make you sleepy."

Her mouth twisted into a painful smile. "Don't worry. I won't miss the telephone."

She went into the kitchen and made herself tea. Thank God that brute Macbride was gone. Thank God she could sit by herself for a while. Her face was very painful and she had a savage headache.

Frank Arbuthnot had hit her so hard she'd been knocked out. She couldn't get the scene out of her mind. The shuttered upstairs room where he was being kept handcuffed to the bed. The sight of him watching her every time she brought food and pushed it to him, with hatred and contempt in his eyes. How easy for that cold-hearted devil Sean Filey to dissect her feelings as if she were a specimen pinned to a board. He spoke of jealousy with clinical detachment. It's killing you, he said. Filey could never imagine the suffering and rejection. Or the humiliation of her desire, that drove her to Arbuthnot when she knew he didn't care for her. Years of living with him in the big house in Meath, with the photographs of his sister Claire mocking her even in the bedroom they shared. Filey would never understand.

"Marie, help me." His voice echoed in her throbbing head. "Help me, Marie, please." There was no hatred in his eyes that morning, only agony and pleading. And that was why she'd gone too close, the gun in her hand lowered instead of pointing at him. When he grabbed at her she had fired. That was the last thing she remembered before the blow from his free hand sent her reeling and crashing unconscious to the ground. And luckily for her, Sean Filey had come, with the gunman, Willie, and found her in the upstairs room. Arbuthnot had escaped and stolen her car from outside, but there was blood on the floor. He had taken the gun with him.

At every moment they expected a news flash that Arbuthnot had been found or had sought refuge with the police. But the radio was silent and the TV had no news. Hopes began to rise that he was wounded and lying in some lane in Marie's car, with the life seeping out of him, unable to seek help. So the search was set up. Men scoured the roads, the look-out phones were rung, the description of man and car circulated. But nothing was found. Arbuthnot had vanished and his sister, Claire Fraser, had left her home in England and was on her way over.

The phone began to shrill and she jumped up, seizing the receiver. Claire's car had been spotted less than half an hour ago, parked under some trees on the old Reynard estate at Cloncarrig; it was still there. Trembling with excitement, Marie dialled Filey's number. He interrupted his patient very courteously while he took the call.

"He must be hiding in the old Reynard place." Marie's words tumbled out. "We'll get them both, Sean. Both!"

"I'll make the arrangements," his voice said in its gently professional way. "Don't worry, I'll let the hospital know."

He turned to his patient and with firmness closed the session. "A very sick patient of mine—suicidal," he explained. "I hope you'll forgive me. I must go at once. My secretary will make another appointment for you."

As soon as the door closed Filey grabbed the telephone. Minutes later he was on his way back to the house at Santry as messages went out to Willie, Macbride, and another expert who'd been brought in specially for the purpose. The hunt was on.

THE SUN WAS HIGH in a sky as clear as a looking glass. It beat down on the green fields of Cloncarrig. From where Claire stood she could see that old Reynard's house was roofless; the windows had fallen in, and a green gravecloth of weeds was creeping up the outside walls. Suddenly tears came into her eyes as she remembered what the house had meant to the Arbuthnots. Friendship and hospitality, the pleasure of good hunting, and the jolly eccentric with the foxy name and bright red hair, building for his afterlife. Neil hadn't seen the point at all when his wife told the story of Tom Reynard and his follies. To him Reynard was an old madman, and the friends who swapped hunting stories about the fox that always vanished on the run at Cloncarrig were drunk or stupid. It was all so Irish, he had complained irritably. Everyone lived in a fantasy world.

Claire hated Neil when he talked like that. It was strange that he should come into her mind so vividly as she looked down on the ruined relic of her youth. Two fields away was the first folly built by old Reynard. Neil seemed to be walking the three miles with her, nudging her with memories she didn't want. It's as if he's still fighting Frank for me, she thought. It was superstitious and silly, but as she made her way across the fields she remembered the dance at Butlers Castle ten long years ago.

The castle had been in its last flush of splendour when she went down with Frank for the weekend of the dance celebrating the famous Olivia's twenty-first birthday. The castle was a Victorian monstrosity. It was cold, of course, and damp in places, but nobody minded and it was always full of people.

Claire had been placed next to one of the English guests at dinner, and as she had predicted, Frank was assigned to Olivia. Claire thought it very funny. She planned to tease him for days afterwards. Her own companion was very attractive, with charming manners, but rather stiff. She was naturally vivacious, and he laughed a lot at what she said and never took his eyes off her.

"You're staying, aren't you?" she asked.

"Yes, Charles asked me over for a week. We're going fishing."

Charles Butler, Olivia's brother, was in his thirties. He dabbled in estate management and made an occasional trip to London on business. He had a lot of friends there, and Neil Fraser was one of them.

"Charles is great fun," Neil said. "Treats everything as a joke."

"And you don't?" she countered.

"You can't afford to if you're a Member of Parliament," he answered.

Claire stared at him. "An MP? Aren't you a bit young?"

He smiled. "Yes. But I always wanted to make a career in politics, and I started as soon as I came down from Oxford. I didn't get in overnight either. I fought two hopeless seats before I was given a by-election with a chance. I've been in the House now for five years."

She looked at him admiringly. He thought she was one of the most beautiful girls he'd ever seen.

"Do you always win in the end?" Claire asked.

"If I want something badly enough," he said.

As soon as the music started, Neil Fraser took her off to dance. He was a good dancer and began to hold her closer and closer. When the music stopped, he guided her to the bar. She noticed that he fended off any other man who came up to them, as if she belonged to him. Claire found it odd and exciting.

They danced again. She saw Frank over Neil's shoulder; he had a fair girl in his arms, and they were talking as they danced. Neil Fraser didn't say a word. He moved with her and held her, and she felt a throb of satisfaction that was a new experience.

When they stopped, he eased through the groups of people and out into the empty hall. "I'm going to kiss you," he said, and she didn't resist. It seemed to last for a long time, and the pleasure of it made her dizzy.

Suddenly he stopped and said, "We'd better go back. I'm going to see you after this weekend, aren't I?"

"If you want to," Claire said.

"I want to very much. Do you ever come to London?"

"I'm going over in September for three months. I'm taking a cooking course."

He smiled at her. "And flower arranging?"

"Yes, how did you know?"

"I guessed," he said gently.

They went back into the ballroom. "Tell me," Neil asked her, "who was that very dark chap who kept staring at us when we were dancing? An old boyfriend? He's over there."

Claire laughed. "Don't be silly. That's my brother, Frank."

"Oh," was all Neil Fraser said.

The next morning, when Claire came down to breakfast, there was no sign of Neil Fraser; she was disappointed when she learned he'd gone off early with Charles Butler. She wanted to ask Frank what he thought of Neil, but there wasn't an opportunity until they were driving back to Riverstown after lunch.

"I only spoke two words to him," Frank said. "When you were upstairs powdering your nose. He took quite a fancy to you."

Claire giggled. "I took one to him as well," she admitted. "He's an MP. Can you believe it? He looked far too young."

"Charles says he is one of the rising stars in the Tory party," Frank remarked. "I can't see an Irish girl fitting into that set-up, can you?"

"Oh, I don't see why not," Claire protested.

"People like him live in a straitjacket compared to us," he said. "They have buttoned-down souls."

She frowned. "If you only spoke two words to him, you certainly formed an opinion."

"I know the type," he said. "And I don't like it."

After that they dropped the subject. Claire soon forgot both Neil Fraser and her brother's judgment of him. Time went by, and all was harmony, as if that summer were a gift from God. Only Claudia felt uneasy watching her daughter and her stepson becoming even more inseparable as adults than they had been as children. But she said nothing; she was a wise woman who believed that things worked out for the best if left alone. Claire was soon going to London for her cooking course. Philip was content with his son, and Frank was busy with plans for his estate in Meath and for a merchant bank in Dublin. The weather was fine, the cattle and horses sleek with the rich grass, and Claire was within a week of going to London. Friday morning opened with a rainstorm. Claudia looked at the weather and decided she would be lazy for once and have breakfast in bed. Philip kissed her goodbye and went off for the day.

Claire stood at the bedroom door and said, "Mum, Frank and I are going on an expedition. We won't be in to lunch."

"What sort of expedition?" Claudia asked.

Claire came close to her. "We've a bet on. I've bet him a fiver we'll get into old Reynard's hideout. Frank says it's all nonsense. We're going over to explore the follies and see. I've made a side bet of twenty pounds that we find a fox's been in one of them."

Claudia smiled. "You're mad. It's absolutely pouring with rain. Have fun, but don't catch cold."

The door closed, and Claudia settled back with the newspaper. She glanced out of the window; the sky was black with malevolent clouds, and the rain struck spitefully at the glass. It was a prophetic morning.

THE LAST DITCH WAS CROSSED and the grey stone folly beckoned Frank and Claire. It was tall and narrow, like a finger pointing upwards. There was a niche set high up in one wall. Too high for any hound to leap, but within the scope of a running fox. They were both soaking wet, but the rain had stopped and the hot Irish sun was drying out the land. Claire was out of breath. They had run across the last field.

The first three follies had been blank stone towers, with slits that were a painted illusion to deceive the eye at a distance. But this one was real, and so was the little entrance to it.

"You owe me a fiver!" Claire shouted as Frank began to climb up the projections in the wall. "Twenty, if a fox has been in there!"

She watched him haul himself up to the edge of the niche.

He called down, "It's big enough to get inside."

"I'll come up too," she said, and began to ascend.

Above her Frank wriggled his way in. Then he leaned out and reached down to help her. "There's a room in here," he said. "And I owe you twenty quid more."

Claire stared at him. "You mean there's been a fox?"

"More than one, by the smell of it. Here, I'll pull you through."

The stench was so strong that Claire gasped. Then, standing in the fusty darkness, they both heard a low, faint growl.

"Stay quiet, Clarry! There's something in here. I'll light my lighter."

By the little gas flame they found the fox crouched in a corner, red eyes glowing in the darkness.

"It's been poisoned, by the look of it," Frank said. "Its pelt will fetch twenty-five pounds these days. Poachers put poison down its earth and wait for the poor creature to come out to die; then they shoot it. I'd shoot them if I could catch them at it!" He came closer, holding the tiny flame above his head. The fox lay dying, its flanks heaving in spasms.

"Oh, Frank," Claire whispered, "I wish we hadn't come."

"I'm glad we did," he said. "You go down and go back to the car. I'll follow in a minute. Go on."

"What are you going to do?" she asked.

"Stop it suffering," he said. "Go on down, please."

She levered herself over the edge of the niche; Frank held her hand until she found toeholds, and then she dropped the last few feet. He turned back into the gloom. He lit the lighter again and found a stone. The red eyes watched him. "Poor old fellow," he said gently. "Be a good lad now, and don't try to bite."

A minute later he caught up with Claire.

"Did you do it?" she asked.

"Yes. I think he knew I was helping him. Maybe it was old Reynard. Come on, don't cry. You've won twenty-five pounds."

"As if I'd take it."

She was very upset. "He was almost human," she went on, "the way he looked up at us. Perhaps we were meant to go today and find him." She paused. "I don't think we should tell anyone about the folly. If the hunt knows a fox can get up there to hide, they'll close it up."

"We won't say anything, not even at home," Frank said.

"It's our secret," Claire said. "What a place! No one would ever find you there."

"No," he agreed, "they wouldn't."

When they got back to Riverstown, Claudia and Philip were having tea. The rain had started again and it was a time to be indoors and snug. They'd lit a fire, although it was early September.

"Hello," Philip greeted them. "Find any foxes? Mummy told me you'd gone off on your wild-goose chase."

"More like a wild-fox chase," Frank answered. "All we did was tramp for miles and get soaked."

Claudia looked up. "There are some letters in the hall. Some for you, Claire, and something from America for you, Frank."

"I'll get them," he said.

Claire was reading a note from the cookery school when something made her glance up. Frank had the letter from America open in his hand.

He said, "This is from my uncle."

Philip put his teacup down. He was frowning. "Uncle? What uncle? What are you talking about?"

A little red crept into Frank's face. "My Ryan uncle. My mother's brother." He spoke quietly, but the tension was palpable. "He says he's bought the Half House. Claudia's old home."

There was a hard set to Philip's mouth and a cold expression in his eyes as he held his son's gaze. "So I heard."

"I must be the only one who didn't know," Frank said. "Why didn't you tell me?"

"Just a moment." Philip left his chair and stood up. He was taller than Frank. "It cropped up in the winter, while you were in America, and besides, we weren't exactly pleased. I don't know why a man who's never seen you should suddenly write to you out of the blue! The best thing you can do is throw the damned letter on the fire!"

Frank said, "Apparently he has seen me. He came here when I was a baby. You were in the army."

Philip said coldly, "If Ryan sneaked into my house behind my back, that's typical. It's a pity he didn't see fit to come and visit your mother after she was married, instead of turning against her like the rest of them."

"He's explained that," Frank said. "He's coming over soon, and he's asked me to meet him."

"No doubt he thinks he'll make capital out of the relationship," Philip snapped. "But it won't help him. Nobody decent round here will have

210

Kevin Ryan in the house. Just let me tell you something about him."

It's happening all over again, Claire thought in horror, the same scene as when Frank said he didn't want to go to Rowden.

Her father was saying, "Kevin Ryan is a gutter politician who's made his career out of raising money for Noraid to pay for the bombings and shootings in the North. He's an IRA front man, backing the murderers who kill innocent people in the name of Irish liberty. You ask why we didn't tell you he'd bought the Half House. Well, I'll tell you why. We were sickened at the thought of people like that living so near us!"

"Philip," Claudia protested, but it was too late.

Frank looked at his father. He said, "That's not the reason. You're ashamed that he's bog Irish and your ex-brother-in-law. You've always been ashamed of me because I'm half Ryan. I'm going to see Senator Ryan. I'll judge him for myself."

Father and son were facing each other, amazingly alike in their anger.

"Frank, I'm warning you," Philip said. "If you take up with people like Ryan, you're not welcome in this house!"

"They're my mother's people," Frank Arbuthnot answered. "As much my family as you are. And you're not going to forbid me to meet anyone. I have my own house if I'm not wanted here."

"Then get out and go to it!" Philip shouted. Twenty-eight years of pent-up antagonism exploded in him at that moment, revealing the hatred he'd hidden even from himself. His son was the mirror image of himself, but with the disquieting look and alien ways of a despised and subject race.

Claire got up; she was trembling. "Dad, if you turn Frank out of this house, then I'm going with him!"

"Oh, for heaven's sake!" Suddenly, shockingly, Claudia exploded. "What a stupid scene you've made over nothing! I'm sick to death of the lot of you! You'd drive any sane person mad." She turned on her daughter. "And as for you, you're going to England next week and that's that. It's time you grew up and stopped holding his hand anyway." And having said that, she flared at her stepson. "Your mother died when you were born; you never even saw her. *I've* been the only mother you've ever known! I've brought you up, Frank, and I've never had a thankyou from anyone. This is my home too, and it's not going to be disrupted like this. Now I'm going upstairs and you can all go to blazes!" As she banged out of the room she burst into tears. It was as if the roof had caved in. Claire had never seen her mother lose her temper. She was the level-headed influence, ready to see the funny side, defuse a clash of temperaments.

Philip looked at his son. "I won't have her upset," he said. "If you want to hobnob with the likes of Ryan, leave Riverstown."

"Frank, please," Claire whispered.

He didn't glance at her. He put the letter into his pocket. "I'll go tomorrow morning," he said.

It was a Thursday in late September when Claire arrived in London; time enough for her to settle into the flat she was sharing before beginning her cooking course on Monday. After Frank's departure the days at Riverstown had been the longest and most miserable of her life. She was shocked to see that her father seemed unmoved.

One occasion peaked in her memory. The morning when Frank said goodbye there was a flat calm after the storm of the night before. He said he was sorry that he and his father couldn't agree on certain issues, but he hoped they'd continue to be friends, and held out his hand to Philip. For one dreadful moment Claire thought her father was going to reject it, but he didn't; he said it was a pity, but this solution was the best. There were tears in Frank's eyes when he embraced her. For a second or two she clung to him with all her strength. He had said goodbye to Claudia.

"I'm glad you made your peace," was all his father said.

Then he was gone, and the next day his clothes and personal belongings were collected and taken to Meath.

The second saddest incident of that wretched time was finding Frank at the airport to see her off. Claudia had driven her in, and there he was, waiting outside the departure lounge, looking thinner and drawn about the face.

"Good God." Her mother didn't look pleased to see him. "This is a surprise..." And then, because she knew how to behave, "How are you, Frank? Have you settled in?"

"I'm fine," he said, turning away from her. "I wanted to see Clarry off. I thought this might amuse you," he said to Claire.

It was a paperback of a book long out of print: *Lady into Fox*.

She looked up at him and smiled. "I'll read it on the flight. I'll write to you, Frank."

"Have a good time," he said, "I've got to go now. Look after yourself."

"I will," she called after him.

He turned and waved and said, "Goodbye, Claudia," as if she were a vague acquaintance. On the flight to London she had opened his going-away present. He had written on the flyleaf, "To remind you of old Reynard. Love, Frank."

Claire took a taxi to the flat in Fulham. She felt depressed and lonely. The more her flatmate, whose name was Jenny, bubbled about the young man who was taking her out the lonelier Claire felt. And at the root of that feeling was the chasm that had opened up inside the family.

Jenny was out on Friday, and Claire spent the evening alone, watching English television, which was full of violent scenes in Northern Ireland. It was odd to see it, because it made what was happening there seem so close. Riverstown was only sixty-odd miles from the border. For all they were aware of the trouble, it might as well have been six hundred. She couldn't forget home and Frank; London and the flat seemed unreal.

212

When the telephone rang the next morning, Jenny answered it, and after a moment banged on Claire's bedroom door. "It's for you. Some dishy-sounding man called Neil Fraser."

And it was because of Neil Fraser that Claire's three months' stay in London ran on to a year. Suddenly her life was exciting, and the awful void of Frank's leaving Riverstown had been filled by this clever, sophisticated man who loved her and showered her with presents and promises of the wonderful life they would have together. She came home at Christmas and Easter and brought Neil back to meet her parents.

She made a lot of friends and met many more through Neil. He was fun, she thought happily, and she was falling in love. His father was a widower and very sweet whenever she went down to stay. Neil had a brilliant political career ahead of him, and she knew people were saying that all he needed was a beautiful young wife and a family to complete the electoral appeal. They were going to be blissfully happy. She was determined to help him and make him proud of her.

KEVIN RYAN CAME BACK to Ireland just before Christmas. His first stop was the Half House. The builders were out and it was being decorated. He was pleased and proud of what he saw. It was a showplace now, with gleaming bathrooms and plumbing that worked. He'd given a decorator a free hand with money, and he'd ransacked Dublin antique shops for Waterford chandeliers and handsome furniture. The pictures—big, heavily framed Irish landscapes—had cost a small fortune, but Kevin was delighted with them. He took a lot of photographs to show people back home in Boston. Then he got into his car and set out for Meath to meet his nephew.

Frank opened the front door himself. He saw a short man with sandy-grey hair, a scarf wound round his neck and a curious forward stoop, as if he were sheltering from a cold wind.

It was Kevin who spoke first. "Frank, I'm your Uncle Kevin," and he held out both hands.

They settled in front of a turf fire, the smell sweet in the large old-fashioned room, one on either side in big armchairs, each with a decent whiskey in his hand.

Frank couldn't stop looking at his uncle. He was like the photograph of his mother, and yet not really. The same thin face and pale eyes. His mother had been delicately pretty. Her brother was wiry, expansive in gesture, with a ready laugh. From the moment he had grasped his uncle's hands, Frank had felt a sympathy between them. Now, sitting opposite him, he felt a warmth and a kinship with an older man for the first time in his life.

"I remember sneaking in to see you," Kevin said. "With our old cousin Mary Donovan. Did you ever know her, Frank?"

"When I was little, yes. She always gave me biscuits."

"She was a grand woman," Kevin announced, forgetting how he had despised her as a slovenly old gossip.

"Yes, she was." Frank nodded, remembering how she'd slipped him his mother's brooch, with the whisper not to tell on her, for it was as much as her job was worth.

"You were a lonely little lad," his uncle went on. "With your poor mother gone and your father away fighting for the English. I said then, one day I'll come back and see Eileen's boy. And so I wrote the letter to you."

At his nephew's insistence Kevin stayed to dinner. He took in the comfort and the shabbiness of a typical upper-class Anglo-Irish house, with its fine glass and silver on the table and holes in the curtains from years of wear. If he'd been his son, Frank couldn't have been more welcoming. It made Kevin feel good, and it wasn't just the drink warming his heart. He recognized the identity that had so alienated Philip. In spite of his English accent and his gentleman's manners, Frank was an Irishman. The Ryan blood was strong in him. Kevin wondered how much of the circumstances of his mother's marriage and her death the young man knew. He decided to enlighten him, a little at a time. He began gently that night.

It was long past midnight when Kevin said goodbye. They'd made a firm date for Frank to go to Boston over Christmas and New Year and stay with him and Mary Rose.

Watching Kevin drive away, Frank saw beyond the swagger of the Irishman made good. He felt elated, excited. He had gambled on meeting his uncle, with his family ties as the stake, and he decided that night that he had won. He had reached out across the class and religious divide of Irish life and touched hands with his mother's people. He knew now that he was closer to them than to the father and stepmother sitting so smugly at Riverstown.

Yet he was sad, because there was no one in his whole big house to talk to about what had happened.

THERE ARE NO SECRETS in Ireland. Philip's friends were not the only ones to hear that there was a rift between him and his son and that Frank had moved to Meath. The cause was known, too. It lost Frank sympathy among his friends and aroused interest among others whom he didn't know, beginning with an invitation to lunch from a well-known writer, an American of Irish descent who'd recently bought a house a few miles away.

It was a Sunday, and Frank's trip to Boston was only ten days off. The writer lived in a big house in a handsome park, with his pretty American wife, who considered him a genius. It was a lavish party, and the atmosphere was stimulating. Frank was soon enjoying himself. A charm-

214

ing professor of history at University College, Dublin treated him to amusing anecdotes and introduced him to a young psychiatrist who'd come back to Ireland after studying for three years at Harvard. The psychiatrist had a beard and a serious manner that Frank found attractive. His name was Sean Filey.

At lunch Frank was seated next to a very pretty, vivacious girl, who paid him a lot of attention. "I was late getting here," she explained. "My car wasn't behaving itself this morning." She added that she lived in Dublin. Her name was Marie Dempster. "Do you live near here?" she asked.

Frank explained that he did and gave the name of the house. She opened her blue eyes very wide.

"Old Lady Blanche Arbuthnot lived there, didn't she?"

"Mrs. Arbuthnot," he corrected. "She was my grandmother."

She looked surprised. "Was she really?"

He smiled at her. "Yes, really. Do you know the house?"

She glanced down; she seemed shy suddenly. "Well, no. I know of it because my father had a little farm not far away. We wouldn't exactly be on the visiting list."

"Then why don't you come over and see it? What about lunch next weekend? After that I'm going to the States for a while."

The girl looked disappointed. "I can't next weekend. I'm going to a concert and I've got friends coming round."

"I'll be in Dublin next Thursday. Could we have dinner?"

"I'd love that," Marie Dempster said.

She didn't drive back to her flat. She drove to the house on the airport road and waited for Sean Filey. The first move had been made.

KEVIN WAS AT LOGAN INTERNATIONAL AIRPORT to meet Frank. "It's great to see you," his uncle said as they walked to the car. "We've a big party arranged for you to meet some of our friends." He wagged his head at Frank and added, "People who'll be useful to you in banking, me boy. Good Irish–Americans with money. We'll have a helluva good time while you're here!"

Frank had never had a welcome like that from his father. The new sensation of warmth and belonging came over him stronger than when he and his uncle had first met.

The Ryans lived in a big modern house in a smart suburb of Boston. When they drew up to the front door it opened and a pretty, brightly dressed woman came to meet them, saying, "Frank? I'm Mary Rose. Welcome to our home," and reaching up, she kissed him. "Now come on in!"

There were four children. Good-looking children in various stages of adolescence and one pretty little red-haired girl who smiled and smiled at him till her father took her on his knee.

"This is Eileen," Kevin said. "Named for your mother. Same red hair, same pale eyes."

Frank smiled at her and thought, This is a real family. This is how I'd want to be with my children. Not like my father.

Mary Rose disappeared into the kitchen and the children went back to the television set. Kevin poured a whiskey and raised his glass. "It's a great day for me, having Eileen's son in my house."

"It's great to be here," Frank responded.

The guests were not expected for several hours, and Kevin and Frank settled down to talk politics. By the time the company arrived, Kevin had established that he and Frank had more than family ties in common. Frank might have an English name, but his sympathies were with his mother's people.

The party in his honour was a lavish buffet for fifty. Mary Rose, gleaming in a black sequined dress and diamond jewellery, greeted their guests. There were politicians, several priests, well-dressed women resplendent in minks and diamonds.

After dinner Kevin gathered a few of the men together in a room he called his den and asked Frank to join them. They talked American politics and business, and the two men Kevin most wanted to impress drew his nephew into a discussion on international banking. Over his nephew's head Kevin received a nod of approval and allowed himself a proud smile. Frank was doing him credit in the closed community of the Boston Irish.

THERE WAS A TELEPHONE MESSAGE from Marie Dempster waiting for Frank when he got back to Ireland. For a moment he couldn't place the name. But it was only a momentary lapse. Of course: the pretty girl he'd taken out to dinner before he went to the States. Marie Dempster. Mrs. Mahoney, his housekeeper, had written everything down in her painstaking hand. Miss Dempster wanted Mr. Frank to telephone as soon as he got back. There were two messages from Claire, asking him to ring her in London. He tried Claire first. The girl she was living with answered. Sorry, Claire was away for the weekend. He felt so disappointed that he didn't call Marie until the next morning.

She sounded pleased to hear from him. "I thought you'd be back by now," she said. "I did enjoy our dinner and I'd love to hear about your trip. Why don't you come here and I'll make dinner for you? Are you busy this Saturday?"

Frank hesitated. He wasn't busy. He had come back from America with a strange feeling of fundamental change in himself. And no one to talk to, because Claire was in England. If she'd been at home, he'd have taken a plane to London.

"No. I've no plans made," he said. "I'd like to come."

216

She gave him the address and said seven, if that wasn't too early. "I'm looking forward to it," she said and then hung up.

It was a flat in a house off Baggot Street. The address was a good one, but he could see there was no money left over for luxuries. He wished he'd thought of bringing her something, but he wasn't used to girls living on their own, with no money to spare.

Over dinner she asked him a few questions about America and then said suddenly, "I'd love to go one day. I'd like to live there and get a really decent job. There's no future for me in the firm I'm in." It was a well-known firm of Dublin lawyers.

He said, "Why not? They're very good people."

She leaned towards him, and her eyes were shining with tears of anger. "Because my name is Dempster and I'm a Catholic," she said. "I've been there four years, Frank, and the job of private secretary to the senior partner is coming vacant. I should have got it. I'm the best secretary they have. But they've brought in a girl from outside. She's from the right background. Church of Ireland and a good Cromwellian name!" She turned away, rummaged in her pocket for a handkerchief, and blew her nose. "I shouldn't have said that to you," she apologized. "But I've been boiling over it for days."

"I'm not surprised," Frank said. "I've never heard of anything like it. It's what you'd expect in the North, but here . . ."

She looked at him. "In the North I wouldn't have got a job with them in the first place," she pointed out. "Up there they're honest about their discrimination. No Catholic need apply."

She seemed very agitated, twisting the handkerchief in her fingers, a bright flush on each cheek. She got up and went through into the cupboard that called itself a kitchen. Frank felt sorry for her, and indignant. He got up and met her as she turned to come back into the room. She looked miserable and anxious. As she said to Sean Filey afterwards, it was the best bit of acting she'd ever done in her life.

"I suppose I've said all the wrong things to you," she said. "Now I'll never see you again."

Frank put both hands on her shoulders. "Don't be silly," he said. "Of course you're angry. I'm planning to open a merchant bank here in Dublin in the not-too-distant future. There'll be a job for you, if you can manage till then."

"You really mean it?" She had beautiful blue eyes, with the heavy dark lashes and eyebrows that are peculiar to the Irish. She glanced downwards and looked shy. Then, unexpectedly, she put her arms round his neck and kissed him. "You mean it, don't you?" she said. "You're a very special man, Frank."

She kissed him again, and he returned her kisses. She was too experienced and subtle to go to bed with him right away. She led him to the sofa and guided him to a pitch of sexual desire. Then she drew back, saying how sorry she was, that she shouldn't have got carried away.

As she'd expected, he didn't insist, but got up and moved away. The perfect gentleman, she thought contemptuously, angered by the fact that she was hot for him despite herself and wouldn't have minded being bundled into bed.

"When will you come down to Meath?" he asked. "You said you'd like to see the house."

"When do you want me to come?"

He was getting his coat on. He smiled at her. She hated him for smiling at her like that. Sean Filey had told her to go slowly. "Be careful. He's clever and he's sophisticated. Get your hook in deep." Filey was wrong. Frank Arbuthnot might be clever, but he wasn't sophisticated or he wouldn't have been fooled by her act.

"Wednesday's a good night," Frank said. "I'll ring you tomorrow. Goodnight, Marie. Thanks for this evening."

She said goodnight and went to bed and dreamed of Wednesday.

Frank felt he'd made rather a fool of himself that night, offering her a job, nearly ending up in bed with her. Next morning he dialled her number to cancel their date, but there was no reply.

He admitted he found her very sexually attractive. She had suddenly appealed to his sympathy and stirred all sorts of muddled emotions in him. And they were muddled. Since his return from America he'd found it a blessing and a curse to be home.

The fine old house at Meath succoured and reproached him at the same time. His grandmother had left it to him, with her fortune. He owed his independence to her. And yet he couldn't bear to see her photographs about the place, because of the picture Kevin Ryan had imprinted on his mind: the image of a cold, contemptuous old patrician scorning her pregnant daughter-in-law and bringing on her premature labour. And above all he missed Claire.

And then, on Monday night, Claire telephoned, and he forgot all about cancelling Marie Dempster.

"Frank, it's me! How are you?" It was so good to hear her voice again. They hadn't been in touch for weeks.

"I'm fine," he said. "It's great to speak to you at last. I phoned, but you were away."

"I was with a friend. A special friend. Listen, he'll be here soon and I'll have to go. But how are you? And how was America?"

"Interesting," he said. "Uncle Kevin was a great help in introducing me to potential backers for the bank. Listen, Clarry, I'd so love to see you. I've got so much to tell you. Please come over, I'll stand you the air fare, but don't tell the parents. I don't think they'd like me paying for you to come and see me."

"Is it still that bad?" she asked. "I hoped maybe things had settled down. Frank, there's nothing wrong, is there?"

"Not wrong, no. I'm fine, but I've got a lot of things on my mind."

Her response was instant. "Of course I'll come. Can you meet me on Friday? I'll let you know the flight."

"You're sure? It would be great to see you."

"I'll be there," Claire said. A few minutes after she hung up, Neil Fraser was at the door. He was taking her to the theatre.

After the theatre, when they were having dinner at the smartest private club in London, she told him that she was going to Ireland that weekend to see her brother, Frank.

He frowned. "But darling," he said, "we're going to stay with the Miltons. It's been arranged for ages. We can't let them down."

She said quietly, "I can't let my brother down. He needs me, Neil. I can go to the Miltons' another time."

He was very angry. James and Pru were not just friends who could be inconvenienced. Milton was one of the prime minister's personal assistants, an important connection for Neil.

"Please, Neil," she continued. "I'm really worried about Frank. I must go over."

Neil loved her too much to see her unhappy. "All right," he said. "You go to Ireland and put your mind at rest."

ONCE SETTLED IN at the old house in Meath, Claire leaned back in one of the big armchairs as the fire roared in the grate. Everything was warm and Irish and familiar. England and Neil seemed a million miles away.

"Oh, Frankie darling," she said, "it's so wonderful to see you! I'd forgotten what a lovely house this is. I haven't been here since you moved into it. Grandmother had great taste. What have you done with all the photographs of her?"

He said quietly, "I've put them away."

"Why? Oh, not because of that old story about your mother? I don't believe it, Frank. I don't believe Grandmother did anything to hurt her. I think Dad went hysterical and had to blame somebody. You ought to put the pictures back. After all, she left everything to you."

"Conscience money," he answered. "I didn't believe the story either. But I heard it in America. It's true, Claire. My mother went into premature labour because of the way Grandmother treated her."

"What good does it do to rake up old wrongs? It's so long ago."

"My uncle told me something else," he said. "It's funny, Claire, but I can't get it out of my mind. The night I was born, I was baptized a Catholic."

She stared at him. "You couldn't have been! Dad was there!"

"The ward sister did it," he explained. "I was very small, and it's common practice among Catholics if the baby's in any danger. It doesn't need a priest to be valid. It's a strange feeling to be brought up one thing and then find out you're something else."

"Brother, dear," she said, trying to sound lighthearted. "If you take any notice of what some old biddy did years ago, you need your head examined! How can you be any different for it?"

He looked at her. "It makes me more Irish."

"We're all Irish," Claire insisted. "Living in England has taught me that. Even Mummy would feel a foreigner if she went back to England now. I certainly do."

"I always did," he countered. "And I went to school and university there. I'm more at home in the States."

"What's got into you, Frank? Is it America? Was Dad right when he told you to leave Kevin Ryan alone? All this business about our grandmother. You've known the story since you were a child, so why is it suddenly an issue? This nonsense about being baptized a Catholic, when you've been brought up Church of Ireland all your life. Can't you tell me what's really the matter?"

She got up and came to him, balancing on the arm of his chair, and slipped her arm round him.

"There was always something about me he hated," she heard him say. "I tried to please him, but nothing worked. He was all right with me on the surface, but at the first opportunity he turned me out. I go to Riverstown once a month or so, and we talk about the farm and cattle prices, like two strangers. And he can't wait for me to go."

"Oh, Frank," she murmured. "I kept hoping it would mend with time. Maybe it will."

"No," he said. "He regrets marrying my mother, falling out with his own family. And so long as I'm around he can't forget it. Can't you see it, Claire? It's like a haunting. She dies, but I survive. Then years later her brother buys Claudia's old home. The Half House going to the Ryans must have crucified him."

"If you go on like this, you'll end up in St. Pat's," Claire said.

"I'm not crazy, Claire, but I feel as if I'm in a vacuum. I'm planning to open a bank in Dublin; there's a lot to do to improve the estate. But nothing has any meaning for me."

"It's leaving home," she said. "That's what makes you feel like this. Thinking Dad doesn't love you."

"Do you think he does? Honestly?"

"I think he's uncomfortable with you," she said after a pause. "He finds it difficult to show his feelings. And he's very obstinate and proud. Frank darling, I've got an idea. Why don't I talk to him about it when I come home next?"

"Haven't you done that already?" he asked her, and she couldn't deny it. She tried to forget that chilling relief in her father when his son had left Riverstown.

"Yes. But you'd just had the row. Time heals everything."

"Not with the Arbuthnots," he said.

They were silent then, watching the flicker of the firelight. She had never known Frank in need like this. He had always been the strong one, giving her security. Now it was her turn to mother him. "Why don't I get us some brandy?" she suggested.

"It makes a good nightcap," he said.

Claire brought him a glass and sat on the floor by his chair.

"I've talked enough about myself," Frank said. "Now I want to hear what you've been doing."

For a moment Claire hesitated. "You remember the Englishman I met at Butlers Castle, the MP?"

He frowned. "Yes, I remember him."

"I've seen a lot of him in London. He seems very keen."

"I'm sure he does," Frank said. "He was pretty keen that night, I remember. Are you keen, too?"

She paused. "I don't know. I was so miserable when I first arrived in London. I nearly came home. Then Neil turned up and started taking me out. He's very nice," she added.

"Please, Clarry, don't rush into anything. I didn't like him; I told you." She sighed. "I know you did."

"He's so English," Frank went on. "Have a good time, but don't get too involved. That kind of man is not for you."

Claire didn't argue. She wasn't going to lie to her brother, but she didn't want to upset him either. He was prejudiced against Neil without knowing anything about him. If she did decide to marry him, Frank would come round. And as Neil hadn't even asked her yet, what was the point of making an issue?

"Your home is Ireland," he said. "You won't be happy anywhere else."

CHAPTER 6

Sean Filey came into the house on the airport road to meet Marie Dempster, who looked nervous. He wondered what had gone wrong with her date with Arbuthnot. That dinner at her flat had been such a success. She had been jubilant when she reported it to him.

"Any coffee?" he asked.

She got up. "I'll make some," she said irritably.

He followed her into the kitchen. "What happened on Wednesday?"

"Nothing. I went down to his house; we talked about this and that, we had dinner, and he said goodbye."

Filey looked up sharply. "Why the change?"

"I don't know," she said flatly. "He was very nice, the perfect gentleman, but his mind wasn't on me, Sean. I tried to get him up to the flat this weekend, but he said no, his sister was coming over from England and he was spending the weekend with her."

Filey knew she had expected to stay the night and consolidate the advantage gained before. He sensed that she was furious and bewildered by the rebuff.

"I told you, this will take time," he said. "Did he say why his sister was coming to see him?"

"No. But it didn't sound like trouble. He sounded happy." Her face darkened.

Filey saw the lowered look and wondered how she could be jealous when she hardly knew the man.

"I'll ring him up and try again," she said. "The sister will have gone home by now." She lit a cigarette. "Sean, I've been thinking about this idea of recruiting him. It sounded great when we discussed it. But I sat in that house the other night and I thought to myself, Is this really going to work? He's from a different world; he's one of *them*. Oh, he plays with the idea of being Irish—it's a big romantic gesture and he's loving it—but how real is it? Could we ever trust him, supposing he does join?"

"He has a role to play for us," Sean Filey said quietly. "We'll trust him as far as it suits us and no further. We need that bank of his, Marie. We need him because he *is* one of them. But don't you contact him. I'll do that. I'm having some friends in for an evening. There's a poet I can get to come and read his verse. Arbuthnot will accept, Marie, and you'll be there. Then it's up to you."

SEAN FILEY LIVED in a comfortable old-fashioned house in Dublin. He arranged his party three weeks ahead, with alternative dates in case Frank Arbuthnot couldn't make one or other. He invited a young poet who was gaining a wide reputation for his verse, and a group of people he hoped would enjoy something different.

He was friendly and relaxed when he spoke to Frank, reminding him of their meeting at the novelist's house. Frank accepted. He wasn't interested in poetry, but he liked Sean Filey. If he was going to be an Irishman, then he would break out of his old circle, with its talk of hunting and land prices, and mix with the Irish.

When he arrived he felt ill at ease, in spite of Sean's efforts. He was introduced to everyone, but they all knew one another and after a few words they drifted away. The poet was a bearded, shabby man. He shook hands limply with Frank, and his eyes slid away, looking for someone else. Twenty minutes after Frank had arrived, Marie walked in. She was out of breath and very flushed, which made her look even prettier.

He heard her say to Sean, "I'm so sorry I'm late, but my car let me down again. I had to take a taxi."

She looked across at Frank and smiled, but she didn't come over immediately. He was suddenly glad to see her. He should have phoned after her visit, but then Claire had arrived and he'd forgotten. He made his way over to her. "Hello, Marie," he greeted her.

"Hello, Frank. I didn't know you were coming. How are you?"

"Fine, thanks."

"I should have thanked you for the lovely evening," she said. "I loved your house."

They sat side by side on hard little chairs, and the poet began to read from his works. There were twenty people in the room, and they sat as still as if they were at a funeral. He read beautifully. The language flowed, full of original imagery. When the reading ended, Frank joined in a loud burst of clapping. From his seat at the back Sean Filey watched him speculatively. He knew the poems well. They had affected him too, the first time he heard them. It was good that Arbuthnot had come under the same spell. Their theme was Ireland. They spoke of beauty and sadness, of longing and reflection, of love that blended into a love deeper than the love of men and women.

"You liked it, didn't you?" Marie said to Frank.

"Yes. He's remarkable."

"Sean discovered him," she explained. "Apart from shrinking people's heads, he's a great one for helping Irish artists. It's funny, I never liked poetry at school. But I like this. It sings, doesn't it?"

Frank said, "But they're sad songs."

"Ireland's been a sad country," she responded. "Who else has a national heroine called Deirdre of the Sorrows?" She looked at her watch. "I'll have to go," she said. "Could you give me a lift home, Frank? My car's on strike again."

"Of course I'll drive you home."

Outside the door in Baggot Street, she turned and said, "Come up for a minute. I'll make us some coffee."

He couldn't have refused if he'd wanted to, and he didn't. Inside her flat, she put her arms round his neck and kissed him. "I nearly didn't go tonight," she said. "Now I'm glad I did."

Frank didn't go home to Meath until the following morning. Marie called Sean Filey during her lunch hour. "I'm seeing him tonight," she told him. "I think we're on."

"Good girl," he said. "Now get yourself the sack. We don't want him forgetting about the job he promised you in his bank."

I'll do better than that, Marie said to herself. I'll work in his bank and I'll move into his house. That way I'll really have him in my hand. And if he makes me happy doing it, why not?

BY CHRISTMAS OF 1971 Claire was engaged to marry Neil Fraser. There would be a spring engagement party and a summer wedding.

I'm going to be happy with Claire for the rest of my life, Neil thought, looking at her across the table. They were dining together at his flat the day after he had proposed.

Claire stretched her hand out, and the ruby and diamond engagement ring sparkled in the light. "I rang my brother to tell him we were engaged," she said.

"Oh? What did he say?" He had a clear memory of the dark Irishman who'd watched them dancing at Butlers Castle.

"He wasn't there," Claire said. "It's funny; a woman answered. It wasn't the housekeeper."

"What's funny about it? Doesn't he have girlfriends?"

"Not the sort who stay in the house when he's not there. She said he was in the States. I wonder who she is."

"How would I know, darling?" Neil said.

She cleared the table and left Neil to the television. She wondered again

who had answered the telephone in Frank's absence. Maybe her parents
would know. It was about time she phoned them again, anyway.

Philip took the call. Afterwards he said to Claudia, "That was Claire; I
called you, but you must have been upstairs."

"Sorry I missed her," she said. "Everything all right?"

"She's fine," Philip said. "Full of beans. Apparently she rang Frank,
and a woman answered. She wanted to know who it was."

Claudia looked up at him. "What did you tell her?"

"I told her I hadn't the faintest idea," he said. "It could have been any
one of the hangers-on he surrounds himself with."

Claudia frowned. "It's probably that Dempster girl, Marie. I gather
she's wormed her way in pretty successfully. Not that it matters. It's time
he had a steady girlfriend." Personally, she didn't care who Frank was
with now that he was out of her house and Claire was happily engaged.
Neil Fraser was a good match: plenty of money, a bright future and, most
important from Claudia's point of view, he was a gentleman.

Philip poked the turf fire. He always did that when he was worried about something. "Isn't this Marie Dempster connected with Eamonn Dempster?"

Claudia had hoped he wouldn't work that out. "I think she's a granddaughter," she said. "But I'm not sure."

"Then he's really mixing with the scum of the earth," Philip said. "The Dempsters have been in the IRA since 1922."

"*She* may not be," Claudia pointed out. "She's a dentist's daughter, I think. Do stop hacking away at the fire, darling, or it'll go out!"

Philip laid down the poker. "I've heard things," he said. "Someone at the club asked me the other day if it was true that Frank was setting up an Irish–American merchant bank and Kevin Ryan was going to be on the board."

"Is he?" Claudia asked. "Why don't you ask him? After all, you're on speaking terms."

"I don't intend to ask," Philip said coldly. "We talk about the farms and the property in Meath, but we've no point of contact beyond that. I just have a feeling he's getting into deep water."

Claudia sighed. "He's a fool," she said. "If he's getting mixed up with people like the Dempsters and that dreadful uncle of his, they'll just use him for all he's worth. He's rich, remember. A rich Anglo with a bad conscience. And an Irish mother to trade on. I wish somebody could talk some sense into him!"

"I've made up my mind," Philip said slowly. "I'm not going to leave him Riverstown. He's irresponsible; I'll change my will."

"You can't disinherit your own son!" Claudia said. "He may change. He may have his fling with these people, and then one day he'll see through them and it'll all be over."

"I love this house," Philip said. "It's been in my family for generations. I'm not going to have it filled with the kind of people he brings into my mother's old home. He won't change, Claudia. He's not one of us. Now don't let's discuss it any more."

"IF ONLY FRANK WAS HERE," Claire said. "Then everything would be perfect. It's such a shame he couldn't get back for the party."

Claudia lit a cigarette. Preparations for the big engagement party and for a summer wedding were taking their toll on her nerves. Now she looked sharply at her daughter and frowned. "He could have come back in time for this if he'd wanted to. Anyway, don't let Neil hear you going on about it. I should think he's sick to death of hearing about Frank."

Claire turned away. Her mother's attitude towards her stepson was openly hostile now. Neil came down the stairs just in time, before Claire said something angry.

"You look super, darling. Doesn't she, Claudia?"

"I think we chose the right dress," was the reply, accompanied by a

226

smile. "Now, come on. I think people are arriving. You two do the honours; nobody's come to see me. And of course your father's disappeared as usual, just before the party starts. I'll go and find him. He hates shaking hands."

Neil slipped his arm round Claire's waist. "Why are you looking so grim—had a row with your mother?"

"No," she said. "She gets on my nerves sometimes, that's all. And I just wish Frank was here."

She'd said it several times. He was surprised to feel hurt.

"Well, you'll have to make do with me," he said.

Claire smiled up at him, and he was happy again. "I think I can manage that," she said.

THREE THOUSAND MILES across the Atlantic Ocean, Kevin Ryan told Mary Rose, "I'm going out tonight. I've a business meeting. You take care of Frankie this evening. Don't wait up for me."

Kevin Ryan's business meeting took place in a large private house twenty miles outside Boston, and went on until after midnight. There were half a dozen men present, shut up in a downstairs room. Whiskey and cigars were on the table. Two prominent citizens of Irish descent who had met Frank Arbuthnot on his previous visits to Boston were among the six at the meeting. A man in his mid-forties presided. He was not American, and he had entered the United States on a false visa.

They discussed the items on the agenda, and the last one concerned the new Boston Irish Bank that was scheduled to open in Dublin in July. It was Kevin Ryan's responsibility, and he had made a detailed report. The Americans present were supplying eighty per cent of the money. Frank Arbuthnot would finance the remaining twenty per cent.

The non-American who presided over the meeting had been born in Northern Ireland, but had spent the last five years living in the Republic under an alias. He was a top Provo leader, and he said, "I'm concerned about Arbuthnot's future brother-in-law. He's a Tory MP, and I don't see how we can risk Frank saying something to his sister that could be passed on."

Kevin gathered himself for the fight. He had been expecting this. He said, "You're wrong, Joe. My nephew is sick about this marriage. He didn't even go home for the big engagement party. I know what he thinks of it. He was overly close to the half-sister. Now she's betrayed him, as he sees it. This cuts the last link with that family of his. If I didn't trust him, I'd be the first to say forget it. Set it up with someone else."

"There isn't anyone else," the Provo leader pointed out. "Arbuthnot's the cover man we need for this. Anyone from our side would be suspect. So we need him, but does he have to know? Won't we have a plant right there beside him in the bank?"

"Eamonn Dempster's granddaughter," Kevin announced. "We all know what the Dempsters did for Irish freedom. She lives with my nephew and she's going to work for him at the bank. I wouldn't be surprised if he married her one day. But answering the question, I'd say he does have to know. There's no way we can get the amount we've in mind through the bank without him finding out. Would you agree with that, Pat?"

"I would," was the reply. "We've got to recruit him and make him one of us. I'm not putting a million dollars into this unless it's making a proper contribution to the cause."

Kevin said, "Leave this to me. Get this sister's weddin' out of the way first. I guarantee he'll join us."

"He's got to commit himself before July," the leader said.

Kevin nodded. "He will," he said. "By the time the bank opens, he'll have taken the oath."

"OH, FRANK, I'M SO GLAD to see you. Why didn't you come to our engagement party?"

"I was up to my eyes in bank business," he said. He had never lied to Claire before. Truth is the first casualty when people drift apart. He'd read that somewhere. They sat in the lounge of the Royal Hibernian Hotel, in Dublin, where he'd booked a table for lunch.

"It was a great party," she said. "Everybody came. But I missed you. It wasn't really bank business, was it? You're not pleased, are you?"

Suddenly there was no need for lies. "That's why I didn't come," he said. "I can't pretend to be happy about the engagement. Are you sure he's the right man for you?"

"Yes," she answered. "I know what I'm doing. I want to marry Neil."

He said slowly, "But do you love him?"

She laid her hand on his. Neil's ring glittered. "I do love him," she said. "We're very happy. The only thing that will spoil it for me is if you and Neil don't get on."

He said, "Then that settles it. So long as he makes you happy, we'll get on fine."

"Now I really am happy," she said. And he knew then that whatever he felt, he must conceal it.

It was a long lunch. He ordered champagne and was told all about the wedding dress and the bridesmaids. In spite of the emptiness in his heart, she made him join in and laugh with her.

"I think this might actually mend things between you and Dad," she said, surprising him.

"Why should it?" Frank asked.

"Because he seems much mellower these days. I thought he'd be fed up with all the fuss, but he's entered into everything. Frank darling, make a **big effort with him and see what happens.**"

228

He said gently, not to disappoint her, "I'll try."

"And by the way," Claire said as they were driving back, "what's this I hear about a live-in girlfriend at Meath?"

"She's a nice girl," Frank explained. "We get on well; she's going to work in the new bank in July."

"She's native Irish, isn't she?"

"Yes, she's Irish," Frank said firmly. "And a Catholic, and her grandfather fought alongside Michael Collins. You can't be more Irish than that!"

"If you're thinking of making it up with Dad—he'd have a fit."

"I'm not thinking of making it up with him, *you* are. And it wouldn't be any of his business, if it was serious. As it happens, it's not. It's a good arrangement and it suits us both, but that's as far as it goes."

"For her, too?" Claire queried.

He sped away from a set of traffic lights. "There are no strings for either Marie or me."

MARIE DEMPSTER LOOKED AT HER WATCH. Lunch with his sister had meant the whole afternoon. It was past five o'clock and Frank hadn't come home from Dublin yet.

She had missed him during his long trip to the States. He always told her to invite friends down to Meath, to treat the house as her own. He didn't want her to be bored or lonely. He never said that he'd be lonely without her. There were times when she thought of him in the bosom of the Ryan family and forgot that she and they were allies. She hated them for having him to themselves, while she waited in Ireland, hoping for an occasional phone call.

Sean Filey kept in close touch with her. As far as he was concerned, she was succeeding past success. And so he would think, she said savagely to herself, with ice water in him instead of blood. Sean knew nothing about love, and love was becoming Marie's problem. Not just passion, but the cruel torment of the spirit that is unrequited love. Frank was often away, and always busy. Today he had stayed out most of the day with his sister, and Marie was consumed with jealousy.

She went upstairs and changed into a pretty dress. Now that she had the use of Frank's money, she bought expensive clothes and went to the best hairdresser in Dublin. She had been a pretty girl, in a provincial way. Now she was glamorous. He was happy with her, she knew that. But she did not hold his heart. After six months of living with him, Marie knew her rival couldn't be fought on ordinary terms. In no way could she compete with a sister. There was a photograph in his bedroom showing them together on a beach. She must have been about fifteen. They were laughing. Marie hated that smooth, smiling image. Now the sister was getting married, and going to live in England permanently. Marie pinned her faith on distance. When Claire wasn't on his doorstep, may be he'd forget about her at last.

She came downstairs, packaged for him, she thought. Six o'clock. She swore out loud. He would come in looking innocent and friendly, unaware of her resentment, which she mustn't ever show him. She wasn't just a jealous mistress who could afford a tantrum. She was part of a conspiracy. If she told him the truth about Filey and his precious Uncle Kevin, that would be the end for her, too. By entangling Frank, she kept him.

She opened the drawing-room door. The room was blazing with the early evening sun. How often had she told that old woman to let the blinds down before the furniture faded? She turned and stormed into the kitchen quarters.

"Why haven't you let the blinds down? Don't you see the sun's pouring in?" She was shouting like a fishwife.

"I was on me way to do it," Biddy Mahoney protested.

"It was rainin' only a little while ago," her husband said, coming to her defence. They'd worked for the Arbuthnots and their kind all their lives. Never before had they been shouted at.

"Don't tell lies to me! Get on and do it this minute!"

There was a pause. She saw in Biddy's face the contempt she didn't dare express. "I'll be drawing the blinds then," Biddy said. She skirted round Marie, moving with maddening slowness and an even more maddening dignity.

Marie had returned to the drawing room when she heard Frank come in. He opened the door.

"Hello," she said. "It must have been a good lunch."

He came in and sat beside her. "Not bad," he said. "I sorted things out, that's the main thing."

He was angry about the marriage; she knew that much. Naturally he would hate to have any member of the English establishment as a brother-in-law. But Marie wondered if there was any man in Ireland he'd consider worthy of that sister.

"So you'll be going to the wedding then?" she asked.

He glanced at her in surprise. "Of course," he said. "Now, tell me what you did today." The subject of Claire was closed.

"I had trouble with Biddy again," she said.

CLAUDIA WAS AT HER DESK, ticking off replies to the wedding invitations. Nearly everyone invited was coming. She heard a tap on the door and said absently, "Yes?"

Biddy Mahoney stood there, wearing her Sunday hat and coat.

"Biddy?" said Claudia. "What are you doing here? Come in."

"I'm sorry to disturb ye, ma'am."

Claudia left her desk. "Sit down, Biddy. What's the matter?"

230

"We've been thrown out of the house," Biddy said.

Claudia could see that the old woman was near tears. She and Jim had looked after that house for years, ever since Blanche Arbuthnot died. "You've been sacked?" she said. "Why?"

"There's a woman livin' there now." Biddy looked embarrassed. "She complained of us, ma'am. She come in the other day, screamin' at me like a banshee over forgettin' somethin', and the next thing is Mr. Frank sends for me and Jim and says he thinks it best we look for work somewhere else."

Claudia exploded. "Surely he didn't just tell you to go?"

"No, he gave us a month's notice and a present. He was generous enough. The girl was smilin' like a cat with the cream in her all the next day. Then he's away for the night, and she comes and tells us to pack up and get out the next mornin'. This very day."

"Have you anywhere to go?" Claudia asked.

"My sister'll have us till we find another place," Biddy answered. "I wanted ye to know the truth, before some lie gets told to ye. Divil a reference we'll get either, if I know her."

"Don't worry," Claudia said. "I'll give you a reference."

"I'm sorry about it, ma'am. It's her comin' to live there that's the cause. She's changed him." Biddy got up and held out her hand.

Claudia shook it. "He certainly has changed," she said, "if he'd be influenced by a creature like that."

At the door Biddy turned back. "There's an old sayin', ma'am. If ye lie down with dirt, ye get up with fleas!"

Claudia couldn't have expressed it better.

THE FIRST THING KEVIN RYAN DID when he arrived at the recently finished Half House was to put in a call to Sean Filey at his office. Kevin was planning a large party to celebrate the opening of the Boston Irish Bank, and there were two members of the Dail he particularly wanted to invite. Filey knew them well. The more support Kevin gathered for the new banking venture, the easier it would be to attract genuine investment on a large scale. And that meant the sums being channelled through from America would be easier to conceal. There was a large shipment of arms and ammunition waiting for payment in the Middle East. That would be the first clandestine transaction, and he intended that Frank Arbuthnot should be responsible for making the payment. Once he had acted as paymaster for a Provo arms deal, he could never go back on his commitment to the cause.

THERE WAS A FAMILY DINNER the night before the wedding. Colonel Jack Fraser, Neil's father, had arrived and made a good impression. Philip liked him. Claudia had begun to relax, like a general in sight of victory.

231

The caterers had been tamed, the flower arrangers had worked miracles in the church, and the big tent outside on the main lawn was a bower of flowers and foliage. Everything was poised for the next day, and there was an air of excitement throughout the household. Philip brought out a bottle of vintage champagne for Colonel Fraser before the rest of the family arrived. They chatted amiably alone in the drawing room for some minutes until Frank joined them. His father introduced him.

"This is my son, Frank, Colonel Fraser. I'll get you a glass of champagne, Frank. This is rather special."

The colonel smiled at him. "I hear you're a banker," he said. There were traces of Neil in him, the same staccato way of speaking that made everything sound like a command.

"Yes," said Frank. "I'm opening a new merchant bank next month in Dublin. It's American-backed, actually."

When Philip returned, Frank excused himself and went over to his sister, who had just come in. "You look great," he said.

"Frank darling," she said. "It's so wonderful to be all together tonight. Look what Dad's given me." She touched the circle of diamonds at her throat. It was a wedding present from Philip. His mother had taken the family heirloom with her rather than surrender it to Eileen Ryan, but she had been too honourable not to will it back to her son. All the Arbuthnot brides for the last hundred years had worn that necklace on their wedding day.

He said, "Aren't you supposed to wear that tomorrow?"

"Neil's given me the most marvellous pearl necklace. He's asked me to wear that instead."

There was a knock on the door. Sheena, the maid, came in to say, "The cars are comin' up the drive, miss," and they exited into the hall to greet the guests. Claire was unashamedly happy. Everyone kissed her and exclaimed over her dress and her father's wedding present.

Frank was disappointed to find himself seated far away from her at dinner, but he dismissed as imagination the feeling that Claudia was keeping them apart. After the meal Claire rushed upstairs to get Neil's pearls, then down again to show them to the guests. If only the bridegroom was different, Frank thought. If only this wedding meant she'd live in Ireland. Couldn't she look at that pompous old Colonel Fraser and see that Neil would end up like him? And why did she have to wear Neil's pearls instead of her own family heirloom?

When he was examining the necklace he was able to whisper to her, "Clarry, don't you know the superstition? Pearls are tears. You should wear Dad's present on your wedding day."

"You've been listening to the housemaids," she teased him. "Tears! Don't be silly, Frank. Besides, I'm wearing that sapphire pin you gave me. It's my 'something blue'."

"Are you? That's very sweet of you."

"It's like taking a bit of you down the aisle with me," she said quietly. "I love Neil, but it won't make any difference to us. You'll always be my best friend."

Philip watched them. How could his daughter be so fond of Frank? He would never understand how his son could inspire that degree of loyalty and affection.

MARIE DEMPSTER WAS AT THE BACK of the crowd that gathered outside the church in Naas. She had slept so badly the night before that the dark glasses were a comfort as well as a disguise. There was no need for Frank to have stayed at Riverstown. Risking a quarrel, she had told him so, reminding him of the way he'd been rejected because he refused to deny his mother's family.

"I don't have your bitter heart," he said. "This is my sister's wedding. Nothing is going to spoil her day. She hopes my father and I will make it up. I don't believe we will. But we'll all be together at home for that one night. If you see it as a betrayal, I see it as just good manners. Now, let's drop the subject."

Marie hadn't mentioned it again. But this morning she'd set out in the car to drive to Naas and see the famous wedding. To see the sister come out of the church in her white finery and stand there smiling, while she skulked in the crowd. It was self-torture, but Marie couldn't help it. There had been a brief shower and some threatening clouds, but they had lifted. The sun was shining as Claire stepped out of the doorway on her new husband's arm.

There was an official photographer, and Claire and Neil stood smiling and posing for a few minutes. Then they got into a big car festooned with white ribbons and drove off. Marie vanished before the guests came pouring out of the church. She couldn't risk Frank seeing her.

The reception went on long after the bride and groom had driven off to Dublin airport to fly to the south of France. Everyone kept saying what a grand party it had been. Claudia was tired, triumphant and happy. Claire was married, and from now on all would be well.

Frank went up to her. "That was a wonderful wedding, Claudia," he said. "You organized it all so well."

"It came together at the end," she said. "She looked a dream. He's such a sweetie; they'll be very happy."

"I hope so," he said. "I can't see my father. I want to say goodbye."

"Oh, must you rush off? Well, it's been a long day. There's Philip, over there talking to Colonel Fraser. Goodbye, Frank."

They didn't kiss or shake hands. "Goodbye, Claudia."

Colonel Fraser said, "Are you leaving? Oh, what a pity. It's been such a wonderful day. Wonderful wedding."

Philip hesitated. He didn't want his son to stay. And yet it mustn't become embarrassing for Neil's father. "Are you sure you can't stay?" he asked. "We've provided some kind of buffet for the hangers-on."

"No, I'm sorry," Frank said. "I've arranged something. I'll see you soon, Dad. Goodbye, Colonel."

"Nice lad," Fraser said. "Strong family likeness between you. I suppose he'll be the next to take the step, eh?"

Philip ignored the remark. He watched his son edge through the groups of guests, pausing to speak and then move on, till he left the marquee. It was at that moment that Philip realized he had lost his daughter, and was suddenly sad.

FRANK DIDN'T GO BACK TO MEATH. He stopped in the gateway of Riverstown and then turned towards Sallins. He too realized Claire was gone. He had noticed the little sapphire pin transferred from her wedding dress to her bright red suit as she came and kissed him goodbye. She wore a flowery hat that pricked his cheek. He would never forget that moment, because it finally changed his life, more fundamentally than his leaving Riverstown. Her love had always been his anchor. It hadn't lessened, but he was losing her. Fraser was taking her away to live in England and things could never be the same.

He drove through Sallins, slowing as he came to the railway bridge. There was the familiar figure of Donny, engrossed in his wait for the train. Donny didn't notice him or wave. Philip's last remark had been a slip of the tongue, Frank realized that. His father would never be cruel in a petty way. "We've provided some kind of buffet for the hangers-on." Still, his father *had* let him go off alone while the spongers were made welcome.

Frank didn't want Marie, who'd be waiting, trying to hide her jealousy, when he got home. He swung left and pulled up in front of the Half House. It looked warm and friendly, with lights blazing in all the windows.

Kevin Ryan opened the door to him. "Frankie!" he exclaimed. "This is a turn-up for the book—come in, come in!"

Frank said simply, "Can I take a drink off you, Uncle?"

Kevin saw the morning suit and knew he'd come directly from the wedding party at Riverstown.

"You can take supper and a bed for the night if you want," he said. The door closed firmly behind them both.

By the time he went to bed, Frank was drunk—anaesthetized was the right description. Feeling no pain, as the English would say, and then bray their empty laughter afterwards. He hated them. He hated the man who had taken his sister from him. He hated his stepmother, because she had encouraged the whole thing. He hated his father, because he hadn't ever been as kind to him as his poor dead mother's brother Kevin. But he didn't feel hurt any more that night, thanks to Kevin's whiskey.

234

THE BOSTON IRISH BANK opened with a large cocktail party on the evening of July 15. The chairmen of the Bank of Ireland and of the Allied Irish Bank were present, as were members of the Dail from both political parties, and investors from the United States. Marie, who had been appointed Frank's personal secretary and assistant, had made all the arrangements.

Sean Filey was among the guests. He stood in the main hall of the handsome Georgian building in Merrion Square with one of the investors from Boston. He noticed how smoothly Marie moved among the guests. She had changed, he thought, changed as fast as only a woman can when she adopts a different life-style. There was little of the Dublin secretary visible in the beautifully dressed woman playing hostess to the top men in Irish business and politics. She looked happy and self-assured. An actress revelling in a star part. Only Filey knew that the audience was just one man. She had become obsessed with Frank Arbuthnot. Everything she did was to gain his approval and draw him closer.

Filey saw the insecurity behind the facade. Most of all he saw the absence of emotional love in Frank Arbuthnot. Generous, yes: she had a red Mercedes, expensive jewellery, even the ultimate bourgeois status symbol, a mink coat. He was kind and considerate. He gave her the type of respect that a man gives to a woman he doesn't love, just because he doesn't love her. Sean was interrupted in his analysis by the American beside him.

"Well, we're off to a helluva good start. Kevin promised and Kevin delivered. He always does."

The opening was a great success. There was wide coverage in the newspapers and on television. The new merchant bank was well supported in Ireland, and its American affiliates were men of wealth and social prominence. Senator Ryan was on the board, but he kept a very low profile. He refused all interviews, saying he was in Ireland as a private citizen. A week after the bank opened, he returned to the States.

At the end of September, Frank Arbuthnot joined his uncle in Boston. Marie stayed in Ireland to finalize the transfer of the money to the Middle East via Italy and finally Lucerne, before Frank arranged its channel through to clients in the bank. The shipment of arms would set out from Holland as soon as the payment was completed. There were new servants at Meath, the Brogans, whom Sean had recommended to Frank. A good couple, Sean told him, very honest and reliable. He did not tell him that the Brogans' son had been arrested for possessing explosives and was known to be a dangerous man.

The money for the arms deal went through, and the shipment came into Ulster via a fishing boat. There was a notable rise in attacks on British troops during the next six months.

Frank Arbuthnot was committed now beyond any hope of opting out.

Over the next few years his life assumed a regular pattern. He made three trips a year to the States on bank business. Once he took Marie with him, and they flew down to Florida for a holiday. But when they were at home, they both worked a five-day week in Merrion Square.

In the meantime, there were regular secret meetings in the house on the airport road. Frank didn't know that Marie's visits to her family or to see old friends were a cover for her attendance at those meetings.

CHAPTER 7

Marie Dempster had been living with Frank Arbuthnot in Meath for five years. She was the mistress of the house and could do what she liked, change what she wanted, and he never demurred. But the photograph of Claire Fraser stood inviolate in its silver frame in the bedroom. Once she had put it away. He hadn't been in the room five minutes before he noticed.

"Don't you dare touch that!" he had exploded at her. She hadn't made that mistake again. But she hated the smiling image more than ever. Frank was isolated from his family: his sister lived in England, and he had been totally rejected by his own father. He should have turned to her and responded to her love for him. But he didn't. He gave her presents and had settled money on her, but he had never said he loved her. As the years passed she had become more jealous and insecure. Every time Frank went over to England to see his sister, Marie nearly went mad. And now, after two miscarriages, Claire was having her first baby and he was due to fly over as soon as it was born.

"DARLING," NEIL FRASER SAID, "what a clever girl you are."

He held Claire's hand. She opened her eyes and smiled at him. He thought she looked more beautiful than ever, but very tired and pale, with a luminous softness that touched him deeply. As deeply as the sight of his baby son.

"He's sweet, isn't he?" she said. "Are you glad it's a boy? I knew you wanted one."

"I'm just glad it's a healthy baby," Neil admitted. "I kept thinking while I was waiting downstairs, I don't care about anything so long as Claire's all right. I love you so much."

She saw that there were tears in his eyes. She was surprised. She had imagined him being proud and pleased, but not like this. He was more emotional than she had ever seen him. I'm very lucky, she thought. I should be glowing with happiness, but I'm not. I'm just very tired. I'll glow tomorrow, I expect.

"Have you rung everyone?" she asked.

He nodded. "Father's delighted, and I got through to Claudia and Philip. They're thrilled. They're flying over tomorrow."

Claire said after a moment, "Did you let Frank know?"

"There wasn't time. I came straight in to see you as soon as I'd spoken to Claudia. I'll do it later."

"Don't worry." She squeezed his hand. "I'll ring him. Why don't you go home, darling? You've been here all night."

He kissed her. "He'll be a great little chap," he murmured. "Now you sleep and I'll be round at lunchtime."

She turned to watch him to the door; he paused before closing it and waved almost shyly at her. Then she was alone. The whole wrenching experience had left her numb and shocked. But she wouldn't say so to Neil. She stretched out her hand and touched the bell. The nurse came in very quickly. Claire said, "I'd like the telephone plugged in, please."

Ten minutes later she was speaking to Frank in Ireland.

"You're an uncle," she said. "Little boy, and he's fine . . . I'm OK. Well, it wasn't much fun. Don't ever have a baby if you can help it . . . No, of course I'm all right. I'm not crying . . . Frank, when are you coming over? I wish you were here now." The tears were rolling down her face, soaking the pillow. "Neil's thrilled. Everyone's thrilled except me . . . I feel as flat as a pancake. I don't know what's the matter with me . . . No, Mum and Dad will be over tomorrow . . . I don't care. I want you to come, please. You're the godfather, remember. How's Ireland? Give it my love." She didn't understand why, but she had never needed him as much as she did now, and he was miles away, across the Irish Sea.

The nurse opened the door. "Mrs. Fraser, I think you should go to sleep now."

Claire didn't have the energy to argue. "I'll ring off now," she said. "Let me know when you're coming. Goodbye, Frank, love."

Marie had been listening to the telephone conversation. She came forward with lying words of congratulation, but Frank didn't seem to hear them.

"There's something wrong," he said.

Hope flared in her. "Oh, no! Your sister's all right, isn't she? Is it the baby?"

"The baby's fine. But Claire was crying when she rang off."

Marie said, "Oh, I shouldn't worry about that. Lots of women cry after they've had a baby. It's quite normal."

"Not Claire. I know my sister. I'd better go to London right away."

"If she's depressed," Marie said after a moment, "surely her husband's the one to deal with it."

He said suddenly, "You're right. But she won't tell him. She'll put a brave face on it. We had a cousin who had post-natal depression. She was ill for three years. I'll speak to him."

At the end of the week Frank flew to London. Claudia and Philip had only just gone back to Ireland, and Claire was about to go home from the hospital. She was feeling a lot better. The sense of sinking misery had stopped, thanks to the prompt treatment that resulted from Frank's warning telephone call to Neil. The pills and the therapy were working, but when she saw Frank the last cloud lifted and she laughed with real joy. She called for the baby and felt quite moved for the first time when she held him. She talked and talked about the birth, as if now she could speak the truth and not pretend that she hadn't hated it and been afraid. Frank stayed beside her, his finger caught in the sleeping baby's tiny fist.

At last Claire sank back and said, "I've nearly burst keeping all that in!" And Frank knew she was not in danger any more.

Outside the room he met Neil. They shook hands, chatted for a while, and then Neil turned and went inside. He saw the brightness in Claire's face, and his heart was light for the first time since the baby's birth. She was better, but his relief was mixed with pain. She had turned to her brother for help. For all they were married, and had a child, Claire still didn't really belong to him.

THE CHILD WAS CHRISTENED Peter Francis Hugh in the old Norman church in Gloucester. Neil's father was there, and Claudia and Philip came over from Ireland for the weekend.

Frank was in America, but he sent a cable and gave a handsome Irish silver mug. He was right not to come; Claire accepted that. Neil was secretly relieved that his son's christening would not be an occasion for an Arbuthnot family confrontation. Frank and his father were not on speaking terms. Personally, he thought it incredible for Philip to cut his only son out of his will because they disagreed about politics, but Ireland was such a mixture of muddle and prejudice that none of it made sense.

Claire was in blooming health after a holiday in Portugal. She was more beautiful than ever, he thought proudly, watching her against the background of a sunny English garden, holding Peter and chatting with her parents. She was the perfect wife for a rising politician. Now that his personal life was settled into a routine—wife, baby, country house and London flat—Neil was concentrating intensely on his career. It was the best way of forgetting that in spite of everything a gap had opened up between him and Claire since the baby's birth. A stranger lurked behind her ready smile. He was aware of it even on this special day, when the sun shone and his child cheeped like a contented nestling in Claire's arms. But he was a man who despised self-pity. Work was the cure for self-doubt.

From the day of the christening Neil set himself a new priority. He was going to rise in the Tory party. His son was almost a year old when Neil Fraser was made a junior minister. One month later there was a story in *The Times* with a photograph of his brother-in-law, Frank Arbuthnot, addressing an audience in New York on behalf of Noraid, with some notorious IRA supporters perched in a row on the platform behind him.

Neil knew Claire had seen it. He waited for her to comment, but she never said a word. She lunched with him at the House of Commons and sat through a debate in the afternoon, as he was making a speech. She was there but not with him, as if she could avoid the issue of what her brother's public statement must mean to Neil's career. After the debate his minister spoke to him privately. He would be expected to make a firm disavowal of his brother-in-law in the House that evening. The issue of security was already being raised in the press, and the powerful pro-Unionist faction in the Tory party, quite apart from the members from Ulster themselves, would hound him unless he could convince them that he and his wife had severed all ties with an avowed enemy of Britain. The words "and your wife" were spoken with emphasis.

On his way home to dinner, before returning to the House, he wondered how he was going to open the subject with Claire.

It was the first serious quarrel they had ever had. It began with Neil being calm and reasonable. He described the interview with the minister and the ordeal he would be facing in a few hours' time. He asked why she had ignored something she knew must have a serious effect upon his political standing. He saw by her face that he wasn't going to get an answer.

He began to shout. "Claire, don't you understand? This isn't some family feud we're talking about—this is my whole career! It's been laid on the line for me. My wife's brother is an open supporter of the Provisional IRA. I've got to condemn him in public in the House."

He paused and tried to calm himself. "You've got to endorse the condemnation," he said. "I've got to say that *we* reject everything Frank says and stands for."

He poured himself a drink and sat down.

"So you're going to make the statement," Claire said. "If you want to include me in it, I can't stop you. I hope it'll be enough."

"Don't you care that what he's done has put me in the most impossible position? No." He shook his head slowly. "He comes first with you, doesn't he?"

He waited, afraid that she might destroy everything between them by telling him the truth. But she didn't. She came over and sat down beside him. "Of course I care about you and what this means to you," she said. "When I saw the paper this morning, I thought, Now Frank's made it all public, and what's Neil going to say? I don't agree with Frank, but I know why he thinks what he is doing is right. I understand the way he feels."

He said slowly, "Supposing you're asked, right out. What are you going to say?"

"That I've nothing to add to my husband's statement."

"It would help if you came to the House this evening. It would strengthen what I've got to say."

"I can't," she said. "I can't sit there and hear my brother denounced. Not even for your career. I'll go to Gloucestershire tonight. You'll do better without me here, till this blows over."

Claire was on her way to the country when Neil made a statement that caught the headlines the next morning. It was one of the most scathing denunciations of the IRA and its methods ever heard in the House of Commons. And as a result of that speech, Neil Fraser emerged with his reputation enhanced.

FRANK NOTICED THAT CLAIRE was pregnant once more as soon as he saw her. She had arrived first in the Gloucestershire pub, and when she got up to meet him her condition was obvious.

They hadn't met for nearly three months. When they did see each other, they varied their meeting places. Sometimes it was London, but he was uneasy about her being recognized there. He didn't want to cause trouble for her with Neil. And trouble there had been after the famous speech, the first time she told Neil that she was seeing her brother. After that, Claire and Frank had made their arrangements in secret.

"Claire," he said. "You're pregnant again!"

"Quite right," she said, and smiled at him. "Nearly five months. Peter is dying for a brother or sister. Remember the fun we used to have when we were little?"

He said gently, "Of course I remember. But are you feeling all right? Not too sick?"

"Not sick at all," Claire answered. "It will be different this time. I've checked with the doctor and I'm going to be fine. All I had was a minor fit of the baby blues, and the minute you came over I cheered up. Tell me, how's everything at home?"

By home she meant Ireland. Riverstown wasn't mentioned by either of them now. It only spoiled their few hours together.

"Much the same as usual," Frank told her. "Nothing really changes. It's very expensive, inflation's gone mad. How are things with you?"

Claire looked at him. "Between Neil and me, you mean? Up and down. That's why I thought another baby would be a good idea. I haven't made him very happy, I'm afraid."

Frank said, "You mean he hasn't made *you* happy. Why don't you pull out before it's too late?"

"You mean leave him? Don't be silly, Frank. I'd never walk out on Neil. Quite apart from Peter and the new baby, what would I do?"

"Come home where you belong," he said slowly. "Start again. I'd look after you. You'd find someone else, who was one of us. I mean it. Life's too short to be unhappy. He'd get over it."

240

"I shouldn't have said anything." She pushed back the chair. "Don't talk to me about leaving him, Frank. I won't. He loves me, and it would break his heart. Come on, let's go and have lunch and talk about something cheerful."

Towards the end of the meal she said, "Frank, I've got to ask you. Are you sure you're right, supporting the Provos now? They've done some terrible things lately. Do you really believe it's the right way?"

He hesitated. "I don't think it's right to go as far as they've gone, no. I've had some pretty basic doubts since the Mountbatten murder. And I've said so."

"Frank, isn't it dangerous saying things like that? If anyone thinks you're changing sides?"

"There's no question of that," Frank insisted. "I believe in a united Ireland. I want to see the British army out of Ulster. There's a war going on up there, whatever people over here try to make out, and the soldiers are fair game." He leaned towards her. "It's killing civilians that shakes me. I'll tell you something."

"What?" she asked.

"I went to see a Catholic priest. Old Father Gorman."

Claire knew the parish priest in Sallins, a kindly old man who had been the spiritual mentor of every servant at Riverstown as far back as she could remember.

"Frank, what on earth did you say to him?"

"I told him about being baptized a Catholic. We talked about my feelings for Ireland and the conflict of not knowing where I really belonged. I asked him if he thought I should study the Catholic faith and see if it would help me."

"I'll bet he jumped at that!" she said.

"No, he didn't. He said that if I was genuinely interested, he'd be glad to give me instruction. But not while I supported violence against my fellow men. I never went back. But I got the message. It wasn't at all what I'd expected."

"Frank, how could Father Gorman cope with the problems of someone like you?"

He said gently, "I thought he coped with them rather well."

"Oh, I wish I didn't live here!" she exclaimed. "If I was near, you wouldn't even have thought of going to see Father Gorman and listening to his mumbo jumbo!" She saw the expression on his face. "I'm sorry, I didn't mean that."

"Of course you meant it; that's the way you were brought up. So was I. Being a Protestant was part of being in the establishment. I remember our father actually saying it about someone he knew who'd changed over: 'No gentleman in Ireland is a Catholic.' I thought, Why not? Just because it's the native religion—the peasant's Church. It's the same old system, them

241

and us. You should try and see things without prejudice and not go on repeating the old bigotry."

Claire fumbled in her bag. Her eyes had filled with tears. "Darling Frank," she said, "I'm so sorry. I'm a tactless idiot. I'll never talk like that again."

He smiled and she was instantly forgiven. "Oh, yes, you will," he countered.

Outside the pub, he helped her into her car. He bent down to the window. "Look after yourself," he said. "And please don't worry about me. I know what I'm doing. Write to me, won't you?"

"Yes, I will." She looked up at him. It always hurt to say goodbye.

He watched the car move off, and waved. He didn't notice the two men sitting in a Ford Escort in the car park. One of them noted the time on his pad. They followed Frank as he drove back to London. Every meeting he made was monitored, but the only ones of significance concerned the junior minister's wife. Sooner or later Neil Fraser would have to be told.

WHEN LUCY WAS BORN, early in 1980, Neil was away on a fact-finding tour of the Middle East. Claire had gone into labour two weeks early. Claudia flew over as soon as she heard; Philip was not feeling well. He had just got over a very bad cold, and he was tired. Claire had had an easy delivery. Neil sent flowers and telephoned, but he couldn't break off his tour. It was a calm and happy occurrence and she liked feeding the little girl. She had been unable to feed Peter.

It was comforting having Claudia there. She moved into the Gloucestershire house and took charge of everything. When Claire came home from the hospital after five days, she was delighted to find a new nanny installed and her mother presiding over the household as if she'd managed it all her life.

Claudia enjoyed herself until Neil came back. Then she was off, she declared, and nothing would persuade her to stay. "The last thing a man wants when he gets back is to find his mother-in-law stuck in front of him," she said.

There had been a letter from Ireland and a big basket of flowers delivered to the house. They came from Frank, but Claudia didn't comment. There was nothing to be said about him now. He had put himself beyond the pale, and she considered his behaviour utterly despicable. Thank goodness Claire was happy with a nice new baby and a fine husband. He really was going to go right up the ladder. One day he might be in line for prime minister.

When Claudia got back to Riverstown, she found Philip in bed. He'd had a dizzy spell while he was walking in the garden. Billy Cavanagh had helped him back to the house, and the doctor advised him to rest. It was

242

nothing to worry about, he insisted. Claudia didn't fuss but spoke to the doctor. The dizzy spell had been a slight heart attack.

Two months later Philip died in his sleep.

"YOU'LL NEVER BELIEVE IT, but he's going to that funeral!"

Sean Filey knew Marie had a furious temper. But this was different. She was slit-eyed with rage. It made her look ugly.

"It's his father," he remarked. "Of course he'll go. Why do you care?" He knew very well why. He knew that the years had fed her jealousy until she was possessed by it and blind to reason.

"His father," she mocked. "A father who cut him out of his will, treated him like dirt all his life. He ought to be celebrating!"

"Perhaps he is," Sean suggested. "Going to the funeral doesn't mean he's sorry. I still don't see what it's got to do with you."

She stared at him and then said something that surprised him.

"Because if he was heart and soul with us, he'd spit on the grave before he went! I'll tell you why it's to do with me, and it's to do with you too. I don't trust him."

Filey said slowly, "What are you saying?"

She slumped into a chair. "You've heard him say we shouldn't hit civilian targets. I've heard him say more than that. He's got doubts, Sean." She raised her head and looked him in the eye.

Filey said quietly, "Why haven't you reported this before?"

She had gone further than she meant to because she was goaded by anger. But it was the truth, and she thought bitterly, Why should I protect him . . . after last night?

"I wanted to be sure," Marie answered. "After we got Mountbatten, he was moody, not himself at all."

"He's still passing the funds through," Filey said. "So he's still useful. But for how long, I wonder? I'll have to report this to the council." He looked at her and said, "You've told me the truth? You're not condemning him for reasons of your own, are you?"

She got up. "If you think that, then go on trusting him till he turns us all in."

When she had gone, Filey stayed on in the house at Santry. He made himself a cup of tea. She was insanely jealous. Jealousy could warp a personality until the person couldn't see truth from lies. Or vengeance from loyalty. But he couldn't deny that recently Arbuthnot had reacted badly to civilian casualties in the North. There was no place for scruples in a desperate struggle. If the shift in Frank Arbuthnot's attitude was fundamental, then something might have to be done about him.

As she drove back to Meath, Marie could not stop thinking about the fight she'd had with Frank the night before. She couldn't forget the dislike in his eyes or the angry dismissal as he slammed out of the room and went to sleep elsewhere. "Keep your tongue off my sister!" he'd shouted. "If you ever say a word against her again, you can get out and stay out!"

Marie knew that she had to try to mend their quarrel. The truth was, she couldn't imagine life without him.

He was not there when she opened the front door. She called, and the housekeeper, Mrs. Brogan, hurried out into the hallway.

"Where's Mr. Arbuthnot?"

"He's away over to Kildare. He'll be in for dinner."

Marie nodded and went upstairs to their bedroom. Kildare. That's a laugh! Claire had arrived for the funeral, that was it. That sister of his had come over, and he'd gone to meet her. She sat down in front of the dressing table. She could have swept all the lotions and bottles onto the floor and smashed the lot.

He'd made her suffer so much. He'd tortured her for years with his love for his sister. Looking in the mirror as if she were face to face with her own soul, a terrible thought came to Marie. She loved Frank, but she'd gone to Sean to do him harm. If Sean believed her, anything might happen. And it might be a relief.

Mrs. Brogan met him when he came in. "Miss Dempster's upstairs. She asked if you'd go up."

He'd spent the day making arrangements for his father's funeral. Claudia was far more shocked by Philip's death than she admitted. Neil couldn't come to the funeral, because it wasn't safe for him to be in Ireland, even for a few hours. Frank sensed how much Claudia wished it was her son-in-law taking the responsibility rather than him. Claire was only flying in and out on the day of the funeral. In spite of himself, Frank was conscious of grief. He had loved the father who had never loved him. He had forgotten about Marie. The night before, he'd slept in a spare room after a sickening scene. She had flared up at him, spewing her poisonous jealousy about his family, lashing out at Claire, whom she had never even met. When he came down next morning she had gone. Now she was back. He supposed he had better go and see what could be salvaged from the relationship. On his part, not very much, he suspected.

He went upstairs. When he came into the room, Marie ran into his arms, begging him to forgive her. There was nothing else he could do. But he refused to let her tempt him into bed. And later, sitting opposite him at dinner, Marie knew that she had lost her only hold on him.

THE SUN SHONE AT PHILIP'S FUNERAL. The service was dignified, with moving readings and Philip's favourite hymn, "Abide with Me". After the burial in Naas cemetery the congregation went to Riverstown for lunch. People were polite to Frank, but not warm. He had betrayed his father's class and lifelong convictions.

The lunch went on until late afternoon. Claire had to fly back to

London, and Claudia was going to friends in Cork, as she couldn't possibly be left alone in the house. As the last of the guests were leaving, Claudia came up to Frank. She looked very haggard and old, in spite of the make-up. She hadn't cried during the funeral. She wasn't the kind of woman to make a public display. She had done her crying in private. "Thank you for arranging everything," she said. "Your father would have been pleased."

He said, "I'm sorry he's dead. I'm sorry so much went wrong between him and me, but I want you to know I'm here if you need anything."

Claudia wished he'd go. He was driving Claire to the airport. She had seemed stunned and silent all through the day. Claudia didn't want to talk to him about his father. The house was full of Philip, as if his spirit had stayed behind. Later it would be gone. Later she could come back and resume her life. He was sorry, he said. He looked unhappy, she admitted. She had noticed their friends giving him the cold shoulder in a subtle way. What a pity, she thought, but bad blood will out. He has only himself to blame for being the outsider on this day. He was so like Philip as a young man, standing in front of her. So alike, and yet quite different.

"Frank," she said, "you know there's nothing for you in the will. But if there's anything you want out of the house, please let me know. Some of the pictures . . ." She let the sentence die.

"Thank you. It's kind of you to offer. But I don't want anything."

"Think about it," Claudia insisted. "You may change your mind. Now, if you're going to drive Claire to the airport, you ought to go."

In the car, Claire took off her black hat. The sun made a bright halo of the blonde hair. "I feel numb," she said. "I can't believe I'll never see him again. I loved him, Frank; you know that. But it was never quite the same after what he did to you. If Mum wills me Riverstown, I'm going to give it straight to you."

"I wouldn't want it. I'm happy at Meath."

"What are your plans?" she asked him.

"Nothing special. I'm very busy. I've a trip planned to the States in the autumn."

Claire looked at him. "You're not going to speak at another rally, are you?"

He didn't answer. "You couldn't get away, I suppose? I'd love to take you round the east coast."

"I don't think Neil would like it. What a stupid world we live in! There we are, me not able to come back to my own country except I've got to fly in and out like a criminal, and you not able to come and stay with me because of my husband's career. We meet in pubs and talk on the phone when he's out. I'm fed up with it, Frank. I'm the perfect minister's wife, with the two regulation children and the manor house with swimming pool. Sometimes I'd give my soul for a bit of Irish mess and madness!"

As he turned in to the airport he saw that her eyes were full of unshed tears.

"With Dad gone and everything different, I feel so lost. And nothing makes up for it. Don't get out; say goodbye to me here. I don't want all that waving goodbye in the departure lounge."

He put an arm round her. "Goodbye, Clarry. You made up to Dad for everything. Remember that and don't grieve. I'll ring you in a couple of days. When's a good time?"

"Any time," Claire said. "I'm finished pretending." She got out of the car and hurried into the airport without looking back.

THREE MEN MET AT THE HOUSE on the airport road: Sean Filey; Jim Quinlan, a dour man who was his superior and a guard on the Irish Railways; and Hugh Macbride, who'd come down from the North for the meeting that Filey had called to discuss Frank Arbuthnot.

Macbride was impatient. "If Arbuthnot's turned lily-livered, get rid of him!"

Filey said coldly, "Your money supply will dry up if we do."

Macbride shouted, "We're already running short of funds. America's dried up since Mountbatten."

Quinlan protested. "Give it a few more months for public opinion to settle," he said. "Noraid will get the cash flowing through to us again."

"We haven't got a few months," Macbride snapped. "With no money coming through, we've had to halt operations. We've been offered a big shipment. It's a new supplier, and he wants the money first. We need a hundred thousand pounds by the end of June. I'm asking you to get the money for us."

"How? A hundred thousand—how the devil are we going to get that?" Quinlan demanded.

Macbride glared at him. "Rob one of your fat Dublin banks."

After a silence Sean Filey said, "You've got banks in Ulster."

"We've got fortresses," Macbride argued. "It'd take an army to get near one of them."

There was another silence. Then Quinlan said, "If we do it, we'll need Arbuthnot to bank the money and launder it."

"A fine time to have doubts about him," Macbride said.

"Doubts or not, he's the only one we've got," Quinlan retorted. "We're not risking our lads just to have them picked up at the border with the money on them. It goes through the usual channels, and your man can be paid in Monte Carlo."

"You'll get the money, then?" Hugh Macbride demanded.

"You'll have it," Quinlan promised. "The how and the where you can leave to us."

The meeting broke up, and Sean offered Quinlan a ride to the centre of

246

Dublin. In the car, Quinlan said, "How much of what Marie said about Arbuthnot do you believe? Can we trust him?"

Sean weighed his answer. "I think she's part right, but only part. He hasn't liked some of the things we've had to do. But he's been straight with me and said so. I think we can rely on him for one more major contribution. After that . . ." He shrugged.

He dropped Quinlan off at Heuston Station and went on to his practice in Fitzwilliam Square.

NEIL'S OFFICIAL CAR met Claire at Heathrow. The driver explained that the minister was delayed in London and would be coming up to Gloucestershire later, by train. When she came into the house, the drawing-room door opened and there was Michael Harvey. And her son Peter, in his pyjamas, holding on to his hand.

"I hope you don't mind," the major said. "Neil asked me to spend a couple of days with you. I got leave unexpectedly."

"I'm so glad you're here," she told Harvey as she came and kissed her son. "You know where I've been."

"I know," he said quietly. "I'm so sorry. Come on, Peter, old chap, you promised to go to bed when your mummy arrived."

She watched her son scamper happily up the stairs. "He's mad about you, Michael," she said. "Let's have a drink, and then I'll go and change out of this awful black."

He gave her an unusually stiff drink, she noticed. He sat down and said, "Neil rang about half an hour ago wanting to know if you'd got back yet. He was very upset he couldn't go with you."

"He shouldn't be," she answered. "He can't go to Ireland even for a funeral, in case someone throws a bomb at him. Any more than I could stay a night with my mother. She had to go to friends. I'm so bored with it all; do let's talk about something else."

When Neil came in, he thought Claire seemed quite relaxed, thanks to Michael Harvey. He was a good buffer when tension rose between them. And he was someone Neil could talk to.

After dinner Claire excused herself and went to bed. The two men stayed up talking. When Neil went upstairs, his wife was asleep and he was careful not to wake her, although what he most wanted was to take her in his arms and ask her all about her father's funeral, to comfort her as deeply as he knew she was hurt. But the moment had eluded him, as it so often did these days, and she slipped a little further away from him as a result.

The following evening, in Michael Harvey's hearing, Claire telephoned Frank in Ireland. Harvey left the room. His two days' unexpected leave was neither leave nor unexpected. He had been chosen, as a friend Neil Fraser trusted, to tell the minister that his wife was meeting Frank Arbuthnot in secret when he came over to England. Harvey saw at that moment that Claire had made it easy for him. He went out to the garden, where Neil was sitting in the warm dusk smoking a cigar.

After they'd spoken Harvey asked, "How much do you tell her about what's going on?"

Neil said slowly, "Confidential stuff, do you mean? Nothing. And she never asks. She's not interested. She'd never pass it on."

"Not intentionally," Harvey said. "But it's amazing what someone can let drop without realizing it."

Neil smoked on in silence. "You say she didn't make any bones about ringing him up just now?" he asked after a time.

"None at all. I think she wanted me to hear. Probably wants you to know, too. That's a very good sign, believe me."

"If you say so. I'm not sure. I should have gone to that funeral. I should have told the security people to stuff it, and gone."

Harvey agreed with him, but he didn't say so. "And what would have happened if you'd been targeted and they'd made their hit? I'll bet there was a plan in case you turned up in Riverstown. Someone, somewhere, was waiting to take a shot at you if you showed up. If Claire's blaming you, then it's time someone pointed out the facts of life to her. Would you like me to do that?"

"Thanks, but no. She'd see it as criticism of her brother."

"WHY DID YOU LIE TO ME?" Neil had joined Claire in their bedroom.

Claire didn't flinch. "I had to; the last time I told you we'd met, you went through the roof. How do you think I feel, not being able to see my brother openly?"

"I don't know how you feel any more. But don't lie to me next time he sneaks over to see you. It'll save a lot of embarrassment."

"All right, then you can tell your spies they don't have to watch me any more."

"They're not my spies," Neil Fraser said. "They're watching your brother because he's an enemy of this country, and a number of people have been killed by the people he supports. I was threatened myself, if you remember. See him if you have to, but don't put me in the position of not knowing, next time."

He closed the door of their room and went out. He hadn't told her that Michael Harvey was his informant.

CHAPTER 8

It took two months for Jim Quinlan to plan the robbery on the Kildare Street branch of the Bank of Ireland, which was to take place early on a Friday afternoon. Sean Filey was informed of the robbery, but not involved in the planning. His role was to watch Arbuthnot, via Marie and the Brogans, and to keep him in line until the money was in hand and could be paid into the Boston Irish Bank. The first thing Sean did was to telephone Kevin Ryan and ask him to cancel Frank's trip to Boston. It would be a big help to a project on hand if Kevin came to Ireland instead. His nephew was in need of moral support. Kevin listened and said he'd think about it. Moral support had only one meaning. Frank was wavering. Kevin wasn't surprised. He remembered how shocked Mary Rose had been by the violence in the North and the murder of the Queen of England's cousin. Kevin had trimmed his sails to the wind of public opinion and cancelled a speaking tour. It might be good for Frank if he went over to Ireland, and good for him too. His own batteries needed recharging. He called Sean Filey back and said he'd come and stay for a few weeks at the Half House. He'd set his nephew straight at the same time.

It was a beautiful spring. The land burgeoned into its dazzling greenery, the hedgerows spilling over with clouds of white may. It was the time of year that Frank loved best. The daffodils would be ablaze at Riverstown now, and the river in full flood. He thought of his home; whatever he had said to Claire, his grandmother's house was no substitute for the place where he had grown up.

And Marie's presence was becoming a burden at Meath. He didn't look forward to coming home with her in the evenings and pretending that their relationship hadn't changed. She grated on him, because she was tense and insincere; most of all he recognized that she was miserably unhappy, and that he was the cause.

It was mid-May, and they were driving back from the Curragh together. As they approached the Sallins railway bridge Frank slowed down.

"There's old Donny. I'll just say hello and give him a few bob."

"Who's Donny?" she asked.

"He's a simple old fellow, loves to stand and watch the train come through from Dublin. He's been on that bridge as long as I can remember. When Claire and I were children we used to give him some of our sweets."

He pulled up. Marie frowned. There was a dirty figure in a torn sweater leaning over the parapet.

Frank called out, "Donny!" and the man turned and waved. His mouth was slack and his eyes were watery. Frank opened the car door.

"Come and say hello," he said to Marie. "It'd make his day."

Marie got out reluctantly.

Frank said, "Donny, this is Miss Dempster, a friend of mine."

He grinned at her, and a trickle of saliva ran down his chin.

She said briefly, "Hello, Donny. Frank darling, come on."

"When's Claire comin' back?" she heard him ask.

"Soon," Frank assured him. "Here's a pound. Buy yourself a packet of cigarettes. Take care now."

"God bless ye," Donny said. "There'll be a train in a minute."

Frank got back into the car. Marie was already in her seat. "Poor devil," he said. "He lives for the sight of a train."

Marie grimaced. "He's so filthy. Why do you bother giving him money? He'll only go to the pub."

"Donny's never been in a pub in his life. He's harmless. Everyone round here knows him."

Frank saw the look of disgust on her face. For all her political convictions, there wasn't room in her heart for one helpless child of nature. He thought suddenly, That's why I could never love her. She has no compassion.

When they got home, he asked her to come into the drawing room and sit down. He gave her a drink.

"Marie," he said quietly, "it's no good between us any more. You know it and I know it. It's time we talked this out." She was very pale. "We've had some wonderful times," he went on, "but it hasn't been right for a long time."

"You're not in love with me," she said. "That's the reason."

"I've never said I was," he reminded her.

"The trouble is, you care more about your sister than me. She's the only one that matters."

Frank didn't move. She waited, having dealt the dagger blow, but nothing happened.

After a moment he said, "I want you out of this house tomorrow. I also want you out of the bank. From tomorrow." He turned and walked out, closing the door behind him.

Marie stood alone in the room, marooned in the silence. He'd given her notice as if she were a servant. For a moment she thought she was going to be sick then and there.

She had aimed at his heart and succeeded only in mortally wounding herself. Upstairs, Frank undressed and went into the spare room to sleep. He didn't know who disgusted him more, Marie, or himself for having been involved with such a woman. By tomorrow she would be gone. And something fundamental would change in his life when she was out of it.

Marie packed some clothes and told the Brogans she was going to visit relatives in Galway. She couldn't take everything in one suitcase. The accumulation of their years together needed trunks. She'd send for the rest later. But now she wanted to get out of the house, to think and plan.

Plan what explanation to give to Sean Filey and his superiors as to why she had lost her position at the Boston Irish Bank. They wouldn't like it if they thought she'd brought it on herself. She'd have to find another reason, something that would take the blame off her and lay it squarely on Arbuthnot. She thought of him as Arbuthnot now. No more as Frank.

Hating him was a relief. She'd make him pay for the rejection, and that insulting dismissal.

As she drove towards Dublin in the smart BMW sports model Frank had bought her for Christmas, the thought came to her that there must be a way to punish that sister as well.

She stayed in a suburban hotel for a whole day before she put a call through to Sean Filey. By that time she had worked out her story to the last detail.

KEVIN HAD ARRIVED at the Half House with Mary Rose. He was happy to be home; the splendid house always gladdened his heart.

One of the first calls to come for him was from Sean Filey. "We've got trouble with your nephew," Filey said. "He's thrown Marie out of the house and the bank. He's in a dangerous frame of mind. And you're the one to steady him."

Kevin hesitated. It sounded bad. Bad for his nephew, too. He was fond of Frank. "I'll call him," he said. "Leave him to me."

"IT'S JUST WONDERFUL to see you, Frank." Mary Rose smiled at him. He was glad to see her and Kevin. They were his family. He could always relax with them.

They had a long lunch, and Kevin eased him into a confidential mood with wine and gentle banter. Then he signalled to Mary Rose that he wanted to be alone with his nephew.

"Things have been bad in the North, I hear," Kevin began.

"They've been bad down here, too," Frank said. Suddenly he spoke his mind. "Killing Mountbatten—why did they do it? Why did they blow up that boat and kill those poor devils? Don't they know that's no way to win public support? What was a war in the North for freedom and justice is becoming more and more a terrorist campaign."

Kevin said reasonably, "I know how you feel, Frank. But let's look at the record. The struggle in the North has been going on for years. People in Britain and America are taking it for granted. It doesn't make the headlines any more. The killing of that fellow Mountbatten and the others—well, it served its purpose. It showed them we can strike anyone, any time, no matter who they are! And we can't give in. We've got to win; don't you see that?"

"Yes," Frank answered. "I do see it. I've helped the cause and I'll go on helping. There's a big payment coming in soon. I'm going to deal with it. Nothing alters my commitment. But I'll speak my mind when I see something rotten creeping into us."

"Speaking your mind to me is one thing, Frank," his uncle said. "But I'd be careful not to shoot your mouth off anywhere else."

Frank said, "Is that a warning? If it is, I won't take it."

Kevin changed his tone. "I'm just giving you advice, that's all. How's Marie?"

"We've split up," Frank said. "And she's left the bank."

"That's a pity. I thought she was a fine girl. Isn't her leaving the bank a bit awkward for you?"

"No. It would have been more awkward having her there."

"What's the next big payment, Frankie?" he asked.

"Sean says it's a hundred thousand pounds," he answered. "It's due in at the end of next week."

Ryan asked the question Frank had asked Sean Filey. "That's a lot of money. Where's it coming from?" He got the answer Frank had been given.

"It's better not to know," his nephew said. "I don't ask for details. The less any one person knows, the safer it is for the others. When I get the cash, I'll put it into a new account at the bank, and transfer it as soon as I know where to send it."

Ryan got up. He thought he had defused the situation. He hoped so; he was fond of his nephew.

ON THE DAY OF THE ROBBERY Sean Filey was with a patient. Jim Quinlan was on duty at Heuston Station. He had arranged the roster so he would be there for the Dublin-to-Cork train. Marie Dempster was at the house at Santry. She would drive out to Sallins at the prearranged time in a rented Ford. She'd taken a flat near Howth Bay, and the sleek BMW had been left there.

Frank was in his office talking to a client who wanted the bank's support for a ceramics company. He heard the wailing sirens in the background but paid no attention.

In the lobby of the Kildare Street branch of the Bank of Ireland the manager lay shot dead. He had played the hero, lunging for an alarm button. A girl was crying hysterically, and police were cordoning off the area and gathering the bank staff into the back rooms. The acrid cordite smell of gunfire lingered in the air. A stolen Renault was hidden in the traffic heading towards Heuston Station. It carried three men, apart from the driver. The hoods were pulled off their heads, the shotgun was on the floor between their feet, and the suitcase with the money crammed into it was stowed in the boot. They heard the sirens too, and one man glanced through the rear window. No one spoke.

The Renault pulled into the station forecourt. The three men got out, nobody hurrying. One of them heaved the suitcase out of the back. A porter lounged nearby.

"Bye now, thanks for the lift," one called out, for the porter's benefit, as the driver set off. Two of the men guarded the suitcase while the other bought three tickets to Cork. They looked relaxed and very ordinary. A number of people were catching the train. The three men, apparently quite unconnected, boarded the train and made their way to the rear.

Quinlan met them. "Follow me," he said. He unlocked the guard's van. The man with the suitcase looked round.

"We had trouble. Declan shot the manager."

Quinlan didn't react. "I'll lock you in; five minutes before Sallins I'll open it. You know what to do then. Good luck."

He went out and they checked their watches. They stood, swaying slightly with the movement of the train.

At the exact time, Quinlan opened the door and glanced in. "Be ready," he said. Then he was gone. The suitcase was taken up, and the three men came out into the corridor. Sallins was just ahead. The first car had passed under the bridge when Quinlan pulled the emergency cord. As the brakes went on and the train screamed under their impact, he raced up to the driver's cabin.

"Bloody yobs!" he shouted. "I saw 'em pull the cord..."

Donny heard the train coming. He couldn't believe it at first, and he craned forward over the edge of the bridge, his mouth stretched into a huge, delighted grin.

It was one thirty, and the rest of Sallins was eating lunch or sitting over a drink in Cargill's Lounge. The shops were shut. It was the hour of the Irish siesta, without the sun. Donny saw the big, beautiful miracle of the train as it approached, and to his astonishment and joy it started to slow down. The Dublin-to-Cork train usually sped through that tiny station. Now it was actually stopping, coming to a slow, slow crawl under the bridge. It was the most exciting moment of his life. For a few seconds he thought it had stopped completely; then it started to move again, gathering speed. As it vanished down the track he saw the three men coming up the steps from the platform.

They'd dropped down from the rear as the train slowed to a near halt. People's heads were poking out of windows way up front, looking ahead for whatever had caused the driver to put on his brakes. No one saw the three men leave the guard's van. Quinlan would come back and relock the door. The incident would be put down to teenagers fooling with the emergency cord, and there'd be no connection with the Dublin bank robbers.

Except that there was a witness up there on the bridge who'd seen them leave the train.

The man called Declan thrust one hand into his coat and bounded up the few steps leading to the bridge. Donny stared at him. He was still grinning, and he didn't see the knife. In a frenzy of rage and fear Declan stabbed him over and over again. Donny didn't even cry out. He died with the memory of the lovely train imprinted on his mind.

The Ford was parked across from the bridge, down a side road. Marie

253

was sitting in the driver's seat. She opened the passenger door, expecting the three men to put the suitcase in and depart.

"Drive us to the next town," she was told, and before she could protest they'd piled into the car and slammed the doors.

"We were seen," was the snapped explanation. "Drive into Naas. We'll get the bus."

Marie turned to the man beside her. "Who saw you?"

"Some auld fella on the bridge. He won't be tellin' anyone. This'll do, here."

They got out when she pulled over to the kerb. The suitcase was on the back seat. One hundred thousand pounds. She'd heard the news flash on the car radio. The bank manager had been murdered. Now there was another man dead. Only when she got back to the house on the airport road did it dawn on her that the witness on the bridge must have been Donny.

That evening, in a little house in Sallins, the neighbours were sitting with Donny's mother. For a long time she had sat with her apron pulled over her face like a shroud, weeping as Irish mothers had done for their sons since time immemorial. Now she had calmed herself. Donny's body had been taken away. There had been words she hardly understood, like "autopsy" and "inquest". But it was murder, she understood that. When one of her daughters whispered to her that Mr. Arbuthnot of Riverstown was outside asking if he might come in, Donny's mother just sat and stared. She broke into a storm of tears as soon as he came into the room.

Frank said gently, "Mrs. Brennan, I heard about Donny on the news. It's a dreadful thing. Whoever did it will be caught, don't worry. They'll pay for it. Donny never hurt anyone in his life."

She let her tears flow, mopping them with her crumpled apron. "He never harmed so much as a fly on the wall. Who'd murder him?"

Frank didn't answer. There'd been a robbery and a murder in a Dublin bank. He remembered hearing the sirens in the early afternoon. By the time he left his office, news on the car radio was linking the robbery with an incident on the Dublin-to-Cork train. He knew, even as he looked into Donny's mother's face, that he would get a call to say the money for the arms shipment was ready for collection.

"Don't worry about anything," he said. "You'll need money for the funeral. I'll see to that. You're not to go borrowing."

Frank drove back to Meath. Mrs. Brogan came out to meet him. "Isn't it terrible news, sir?" she said. "That poor man murdered in Dublin?"

"Yes, terrible," he said, and went into the study and shut the door. He switched on the television for the latest news.

Mrs. Brogan went back to her husband. "Did ye see the face on him?" she demanded. "White to the gills. Maybe it's robbin' the bank he doesn't like—too close to home."

Brogan said, "It looks like our lads, Mary."

"I'd say so," she said. "Good luck to 'em. I'll say a little prayer they won't be caught."

"YOU DON'T UNDERSTAND." Marie's voice rose. "He stopped the car to give that dirty old creature money. He'll go mad over this!"

Sean said, "You don't need to shout. Arbuthnot won't like it, but he's agreed to take the money and pay it to the supplier in Monte Carlo. He's in up to his neck."

"He'll give us away," she said. "That'll buy him immunity."

"From Dublin, maybe. But not from us. He knows what happens to informers."

She said bitterly, "He's not afraid of us. He's never in his life had to keep his mouth shut for fear of anyone. I told you why we broke up. I stood up for what we were doing, and he raved at me. Murderers, cowards . . . that's what he called our people in the North, Sean. But you'd rather risk everything than listen to me!"

He swung round on her. "I know what you told me. But I don't believe you, Marie. You're jealous because he doesn't love you, and now you'd like to see him dead! But I won't kill him to please you. Not till I know he's a real danger."

"Ask him to accept the money. See what he says," she taunted.

"I'm going to," he answered. "I'm going to Meath on Monday. Now shut up. I've had enough." He went out, banging the door.

FRANK WENT TO HIS OFFICE IN DUBLIN on Monday as usual. The staff thought he seemed withdrawn, as if he had something on his mind. He told his secretary to cancel the appointment with Dr. Filey at Meath that evening. He had to stay in town on business.

He read the newspaper reports. The public was roused. The IRA was being accused in the media; the circumstantial evidence was growing, linking the murder of the retarded man at Sallins to the escaping robbers, who feared he would identify them. Nothing could be proved unless one of the killers was caught. But there were no clues. They weren't going to be caught.

Kevin Ryan telephoned. Frank didn't take the call. He didn't want to talk to his uncle. He knew the moment of decision was upon him.

There were violent, ruthless men within the framework of the Provisional IRA. And they were part of a horrible scenario of vengeance and terror in the North. Now, that terror had struck two streets distant, and knifed a helpless old man because he happened to be in the way. He wouldn't touch the money until the men responsible for killing Donny had been punished by their own people, and he'd been given proof of it. If they refused—he had made up his mind what to do.

He left Dublin and drove to Riverstown. Claudia was in the study. She flushed angrily when he was shown in. "Why do you burst in here without even ringing up?" she asked.

Frank said, "Because I knew you wouldn't see me. I've come about Donny, Claudia. I want to do something for his family."

"Why don't your friends in the IRA provide for them?" she said bitterly. "After all, they killed the poor devil."

"It's not proved," he said, but it sounded feeble.

She shrugged contemptuously. "Everyone in Sallins knows it was them. That's why nobody's come forward. You make me sick, Frank, talking about helping the family. You and your speeches in New York and your public support for the murderers—what do you want to do, salve your conscience with money?"

"I want to offer a reward for information," he said, "and set up a proper fund for Mrs. Brennan. I want you to join me, Claudia, and get your friends to contribute too. If we offer enough, someone will inform on whoever did this. They always do."

"So it's said. Offer them enough and they'll betray their nearest and dearest. Why don't you get your charming uncle to put his hand in his pocket for this?"

"Then you won't help?" Frank said.

"No. I'm sorry about Donny. But I'm not going to get a bomb thrown through my window just to make you feel better. If your chickens are coming home to roost, then it's about time."

He left the house. She stood by the window and watched him get into his car and drive away. Suddenly a flash of premonition swept over her, a sense of tragedy so strong that she opened the window and tried to call him back. But the next moment the car had disappeared.

By the following morning the story was being whispered throughout Sallins. Not only had Frank Arbuthnot gone to see Donny's mother and paid for the funeral, but he was going to pay big money for information about who'd done the killing as well.

The report came direct to Sean Filey via Joe Burns, who'd heard it in the Gardai station. He didn't dare contact Jim Quinlan. Quinlan thought he was being watched. Kevin Ryan couldn't be trusted either, if he felt his nephew might be at risk. Filey had to deal with this alone. He had suffered two days of suspense after Frank cancelled their meeting. The excuse could have been genuine. He had tried to believe it was, if only to allay his own fears.

Then he got the call from young Burns, and he knew he had to act. He phoned Mrs. Brogan.

"Is Mr. Arbuthnot expected home tonight?"

"He is," she answered. "He's dining in."

"Good," Sean said. "I'm on my way over."

"WHAT YOU'RE ASKING is impossible."

"I'm not asking," Frank Arbuthnot said. "I'm demanding it. I want the men who murdered Donny Brennan punished. And I want proof of it, Sean. Nothing else will do."

They were standing in the drawing room at Meath, and Filey was conscious of the difference in their height. He felt overshadowed for the first time in their long relationship. He had never lost the initiative before. Now it had been wrested from him by the man he had manipulated and despised. He felt a conscious hatred of Frank, and recognized that it had been there from the beginning.

"You really mean to tell me that the life of one half-wit means more to you than our victory in the North?"

"There is no victory in the North," Frank retorted. "There's just more killing, more violence. And never mind who gets hurt."

"That's oversimplifying," Sean countered. "Every man's life is important. But sacrifices have to be made. Be reasonable, Frank. They had to do it. He could have identified them!"

Frank said quietly, "Donny couldn't identify his own mother. Isn't there any limit when it comes to killing in cold blood? Is it always right, because somehow it's part of the fight for Irish freedom?"

Sean Filey knew the argument was lost. He threw down his challenge. "Whatever we have to do, we'll do," he said.

"Then you can count me out," he heard Frank say. "You can find someone else to deal with that money. I wouldn't touch it."

"You're breaking your oath, Frank. You realize that?"

"Yes. But you needn't be afraid I'll go to the police. There are other ways of helping them catch those swine. I won't betray you or anyone I've worked with. You can be sure of that. Would you like a drink?"

"I don't drink with traitors," Filey said.

"Only with murderers!" was the retort, as he went out.

It was very quiet in the room. The gentle ticking of a fine mantel clock sounded like gunshots in the silence.

Frank went to the phone and dialled a number in England. "Claire? It's me," he said when she answered. "I've got something to tell you. I think you'll be glad . . ." And while she asked him worried questions he thought of a joke to ease her mind. "And anyway, I can always hole up in our secret place. Remember Reynard and his folly?" And then he said goodbye, God bless you, and hung up.

They wouldn't dare touch him. They might talk about it among themselves, but they wouldn't dare.

FILEY DIDN'T INTERRUPT. He let Marie talk, filling out the details of her plan. She couldn't sit still. She was walking round the kitchen, flushed and bright-eyed, and everything she said made sense.

"If you kidnap him," Marie said, "she'll come here trying to find him."

Filey said, "You really think she'd take that risk?"

"I know it," Marie declared. "I've listened to them talk on the phone. I've read the letters she writes him. She'll come."

Filey imagined that jealous spying carried on over the years. "Did you ever say anything about this to him?" he asked.

"Yes," she admitted. "That's why he threw me out, Sean."

"I thought it might be," he said. "Not that it matters now that he's turned against us. I'll talk to Macbride."

"Why?" she demanded. "We've got enough people—we can keep him here till we get her."

"I have to bring Macbride in," Sean explained. "It's too risky for our lads to take the money to the North. He'll have to make his own arrangements. A boat would be the best way. And he can keep Quinlan informed. I'll get on to him. Meanwhile, we've got to work out the timing and a place to take Arbuthnot."

"I know his routine by heart," she said. "I can do that. We'll need someone to make the upstairs room secure."

By the next morning a bed had been moved into the upstairs room, the window had been whitewashed, and a strong padlock had been fitted to the door.

Macbride had asked one question only. "How much more time have we got?"

"Not much," Filey answered. "He could spill his guts to the Gardai any day."

"Good luck," said Macbride. "That sister'd be a big fish to catch."

CHAPTER 9

There was a car park behind the bank. It was overlooked by blank walls and was marked "Private", with spaces reserved for senior employees.

Frank turned into the space reserved for him and glanced at his watch. Nine forty. Not bad, considering the traffic. All the other spaces were full. He didn't even notice the black Peugeot. He reached behind him for his briefcase and got out. At the same moment Willie left the stolen Peugeot. He came up to Frank.

"Mornin'," he said. "It's Mr. Arbuthnot, is it?"

"Yes."

Pat straightened up from where he'd been crouching, brought the cosh up and then down with all his force onto the back of Frank's head. Willie caught him as he went down. The boot of the Peugeot sprang open, and the two men had him bundled inside in a few seconds.

They got in, started the engine, and drove away.

MARIE WATCHED FROM BEHIND the curtain as the car drove up to the house. She saw Frank briefly, manhandled in through the front door, and heard the scuffle of resistance as Pat and Willie forced him up the stairs.

She stood very still, her heart hammering with a savage excitement. All she could think of was him imprisoned upstairs, at her mercy now, as she had so often been at his. She wondered if he'd beg. No, she thought, not for himself. But wait until we bring *her* face to face with him. He'll beg then, and I'll be there watching.

Willie handcuffed Frank, locking one cuff round his wrist and snapping the other round the bedpost. He looked down at him while Pat stood in the rear holding a gun. "Listen to me," Willie snarled. "Open yer trap to make a sound and I'll be up here to knock the teeth down yer throat."

Then he went out. Pat lingered in the doorway for a moment and levelled the gun at Frank. He didn't say a word. He just looked, and the look said everything. It was more terrifying than Willie's threats. Then Frank was alone.

He had a blinding pain where he'd been hit over the head. He felt dizzy and nauseated. He sank back and closed his eyes. He couldn't remember anything before he came to in the black, cramped space, and found himself blindfolded and tied up. Concussion, he thought, that's the headache. Stay quiet, he thought. You can't do anything like this. They haven't killed you. Remember that. They want something from you first. Slowly he stilled the fear that threatened to turn into panic.

Downstairs, in the sitting room, Sean Filey was explaining the plan to his men. "Marie'll be coming in and out. She'll see to the food. You two take turns guarding Arbuthnot. I'll be over tomorrow. Watch yourselves, meantime."

Pat stayed the first night. He went up in the late afternoon, opened the door, and stared at the man lying on his back on the bed. He was breathing and seemed asleep.

Frank watched the dim figure through a slit of eyelid. The nausea had stopped, but his head was a continuous, throbbing ache. The door closed again, and he could hear the man's footsteps going down the stairs. Frank lay still, willing himself to sleep.

When he woke, he saw that someone had left a lamp burning in a corner, too far away for him to reach. There was a chamber pot and a jug of water with a tin mug placed beside the bed. His head ached, but he felt no dizziness when he sat up. His handcuffed arm was very stiff. There was no carpeting, just bare boards. He lay back, listening. The floor was thin, but he could hear only a murmur of voices from below. He couldn't isolate any words. If he could make a hole, there was a chance . . . But his pockets had been emptied. There was nothing he could use.

He passed the night in fits of sleeping and starts of waking panic, when he dreamed the door was opening and the man with that murderous look was standing there. But when it did open, it was late morning and it was Marie Dempster who stood and smiled at him, with a tray in her hands. The gunman was just behind her.

"How are you feeling now, Frank?" she asked. "I've brought you a bite of breakfast."

THE ALARM HAD BEEN RAISED by midafternoon. The girl who'd replaced Marie as Frank's secretary phoned to Meath when he didn't come in, because he had clients waiting. He had left for Dublin at his usual time, she was told. The senior investment consultant advised her to contact the police and the hospitals, in case he'd been in an accident. A detective came over, took details, found Frank's car, and went back to report.

The item was on the early TV news. Sean Filey watched at home. "Mr. Frank Arbuthnot, prominent merchant banker, disappeared after leaving his car in the car park outside the Boston Irish Bank this morning. Mr. Arbuthnot left his Meath mansion at eight thirty this morning and has not been seen since..."

Filey switched off the set. Arbuthnot had been swallowed up as if he'd stepped into a bog. And a bog was where he would end as soon as they had Claire Fraser in their hands.

Up at Riverstown, Claudia saw a news programme reporting Frank's disappearance. "Your chickens are coming home to roost..." she had said. It looked like a terrible prophecy now. And then came the call she'd been dreading. The call from Claire in Gloucestershire.

CLAIRE HAD JUST BROUGHT PETER back from a birthday party. She took him upstairs to the nursery, where the nanny was waiting to bath him. Lucy was asleep in her cot.

"I'll come and say goodnight after he's had his supper," Claire said. She went back downstairs and tucked herself up on the sofa. She switched on the BBC six-o'clock news.

Because of the family connection, Neil had been told about his brother-in-law's disappearance before it became public. He drove flat out to get home to tell Claire himself. As soon as he came into the drawing room and saw her stricken face, he knew that she'd already heard.

He hurried towards her and put his arms round her. "Oh, darling, I know. I know. Don't cry."

"I'll die if anything's happened to him," she said. "It's the IRA. I warned him; I begged him. Oh, my God, my God..."

"Claire, he could have gone off somewhere without telling anyone. Don't work yourself up till we know more."

She wrenched away from him. "Oh, it's easy for you to say that. They'll kill him. I know they will!"

He couldn't calm her. Nothing he said seemed to penetrate at all. In the end he said, "You stay here. I'll ring up London and see what I can find out. They may have more news."

For the first time she seemed to listen. "Will you? Will you do that? Please."

When he came back, her face was blotched and the tears were still running unchecked. He gave her his handkerchief and slipped his arm round her. This time she didn't pull away.

"I've spoken to people who'd know the full details," he said. "It does look as if Frank's been kidnapped. It could be for ransom." He didn't mention the other suggestion.

"It may be murder," Neil had been told. "He's been putting the Provos' backs up lately. If they don't find his body by tomorrow, then it could be a ransom job. Let's hope it is, for Mrs. Fraser's sake."

Claire wiped her eyes and said, "I want to ring my mother." Neil went to the telephone and dialled for her.

"Don't cry," Claudia said. "It doesn't help to upset yourself. He may turn up. You've got to keep calm and think of Neil and the children, darling. The Gardai came round a little while ago, and they've promised to let me know if anything comes through. Don't worry; he's probably all right."

"No, he isn't, Mother," Claire said, "and you know it. He rang me and told me he was finished with the IRA." There was a pause. Then she said, "Mother, I'm coming over."

She heard Neil say, "No!" very loudly in the background.

"That would be ridiculous." Claudia spoke sharply. "Rushing over and leaving your husband and children. It wouldn't be safe, and you're not staying here. I'm not either, till this clears up. I'm going to Maura Keys, in Cork. Put Neil on, please, darling."

Claire said distinctly, "No, I won't. You'll only gang up together. Poor Frank. My poor brother. Nobody gives a damn about him except me." Then she hung up.

Neil came towards her. "Claire, please, darling."

"They're merciless, Neil," she said. "They won't just kill him. If they think he's betrayed them, they'll torture him."

"Has he betrayed them? Why didn't you tell me?"

"We don't talk about him," she pointed out. "He phoned me to say he was finished with the IRA. They can't touch me, that's what he said. Oh, Neil, I'm so frightened of waking up in the morning and hearing something dreadful."

"You won't," he assured her. "Our people said tonight that no news will be good news. They're usually right."

That night he lay awake beside her. If Frank's dead, he thought, I've probably lost her. She'll never get over it.

In the morning she awoke before Neil and switched on the radio. Frank's disappearance was not mentioned. She lay back against the pillows. No news will be good news, Neil had said. What had Frank said when they spoke last . . . how long ago? It was only days, but it seemed like a lifetime. "I can always hole up in our secret place. Remember Reynard and his folly?" She turned and grabbed Neil by the shoulder.

"Wake up! Oh, wake up, darling."

He started up, alarmed, and saw by her look that it wasn't bad news.

"He may be all right," she said. "He may have gone into hiding! If he was threatened, that's what he did! Oh, Neil, it's a chance. If he's not found and there's no ransom demand or communiqué from those brutes, it's a very good chance! He even said something like that. I was in such a state last night I forgot all about it."

"Well, maybe that's the explanation. If he thought they were going after him, it makes sense. But where would he go?"

It was their secret. She wouldn't mention it to Neil. He'd dismiss the idea as a piece of Irish lunacy, and she couldn't afford that. If he took her last hope away, she'd never forgive him.

"He didn't say," she said.

MARIE LAID THE TRAY DOWN on the bed. It was the morning of the third day. Frank hadn't spoken a word or responded to her taunting. The silence maddened her.

"The police came to see me yesterday," she said, mocking him. "I told them we'd not seen each other for weeks. I said I was so sorry, but I'd no *idea* where you might be."

Willie was sick of standing there with the gun while Marie jeered. "Come on," he told her. "Come on."

There was a routine. Marie brought him food twice a day, then left, giving him ten minutes alone to eat before Willie or the sinister Pat came in and collected the tray.

Frank couldn't shift the frame of the bed. The handcuffs were a sophisticated type that couldn't be picked open, even if he'd had anything to pick them with. But he'd made a small hole between the floorboards with the fork that came with his meals. He didn't try to keep it; that would have been noticed immediately.

He ate the food quickly. It was a slab of stale ham, with a hunk of bread and rancid margarine. Then he eased himself to the edge of the bed and dug away at the wood. When he heard them coming he lay back and pretended to be sleeping. By the evening, if he got the fork again, he might be able to distinguish what was being said downstairs.

But the evening came, and Marie wasn't there. Pat brought him a bowl of soup and a spoon. It had a blunt end that wouldn't go between the floorboards.

THE WEEKEND PASSED. Claire had stayed by the television set watching every news bulletin. Neil had assured her they'd be told before anything was released to the media, but she insisted on sitting by the TV. Neil played with Peter.

At the end of that long, agonizing Sunday, Claire said to Neil, "I think Frank's gone to ground. How can I find out?"

"You can't," he said. "You'll just have to be patient and keep your spirits up."

A major Sunday newspaper carried the story of Frank's IRA associations. Claire threw the paper down in helpless rage. "What a pack of lies! All that stuff about millionaires and giving money to the Provos! I've never read such filthy lies in my life."

"I'm not exactly pleased with it myself," Neil pointed out.

"It can't hurt you. Stop thinking of your career for five minutes, can't you? Everyone knows what you think about Ireland; you've said it often enough. They've made my brother out as some kind of thug." Then, seeing Peter, she said, "Oh, please, Peter, not now. Go back to the nursery; Mummy's got a headache ... no, Peter, I said no. Where on earth is Iris?"

And then Neil's patience snapped for the first time. "There's no need to take it out on him. He doesn't know what's happened. You've made the child cry."

"Just because he can't have his own way. And don't talk to me like that in front of the children."

He ushered the bewildered little boy out, calling for his nanny. Then he came back into the room. Claire was chain-smoking. She had hardly eaten since Thursday night. She looked pale and ill, but by now he was too angry to feel sorry for her. Nothing counted with her but that half-brother. Nothing!

"You may as well know I've decided to go to Ireland," she said.

"It would be insane to go there at this time. I absolutely forbid it."

"Because it would look bad in the press? Bad for you I mean?"

"I don't want you going to Ireland because you could be in real danger. You can't do that, because of Peter and Lucy, even if you don't care about me."

"I can't stay here not knowing what's become of my brother. If you loved me, Neil, you wouldn't expect me to."

"I love you," he said. "But I expect you to put your family first. Your own mother said the same."

"She's not Frank's mother. I'm the only person in the world who loves him. I'm the only one he's got."

"He's been coming between us ever since we married. I've had enough. If you walk out now, it's for good."

She didn't answer. She walked past him out of the room, and that night they slept in different bedrooms. He left for London on Monday morning

264

without seeing her again. She drove Peter to nursery school and played with Lucy for an hour. Then she hired a car in a nearby village and set out to catch the night boat to Dublin.

KEVIN AND MARY ROSE PACKED UP and left the Half House to fly home to the States a week early. The headlines about Frank's disappearance glared at them from every newspaper. They didn't speak on the drive to the airport. Mary Rose was pink around the eyes; she was still trying to come to terms with her husband of nearly thirty years, the man who'd said of his own flesh and blood, "He's turned traitor. He deserves all he gets, and that's an end of it! No more, Rose, just shut your mouth, I tell you!"

As the plane taxied and took off Kevin Ryan looked out of the little window and watched the grey shreds of cloud gradually change to a dazzling, sun-filled blue. He felt bitter, as if there were bile in his mouth he couldn't spit out. Bitter and old. And the explanations lay ahead of him. There was no greater shame than betrayal by a member of the family. He had to fan his anger. It kept the sorrow at bay.

FRANK GOT THE FORK BACK on Sunday. It was thrust into a plateful of stew. He could hardly wait for the brutish Willie to go out. Then he was over the side of the bed, picking away at the gap between the boards. By now there was a sizable hole. He got back on the bed and swallowed half the tepid mess before the plate was taken away. He'd be alone until the evening now.

They'd taken his watch, so he had no idea of time. His arm was numb from the pressure of the metal cuff round his wrist. The hours passed. He heard a noise and the door opened.

"I've brought your supper," Marie announced. The gunman, Pat this time, stood behind her, the distant light in the passage glinting on the levelled gun.

She moved towards him holding the tray. "Willie says you didn't finish your lunch," she said admonishingly. He refused to look at her. "Answer me when I speak or I'll take your food away!"

He couldn't let that happen. "Don't," he said. "I'm hungry."

A smile touched her lips. "Ready to speak to me, are you?"

He had to get the fork once more. "Why are you doing this?"

She said in a shrill voice, "Because you're a dirty betrayer. Turned against us on account of that loony at Sallins. That's all Ireland means to you. Take your dinner. I hope it chokes you!"

She banged the tray down on the foot of the bed. Then she was gone and the door was shut and locked. He worked feverishly at the hole in the floor. Then he hurriedly ate the food.

Pat came to take the plate away. He didn't come close, like Willie. He was a real professional. "Put that tray on the ground. Now push it over. Use your foot." He was well beyond reach when he picked it up. Then he was gone.

Frank sat quietly for a few moments. He was going to be killed. He knew that the man who would pull the trigger had just left him. He could sense his impatience. But why the delay?

He could hear voices below him. Straining to the limit, he managed to get his head down and his left ear close to the hole he had made.

Marie and Pat were talking in the room below. "How long are we goin' to keep him up there?" Pat demanded.

Marie said irritably, "Till she comes. I've told you. Sean's told you. Stop asking, damn it. You'll get your chance."

"What happens if she don't come?" he said.

"She'll come looking for him," Marie snapped. "His sister won't stay snug in England when he might be in trouble! They've a close relationship, those two. I ought to know."

Frank got back on the bed. He wrenched and wrenched in helpless fury at the handcuffs. Claire. That was what they were waiting for. She was the prize. To kidnap and murder a British cabinet minister's wife would be a propaganda coup, like the murder of Mountbatten.

The night passed. He lay in mental agony until he heard sounds from below. They were awake and moving around. He eased over the edge of the bed again to listen.

"I'll be off then," Pat said. He'd finished his breakfast.

"Willie's not here yet," Marie pointed out.

"I can't wait. I've me job to get to. Here, give him the gun and the key to the cuffs. Don't go near Arbuthnot till Willie gets here!"

Frank stayed very still. He heard a door closing. She was alone in the house. She had the gun and the key to his handcuffs. A chance in a million that he could get her to come upstairs before Willie got there, but he had to try. He let his body fall heavily to the floor.

The sudden noise made Marie jump to her feet. She heard her name being called, "Marie! Marie . . ." It ended in a moan of agony, and then came piteous cries, "Marie . . . help me." She picked up the gun, slipped the safety catch off and ran upstairs.

He was lying on the floor, grotesquely twisted, the pinioned arm at a horrible angle. He cried out as she entered the room. She held the gun pointed at him.

"My arm's broken," he moaned, and then lolled back as if he were fainting. "Help me. . . ."

She came towards him, and as she drew near she unconsciously lowered the gun.

It was too late for her to move back. His left fist lashed out with every vestige of strength. At the same moment she pulled the trigger. His blow

266

caught her on the side of the face and threw her backwards, crashing against the wall. She was knocked out instantly. The gun clattered to the floor.

He heaved and pulled at the heavy bed, inching to within reach of where she lay. She had a cardigan on. The pockets were empty. She'd have put the key to the handcuffs in her handbag. At any moment the thug, Willie, would arrive.

Frank manoeuvred the bed backwards, reaching for the gun. He had to take the only chance left. He brought the muzzle up to the lock mechanism on the handcuff round the bedpost and pulled the trigger.

The bullet shot the locking device to pieces and ricocheted off the wall into his side, where he felt a sharp blow. He didn't notice the pain in his calf, where Marie's bullet had grazed the skin. He knew only that he might have seconds at most to get out of the house. He was down the stairs and at the front door.

There was a car parked outside. The BMW he'd given Marie as a Christmas present. The keys. He had to have the keys. They'd be in her handbag. He found it on the kitchen table, and the keys were in it. So were the keys to the handcuffs.

He ran to the car. He slid into the front seat and winced as a spasm of pain tore through him. Then he turned the key and the engine was alive. He was out of the drive and on the road. He still didn't know where he was.

The phone in the house began to ring. It rang and rang, and no one answered. Sean Filey knew that something had gone wrong. Willie hadn't been able to start his car. He'd called Marie and got no answer. Then he'd called Sean, who was now trying her.

Sean didn't waste any more time. He called Willie back. "I'm coming to get you," he said. "Be on the doorstep." It would be no use for Sean to go to the house alone. He was unarmed. Getting Willie was a ten-minute detour, but he had to do it.

Frank slowed at a crossroads. He recognized the building on the corner and knew where he was. He hesitated when he saw a red car coming towards him with Willie at the wheel. To be caught now, at the last moment . . . A very sharp pain ran through him, and a feeling of dizziness. He had to escape, to outrun that car and get to safety somewhere. If they caught him, he couldn't warn Claire. He swung the wheel and sent his car hurtling down the road towards Kells. The red car turned after him.

MARIE REGAINED CONSCIOUSNESS. She moaned, and felt her face. Slowly, with much pain, she managed to get to her feet. Frank was gone. A shattered handcuff was lying on the floor. Her gun was gone. But there were bloodstains. She must have hit him. And then she heard Sean and Willie calling her from below. Frank had escaped. But she'd wounded him. That would save her life.

FRANK DROVE DOWN THE TWISTING, potholed country roads at desperate speed, hoping for the green Gardai sign, but he couldn't see one. The red car with Willie in it was still in sight. He was in constant pain when he breathed now, and fighting the dizziness that came and went.

Near Kells he came to the main road, and the red car came into view behind. Straight ahead was a sign: "Cloncarrig". The location of Reynard's old house. The folly, the secret place where nobody could find him. The perfect hideaway. He went flying across the road and saw the house loom up on the right. His head felt light. There was a track off the road. The folly with the secret room was only one field away. He pulled onto the track and stopped the car. He had to reach the folly. Once there he would be safe. They wouldn't find him and Claire there. He got out and started to walk.

The red car he'd been escaping from sat at the junction with the main road, waiting until there was a break in the traffic. The driver was not Willie. He was a farmer, and he kept muttering to himself that people who drove like that crazy fella shouldn't be allowed on the roads.

Frank kept the grey stone tower in sight as he fought to stay on his feet and cross the field. Twice he fell and dragged himself upright. He had to escape them. If he didn't, they'd capture his sister. She'd been so upset about the dead fox . . . He pulled his straying thoughts back to the present. Only a little further. The ditch ahead, and then he would be there. The ditch was steep, and he slithered to the bottom and lay gasping. Get up, on hands and knees. Crawl till you reach the top of it. Never mind the brambles.

Now, just a little further. There's the base of the folly. Now all you've got to do is get yourself up to that little entrance. He pulled himself up the first few feet, clung, almost fell backwards, and then found the final toehold. He reached the dark sanctuary of the window and slid through it onto the floor. He lost consciousness.

As he came to, he heard his father talking to him, and he wasn't angry. Frank couldn't understand what was said, because it was a murmur, like listening to people in another room. He thought once he saw his mother. Young and pale, with the fine red hair in the photograph.

A night passed—he dreamed of his mother, and of his father again. Then Claudia; she faded, and it was his Uncle Kevin in her place. He wanted Claire. They were going fishing and they'd be late. He called her, and she came dancing through the darkness to him, all legs and pigtails flying, and he smiled in his delirium. He felt no pain, no sense of dying. He drifted from waking dream to fitful sleep, immobile, unaware of cold or damp. The stillness prolonged his life for another day and night.

Two teenagers found the BMW, with the keys in it. They crashed it at ninety miles an hour on the main road to Dublin. Both were killed, and the BMW was burned out.

CHAPTER 10

As Claire set out to find him from the opposite end of the estate, crossing fields and ditches, Frank was still back in time, floating between dream and reality. He was out hunting, following the hounds with Claire close behind.

Life was full of happy days. It was bright sunlight outside the narrow window. He opened his eyes. There was a marvellous sense of peace. And then he heard her voice, clear and urgent, coming from below.

"Frank? Frank, are you there, Frank?"

"Clarry. I'm here. Come quickly."

AN ARTICULATED LORRY HAD JACKKNIFED on the Dundalk road. It sat across the road like a stranded elephant, its driver arguing with two policemen and a posse of infuriated motorists.

Michael Harvey didn't waste time. He pulled up, leaped out of the car, and went up to one of the uniformed Gardai.

"What's the quickest way to Kells? I've a job waitin' an' I'll lose it if I'm stuck behind this fella for too long."

"Reverse back there and take the second to your right," the officer said. "Follow the signs to Clonkelty."

Harvey grunted his thanks and ran back to the car, cursing the delay. Billy Cavanagh was dead, and if the killers were ahead of him, then there was little hope of him doing anything. They'd reach Claire Fraser, and she'd be gone by the time he arrived. He was a man who'd learned to trust his instincts. On more than one occasion they had warned him and saved his life. They didn't warn him now. He felt somehow that luck was with him, that Cavanagh had either not known, or had died rather than disclose, where Claire was heading.

It was crazy, no question about that. So crazy that only someone born and bred in the country would have taken it seriously. A man on the run for his life taking refuge in a fox's hide. No crazier than the eccentric hunter who had built the hide as a refuge for himself in his reincarnated form. Michael Harvey knew the country and the people, and he knew that the Arbuthnot brother and sister would make use of the place Claire had told him about.

If he had guessed wrong, and the tale Claire had told him by a swimming pool in the heart of Gloucestershire was just a tale, then he had come over for nothing. But once committed to a course, Michael Harvey had been trained not to doubt. He swung round a corner into the town of Kells. Cloncarrig was some six or so miles beyond. But he didn't know where Reynard's old house would be. And he had to find the house before he could track down the folly Claire had described. He stopped at a seedy roadside lounge named Loughlin's, and sauntered in. A man in shirtsleeves and braces was reading the *Sporting Life* behind the bar. Two old women were drinking Guinness in a far corner.

Harvey bought cigarettes and asked where the old Reynard house might be. The man stared at him. "It's over at Cloncarrig," he said. "But it's empty. Been empty for years."

"Can you see it from the road?" Harvey asked.

"No. It's set back up a drive. It's fallen down by now, I'd think."

Harvey thanked him, got back into his car and drove on, almost missing the faded little signpost to Cloncarrig. It was a hamlet, a cluster of stone houses on either side of the street. Then the hamlet was gone, like a dream blinked away, and the road was open before him, with fields and belts of tall trees.

"Up a drive," the bartender had said. That meant an entrance. He saw something on the left, and slowed. There had been gates, but they'd gone. Only the tall stone piers were left, robed in triumphant ivy. He turned the car in and found a muddy drive. A wind had blown down some branches from the trees on either side. Light, twiggy things; the car passed over them. As another car had done, he noticed, seeing the broken branches.

He had to put his car out of sight. He saw the house and drove round to the back, under a handsome archway, through the trees and crowded bushes that had become a jungle, and there were the garages and, beyond, what had once been the stable block. He drove in under shelter; there was a door that would actually close if heaved by brute force across the entrance.

He took the automatic rifle out of the boot, packed the ammunition in the pockets of his anorak, checked the gun and lodged it in his shoulder holster. Then, with the car hidden, he skirted the old mansion and came out on the west side, facing a sheet of grey-green water that had once been a fine lake. Beyond it, like a pencil tip writing in the sky, Harvey saw the first of the follies, two long fields away. He set off at a slow, jogging run that covered the ground at a surprising rate.

MARIE DEMPSTER SAT ON THE SOFA in the house at Santry. Pat, the professional, with the brutish Willie driving, had set off for Kells. And behind them, in a separate car, Hugh Macbride was following as backup.

"Macbride can make trouble for me," she said bitterly to Sean Filey. She touched her bruised face with a timid finger. "He'll find a way to blame me if they don't find her."

Sean knew that she was afraid.

"The Reynard place, where her car was found, is empty and derelict. The sister knows Arbuthnot better than anyone in the world. If she's gone there, it's because she expects to find him. We'll get them both." He looked at his watch. "I have to see a patient. Phone me at my consulting room if anything comes up."

"And what about me?" she demanded.

"Wait here. When they're brought in, you'll be on the welcoming committee."

He left, and she was alone, she didn't know for how long. She couldn't sit still. She walked in and out of the rooms, and climbed the stairs and to the room where he'd been kept. "Oh, Frank," she said aloud. "How I do hate you. If you'd loved me, none of this would have happened."

After Frank's escape she had been questioned, and not just by Sean, but by men she had never seen before. Sean Filey was her salvation. She had been tried and acquitted. Only the northerner, Macbride, coming hotfoot from Belfast, had asked the same questions all over again, and said the same as her inquisitors from the Council in the Republic. Why had a woman been left in charge of Arbuthnot, armed or not? It was a man's job, as the outcome proved. Filey's answer had been truthful; he never lied, she knew that. He wouldn't have lied to save her either. She'd been left alone because the man who'd guarded Arbuthnot the night before had gone home, expecting Willie to arrive. But Willie's car had broken down and in the end Filey himself had had to drive over to collect him and bring him to the house. Nobody could be blamed.

She leaned against the door frame and began to cry. No tears came, only the anguished sobs of a woman suffering past endurance. And then the storm was over. Filey was right; she'd never be at peace till Arbuthnot was dead. Maybe then she would stop loving him.

She went back down the stairs to sit and wait.

HUGH MACBRIDE FOLLOWED Willie and Pat at a safe distance. They didn't impress him. Willie had managed to kill the Cavanagh fellow at Riverstown and get nothing out of him for his pains. Macbride would be close enough when the action started to take over if necessary.

There was heavy traffic, unexpected at that time of the afternoon. Macbride scowled, moving a few yards at a time. Willie's grey Cortina was ahead of him, likewise slowed to a crawl. He found the reason on the Dundalk road. A huge lorry had come to grief and been moved far enough over to allow one lane of traffic, under the control of a policeman. Once past the obstacle, the cars picked up speed.

Turning down the road into Kells, he saw Willie's indicator flashing. The Cortina pulled over, and Pat got out and walked back to Macbride. He put his head through the open window.

"Willie's goin' to make sure of the way," he said.

Willie went into Loughlin's Lounge. The car with Billy Cavanagh's licence plates had been sighted under some trees on the old Reynard estate by a man out walking his dogs. But the estate was off the main road. Willie didn't buy cigarettes, as Major Harvey had done. The same man was behind the bar.

Willie said, "I'm lookin' for a place called Mount Reynard. D'ye know it?"

The man nodded. "I do," he replied. "You're the second asking about it today."

Willie stiffened. "A woman, was it?"

"Not at all. A youngish fella. I told him the way."

"Was he a dark sort of a fella?"

"Not dark at all," the barman said. "More reddish. Is there anythin' you're wantin'?"

"Only what I asked," said Willie. "The best way to get there."

The barman gave the directions and watched Willie hurry out.

"There's someone else gone ahead of us," Willie told Macbride. "A man, askin' the way." He saw the question coming. "Not *him*. Ginger-haired, the barman says."

"Forewarned is forearmed," Macbride snapped. "Let's go."

They set off. Another man asking the way to a derelict house on the same day. Coincidence? Maybe. Macbride didn't like coincidences. They usually meant that things had gone wrong.

At Cloncarrig, Macbride told them to leave the cars and spread out. When they reached Reynard's old house, he sent Willie to scour the fields; Pat stayed by the Fraser woman's hidden car; and Macbride elected to search the house and outbuildings.

He moved through the first floor, his gun in his hand. No one could go upstairs because the staircase had collapsed. He made his way down to the basement, sloshing in rainwater and rubbish. He had a nose for people in hiding, and he knew that the sister and Arbuthnot were not in the house. When he started to search the outbuildings, he opened the one door that was shut, and through the gloom he saw the outline of a car.

They weren't in the house, the stables or the garages. Willie was looking for them in the open; Pat was poised to take them if they tried to reach Claire's car. And he would stay by this car and wait for the man who had gone ahead of them to Loughlin's Lounge and asked the way to the same abandoned house.

It was Willie who saw her. He stopped and stared at the little figure hurrying along the rise in the next field, too far away to identify, but clearly a woman. He gave a grunt of excitement, checked his gun and set off. He couldn't move very fast, because he was a heavy man with a Guinness belly on him. He could fight like a bull at close quarters, but he wasn't made for running. He was over the rise himself and scrambling through the muddy, overgrown ditch when he saw the grey stone tower and the woman set on the side of it like a fly. Then she was gone, and he knew that he'd soon have the both of them.

IT WAS DARK, and she could scarcely see her brother's face. It was a pale blur against her breast. She stroked his hair, not knowing that she did so. His body was heavy in her arms.

"I knew you'd come," he said. "They mustn't find you, Clarry."

"They won't," she promised. "I'll get help. I'll get you out, my darling brother."

"Don't be silly." He smiled up at her. "I'm not going anywhere. I was shot . . . I can't remember much about it. I think it was Marie . . . or maybe it was my own fault. It doesn't matter now."

"Oh Frank, oh God, what can I do? Does it hurt terribly?" He didn't hear the anguish in her voice because at times it faded. The last question was a murmur, and he tried to reassure her.

"No, no, I don't feel anything. Just tired, Clarry. She was so jealous of you—that's what made her do it. She knew I loved you the best . . ." He closed his eyes.

She wept and her tears fell on him.

Then he moved in sudden agitation, his mind clear. Fear for her had brought everything into focus again.

"You've got to get away, they mustn't find you . . . It was you they wanted," he mumbled. "I was just the bait . . . You must go home, where you'll be safe . . . Don't try to get to the boat or the airport. Go to the Gardai. They'll protect you . . . Promise me."

"I promise," she said. She leaned her cheek against his hair.

"I'm so glad you came," she heard him say. "I don't mind anything now."

She went on holding him after he died. She stroked his hair and held his lifeless hand. She thought she saw a heap of whitened bones in the corner and remembered the fox of long ago. And then she heard the shout from below.

"Come on out or I'll come up and blast the two of ye!"

She froze in terror. They'd found her. She eased away from her brother and loaded the revolver which she'd brought from Riverstown with its clip of ammunition.

"Are ye comin' out of there?" the bellow came again.

Claire braced herself against the wall, holding the gun in both hands. Frank had taught her to shoot when they were children. If she hesitated, there'd be no second chance. They'd killed Frank. The man's head came above the level of the opening, and she fired.

As Willie had seen Claire, so Michael Harvey had seen Willie's clumsy figure lumbering across the field. Harvey's easy jogging became a run. He eased the automatic from its holster and gained rapidly on the slow-moving target. There was the last of the four towers looming ahead, bathed in brilliant sunshine, and the man was at the base of it. His shouts floated back to Harvey. Claire Fraser was inside the folly. He stopped. The man was climbing. Harvey brought the automatic rifle up to his shoulder and took aim. The crack of a shot split the silence. The man fell backwards before Michael Harvey had had time to fire.

As Harvey ran up to the folly he saw the dead man, and Claire Fraser standing there with a heavy, old-fashioned army revolver in her right hand. When she saw him, she raised it.

He shouted, "Claire—it's me! Michael Harvey!"

She lowered the gun and he ran up to her and stopped her from falling in a faint over the ugly corpse lying at her feet.

Pat heard the distant gunshot. He was hidden behind Claire's hired car, under the beech trees. He didn't dare disobey his orders and move out of cover to see what was happening. He didn't want to be in the wrong place with someone like Macbride.

There wasn't time for Claire to feel faint. Harvey guided her to the perimeter of the field, trying to keep in the shelter of the hedges. He asked one question only: "Did you find your brother?" and heard her answer as they hurried, bent low, Claire stumbling under his relentless urging.

"Yes. He was there. He's dead."

He saw the tears streaming down her face, but he wouldn't let her stop to rest.

"There's more than one gunman," he said. "They'll have heard that shot ... Keep going now, come on."

He knew how to use cover; it took longer than the direct way across the open fields, but no watcher would have seen them. He asked one other question. Where had she left her car?

She told him it was in a clump of trees, far over to the left. No doubt it had been seen and reported. If he knew the form, there'd be a man waiting by that car in case she went back to it. He decided to head for the garage where his own car was hidden.

When they reached the house itself, he kept close to the outside wall, hissing at her to keep flat in the shelter of it. He had his automatic rifle at the ready. They rounded the rear of the old mansion. It was very quiet. The garages were through the archway.

Macbride looked at his watch in the darkness. The dial glowed; he'd been an hour waiting beside the car. He'd checked it. A change of clothes in the back. English clothes. As he'd thought. They'd sent someone over to find her. He waited with his gun in his hand ready for the door to open and the man to be silhouetted against the light. If he had the woman with him, too bad.

"You stay here," Harvey said softly. "And don't move. My car's in there."

From the archway Claire watched him creep towards the line of half-open doors, many of them loose on broken hinges. And then he stopped. Before he left, he'd pulled the door across to hide his car; the drag marks were on the ground, scored deep into the dirt. A second set of marks overlapped them. Someone else had been there.

He knew that whoever it was was hiding in there, waiting for him to show himself. He grabbed the door and pulled. It lurched, unbalanced by its own weight and lack of support. Harvey dropped flat as it fell off its hinge. He saw the figure of Hugh Macbride crouched in the corner, his gun levelled in both hands. He fired before Macbride got off a single shot. Macbride was dead before he fell.

THEY DIDN'T DRIVE TO THE AIRPORT. They drove to a car-hire office in the centre of Dublin, where Harvey changed his car for another make. He disappeared for several minutes, leaving Claire sitting in the office with a cup of tea and a man who never spoke a word. When he came back, he'd changed his clothes to the corduroys and jacket he'd worn when he left England. He spoke to the man behind the desk. "Thanks, Bob." He nodded to Claire. "I've fixed a private plane," he told her. "We'll drive straight out to the airport now."

She couldn't think or feel. They arrived at the airport and she followed him obediently, boarded the Piper Comanche and strapped herself into the seat beside him.

"How long before we get to London?"

"We're not going to London," he said. "We're going to Belfast. There's some decent transport waiting there."

He squeezed her hand. She was freezing cold.

"It's all over," he said. "You were very good. You'll be home and safe with Neil and the kids in a few hours."

THE CALL FROM BELFAST had come through to Neil's office. His secretary didn't even knock. She came bursting in to give him the message. "Direct, via the army. Mrs. Fraser is on her way home and will be landing at RAF Highmore at six o'clock. Major Harvey is with her."

The secretary couldn't help herself. She said, "Oh, Minister, thank God!" and blinked back tears. She couldn't be sure, as she hurried out in embarrassment, but he looked as if he were doing the same.

IN BELFAST, CLAIRE was given a sedative. It was very mild, the doctor assured her. Just enough to take the edge off, after what she'd gone through. She was offered sandwiches, which she couldn't eat, and coffee. The coffee was a godsend.

Now she and Michael Harvey sat side by side in an army transport plane.

"Claire," he said, "I meant it, you were marvellous. But now you've got to put it all behind you and get on with your life."

She turned to him. "I don't want to go home," she said.

Michael Harvey drew a deep breath. He was fond of her. He admired her courage. But suddenly he was very angry.

"What about Neil?" he demanded. "He'll be there waiting for you. What are you going to do, walk away from him?"

"I don't know," she answered. "I don't know what to do or where to go now." A tear ran down her cheek.

Harvey said quietly, "Then I'll tell you what you do. You go back to your husband, who loves you, and your two little children. Your brother's dead. If you walk out now you'll spend the rest of your life looking for him. But you'll never find him. There'll be another man and that won't work either. Nothing would have worked so long as he was alive. And you know it."

She put her hands to her face. He didn't spare her.

"That chapter's closed," he said. "Go back and make it up to Neil and the kids, Claire. It's the only way you'll be happy in the end."

She didn't answer. As they were about to land she said, "I don't want Frank moved. I want him left where he is. I don't want anyone disturbing him."

Harvey nodded. "I said in my report that he was dead. I didn't say where. It's up to you."

"Thank you, Michael," Claire said simply. "Thank you for everything. Not just for saving my life."

The plane taxied to a halt. "If you want to thank me," he answered, "go out and meet your husband."

He let her leave the aircraft first. He saw Neil waiting on the tarmac.

Claire had seen him too. She began to walk towards him. Moments later they were locked together.

THE BODIES OF HUGH MACBRIDE and Willie were discovered by Pat. They were taken away by their own people, who considered them heroes. They were given a military funeral in a lonely graveyard far to the north. Shots were fired over their graves, and the tricolour flag of Ireland draped their coffins.

Sean Filey was tipped off that he was being watched by the Dublin Special Branch. There wasn't enough evidence to bring him to trial on a charge of kidnapping Frank Arbuthnot, and Claire couldn't be involved. But his name and Marie Dempster's were passed to the Irish government as dangerous subversives. Filey applied for a visa to visit the United States for a conference of psychiatrists in Cincinnati. He decided to accept an appointment for a two-year fellowship at an American university, and his practice in Dublin was closed down.

Marie Dempster was shot dead as she drove back from a party to her flat in Howth. The catastrophe that had cost the life of Hugh Macbride was not to go unpunished. The sentence had been pronounced upon her in the

North. It was generally agreed up there that she must have connived at Arbuthnot's escape.

Joe Burns applied for and got a transfer to a Gardai station in Trim. The family couldn't understand why he wanted to go. A better chance of promotion, he explained. He wasn't a nervous man, and he didn't have a twinge of conscience, but he didn't like driving past old Cavanagh's empty cottage of an evening.

EPILOGUE

"Mummy," the little boy said, "I'm looking forward to Christmas."

Claire smiled down at him. He liked to sit beside her on the sofa in front of the big open fire when he came back from school.

"So am I, Peter. It'll be nice to have Granny with us, won't it?"

"Yes." He nodded happily. Claudia had a brisk no-nonsense attitude towards children, and they loved it. She was affectionate but firm. "Is she coming for long?" he asked.

"Quite long," Claire answered. "She's going to look for a house near us. That'll be nice too."

A year ago she would have been impatient and brushed the questions aside. His dark eyes were always searching her face for reassurance. A lot had changed since her life had ended, that summer in Ireland, and begun again in the months that followed. Slowly, and painfully sometimes, with an ache of sadness.

It hadn't been easy for Neil or for her, but a new kind of love was growing between them. It had started as he held her on the windy tarmac on the military airfield.

"My darling, thank God, thank God ..." was all he had said.

And she said simply, "I'm so sorry, Neil."

Peter edged a little closer to his mother. "Will Granny be with us when the new baby comes?"

"I'm sure she will," Claire answered. "It'll be nice to have a baby, won't it? Lucy's growing up so fast."

He didn't say anything for a moment. He had very dark hair, and she ran her hand gently over his head.

"You won't love it better than Lucy and me, will you?"

She turned him to look at her. He glanced downwards and away, so that her heart turned over in recognition. "You'll never find him," Michael Harvey had warned her. He was right about everything else, but wrong about that. The Arbuthnot genes were strong in her son.

"No," Claire said firmly. "I'll never love anyone better than you and Lucy. Now, I think that's Daddy's car outside. Let's go and meet him, shall we?"

277

SNOW FELL IN IRELAND that winter. There was no hunting. No foxes ran at the old Reynard estate any more. For many years the Flanagans had refused the hunt permission to cross their land.

Snow fell at Riverstown, and it was so cold that part of the river froze. There was a new bus stop put up on the Naas road, and two women waited there, huddled against the driving wind. Such a winter was unknown. Everybody talked about it. It was grand for the children, throwing snowballs.

One woman was old; the other, young. They worked at a very grand stud farm about a mile up the road, cooking and cleaning for the family. There was a large "For Sale" sign nailed up beside the gates of Riverstown. The young woman looked at it, pulling her collar close round her neck.

"I heard the missus say she'd gone to England," she remarked.

"She has so," the old woman said. "The trouble was too much for her."

"The Arbuthnots were here a long time," the girl said.

"Maybe so," the old woman muttered. "They come. But in the end they go. Thanks be to God, here comes the bus."

EVELYN ANTHONY

In creating the character of Frank Arbuthnot in *No Enemy but Time*, Evelyn Anthony has drawn on personal experience, for she too had an Irish Catholic mother and an English Protestant father. Born in England, she has spent most of her life here, but from 1976 to 1982 she and her husband lived in County Kildare, in the Republic of Ireland. She remembers that although they were "received most kindly both by Anglo-Irish friends and by the Irish themselves, all the old conflicts and divisions seemed to lie just under the surface." The continuing conflict there makes her sad, she says. "There's so much that's marvellous about Ireland. If only class and religious prejudices could be swept away, it would be the most perfect country to live in."

The author of twenty-nine books, including the recent, popular Condensed Books selection, *Voices on the Wind*, Evelyn Anthony says that writing her latest novel was "very traumatic and emotional. I was worried when I started it because people said, 'This is a recipe for disaster. You'll just antagonize everybody.' But I thought, if I don't do this, I'll never be happy. I really wanted to do it."

What she likes doing when she's not writing, is spending time in her beautiful Tudor home in Essex, which she and her husband have lovingly restored and filled with sixteenth century furnishings and paintings. They open it to the public to raise money for charity at least twice a year. With her six children now grown up, Evelyn Anthony can indulge her passion for gardening and watching old films on TV. She already has an idea for her next novel, but says, "I'm not working on it yet. Writing *No Enemy but Time* left me a bit drained. I need a few months to recharge before attempting anything else."

TO KILL THE
POTEMKIN

A CONDENSATION OF THE BOOK BY

Mark Joseph

ILLUSTRATED BY HARRY SCHAARE

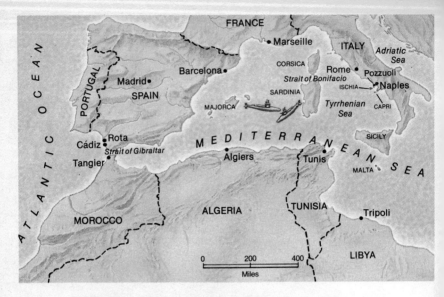

Jack Sorensen, the best sonarman in the US navy, has an almost uncanny talent for identifying the jumbled sounds of the ocean's depths.

To him, the task of manoeuvring the nuclear attack sub *Barracuda* is an exhilarating game requiring nerves of steel and unshakeable concentration—a game played hundreds of feet below the surface of the sea.

Cowboys and Cossacks, Sorensen calls it, and the object is to locate the Russians before they locate you. So far, Sorensen's team has been winning hands down.

But now *Barracuda* has come up against a new opponent, an experimental Russian sub called *Potemkin*. And suddenly, the game is being played for real . . .

Prologue

On May 27, 1968, at one o'clock in the afternoon, the USS *Scorpion*, a nuclear submarine with ninety-nine men aboard, was due to arrive at her home port of Norfolk, Virginia, after a ninety-day patrol. The families of the crew were waiting on the dock. At about three o'clock a navy public relations officer announced that *Scorpion* was overdue. She had last communicated on May 21, when she filed a routine position report from fifty miles south of the Azores, in mid-Atlantic.

After several more hours, the navy undertook a massive search of the waters around Norfolk. Over the next few days the search was widened into the deep Atlantic. On June 5 the navy declared *Scorpion* presumed lost with all hands, and on June 30 her name was struck from the navy list.

The loss of *Scorpion* was the worst disaster to befall a fully armed United States navy warship on patrol since the end of World War Two.

The USS *Scorpion*, SSN 589, one of six Skipjack class submarines, was two hundred and fifty-two feet long and thirty-one feet wide. An attack submarine, a hunter-killer, she carried no ballistic missiles. She was armed with torpedoes of various types, including several with nuclear warheads. Her crew represented the highest level of training of any military unit in the armed forces of the United States. They were the navy's elite.

Their loss went largely unnoticed. In May 1968 American soldiers and sailors were dying every day in Vietnam. Students at Columbia and elsewhere were laying siege to their universities. The cultural revolution in China, and the death the previous month of Dr. Martin Luther King, Jr., crowded the front pages of America's newspapers.

On June 5, 1968, a naval court of inquiry convened in Norfolk and took testimony in secret from more than ninety witnesses. On August 5 it was reported that technicians at a US navy SOSUS (Sound Surveillance System) listening station in Greece had made a tape recording of an implosion in mid-Atlantic on May 21.

The search in the deep Atlantic began in earnest. Using sonars, magnetometers, lights and cameras, an oceanographic research vessel was assigned the task of finding the wreck.

Finally, on October 29, the *Scorpion* was found, under eleven thousand feet of water, four hundred miles from her last reported position.

The court reconvened in November, examined the evidence, and declared that "the certain cause of the loss of the *Scorpion* cannot be ascertained." The death of SSN 589 became an official mystery.

During the early months of 1968 multiple submarine disasters were reported in the press. On February 25 the Israeli sub *Dakar* disappeared in the Mediterranean. On April 11 a Soviet navy Golf II class submarine sank in the Pacific. *Scorpion* imploded and sank on May 21. Were all these events coincidence? Answers may lie deep in the archives of all the navies involved. The essence of submarine warfare is secrecy and stealth, and submarine operations rank among the most carefully guarded secrets of all military powers. In the US navy, submariners are said to belong to the Silent Service.

Nevertheless, as in all navies, there is gossip. Rumours circulate for years. Was there a sub war in the late 1960s, when the Soviet navy was making frantic efforts to catch and technologically surpass the US navy?

The story that follows is fiction. The ships and the men who sail them are imaginary, but their time and the nature of their struggle are real. Then, as now, the submarine forces of the United States navy and the Soviet navy confronted one another under the oceans of the earth, playing a deadly game of nuclear war. What happened then, if it happened at all, may happen again . . .

Chapter 1

Twin dolphins faced each other across Sorensen's chest. Sailors called them dolphins, but the strange creatures tattooed on Sorensen's skin scarcely resembled the small singing whales that live in the sea. Their eyes bulged and their mouths gaped, as if they were about to devour the submarine making way between them. The sub, an old-fashioned diesel-electric with knife-edged prow and crude sonar dome, appeared to drive straight out of Sorensen's heart. Over the years the tattoo had faded, but the legend that curved over the sub was still legible: SSN 593.

Sorensen was a big man; with his wide shoulders and lean swimmer's muscles, he radiated tension like a sheathed sword.

The girl was enjoying herself. Ordinarily, she took little notice of the men who came from the navy base. Sorensen was different. He spent a lot of money and he treated her right. She liked the way his lopsided smile slanted across his face when he grinned. His hair was longer than regulation and slicked back over large ears. His skin was tanned and healthy.

She giggled. "You submarine guys are all a little crazy, you know? But you're the only one I ever saw with a tan. You look like one of them California surfers."

"Hardly likely. I'm from Oakland. That's California, but the only beach is a mudflat where people shoot ducks."

"Is that your ship on your chest? SSN 593?"

"USS *Barracuda*. The one and only." He paused. "What time is it?"

"Three am."

"Listen, be a good girl and let me sleep. Wake me up at four."

"Sure, sailor."

Sorensen closed his eyes and listened to the night. He strained to hear the sounds of the harbour, but they were too far away, lost in the low rumble of a sleeping city. Gradually the sounds of Chesapeake Bay were replaced by the ocean sounds inside his head. Submarine sounds, underwater sounds, sonar beacons. He fell asleep and dreamed he was a steel fish with a nuclear heart, swimming effortlessly through the vast blackness of the sea.

Asleep, he became *Barracuda*. The ship's technology became an extension of his senses; her sonars were like his own ears, plunging him into a world of pure sound: the open sea, a noisy place. Whales signal across thousands of miles. Surface ships clutter up the medium with their struggle against wind, waves and turbulence. As *Barracuda*, perfect and invulnerable lord of the deep, Sorensen ignored them all. He was searching for one unforgettable sound. It was another sub, sometimes far away, sometimes nearby, but always elusive. The sound faded in and out, one moment barely audible, an instant later roaring in his ears. It was deeper in pitch than that of any other sub in Sorensen's experience, and conveyed a sense of raw power and terrible menace.

This time it was closer than ever before, so close he could hear men breathing inside. They wore black uniforms. One of them was the sonar operator, sitting at a console. Sorensen listened to his beating heart, and when the man turned round, Sorensen saw his own face.

AFTER AN HOUR the girl gently shook his shoulder. "Jack, wake up."

"Go 'way."

"Listen, you told me to wake you up at four."

She heard him sigh. "OK. Give me a minute."

Awake, he realized the dream would never end. Perhaps he had lived under water too long. On each patrol *Barracuda* seemed to get closer to the Russians. Or maybe the Russians were getting closer to him.

"Did you have a bad dream?" the girl asked.

"Why? Did I say anything?"

"You said, 'It's a Russian,' but the rest was mumbo jumbo."

He slapped himself on the cheek. "Shut up, Sorensen. You talk too much." He stood up and grinned. "I must be getting old."

Through an open window he heard trucks passing on a highway, the only sounds of a city asleep. The ocean never slept. Under water there was neither night nor day, only the passing of the watches and the blinking numbers on a digital chronometer.

It was time to go. *Barracuda* sailed at dawn. While he was putting on his uniform, there was a knock on the door.

"Sorensen, you in there?" The voice was pure East Los Angeles.

"Who's that?" the girl asked.

"Open it up," Sorensen said.

Manuel Lopez stood in the corridor, two hundred and fifty pounds of Mexican torpedoman dressed in the full regalia of a chief petty officer.

"Come on, Ace. You're late. The shore patrol has kindly lent me a car and a driver. He's waiting downstairs."

"How d'you know I was here?"

"I'm chief of the boat, Sorensen. It's my job to know where every one of you guys is, every minute. Let's go."

Sorensen looked at himself in the mirror. He needed a shave and his uniform was rumpled. He drew himself to attention, placed his hat two fingers above his eyebrows, and saluted.

SORENSEN SAT IN THE BACK of the jeep, peering at the shabby streets and rotting Victorian houses of Norfolk. To him, Norfolk, Virginia was a target, a blip on a Soviet attack console, and when he was there, he felt naked and exposed, like a sub on the surface.

The jeep turned a corner and he caught a glimpse of lights on the river and the darkness of the Atlantic beyond.

"What's the word, Chief? We got us a Russkie out there?"

Lopez shook his head. "Nah. There was one sub that tried to get in yesterday, but Ivan hasn't figured out yet that we can track him anywhere in the Atlantic. We let this November class get in as near as fifty miles offshore, but *Mako* flushed her last night. She won't be back."

"Why didn't they leave it for us?"

"You're nuts, Sorensen, you know that? All you ever want to do is chase the Russians around the ocean. Me, I just like a nice quiet patrol with no excitement."

286

"That's because you're a torpedoman, Lopez. It makes you nervous to think that some day you may have to fire one of those things."

"This is my last patrol, Sorensen. I been down below for twenty years and I've never fired a war shot yet. I want to go out the same way."

"I'm gonna miss you, Chief."

"You won't miss me, Ace. You'll be too busy playing Cowboys and Cossacks to think about me in LA, lyin' around the pool sippin' a cold beer." Lopez laughed, his gold teeth glinting in the street light.

Traffic picked up as they neared the navy base. The early shift was going to work in the dark. The shore-patrol driver stopped at the gate, and the marine guard waved them through.

Sorensen said, "I heard a nasty rumour, Chief. I heard they assigned thirteen apprentice seamen to the ship yesterday."

Lopez turned round to face the back seat. "You heard wrong. They're not all apprentices. Yours is a third class."

"Mine? What do you mean, mine?" Sorensen groaned.

"That's the way it is. You get Sonarman Third Class Michael Fogarty."

"I don't suppose he's qualified in subs?"

"You suppose right. But I hear he's another hotshot, just like you, Ace. He's your baby, you keep him in line."

The first red splashes of dawn appeared as the jeep wound its way through the base. Two hundred people lined the submarine pier. Families clustered round their sailors, mothers patted flat their sons' collars, little boys saluted their fathers. One by one the sailors kissed their wives and children and disappeared down the hatch.

There was a commotion as the crowd parted before the jeep. Lopez and the driver sat in front, faces impassive, eyes straight ahead. From the back seat Sorensen waved his hat to the crowd like an astronaut on parade. "I love ya, I love ya," he shouted to the kids.

Out of the side of his mouth Lopez growled, "Shut up, Sorensen. You ain't no movie star."

Sorensen smiled and continued to wave. The kids waved back.

The jeep stopped at the gangway. Straining at her lines, *Barracuda* rode low in the water. She had the look of a great black shark, a predator of the deep come momentarily into the light. Bunting hung from the gangway, and for a moment the white stars in the fabric shimmered red.

Sorensen smartly squared his hat and climbed out of the jeep. Reaching inside his jumper pocket, he extracted a five dollar bill and dropped it in the shore patrolman's lap.

"Thanks for the lift, pal. This is my stop."

FROM HIS PERCH ON THE BRIDGE Captain John Springfield watched the proceedings on the pier. The tall, slender Texan had been in command of *Barracuda* for eighteen months, long enough, he thought, to have become

287

intimately acquainted with the ship and her crew. He scrutinized the sailors as they went aboard. Torpedomen, yeomen, reactor technicians, the quartermaster. The eldest was the steward, forty-three-year-old Jimmy "Cakes" Colby. The youngest was an eighteen-year-old seaman apprentice, Duane Hicks. Springfield himself was thirty-five.

He watched Sorensen come aboard. At sea Sorensen was perfectly disciplined. Ashore—well . . .

The ship tugged gently at her lines. The tide had peaked, stopped for an instant and was now ebbing back to the sea. A naval band struck up "The Stars and Stripes Forever", and a flurry of butterflies churned Springfield's stomach.

IN THE CONTROL ROOM the Executive Officer, Lieutenant Commander Leo Pisaro, was going through the departure checklist when Sorensen came through the hatch.

"Good afternoon, Sorensen, good of you to join us."

Sorensen snapped to attention. "Petty Officer First Class Sorensen reporting for duty, sir."

Pisaro was starkly bald, swarthy, tenacious. His jumpsuit was covered with insignia, a patchwork of blazing lightning bolts, missiles, guns, swords and engines of destruction. The newest and most prominent patch was a sub whose bow tapered into the snout of a great barracuda. "SSN 593," it read. "Shipkiller."

"You're four hours late, Sorensen. It's a good thing Chief Lopez knew where to find you."

"Yes, sir."

Pisaro shook his head, smiling to himself. Every cruise was the same. Either the shore patrol or the civilian police would drag Sorensen back to the ship, and he would stand in the control room with that stupid grin on his face. His uniform was a mess.

One thing was certain: Sorensen could go into the sonar room right now, sit down at his console and drive the ship to Naples.

"All right. Get out of your blues. Take a shower. I want you in sonar in fifteen minutes."

Sorensen descended two decks to the forward crew quarters. The compartment was crowded with boisterous sailors changing into ship-board uniforms—dark-blue nylon jumpsuits and rubber-soled shoes.

"What say, Ace? Where the hell you been?"

Sorensen searched the bunks for the owner of the Southern drawl. A freckle-faced redhead peeked out from behind a technical manual.

"Hey, Willie Joe."

"Where you been, man?"

"Tokyo."

"Tokyo, Japan?"

"That's the one."

Sonarman Second Class Willie Joe Black laid down his book and yellow felt-tipped pen. "Tell me something, Ace. Why did you go to Japan with just three days' liberty?"

"I got a friend over there, an old pal from sub school who lives there. He's what you might call an advanced gadget freak. He likes to make toys a few years before anybody else."

"So what did he make for you?"

"This." Sorensen tossed a tape recorder onto Willie Joe's bunk.

"What is it?"

Sorensen pushed a button and out came the Beatles' "Can't Buy Me Love". Throughout the compartment, heads swivelled towards the music.

"It's a tape recorder, the smallest in the world. Rechargeable battery, ultrathin tape, the works."

Shaking his head in amazement, Willie Joe picked up his pen and resumed his study of advanced hydraulics.

The Beatles went into "Back in the USSR". Sorensen looked round at the faces shining in the bright fluorescent lights. He recognized all but one of the sailors.

"Willie Joe," he said, "I hear we got a green pea."

"That's right."

"Did you check him out?"

"No, he just got here." Willie Joe nodded his head in the direction of the young sailor standing in the passageway, hands stuffed into the pockets of his jumpsuit, staring at the maze of piping and cables that ran through the top of the compartment. He didn't appear shy, but he hung back from the crowd round Willie Joe's bunk and the little tape recorder. He had a pretty face and a look that wasn't so much cocky as confident.

Fogarty felt Sorensen's eyes looking him up and down. He turned to meet Sorensen's stare. Sorensen walked over to him. "Fogarty, right?"

"Right." Fogarty smiled. "You must be Sorensen."

"That's me."

"I heard about you in sonar school. They played us tapes of all the different Soviet subs and told us you're the guy who made the tapes. They said you've collected more signatures of Soviet subs than anyone else."

"That's what they told you? It wasn't me, kid. It was *Barracuda*. Willie Joe there, he's done his share too. It's the luck of the draw. Whatever we do here, we do together."

Fogarty nodded. "That makes me the luckiest guy in the navy. I asked for this ship."

"You must believe in miracles. I'll tell you straight, kid. *Barracuda* is going to get a special assignment in Naples, and they've put you and all these other apprentices on this ship to foul us up and get in our way."

Sorensen was a good four inches taller than Fogarty, and his narrowed, unsmiling eyes bore down now on the younger man. When he saw that Fogarty didn't flinch, kept cool, he relaxed.

"Tell me something Fogarty. Why'd you ask for this ship?"

"Because of you, Sorensen. I wanted to learn from the best."

"You mean you don't know everything yet?"

Fogarty seemed to blush, and shook his head. Sorensen punched him in the shoulder and was surprised to find the muscle hard as steel. "All right, kid. Welcome aboard."

Sorensen retrieved his tape recorder, switched it off and put it in his locker. "Show's over for today, gents. Tune in tomorrow."

He stripped off his blues and stashed them in his locker. In shorts he paraded through the compartment, and whistling "We all live in a yellow submarine", he headed for the showers.

A YEAR OUT OF NAVAL COLLEGE and fresh from Nuclear Power School, Lieutenant Fred Hoek was making his second patrol. Twenty-three years old, overweight and plagued by pimples, Hoek was the ninth sonar officer to serve on *Barracuda* in eight years.

He was standing at attention in the Executive Officer's tiny cabin, watching Pisaro shuffle papers. Pisaro's thick lips and large teeth made Hoek nervous.

"At ease, Lieutenant. Sit down."

Hoek sat at attention. Pisaro stacked his papers in a neat pile. "You're going to be wearing two hats this cruise, Lieutenant, weapons and sonar. Did you go down to the torpedo room and have a chat with the boys down there?"

"Yes, sir."

"All right, have you looked through the sonarmen's records?"

"Yes, sir. Davic and Black are solid, hardworking men. Davic is, ah, unusual."

"He wants to go to work for the CIA when his enlistment is up. He knows quite a lot about the Russians."

"Yes, sir. Black is up for first class, so he's going to be a bookworm this cruise."

"Willie Joe Black is a top-notch technician. On any other ship he'd be the leading sonarman. I expect him to get his promotion and move on." Pisaro lit a cigarette. "That brings us to Petty Officer Sorensen. Did you go through his records carefully?"

"Yes, sir."

"And what do you think, Lieutenant?"

"Well, Commander, he's clearly a genius at sonar, but otherwise, he's somewhat unconventional."

"Somewhat? He's a maniac." Pisaro burst out laughing. "OK, Lieutenant. You're very young, and I'll give you the benefit of the doubt. A short lectúre: the strength of the navy is our senior petty officers. You don't see many of them around the Naval Academy. They're called men."

"Yes, sir."

"Petty Officer Sorensen knows more about sonar than you or I ever will. Sonar is an art. Every sound is a question of interpretation, and Sorensen has an uncanny feel for it. Don't ask me how. I doubt if he can explain it himself. If he is, as you say, unconventional, we tolerate that down here. As long as a man does his job, we leave him alone."

"Yes, sir."

"All right. Now, the new man. Fogarty. Sorensen will look after him. Here's one more short lecture: this is an experienced crew. They've been through a lot together. When we close the hatch and dive, we're all alone. We're at war with the sea every second, and not far from the same with the Russians. Under those conditions there is no such thing as a routine patrol. That's all. Dismissed."

HOEK FOUND THE SONARMEN waiting in the control room.

"Good morning, sir," Sorensen said.

"Good morning." Hoek cleared his throat, realizing that nothing he had learned at the academy had prepared him adequately for this moment. He saw Sorensen's eyes testing him. Next to Sorensen, Willie Joe looked like a puppy dog, anxious to please. Then came Davic, a scowl firmly etched across his plump face. At the end of the line was Fogarty, looking straight ahead.

Hoek cleared his throat again. "Our transit time to Naples will be ten days. We don't expect to encounter any problems, but let's keep our ears alert and our eyes on the screen."

Sorensen rolled his eyes. It was a tradition in the Submarine Service for the most junior officer on a ship to be assigned the duties of sonar officer. Sorensen reckoned the only things these young lieutenants had in common were a bad complexion and a drive to become admirals.

Hoek continued, "There is one thing to note. Crossing the Atlantic, we will be participating in a test of a new SOSUS deep-water submarine detection system. As you know, the bottom of our coastal waters has been seeded with passive sonars for ten years. This new extension of the system will enable us to track any sub in the North Atlantic. The hydrophones are laid out in a grid centred in the Azores. It's similar to the system we've been operating in the Caribbean for the last year. As far as we know, the Russians don't know anything about it. Any questions?"

Sorensen shook his head.

"OK, Chief Lopez has assigned the watches. Sorensen, you take the first watch, Willie Joe the second, Davic the third. Sorensen, you will be responsible for training the new man, Third Class Fogarty."

"Yes, sir."

Nearby, Commander Pisaro, who also served as navigation officer, was making a similar speech as he stood before the assembled helmsmen, planesmen and quartermaster. When he had finished he spoke out for the benefit of the entire control room. "Set the manoeuvring watch and let's go."

THE SONAR ROOM WAS AMIDSHIPS, next to the control room. It contained three operators' consoles, each with a keyboard and display screen as well as a cabinet for tools and parts.

Fogarty followed Sorensen into the tiny chamber and looked closely at the banks of loudspeakers and tape recorders mounted on the bulkheads. Layers of acoustic tile and cork insulated the compartment from noise in the control room and the machinery aft.

The colours were drab and military. The air-conditioner never completely cleaned out the smell of cigarette smoke and sweat. Years earlier, Sorensen had taped up a photo of his hero, John Kennedy. It was still there, yellow and ragged, partially obscured by fleshy pinups and a photograph of Sergei Gorshkov, admiral of the fleet of the Soviet Union. A large chart displayed line drawings of the several classes of Soviet submarines: Whiskey, Hotel, Echo, Golf, November and the new Viktor.

Sorensen put on his earphones. His fingers danced over the keyboard and activated the array of sixteen hydrophones, each a foot in diameter, mounted on the hull around the bow and down the sides of the ship. The hydrophones—the passive "listening" sonars—were sensitive microphones that collected sounds that travelled through the water, sometimes across great distances.

He listened to the familiar sounds of *Barracuda*'s machinery, the pulse of pumps and the throttling steam. He heard the underwater beacons, fixed to the bottom of Chesapeake Bay, that would guide the ship through the channel and into the Atlantic. Satisfied that all was in order, he took off his earphones and looked at Fogarty.

To his surprise, Fogarty's eyes were closed. He was literally all ears. "What do you hear?" Sorensen asked.

"*Barracuda*."

"And what does she sound like?"

Fogarty opened his eyes and smiled. His eyes were dark brown, almost black. There was a hint of controlled tension in them.

"She sounds like World War Three."

Sorensen laughed. "OK, wise guy, test BQR-2, passive array."

"Testing BQR-2, passive array." Fogarty checked the circuits which connected the hydrophones to his console. "Test positive. All circuits functioning."

"Test active array."

Fogarty punched more buttons, activating the transducers mounted in the centre of each hydrophone. The transducers created the familiar sonar "pings" that radiated through the water and, if they struck an object, returned as an echo heard by the hydrophones. This "echo-ranger" was used only in special circumstances, since each time it was activated it revealed the sub's location.

"Testing active array. Test positive."

"Test target-seeking frequency." In combat the target-seeking frequency was created by a special transducer, to locate and pinpoint a target. To the target it was the sound of doom, followed immediately by a torpedo.

"Testing target-seeking frequency. Test positive."

Sorensen lit a cigarette. "How'd you do in sonar school, kid?"

Fogarty flushed. It seemed he did that easily. "I was first in the class."

"Good for you. You look like a smart kid. Where you from?"

"Minnesota."

"A child of the frozen north, huh? OK, read the notice on the door. Read it out loud."

Fogarty twisted round in his seat and read out, " 'Warning! This is a Secure Area. Any Unauthorized Use of Classified Material will Result in Imprisonment and Forfeiture of Pay. Removal of Classified Material is a Violation of the National Security Act.' "

"That's not all," Sorensen said.

At the bottom was an addition, scribbled in large block letters. Fogarty read, " 'LEAVE YOUR MIND BEHIND.' "

"That's what you do when you come in here," Sorensen said.

ON THE BRIDGE CAPTAIN SPRINGFIELD told the lookouts to be sharp. Two tugs stood off the bow, but Springfield intended to take his ship into the channel without assistance.

"Deck party, stand by to cast off lines," he shouted to the sailors fore and aft. He watched the shore as the ship drifted with the wind and current. Some people on the pier began to cheer and wave.

When *Barracuda* cleared the dock and there was no danger of fouling her huge propeller, the captain ordered, "All ahead slow."

Sorensen and Fogarty listened intently to the sounds coming through their earphones. They heard the *whoosh* of water as it began to wash over the hull, and every revolution of the prop, which would be audible until they submerged to four hundred feet. Ungainly on the surface, the ship rolled and pitched slightly as they headed for the channel.

"Sonar to control. Do you have the beacon on the repeater?" The repeater was the sonar console in the control room that duplicated what the sonarmen saw and heard.

It was Pisaro who replied, "Control to sonar. We have it."

Twenty minutes after leaving the pier the captain and the lookouts came down from the sail. The sail, which was called the conning tower in earlier submarines, also housed the ship's bridge. Springfield closed the hatch.

"Prepare to dive," said the captain. "Take her down, Leo."

Barracuda angled over and slid silently beneath the sea.

Chapter 2

Barracuda steamed through the Atlantic at twenty-four knots, four hundred feet beneath the surface. There were no wind, no waves, no turbulence. As the prop turned, the ship moved ahead with maximum efficiency. Three precise inertial navigation gyroscopes recorded every movement of the ship in three dimensions. Without contacting the surface, the navigation computer determined *Barracuda*'s exact position.

The crew settled into the patrol routine of repetitious drills—damage-control drill, collision drill, atmosphere systems failure drill, weapons drill. Muzak wafted through the ship and air-conditioners maintained a comfortable seventy-two degrees.

From the conning station the captain looked round the brilliantly illuminated control room. The greenish hue of fluorescent lighting, accentuated by the display screens, gave the compartment an unearthly glow. "Lieutenant Hoek," he said to the weapons officer, "you have the conn."

Fred Hoek moved his heavy frame up to the conning station, and Springfield strolled over to the displays that monitored the nuclear chain reaction taking place fifteen feet away. Instinctively he fondled his film badge, a strip of sensitive celluloid that measured radiation. Like everyone else, the captain turned in his badge once a month to a medical orderly, who processed the film in the darkroom and determined how much radiation each crew member was receiving.

IN THE STERN OF THE SHIP, in the steering machinery room, Machinist's Mate Barnes was standing his watch amid the jungle of pipes and compressors that moved the rudder and stern planes. Barnes worked at a lathe, turning parts for the constant maintenance and repair of the ship's intricate machinery. From the engine room came the high whine of turbines and the throttling noises of high pressure steam.

"Howdy, Barnes." It was Sorensen, standing in the hatch in a pair of red Bermuda shorts, flip-flops and wrap-around sunglasses. He walked over to a small door with a brass plaque that read: WELCOME TO SORENSEN'S BEACH. NO VOLLEYBALL ALLOWED. PLEASE KNOCK. Sorensen went in without knocking.

Designated in the ship's plans as storage space for electronic parts, Sorensen's Beach was barely six and a half feet long by four feet wide.

Stooping under the low ceiling, he switched on a pair of bright sunlamps and pulled a plastic mat and a wooden beach chair out of a cupboard. Taped to the door was a travel poster. California. Sun, surf, sand.

"Tide's in." He turned on the tape recorder and out flowed the mellow tones of Dave Brubeck's "Home at Last". From a pile of magazines he grabbed the one on top, *Newsweek*. Bad news. Riot, revolution, war.

The chaos of life ashore made him crazy. Millions of half-wits running around in confusion, like an ant colony gone berserk. Under water, the madness disappeared. Inside *Barracuda*'s pressure hull Sorensen had found a purpose and an identity. On the ship life was orderly, pure, simple. The sub demanded total discipline and absolute dedication. Every man had a job to do and did it with his whole being or not at all.

Few could give that much, but certain men thrived in the artificial environment of a submarine. For Sorensen it was liberation. He had joined the navy on his eighteenth birthday and never looked back. Now, after ten years, he realized that he couldn't stay below for ever. For one thing, navy regulations were against it and eventually he would be promoted to chief and stuck in a sonar school somewhere.

IN THE TORPEDO ROOM Chief Lopez was feeding a fly to his pet, a brown Mexican scorpion named Zapata. The scorpion lived in a glass cage mounted over the firing console, and was the subject of many legends.

In the galley the Filipino cook, Stanley Real, had worked for hours on a *sauce demi-glace*. Stanley fancied himself a *chef de cuisine* rather than a naval cook. He was trying to explain the difference to Cakes Colby, the steward. "This sauce, it is cook for three days."

Cakes thought Stanley's fuss over the sauce was ludicrous.

"It looks like gravy to me, Stanley."

Cakes was making his last cruise. The only member of the crew to have served in World War Two, he had seen a lot of cooks in twenty-five years, but never one like Stanley Real.

In the forward crew quarters Fogarty lay sleepless in his bunk. In two days his world had changed so completely that he seemed to have forgotten who he was. The discipline of the sub often required him to react without thinking. On a submarine there was no margin for error. A moment's hesitation could mean disaster. Fogarty knew that in time the discipline would become automatic, but the learning was painful. He was being bombarded by information. A whole new world was being revealed to him in the sonar room—the sea and all its multifarious sounds—and he was close to overload.

Sitting watches with Sorensen was an exacting experience. In his casual way, Sorensen was a perfectionist who never tolerated mistakes. Off watch, Fogarty found himself running through the sound signatures of Soviet submarines, retrieving them from memory. Night and day had been replaced by the rotation of the watches. He knew it was five o'clock in the morning and four hundred feet up there was weather, a sunrise, a sky—but on *Barracuda* there was only machinery, a handful of radioactive metal and one hundred men.

The compartment was dark. His bunk was a tidy cocoon. To his right he could feel the acoustic rubber insulation that lined the pressure hull. To his left, a flimsy grey curtain gave him a sense of seclusion. He heard the whirr of air-conditioners, and the sounds of sleeping men.

All his life he had waited to get on a nuclear-powered sub. When *Nautilus*, the world's first nuclear-propelled submarine, went under the polar ice cap and surfaced at the North Pole, Fogarty had made up his mind that he was going to become a submariner. He read *20,000 Leagues Under the Sea* so many times that his paperback copy fell apart.

At an early age he had learned to distinguish the different types of submarines. First, there were the SSNs, fast attack subs, hunter-killers like *Nautilus* and *Barracuda*. Then there were the FBMs, the Fleet Ballistic Missile subs. The missile subs had frightened him. The idea of a ship that could by itself destroy a civilization drove a wedge of doubt into his adolescent mind. Though he never wavered from his ambition to join the Submarine Service, he grew increasingly haunted by dark visions of nuclear war. But, in the end, nothing was going to keep him off a sub.

Now, here he was, breathing air-conditioned air and sitting watches with the great Sorensen himself. In sonar school the gossip had been that Sorensen was the only American enlisted man whose name was known to the Russians. He doubted that, but in any case it wasn't Sorensen the legend but Sorensen the taskmaster he had to deal with.

Leave your mind behind.

IN THE MANOEUVRING ROOM Master Chief Alexander Wong, the head nuclear engineer, and the other three men on watch were discussing the highly paid civilian jobs waiting for them when they got out of the navy. When the captain walked in, though, they stopped talking and stared at their displays. Springfield stood in silence. Then, without warning, he reached over Wong's shoulder to the main control panel and flipped a bright red switch. The neutron chain reaction came to a complete stop. The ship would soon be without main propulsion power, and begin to sink.

The reactor-control team responded instantly. Wong grabbed the intercom. "This is a drill, this is a drill. Reactor scram, reactor scram. All hands to damage-control stations. All hands to damage-control stations. This is a drill." Alarms began sounding in every compartment. In the forward crew quarters Pisaro stood in the hatch. "This is a drill. Hit the deck." Sleepy sailors stumbled out of their bunks and into their shoes. Many slept in their clothes, ready for such a moment.

The passageway was jammed. The new seamen collided with one another in the hatches and banged into hard steel at the turns. Grunts and howls of pain rattled around in the dim light.

Damage-control teams put on asbestos suits and checked fire extinguishers. Everything loose was fastened down and double-checked.

In the galley Stanley was indignant. The cook could not have explained the physics of a reactor scram, but he knew that with no power for his stove his sauce was ruined. He slopped the brown fluid into a plastic bag and swore in a Filipino dialect.

Sorensen moved rapidly through the ship on bare feet, one step ahead of the confusion. In the control room Lieutenant Hoek still had the conn. He gave the commands to recover from the reactor scram, a sailor spun a valve and compressed air was forced into the ballast tanks, expelling the water into the sea. The rate of descent was slackened.

"Blow after tanks. Slowly, very slowly. Let's not spill the coffee."

Willie Joe was on duty in the sonar room when Sorensen burst in. The screens were clear. There was nothing around them but ocean, nine thousand feet of it under the keel.

"OK, go," Sorensen said. Willie Joe quickly changed into a white asbestos suit and hurried to his damage-control station.

Fogarty came in. Sorensen frowned.

"You have to get in here quicker than that, Fogarty. Much quicker. If people are in your way, jump over them, run through them."

"Aye aye."

The ship was still going down. Fogarty stared at the digital fathometer: six hundred and fifty, seven hundred, seven hundred and fifty feet. His face remained impassive. The sea didn't frighten him.

Sorensen liked his nerve.

At eight hundred feet the ship levelled off and stopped. The sea was quiet.

"Tell me what you hear," Sorensen said.

"The turbogenerator," Fogarty replied.

"That's all?" Sorensen punched a button and the overhead loudspeakers came on. An intermittent scratching sound came from the sea.

"What's that?" Sorensen asked.

Fogarty listened. "I don't know."

"Turtles," Sorensen said cheerfully. "Fishing at one hundred and fifty feet."

"Attention all hands," Hoek's voice came through the intercom. "Prepare for slow speed."

The ship began to move. The turtle sounds faded. A moment later weird beeps and hoots came through the speakers.

"Whales," Sorensen said, and began to hoot and beep himself. Every few seconds his fingers reached for the keyboard as he altered the

combination of arrays and filters, playing the sea like a vast water organ.

Fogarty said, "In sonar school they told us to filter out whales. They called all marine noises signal interference."

"Forget school, Fogarty. This is the real ocean. If you're going to be a good sonarman, you listen to everything, and you think about everything you hear. Are you following me?"

"I am."

"Tell me, Fogarty, how come you volunteered for subs?"

Fogarty shrugged. "I've wanted to get on one of these things since I was a little kid. That's the truth."

Sorensen nodded. "I see. A genuine sub freak. I suppose you were first in your class in sub school, too."

Fogarty shook his head. "No. Second."

"Shame on you."

Fogarty smiled. "What about you, Sorensen? Why are you here?"

"I had no sense, no real education, although I read a lot. I got married when I was seventeen. I needed a job, so on my eighteenth birthday I walked into a navy recruiter's office and said, 'Man, I built my first sonar when I was twelve out of a microphone, a plastic bag and a tube of rubber cement.' He said, 'Son, sign on the dotted line.' I signed. I was fresh meat for the fleet."

Sorensen paused to light a cigarette, and Fogarty asked, "Where's your wife?"

"She divorced me when I reenlisted. She hated the navy. A few years ago, the night before the ship was leaving she told me she'd be gone when I got back. I didn't blame her. She was looking at two months of lonely nights in a crummy naval town. I think she went back to California."

THEY CONTINUED AT SLOW SPEED for two hours. Sorensen assigned Fogarty the elaborate, time-consuming task of checking all the circuits that ran from the sonar room to the torpedo room in the bow.

Alone in the sonar room, Sorensen popped open his console and gazed at the maze of circuitry. Over the years he had modified it extensively, sometimes without authorization.

On his trip to Japan he had acquired not one but two of the miniature tape recorders, one of which he now inserted into a disguised panel.

Chapter 3

The Strait of Gibraltar forms one of the great bottlenecks in the world ocean. Historically, control of the Strait has meant control of the Mediterranean. Since the end of World War Two the US navy has considered "the sea in the middle of the earth" an American lake.

Seven days after leaving Norfolk, *Barracuda* approached the Strait at slow speed. In the sonar room Sorensen listened to the sonic beacon fixed to the bottom of the Strait, which guided submerged ships through the deep channel. He locked on and the ship slowly passed into the Mediterranean.

Presently they heard engine noise from another sub nearby. Before Sorensen could ask, Fogarty said, "British. HMS *Valiant*."

"Very good, very good indeed."

TWO DAYS LATER *BARRACUDA* was two hundred and fifty miles from Naples. Springfield and Pisaro studied the display screen on the navigation console, which showed an electronic chart of the Tyrrhenian Sea between Sardinia and the Bay of Naples. A blip in the centre of the screen represented the ship. A flickering digital readout reported the changing longitude and latitude.

Springfield had ordered a burst of speed. Driving *Barracuda* at forty-seven knots was like flying blind under water. The noise rendered her listening sonars useless, and there was danger of colliding with another submerged vessel. Every fifty miles Springfield slowed the sub to a crawl and quietened all machinery to allow the sonar operators to "clear baffles", the blind spots in her sonar. While the ship slowly turned three hundred and sixty degrees, the sonarmen listened through the hydrophones, the passive sonars.

Pisaro blew cigarette smoke away from the console. "There's supposed to be a storm up above," Springfield said to him. "If we're going to hear anything, we'd better get Sorensen up here."

"Aye aye, skipper." Pisaro spoke into the intercom. "Control to engineering. Listen, Chief, send somebody aft to drag Sorensen back into the real world. I want him in sonar."

"Engineering to control. Aye aye. The Ace will be in place."

IN THE SONAR ROOM Sonarman Second Class Emile Davic sat at his operator's console. He was alone.

Three hours into his watch, Davic sipped a sixth cup of coffee and daydreamed about food in Naples. Davic hated Naples: it was dirty and reminded him of the worst parts of New York, but he relished the food.

As a boy of twelve Davic had emigrated with his mother from Budapest to Brooklyn. Eventually he became naturalized, but he never became "American". He didn't know how to have fun, and devoted his life to the study of modern languages and the cultivation of a bitter hatred of the Russians. Anything else seemed frivolous.

He had joined the Submarine Service to get as close to the Soviets as possible. When World War Three started, Davic didn't want to miss it. To him, serving on the sub was a solemn obligation. He considered himself a

300

dedicated cold warrior and regarded anyone less fanatic than himself as a fool. Naturally, he despised Sorensen, whose open irreverence Davic found intolerable. Sorensen acted as if *Barracuda* were his personal property, provided by the navy for his amusement. In spite of himself, Davic envied Sorensen his talent and was jealous of his privileges.

Davic was now contemplating the photo of Admiral Gorshkov. He was the one who had taped the Russian's stony-faced portrait to the bulkhead. Gorshkov, architect of the modern Soviet navy, was the officer who had dragged the Russian fleet out of the nineteenth century and transformed it into a blue-water force. And that frightened Davic, who as a young boy had witnessed Soviet tanks in Budapest. He kept the photograph of Sergei Gorshkov as a reminder.

MACHINIST BARNES BANGED ON THE DOOR to Sorensen's Beach.

The door opened. Dripping sweat, Sorensen stuck his head out. "What's up?"

"They want you in sonar."

"Where are we?"

"I don't know. Switzerland?"

"Listen, Barnes, did you make my little box yet?"

"Your little watertight box? It's next."

"I gotta have it tomorrow in Naples. Skipper's orders."

"Not to worry. What's it for, anyway?"

"You got me, sport." Sorensen took off his sunglasses and winked.

THE DOOR TO THE SONAR ROOM jerked open and Sorensen suddenly filled the tiny space. He sat down at the supervisor's console, logged in and adjusted a headset over his ears.

"Just carry on," he said to Davic. Sorensen didn't look at the screen. He closed his eyes and listened.

Barracuda was following a standard NATO deep-water route off Sardinia. The deep waters of the Mediterranean constituted a notoriously fickle sonar environment. Sound waves were bounced up and down by thermal layers and distorted by sea mounts and an uneven bottom. It was impossible to determine the range of a contact unless it was moving.

"Control to sonar, prepare for three-sixty-degree revolution."

"Sonar to control. Aye aye," Davic replied.

As the ship slowed, the machinery quietened and the screens gradually cleared. The ship banked slightly as it turned. A third of the way through the turn, they clearly heard a propeller rotating on the surface. Sorensen estimated the range as five miles.

"Sonar to control. Contact on the surface, bearing one one seven. Speed two knots."

"Control to helm. Make our course bearing one one seven."

"Course one one seven, aye."

The ship turned back to the left and once again the sonar operators heard the propeller.

"All stop," ordered the captain.

The sub drifted, listening. Sorensen heard a second propeller. Twin screws. A small ship was barely making way on the surface.

"It's your watch, Davic," Sorensen said. "What do you think it is?"

As Davic logged the contact into the computer he mumbled, "It could be anything: a coastal freighter, a fisherman?"

Sorensen opened his eyes and began watching the screen, listening intently. NATO routes avoided commercial shipping lanes and fishing grounds. He had a hunch. "Fee fie foe fum, I smell the blood of a Russian bum. Davic," he said, "that's a Soviet surveillance ship up there, a trawler, and he's got us pegged for sure."

"What makes you think so?"

"Tomorrow, the Sixth Fleet is going to sail from Naples, right up this alley. Now, if I was your friend Admiral Gorshkov, I'd wait for those ships right about here."

Before Sorensen could go on, a streak flickered across the extreme edge of the sonar screen, a faint electronic shadow. Sorensen snapped to attention. The trawler had company.

Deftly Sorensen locked his sonars on bearing one one seven, and immediately heard the throb of a saltwater pump, the type of pump that circulates seawater round a steam condenser, the unmistakable signature of a nuclear reactor. A nuclear submarine was hovering under the trawler, listening to *Barracuda*.

"Bingo," he said. "Sonar to control. We have another contact, bearing one one seven, range estimated ten thousand yards, speed zero zero. Contact is submerged. Repeat, contact is submerged."

"Control to sonar," said Pisaro's voice, "the repeater shows nothing." Pisaro paused for a moment. "Wait a minute, wait a minute. That's impossible. No Russkie sub has been reported in this sector of the Med. How in hell did he get in here?"

The faint streak returned at the same bearing, directly below the trawler. Pisaro swore. "Quartermaster, sound general quarters."

Throughout the ship loudspeakers drove one hundred men into furious but disciplined activity. "General quarters, general quarters. All hands man battle stations. This is not a drill. Man battle stations."

Davic stood up and took off his headset. His battle station was forward, as part of a damage-control team. He opened a cupboard and pulled on a white asbestos suit. Inside the plexiglass faceplate he looked like a chubby astronaut. "I would prefer to remain in the sonar room," he said into the microphone inside his helmet.

"Look, Davic, I don't assign the stations. Lopez does."

"That's *my* Russian, Sorensen," Davic shouted.

"Sure, he's all yours. He's in your log. Don't worry, you'll get your chance to go toe-to-toe with him."

Davic muttered a Hungarian curse and went out.

A moment later Fogarty rushed in, sat down and put on his earphones. He heard a deep throb, an unnatural predatory growl, and suddenly he was very alert. He was hearing his first Russian.

"What's he doing?" he asked Sorensen.

"Our friend Ivan is just sitting there listening to us with a big fat smile on his face. The joke's on us."

Fogarty watched the resolution of the streak improve as the range closed. Invisible to the rest of the world, the two subs drifted, five miles apart, listening warily for the slightest hint of a wrong move.

"Well," Sorensen said, "the game is on."

"What game?" Fogarty asked.

"*The* game. The game we play with the Russians. Cowboys and Cossacks." Fogarty stared at him. "Call it practice for World War Three." Sorensen switched on the overhead speakers and took off his earphones. "His weapons-control system is locked right on your beating heart," he said with a smile.

"Control to sonar. Prepare to lock on weapons-control."

"Sonar to control. Prepare to lock on weapons-control, aye." Sorensen pushed a sequence of buttons on his console and the sonar signals were ready to be fed into the weapons-guidance systems.

When Fogarty practised this drill it had always made him nervous. Now, faced with an actual adversary, he was surprised to discover how calm he felt.

"Control to weapons. Lock on sonar."

Hoek's voice came through the intercom. "Weapons to control. Lock on sonar, aye." The torpedo room crew was standing by.

"Load tube number one, Mark thirty-seven, conventional warhead, wire-guided."

"Load tube number one, aye."

Barracuda dipped slightly forward as the weight of a torpedo was shifted into a tube. A trim tank automatically compensated and the ship levelled.

Fogarty shook his head. "This is like playing with a loaded gun."

"Indeed it is. That's the spice that makes it so tasty."

"What if someone screws up? We could have a war down here and nobody would ever know it."

"Nobody wants to start a war. Not today."

Fogarty still felt strangely calm. A torpedo could not be fired until the tube was flooded, a provocative act that would be heard by the Russian sonar operators.

He tried to imagine the Russian sub. He had seen them on film. They looked mean, warlike. As for the men inside, he had only the residue of a lifetime of propaganda that pictured them as an enemy ...

"Well," Sorensen said, "what class of sub do you think it is?"

"I don't know. Most of their attack subs are November class."

"She's starting to move. Sonar to control, contact is moving."

"Control to sonar." Springfield's voice replaced Leo Pisaro's. "Try to get a signature. All ahead slow."

The instant *Barracuda* moved the Russian took off, making a great deal of noise as his speed increased. The streak on the screen resolved into a blip. Sorensen heard the unmistakable sounds of Soviet machinery, but it was not the classic signature of a November. He switched on the signature program that compared the sounds of the contact sub with the recorded sounds of known Soviet submarines stored in the program.

"It's a Viktor," he said, a good fifteen seconds before the computer verified his judgment.

Fogarty glanced at the chart. "One of the new ones," he said.

"Yeah. We don't know much about these Viktors. They can go deep, but they make a lot of noise."

Springfield and Pisaro were alarmed by the Russian's unexpected appearance in the Mediterranean. How did he get through the Strait of Gibraltar undetected?

"Leo," Springfield said quietly, "move in on him. All ahead half."

As the *Barracuda* began to accelerate, the Russian went into a steep dive, machinery roaring like breaking surf. The blip accelerated across Sorensen's screen at a fantastic rate. *Barracuda*, the fastest submarine in the US navy, was being left behind.

Abruptly Sorensen snatched off his earphones and reached over to yank Fogarty's away from his ears. He was too late. The high pitch of a powerful target-seeking sonar erupted in the young sonarman's ears. He winced with pain, and swore. It was his first sonar lashing.

"Welcome to the wonderful world of sub wars," Sorensen said to him.

Fogarty poked at his ears, his face contorted with pain.

"When Ivan stings your ears like that, it means he could have put a torpedo between your eyes. Bang bang, you're dead. Our friend heard us a long time before we heard him."

The Russian descended to twenty-one hundred feet and the sound abruptly ceased. The sub disappeared.

Sorensen stared at his blank screen. "I don't believe it. She vanished below a deep thermal. Sonar to control. We've lost him, Captain. He's gone."

There was shocked silence in the control room. A deep thermal layer deflected the down-searching sonars at twenty-one hundred feet, but no one wanted to admit that a Soviet sub could go beyond that depth.

Springfield was shaken. The Viktor had revealed herself as a far more formidable opponent than he had been taught to expect. For three hours they searched, but finally he gave up.

Sorensen was intrigued. In the grand game of Cowboys and Cossacks the Viktor was a new challenge. "Score one for Ivan," he said. "We lost this round."

Fogarty was still poking at his ears. "That was a slap in the face. I didn't like it."

"Don't take it personally, Fogarty. Sooner or later you'll get to do it to him, or to one of his pals. The only thing that bothers me is that he got away. That Viktor went deep. And fast."

"You really like this, don't you?" Fogarty said.

"Sure I do. There's nothing else like it in the world. This is what it's all about. We chase the Russians around the ocean, then they chase us, then we chase them some more. After all, kid, it's just a game, isn't it?"

"It may be just a game, Sorensen, but the stakes seem pretty high. If it gets out of hand we could have a war."

"Well, try to remember the other guys have as much to lose as we do."

Fogarty shrugged and looked away.

"Lighten up, kid," Sorensen said. "I'm not going to bug you about what you believe or don't. You do your job, you keep your ears sharp, and you're going to be all right. I think maybe you've got a conscience, and that's OK. But under water, what you believe doesn't count, only what you do, how you react. The rest of the world doesn't exist."

" 'Leave your mind behind.' "

"You got it."

THE NEXT MORNING Springfield prepared to take his ship into the Bay of Naples. Surfacing near a crowded harbour was always undertaken with great caution.

Fogarty was at the operator's console as the sub made a slow three-hundred-and-sixty-degree turn, echo-ranging to make certain the surface was clear of shipping before raising the periscope.

When Springfield gave the order to surface, *Barracuda* surged out of the sea, a silent monster of the deep. Her surface was a mottled black, like the skin of a whale. The only sound was the hiss of water breaking over her bow. She steamed into the Bay of Naples and tied up outside the breakwater.

Nearby, *Kitty Hawk*, flagship of the Sixth Fleet, was preparing for departure later that afternoon. From high up on the superstructure of the massive aircraft carrier, a sailor looked down at the tiny submarine. Compared to the manifest might of *Kitty Hawk*, the sub appeared insignificant. With a dorsal fin and a tail protruding from the water, *Barracuda* looked like a fish to him, at worst a harmless little shark.

Chapter 4

Jaded, polluted Naples spilled down the mountains to the bay, home port of the US Sixth Fleet. Down by the breakwater, a canopy stretched from *Barracuda*'s tender over the top of her sail, veiling her profile from Soviet spy satellites overhead.

In the sonar room Sorensen was assembling a sonic beacon in the watertight, pressure-proof, stainless steel box made by Barnes. He tinkered with a soldering gun and a tiny screwdriver, then torqued down the pressure seals and threw the switch. The box began to beep.

Lopez looked in from the control room. "Sorensen, Commander Pisaro wants to see you and your gizmo."

Sorensen turned off the box and headed for Pisaro's cabin.

"C'mon in, Ace," Pisaro said, responding to Sorensen's knock.

Spread out on the table was a chart of the Bay of Naples and the adjacent Gulf of Pozzuoli to the north.

"At ease, Sorensen. You been topside yet?"

"No, sir. Too busy."

"I wonder if it's a nice day. Naples can be a nice place. My grandfather came from Naples."

Sorensen asked, "Will there be liberty here, sir?"

Pisaro ran his hands over his scalp. "No liberty. We're going to be here less than twenty-four hours. Now, let's see your handiwork." He reached for the beacon and switched it on, listened to it for a moment and turned it off. "Is it going to work?"

"I can't say, sir. I haven't had it in the water."

"Well, then." Pisaro looked over his chart and jabbed his finger at a spot in the middle of the Gulf of Pozzuoli. "It's got to go one hundred and twenty feet down. Can you handle that?"

Sorensen peered at the chart and nodded. "No problem."

"OK, you need to take someone with you. Who's it going to be?"

"Fogarty."

"The kid? Is he qualified for scuba?" Pisaro opened his personnel files and pulled out Fogarty's records. "So he is. Is he any good at sonar?"

"He's a sharp cookie, Commander. He's got good ears."

Pisaro studied the file. "There's something about him I can't put my finger on. He's kind of sullen. I don't think he really likes the military."

"For cryin' out loud, Commander, I don't like the military. I don't think you like it very much. If you'll pardon my saying so."

Pisaro pretended not to hear this. He went on reading Fogarty's file. "Why can't I get more guys like Willie Joe? Just a good old boy who loves his submarine. Instead, I get the likes of you and this Fogarty. Get outta here. Go swimming."

IN WET SUITS SORENSEN AND FOGARTY popped out of the after hatch and carefully made their way along the deck. From the portside forward diving plane Hoek was supervising the loading of dummy torpedoes for a forthcoming fleet exercise. Each torpedo was equipped with a reel of fine wire, miles long, that remained attached to the submarine when the weapon was fired. By means of an electronic pulse transmitted along the wire, the weapons officer could guide the torpedo to its target. The gleaming weapons were painted brilliant orange to indicate they were unarmed.

The two sonarmen dropped into a waiting rubber boat. Sorensen cranked up the outboard motor and they went skimming across the water, heading for the Gulf of Pozzuoli. The bay was calm. Shadows crept down the slopes of Vesuvius. The air was heavy with diesel oil and thyme.

Fogarty was awestruck by the crumbling magnificence of Naples. After ten days under water he seemed to have surfaced in paradise. Waving his arms, he shouted into the wind, "It's like a dream, it's beautiful."

"You know what they say, kid. See Naples and die."

As they rounded the point and entered the gulf, Sorensen slowed to get his bearings. Fogarty chattered excitedly.

"C'mon, Sorensen. Which one is Vesuvius?"

"How do I know? The one blowing smoke rings."

"Where's Pompeii? It's supposed to be around here."

Sorensen became annoyed. "Look, Fogarty, I know this is all new to you, but try to restrain yourself. I'm not a tour guide and we've got a little job to do." He started putting on his scuba gear. "C'mon, sailor, drop anchor. We're here." He zipped up his wet suit with a flourish.

Slipping into the water, Sorensen and Fogarty followed the anchor rope to the bottom. Murky green light filtered down into the gulf and they could see the debris of centuries littering the seabed. Sorensen consulted his compass. He carried the sonic beacon and Fogarty a magnet.

It didn't take long to find their objective—a dark shape looming up from the deep, the mangled hulk of a World War Two German submarine. The stern was half buried in the silt, and the rest of the wreck was covered with algae and rust. On the conning tower they read: *U-62.*

Sorensen took the magnet from Fogarty, swam to the sub and attached the beacon to the hull. He switched it on, and they listened to the beep.

They swam slowly round the wreck. Half the bow was torn away, and round the edges of the gaping hole the metal was twisted outwards. In one awful moment a torpedo had exploded inside the boat, sinking it instantly.

BACK IN THE CREW QUARTERS of *Barracuda* Sorensen whistled cheerfully as he rummaged around in his tiny locker for a cigarette. Fogarty lay on his bunk and glowered at the bulkhead.

"What's the matter with you? Some folks would pay a fortune to go scuba diving in the Med."

"Sorensen, there were dead men on that boat—"

"Maybe, maybe not. The ocean is full of dead men and sunken ships. Their wars are over."

"They were sailors just like you and me—"

"They were not like you and me. They were the enemy. C'mon, Fogarty, lighten up. You think too much. It isn't going to make your life any easier, I guarantee you." Sorensen grinned. "At least on this ship we might get a chance to destroy a Russian missile sub before she blows up New York City."

"And until then?"

"Hey, man, we all live in our little yellow submarine. Relax, try thinking of yourself as a pioneer exploring life under water. You get a nice clean, comfortable air-conditioned submarine to drive you around, all meals provided. You get the best toys and the best talent to operate them. And for excitement you get to play Cowboys and Cossacks with the Russians. Some deal, right?"

"A forty-million-dollar submarine designed to kill people isn't a toy."

"Well, we haven't killed anybody yet. Listen, Fogarty," Sorensen said, his voice lowering, "as long as you are on this ship, I'm your supervisor. For some stupid reason I like you. I think you will turn into a fine sonar operator, so I'm giving you some advice. Just keep your mouth shut and do your job, and you'll be all right. You hear me, sailor?"

Fogarty kept his mouth shut. Sorensen looked at him, then broke into a smile and slapped him on the back.

"Hey, OK, now get in gear. We have to report to Pisaro."

THE SHIP BUZZED with excitement. The word had been passed that an admiral was coming aboard to give *Barracuda* a special assignment. Sorensen and Fogarty were passing through the control room when Pisaro called out, "Attention!"

Instantly the control room was transformed into a parade ground. Moments later, two men passed through the hatch.

"At ease," said Pisaro.

Fogarty saw a short, pudgy man of sixty in a flowered Hawaiian shirt, flat black sunglasses and a salt-and-pepper beard that wrapped round his jowls like a mask.

"Who is *that?*" he whispered to Sorensen.

"Netts," said Sorensen. "Vice-Admiral Edward P. Netts."

"Never heard of him," Fogarty said.

"The Russians have."

The man accompanying the admiral was impeccably dressed in custom-tailored dress uniform.

"Who's that?" Fogarty asked.

"His aide, Commander Billings. I expect he'll be with us for a few days."

Netts looked round the control room and spotted Sorensen. Quietly, to avoid being overheard by the other men in the compartment, he asked Sorensen about the Viktor they had encountered. "I understand it went below two thousand feet. Is that true?"

"Yes, sir. It did, indeed."

Netts mulled over the unhappy implications. "Is the beacon planted on *U-62*?" he asked.

"Yes, sir."

"Did you go over the plan with the skipper?"

"Yes, sir. It's going to be a piece of cake, Admiral."

"All right"—Netts turned to Pisaro—"let's get on with it."

At the navigation console the quartermaster was taking a satellite feed of up-to-date information on tide, current, wind and sea conditions. At the attack console Hoek took another satellite feed, which showed *Kitty Hawk* and her escorts on a radar screen. The fleet had sailed and was now three hundred miles from Naples, fifty miles off the southern tip of Sardinia.

Netts stared at the screen. "Do they have company?"

"Yes, sir, they sure do," said Hoek, punching buttons. Two more blips appeared, Russian surface ships trailing the rearmost destroyer.

"What about subs? Any sign of the Viktor you met?"

"Not so far."

"Well, let's hope it stays that way, but don't bet on it. Can you show me Naples?" asked Netts.

"Certainly, Admiral." Hoek punched more buttons and the screen showed the navigation chart. Scattered among the freighters and ferries that appeared as blips were the buoys that marked the channel. Netts studied the screen.

"Lieutenant, there's going to be a sub waiting for you out there, as part of the exercise, probably ten or twelve miles out. There might even be two. I wouldn't be surprised if one of them is under one of those buoys. I suggest that you plot an attack course for every buoy more than ten miles out, just in case one of them moves."

"Aye aye," replied Hoek as he began energetically to push buttons. Hoek was ready for a fight. His breath was short, his chest felt constricted. He was due for a physical when *Barracuda* returned to Norfolk, and he knew he would never pass. This was his last patrol, and he wanted some memories to take ashore.

Netts led his party down a ladder and entered the torpedo room. He swept the room with a scowl, taking in the fourteen dummy torpedoes stacked neatly in racks. The eight members of the torpedo gang stood at attention in his presence.

Netts said to Lopez, "Chief, did you run checks on these fish yourself?"

"Yes, sir!"

"You happy?"

Lopez hesitated. "Sir, I don't like to go on patrol without no live torpedoes, sir!"

Netts's mood changed. "At ease, men," he said. "I understand your point, Chief, but this is not a patrol, it's an exercise."

"Sir, what if a war starts during the exercise?"

Netts crossed over to the attack console and tapped Zapata's cage. "In that case, Chief, you'll go up to the surface and set this nasty little scorpion onto the Russians."

SORENSEN AND FOGARTY were sitting in the mess with forty other sailors when the loudspeaker piped attention. "Attention all hands, attention all hands. The captain is going to address the crew."

Springfield's voice resounded throughout the ship. "As I am sure all of you are aware, we have a distinguished visitor aboard. Admiral Netts has come from the office of the Chief of Naval Operations to give *Barracuda* a special assignment, and he is going to tell you about it now."

"Gentlemen," said Netts, "today, on all the oceans of the world, we face a far more powerful and dangerous adversary than the ones we defeated in the Second World War. In the last decade, under the leadership of Admiral Gorshkov, the Soviet navy has become the second most powerful navy in the world. If the Russians were to attack us today I can tell you we would have a hell of a time stopping them.

"If I were Admiral Gorshkov and I were planning an attack on the US navy, the first thing I would do would be to sink as many American missile submarines as I could find. In all likelihood, I wouldn't find many, if any at all. Therefore, I would attack what I could find. And that, gentlemen, means aircraft carriers. You just can't hide them.

"Our navy has spent and spent building aircraft carriers and carrier groups, and intends to spend more. In my opinion, this is wrong. Terribly wrong. If war with the Russians comes, those carriers will be sitting ducks. They will be blown out of the water in the first fifteen minutes of the war, and then it will be up to the submarine forces to carry on the fight.

"Why am I telling you all this? Because in the next five days your mission will be to prove the truth of it to my superiors in Washington. You will be playing the role of a Soviet crew, and *Barracuda* will act as though it were part of the Black Sea Fleet. This ship is going to demonstrate that one Russian submarine can penetrate the defences of an entire carrier group and sink the queen bee. You can't put a live charge into *Kitty Hawk*, but you can smash a pair of dummies into her hull and give everybody on her flight deck a good soaking.

"The future of the navy is at stake here. Captain Springfield will have absolute discretion to go where he wants, as deep as he wants and as fast as he wants. You men will do whatever it takes to sink the *Hawk*.

"That is all. God bless you."

When the speech ended a cheer erupted in the mess. Only Sorensen kept silent. He slammed his coffee cup onto the table and stood up. The noise instantly quietened.

"You people are crazy," he said. "This isn't going to be a joyride. The fleet will have six subs looking for us." He looked over the young faces in the mess. "And while half the US navy is chasing us round in circles, there's still a *real* Russian sub loose out there. It's going to get crowded down there. Eight subs in one tiny piece of ocean, seven of them and us. Keep it in mind."

IN THE SONAR ROOM later Fogarty said, "Willie Joe, what's with Sorensen?"

"He figures anything but chasing Russians is a waste of time."

"Do you?"

"I just put in my time, man. It don't make any difference to me."

Sorensen came in muttering. "All right," he said. "If we're going to do this, we're going to do it right. Willie Joe, run signature programs for *Swordfish*, *Shark*, *Seawolf*, *Mako*, *Dragonfish* and *Stingray*."

All over the ship, division heads were logging in the first watch. In the control room the captain went through the departure checklist.

The game began.

Chapter 5

On the stroke of midnight an inbound tanker passed a large red navigation buoy eleven miles outside the Naples breakwater. The sailors on the tanker's bridge scarcely glanced at it, and no one noticed a much smaller float that had attached itself magnetically to it. Eight inches in diameter, the float had a two-foot-long antenna extending into the air and a thin wire descending into the depths. At the far end of the wire, one hundred and fifty feet down, USS *Mako* hovered in ambush.

She had been on station for six hours, waiting for the message from the Sixth Fleet shore command that would announce *Barracuda*'s departure. Having spent a dozen patrols lying off Soviet ports waiting for Russian submarines, the crew was accustomed to picket duty.

The tide had turned and *Barracuda* was about to exit from the bay under the tanker's sound screen, which would foul the water with noise pollution. Like everyone else on *Mako*, Captain Flowers wished for *Barracuda*'s ultimate success, but regretted that if it came it would be at his own expense. His orders were to stop *Barracuda* the moment she emerged from the channel and thus put a quick end to "Netts's Folly".

"Radio to control. Target under way." Flowers wasted no time. Should *Barracuda* elude the picket and reach blue water, she could out-run *Mako* and reach the fleet in thirty hours. "Cut loose that buoy," he ordered. "Control to weapons, he's moving. Load dummies in tubes one and two."

The rules of the war game established a combat-free zone within a radius of ten miles round Naples. Outside the ten-mile limit, a submarine "kill" would be registered by the firing of a dummy torpedo and a sonar blast, to be judged as a hit or a miss by umpires aboard each ship. Torpedoes fired at other submarines would contain no propellant. Immediately after being ejected from the tubes, they would sink. Only the torpedoes *Barracuda* fired at *Kitty Hawk* would make a run to the target. With no warhead the fish would bounce off the huge hull of the carrier, causing no significant damage.

"Control to sonar, listen out. He's moving."

With her more sophisticated sonars and computers, plus the element of surprise, *Mako* seemed to have every advantage. Her sonarmen expected *Barracuda* to proceed seven or eight miles into the bay and swim under their noses.

"Sonar to control. We have her, bearing three four six. Course one two three. Speed four knots. Range nineteen thousand yards. She's turning, Captain"—the operator's voice suddenly rose in astonishment—"she's *submerging!*"

The sonar operators listened to *Barracuda*'s machinery as she sub-merged. The sounds were muddled by the tanker that was now between the two subs. Suddenly the machinery noises stopped. They heard the tanker, the ping of the fixed beacon that guided ships in and out of the harbour, but no submarine.

"Sonar to control. We lost her. She disappeared."

Mako's Executive Officer, Commander Poland, said, "She's gone turboelectric. She's trying to sneak out on the quiet."

Captain Flowers nodded, knowing that during such exercises ballistic missile submarines occasionally left port under turboelectric power in order to evade a waiting attack sub. "The question is," said Flowers, "does Springfield come after us or try to escape?"

"I think he'll run." Pointing at the electronic chart that displayed the Bay of Naples and the islands of Procida, Ischia and Capri just offshore, Poland said, "If Springfield can get behind one of the islands and block our sonar, he can escape. The channel between Capri and the mainland is the deepest and the safest for passage. I reckon he'll go south, here, round Capri. He's already moving in that direction."

"All right," said Flowers. "We have to go somewhere and Capri is as good a place as any. We can't stay here now that he knows where we are."

ORIGINALLY SPRINGFIELD HAD PROPOSED to Netts that *Barracuda* should make a run for Capri, counting on her speed to get her past any picket. Netts rejected that as too obvious. He suggested that Springfield hide in the Gulf of Pozzuoli until the picket was "sunk" or gave up and returned to the fleet. Then *Barracuda* could run north, pass through the Strait of Bonifacio between Sardinia and Corsica, sail down the west coast of Sardinia and surprise the fleet with an attack from the north.

The plan was dangerous. First *Barracuda* had to manoeuvre in the bay, and then in the shallow gulf, without colliding with a submerged obstacle. To do this it was necessary to echo-range and thereby announce her location to *Mako*. Both Springfield and Netts found this unacceptable.

Sorensen had provided the solution. The Bay of Naples was seeded with fixed sonars that transmitted sonic beacons on regular frequencies to guide ships in and out of port at times of low visibility. Sorensen demonstrated how it was possible to echo-range on the same frequency as one of the beacons. "All we have to do," Sorensen told the captain, "is time the pulse to coincide with the moment *Barracuda* is directly in line between a beacon and the picket. If it doesn't work, we'll still be inside the ten-mile limit and he can't shoot us."

"If it doesn't work, Sorensen," Springfield said, "this exercise will be over in five minutes, not five days."

WHEN *BARRACUDA* SUBMERGED, less than a mile out into the bay, Sorensen immediately picked up garbled but distinct sounds of a submarine's coolant pumps throbbing ten miles away. He logged it and told Hoek that the sub was hovering, but the sound was too much distorted by other noises in the channel for an absolute fix. Hoek, watching the sonar display on his attack console, guessed that the sub was under buoy number five, and busily plotted an attack.

When *Barracuda* was lined up between a beacon and buoy number five, Springfield ordered sonar to echo-range once on the beacon's frequency. Sorensen sent one narrow-beamed pulse of sound out into the channel. A single blip appeared on the screen: a sub lying at radio depth.

Sorensen recognized her signature. "It's *Mako*," he said, a split second before the computer.

Springfield ordered, "All stop."

With a clear picture of the traffic in the harbour, *Barracuda* carefully crept north round the point of La Gaiola and into the Gulf of Pozzuoli. Sorensen informed Springfield that *Mako* had begun moving on a southerly course. Making a great deal of noise with her own machinery, *Mako* apparently did not notice *Barracuda*'s manoeuvre.

As soon as *Barracuda* cleared the point, Sorensen picked up the signal from the beacon attached to the hull of *U-62*. Using the beacon as a guide, Springfield cautiously manoeuvred into a position that allowed the rusting hulk of the dead German sub to shield *Barracuda* from probing sonars. They hovered there, just above the bottom.

Sorensen stood at his console, listening to *Mako* conducting her search. After a few minutes she disappeared behind Capri.

"Control to weapons. Load a dummy in tube number one," Springfield ordered.

"Weapons, aye. Loading dummy."

In the torpedo room Lopez's men loaded a dummy Mark 37 wire-guided torpedo into tube number one.

"Flood tube."

"Flooding tube, aye."

Sorensen and Fogarty heard seawater rush into the torpedo tube. The ship tilted forward, then came back to dead level.

"Now, be quiet," Sorensen said to Fogarty. "This is a special treat. It's not often we get to lie quietly in shallow water like this. You never know what you might hear." Suddenly he sat up with a jerk. "Sonar to control," he said into his intercom. "Lieutenant, *Mako* is coming back this way."

In the control room every officer experienced a rush of adrenalin. *Mako* was going to pass right across *Barracuda*'s bow and give her the chance of a clean shot. Hoek was tracking the target on his weapons console, waiting for *Mako* to pass beyond the ten-mile limit.

"Sorensen," said Hoek, "get ready. When I give the order to fire, you give them a blast with the target-seeking frequency."

"Yes, sir, Mr. Hoek." Sorensen nodded to Fogarty. "You do it, kid. You blast 'em."

Fogarty watched the screen. Sorensen held up his thumb. "Go."

"Sonar to weapons," Fogarty said. "Lock on weapons guidance."

"Weapons guidance locked on sonar," said Hoek over the intercom. "Tracking target. Five, four, three, two, one. Fire."

The ship bucked as it spat out a dummy torpedo, which immediately sank into the mud of the bay.

Hoek yelled through the intercom, "Sorensen, what's the matter with you? Hit them with the target sonar."

Fogarty stared at his console. Remembering his own recent sonar lashing, he couldn't help thinking of the sonar operators whose eardrums were about to take a pounding. Reluctantly, he pushed the echo-ranger button on his console.

Glaring at Fogarty, Sorensen said, "The next time you hesitate on a direct order will be your last."

Twelve seconds later two men were screaming in *Mako*'s sonar room, and three more in her control room.

On *Barracuda* there were cheers. *Mako* was now *hors de combat*. The umpire aboard *Mako* immediately noted the "kill", as did Billings,

Admiral Netts's aide, who was the umpire aboard *Barracuda*. Both ships sent up radio buoys.

"Well done," signalled Flowers. "Congratulations."

"Sorry about your men," answered Springfield. "Buy you a drink in Norfolk."

"Sink the *Hawk* and I'll buy you one."

Springfield retracted his buoy. "All ahead full," he ordered, and *Barracuda* lunged forward like a dolphin. She raced through the Tyrrhenian Sea, heading for the Strait of Bonifacio, which led out into the Mediterranean.

FOR THREE DAYS AND NIGHTS Admiral Horning, commodore of the carrier group, had directed the search for the elusive *Barracuda*. *Mako* had vanished, obviously "sunk". From the operations centre on *Kitty Hawk* Horning had plumbed the depths with sonars and magnometers, crisscrossed the surface with frigates and destroyers, helicopters and antisubmarine planes. Five of his own submarines prowled under and around his armada, hydrophones open to every gurgle, yet *Barracuda* remained undetected. Springfield had eluded the trap set by *Mako* and had disappeared. And as if that weren't enough, Horning had Netts gloating in the wardroom.

On the morning of the fourth day, after a sleepless night, Horning reflected that it was twenty-five years since he had felt so rotten. During World War Two, as commander of a destroyer, he had escorted convoys of merchant ships across the North Atlantic through deadly wolfpacks of German U-boats. In that war an enemy submarine presented a terrible menace, but one he could deal with. Diesel-electric subs spent most of their time on the surface, submerging only to hide, attack or escape intolerable weather. Under water, they were slow and at the mercy of short supplies of air, water and battery-power.

A nuclear-propelled attack submarine was another matter entirely. A nuke remained under water virtually all the time. It made fresh water by desalinating seawater, and oxygen by electrolysis of the fresh water. As for sheer power, it was incomparable. The reactor core in *Barracuda* was good for one hundred thousand miles, and she could outrun any ship in the fleet.

On entering the operations centre he stood quietly to one side, observing the anxious, strained faces of his officers. For an instant he looked directly at Captain Lewis, commander of the carrier. The haggard, unshaven man shook his head. No luck, no change, no *Barracuda*.

Netts was there, out of uniform, silently watching. "Good morning, Admiral. Sleep well?" he said, making no effort to keep the sarcasm out of his voice.

"Well, where's your pet submarine, Mr. Netts? I haven't seen any torpedoes streaking through these waters."

"Perhaps we should contact the manufacturer. Faulty torpedoes are a terrible thing."

Horning bit his lip. "Perhaps we should wait until we see Commander Billings's report."

"Fine," said Netts, who turned his attention to the dawn breaking in pink streaks off the flight deck.

No other ship was visible. *Barracuda*'s mission was to simulate a nuclear attack. To avoid having a ship damaged or sunk by a blast that destroyed another, Horning had spread his perimeters to the maximum, with no ship within five miles of another. This dispersal also allowed him to search the widest possible area. On the bulkhead a large screen displayed the fleet's order of battle. While the location of each surface ship was shown with precision, in the form of an electronic silhouette, the whereabouts of each escort submarine could only be estimated.

Horning had not guessed that *Barracuda* had run the Strait of Bonifacio and was preparing an attack from the north. Two of the fleet's subs were on station fifty miles south, hoping to intercept *Barracuda*'s approach from that direction. *Swordfish*, *Stingray* and *Dragonfish* were roving under and around the armada.

Netts, however, knew that *Springfield*'s plan was to position *Barracuda* in front of the fleet, lie quietly at depth and wait for the advance ships to pass directly over her. If the advance ships made contact, she would try to outrun them and attack the carrier before they got a fix. Netts stared out to sea, hoping that at any minute now a pair of torpedoes would streak out of the north and slam into the hulking *Kitty Hawk*.

THERE WAS A STILLNESS in *Barracuda*.

The captain had slipped under a thermal layer of warm water that deflected sonar pulses searching from above, and for twelve hours the submarine had hovered, a thousand feet down. She was rigged for quiet. The noisy air-conditioning system was reduced to the minimum and the temperature had risen to eighty-three degrees. The fresh-water still, which made a terrible racket, was shut down, so no one could shower. The ship was rank.

In the sonar room Willie Joe was on watch. Fifteen miles away *Kitty Hawk* was steaming north, directly towards *Barracuda*. In the control room Captain Springfield, Pisaro, Billings and Hoek watched the repeater and listened through headphones to the muffled sound of the nearest destroyer, distorted by the thermal.

Then there was another, more ominous, sound, much closer.

"SORENSEN!"

The high, brittle voice belonged to Lieutenant Hoek, who was standing in the hatch of the forward crew quarters. "You and Fogarty in the sonar

316

room, on the double." He lowered his voice. "We have a sub," he said, eyes gleaming. "It's *Swordfish*. We're going to get right on her tail."

"Well, what do you know, Lieutenant. Sounds like fun," said Sorensen. He winked at Fogarty as they followed Hoek through the hatch.

Throughout the ship loudspeakers whispered, "General quarters. General quarters. All hands man battle stations, nuclear."

That did not sound like fun.

Chapter 6

In the control room of the Soviet submarine *Potemkin* nine men were crowded into a space designed for six. After seventy-three days at sea, the moment of truth was at hand.

Standing behind Popov, the sonar operator, Captain Nikolai Federov calmly gave the orders to manoeuvre *Potemkin* under the perimeter of ships that surrounded *Kitty Hawk*.

All eyes were on the sonar screen, where a splendid array of blips represented the US Sixth Fleet.

Potemkin was an Alpha-class experimental submarine. Her sleek hull was constructed of an alloy of titanium, a rare, strong, lightweight metal. The use of titanium in place of steel enabled *Potemkin* to cruise at fifty knots, a speed that had been thought impossible, and at a depth below four thousand feet. No other sub in the world could go that deep.

Potemkin was the most secret ship in the Soviet navy. Only those in the highest echelons of command were aware of her presence in the Mediterranean. Federov had slipped through the Strait by going deeper than the NATO sonar operators expected, positioning himself under a tanker and drifting through with the current and short bursts of electric power.

During the cruise, the longest submerged patrol in Soviet history, *Potemkin* had exceeded her design specifications. Federov had tested her depth and speed, her weapons, sonars and electronics, all with glorious results. As he approached the American fleet, at a depth of only four hundred feet, his orders were to test the ultimate effectiveness of one more system: Acoustical Reproductive Device Number Seven.

A tape recorder was mounted above the sonar console. Transfixed, the men in the control room listened as the reels spun out the song of the *Swordfish*. The taped signature of the American sub was the heart of a complex apparatus designed to make American sonar operators think *Potemkin* was one of their own. An earlier test had demonstrated that the device could make the Americans believe *Potemkin* was a Viktor.

Federov was not fond of Acoustical Reproduction Device Number Seven. For ten weeks he had eluded detection without it. With the aid of the thermal that lay beneath him, he believed he could station *Potemkin* directly under *Kitty Hawk* without the Americans suspecting he was there.

But orders were orders, the tape was rolling, the special sound-absorbent silicon packing that quietened *Potemkin*'s turbine was in place, and she was running shallow and slow, just as *Swordfish* would do, as part of the American defence.

On the sonar screen the nearest blip, a destroyer, turned towards *Potemkin*. A moment later everyone on board heard the ping of the American's echo-ranger.

Federov looked round the control room at the tense bearded and sweating faces. "Destroyer range?"

"Five thousand metres," said Popov. "He's ... he's turning back, Captain."

On the screen the blip revolved back to its original course.

"It's working," gloated the First Officer Kurnachov, who was officially responsible for Acoustical Reproduction Device Number Seven. Kurnachov was also the political officer, the representative of the Party, and he had great faith in the prowess of Soviet technology.

"The only thing I regret, Captain First Rank Federov, is that we cannot surface and reveal the Alpha to the Americans, to throw it in their faces. Their metallurgists can't build a submarine of titanium. They would give anything to photograph our pretty ship."

Federov said nothing. He was weary of playing war with the Americans. He wanted either to make war or peace, put an end to the purgatory of waiting. He had spent fifteen years in subs, fifteen years in the lightless, heartless, impersonal ocean that had swallowed him, his ship and his crew. And all the time the hostile, menacing sea was relentlessly testing every square millimetre of the pressure hull, looking for the weak spot, the casual error of some drunken shipyard worker, some lazy quality control inspector ... *Nyet*, his mind was wandering.

"Range to *Kitty Hawk*?"

"Twenty thousand metres."

Suddenly Popov was out of his seat, his eyes fixed on the screen.

"Captain, there's another sub ... he's right under us!"

"GENERAL QUARTERS. GENERAL QUARTERS. All hands man battle stations, nuclear." The whispered announcement over *Barracuda*'s loud-speakers sent the crew rushing through the ship.

Willie Joe was positive the sub they had picked up was *Swordfish*. The computer had verified his judgment.

Springfield's plan of attack was quite simple. As *Swordfish* passed overhead, *Barracuda* would rise into the blind spot of her sonar and follow directly behind her prop. Sonars of surface ships would read the two subs as one. When they reached optimum range Springfield would launch a pair of fish at *Kitty Hawk*, then attempt to "sink" *Swordfish*.

"Range to *Kitty Hawk*?"

"Eighteen thousand yards," replied Hoek, reading from the screen on his attack console.

"Range to *Swordfish*?"

"Two hundred yards."

"Torpedo room, load torpedoes in tubes one and four."

In the torpedo room Lopez and his crew carefully slid Mark 45s into the two uppermost torpedo tubes.

From the moment Sorensen sat down to listen to the approaching sub, he sensed that something was peculiar. He checked Willie Joe's log and punched up the signature program for *Swordfish*.

Apparently oblivious to *Barracuda*'s presence, the sub was almost on top of them. He discerned the sounds of coolant pumps, reduction gears, secondary pumps and the odd cadence of a faulty bearing on one saltwater pump that had been a chronic problem on *Swordfish* for years.

He bumped Fogarty with his elbow to get his attention. On a notepad he scribbled SWORDFISH. Fogarty nodded. Sorensen smiled his most wicked smile, drew a line through the word SWORDFISH and sketched a hammer and sickle.

Fogarty paled. "You sure?"

Sorensen nodded. "Listen up. This is a Russian submarine."

Fogarty listened. It sounded like *Swordfish* to him. Sorensen played the *Swordfish* signature program, and then Fogarty heard the difference too.

With every revolution of the Russian prop, *Kitty Hawk* and the war game faded into insignificance.

Sorensen spoke into the intercom. "Lieutenant Hoek, can you step in here a moment, sir?"

Hoek entered the sonar room. "Yes, Sorensen?"

"I know the *Swordfish*, sir. I know every sound she makes. She's a noisy boat, but not as noisy as she was before her last refit. They fixed the bearings in her saltwater pumps. What we are listening to here is the way *Swordfish* *used* to sound, not the way she sounds now. Somebody wants us to think that's one of our subs out there, but it isn't."

Hoek's eyes lit up. "It's the Russians." He could hardly contain himself. He rushed back to the control room. Seconds later the captain made a rare appearance in the sonar room.

"What do you think, Sorensen?"

"It's gotta be a Russkie, sir, probably that same Viktor we ran into on the way out here. It sure as hell isn't the old *Swordfish*. They fixed that pump for sure. That boat has some kind of gadget rigged to make it sound like *Swordfish*. She fooled those destroyers."

"Play the tape."

Springfield listened. The distinction was obvious.

"All right, carry on. Good work, Sorensen."

319

As the Russian sub passed directly overhead, the sound was an exact imitation of *Swordfish* before her pumps were repaired.

"Attention, all hands. This is the captain. Prepare for steep angles. Take us up, Leo. We have to assume she knows we're here, and that she's testing her cover on us. For a moment we'll let her think it works. Put us in her blind spot. Keep right on her."

Pisaro pushed a sequence of buttons on his diving panel and *Barracuda* rose directly behind *Potemkin*. She matched the Russian's speed and began to follow, two hundred yards behind.

As far as Springfield was concerned the war game was suspended. They would stay on the tail of the Russian sub until they either obtained a positive identification, or lost it.

"Speed of target increasing to twenty-one knots," came Pisaro's voice.

"Mr. Pisaro, make our speed twenty-one knots. Torpedo room, unload torpedoes. We're not playing games any more. Engineering, prepare for high power. Keep right after her, Mr. Pisaro, keep right on her tail."

"IDENTIFY HIM, IF YOU PLEASE, Mr. Popov."

"It's a Skipjack class, Captain. It must be *Barracuda*."

When the *Barracuda* rose up and began to follow, Federov deduced that he had come upon the sub that was playing the role of attacker in the American war game he had been ordered to penetrate. It was quite a situation—he was pretending to be an American and he was being followed by an American pretending to be a Soviet.

"First Officer Kurnachov, I think we have completed our test of Acoustical Reproduction Device Number Seven. I am not certain the American submarine following us has been fooled by our tricks."

"I disagree, Comrade Captain," Kurnachov said. "I believe we have fooled him. He follows because he believes we are *Swordfish*. In any case your course is taking him towards the carrier that is his target."

"Then we shall have to take him somewhere else, Comrade First Officer Captain Second Rank Kurnachov." Federov loved to give him his full ridiculous due. "Right full rudder. Increase speed to thirty knots. Bearing one seven seven. Depth three hundred metres. Ten degrees down."

Kurnachov was shocked. "Captain, Acoustical Reproduction Device Number Seven has never been tested at over twenty-four knots."

"Then consider this a test."

Potemkin abruptly tilted downwards and accelerated into the depths.

In the engine room the chief engineer watched awestruck as the silicon packing on the turbine slowly turned into a pool of glassy liquid. The quiet hum of the whirring blades was transformed into a deep roar.

"Captain," the engineer said into his microphone, "we have to stop the turbine. The packing has melted!"

One hundred and fifty feet away the noise burst into the quiet of the

320

control room. The captain glared across at the first officer. "All stop. Quiet in the boat."

The noise ceased. The turbine came to a halt. *Potemkin* continued to plunge on momentum. Kurnachov jumped up from his seat and went across the control room towards the engine room.

"First Officer Kurnachov," Federov said, "return to your diving panel. Where do you think you are? Right full rudder. Zero angle on the diving planes." Gradually, the ship levelled off and slowly came to a halt.

"Engine room, damage report."

"The packing melted, Captain, but the turbine is all right."

"Popov, do you hear the American sub?"

"No, sir. I hear the aircraft carrier. Range eight thousand two hundred metres and closing."

Turning on Kurnachov, Federov ordered the first officer to accompany him to his cabin. There, the captain locked the door. "Mr. Kurnachov, if you ever move from your station again, I'll have you before a court-martial. As for Acoustical Reproduction Device Number Seven, it is now useless."

"Comrade Captain," Kurnachov said, "I believe you deliberately increased the speed of this ship to sabotage the device."

"You can believe whatever you want to believe. I am growing impatient with you, Kurnachov. My responsibility is to carry out my mission and return my ship and crew safely home. The Americans know nothing about the Alpha. At worst they think we are a Viktor. We must disappear before they collect too much information. If you want to relieve me and take command of *Potemkin*, do it now. You have the entire American Sixth Fleet above you and an American submarine on your tail. You have a jittery crew that has been at sea far too long. This would be an excellent moment to demonstrate your seamanship."

The captain unlocked the door and returned to the control room. Kurnachov began formulating his report on the captain's remarks. Then he reconsidered. He would act.

SORENSEN WAS ASTOUNDED at the Russian sub's rate of acceleration. *Barracuda* was the fastest submarine in the US navy, but the Russian ship had taken off like a sports car.

Springfield ordered a steep dive and increased speed. *Barracuda* angled over and rocketed down.

Thirty seconds into the dive the Russian sub erupted with a sudden burst of noise that caused Sorensen to jump out of his seat. Then, abruptly, there was no noise at all.

Springfield ordered, "All stop." Drifting on momentum, *Barracuda* descended through a thermal layer and unwittingly passed under *Potemkin*. At thirteen hundred feet, very close to her test depth, she came to a

halt. The Russian was not on the screens. She was in a blind spot, above *Barracuda*, obscured by the thermal. Fear of collision swept through the control room.

Since Springfield did not know the Russian's location, he intended to let her know where *Barracuda* was. "Control to sonar. Echo-range."

The broad beam swept all round, but there was no contact.

Sorensen hammered on his console. "C'mon, Ivan, make some noise."

"CAPTAIN FIRST RANK Nikolai Petrovitch Federov, by the authority invested in me, I relieve you of command of *Potemkin*. Return to your cabin at once."

Face flushed, sweating, black eyes too bright, Kurnachov held a pistol. Still standing over the sonar console, Federov's first impluse was to laugh. Then Kurnachov cocked the hammer.

"Put the gun away, Kurnachov, before you blow a hole in the ship and kill us all."

Everyone in the control room remained at his station. With dignity Federov assumed a military bearing and left the control room without another word.

Still brandishing the pistol, Kurnachov paced round the control room, unsure what to do. After a minute he called out, "Stern planes, down twenty degrees. Reverse engines. Slow revolutions."

The hull shuddered once as the turbine started to revolve. The ship began to angle down at the stern and descend backwards into the unknown. Kurnachov felt giddy with power. He was in command for the first time in his life. He had, he believed, saved *Potemkin*.

"SONAR TO CONTROL, sonar to control," Sorensen's voice shouted over the intercom, "I hear him, Captain, he's right on top of us. He's backing down out of the thermal. *Left full rudder*."

The helmsman was cranking his joystick before Springfield could give the order. Barely making way, *Barracuda* slowly turned to the left.

For one terrible moment everyone froze as *Potemkin*'s portside stern plane brushed *Barracuda*'s bow. The impact reverberated through *Barracuda*'s hull like a giant gong.

Collision alarms began screaming, circuits popped, sirens went off. In the torpedo room the solid steel bulkhead bulged into the compartment and snapped back into place with a thundering bang. Lopez braced himself, praying for the pressure hull to hold. Making a grinding noise, the keel of the Russian sub slid down the starboard side of the hull, rolling *Barracuda* over to the right and sending men sprawling. There was a lurch, another metallic crunch ... and the ships separated.

Barracuda swung back to the left and righted herself. Zapata's glass cage slid from the top of the fire-control panel to the steel floor and shattered. Miraculously uninjured, the scorpion skittered away and hid in the shadows of the torpedo racks.

Lopez rushed to the fire-control panel and saw that one of the outer-tube door indicators had changed from green to red. Tube number four was ruptured, having been the exact point of impact from the tip of the Russian sub's stern plane. Lopez was certain the tube's inner door would burst open. "Torpedo room to control. Tube number four open to sea."

In the control room an indicator light on Pisaro's diving panel changed from green to red. He blanched. "Torpedo tube number four open to sea," he said, making the greatest effort to sound calm.

"Blow all ballast tanks, surface," ordered the captain.

The sub slowly began to rise.

"Fire yellow distress rocket."

"Rocket away."

"Control to torpedo room, damage report."

"Torpedo room to control. Tube number four open to sea. Inner door is holding. We've got a small electrical fire here."

"Attention all hands. Damage-control team to torpedo room, on the double. Sonar, where's the Russian?"

Sorensen switched on the active sonar. Instantly, an erratically pulsating sphere of sound expanded around *Barracuda*.

He stared at his screen. It took him a moment to realize that the sonars on the starboard side of the hull were damaged. He played with his console to compensate. "Fogarty, switch to bottom scanners. Sonar to control. I hear no reactor noises. He's lost power."

Fogarty activated the down-searching bottom scanners and made contact. "Oh no," he said, and closed his eyes.

Sorensen looked at Fogarty's screen and slowly removed his headphones. He switched on the overhead speakers. Shaking his head he said, very quietly, "Sonar to control, he's sinking. He's already down to two thousand feet. He's going down without power. He can't blow his tanks."

Sorensen began to fidget. Somehow, the collision had left the Soviet sub without power, he guessed. It would sink until the pressure of the sea became too great, then it would implode. What they had feared would happen to them was about to happen to the Russians. In a few seconds their hull would rupture and the sea would come crashing in.

Springfield entered the sonar room and stared at the screen in disbelief. The sub was already far deeper than any other submarine had ever dived. He imagined the scene aboard the Russian sub ... the men in there knowing they had only moments to live, some praying, others weeping or gone mad with panic and fear. But most, he was sure, were trying their best to get power to the pumps to blow her tanks and make her rise ...

"Good God!" said Sorensen. "They've fired a torpedo."

He stood up and backed away from the console. On the screen the slowly sinking blip divided into two. They heard the whine of an electric motor. A guide wire between the blips was clearly visible. Someone aboard the doomed sub was attempting to steer the torpedo.

Springfield shouted, "Evasive manoeuvres. All ahead full. Right full rudder." But before the helm could respond, the torpedo went awry, and plunged straight down to four thousand feet.

While all eyes were on the torpedo, they heard the sound of the Russian sub imploding—painfully loud cracks separated by a fraction of a second as each of the ship's compartments ruptured in close sequence. The sea would now be pouring through the fractured pressure hull, blowing out the bulkheads between the individually pressurized compartments, until everything was smashed into tiny fragments.

"My God, my God . . ." Springfield said, over and over. "Did you get it all on tape, Sorensen?"

"Yes, sir."

"Seal that tape and bring it to my cabin. You people in here are not to say a word about this to anyone. Understood?"

"Aye aye, sir."

Springfield returned to the control room. "Take her up to the surface, Leo. We'll have to send off a message to ComSubLant. You have the conn. I'm going to inspect the torpedo room."

Chapter 7

The operations centre on *Kitty Hawk* had tracked the entire encounter between the two subs on the sonar screen. Now everyone on the bridge saw the distress rocket break the surface a mile away, streak into the sky and explode into a yellow cloud.

A moment later, in the midst of a boiling white sea, *Barracuda* bobbed to the surface. A hatch in the sail opened, and two men in scuba gear climbed out and jumped into the sea. Admiral Netts held his breath, waiting for the hatches in the hull to open. If the sub were about to sink, the crew would scramble out. Instead, the hatches stayed closed and a blinking light on the bridge began flashing a message: COLLISION WITH SUBMARINE. IDENTITY UNKNOWN. SPRINGFIELD.

Springfield had signalled with lights rather than radio so as to keep his transmission out of the hands of the Soviet trawlers trailing the fleet.

Admiral Horning was furious. The destroyers had let Springfield slip through the perimeter. No ship had fired at *Barracuda*, and she had not launched her weapons, so the war game was technically a stalemate, but Horning knew he had lost. All hell had broken loose down below, then *Barracuda* had reared up out of the sea like a nuclear sea monster only two thousand yards from his flagship.

As dozens of reports came in from the fleet, the communications officers were trying desperately to make sense out of the confusion. Several ships reported the sounds of bulkheads bursting as a ship sank. Yet all of the fleet's subs were accounted for.

Netts was stunned. "What the hell is going on here?" he said to Horning.

"I think your Captain Springfield has got some explaining to do."

FIFTEEN MINUTES AFTER *Barracuda* surfaced the divers reported that the damage to the outer hull was minor. Springfield signalled to the carrier that his ship was seaworthy, and that he and Commander Billings wished to board *Kitty Hawk*.

Before he left the sub, Springfield spoke to the crew.

"Attention all hands, this is the captain. I want to take this opportunity to congratulate each one of you for an outstanding performance during this action. In particular I want to mention Chief Lopez and the entire torpedo gang who put their lives at risk to save ours, and Sonarman Sorensen, whose quick reaction saved the ship from certain destruction. That is all."

THE SONAR ROOM WAS A SHAMBLES. Technical manuals were scattered over the deck. The cabinet had fallen over and spilled thousands of tiny electronic parts. A cup of coffee had splashed over Fogarty's console.

Sorensen was still wound up with tension. The sound of the Soviet submarine—the mystery sub—plunging straight towards him reverberated in his ears, a sound he would never forget.

He looked at Fogarty, who was pale and drenched with sweat.

Fogarty's hands were trembling as he lit a cigarette. "What did he do? Ram us on purpose?"

"I don't think so. Sub drivers aren't generally suicidal. This was just bad seamanship."

"The waiting. Sinking, knowing they were going to die ..." Fogarty stammered. "It could've been us."

"But it wasn't. Maybe next time."

"Do you think the Russians know?"

"I don't think so, not yet. But sooner or later they'll find out."

"Then what?"

"Then maybe we have sub wars. Who knows?"

Sorensen began to run checks on all the equipment. Fogarty knelt down and began sorting through the spilled diodes and transistors.

Ten minutes later Davic and Willie Joe came in to relieve Sorensen and Fogarty. Davic's dream had come true. *Barracuda* had finally sunk a Russian sub.

"Sorensen, is it true? Was it the Viktor? Did it sink?"

"Sorry Davic, the log is sealed. Captain's orders."

But Davic could see in Sorensen's eyes that it was true, and that was good enough. On the profile sheet of Soviet subs he scrawled an X over the drawing of the Viktor.

SORENSEN HAD HEARD the ultimate sound effect. The collision and the implosion of the Russian sub were engraved in his brain. Just to make sure, however, he had recorded the entire sequence of events on his own machine. In the seclusion of Sorensen's Beach he played the tape over and over. Several questions began to nag at him. Why did the Russians fire a torpedo? Were they trying to sink *Barracuda* or *Kitty Hawk*? The sub imploded below three thousand feet, an incredible depth. How could the Russians go so deep? Was the collision an accident, or did the Russians ram them intentionally? No sane captain would do that, but no sane captain would fire a torpedo either.

He tried to picture the wreck of the Russian sub. Eight thousand feet down, he knew, there was no light, no perceptible movement in the water, nothing but pressure beyond imagination. In the cold black desert of the ocean bottom, pieces of the shattered sub would by now have settled over a debris field many miles square. All those men. It chilled his heart.

"ATTENTION ALL HANDS, this is the captain. We have been ordered to put in to the naval station at Rota for repairs. Transit time will be forty-eight hours. Our depth will be restricted to two hundred feet. Prepare for manoeuvring. That is all."

In the torpedo room Chief Lopez discovered that Zapata was missing. He cleaned up the broken glass from the cage and searched the compartment thoroughly, but the scorpion was nowhere to be found. Lopez felt queasy. A sub had thousands of nooks and crannies where a bug could hide. It was only a matter of time before someone got stung. Lopez was sure it would be him.

Several hours after they were under way, Lopez reported Zapata to the Executive Officer as "missing in action".

Pisaro blinked, not sure whether to laugh or show concern. The scorpion was not all that dangerous. Its sting was hardly worse than a bee's.

"How long can that thing live with nothing to eat, Chief?"

"Months, Commander. Maybe a year."

"All right. Organize a search. Give the crew something to take their minds off the collision.

Lopez drew a crude picture of a scorpion adorned with a Mexican sombrero and crossed cartridge belts, and printed a wanted poster on the ship's duplicating machine. He offered a reward of twenty-five dollars for the return of Zapata, dead or alive, and organized search-and-destroy patrols. For twenty-four hours sailors armed with torches and hastily constructed nets systematically ripped out every panel, emptied every locker, tossed every bunk. By the time they reached Gibraltar every cubic inch of the ship had been searched twice, but Zapata remained AWOL.

Lopez now reported Zapata's continued absence to Pisaro. "I think he's still in the torpedo room, sir. I don't see how he could get out. The hatch has been closed since the collision, except when someone goes in or out."

"Don't worry about it, Chief. Zapata is a survivor, I'd bet on it."

THE SHIP LOCKED on to a NATO submarine beacon and passed submerged through the Strait of Gibraltar into the Atlantic. She then turned north towards the Bay of Cádiz and the huge Spanish naval base at Rota. At dawn the sub reduced speed and began to rise from cruising depth.

Springfield went aloft to pilot the ship. As they followed a radar beacon into the inner harbour a cool mist rose off the bay. Inside the breakwater at Rota, opposite Cádiz, the Spanish aircraft carrier *Dédalo* loomed over the smaller ships and tugs that lined the piers.

A tug pushed *Barracuda* against a massive floating dry dock, and lines were secured fore and aft. Two days had passed since the collision, and the Russians had not uttered a word about their missing sub.

IN *POTEMKIN* THE COLLISION had sent men and machinery flying about as though bewitched by poltergeists. Kurnachov had cracked his head against a periscope housing and fallen unconscious to the deck.

Potemkin had revolved 360 degrees around her keel, turning completely upside down before righting herself. The prop was no longer turning, but the stern planes were angled down and the ship was sinking.

Federov had groped his way out of his cabin, through the darkened passageway and into the control room. There, after stumbling over the prostrate Kurnachov, he discovered that the lights on the diving panel were still green—the pressure hull was intact.

"Stern planes up to zero degrees," Federov ordered. "Seal the hatches. I want damage reports."

Federov's return to the control room inspired the crew to shake off their daze and follow orders. The intercom still operated. "This is the steering machinery room. Portside stern plane fails to respond. Attempting to operate manually."

"This is electrical engineering. All systems functioning on emergency power."

"This is reactor control. We have steam. Injection pressure normal."

The instruments popped back to life. With a glance, Federov realized that the most obvious danger came from the atmosphere machinery. The carbon dioxide scrubber and carbon burners were not functioning.

"All hands put on gas masks and oxygen tanks."

Slowly, air was bled into the ballast tank, and the bubble in the buoyancy gauge rose to the centre. The rate of descent slackened.

At three thousand feet the engineers were able to crank the stern plane up to zero degrees. The carbon monoxide burners were reignited. Only the carbon dioxide scrubber remained out of action.

"Torpedo room, load Acoustical Decoy Number Five. Flood tanks. Sonar, where is the American sub?"

"Rising, Captain, almost on the surface."

"Fire decoy, maximum speed, down angle twenty degrees. All hands prepare for decoy concussion."

WHEN KURNACHOV WOKE UP in his cabin, his head was bandaged and his left arm encased in plaster. When he tried to sit up he discovered a manacle on his ankle that chained him to his bunk.

All insignia of rank had been removed from his uniform. He sank back to consider his fate ...

Several hours later Federov brought him a tray of sausage and *kasha*.

"Release me," Kurnachov demanded. "I am still master of this ship."

Federov set down the tray.

"Former Captain Second Rank Kurnachov"—he spat the words—"you have demonstrated an incredible lack of seamanship, provoked the Americans, compromised the secrecy of *Potemkin* and abused your authority. All these will be included in the charges against you."

CHIEF ENGINEER ALEXIS ROLONOV, son of a Leningrad shipyard worker, had spent a large part of his life covered with grease. As he sat in Federov's cabin, a black streak across his forehead, his hands were coated with a fine film of oil. He and the captain were old shipmates.

"How goes the portside stern plane?" Federov asked.

"The hydraulic system is ruined, but it can be operated manually."

"The reactor?"

"We can start it any time."

"And the carbon dioxide scrubber?"

"That's going to get serious. The lithium hydroxide filters were spilled and scattered. We have only partial function. Normal carbon dioxide concentration is two per cent. We're now up to three per cent. Without filters, four days, five at the most, then it's going to be carbon dioxide narcosis."

Federov pulled out his flask of vodka, swallowed two mouthfuls and passed it to Alexis.

"How are the injured men?" the engineer asked.

"They're going to die if we don't get them off this ship, which we can't do in the immediate future. Gorshkov wanted a one-hundred-day cruise and he's going to get it, but we may all be dead."

"Well, we are making history—"

"To hell with history. *Potemkin* was rushed through production too quickly. Inadequate sea trials, insufficient training for the crew, too many gadgets and no backup systems. In another three years these titanium subs will own the seas, but now, thanks to our comrade political officer, we've shown our hand. I'd like to strangle him."

"What are we going to do about the carbon dioxide?"

"What are you going to suggest, Alexis? That I surface? No. We are not going to surface. Our orders are to avoid detection at all costs, even if we have to scuttle *Potemkin* ourselves. We are going through Gibraltar."

"But the scrubber, Captain? We need the filters."

"We can snorkel. We can escape detection by running very slow, very quiet and very deep."

"And if we're detected?"

Federov ignored the question and turned his attention to a chart.

RUNNING *POTEMKIN* ON MINIMAL REACTOR POWER and maintaining a depth of below three thousand feet, Federov manoeuvred his ship towards Gibraltar. He hugged the North African coast, taking care to avoid major shipping lanes and NATO operations areas. No one was looking for him at that depth, and even if they were, he believed, their sonars would not find him. He'd heard vague rumours of an advanced American sonar system but he tended to discount them.

After five days the carbon dioxide concentration was four per cent. The crew was breathing at an increased rate, pumping more and more carbon dioxide into the atmosphere. The men were weakening, and their resistance to infection was crumbling. An outbreak of colds ravaged the engineers.

To vent the sub's noxious atmosphere Federov had to snorkel, rising almost to the surface and pushing a tube into the ocean air, through which to pump out the carbon dioxide-rich atmosphere and suck in fresh air. He cursed his bad luck. The failure of one simple subsystem had reduced *Potemkin* to a primitive submersible craft. They needed air!

As the fifth day drew to a close, *Potemkin* was fifty miles off the Algerian coast. In no more than four hours the carbon dioxide concentration would reach a point of extremely dangerous toxicity. Federov studied his charts. It seemed as safe a place as he would find.

"Prepare to surface," he ordered. "Ready the snorkel. Alexis, take us up to one hundred and fifty metres."

Potemkin rose slowly from the depths. At five hundred feet Popov intoned, "Contact, subsurface. Two screws, diesel-electric. Range five thousand metres."

On the sonar screen the sub was a two-dimensional streak on one quadrant of the screen, above and ahead of *Potemkin*, going slowly.

"Identify, please, Popov."

"French, Daphné class. Probably *Sirène*," reported Popov.

In the engineering room four coughing, sneezing men cranked down the stern planes, and *Potemkin* descended.

Federov spoke quietly into the command intercom. "Torpedo room, load tubes one and two—"

"Nikolai, you can't shoot him, you can't know if—"

"If he's looking for us, Alexis, what choice do I have? If this French captain reports our position, more will come looking. The British will blockade the Strait of Gibraltar. We will have no escape. And we will all die here if we do not snorkel. . ."

"Range to target, five thousand seven hundred metres," came a voice from the torpedo room.

"Flood tubes."

FOR A MOMENT ABOARD *Sirène*, just a fleeting moment, the sonarman thought he saw a blip on his screen, but it was too slight, too faint, and he well remembered how once before he had been severely reprimanded for sounding a false alarm . . . and now whatever it was, if it was ever anything, had disappeared.

At eight hundred metres, having gone quickly down from five hundred feet, *Potemkin* was too deep for discovery by the Frenchman's sonars. But it was not safe, not unless the French ship cleared the area.

"Range to contact?" Federov asked.

"Range five thousand nine hundred metres, Captain," said Popov. "He seems to be moving . . ."

Keep moving, *please*, Federov silently intoned to himself. And as he did, a tired and disgruntled Frenchman some eight hundred metres above him leaned back from his console, sighing mightily, and made the easy decision not to report what he probably had not seen, thereby allowing the *Sirène* to proceed.

An hour later *Potemkin* rose to a depth of sixty feet. The snorkel and a radar antenna broke the surface for half an hour and then disappeared. A lonely old Tunisian fisherman saw what he thought was a strange blue light in the sea and called his mate, who was asleep. By the time he had woken up and arrived on deck, the strange light was gone. The fisherman never mentioned it to anyone else.

Chapter 8

Seventy crewmen were transferred to barracks ashore, leaving a skeleton crew of twenty-nine men on *Barracuda* to supervise the repairs to the bow.

A canopy was stretched from the side of the floating dry dock over the sail, the gates locked, and the water pumped out. Gently, the sub settled onto the steel braces of the huge repair ship. Naked, with the entire two hundred and fifty-two feet of teardrop hull exposed, *Barracuda* was a beached leviathan of massive proportions.

A team of specialists was flown in from the US naval shipyard. They turned on portable floodlights and began to erect scaffolding over the bow, and eighty feet down the starboard side, where the Russian sub had scraped along the hull.

Sorensen went up on deck to get a look at the damaged sonars. For half an hour he lay on his stomach, spreadeagled over the hull, trying to match what he saw with what he had heard during the collision. The point of impact was directly in the centre of a torpedo tube door. The Soviet sub had sideswiped two torpedo doors and six sonar transducers.

He tried to imagine what had happened to the Russian sub. How had she sustained enough damage to sink and implode? Was her hull ruptured? Did she lose her prop? He climbed back through the hatch and into the ship, his mind racing through the possibilities. He stood in the control room, watching the electricians, pondering what to do. Finally, he knocked on Pisaro's door.

"Come in. What is it, Ace?"

"Sir, I request permission to listen to the tape of the collision. I would like you to listen with me, Mr. Pisaro. You'll hear why."

Pisaro agreed, and a minute later Sorensen and he were alone in the sonar room. Pisaro broke the seal on the reel of tape, and Sorensen threaded it into one of the big recorders.

They listened to the voices on the command intercom, and the machinery noises, and then the clash of the collision reverberated round the room, followed by the torpedo motor and the implosions. When it ended, Sorensen reversed the tape to the point where the Russian fired the torpedo, and again they listened to the high whine of the torpedo's gas turbine motor.

"What does it sound like to you, sir?"

"It sounds like a Russian torpedo, Sorensen."

"It appears that way, sir. But I wouldn't swear that is a torpedo."

"What else could it have been?"

"I don't know, but I don't trust any of the sounds I heard from that sub. I believe everything that boat did was an acoustic trick. I want to edit the tape."

"All right. Do it."

Sorensen quickly made a copy of the tape and gave the original back to Pisaro. He ran the duplicate forward to where the Russian fired the torpedo, then played it at a slow speed up to the sound of the first implosion, where he stopped it. With the filters built into his console he laboriously removed each implosion and explosion from the tape, then

332

took out the sounds of the ship breaking up. It was tedious work but at last he had a tape of the sounds that were left.

They listened to the edited tape, and the torpedo motor was still there. It was faint, but it was clear, and the sound continued right to the end of the tape.

"Commander," asked Sorensen, "what do you know about Russian torpedoes? If they're wire-guided and the wire breaks, what happens?"

"I don't know. With ours, the motor stops and the torpedo sinks. Can't have a torpedo run wild."

"But what if the Russian sub is still alive, sir? Maybe she never sank. Maybe the torpedo we just heard wasn't a torpedo at all, but the sub itself. What if the implosions were faked?"

Pisaro swore softly. "I'll have to show this to the skipper right away."

AFTER PISARO HAD LEFT, Sorensen popped open his console and removed the tape from his concealed recorder. He was about to take it back to Sorensen's Beach when Fogarty came in, slumped in his seat and stared, brooding, at the X drawn through the Viktor on the profile sheet.

"What's buggin' you, kid?"

"What do you think, Sorensen? Is this going to get us into a war?"

"Fogarty, the Russians are not going to start World War Three over one lost sub. Besides, it was an accident."

"The Russians might not see it that way. But I think if the whole affair were made public, that might defuse the situation."

"What good would knowing about this do anybody? It would just get people excited."

"The people at home have the right to know," Fogarty said.

"They do? Since when? What if people knew about all this stuff? All this secret stuff and all the games with the Russians. Look, here's Joe Blow sitting at home watching his TV and he hears, 'Sub Sinks. War Threatens', and he goes nuts. And when you tell him, you also tell the guy watching the news in Moscow. He learns that a bunch of his comrades are lying dead on the bottom, and he starts screaming for war. It works both ways. If it was us down there, half the United States Senate would vote to nuke the Russians in a minute. So we don't tell people anything. It may be wrong, but the other way is worse."

"So we just forget about it, like it never happened?"

"Look at it this way, Fogarty. If the Russians were going to start a war over this they already would've done it."

"Maybe they don't know about it yet."

"Don't bet on it. They know more than you think, and so do we." Sorensen bit his tongue. He thought about telling Fogarty that he now had evidence that maybe the Russian sub hadn't sunk. But he wasn't positive, not yet, and he wanted his point to sink in.

AFTER A WEEK IN DRY DOCK, the welding of the bow was completed and new sonars and torpedo doors installed.

Sorensen and Fogarty were in the control room, pulling hundreds of feet of inch-thick cable up from the torpedo room and arranging it in coils.

Fogarty wiped his brow. "I sure could go for a cold beer."

Sorensen dropped the cable. "That's the most sensible thing I've heard you say since you've been aboard. I could go for a dozen, myself."

"You been in Rota before?"

"Once. It's just another navy town, kid. Don't get your hopes up."

For an hour they dragged the coils out of the ship and stacked them on the pier. When the last coil was placed on top of the pile they lounged on the pier and watched the engineers work.

A light warm rain started to fall. They could see the lights on the Russian trawler as it moved along its picket line from Cádiz to Rota.

"What are they so interested in?" Fogarty asked.

"The *Vallejo*," Sorensen replied. "What else?"

The USS *Mariano G. Vallejo*, a missile submarine, was berthed at the next pier. Her sixteen Polaris A–3 missiles and their warheads represented more firepower than all the bullets and bombs in all the wars in history. She was, in navy jargon, a "boomer".

A moment later, they heard the quartermaster's voice blaring from the loudspeakers on the pier. "Now hear this. Liberty call, liberty call. Liberty for the first division will commence at twenty hundred hours. Cards will be good for twenty-four hours. Be advised that all personnel are restricted to the town of Rota. The city of Cádiz is off limits. That is all."

"That's us," said Sorensen. "Let's go get that beer."

NOTHING LOOKS MORE LIKE a sailor than a sailor on liberty in civilian clothes. Fogarty had the haircut, the creased Levis and the all-American smile. Even Sorensen, who took pains to look like anything but a GI, was doomed to failure. The wrap-around sunglasses and custom-made cowboy boots helped, but there was nothing he could do about his swagger, or his natural tendency to walk in step with his buddy.

The main gate to the naval station was in the middle of the town. Sorensen and Fogarty flashed IDs at the American and Spanish marine guards in the sentry box and passed through the barriers.

Directly opposite the gate, at the foot of the Avenida de Sevilla, they stood surveying the scene. A string of seedy bars and cheap hotels tailed away from the gate, their faint light barely illuminating the dank slum. The rain had stopped, and the cobbled streets glistened. Trucks and motor scooters buzzed past, sending a fine spray into the night. A few sailors in white hats, and many more in civilian clothes, milled from bar to bar.

"So this is Spain," said Fogarty, staring into the darkness.

"What are we, tourists?" Sorensen said. "C'mon."

334

They strolled up the Avenida de Sevilla. A hundred yards from the gate they stopped in front of *El Farolito*, "The Little Lighthouse", and pushed through the door. A blast of loud rock and roll greeted them. They stood for a moment on a small landing, looking down into the subterranean bar, while their eyes grew accustomed to the cherry glow of the lighting. A white hat flew through the air and landed on a table full of beer bottles. In the rear a pair of castanets danced above a ring of clapping sailors. They picked their way through the crowd to the bar.

"*Dos cervezas*," said Sorensen.

"You can talk American here, Mac."

"OK, pal. Two cold ones."

Two bottles appeared on the bar. "You fellas off the *Barracuda*?" They nodded.

"Hear you're in for repairs?"

More nods.

"Hear you sank a Russian boat?"

Sorensen did his best to look surprised. "Where d'you hear that?"

"The word gets around." He moved on down the bar.

Sorensen laughed. "You want to tell the world about the collision? Seems the world already knows. So much for naval security. Drink up, Fogarty. To freedom, truth, justice and the right to know."

Sorensen threw back his head and downed half a bottle of beer.

Fogarty looked round. It was a large L-shaped room with sawdust on the floor and a high ceiling obscured by smoke. Several of his shipmates were lying in the sawdust. Others were dancing to the thumping tempo of rock music. Here and there in booths and at tables clusters of Spanish men and women aloofly watched the action. Gipsies meandered through the crowd selling switchblades and watches.

Sorensen waved Fogarty to a table.

"Nice party, hey, kid?"

Fogarty shrugged. "It's all right."

Sorensen laughed. "Relax, Fogarty. Have yourself a good time. You're a good boy, aren't you? All your life you've been a good boy. I'd bet anything that you've never been in trouble. I mean, real trouble. You believe in peace, love, all that."

"I don't have to prove that I can break a few bones, if that's what you mean."

"How about a few Russian bones, Fogarty? Would you break them if you had to?"

"I hope I don't have to."

"So do I, kid, and don't forget it. But the question is, what are you going to do if and when it comes to the crunch?"

Fogarty shrugged again.

The party in El Farolito was still going full blast. In the back room a lone dancer went through the motions of flamenco in slow motion, kicking the floor and snapping castanets to music only she could hear.

"See you later," Sorensen said to Fogarty. He carried his drink across the bar to the table nearest her and sat down. At first she appeared not to notice him. Then she slowly danced around his table. They exchanged a few words, then left together. Sorensen waved to Fogarty on the way out.

FOGARTY DRANK ALONE for an hour. He wasn't sure about how to approach the women. He wasn't interested in fat gipsies, and was ready to stumble back to the hotel where he and Sorensen were staying, but he was so drunk he could hardly walk. One of the women from El Farolito helped him up the stairs and out of the bar, and got a taxi to take him the short distance to the hotel.

SORENSEN LAY IN BED listening to the sound of a morning maid slowly working up the marble stairs to the third floor. Somewhere in the hotel a radio came to life and a muffled female voice sang a slow ballad.

He got out of bed and pulled on his clothes, went into the corridor and knocked on Fogarty's door. No answer. He put his ear to the door, smiled and went downstairs for breakfast.

In the afternoon, El Farolito was taken over by the crew of *Vallejo*. This was their last blowout before the big missile sub began a sixty-day cruise under the Med, and they pulled out all the stops. When Sorensen came in a radio was going full blast, filling the room with music from the Armed Forces Radio Network.

About two o'clock Sorensen pushed up to the bar and ordered a beer. The bartender pointed across the room and said, "There's a fella lookin' for you."

Sorensen looked round and noticed a man in a tweed jacket sitting in a booth, away from the crowd.

It was Admiral Netts, sitting alone with a bottle of brandy and two glasses. He gestured for Sorensen to sit.

"Afternoon, Admiral."

"Don't salute, Sorensen, I'm not in uniform, so let's skip the formalities. What happened down there?"

"You mean during the collision, sir?"

"Of course I mean during the collision. What was he up to, that damned Russian?"

Sorensen hesitated. The din from the rowdy sailors swirled around him.

"Have a drink," said Netts, pushing the bottle and a glass across the table. "Just tell me what you know about this Russian sub."

"It's hard to say, sir. They seemed to be testing acoustical systems."

"Submarine disinformation, deception, fakery, tricks?"

"Yes, sir. That's about the size of it. Dirty tricks."

Netts lowered his voice. "I listened to the tape you made for Commander Pisaro, but I don't quite know what to make of it."

"I'd like to ask you a question, sir. Have the Russians said anything about their missing sub?"

"No. As a matter of fact they aren't even searching for it at all. No reconnaissance ships, nothing. That's what I don't understand"

Sorensen drank his glass of brandy and poured another. "Admiral, I'm not convinced that boat sank. I mean, we all heard the implosions, but we heard a lot of things that turned out to be something else. Fact is, I think they faked it. I don't know how, I can't *prove* it—"

Netts cocked an eyebrow, questioning. "Sorensen, do you know what you're saying? That sub was four thousand feet deep."

"Yes, sir. Four thousand one hundred and thirty-five to be exact."

A strange smile flickered across the admiral's face, a Cheshire-cat smile. "You're saying the Russians have built a submarine that can go that deep. If so, it's a revolution in hull technology."

"Yes, sir, I know. It's bad news."

"If that's the case we need to know more about this submarine. Hull sections involved in the collision with the Russian sub have been cut out of *Barracuda* and sent to Washington for analysis, but meanwhile *Barracuda* is going back to sea. You and Springfield are going to find this Russian sub, record every sound she makes and then do everything you can to force her to the surface and take her picture."

"Do you know where she is, Admiral?"

"No. She got into the Med without our detecting her at Gibraltar, but she hasn't passed back into the Atlantic. The new SOSUS net that *Barracuda* tested will pick her up right away. When she does go back into the Atlantic, we'll be all over her. I have great faith in you, Sorensen. You're an asset to the navy."

"Thank you, sir. I'm flattered you should say so."

"Have you ever thought about accepting a commission?"

"No, sir. I like it fine where I am."

"You think about it."

Sorensen nodded, knowing he wouldn't think about it at all. Netts pushed the bottle across the table and stood up.

"Drink up, then, and I'll see you in Norfolk."

Sorensen watched the admiral's back move away and out of the door.

Chapter 9

Sorensen returned to the decrepit hotel off the Avenida de Sevilla, and knocked on Fogarty's door.

Fogarty was asleep, dreaming he was inside the sinking Russian sub.

Blaming him for their fate, the Russians were stuffing him into a torpedo tube ...

Sorensen pounded on the door and woke him up. "Fogarty, you in there?"

"Yeah, just a minute ..."

Fogarty unlocked the door. His eyes were red and puffy.

Sorensen walked into the room and flopped on a chair. "You all right?" he asked.

"I drank too much."

"We're due back on the ship in a couple of hours," Sorensen said. "Want to go back to El Farolito? There's a party on."

Fogarty tried to shake his head, but the motion made him woozy. Sorensen shrugged and shoved a Bob Dylan tape into his miniature recorder. While Fogarty closed his eyes and listened to the music, Sorensen opened the windows and stepped onto the balcony. Below, the street was nearly deserted. It was three in the afternoon, the hour of siesta. Sorensen went back into the room and pushed the rewind button on his recorder.

"You know, Fogarty, I think you're going to be a good sonarman. You've got good ears."

"Thank you. Coming from you, that's a real compliment."

"Well, I want to give you a little test. I want to find out just how good you are. But to do that I have to let you in on a little secret."

Fogarty sat up straight and squinted in the dim sunlight coming through the windows. "What kind of secret?"

"Personal. That means I personally will strangle you if you tell anyone." He retrieved his tape recorder, took out Bob Dylan and put in a new tape. "I wired this recorder into my console in the sonar room."

"But that's illegal."

Sorensen grinned. "Yeah, that's my secret, and now it's yours too. If I did everything the navy's way I couldn't do my job. This way I can listen to any tape, any old time I want. Now, listen to this."

Sorensen proceeded to play the original, unedited, tape of the collision. Fogarty recognized it immediately. He heard the voices on the command intercom, then the crunch of metal on metal. Coming through the miniature speaker in the recorder it didn't sound quite so terrifying.

Sorensen flipped over the tape and punched the play button. Once more they heard the Russian sub sinking. The torpedo motor howled across the sea. But this time there were no explosions, no bursting bulkheads. The torpedo motor continued for several seconds, and then the tape ended.

"What did you do to the tape?"

"That's the test, Fogarty. You tell me."

Fogarty laughed nervously. "What kind of a game is this, Ace?"

"This is the home version of Cowboys and Cossacks. C'mon, Fogarty, tell me what you hear."

338

Fogarty said, "You took out the implosions. What's left is the torpedo. You're trying to find out what happened to that."

"Could be. What do you think happened to it?"

"It was wire-guided. It sank when the wire broke."

"You sure?"

"No ... the motor keeps running."

"Very good. What else?"

"Maybe it's not a torpedo."

"Real good. So what is it?"

"A decoy?"

"Nope."

Fogarty picked up the recorder, carried it to the bed, sat down and listened once more. The motor churned out a highpitched whine that reminded him of the little electric motors he used to put in his model subs.

And suddenly, he understood. Or did he? "You want me to believe that it's the sub? It never sank?" When Sorensen didn't reply, he sat perfectly still for a minute. Finally he said, "I can't believe it."

"You don't want to believe it, but it's true."

"But it went down to four thousand feet. No sub can go that deep."

"This one did."

"It's impossible."

"Fogarty, can't you shake your mind loose? It used to be impossible, but it isn't any more."

"It just doesn't make sense—"

"Then tell me why the Russians aren't looking for their missing sub."

"How do you know that?"

"Netts told me," Sorensen said cheerfully. "He came all the way from Washington just to chat with the Ace. You like that?"

"You talked to Admiral Netts?"

"Sure. I'm a big hero, remember?"

"Why would the Russians fake the sinking of their own ship?"

"First, to make enough noise to cover their exit. And, if we thought she was sunk, we wouldn't look for her. Come on, Fogarty, *think*."

"So it was a trick."

"Looks like it, kid."

"I grieved for those people—"

"I know you did. An honourable thing to do."

"How long have you known?"

"Since I played what you just heard. The skipper is going to tell the crew about it tonight. Then we're going after her; and we'll find her."

"How can you be so sure?"

Sorensen looked at Fogarty. "Because of the new system, the deep submergence sonars. SOSUS, they're called. The way they work is simple. They laid down cable, ordinary undersea telephone cable, only every twenty miles they spliced in a hydrophone. We now have a grid of cables with a total of thirty-six hundred hydrophones in the Atlantic. Some spots, like the Caribbean and the Iceland-Greenland-UK gap, are saturated with phones. It means we ought to be able to track this sub, wherever she goes. The game is going to get very interesting. When we go back to sea tonight we have to be ready for anything."

Fogarty picked up the miniature tape recorder and weighed it in his hands. He was scared, but he figured that was only natural. He remembered hearing what he had thought was the torpedo charging through the water directly at him . . .

LOPEZ WAS STANDING at the foot of the submarine pier when Sorensen and Fogarty arrived. "All right, you're the last ones. Let's go."

The pier was crowded with sailors and technicians preparing *Barracuda* and *Vallejo* for departure. As they walked along Sorensen said, "What's happening in the real world, Chief? Any traffic out there?" He waved his arm in the direction of the Atlantic.

"Seems the whole ocean is full of Russians. It's gonna be hot. The skipper wants to see you right away. Go change."

Sorensen showered, changed into a jumpsuit and knocked on Springfield's door.

"Come in."

"Chief Lopez said you wanted to see me, sir."

"Sit down, Sorensen. Coffee?"

"Thank you, sir. Black."

Springfield poured two cups of coffee and handed one to Sorensen. "I understand you spoke with Admiral Netts."

"Yes, sir."

"He wants to give you a commission."

Sorensen rattled his coffee cup. "We've been through this before, Captain."

"And you've turned us down each time."

"Yes, sir. I like it fine where I am."

"I told Netts you would say that, but there's a hitch. You can't stay where you are. None of us can. *Barracuda* is going back for a major refit and they're going to disband the crew. We're assigning you to *Guitarro* and promoting you. You'll be chief of the boat."

Sorensen almost dropped his coffee.

"Chief of the boat? You're putting me on, skipper? No sonarman in the navy is chief of the boat."

Springfield smiled. "Some naval traditions are flexible. Netts is willing to make an exception in your case."

"You said *Guitarro*? I never heard of her."

"She's a new attack sub, still on the stocks. You'll have the most advanced electronics and sonars. Space on the boat has already been designated as Sorensen's Beach."

Sorensen hadn't expected this, and he wasn't sure how he felt about it. A new ship, a new crew, a new captain and chief of the boat all at once. Too much ...

"I don't know what to say, Captain. I'll have to think about it."

"That's fine, Sorensen. You think about it as long as you like. Right now we have more immediate concerns. Admiral Netts tells me that in your opinion the Russian sub never sank, that it was an acoustic trick of some sort."

"Skipper, what we thought was the torpedo was the sub itself. I think they fired some kind of decoy that sank and imploded."

Springfield tapped a pencil on his desk. "That means we have to assume that sub is still loose. We don't know where it is or what shape it's in but we do know it got into the Mediterranean undetected, and as far as we know it hasn't come out."

"If it got in, sir, I wouldn't be surprised if it can get out."

"Well ... we've increased the number of patrols through the Strait and beefed up the fixed arrays, but this sub isn't our only problem. Four days ago three more Soviet attack subs passed through the Iceland gap and headed south into the Atlantic. We're tracking them through the North Atlantic with SOSUS right now. One of them is riding a picket line about thirty miles out. Clearly the Russians believe they can penetrate the Med, and go after our big missile subs. We think they're going after *Vallejo*, so the first thing we're going to do is help *Vallejo* shake her tail. When she is clear, we're going on station outside the Strait. If we're lucky, we'll catch the mystery boat coming out. Any questions?"

"Yes, sir. Is there a designation for the new sub?"

"Alpha."

"It's one hell of a sub, sir."

"It is. No question about that."

"We'll keep sharp ears, skipper."

"Very well. Get ready to take her out."

SIPPING ALKA-SELTZER, Sorensen was running circuit checks on the new sonars when Fogarty came into the sonar room and sat down. Fogarty switched on his screen and punched up the bottom scanners.

"How's your hangover, kid?"

"Awful."

Sorensen punched him lightly on the shoulder. "Relax, Fogarty, we're home. What's the depth under our keel?"

"Thirty-four feet."

"All right. Sharpen your spurs, cowboy. Here we go."

They heard Pisaro's voice come through the intercom: "Attention all

341

hands, attention all hands. Manoeuvring stations, manoeuvring stations. Prepare for slow speed."

The reactor was hot, the steam lines were charged, the course was plotted, captain and lookouts were on the bridge. Overhead, the night sky was cloudy. On the pier opposite, the captain of *Vallejo* prepared to follow *Barracuda* into the bay. Springfield waved and ordered the bow and stern lines away.

"All ahead slow."

With a shudder the ship moved away from the pier, passed outside the breakwaters and slipped by the Russian trawler. Springfield turned his ship into the moderate sea and headed for deep water.

"Strike the colours," he said. "Clear the bridge. Rig for dive."

No band played. No crowd waved goodbye. *Barracuda* steamed out of Rota in the dead of night and slipped furtively into the Atlantic.

Chapter 10

In the torpedo room Lopez checked the serial numbers of the live torpedoes against the log and cheerfully dusted off the warheads. Once again fully armed, *Barracuda* carried twenty Mark 37 torpedoes with conventional high-explosive warheads, in both wire-guided and acoustic-homing modes, four Mark 45 torpedoes with quarter-kiloton tactical nuclear warheads, and two chaff decoys designed to confound and mislead an enemy torpedo. Lopez hummed a happy tune.

The young torpedomen gathered round a plaque newly installed over the firing console: "Zapata, Missing In Action".

Johnson, the mate, was scrutinizing the new plating in the curved snout of the compartment. Patches of fresh grey paint still glistened in the bright light, but the welds were invisible. A thin, wiry man, Johnson had a voice like two stones scraping together.

"Lopez, the word is that a Russian sub is riding a picket line thirty miles out."

"That's right. They do it all the time."

"Yeah, but this one's waiting for us."

Lopez watched the torpedomen rivet their eyes on the mate.

"They want revenge because we sank their boat."

"They're waiting for the *Vallejo*."

"How do you know, Lopez? Maybe they want to even the score."

"Johnson, you've got a big mouth. All of you, listen. The Russians aren't interested in us. Don't worry about it. When we get back to Norfolk, all of you will get thirty days' leave. Think about that and forget the Russians."

The torpedomen appeared unconvinced, but none spoke.

342

A moment later the ship began to submerge. As the hull compressed, the torpedomen gasped at every creak and groan. All eyes were on the new torpedo doors. Every weld had been X-rayed twice, and the repair team had taken the ship for a trial dive to eight hundred feet, but Lopez had sealed the hatch and prepared for the worst. When Springfield adjusted the trim and levelled the ship, all systems were functioning normally. The torpedomen cheered.

THE CAPTAIN REDUCED SPEED to a crawl and began to circle. In the sonar room Sorensen closed his eyes and pressed his earphones tight against his ears, listening for the picket. Slowly *Barracuda* swung back towards the bay where *Vallejo* was due to emerge in ninety minutes.

Sorensen took off his headset and turned on the speakers. Fogarty watched the blank screen, giving a little start each time the brief sound of a distant surface ship flashed across it.

"What's the matter, Fogarty? You jumpy? Relax. This Russian isn't going to pull any dirty tricks. It's our turn."

Fogarty rubbed his eyes and stretched. "It's been a long day and I could use some sleep."

Sorensen glanced at the chronometer in his console. "You'll have plenty of time to sleep when this cruise is over. Meanwhile, we have to try out the new down-searching passive array they installed in Rota. And get us some coffee. Let's stay awake."

In the galley Fogarty found Cakes, the steward, sipping tea with Stanley, the Filipino cook.

"I hear the Russians put out a contract on *Barracuda*," Stanley was saying. "They want us bad. Just like the Mafia."

Cakes laughed. "Why put a contract on us, Stanley?"

Stanley put a finger to his lips and whispered, "We sink their ship, kill their sailors. They want an eye for a tooth."

Fogarty laughed. He poured two cups of coffee and, balancing them precariously, returned to the sonar room where he found Davic and Willie Joe crowded round Sorensen's console.

Barracuda was at four hundred feet. A school of tuna passed under the ship at a thousand feet, turning the screen into a swirl of green dots. Sorensen took his coffee from Fogarty, punched a button, and most of the fish disappeared. "This new sonar is computer-enhanced. It compensates for the thermals," he said. "Not completely, not perfectly, but it helps."

"What's the point?" Davic asked. "No sub goes that deep anyway."

Sorensen said, "I dunno, Davic. You never can tell. Go ahead and sit down. You're going to have to learn how to use this."

Davic and Willie Joe each took a turn, and Fogarty was taking his when the overhead speakers came to life. "Attention all hands. This is the captain. Now that we have put to sea, I am authorized to read you a communication from Admiral Netts. It is dated yesterday and addressed to all the officers and men of *Barracuda*. The message is as follows:

"Gentlemen, I wish to commend all of you for an outstanding performance during the exercise that resulted in your unfortunate collision with a Soviet submarine. As many of you know, it was believed at the time that the Soviet submarine sank. I wish for all of you to know that, to the best of our knowledge, this was not the case. It is probable that the submarine is still operating in the Mediterranean, but eventually she must pass through the Strait of Gibraltar and into the Atlantic. Once *Vallejo* is clear of a reported Russian picket and free to begin her patrol in the Mediterranean, *Barracuda*'s orders are to remain on-station on the Atlantic side of the Strait of Gibraltar and wait for the Soviet submarine to attempt to leave the Med. You cannot stop her, but you will follow her and use every means at your disposal to collect as much information about her as possible. Good luck and good hunting. Signed, Edward P. Netts.

"That is all."

Stunned silence greeted the captain's speech. In every compartment every sailor was thinking the same thing, but in the torpedo room Johnson, the mate, said it aloud. "The ship that hit us is still alive. Alive and kicking and maybe after us."

In the sonar room Davic blanched. "She is not sunk? Sorensen, what does this mean?"

"It means it was hit and run."

"But the implosions . . ."

"Faked."

"You *knew* about this?"

"What if I did? Now you know about it too. And I'll give you all something to think about. This is a new class of ship that can go down to at least four thousand feet, maybe deeper."

Davic gasped. "What is it? A bathysphere?"

"No, it's an attack boat, class name Alpha. She's a noisy devil. We have her signature. We got it just before the collision."

"If she's so noisy," Willie Joe asked, "why can't anybody find her?"

"That's a good question. My guess is she's been running slow and deep, maybe on electric power, but she has to come up to pass through the Strait. She got in because we weren't looking for her."

"Where is she?" Davic persisted. "Is she coming after us?"

"I don't think so, Davic. I figure all they want is to get that sub out of the Med and on her way home." At least I hope that's all, he added to himself. And then, as much to reassure himself as the others, he said, "We're not at war with these people. Now, let's get on with this test. This new sonar just might help us detect a deep-running sub."

344

EXACTLY ON SCHEDULE they heard the thrashing sounds of a submarine.

"Sonar to control. Contact bearing zero seven two degrees, speed twelve knots, course two eight eight, range eight miles. It's *Vallejo*, skipper."

"Very well, sonar. All hands man manoeuvring stations."

Davic and Willie Joe took their asbestos suits and went forward to their damage-control stations.

Barracuda accelerated, her course parallel to that of the big missile ship emerging from the bay. The two subs swept past each other a hundred yards apart, frothing the sea like a pod of whales, then turned and steamed past one another again. They crisscrossed back and forth twice more.

Fogarty shook his head. "Why don't we just send the Russians a telegram telling them where we are? Can't they tell us apart?"

"No. Our signatures are almost identical, and for the moment we're the bait. We want this Russkie to come after us so *Vallejo* can escape. That's the name of the game, to help *Vallejo* shake her tail. Hang on. You'll see."

"Maybe the picket is the Alpha."

Sorensen let his face fold slowly into a smile. "And if it is? Is that what's making you nervous?"

Fogarty shrugged, trying to maintain a casual air. "He rammed us once. I'd rather not give him a second chance."

"You know what I think, Fogarty? I think you're sore at the Russians. I think you're ready to make war."

"I'm not crazy, Sorensen."

"I hope not."

"Except this is a war now, Sorensen ... an electronic war of nerves ..."

"It's Cowboys and Cossacks, Fogarty. It's just a game. Believe it."

HALF AN HOUR INTO THE EXERCISE, at a precisely timed moment, both subs suddenly went quiet and drifted, their momentum carrying them in opposite directions.

Sorensen's fingers stabbed at his keyboard. In the abrupt silence that followed the shutdown of machinery he heard a faint mechanical rumble. An instant later, it stopped.

"Got her. That's it. Sonar to control. Contact bearing two three zero degrees. No range, but she's not too close. She's holding still, skipper. No identification yet."

In the control room the bearing of the Soviet sub appeared on the navigation and weapons screens.

"Bingo," said Lieutenant Hoek.

"Where is *Vallejo*?" Springfield asked.

"Right here, skipper," Pisaro answered, pointing to a blip on his chart.

Vallejo was making a wide turn to the right, away from *Barracuda*, and descending to one thousand feet.

Springfield spoke quietly into his microphone. "Attention all hands. Prepare for quiet running. Quiet in the boat."

In the sonar room the air-conditioner stopped whirring. Sorensen said quietly to Fogarty, "We're going to try to make this Ivan think we're *Vallejo*. We're going to go north. If the Russian takes the bait and follows us, then *Vallejo* is clear."

Sorensen played the brief tape of the picket, backed it up and ran it through a series of filters that corrected the distortion and removed extraneous sound. Then he ran it through the signature program.

"OK, Fogarty, what is it?"

"I'm not sure, but it's Soviet."

"How do you know?"

"He moved when we moved, and stopped when we stopped," Fogarty said. "He's hostile. He's up above four hundred feet trying to listen to us, trying to decide which one to follow. November class. It's not the Alpha."

November flashed up on the computer screen.

"Very good, Fogarty. See, there's nothing so mysterious about these Russians and their noisy boats. Let's play the tape again. It *could* be the Alpha simulating a November."

While the tape was running, Sorensen stood up and looked at the chart of Soviet subs. He tapped the drawing of the November class attack subs. "Wait a minute, wait a minute, I recognize that boat. That's our old friend *Arkangel*. They must've pulled that thing out of mothballs. Wow, we don't need sonars to pick up *Arkangel*. All we need is a Geiger counter."

"What do you mean?"

"I mean, that is a hot boat. She's so radioactive I bet she glows in the dark. I sure wouldn't want to be on it. Those Russian sailors get more radiation in a month than we'll get in five hundred years. Sonar to control, we have a signature. November class. It's *Arkangel*."

"Very well, sonar. Control to communications."

"Communications, aye."

"Prepare to send up a radio buoy on my order. Message as follows: Hostile contact thirty-six degrees thirty-four minutes north, six degrees forty-one minutes west. Priority one."

"Priority one, aye."

They waited in silence, drifting slowly in the slight current. *Vallejo* was three miles south, six hundred feet deeper, and also drifting. The Russian was eight miles west and making no noise. Sorensen hunched over his console, quietly humming and beeping along with the faint sounds of marine life that came through his earphones.

AFTER TWO HOURS Sorensen was ready to have Fogarty relieved. He whispered, "You're through, kid. Hit the sack."

Fogarty shook his head.

346

"That's an order. Get outta—"

"Attention all hands. General quarters, general quarters. Man battle stations, man battle stations. Prepare for manoeuvring."

On the screen they could see *Vallejo* already moving.

"OK, Fogarty, I guess you'll have to stay put. You awake?"

"Never felt better in my life."

The ship shuddered once and began to move. *Vallejo* was heading south and *Barracuda* north. The Russian hesitated, then moved towards *Vallejo*.

"Dammit," Sorensen said. "She didn't take the bait."

In the control room Springfield called communications. "Send up the radio buoy."

"Communications to control. Buoy away."

A small float detached itself from the ship and rose to the surface. A powerful radio beamed an encoded, enciphered, compressed and scrambled message to Rota. Thirty seconds later an alarm sounded on the Spanish aircraft carrier *Dédalo*, and helicopter rotors started churning up the night.

"Control to weapons."

"Weapons, aye."

"Lieutenant, load tubes three and six. Conventional warheads, wire-guided."

Hoek could sense his blood pressure rising. He began to sweat. "Conventional warheads, wire-guided, aye. Weapons to torpedo room."

"Torpedo room, aye."

"Chief, load tubes three and six with Mark thirty-sevens, Mod three. This is not a drill. Repeat, this is not a drill."

Lopez pushed a button on his console and a red light began to blink in the torpedo room. The torpedomen jumped to attention.

"Johnson," Lopez yelled across the room, "load three and six. This ... is ... not ... a ... drill."

The torpedomen unbolted two torpedoes from their bays and slipped them into tubes. When the inner doors were locked, the targeting computer began feeding data to the warheads.

"Control to weapons, lock on sonar."

"Lock on sonar, aye."

Hoek punched buttons on his console and the signature of the November was fed into the torpedoes.

"Flood tubes."

"Flood tubes, aye."

Fogarty listened to the sound of seawater rushing into the torpedo tubes. "We can't sink her," he muttered, "she's in international waters."

"There is no way the skipper is going to let *Arkangel* or any other Russian sub put a tail on one of our nuclear missile subs. Not allowed. No way. We know it, and the captain of *Arkangel* knows it. Suppose the

Russians had a tail on every one of our boomers? They could sink all of them at once. Result—no second strike, no deterrence. So we don't even give them a chance. Just like they wouldn't give us a chance."

"Control to sonar. Echo-range, maximum power, target-seeking frequency. Let him have it, Ace."

Sorensen nodded, and Fogarty took a deep breath. The Russian on his screen had become much more than a blip. In a fraction of a second Fogarty remembered his first sonar lashing, the collision, and Sorensen's tape. He was ready. His onetime concern for the Russians was gone. Deliberately he locked the echo-ranger on the Russian sub, turned it up to maximum power, and pushed the button. The echo came back with a resounding ping.

In the control room every screen came alive with incoming data from the target. Each man was holding his breath. They were alone, no longer a so-called "instrument of national policy" but a state unto themselves in the open sea. In a matter of moments they might be dead, or worse.

This time the Russians did not hesitate. The single ping from the target-seeking sonar meant the next thing they would hear would be a torpedo. *Arkangel* made an abrupt ninety-degree turn and suddenly the sea erupted with the roar of her machinery. She cut loose all her raw power, and in a matter of seconds she was heading due west at thirty knots, leaving *Vallejo* free to begin her patrol unmolested.

It happened so fast, no one had time to feel relief. Fogarty's heart was banging his ribs hard enough to make his chest hurt.

Sorensen was standing with his face an inch from the screen. "That was close," he mumbled. "That was awfully damn close."

He sat down and lit a cigarette with unsteady fingers.

"Is it over?" Fogarty said.

"Yeah, it's over. She did the prudent thing, you might say, under the circumstances. She was outnumbered, after all." He grinned. "You sure put the fear of God into them, Fogarty. You put the fear of God into *me*."

Fogarty stood up and took off his earphones. He was flexing his hand muscles, snapping his fingers over and over from a fist into a straight edge. Sorensen saw the glint still flickering in his eyes.

"Take it easy, kid, it's over."

Fogarty shook his head. "They'll come back, they'll always come back, and we'll chase 'em and—"

"*And* as long as we win the battles, we don't have to win the war."

"Listen, Sorensen, you told me to shape up and do my job. So I'm doing it. OK?"

"Sure, OK, killer." He smiled when he said it. "But don't turn into another Davic. Stay cool."

"There's nothing *cool* about a target-seeking sonar. It's about as hot as you can get."

"It's sure as hot as I ever want to see it. Listen, you scared yourself, you scared me. It's OK, sooner or later we all scare ourselves down here. We all feel like killers sometimes. You just got to put the beast back in his cage and keep him there. You're tired, you've had a busy day. Go get yourself some sleep."

Fogarty reached for the door and smiled. "OK, cowboy. Whatever you say."

He opened the door to find Pisaro about to move in from the control room. As Fogarty stepped past him, Pisaro shut the door and sat down next to Sorensen. "Pretty hairy, wouldn't you say, Ace?"

"I'd say, Commander."

"Did the kid do OK?"

"He's not ready to stand watch by himself. He got pretty excited; but he'll get used to it, as much as anybody ever does."

"Look, Ace, are you positive that was *Arkangel*?"

"Yes, sir. That was old dirty Ivan, in person, polluting the Atlantic."

"No more dirty tricks?"

"I don't think so, sir. Not this time."

"All right. We're going to run a rearguard for *Vallejo* until she clears the Strait. You're relieved. Davic is on his way in here. Go and get yourself some grub."

THE LONGITUDE AND LATITUDE readouts on the navigation console stopped flickering and came to rest. *Barracuda* hovered six hundred feet deep at the edge of the Atlantic. Above her, dozens of ships passed through one of the busiest waterways of the world, oblivious of her presence.

"Attention all hands, this is the captain. We are now on station four miles west of the Strait of Gibraltar. We might be here quite some time, waiting for the Alpha. When she emerges, our orders are to track her into the Atlantic. Be advised that three other Soviet subs have been detected in the eastern North Atlantic. One of them is certainly *Arkangel*. Twelve hours ago they were reported approximately three hundred miles northeast of Rota. Prepare for combat drills. That is all."

For two days Springfield ran the crew through repeated drills, using the endless stream of ships that passed through the Strait as simulated targets. As the third day began, Willie Joe was spending his watch tracking a giant container ship and feeding data to Hoek, who was sitting at the weapons console. Hoek thought he'd died and gone to weapons officers' heaven. In two days he had pretended to sink more tonnage than was sunk in all the wars of the twentieth century.

The container ship passed a mile away; Hoek happily simulated her destruction, sending tens of thousands of imaginary Japanese television sets to the bottom.

The rest of the sonar gang were in the mess. They filed through the chow line, carried trays of roast chicken, peas and mashed potatoes to one of the tables and squeezed in next to the torpedomen. It was a lively mess. There was talk of home, of wives and girlfriends and kids.

"Say, Fogarty," Sorensen said, "you have any plans for the thirty days' liberty we have coming up?"

"I thought I'd go home and see my dad."

"You ever been to Japan?" Sorensen asked.

"Nope. Too far away."

"Hey, man, you're in the navy. You can hop a military flight anywhere, any time. Look, I want a new tape recorder. Wanna go to Japan with me to get one?"

"Maybe. I'll think about it."

"Well, you do that. Think about having a little fun. A woman walking on your back with tiny feet is very nice."

"By the way, don't you ever go home, Sorensen?"

"Home?"

"Oakland."

"This is home, Fogarty. I don't recommend it for everybody, but it's got its advantages. Most of these guys have families, or did. They all have trouble with their wives and more than half get divorced. They have kids they never see and parents who don't know where they are. Home for them is mostly a quarter on some navy base, with a busted washing machine and a Pontiac that burns oil. I tried it and it didn't work. Up there I'm a misfit. Down here I'm at least a well-adjusted misfit."

That drew a few knowing guffaws from the table. Sorensen went on to describe a night in Tokyo's Ginza, and everyone listened except Davic, who propped a Russian magazine against a water tumbler and methodically turned the pages.

Watching Davic, Fogarty picked at his chicken and let his curiosity grow. When Sorensen finished his story, Fogarty asked, "What are you reading, Davic?"

"An article on Czechoslovakia."

"That's interesting. What's it say?"

Sorensen now turned to listen.

"It says, 'The Soviet cultural attaché left the Spring Art Festival in Prague in indignation, after he learned that the colourful abstractions presented by several artists could be interpreted as anti-Soviet propaganda.'"

"My goodness, how rude," cried Sorensen.

"What happened to the artists?" Fogarty asked.

"It doesn't say. But for them, the *gulag*."

"Davic," Sorensen said, "I know a lot of guys who don't like the Russians, but you—it's like an obsession with you."

350

Davic folded up his magazine and leaned across the table. "Does that bother you, Sorensen?"

"Yes."

"Why?"

"We're supposed to be professionals. Too much emotion can foul up a decision."

"You want to know why I hate them? They killed my father in Budapest when I was twelve years old."

Sorensen felt a little sheepish. "What happened?"

No one had ever heard Davic say much more than a couple of words at a time—usually a grouse of some kind. When he saw that all hands at the table were listening, he decided he'd go ahead and tell his story.

"It was in nineteen fifty-six, during the uprising. My family had a small grocery in Budapest. When the Russian tanks entered the city my father tried to keep me inside, but I wanted to watch the tanks and hear the roar of the guns. I was across the street when the first tank came past our block.

"A gang of boys attacked the tank with rocks. One threw a Molotov cocktail that just smashed against the side of the huge tank and shattered. The gunner fired one shot over their heads to frighten them away.

"The shell landed in the store. Two soldiers climbed out of the tank and went in. When they came out, their arms were full of groceries, as much as they could carry. When the tank finally left I went into the store. They hadn't even moved my father's body out of the way. They'd just pushed a few broken crates over him to get at the rest ..." Davic's voice quivered.

"That's real bad, Davic," Sorensen said quietly. "But even for that you can't want to nuke all the people in Moscow—"

"*Yes*," Davic said, "and Leningrad and Kiev and Odessa too. The Russians have been doing the same thing for hundreds of years. The communists are no different from the tsars. They rule through fear. They treat the whole world like my father's grocery store. What's the matter with you, Sorensen? Are you blind? We sit and watch their power grow every day. The only way to save ourselves is to stop them now ..."

Davic sat back and looked round the mess. All conversation had ceased. Every sailor was looking at him.

Johnson, sitting at the far end of the table among the torpedomen, leaned over and said, "Right on, Davic."

Davic nodded and smiled. It was the first show of approval since he'd been aboard and it was heady stuff. Sorensen thought he caught a couple more heads nodding. Fogarty stood up and was about to walk out of the mess.

"Stay put, kid. Look the old monster in the eye. It's the best way to put it back in its cage."

Pisaro, passing through the galley, had overheard some of the exchange. "Gentlemen, let's try to keep it cool. You too, Davic."

"Yes, sir. Aye aye, sir."

"World War Three hasn't started yet. Our job is to see that it doesn't." And he left the mess, shaking his head.

IN SONAR, WILLIE JOE was chatting over the intercom with Hoek. "How many is that, Lieutenant?"

"Let's see. That makes one eight eight. The last one was a big one."

"When's the next sub scheduled to come through?"

"We've got an Italian due in three hours."

"OK, I've got a tanker on the screen. Let's take it."

"My treat," said Hoek, and three minutes later enough hypothetical crude oil was spilled to pollute the Strait for a hundred years.

As the noise from the tanker faded, a bright streak flashed across Willie Joe's screen. He blinked, and rechecked the list of expected submarines scheduled to pass through the Strait. Through his earphones he heard distinct propulsion noises. An unscheduled submarine was approaching the Strait from the west.

"Do you see him, Lieutenant? That's not our Italian."

"Agreed."

"Sonar to control, we have a contact. Bearing two five five, course one two one, speed three zero knots, range ten miles and closing."

"Control to sonar. Do you have identification?"

"Sonar to control. Soviet November class. It's *Arkangel*."

"Attention all hands. Attention all hands. General quarters, general quarters. Man battle stations, man battle stations. Control to radio, send up a buoy."

In ten seconds the mess was empty. Sorensen and Fogarty were in the sonar room.

Willie Joe stood up. "She's all yours, Ace."

"Who is it?" Sorensen asked, sitting down.

"Who else? *Arkangel*," said Willie Joe on his way out. "If she's after *Vallejo*, she's three days late."

As Sorensen sat down, a second streak appeared on the screen, diverging at a slight angle.

"Sonar to control, we have another contact. Same bearing, same course, same speed."

Then a third streak appeared. The sound of the three subs together was as loud as Niagara Falls. Sorensen had never heard anything like it. He said to Fogarty, "Those Russians are storming into the Mediterranean like—"

"Like Cossacks?"

The Russians were following the eastbound NATO beacon through the Strait, the lead ship, *Arkangel*, directly astride it, the others following on either side.

353

Sorensen sat back in his chair, staring at the screen as the subs passed from right to left, three miles south. The Russians blew through the Strait and into the Med in a remarkable display of arrogance and power.

Fogarty hunched over and watched his screen. "If this were chess," he said, "I'd say this looks like a sacrifice."

"Could be, Fogarty. Could be. But this ain't chess. It's boys playing with boats. I don't know what's worse, Davic or these maniacs."

Springfield sent up a radio buoy and made his report. Thirty seconds after it was received in Rota the message was relayed to Gibraltar, and British anti-submarine helicopters were soon in the air. Quickly outdistancing the Russian subs, they raced over the sea and dropped a cordon of sonar buoys in the path of the intruders. The hydrophones, dangling two hundred feet below the buoys, easily picked up the roar of the three subs. Within the hour the anti-submarine forces of the Sixth Fleet, still in Naples, were brought to bear on the noisy Russian subs.

Barracuda remained on station, west of the Strait.

"I'm no Davic," Fogarty said, "but I don't see why we don't track them instead of just sitting here and letting the blood pressure build."

"If this is a sacrifice, as you say," Sorensen said, "there's no reason for us to play their game. These old Russian subs are so noisy they won't be able to hide. The Brits will take care of tracking them, seeing they behave. We don't care about *Arkangel* or those other boats. We want the Alpha, and we're going to sit here until she comes through."

Chapter 11

The interior of *Potemkin* smelled like Lubyanka prison. She had been running slow and quiet since the collision, and since the fresh-water still had been shut down, no one could shave or bathe. *Potemkin* had now been at sea eighty-four days and the men looked like shaggy, grimy albinos. Twelve days of running slow and deep, breathing poisoned air, had rubbed them raw. In the engineering compartment the reactor operators were suffering from the first symptoms of radiation sickness. Only Federov's outward calm kept them under control.

Weeks before, when *Potemkin* had passed eastbound into the Med, Federov had taken advantage of the tide and current conditions, plus the fortuitous passing of a huge tanker, and drifted in silence over the bottom-mounted sonars and past the British picket sub.

No such combination of circumstances would aid *Potemkin*'s escape back into the Atlantic. The currents were against her, and she would have to use her engines in the Strait. Any bottom sonars were certain to pick up her passage. Operators on shore would alert the anti-submarine forces, and the picket subs would tail her into the Atlantic.

Before *Potemkin* sailed from Murmansk, Admiral Gorshkov had foreseen the difficulty of *Potemkin*'s exit from the Mediterranean and had ordered the three subs, *Murmansk*, *Odessa* and *Arkangel*, to pass through the Strait at a prearranged time as a diversion to draw off the pickets. But who knew if it would work?

FROM TIME TO TIME the ship's surgeon changed Kurnachov's bandage and emptied his chamber pot. Federov brought him meals, but no one spoke to him. Even in his own mind Kurnachov had become a nonperson. When he looked in the mirror, he saw a dead man.

Potemkin moved slowly, making wide turns and stopping frequently. Kurnachov, who was still chained to his bunk, assumed that they were on course for Gibraltar and home. After ten or eleven days—Kurnachov wasn't sure of the exact number—the ship halted and remained stationary for several hours. When Federov brought him a meal he asked, "Where are we?"

"Thirty kilometres east of Gibraltar," Federov said as he reached the door.

"Please," Kurnachov said. "Don't go. Give me a moment. The silence is torture."

Federov turned cold eyes on his prisoner. Listless, Kurnachov sat on his bunk and looked away. Federov took a chair. "All right, what do you want to know?"

"After the collision, what happened to the American submarine?"

"You failed to sink it, Kurnachov. You only succeeded in making them angry."

"How did we escape?"

"We fired a decoy, Acoustical Reproduction Device Number Five, which confused them. At first, they were convinced we sank. However, I don't believe their conviction will remain firm."

There was a lingering silence. Finally, Kurnachov said, "Must I remain here alone?"

"Several men were injured during the collision and one died. If I let you out, the crew will attack you."

"That might be preferable to what's waiting for me . . ."

After Federov left, Kurnachov prolonged his meal as if it were his last. Lifelong devotion to the party could not help him now. There would be a trial; then he would be shot.

ON POPOV'S SONAR SCREEN three streaks radiated from the west.

"Captain, I have a contact. They're right on schedule. *Murmansk*, *Odessa* and *Arkangel*."

The trio of Soviet submarines roared past, followed at close quarters by a NATO picket boat.

"One more and we're home free," said Alexis, the engineer who was now first officer in place of Kurnachov.

For an hour they waited for the second NATO picket to come through, but the submarine west of the Strait remained on station. When it did not arrive, Federov knew the gambit to draw off the subs guarding the Strait had failed.

"Take us up," he ordered. "We have to go through. We'll die here. Depth two hundred metres, all ahead slow."

"All ahead slow," Alexis repeated.

For the first time since the collision, *Potemkin* switched from quiet emergency electrical power, and its great nuclear engines rumbled to life. Without its sound-absorbent silicon packing and Acoustical Reproduction Device Number Seven the Alpha became the noisiest submarine in the sea.

The bottom sonars in the Strait immediately recorded her presence. Halfway through the Strait Popov heard the first ping of active sonar. Others followed in rapid succession and seemed to come from all directions at once.

"They've locked onto us, Captain."

"Make revolutions for thirty knots," ordered Federov. "There's no point in being coy."

In the engine room the crewmen put cotton-wool balls into their ears. The steam pumps began to hammer and the turbine wailed like a jet engine.

In the turbulent waters of the Strait, *Potemkin* pitched and bounced like a surface ship. When she reached thirty knots, Federov shouted above the racket, "Increase speed. Thirty-five knots."

Through the Strait, opposite the Bay of Tangiers, Federov ordered, "Make revolutions for full speed. Fifty knots. Let him chase us all the way to the Azores."

TO SORENSEN, FOUR MILES AWAY, *Potemkin* sounded like a tank division smashing through a forest. Alone, it was almost as noisy as all the three subs that had passed through in the other direction.

"Listen up, Fogarty. Tell me what you hear."

"An earthquake? World War Two and a half?"

"You're such a clever boy ... Is this *Arkangel* coming back?"

Fogarty took off his headset and turned on the overhead speakers. "No more games, Sorensen. It's the Alpha."

"*Right*. Sonar to control, contact bearing zero niner two degrees, range seven five zero zero yards, course two seven zero, speed four four knots."

"Control to sonar, say speed again."

"Speed, four four knots, sir, and increasing. Four seven, four niner, five zero knots. Holding steady at five zero knots."

"Holy smoke!" said Pisaro. "I should have joined the air force. We need afterburners to catch that thing."

"Control to sonar. Sorensen, do you have identification?"

"Yes, sir. It's our boy."

"Quartermaster, run sonar through the intercom."

"Aye aye, sir."

A moment later every sailor on *Barracuda* could hear the roar of *Potemkin*.

"Attention all hands, this is the captain. Gentlemen, you all hear the sound of a submarine operating in close proximity to us. Listen good. That's the same submarine that collided with us. As you know, our orders are to track her, record every sound she makes and, if possible, surprise her on the surface and take her pretty picture. If we're going to be up against subs like this one for the next twenty years, we need to know everything about her."

As *Potemkin* swept across *Barracuda*'s bow, heading due west into the Atlantic, the roar of her machinery was audible directly through the hull without benefit of hydrophones.

"Control to engineering."

"Engineering, aye."

"Chief, give me one hundred per cent. Let her rip. All ahead flank, course two seven zero. Right full rudder."

Barracuda nosed into *Potemkin*'s wake and accelerated after the speeding Russian. By the time *Barracuda* reached her flank speed of forty-seven knots, the distance between the subs had increased to nine miles.

At flank speed, every system in the ship was strained to the limit. In engineering the heat from the steam lines caused the temperature to rise to ninety degrees. Stripped to the waist, Chief Wong methodically tested every gauge, checked every calculation to coax every ounce of power from the turbines. *Potemkin* still continued to pull away.

Hour after hour, the Alpha struck further into the Atlantic, deepening the frustration of her pursuers. Sorensen stood in front of his console, arms folded, nodding as if in a trance. On the screen the Russian remained a solid blip in the west, a sun that refused to set. Finally he said to Fogarty, "I used to have bad dreams about that sub. I used to wake up with the sound of her engines clanging in my ears. The mystery sub. Well, it ain't a mystery any more. This nightmare is reality."

"You scared, Ace?"

"You're damned right. This Alpha is fast and goes deep. But you know what's worst of all? If the Russians believe in it so much, they'll think that it's worth anything to keep its secrets from us."

As *Potemkin* raced dead ahead, steadily increasing her lead, the solid blip on *Barracuda*'s screens began to deteriorate.

After four hours, more than two hundred miles into the Atlantic,

Potemkin began to descend. Without decreasing speed she went down to fifteen hundred feet, putting a thermal layer between herself and *Barracuda*.

"Sonar to control, contact is growing indistinct. He's going down, recommend descent to eight hundred feet."

"Very well, sonar, if you think it'll help."

Barracuda nosed over and descended another four hundred feet. Sorensen pursed his lips and watched his screen. "Damn," he swore. "We're going to lose her."

Fogarty asked, "How can we lose her if she's making this much noise?"

"She's twenty-one miles ahead of us now, and we're getting echoes, reverberations and a deteriorating signal. We may hear machinery noises, but we won't know exactly where they are coming from. She can fire a decoy, go silent, go deep. If she continues at fifty knots she'll be completely out of range in five hours and we won't hear a thing."

"But what about the bottom sonars?"

Sorensen nodded. "They'll track her all right, but they can only locate her within fifty miles. They can get an exact fix only when she passes over one of the cables. She's hell-bent on running away from us. She isn't going to stop for anything, and I guess neither are we until we lose her. Sooner or later that Russian captain is going to learn that we are the boat he hit, and that, my friend, is going to put him right on the edge."

POTEMKIN CONTINUED WEST for another seven hours, during which time the distance between the two subs stretched to over forty miles. The roar of the Russian sub gradually deteriorated into a faint buzz, then an erratic hum. Willie Joe was on watch when *Potemkin* finally disappeared from the screens.

"Sonar to control," said Willie Joe. "She's gone."

"Control to sonar. Very well. Prepare for slow speed. Prepare to send up a buoy."

Barracuda slowly circled and sent up a radio buoy. Springfield transmitted a position report and the last known location of *Potemkin*. A moment later Norfolk flashed a reply that Springfield and Pisaro took into the captain's cabin to decode. The message reported that the bottom sonars had successfully tracked both subs into the Atlantic. The Alpha was still heading due west at great speed, generating enough noise to make her easy to track as she passed over the sonar-seeded cables that radiated out from the Azores.

Springfield spread out a chart of the North Atlantic. A chain of marine mountains, the mid-Atlantic ridge, ran north and south, splitting the ocean in half. A deep-running submarine could hide indefinitely among the mountain peaks, and travel north and south through the deep valleys.

Pisaro said, "My guess is, this Russian skipper will go north, try to break through the Iceland gap and go under the ice."

"I'm not so sure, Leo. If he were heading for the ice pack he'd already be making a northerly course. There's no way he could have escaped the collision with no damage at all. He must be hurt. So he can't go under the ice. Plus, he's been at sea a long time. He's probably got sailors who are tired, anaemic, maybe with radiation sickness. He needs a new crew."

Springfield tapped the chart in the region of the Caribbean. "He isn't going north, Leo. He's going south. He's trying to make it to Cuba."

Pisaro shook his head. "Into their ballistic missile sub base? He wouldn't lead us into that. They think we don't know about it."

"I agree. But he might try to rendezvous at sea with a missile sub coming out of the Puerto Rica Trench."

"Do you *really* think they would pull a missile sub off-station for a rendezvous?" Pisaro said.

"This Alpha apparently means a great deal to them, and she's in trouble. They think they can bring the boomer out quietly, rendezvous with the Alpha and slip straight back into the Puerto Rica Trench. If we catch them red-handed, photograph the missile sub on the surface and then follow it, it will never be able to return to the Caribbean. This way, we'll get them out of the area for good without provoking a crisis. The price will be that we'll have to reveal to them the new system of bottom sonars in the Atlantic. Still, once they realize we can track them anywhere, maybe they'll pull back into their home waters. Whatever, I believe this Alpha is going to lead us right to the big boy. That's some bonus."

ABOARD *POTEMKIN* FEDEROV stood before the reactor displays in the engineering room, his face impassive. The sailors wore no radiation badges, but Federov had managed to acquire a US navy dosimeter that he kept secret. It verified what he knew already: he was expendable. He was condemned as surely as Kurnachov. The radiation would kill him slowly. A genuine patriot, Federov considered the loss of his life a proper sacrifice, but meaningful only if he returned his ship safely home. *Potemkin* was everything—the future of the Soviet navy.

He moved to the atmosphere displays. The carbon dioxide concentration was an uncomfortable three-and-a-half per cent. Half the crew had headaches, miserably aggravated by the rattle and vibration of the racing turbines. Comfort had been sacrificed to demonstrate *Potemkin's* durability.

Federov was reasonably certain the American picket sub had followed him into the Atlantic, but for how long and how far he didn't know. After two hours he decided it was safe to change course. *Potemkin* made a wide turn to the left and continued southwest another three hours. Finally, he ordered, "All stop."

In the abrupt silence the men heard their own laboured breathing.

"We're going to snorkel. Take us up, Alexis. Snorkel depth."

For thirty minutes the snorkel projected above the surface. The carbon dioxide-laden atmosphere inside the ship was pumped out and replaced with fresh ocean air. While the ventilation was taking place, Federov remained in his cabin with Alexis and studied charts of the Atlantic.

"We must have new carbon dioxide filters if we are to make it to Murmansk," he said. "Once under the ice pack we can't snorkel. *Potemkin* is many things, but an icebreaker she is not. The sail is not sufficiently hardened to crack through a layer of ice."

"Who can help us?" Alexis asked. "We have no tenders in the Atlantic."

"I know. We have better than a tender. As first officer you are entitled to learn a few secrets, my friend."

Federov unlocked his safe and removed a sealed set of documents that contained the disposition of all Soviet navy vessels throughout the world. He broke the seal, unfolded a chart of the Caribbean and put his thumb on Cuba.

"We can't go *there*—"

"You're right, but *Dherzinski* is operating from there, and he can meet us here, where the Americans least expect it."

Federov moved his thumb to a spot fifteen hundred miles southwest of the Azores.

FIFTEEN HUNDRED MILES FURTHER WEST, *Dherzinski*, a Soviet fleet ballistic missile submarine of the Hotel class, squatted under a half mile of water in the Puerto Rica Trench, the deepest part of the Atlantic. Inside her elongated sail three huge Serb missiles, armed with hydrogen warheads, were aimed at Washington DC, Norfolk, Virginia and Charleston, South Carolina. *Dherzinski*'s presence so close to the North American mainland and her supply base in Cuba were among the most carefully guarded secrets in the Soviet navy, second only to the existence of the submarine *Potemkin*.

For a year *Dherzinski* had operated regular twenty-one-day patrols out of Havana, moving in and out of the harbour by steaming directly under Soviet cargo vessels. The huge sub, three hundred and twenty-eight feet long, never surfaced, and the US satellites which frequently passed over Cuba never photographed her. Submerged in the harbour, moored under a Soviet freighter with a false bottom, she took aboard supplies and new crewmen via a submersible elevator that clamped over her forward hatch. The sailors never went into Havana. When they left the ship, they were taken directly to an airstrip and flown to the Soviet Union.

Captain First Rank Olonov had seen neither the sun nor the stars in over a year. Seventeen times he had piloted his ship into the harbour, stopped under the freighter and watched his crewmen go through the hatch and into the watertight elevator. The lift went up, paused, then returned full of strangers, and *Dherzinski* went back on patrol.

Olonov was in his cabin reading when the nervous voice of the senior radio operator called him to the radio room.

Annoyed, Olonov went to see why the radioman had interrupted him. "What is it?" he demanded.

"A very low frequency message is arriving from Leningrad."

"Which code?"

"Priority one-time, book three."

Olonov blinked and tried to swallow. His throat was dry. The code was the one to be used in the event of war. Only he or the first officer could decode the message. Olonov locked himself in his cabin and rendered the transmission into Russian:

> Olonov: *Dherzinski*: Rendezvous on surface 52° W 33° N. plus 36 hours. Sonic code 2. Supply lithium hydroxide filters for CO_2 scrubber M7. Take eight casualties. Supply eight reactor technicians. Gorshkov.

Olonov's first reaction was relief: the message was not an order to launch his missiles. But it was almost as bad. He summoned First Officer Piznoshov.

"A rendezvous on the surface? With one of our subs?" said Piznoshov vehemently. "Gorshkov himself has ordered *Dherzinski* to surface? It's crazy."

"I know," Olonov said. "Obviously the scrubber failed on this ship, and they have a reactor problem. It's happened before."

"Yes, but Gorshkov has never pulled a missile sub off station. Never. Right now *Dherzinski* is the most important ship in the Soviet navy—"

"Perhaps not."

Olonov was not officially aware of *Potemkin*'s existence, but he had heard rumours of a titanium-hulled attack sub.

"If the scrubber on this mysterious submarine has failed, why doesn't he simply snorkel back to Murmansk? Why compromise *Dherzinski*?"

"Ours is not to reason why, Comrade First Officer, but I have a rather good idea of what this is all about. And there is no question but that we have an appointment thirty-five hours and twenty minutes from now. Prepare to make way."

TWENTY-TWO HOURS AFTER contact was lost with *Potemkin*, *Barracuda* was one hundred miles south of the Azores.

"Take us up, Mr. Pisaro," ordered Captain Springfield. "We're going to transmit a position report."

"Aye aye, sir."

"Control to engineering, all stop."

A moment later the roar of *Barracuda*'s propulsion plant slackened, and the ship rocked in its own turbulence.

"Sonar to control. All clear."

"Very well, sonar. Radio depth. Take us up, Leo."

Above, on the surface, it was seven minutes after midnight, May 21. A new day greeted the ancient sky, whose stars gleamed like pearls above the clean ocean air. To the west, America tossed and turned in troubled sleep. Much further west, in southeast Asia, soldiers died in the noonday sun. To the east in the Soviet Union tank battalions prepared for the invasion of Czechoslovakia, scheduled for later in the summer. Much further east, Red Guards burned books in the Great Square in Peking.

They were far into the Atlantic now, alone in the great ocean. Sorensen heard no ships, no whales, no sign of life. Fogarty was in the control room, learning from Hoek how to track a target on the weapons console. Sorensen felt weary. He had sat through three consecutive watches and was an hour into a fourth, obstinately refusing to relinquish the console to less experienced hands while there was a possibility of *Barracuda* chancing on the Alpha. The cards, he thought, were in *Barracuda*'s favour. The North Atlantic was the US navy's *mare nostrum*. They could track the Alpha just about all the way to Murmansk if they had to. Of course the closer they came to Mother Russia, the greater the risk. Not that the tracking itself wasn't a risk. But that was the order—track, observe, photograph.

Aye aye, sir.

A moment later *Barracuda*'s radio antenna broke the surface and a message flashed the ship's position to Norfolk. A radio operator in Virginia immediately sent a reply. Springfield and Pisaro decoded the message in the captain's cabin.

ComSubLant: *Barracuda* SSN 593: Soviet Alpha class SSN detected by SOSUS GMT 2200 HRS 052068 lat 35° N long 30° W. Course two three zero. Speed unknown. Spectrographic analysis of *Barracuda* hull fragments show traces of titanium. Soviet FBM Hotel class *Dherzinski* detected by SOSUS GMT 2330 Hours 052068 lat 27° N long 53° W. Speed three zero knots, course zero five zero. Proceed on course two three zero. Intercept, photograph, track *Dherzinski*. If she returns to Cuban waters, notify ComSubLant immediately. Netts.

"We hit the bull's-eye!" Pisaro said excitedly. "*Dherzinski*'s coming right at us. She must be going for a rendezvous with the Alpha. We're going to catch up with them both."

Springfield tried to sound calm. "Call the officers into the ward room. We need to brief everyone. Meanwhile, set course two three zero. All ahead full. Let's not waste time."

LIEUTENANT HOEK WENT DIRECTLY from the officers' briefing to the sonar room, where he found Sorensen mesmerized by the blank screen.

"You trying to set a world record for consecutive watches, Ace? You've been in here for thirteen hours."

"What's the word from Norfolk, Lieutenant?"

"They picked up the Alpha three hours ago. She was two hundred and twelve miles southwest of our present position."

"That it?"

"No. They found traces of titanium in the hull sections cut out of the bow."

"Titanium? Well, I'll be damned. That explains how they go so deep and how they survived the collision. Titanium—that stuff is unbelievably hard. What else, Lieutenant?"

"They're tracking *Dherzinski*. She's coming this way."

"*Dherzinski*? That's the boomer out of Cuba. We put a tail on her for a couple of days last year. Talk about out of the frying pan into the fire. Do you know what this means, Lieutenant?"

"You're damn right I know what it means."

"The Russians aren't going to like this."

"Well, the hell with them. They've been throwing their weight around, it's time we got them to back down . . . Look, Ace, you're beat. Willie Joe is on his way in. Take a break, get outta here."

"Aye aye, sir."

Sorensen stood up, stretched, and went out. He paused in the control room to watch Fogarty practise on the weapons console. In the centre of the screen a pulsing red blip simulated a target, a Soviet FBM. Red speckles danced in Fogarty's eyes as he jabbed a finger at his keyboard. The red blip disappeared. "Very good, Fogarty. Only, that time we nuked ourselves too. That gets you a posthumous Navy Cross."

Unaware that Sorensen had been observing him, Fogarty swivelled round in his seat. "It's just the simulator, Sorensen. Like you like to say, cool it."

"Yeah, right. In a few hours you won't need a simulator. You're going to have a real boomer on the screen. You'd better pull out all the Soviet FBM tapes. You'll like the *Dherzinski* tape. I made it last year."

Sorensen shuffled through the passageways aft to Sorensen's Beach, snapped on the sunlamps, put on his wrap-around Italian sunglasses, stripped off his jumpsuit and began doing pushups in his red Bermudas. He wanted to flush the Russians out of his pores.

After five minutes he stopped, opened the cupboard and pulled out the deckchair. Casually he unfolded the chair, set it on the deck and dug into the stack of magazines. As he was about to sit down he glanced round—and there was the long-lost Zapata.

The scorpion eyed him, tail aquiver.

"Hey, I almost sat on you."

He didn't know whether to kill it, catch it or walk out and leave it. Before he could make up his mind, Zapata scrambled off the chair and disappeared under the pipes at the rear of the compartment.

Sorensen got down on hands and knees and searched the shadows under the machinery, but the little arachnid was invisible. Cautiously, he backed up to the chair and stretched out, keeping one eye on the pipes beyond his feet. "I'll make a deal with you, bug. Stay out of sight and I won't step on you."

The heat from the lamps felt good. After a few minutes of lying perfectly still, Sorensen noticed the scorpion crawling out of the shadow of a pipe. It came to rest in a pool of warm light.

"You little devil, I get it," said Sorensen to Zapata. "You found your way in here because it's warm. Those steam pipes are real cosy, aren't they? Like the desert. I bet you miss the desert. Maybe I should take you down to Mexico and turn you loose. Would you like that, or would you rather go back and live with Lopez in the torpedo room? You don't have to make up your mind until we get back to Norfolk, but you can't stay on this boat. She's going into the yard. They're going to cut her into pieces, rip her guts out and use her for target practice. The only *Barracuda* left will be this one right here." Sorensen tapped himself on his tattoo.

He grabbed a magazine. *National Geographic*. He flipped through it, knowing he would never find the article he wanted to read ... "Inside the Newest Soviet Submarine—the Alpha, a Marvel of the Deep". He wondered what its name was. They didn't have one called *Joseph Stalin*, so perhaps it was that. He had hoped he could forget about the Russians for an hour but apparently he couldn't. Whenever he pushed them out of his mind for five minutes, one popped up again where it wasn't expected— sort of like old Zapata there.

It was, it seemed, finally getting to him. As a young man, hardly more than a boy, he had found a perfect niche for his talent. His temperament was suited to life under water. He enjoyed it so much he never questioned it. Now, for the first time in his life, he was confused by doubts. By fears. Yes, the Ace was afraid. He began to speak again to Zapata.

"Listen up, bug. They want to make me chief of the boat. What do you make of that? If I was chief, for once things would get done right. No muzak on my boat, no way. Better movies too. Man, being chief is better than being captain.

"Would you like to hear a secret? I'll tell you why I really joined the navy. When I was a kid in Oakland my dad used to take me to watch the Giants play in San Francisco. We'd go to watch Willie Mays. Willie was different. He was the best. He never let up and never gave less than one hundred per cent. When he stepped between the white lines he was *all* there, and I wanted to be like him.

"After the game we went downtown to eat. Market Street was always jammed with sailors. I thought they were pretty sharp in their uniforms and cocky hats. They all strutted up and down the sidewalk like recruiting posters. On that day I figured the next best thing to being a ballplayer was to be a sailor. So, here I am, and you want to know something? I'm the best at what I do. Like Willie Mays. I ain't braggin', it's the truth. Anyway, in this life nothing matters except the ship, a set of earphones, and the screen. Well, they're taking the ship away and want to give me a new one. I've done my bit, just like *Barracuda*. Me and the ship, we're finishing together . . . That Netts, he's trying to hand me a line of baloney. He knows I can make thirty, forty grand a year in any sound studio in the world, so he wants to make me chief of the boat. And then what? Another five years of Cowboys and Cossacks? Making the world safe for World War Three? Well, old buddy, I ain't gonna be no chief of no boat. I'll get my own studio somewhere. Sorensen Sound, three hundred dollars an hour. No more chasing around. Besides, nobody in his right mind wants to live under water. So why am I doing this?" He grinned. "I know why, because I'm alive down here. I also love it. Well, I'd better learn to live topside, love something else."

Sorensen noticed that Zapata was ignoring him. "Listen up, bug. I'm talking to you. I've done my job. This kid Fogarty has talent, let him be the new Sorensen, ace of the fleet. The next ten years can be his. I don't need any more Cowboys and Cossacks. You and me, Zapata, we're going to fade into the sunset . . ."

Sorensen closed his eyes and for the first time in years he slept without nightmares. Zapata basked silently in the light, observing him.

TWENTY-FOUR HOURS LATER Sorensen and Fogarty mustered in the sonar room for their next watch. Sorensen had slept too long under the sunlamps and was sunburnt.

Barracuda was running slow and quiet. Two more messages had been received from Norfolk. *Dherzinski* continued on the same course, but between the first and second messages the Alpha had disappeared five hundred miles southwest of the Azores.

Figuring the Alpha was waiting at the rendezvous point for *Dherzinski*, Springfield set a course south and parallel to the projected track of the huge missile sub, which he calculated was less than fifty miles away.

Between watches, Fogarty had spent hours listening to tapes of Soviet FBMs. He had listened to the tape of *Dherzinski* several times.

"Say, Ace, how long has this boomer been making patrols out of Cuba?"

"A year."

"How did she get in there in the first place?"

"She must have crossed the Pacific from Vladivostok, passed round

365

Cape Horn and come up through the South Atlantic. I'll tell you one thing, I bet her skipper is unhappy right now. I bet he'd like to put a fish into the Alpha himself for making him risk exposure."

For three hours they listened and drank coffee. They heard a lone whale sing a mournful song, but no surface ships and no submarines.

Sorensen yawned and stretched.

"You sound tired, Ace."

"It's not that, Fogarty. They want to promote me to chief and put me on a new boat in the Pacific."

"Congratulations. A lifer like you, what more could you ask for?"

"I'm going to turn it down."

Fogarty was stunned. "I don't believe it. Not you, not the great Sorensen."

"Yeah, well, I'm going to be the *former* great." He pointed to the speakers, which were churning out the signature of *Dherzinski*. "I don't want to hear one of those things ever again."

"What do you mean? This is what it's all about, isn't it?"

"It sure is, but this is it for me. You can look after the Russians, you're going to be the hotshot."

"Me? Come on, Ace."

"Look, Fogarty, you're good enough. You've got it. And you'll fight if you have to. You're gonna be bad, dude."

Fogarty was embarrassed, partly for being pleased at Sorensen's words.

"Am I right or am I right?"

"We'll see ... but what about you, Sorensen? What are you going to do?"

"Sorensen Sound Effects, three hundred an hour ... But first we're going fishing for a big fish, and hope we don't get hooked."

THEY WERE ALMOST AT THE END of their watch when Fogarty saw the streak flash across his screen. He recognized it the instant he heard it.

"Contact, bearing two eight eight, range fourteen thousand yards, course zero seven six, speed eighteen knots, identification, Soviet Hotel class FBM, *Dherzinski*."

Sorensen barely glanced at the screen. "OK, champ, feed it to the skipper."

"Sonar to control," said Fogarty, repeating the data over the intercom.

"All stop. Quiet in the boat," ordered Springfield.

The sonar screens immediately cleared as *Barracuda* glided to a stop. Fogarty closed his eyes and listened to the rumble of machinery moving through the ocean. *Dherzinski*'s missiles, like *Vallejo*'s, represented Fogarty's worst nightmare. And it popped into his head that one way to get rid of them would be to sink *Dherzinski* right now—and that thought made him sweat. What was happening to him?

Sorensen lit a cigarette and blew smoke at the air-conditioner.

"Does she know we're here?" Fogarty asked him.

"I don't think so. We're too quiet. If she hears us, her commander will take evasive action, or threaten us."

"What are we going to do?"

"Follow her. She'll lead us to the Alpha. In a few hours we're going to be on top of the two most secret ships in the Soviet navy. *Dherzinski* must need something from the Alpha. Or vice-versa. Otherwise they'd never pull her off station. If we're lucky we'll catch them together on the surface."

"What will they do?"

"I don't read minds, kid. But I do know Springfield will do his job, which won't win us the Order of Lenin—"

"Control to sonar. We're going to play tag. Let's keep our range between ten thousand and twelve thousand yards."

"Sonar to control, aye aye."

Barracuda fell in behind *Dherzinski* and began to follow the huge missile sub at a distance of six miles. Steaming on an easterly course, *Dherzinski* rolled through the sea like a leviathan, her computers continuously tracking targets on the east coast of the United States, fourteen hundred miles away.

Sorensen quietly listened to the sounds of machinery, then spoke up. "You know, Fogarty, as of now we're tailing a part of the strategic deterrence of the Soviet Union. She's got the capacity to hit our coast cities, and she's in our sights. If she so much as floods a missile tube . . . well, we can't give her a chance to launch a missile."

Fogarty stared at the blip on his screen.

FIFTY MILES AWAY *POTEMKIN* hovered six hundred feet down, waiting for *Dherzinski*. The atmosphere inside the sub was again fetid. Seven reactor engineers with virulent colds were growing steadily worse. The constant bombardment by neutron radiation was killing the marrow in their bones. They were going to be transferred to *Dherzinski* and replaced with engineers from the FBM, and it had better happen fast.

Popov's voice came through the intercom speakers. "This is sonar calling the captain. We have made contact with *Dherzinski*."

Federov rushed to the control room and stood over Popov at the sonar console. *Dherzinski* was beaming a sonic signal over the prearranged frequency that *Potemkin* was to use as a homing device.

"Prepare to surface. All ahead slow," ordered Federov. "Alexis, put life jackets on the men to be transferred. I'm sending along a sealed copy of the log with an account of Kurnachov's actions, for Gorshkov's eyes only. I want your signature on it."

"Yes, Captain."

ON *BARRACUDA* SORENSEN and Fogarty heard *Dherzinski*'s signal.

"Sonar to control. *Dherzinski* is echo-ranging."

"Very well, sonar. Slow speed. We must be near the Alpha. If *Dherzinski* starts to circle, we'll go round with her."

Sorensen stood up. "Any second now *Dherzinski*'s echo-ranger will pick up the Alpha. When the echo bounces back, we should hear it. That's when one of them might pick us up. Cross your fingers. If they hear us they'll never surface. And that means we can't get the pretty pictures the admiral wants."

Tension crept through the ship. In the control room Springfield said, "She's turning. Go left three degrees." A second blip appeared on the screens. "There it is. All stop."

The two Russian subs were a mile apart, six miles from *Barracuda*. Slowly the two blips moved together.

"General quarters, general quarters. All hands prepare for manoeuvring. Control to weapons. Load tubes two and four with Mark thirty-sevens, acoustic homing."

"If they discover us right now," said Pisaro, "I think they'll shoot ..."

Springfield silently agreed. "Leo, if we hear a target-seeking sonar, we've got to turn tail. Tell the quartermaster to load the camera. When we raise the scopes, you blow off your film in a hurry. As soon as you're done, we back off. We're not going to invite this Alpha driver to be a hero of the Soviet Union at our expense. All ahead slow."

Barracuda inched towards the hovering subs. When the distance was reduced to a mile Sorensen heard strange garbled noises. The Russians were communicating on an underwater telephone.

"Sonar to control, they're talking."

"Very well, sonar. We're sending Davic in."

A moment later Davic pushed through the door into the sonar room. Sorensen greeted him with a big smile. "You're on, Davic. Listen up."

Davic squeezed into the third console, put on a headset and shook his head. "It's breaking up. They're too far away. Wait a minute, wait a minute, I'm getting something—something about carbon dioxide ... lithium ... now I've lost it again."

Fogarty said, "One of them is blowing her tanks. It's *Dherzinski*, she's rising. Now the Alpha. They're both surfacing."

Sorensen watched the screen. "OK, it seems they still don't know we're here. Sonar to control. They're surfacing."

"All ahead slow. Helm, take us in to one thousand yards. Periscope depth, gear for red," ordered Springfield.

The lights in the control room switched from green fluorescence to red.

"Take her up. Quartermaster, rig the camera to number one scope."

"Aye aye, sir. It's going to be dark up there."

"Switch on light intensifiers. We'll activate the infrared system."

"Aye aye, skipper."

"Control to engineering. Chief, increase steam to ninety per cent. We may have to get out of here in a hurry. Up scopes."

Barracuda angled up, and at sixty feet the periscopes broke the surface. Springfield bent over the binocular eyepiece of the number two scope.

OLONOV STOOD ON THE BRIDGE on *Dherzinski*'s squat ugly sail, looking at the short, sleek sub rocking twenty metres away in the gentle sea. He shouted through a bullhorn, "Who are you?"

"This is *Potemkin*," came Federov's reply. "Do you have the lithium hydroxide?"

Olonov's mood was dark. "So you're Federov, Gorshkov's fair-haired boy. Prince of the Northern Fleet. Pleased to make your acquaintance."

Federov did not appreciate the sarcasm. "Send across the lifeline."

It was thirty years since Olonov had worked as a deckhand. Alone on the bridge of *Dherzinski* he managed to fire the small rocket that catapulted the rope across the void. Federov secured the line to a cleat and spoke into his headset.

"Send up the first sick man. Get the others ready."

Olonov secured the bag of crystals to the line and Federov slowly pulled it across. When the precious chemical was safely aboard *Potemkin*, Federov tied one of the unconscious sailors into a litter, stuffed the copy of the log into his jacket, and Olonov began to pull the crewman towards *Dherzinski*.

The man was suspended over the sea when Federov heard Popov's voice on the intercom. Radar had picked up periscopes at a distance of one kilometre.

Federov was furious at Olonov for letting himself be picked up and trailed, thereby compromising *Potemkin*. He spoke to Popov again. "Do we have identification?"

"None, Captain. We never heard him. But now we have periscopes on radar—"

"Alexis, prepare to dive. Load torpedoes and flood tubes, *now*." He shouted into the bullhorn, "Olonov, get that man aboard. You dive first and proceed due north exactly five hundred kilometres. We'll rendezvous again in twenty-four hours to finish the transfers."

Olonov was equally dismayed. He too was risking exposure, and possibly being cut off from retreating back to the Cuban lair. Through infrared binoculars he could now see the periscopes. *Dherzinski* was compromised.

IT WAS THREE O'CLOCK in the morning. Through the binocular lenses of his periscope Springfield saw a mottled shape half a mile away, rolling in the sea. *Dherzinski*. One man stood on top of her low stubby sail wrestling with a lifeline. As the big ship rocked in the waves, Springfield saw that the line stretched across to another much smaller submarine.

"Leo, start the camera." Pisaro put his eyes to the Nikon's viewfinder and activated the motordrive. The camera began taking rapid-fire pictures.

"We got a Hotel class boomer and what has to be the Alpha," said Pisaro. "They're not acting like they know we're here."

"Then they'll know any minute," Springfield replied. "Their radar will pick up the 'scopes. *Dherzinski* is sending a container across. They've got a man rigged to the lifeline."

"Sonar to control. They're echo-ranging. They've got us."

"Radar to control. They've picked up the periscopes."

"They're cutting loose the lifeline," Pisaro announced. "They're closing the hatches."

"Attention all hands. This is the captain. Prepare for steep angles and deep submergence. Control to radio, prepare a position report and the following message: Soviet Hotel class FBM *Dherzinski* and Soviet Alpha class SSN photographed on surface. Will follow FBM according to orders."

"Sonar to control. One sub is flooding her tanks, she's making way. It's *Dherzinski*."

"Steady now," said Springfield. "We'll wait until the Alpha is down before we transmit. We don't want them to intercept our message. Control to sonar. Keep track of the boomer. We'll want to pick up its trail fast, as soon as we're sure the Alpha isn't on our tail."

"Sonar to control, echo-ranging. *Dherzinski* is making six knots. The Alpha is holding steady on the surface."

Through his periscope Springfield saw Federov staring back at him through infrared binoculars. He knew the Russian was waiting for him to transmit.

"Sonar to control, the Alpha is flooding torpedo tubes."

"Steady as she goes. He won't fire from the surface. That's suicide. Control to weapons. Flood tubes."

"Weapons to control. Flooding tubes."

"Mr. Hoek, programme your fish to home on the Alpha. But go easy on the trigger, Lieutenant. Very easy. Give him a chance to back off."

In the sonar room Davic was yelling at the blip on his screen. "Shoot him. Shoot him *now*—"

Fogarty turned on him. "Shut up, Davic. Just shut up."

Sorensen wheeled round, barely restraining himself. "Get out of here, Davic. Take your white suit and go to your damage-control station. *Now!*"

Davic hesitated for a moment, then put on his asbestos suit and left, trailing an untranslatable curse.

Chapter 12

Federov gazed through binoculars at the four thin vertical lines that poked out of the sea a half mile away—radar and radio antennae and two periscopes. He still had no positive identification but he felt certain it was *Barracuda*—who had a better motive?

He had outrun *Barracuda*, outdived it, outmanoeuvred it, but he had not escaped it. They were good, damn them. The very stealth of the American submarine disturbed him. This was no chance encounter: the Americans had tracked him—precisely how, he wasn't certain. He had no doubt that the American commander was taking his picture, and he could not allow that film to be delivered to the Pentagon. His orders had been given to him by Gorshkov in person—under no circumstances was he to permit discovery of this top-secret submarine.

Well, he had been discovered. Now he had to take action. *Barracuda* must be silenced.

But first he had to do what he could to drive off *Barracuda*, to make possible *Dherzinski*'s escape, and then, using *Potemkin*'s depth and speed, try to recover his advantage. Both sides knew the rules: the FBMs of both navies were supposed to be untouchable. Yet now both sides had violated that unspoken understanding. His side by dispatching *Dherzinski* from its hidden station, and the Americans by persisting in tailing the FBM and even, no doubt, photographing it just as they had *Potemkin*.

He knew the action he must take. He would make a threatening gesture, then submerge. To attack from the surface would give the American an opportunity to shoot back and possibly destroy the *Potemkin*. Secretly, in a corner of his mind, he wished the American would escape, save him from what he must do—and then quickly he shook his head, forcing himself to concentrate on his mission.

He spoke into his headset. "Radio, did the American transmit?"

"No, sir, not yet."

He took a deep breath, wiped his eyes. "Range to target."

"Range one thousand metres."

"Start torpedo-guidance sonar."

"Guidance on."

And silently he screamed across the sea at the periscopes, at the American captain, at Gorshkov ... *This is madness* ...

IN *BARRACUDA*'S SONAR ROOM Sorensen and Fogarty snatched away their earphones just in time. The screech of the Russian targeting sonar erupted from the loudspeakers.

"Sonar to control, she's activated her target frequency."

"Down scopes. Retract antennae. All ahead full. Take us down to four

371

hundred feet, Mr. Pisaro. All hands prepare for evasive manoeuvres."

In the manoeuvring room Chief Wong opened the main steam valve all the way, and *Barracuda*'s prop suddenly turned the sea to foam. The ship banked, tilted forward, and shot down into the depths.

Springfield watched the depth gauge as *Barracuda* rapidly approached four hundred feet.

"Helm, make our course zero four five. Depth, eight hundred feet. We'll go under the thermal and give him a run for his money. We have positive proof of her existence, Leo. I tell you, she's going to come after us. Control to sonar, where's *Dherzinski* now?"

"Sonar to control. Five thousand, two hundred yards. Speed fifteen knots and increasing. She's submerging now, but I'm about to lose them both above the thermal. The Alpha is still on the surface."

Barracuda descended to eight hundred feet, turned northeast, and began to move away from *Potemkin*.

FEDEROV SCRAMBLED OFF THE BRIDGE, down the ladder and into the control room. One glance at the diving panel told him that all the hatches were sealed.

"Identification, Popov."

"It's *Barracuda*, Captain."

As he had thought. "What's her course?"

"Zero four five. She's running away. I'm about to lose her under a thermal."

"We must catch her." In order to stop those pictures of *Potemkin* from being delivered, and to ensure *Dherzinski* getting safely back to her lair . . . "Belay torpedo guidance. We're going right down there with him. Engineering, this is the captain. Fast dive. Take us down to three hundred metres. Flood tanks, now."

Alexis opened all the saltwater vents and *Potemkin* dropped like an anchor, an extremely dangerous manoeuvre. One hundred and fifty metres down Federov ordered, "Blow tanks. Neutral buoyancy. Alexis, stop us at three hundred metres."

Potemkin gradually stopped sinking.

"Popov, is *Barracuda* back on your screen?"

"Yes, sir, we're under the thermal now—there she is, bearing zero four five. Speed fifteen knots and increasing. And there's *Dherzinski*." On Popov's screen *Dherzinski* was steaming due north.

Alexis appeared in the control room. "Captain," he said quietly, so as not to be overheard by the others, "are we going to try to rendezvous with *Dherzinski* again? We have to get these sick men off the ship. They're too sick to work, and I need engineers."

Federov spoke without looking at him. "We must eliminate the American sub first. There is no other way."

372

"This American is no fool, Nikolai, and his boat is very quiet ..."

"All ahead two thirds," was Federov's reply. "Course zero four five. We're right on his stern now."

IN THE SONAR ROOM OF *BARRACUDA* Sorensen swore at the screen. The Alpha had gone down swiftly, using her titanium hull to best advantage. Thirty seconds later, she disappeared. "Sonar to control, the Alpha is gone. Her last recorded depth on the down-searching scanner estimated one thousand feet. I don't know where she is."

"Very well, sonar. Control to engineering, prepare for slow speed. All ahead slow. Go right twenty degrees."

Ninety seconds into the turn, the Alpha reappeared on the screen.

"I knew it," said Sorensen. "Sonar to control. Contact bearing one four eight. Range three two five zero yards and closing. Speed twenty-four knots, depth one thousand feet."

"Very well, sonar. We have her on the repeater."

Springfield crossed the control room to the weapons console and stood behind Hoek. "We've got to threaten him, give him second thoughts. Make him back off ... otherwise the bastard will try to finish us ... Control to sonar. Prepare to activate target-seeking sonar."

As Sorensen punched at his keyboard, Fogarty felt as if he were in suspended animation. Was the impossible about to happen? Was no one going to back down?

The Alpha abruptly slowed and turned sharply to the right.

Sorensen reacted instantly, realizing that the Alpha's action meant she was about to shoot. "Sonar to control, recommend evasive action."

"Helm, left full rudder! All ahead full. Thirty degrees up angle! Sonar, activate torpedo-detection frequency!"

POTEMKIN'S TORPEDO ROOM was portside amidships. Federov wheeled to the right, reversed his prop and stopped dead in the water. "Fire acoustic-homing torpedo."

Alexis hesitated, then stuck his thumb onto the red button on his console. A gas-turbine-propelled torpedo shot out of a tube. The projectile took off after *Barracuda* at forty knots, the onboard ultrasonic echo-ranging sonar probing the sea for its target. The instant the torpedo was away, Federov ordered, "Stern planes, maximum down angle, all ahead one third. Take us down to one thousand three hundred metres." He must not give *Barracuda* a chance to find him and shoot back. He must not think of the torpedo he had loosed. He must not think.

"INCOMING! TORPEDO, bearing one eight zero!"

Barracuda was racing upwards at thirty degrees, trying to rise into a cooler layer of water. Springfield was counting on the torpedo's searching in a normal down-spiralling pattern. He calculated he had ten minutes before the torpedo either ran out of fuel or outpaced *Barracuda* and ran up her stern.

"Control to weapons, load chaff decoy."

"Weapons to control, understand load chaff decoy."

When *Barracuda* was at four hundred feet, Springfield ordered, "Zero angle on the planes. Fire decoy."

"Decoy away."

A jet of compressed air pushed the decoy out of the tube, and it promptly began to emit electronic pulses that imitated *Barracuda*'s target-frequency sonar. The decoy spiralled down as *Barracuda* continued up.

The Russian torpedo had remained at eight hundred feet, its sonar confused by the reflecting nature of the ceiling of the thermal layer. When it heard the decoy it zeroed in. Two minutes after the decoy was fired, Sorensen and Fogarty heard the explosion.

"It worked!" Sorensen exclaimed. "Keep your eyes on the screen, kid. There may be another one."

In the control room there was momentary relief. When the torpedo destroyed the decoy, even Springfield allowed himself a minor celebration. A moment later, however, it was replaced by quiet fury. "Leo, take us down to fifteen hundred feet. We've got to get this bastard before he gets us. He fired first."

"ONE THOUSAND THREE HUNDRED metres and holding."

Potemkin was steaming at twelve knots, 4,264 feet beneath the surface. At that tremendous depth she was in a deep sound channel between two thermals, and her own thundering noise rendered Popov's sonars ineffective. He could hear neither *Barracuda*, nor the torpedo, but he did hear the unmistakable sound of an explosion.

"Captain, we got him—"

Federov looked at the screen and at Alexis, who was shaking his head. "Don't be too sure, Popov. We don't know what we hit."

SORENSEN WAS STANDING at his console, working the downsearching sonars. "C'mon, Ivan, come and see what damage you did. C'mon ..." And then, to Springfield, "Sonar to control. Recommend all stop and quiet in the boat."

"Attention all hands. All stop. Quiet in the boat."

Barracuda hovered at fifteen hundred feet. Fogarty expected another torpedo, Sorensen did not. The down-searching sonars were acutely sensitive to frequencies that refracted through the various thermal layers.

A fuzzy splash of illumination appeared on one side of the screen. "There she is. Sonar to control. Contact, range six thousand yards, depth four thousand two hundred feet, bearing one one three, speed twelve knots. She's coming right at us, Captain, but she's deep."

Fogarty slammed his fist on the console. "But we can't shoot her that deep with our regular torpedoes. A Mark thirty-seven will implode at twenty-five hundred feet."

Sorensen nodded. "You're right, Fogarty, but when this Alpha took a shot at us, I figure he was asking for a nuke. Our job now is to survive . . . and his is to see we don't."

Fogarty stared at the screen. "We wouldn't . . . Springfield wouldn't . . . we can't—"

"Fogarty, prepare to feed the guidance system on a Mark forty-five."

Fogarty hesitated. Sorensen just stared at him, and Fogarty, numb, began punching buttons.

"Attention all hands. Battle stations, nuclear. Control to weapons, load tube six with a Mark forty-five."

In the torpedo room Lopez bit through his cigar. He stood up and crossed himself. "Johnson, cut loose a Mark forty-five. Open the door."

Four torpedomen moved along the rack and unbolted the torpedo from its mooring. A fifth opened the torpedo door. Carefully, they slid it onto the guides, and pushed it into the tube. Lopez closed the electronic locks in the proper sequence and ran the circuit tests. "Torpedo room to control," he said into his headset, "Mark forty-five loaded in tube six."

"Control to weapons, arm warhead."

Hoek was having trouble breathing. He responded in a scarcely audible whisper and pushed the coded numbers into his keyboard. "Mark forty-five warhead armed and ready."

"Flood tube."

"Flooding tube, aye."

In the sonar room Sorensen and Fogarty could only listen to the commands as they passed back and forth over the intercom.

Chapter 13

Federov watched the sonar console.

Barracuda was not on the screen. Federov didn't know if she was sunk or whether signal interference in the deep sound channel prevented him from hearing her. He had heard neither implosions nor a train of debris settling towards the bottom.

"Prepare for manoeuvring. Slow speed. Let's be quiet."

ON SORENSEN'S SCREEN the Alpha decreased speed and became quieter.

"Sonar to control, range now four thousand yards and holding. He's looking for us. Depth three eight zero zero feet."

"Control to sonar, activate target-seeking sonar." And pray he comes to his senses and backs off ...

Sorensen looked at Fogarty, punched the button and a wave of high-pitched sound pulsed out of *Barracuda*'s bow in a narrow sound ray aimed directly at *Potemkin*.

POPOV SCREAMED WITH PAIN, his eardrums ruptured by *Barracuda*'s target-seeking sonar. Federov rushed to the sonar console. The pulse of sound that appeared as a bright streak on the screen was like a sharp jab in his guts. Their sonar had found him.

"All ahead full. Right full rudder."

For thirty seconds *Potemkin*'s engines pushed her through a sharp turn. "All stop," commanded Federov. "Level the planes."

The American target-seeking sonar gave him an exact fix on *Barracuda*. *Potemkin* was gliding back towards the American's position. The question

rattling through his mind was whether or not the American torpedoes had an enhanced capability, like their sonars.

His choices were to back off and run, or fight. If he ran, *Dherzinski* would never escape, the *Potemkin* would be fatally compromised by film and *Barracuda* would surface and report that *Potemkin* had already fired one torpedo. Which would bring out the whole damn United States navy to hunt him down ... He looked at his friend Alexis, who had taken his position at the firing console.

"Activate targeting sonar."

The waiting was over.

"Targeting sonar activated. I'm getting one signal, Captain, from *Barracuda*. He hasn't fired."

Federov moved to the weapons station. This was his to do. "Alexis, take the helm."

"Yes, sir."

Federov pushed the button. "Torpedo away."

He steered the torpedo towards *Barracuda* at forty knots, trailing its guide wire behind it.

BARRACUDA'S SONAR SCREENS blazed with red blips. "Sonar to control, he's fired a torpedo, wire-guided, speed forty knots. Torpedo range three seven zero zero yards and closing."

No more hesitation. No more options. The Russian had not backed off. "All stop. Prepare to fire Mark forty-five. Set detonation for maximum depth."

Hoek watched on his screen as the single red blip that was *Potemkin* began to blink. His hand trembled over the keys, then a spike of pain shot down his left arm. He could barely whisper, "Set detonation for maximum depth, aye."

"Fire one."

Hoek reached for the button, but his hand never made it. Clutching his chest, gasping for breath, he fell to the deck.

"Good God, I think he's had a heart attack," Springfield shouted, and ran towards the weapons console. He punched the buttons. "Chief, fire one."

Lopez muttered a prayer and pushed the button. The Mark 45 leaped out of the tube and immediately nosed over for a fast run to maximum depth.

The warhead would explode in two minutes. By then *Barracuda* should be three miles away, and at that distance she should withstand the shock wave that would pass through the water like a nuclear-powered tidal wave—except that the Russian torpedo was still coming at them.

Springfield looked at Hoek lying behind the weapons station. The quartermaster was bending over him, pumping his chest. *Barracuda* was coming round in a tight turn at speed and they were leaning into the deck. Torpedo alarms were sounding, but to Springfield it was almost as if they were echoes from another ship in another ocean on another planet.

Suddenly the door to the sonar room opened and Sorensen stood there, looking round the control room, eyes blazing. The torpedo was gaining on them, he said.

POPOV HAD FAINTED from the acute pain of his ruptured eardrums. Federov snatched away his earphones and pressed them to his own ears. On the screen he saw *Barracuda* fire a torpedo, turn one hundred and eighty degrees, then begin to accelerate away. Could *Barracuda* outrun his torpedo? For a brief moment he continued to guide the missile, but then heard the active sonar in the Mark 45—it was unlike any sonar he had ever heard. And then he knew. The American torpedo was diving, was already below two thousand feet.

"Evasive action," he ordered. "Left full rudder. Dive! Dive! Flank speed! It's nuclear!"

Potemkin turned and accelerated, and the forward motion was enough to snap the torpedo's guide wire. The fish was now on its own. Federov no longer had control of it.

"THE WIRE'S CUT!" shouted Pisaro. "It's running wild." On the sonar screens the Russian torpedo went awry.

Barracuda's control room dared to hope.

Sorensen, standing in the control room door, turned back to Fogarty. His face said he was not ready to celebrate.

"Quiet on the boat," Springfield ordered. "Right full rudder. Engineering, give it all you've got."

THE ECHO-RANGER in the Mark 45 torpedo immediately recognized *Potemkin*, ignoring the frequencies of *Barracuda* and the Russian torpedo.

The two torpedoes sped past each other, missing a collision by fifty yards. The Mark 45 closed on *Potemkin*.

INSIDE THE RUSSIAN TORPEDO a relay snapped and the guidance system switched to an active sonar homing system. The transducer heard and recognized the surge of sound from *Barracuda*'s pumps, and the on-board computer smoothly turned the rudder to the left. The torpedo homed in on *Barracuda*'s engine room compartment.

SORENSEN HEARD THE TORPEDO'S highpitched homing sonar as it bounced off *Barracuda*'s hull. *Barracuda*'s speed was now up to twenty knots, but the torpedo was rapidly closing the gap. Three minutes, four? He stood up, took off his earphones and turned off the overhead speakers.

"I guess I'll be going to the beach. What say, kid, join me?"

Fogarty was unable to speak. He found himself rising like a zombie to follow Sorensen. He felt nothing as they moved through the control room, barely heard Springfield order in an expressionless voice, "Flank speed, stern planes down twenty degrees, sail planes down twenty degrees."

The planesman was staring at the sonar repeater, not able to accept what he saw. The radiomen were trying to send up a communications buoy. Pisaro looked as though he had swallowed his tongue. Cakes was frozen in a hatchway, a tray of coffee in his hands. The tray slipped out of his grasp and crashed to the deck. He stayed immobile.

Sorensen and Fogarty proceeded aft.

In the manoeuvring room there was silence. The men monitored their instruments with undistracted attention. After all, the system had never been pushed to the limit. A technician's dream come true.

Sorensen peeled off his jumpsuit and entered Sorensen's Beach in his red Bermuda shorts. He switched on the sunlamps and put on his sunglasses. Fogarty came in. They pulled out the mat and sat there. Zapata crawled out of the shadows and looked at them.

THE MARK 45 REACHED its maximum depth six hundred feet above *Potemkin*. A spherical shell of high explosive ignited, imploding a sphere of plutonium which instantly reached a critical mass.

The warhead exploded.

In a millionth of a second a fireball thirty yards in diameter erupted into a mass of superheated steam. The sudden impulse of energy pushed out a shock wave that slammed into *Potemkin* with the force of a freight train. Her titanium hull was not designed to withstand that much asymmetric overpressure and ruptured in a dozen places. At four thousand feet the pressure of one hundred and twenty-two atmospheres killed *Potemkin* in eight seconds. Federov's last thought was of the hand of God grabbing his ship and crushing it in His fist.

The giant bubble of highly radioactive water vapour continued to expand, pushing above it a waterspout that rose one hundred feet into the air. The bubble rose swiftly to the surface, where it erupted over an area the size of a football field. A great wave radiated over the surface, and the steam was slowly diluted and dispersed in the atmosphere. When the waterspout fell back into the sea after a few seconds, all visible traces of a nuclear explosion vanished. All that remained was the sonic record heard by SOSUS and the sonar operators on *Dherzinski*, twenty miles away.

SORENSEN AND FOGARTY heard the explosion at the same time that the shock wave rolled through *Barracuda*.

Fogarty sat perfectly still, his mind numbed, seeing only a picture of his toy submarine diving into Lake Minnesota.

The Russian torpedo did not function perfectly. It struck *Barracuda* twenty feet forward of the reactor.

Exploding on impact, the warhead punched a hole six feet in diameter in the pressure hull, directly into the control room. Cracks radiating from the rupture opened around the circumference of the hull. *Barracuda* broke in half. Eight thousandths of a second after the explosion ripped *Barracuda* in two, the sea and the laws of physics finished her.

Chapter 14

A plain, unmarked Mercedes was waiting for Netts when he stepped off the plane at the airstrip near Hamburg. Three days had passed since *Barracuda* and *Potemkin* had destroyed one another.

A young lieutenant stood on the tarmac, holding open the rear door. The admiral waved the lieutenant aside, slid into the driver's seat and drove south along the west bank of the Elbe.

It was a fine spring morning and the river was wide and beautiful. In that part of central Germany the Elbe is the border between East and West. Netts drove through Lauenberg, an ancient town of long slate roofs, and stopped when he reached a single-lane bridge that crossed the river. Two West German border patrolmen, whose usual station was at the foot of the bridge, sat in a jeep a discreet distance away.

On the other side of the river another Mercedes was parked, behind a lowered crossing gate. In the middle of the bridge, alone, stood Sergei Gorshkov, admiral of the fleet of the Soviet Union.

Netts joined him on the bridge. They had never met before. Netts looked at him, not trusting himself to speak.

Gorshkov was a tall, heavy man dressed in a dark, well-cut suit. His face was bland. He spoke in heavily accented but otherwise good English. "I am pleased you agreed to meet."

"I thought it prudent. Tell me what you have to say."

"You will not inform your press agencies of what has happened?"

"Of course not." No need to get such an assurance in return. Everything *Potemkin* had done had been precisely in order to keep the secret of its existence and of *Dherzinski*'s presence in the Caribbean.

"*Dherzinski* is returning home. She is no longer in position—"

"We know. She passed through the Iceland gap this morning. Admiral, your captain sank my ship. He committed an unprovoked act of war. You are responsible—"

"It was not unprovoked. Your ship came within a kilometre of *Dherzinski*—"

"*Dherzinski* was in our waters. In any case, you know now that your attempt to violate our Cuban agreement is ended. Your patrols in the Caribbean have been terminated. But I don't think you were so concerned about *Dherzinski*. I think you were trying to protect your new class of attack submarines. What was the name of the ship that sank *Barracuda*?"

"*Potemkin*."

"How apt. Named for a tsarist prince. You Russians never forget who you are. Why were you so anxious to protect *Potemkin*?"

Gorshkov smiled. "Admiral Netts, I am sure you would not ask such a question unless you knew the answer. Your technicians have spectroscopes. By now they will have examined the sections of the bow removed from *Barracuda* after the collision, and found traces of titanium." Gorshkov added, "We do not want to sink your ships. We want to put a stop to this before it gets out of control."

"You're buying time, Admiral. You want to delay until you have a fleet of deep-diving titanium subs."

Gorshkov's face was still bland, almost affable. "You're a gambler, Admiral Netts. I would enjoy playing poker with you. But, as it is, we have each lost a submarine, and neither of us wishes to lose another. Or be provoked into a war."

They both turned to the river. Gorshkov said, "And so, it is agreed that neither of us will speak of what has happened, or of this meeting?"

Netts nodded curtly. "I have already said so. *Barracuda* disappeared, causes unknown."

"For us, it is simple. *Potemkin* never existed."

They did not shake hands on the bargain. Self-interest sealed it, for now. They would have no war today.

Below them a barge whistle shrilled. They faced each other for a moment, then turned and walked off in opposite directions.

The game was over.

The game had just begun.

MARK JOSEPH

Hanging on a wall in "The Horse and Cow", a bar near the Mare Island Naval Shipyard in Vallejo, California, are two glass-covered plaques. One honours the nuclear submarine USS *Thresher*, which sank mysteriously in 1963 carrying one hundred and twenty-nine men to the bottom of the Atlantic. That tragedy—the worst submarine disaster in US history—produced a huge public outcry and nationwide mourning. The other plaque honours USS *Scorpion*, a submarine that sank in 1968. Its loss received far less attention, and continues to be cloaked in official secrecy.

Mark Joseph first saw the two plaques on a visit to "The Horse and Cow" in 1980. "I knew about the *Thresher*," he says, but he wondered what happened to the *Scorpion* and started asking questions of the navy personnel who frequented the bar. From the answers he received—part gossip, part speculation, and a few scant facts—Joseph says, "I knew I had the makings of a book."

The forty-year-old author grew up in Vallejo and attended high school in nearby San Francisco. He was a teacher for a short time, but found that driving a taxi on the night shift allowed him more time for writing. During those years he turned out short stories and also worked as a writer-editor for a small local magazine. "But I always wanted to be a novelist," he explains.

Then came Joseph's visit to "The Horse and Cow", and the inspiration for his first novel was born. *To Kill the Potemkin* took five years to research, during which time Joseph made repeated requests to the Navy Department for declassified data about the sinking of *Scorpion*. The navy, however, often failed to respond or, at best, sent only limited information. The full story, it seems, is still too sensitive to be made public.

Mark Joseph lives with his wife Nancy and his five-year-old son Jesse in San Francisco. He says he has ideas for at least three more novels, though none of them is about submarines or the navy. But who knows what another visit to "The Horse and Cow" might bring?

TREE
OF
GOLD

A CONDENSATION OF THE BOOK BY
Rosalind Laker

ILLUSTRATED BY JOHN THOMPSON

As the daughter of one of Lyons' most distinguished silkmakers, Gabrielle Roche has always known that the silk trade would dominate her life. Thus it seems only natural that she should wed the cool and businesslike Emile Valmont in order that his silk farm may be profitably linked to her family's silk mill. A perfect match.

But that perfection is shaken on the morning of her wedding day by a chance encounter with handsome Nicolas Devaux, son of her father's bitterest rival. With just one look, her love for Nicolas is sealed—even as she drives away in her carriage to meet the man she must marry . . .

Filled with a wealth of colourful historical detail, *Tree of Gold* is a gloriously memorable saga of destiny and romance.

CHAPTER ONE

Nobody could have foreseen the danger. Least of all Gabrielle Roche, who was being driven to her wedding through the narrow medieval streets of the Croix-Rousse, the silk weavers' district of Lyons. It was the first day of spring, 1804. The sky was a clear morning blue, with a few harmless white clouds drifting light as dandelion down. The sunshine slanted down the stone walls of the ancient buildings, leaving in shadow the deep-set, black-timbered doorways, and gleaming across the worn slabs of dark alleyways leading to inner courtyards.

At street level, the windows of every house were wide and high, allowing plenty of light to enter the weaving workshops and loom rooms. And now, as the wedding carriage passed, the square windowpanes reflected back the day's brilliance with prism colours. In its wake the carriage left the scent of the garlands, tied with love knots of satin ribbon, that bobbed on the horses' harnesses and swayed around the domed roof.

Gabrielle, outwardly the traditional bride—young, composed and ethereal—put her bouquet down on the seat beside her. "We'll see our weavers soon now," she remarked eagerly to her elder brother, who was escorting her to the ceremony. "I must be ready to wave to them."

Henri Roche sat squarely opposite her. At thirty-six he was fifteen years her senior, an overweight, abrasive man, and at her words his mouth compressed into a line of irritability. The weavers were of no interest to him except when they were working. He disliked the fact that his sister had asked that the driver keep a moderate pace throughout this district in order that she might make her farewells without haste to a part of her life that had come to an end. In his opinion she should never have been allowed to visit the weavers' homes as a child, and take instruction like a common apprentice. Left motherless from birth, she had become an undisciplined young girl with a mind of her own.

"I hope this won't take long," he commented impatiently.

"You need have no fear of that," Gabrielle replied. "Time is too valuable to these hardworking people. You should know that, after all your years in the silk trade."

Word of her approach had preceded her. The noise of the looms in these houses was stilled briefly as the weavers who served Maison Roche came out to cheer and wave as she went by. Gabrielle stood to call from the open window of the carriage, knowing each weaver by name. Silk was in her blood as it was in theirs, and they respected her for it.

"Oh, thank you so much!" Gabrielle caught nosegays of wild flowers that were thrown to her, the petals scattering over the carriage floor.

"We're going to be late," Henri informed her sharply.

Unconcerned, she continued to wave back to the family group at each doorstep. The craft of weaving involved the whole household, from the grandparents down to the youngest child, with family life invariably centred around the loom that occupied a large section of their living space. Weavers were a stubborn, independent breed of people, and Gabrielle considered herself fortunate to have been accepted into their community.

She gave a final wave and resumed her seat in a rustle of oyster silk, the Chantilly lace of her wedding cap wafting light as a cobweb on her luxuriant chestnut hair, which she wore drawn into a topknot, with curls at her forehead and at the nape of her swanlike neck. Pearl eardrops danced from the lobes of her pretty ears. A smile hid the pang the partings had given her.

"We can proceed at a faster rate, now," she said. Henri grunted. He gave the ceiling of the carriage a sharp rap with his cane, and a sudden burst of speed made Gabrielle clutch the seat to steady herself.

Although Henri viewed his sister as a nuisance that he wanted out of the family home as much for the sake of his wife, Yvonne, as for his own, he conceded that her looks, particularly on this day in her wedding garments, were pleasing. Slightly above average height, possessed of a provocatively beautiful figure and a clear, warm voice, she had long-lashed violet-blue eyes set attractively wide apart. She was also lively and vivacious. Now she was about to wed a solemn intellectual, the owner of a silk farm, who had no liking for the social pleasures of city life that she had always enjoyed. As far as Henri was concerned, she was getting exactly what she deserved. Consulting his gold fob watch, he gave another rap of his cane as a spur to greater speed.

Neither he nor Gabrielle heard the warning shout to their coachman, from a bystander who was able to see beyond the Renaissance archway through which their carriage was about to pass.

"Look out, citizen!"

It was too late. Seconds later Gabrielle was tossed from her seat onto the floor as the wheels of the carriage collided and locked with those of another that had emerged ponderously from the archway. In the impact, Henri was thrown into a corner, where he held his breath, his eyes tightly closed, as the carriage teetered precariously. It hung suspended at a sharp angle for timeless moments until the terrified horses, straining to bolt, jerked it free. As it crashed down again onto its wheels Henri fell across Gabrielle, half crushing her with his weight. Managing to get up again, he was concerned for his sister.

"Are you harmed?" he demanded, hoarse with anxiety.

"I'm perfectly all right," she answered breathlessly. "Make sure nobody else is hurt."

He helped her back onto the seat, and she accepted his support thankfully, more shaken than she had at first realized. In looking out of the window then, she saw what he had already seen: she sat as though frozen, taking automatically, with nerveless fingers, the bruised nosegay that he had rescued from the floor.

They had collided with a carriage in a funeral cortege, its sides hung with funereal drapery, its black horses plunging their plumed heads in snorting agitation. The mourners had broken rank from the procession at the rear to swarm forward and view the situation, a crowd in sober clothes, some red-eyed from grief momentarily forgotten in current outrage at what had occurred. As Henri prepared to alight, already fuming about the damage to his carriage, Gabrielle put a white-gloved hand on his arm.

"Do apologize to the bereaved family," she urged. "It must have been our coachman's fault."

His face contorted with temper. "Indeed I shall not! I've just realized whose funeral this is. I had heard that Louis Devaux was being brought home from Paris by his only son for burial today."

An icy chill slid down her spine. The family feud between the Roche and Devaux silk merchants was of long standing. It had had its origin in a business quarrel, and succeeding generations had been virulent and bitter rivals for commissions in the city of Lyons. Then the Revolution had given the feud a new and deadly twist, dividing the moderate Roches from the extremist Devaux along political lines. Gabrielle shivered. Now, on this of all days, the feud had reached out a macabre hand to touch her in her wedding finery.

Suddenly she stiffened; a rearing horse in the funeral cortege had been seized by its bridle, revealing to her gaze for the first time today the deceased's son, Nicolas Devaux. She had seen him once before, although at the time he had not seen her, a frightened little girl watching from an upstairs window. He had stood belligerently before her father's house, a lean boy of fifteen with curly black hair, yelling his defiance of the Roche family and all it represented of the old France. His father had dragged him away, afraid he would be killed by the pistol being aimed by Henri Roche from the window.

That had been in 1793, when Lyons had been besieged and then half demolished during Robespierre's Reign of Terror—the time when the Devaux had closed their mill and fled to join the extremists.

Eleven years had gone by since then, and yet there was no mistaking the gaunt, sculptured face, the bold straight nose, the well-shaped mouth and the strong jaw, all of which had made Nicolas, with the passing of time, into a man of arresting appearance. The wild revolutionary had been tempered to a virile and forceful presence.

The horse he was handling settled down at last. In the same instant his eyes met Gabrielle's. It was a penetrating stare that bored into her, as if he were drawing the very essence of her into himself. Her old fear of him resurfaced, but with a dimension of excitement that caused her pulse to race. She forgot completely that she was a bride on her way to her wedding, and he, for his part, had become equally oblivious of his surroundings and why he was there.

He moved in front of the horses as if to come across to her. But Henri, stalking forward, grabbed Nicolas Devaux's sleeve and hauled him round. "You, Devaux have always caused trouble in this city!" he cried. "Living or dead, anyone bearing your detestable name is not wanted here! Do you see what damage your hearse has done to our carriage?"

Nicolas threw off Henri's grasp, his black brows drawing together ominously. "It seems the Roches have learned neither manners nor tolerance since I was last in Lyons!"

Henri made a bullying gesture. "Damnation to you! Your late father is already damned!" Turning his back, he retraced his steps to the carriage, which dipped under his weight as he stepped back inside. Before the coachman could close the door, it was wrenched wide again as Nicolas leaned in and seized the lapels of Henri's coat. "No man shall insult my father's memory. You'll give me satisfaction over this!"

Gabrielle gave a cry of dismay, sick with shame for her brother's actions. "No, please," she implored. "The collision was our fault, and words have been spoken hastily."

Nicolas neither looked at her nor eased his grip on her brother. "That doesn't excuse a lack of respect for the dead."

She continued her attempt to intercede. "I'm on my way to my wedding. For that reason alone, I beg you to forgive what has taken place and retract your demand for satisfaction."

390

He answered her fiercely. "You'd be well advised to leave this carriage and escape the marriage, mademoiselle. You'll have no happiness in wedlock with this fellow."

"He's not my bridegroom! He's my elder brother and my escort. I'm Gabrielle Roche, and I apologize fully on his behalf." Her voice rang with appeal. "Surely, on this day of days, amends can be made."

To her relief Nicolas released her brother then, throwing him back in the seat and turning towards her again. The look he gave her was much as before, awakening the same response in her of mingled pleasure and trepidation. He spoke with care.

"I accept your apology on your brother's behalf, Mademoiselle Roche. But I repeat the advice I gave about escaping your marriage today. Wait awhile. Mistakes are made all too easily."

Her one thought was to get Henri away from the confrontation as quickly as possible. "I shall do what is best, Monsieur Devaux. Don't let us delay you any longer. I'm thankful this has been resolved peacefully."

He raised a questioning eyebrow as he stepped down to the cobbles. The very air seemed charged between them. "Has it?"

"Goodbye, Monsieur Devaux," she heard herself say.

He bowed to her and turned away. The carriage door was shut. As the wheels rolled forward Henri exploded with rage. "What infernal impudence! Bad blood, that's what that family has always had!"

Nicolas, meanwhile, returned to his position leading the procession of mourners. He turned his head, and his mesmerizing gaze held Gabrielle's once more as the wheels of her carriage began to spin across the cobbles. Her face was framed for him, like a lovely portrait, in the carriage window. Then, abruptly, and with a sudden burst of speed, she was swept from his sight.

Gabrielle sank back against the velvet upholstery, dazed but stimulated, laughter and tears welling up in her. Opposite her, Henri splayed his hands across his heavy thighs, which strained the burgundy doeskin of his pantaloons.

"You're looking pale." He attempted to soften the blunt manner he usually used towards her, knowing that bridal nerves often did unpredictable things to women. "Try to forget the little contretemps that took place. Remember that Emile is waiting for you."

She gave a little nod, and turned her head to look unseeingly at the passing wineshops and small cafes. Her brother's advice was not easy to follow. The look Nicolas had given her was not what a bride should receive from a man other than the groom on the day of her wedding. She must forget the whole incident, concentrate on other things as the last quarter of an hour of her single state drew to a close.

Since she was sixteen there had always been men wanting to marry her, but she had always been determined to make her own choice when the time came, in spite of tyrannical pressure from her father. The battle to retain her independence had been hard. Henri and his self-centred wife, Yvonne, had ranged themselves with her father against her. Her only allies had been the younger of her two brothers, Jules, and his sweet-natured wife, Hélène. Unfortunately, Jules was in the army and rarely at home. As for Hélène, although she was the one who waited most upon her cantankerous father-in-law, Dominique Roche, she had no influence with him on his daughter's behalf.

Gabrielle's hope had always been that she might take some official part in the manufacture of Roche silk, and to this end she had learned every stage of the procedure. It was not surprising that she looked beyond docile domesticity, for at the most impressionable time of her life she had experienced the full turmoil of the Revolution. The cry of liberty had been an echo of her own demands for the right to decide her future.

Lyons had suffered more than most cities in the Revolution. Since medieval times it had been a great international trading centre in cloth, although it was not until the introduction of silkworms into France in the fifteenth century that silk weaving took hold and flourished. At that time royal privileges had given Lyons complete control over all the raw silk in the land, and the city continued to rise until the Revolution brought disaster to its luxury-based trade.

With these long traditions of supplying the rich and the noble, the people of Lyons had revolted against the new revolutionary regime that wished to redistribute wealth. Government forces had then moved against the city, and a siege began that brought starvation to its people. After holding out for two months, Lyons raised the white flag of surrender, in the hope of mercy.

It was not forthcoming. As a punishment the city was condemned to demolition, an ignominious fate. Every day smoke and dust from fires and explosions drifted in dark clouds across the peninsula on which the city stood, at the confluence of the Saône and the Rhône rivers. No area escaped the butchering of Frenchmen by Frenchmen. The destruction and slaughter went on for two months and took more than two thousand lives, until in Paris the tyrant Robespierre fell from power and the Reign of Terror came to an end.

By then there were no Devaux of the silk world left in Lyons, for Dominique Roche had seized the chance to rid himself of his old enemies by denouncing them as extremists who were in league with the government forces against the Lyonnais. Louis Devaux had had to flee for his life, taking his wife and son, Nicolas, with him. No Devaux had returned to Lyons until this day, and Gabrielle hoped Nicolas would leave after the funeral as speedily as he had left last time. It would be best for her never to see him again. He was too disturbing.

"We're here," Henri said, breaking into her thoughts. They had stopped by the stone steps of their destination, one of the many churches that had been turned into public assembly halls since the Revolution. Gabrielle smoothed the gathers of her gown carefully into place. For all its delicate appearance, silk was a hardy fabric, and it had suffered no harm through her fall to the carriage floor. The current fashion of skirts flowing from a high waistline suited her well. On the steps Henri offered her his arm, and they disappeared into the entrance.

Inside, an orchestra was playing in what had once been a side chapel. All marriage ceremonies were civil ones now, but she and Emile planned to receive a religious blessing at another time.

There was a stir of movement among those present at the bride's arrival, and she caught an affectionate grin from her brother Jules. Sandy-haired and freckled, still retaining his boyish looks in spite of extensive service on foreign battlefields, he was tall and dashing in his grey-and-red hussar's uniform, his plumed fur hat held military-fashion in the crook of his arm. By his side, Hélène was smiling, dimples playing, happy in the occasion and in having her husband home again, however short his leave might be. She wore a fashionable turban of amber gauze that echoed the colour of her eyes and set off the raven black of her smoothly dressed hair. Gabrielle was heartened by the warm expressions of these two who meant the most to her.

She looked beyond them to the head of the aisle, where Emile waited. His dark brown hair was winged with grey, and shining in the sun's rays that poured down on him through a stained-glass window. Behind him the tricolour flamed blue, white and red.

She returned Emile's steady gaze as she advanced step by gliding step towards him, her gown whispering about her. From the first he had pleased her with his meditative grey eyes, his lean, sensitive face, his deep, attractive voice and his quiet demeanour. She felt that with this intelligent older man she would be able to forget once and for all the swift, sweet love she had shared with Philippe, a weaver's son—an affair crushed by her father. She had been seventeen, and it had taken her a long time to recover from that youthful anguish.

Love, as she had once expected to find it, did not enter into this union, any more than it did into most marriages of convenience. But she did want her marriage to Emile to be a good one. Although divorce had become commonplace since the Revolution, she was resolved that there should be no broken vows for her, and she knew Emile felt the same way. Now he was coming forward to meet her.

"My dear Gabrielle." He seized her hand and linked his fingers with hers as they turned together to face the magistrate.

"Citizen Emile Valmont and Citizeness Gabrielle Roche, you have come before the law of France to be joined in wedlock."

The ceremony went well until she removed her glove to receive the

393

ring. As Emile made to slip the gold band onto her finger, she jerked her hand back involuntarily. She was aghast at her own action. A look of surprise passed across Emile's face, but he remained in control, simply tightening his hold on her fingers. Nobody else, except the magistrate, was aware of the instinctive last bid she had made for freedom.

Emile now bent his head to kiss her lips with reassurance and promise. Her panic ebbed away as if it had never been.

Well-wishers surrounded them. Her first kiss on the cheek was from Hélène. "May you always be happy, dearest Gabrielle."

"I echo my wife's sentiments, little sister." Jules embraced Gabrielle affectionately. With an age gap of only four years between them, they had always been close.

"How I wish your leave could have begun sooner," she said to him. "I've hardly had a chance to talk to you."

"I'll bring Hélène out to visit you before I leave," he promised.

That cheered her immensely. Then she turned to receive kisses and embraces from the rest of her family and friends. Yvonne, Henri's wife, was as usual the height of elegance, wearing a dress of yellow-striped silk, with a large diamond brooch at her throat, and a hat ornamented with tall plumes. She exuded a strong perfume as she leaned forward to kiss the bride. "My good wishes. Your bridal gown is quite charming." Her glance was uncertain. "Oyster is not a shade that is easy to wear, although with my complexion I could get away with it."

· Gabrielle hid her amusement; even at another woman's wedding, Yvonne could not cease to be completely self-absorbed.

More people came forward, and it took a little while before the bride and groom were able to leave the assembly hall and enter the waiting carriage. Observing the old custom that the couple must make a grand entrance at the wedding feast, they were to be driven by a long route to her father's house, giving everyone else the chance to arrive first.

After waving to those gathered on the steps of the assembly hall, Gabrielle turned her head to look at her bridegroom, sitting at her side. He was gazing composedly out of the window at the passing scene, his fine profile etched almost coinlike against the sun. She would have liked to talk, but guessed he was thankful for this quiet respite before facing the feast and chatter that lay ahead. There would be plenty of opportunity to converse, and even argue points of view with him, in the future, particularly whenever she should praise Napoleon Bonaparte for all he and Madame Josephine had done to stimulate the Lyons silk trade by refurbishing the palaces of France.

Emile did not share Gabrielle's enthusiasm for Napoleon, yet he was always ready to listen to her opinions. That was why over the past months Emile had gradually won her trust and respect. There were depths in him that she still had to plumb, for they had had almost no time on their own; Hélène had always been present as chaperone. Only on the evening when he had proposed to her had they been alone together.

There had been moments when she thought she glimpsed in Emile a deep passion. Yet never once had he mentioned the word love. She would have liked him to hold her hand now on this drive, as he had done during the marriage ceremony. To encourage him she placed her hand with its new gold band palm downwards on the seat between them. He did not appear to notice.

They arrived at her father's house in the Rue Clémont. It was a spacious residence—as much a showpiece as a home, since business associates and buyers were received there. Two offices, used by Dominique and Henri respectively, as well as design rooms, were situated to the rear of the house. Every one of the main salons and upper rooms was hung with panels of Roche silk; the designs ranged from spectacular in the Grand Salon to modest in the smaller salons.

During the Revolution the house had escaped damage except for a few broken windows. Shortly afterwards Henri had married Yvonne and brought her home to live. Later, Hélène had been the second bride to take up residence in her father-in-law's house, for with Jules away on active service most of the time, there was as yet no chance for them to build a home of their own.

In the Grand Salon Dominique Roche had received his guests and was awaiting the arrival of the bride and groom.

The walls of the room blazed with richly hued silks which dazzled and beguiled the eye, showing that Maison Roche could match and outweave its rivals. From the looms under Dominique's control came some of the most sumptuous fabrics to be found anywhere in the world. Damask, moirés that shimmered like rippling water, velvets soft as a cat's fur, satins, gros de Tours, lampas, silk brochés, all of them proof that it was Lyons silk that made France superior to all other lands in the manufacture of exquisite fabrics.

Dominique was seated in his great carved chair, with its seat and back of peacock brocade. Since a fall three years before, when he had damaged his hip, lack of exercise and his enormous appetite had increased his already considerable weight. Yet, in spite of being confined to his chair, he missed nothing that went on in his house or in his business domain. He used his wits now as never before to ensure that his elder son, impatient for full control, did not take over on any pretext.

"Emile and Gabrielle have arrived," said Hélène, lowering her smiling face towards his.

"Good girl." He nodded, closing his hand paternally over hers. He could always rely upon Hélène to keep him notified of any developments, but it was her being the wife of his favourite son that had truly endeared her to him. Unlike Henri and himself, Jules never bore malice;

he had his late mother's light-hearted temperament as well as her charm. For Dominique it had been a bitter disappointment when Jules had announced his intention to go into the army and not into the silk business. He accepted his son's decision, but made his own secret plan to bring Jules into Maison Roche when his soldiering days were done.

"Monsieur and Madame Valmont." The bridal couple were announced, and as they came through the doorway applause broke out, rippling round the silken walls. A belligerent expression dominated Dominique's loose-jowled face. He felt the old resentment of his daughter rise up in him, for no reason other than that she was alive and his beloved wife was long since gone, because of her. On the day of Gabrielle's birth he had not so much as glanced in her cradle.

Today, as through a veil of memory, Dominique could glimpse again Marguerite, the only woman he had ever loved, in Gabrielle's dramatic beauty, her chestnut curls, her movements and her grace. As she curtsied to him while her husband bowed, he ignored her. "So, now you are my son-in-law," he declared heartily to Emile. "May good fortune go with you and your bride."

Emile bowed again. "I thank you for your kind words."

Dominique, shifting in his chair, signalled that he was ready to rise from it. Leaning heavily on a walking stick, he would let no one but Jules help him into the adjoining dining salon, where the wedding feast was set out against a glittering backdrop of damask, silver and crystal.

Gabrielle followed with Emile, the rest of the company falling in behind. Her father's deliberate slight had struck deep, on this day in particular. Yet the fact that she had a will to match his meant that he had never broken her. She sometimes wondered if her passion for silk had its origin in a childhood of yearning to break through Dominique's hostility. Whatever its beginnings, she loved silk now for its own sake, and she regarded it as the most beautiful fabric in existence. Her life in the future, she knew, would be spent at the Valmont silk farm, a successful business located at a charming country estate outside Lyons.

The feasting lasted several hours. It was early evening when Gabrielle finally went upstairs with Hélène, who helped her change out of her bridal attire into a lilac travelling dress and coat. The journey to her new home would take no more than an hour.

"Here are your gloves." Hélène held them out to her.

Gabrielle took them and then caught her sister-in-law's hands in a tight clasp. "I shall miss you so much. Please visit me often when Jules's leave is over. It will be lonely without your company."

"You're forgetting, you'll have Emile now."

A shuttered look came over Gabrielle's face. She withdrew her hands and began to put on her gloves. "Yes, so I shall."

Hélène watched her. It was almost possible to believe that Gabrielle was experiencing qualms, in total contrast to her self-assurance that morning while dressing for the ceremony. It seemed to Hélène that something had happened to her sister-in-law between her leaving the house and returning; perhaps the accident with the funeral cortege had upset her more than anyone had realized.

"Are you ready?" she prompted the bride gently.

Gabrielle embraced Hélène and, with a smile arranged on her lips, swept ahead out of the room and down the stairs to the hall, where Emile was waiting for her and where everyone was gathered to send them on their way. Even Dominique was there, leaning on his stick, with Jules at his side. She and Emile departed in the usual noisy excitement that accompanies the going away of newlyweds.

IN ANOTHER PART OF THE CITY, Nicolas Devaux shook the hands of departing mourners. They all knew him as if the eleven years since he had left Lyons had been only as many days.

As the last carriage left, he went back into the building to confirm that he would be staying overnight. Then, lantern in hand, he set off for an address he had not seen since his family had departed from it in haste. It was in the Croix-Rousse quarter, where earlier that day the Roche carriage had halted the cortege, like a last dart thrown at his father's memory.

He ascended a flight of steps to reach a narrow cobbled street, and followed its winding slope upwards. From the windows of the high stone houses which stood on either side there wafted the aromas of garlic and soup and wine, as people sat at supper.

It was all familiar to him, for he had spent his boyhood in these streets. Unlike the Roches who, a couple of generations before, had moved from the crowded heights to an elegant district, the Devaux had remained at the heart of the industry, in an ancient house whose black facade hid a treasure trove of silks within.

His old home came into sight. From his coat pocket Nicolas removed the key that was about to take him into the past. What would he find after all these years? Preparing himself for the worst, he turned the key and let the door swing wide.

The beam of his lantern showed him the chequered marble floor and the staircase rising beyond. He stepped inside and closed the door behind him. The house smelled musty and neglected. But paintings still hung on the walls, and none of the hall chairs was overturned. No sign of disorder yet. He opened one of the double doors leading to the main salon.

The damage there was worse than anything he had envisaged. The silk panels that covered the walls had been slashed to pieces. Gilded chairs lay in splinters, the stuffing ripped out of the silk brocade. He was appalled at the wanton destruction, for the finest Devaux silk had gone into this room. Stepping over the debris, he went to another pair of doors that led into a long, narrow room known as the gallery; it contained many portraits and pictures, all woven in silk. Not one had escaped. It was as though somebody had run the length of the gallery, bludgeoning each one with a spiked instrument.

The gallery opened into his father's office which, he was relieved to see, had been left untouched. So had the adjoining design room, with its brushes and paints and coloured inks ranged neatly in rows, half-finished designs on the sloping desk boards.

He went out into an inner courtyard, and unlocked a door that led to the mill. Holding the lantern high, he sent its glow over sixty looms that stood dark and skeletal in four rows. Axes had been used on the sturdy looms, which bore raw gashes like wounds in the timeworn wood.

Moving slowly down one of the aisles between the looms, he remembered how he had been put to every task in this place, for his father had been determined that there should be no gaps in his knowledge of weaving. In early boyhood he had taken his turn under a loom, retying the threads as they broke, a gruelling and exhausting task allotted to children. Fingers became sore and limbs cramped, and it was not unusual to see children weeping as they worked.

He completed his tour of the workshop, sometimes stepping accidentally on one of the hundreds of bobbins and shuttles that had been thrown across the floor. He had no sooner returned to the house than a knock sounded on the front door. Opening it, he was met by the sight of a short, grizzled old man in the weaver's garb of belted loose tunic and trousers, and a cap topped with a full, soft crown. The visitor seized Nicolas's hand in a gnarled clasp and pumped it heartily.

"It is you, then, Citizen Devaux. I thought I had seen you come home to your roots at last."

Nicolas grinned broadly. "Jean-Baptiste Rouband! After all these years! Come in! If it hadn't been for your timely warning when my father and I were marked men, I shouldn't be here today." He threw an arm round the old man's shoulder. "This calls for a bottle of wine."

"Have you looked in the cellar yet?"

"There's been no time." Nicolas flung a hand in the direction of the open door of the salon. His tone bitter, he said, "See the damage that was done here in the name of law and order. The workshop has also suffered."

Jean-Baptiste took a few paces into the salon. "It's bad, but nothing that can't be put right. In any case, the law didn't do it."

"Then who did?"

The old man turned. "It was Dominique Roche's men. They broke in after you escaped. They would have done more damage if some of your weavers hadn't moved in to drive them out."

Nicolas, for the second time that day, felt an uncontrollable fury against the name of Roche. "I should have guessed it wasn't enough to put our lives in jeopardy! He had to destroy our home and mill."

"How did your mother stand up to the escape?"

"Not at all, I'm sad to say. She had been sick for several weeks and having to leave her home in those circumstances hastened her death. There is no doubt about that." Nicolas moved restlessly, pacing to and fro. "I tell you, I have a heavy score against the Roches, and today more has been added to it."

"If you wouldn't be offended," Jean-Baptiste ventured warily, "I'd like to ask whether Dominique Roche's charge that your family collaborated with Robespierre's Reign of Terror could have been upheld if it had been taken into the Lyons courts?"

"Very possibly!" Nicolas did not hedge. "Feelings were running high at the time, and it would have been hard to find an unbiased judge." He stopped pacing. "That's enough gloomy talk for today. Let's see what can be found in the wine cellar."

He led the way down to the cellar. They were in for a pleasant discovery. Nothing there had been looted. Armed with bottles and glasses, the two men came back upstairs and settled themselves in what had been the family salon.

"When shall you be starting up the looms again, Citizen Devaux?" the old man asked.

Nicolas, reclining in a comfortable chair, regarded the weaver over the rim of his glass. "What makes you think I should want to live here again? After serving four years in the army, I rejoined my father in Paris, where we went into silk negotiating together. Now I control a number of looms in the outskirts of Paris. It suits me very well."

"Silk isn't silk if it isn't woven in Lyons. Parisian silk? Bah!" Jean-Baptiste's contempt needed the leavening of a refill of his glass; he took a gulp. Then he added, "You needn't fear that the mud slung at your good name will stick. Times have changed."

"If I decide to come back to Lyons," Nicolas said, "it would be to reestablish myself in my own right. As for Parisian silk, which you so despise, I recently fulfilled a commission that was part of the refurbishing of the Tuileries."

The old man grunted. "You'd still do better in your own city." Cunningly, he added an inducement. "Maison Roche is hoping to secure good commissions from Napoleon Bonaparte before long."

Nicolas narrowed his eyes. "So the Roches are in the running, are they? Maybe it *is* time for Maison Devaux to reopen."

"Well said!" Jean-Baptiste slapped his knee in triumph. "You mean it, I can see that! It's the best news I've heard in a long while." Putting his glass aside, he seized a bottle by its neck to swallow its contents jubilantly. He remembered little after that, and had no recollection of Nicolas helping him home.

Returning to his hotel, Nicolas guessed that Jean-Baptiste would always boast of being instrumental in restoring Devaux silk to Lyons. The truth was that it had been in his mind all day that he might return, and reestablish himself as one of the manufacturers known collectively as *La Grande Fabrique*. The silk trade was recovering at last from the Revolution, and he found himself wanting to return to the heart of it, to this place where his forebears had produced the best of Lyons silk.

Once in his room, his thoughts went to the bride he had met that day. In the aftermath of that clash of locking wheels he had looked at her and wanted her and thought himself demented, that in the midst of his father's funeral, he should be seized by desire. Never in his life had he been so enthralled on sight by any woman. And he had sensed a response in her, making the rapport between them complete.

At the funeral reception a local mourner had given him valuable information about her, including the name of her bridegroom. If ever the chance presented itself, Nicolas intended to see her again.

BY CANDLELIGHT GABRIELLE prepared for bed. She was being assisted by the maid whom Emile had employed to wait on her. She had never had a personal servant before, and it was a novelty having someone to put away her clothes and brush her hair.

She had made only one visit to Emile's house prior to her marriage and had liked it at first sight. Built of mellow stone, sun-baked to a golden hue, it dated back a hundred years or more and had well-proportioned rooms.

Now that she was upstairs for the first time, she could tell that extensive redecoration had been done for her benefit, for the white paintwork of the bedchamber smelled pristine and the wallpaper was patterned prettily with blossoms from her favourite tree, the mimosa. The bed, also new, had a circular canopy from which filmy draperies looped down over the head and the foot, creating a tentlike look.

She liked everything about her new home. She felt safe in it, although it had never been her policy to seek security.

"Is there anything more, madame?" the maid asked.

She shook her head. "No, thank you. You may go."

Left on her own, Gabrielle crossed to the window and looked out. The moon was bright, and she could see beyond the formal flower gardens to the copse of trees that hid the silk farm beyond. On the day she came to visit, Emile had shown her the white stone silk-sheds with terracotta tiles, where thousands of eggs were being stored in a cold cellar until the time of hatching. After the hatching, the whole cycle of sericulture—the raising of silkworms for the production of raw silk—would begin again.

As a child, Gabrielle's favourite story had been that of the origins of silk: one day, when the Chinese empress Hsi Ling-shi was taking tea in her garden, in 2640 BC, she noticed that a cocoon had dropped into her cup. Seeing a fine thread loosened from it, she pulled it gently and, surprised to find it continuous, began to reel it onto a twig. It proved to be several thousand feet long, and realizing its potential, the empress introduced sericulture on a large scale. For Gabrielle it had always been easy to feel akin to the empress in her love of silk.

Holding back the curtain and looking westwards, she could see the mulberry plantation spread out under the stars, the trees kept to size as bushes. Since silkworms were entirely dependent on mulberry leaves for their sustenance, it was no wonder that the mulberry had become known worldwide as the "Tree of Gold", a magical name that appealed to her.

Emile, having come up the stairs, passed the bedchamber door to go into his dressing room. As he made ready for bed he was clear in his mind as to how it should be between Gabrielle and himself on their wedding night. He accepted that she did not love him. If he had needed proof, he had had it during the marriage ceremony when she had momentarily pulled her hand away from his ring. The hurt of it had been like a dagger thrust, the pain made worse by his desire for her. He planned to win her love gradually. He would rush nothing.

She was in bed when he entered the room, her hair copper bright in the candlelight. Taking the silver candlesnuffer, he put out the flame, then turned back the bedcovers and got in beside her. Trembling with restraint, he leaned over to cup her face with his hand and kiss her gently.

"Goodnight, my dear Gabrielle. Sleep well." Then, as he was about to withdraw to the far side of the bed, she flung her arms round his neck, pressing herself to him.

"What's wrong?" she cried in bewilderment. "I'm glad to be your wife."

He uttered a groan of joy, taking her mouth in passion. He found her generous and responsive, and he believed he had awakened a need of him in her that boded well for their married life. If she lay awake after he slept, he did not know it.

CHAPTER TWO

Ten days went by before Jules and Hélène made their promised visit. Gabrielle ran down the front steps of the house to meet them, her arms held wide, her muslin gown billowing behind her.

"Welcome! Both of you! I've been watching the road for you."

Jules, alighting from the carriage first, greeted Gabrielle exuberantly.

"Then here's your reward!" He caught his sister by the waist to swing her around, she laughing in protest, as if they were still in their nursery days.

Emile, emerging from the house at a more sober pace, creased his brows at this buoyant display of affection. He did not feel ready yet to share his lovely young wife with others. But with inherent courtesy he went forward to receive his company. "I endorse my wife's welcome," he said to them. "We are privileged that you can spend some time with us."

As the servants carried in the baggage, Emile took Jules through to the salon to offer him wine after the journey, while Gabrielle showed Hélène upstairs to the guestroom.

"We shall be most comfortable here," Hélène remarked as she glanced round at the blue-and-white-striped wallpaper and the bed with its gilded mouldings.

Gabrielle took her coat and bonnet from her. "How is Father?"

Hélène's dimples appeared. "He's difficult," she admitted. "He doesn't like to lose sight of Jules when he is at home, so it was quite difficult to get away. But Jules insisted."

"I'm glad. Father wants to rule everybody's life." Gabrielle sighed. "You are now his housekeeper, companion, nurse and slave. His hold on you is getting tighter and tighter. But enough about family frictions. Let's rejoin the men. They'll be wondering what has happened to us."

Jules and Hélène stayed for three days, and the time went by all too quickly for Gabrielle. The opportunity for which she had been waiting did not come until the final evening, when Emile invited Hélène to view his collection of rare silk moths from India and the Far East.

"At last a chance to talk to you alone," Jules said to Gabrielle.

"And I to you," she replied. "I know you've never wanted Hélène to endure the hardships of following you on campaign, but now she should go with you, or you should buy a home for her. She deserves to have time to herself instead of being the mainstay of a house where she is never left in peace. Her duties have doubled since I married Emile."

Jules took her by the elbow and led her to a sofa, where they sat down together. "Hélène and I have talked the matter over," he began. "She does not want to move into a place where she would have little more to do than worry about me. It does her good to be busy. She also believes that Father needs her, and it pleases me that my wife can be a comfort to him." He saw a shadow pass over his sister's face. "I didn't mean to hurt you. I'm probably the only one, with the exception of Hélène, who knows that, in spite of everything, you do care about Father."

She gave a little shrug of resignation. "The filial bond is not easily broken. He is an extraordinary man, and I admire the power he wields. I should like to have it myself."

"Henri is the one who will inherit the power one day, which brings me to something else. Father has deteriorated in health. We must face the possibility that his life might not last as long as we would wish. When he does go, Hélène must not remain in the house. I don't want my dear wife to spend the rest of her life in submission to Yvonne."

"Why should she?" Gabrielle exclaimed. "These wars will end one day, and you'll be home to stay." She saw how the boyish look had gone from his face to reveal the soldier beneath.

"There's no guarantee that I'll be among those to survive."

"Don't say that," she implored.

"I have to speak of it. You see, we believe Hélène may already have conceived a child. If it is so, it means she would be more vulnerable than ever, being left a widow with a baby." He reached out to grip his sister's hand. "Will you promise me that you'll get her away from our father's house if, when he dies, I'm no longer able to protect her?"

"You know I will!" The promise burst from her. "I just hope and pray that particular duty never comes my way."

Some of his usual cheerfulness returned, and he smiled broadly.

All that had been said filled Gabrielle's thoughts as she stood with her husband to wave farewell to Jules and Hélène next day. When the carriage was lost from sight, she sighed and turned to walk back into the house with Emile, only to find he had not waited for her. During the next few days he was cool and withdrawn, and she realized with dismay that he had felt neglected. He was the last person she would ever have suspected of being jealous for her attention, and it was a relief to her when he recovered from his moodiness by the end of the week.

The spring of 1804 gave way to summer. Their marriage followed a smooth path, so that a sudden and unexpected confrontation between them was something of a shock to her. It occurred not long after the thousands of silkworms had hatched, bringing a bustle of activity throughout the silk farm.

Emile came into one of the smaller silk-sheds, where Gabrielle was laying out a fresh supply of mulberry leaves over netting that had been fastened across each tray of larvae. Silkworms are voracious eaters; it takes a ton of leaves to feed the worms that come from just one ounce of eggs. That same ounce eventually produces more than seventeen thousand miles of silk.

Emile watched Gabrielle for a moment, then informed her crisply, "You are spending far too much time in these buildings, and not enough on domestic duties."

"That's an unjust accusation!" she protested indignantly. She stood facing him in the aisle between the shelves of trays. "I should have thought, Emile, that you'd be pleased that I'm taking such an interest in our means of livelihood."

"I am, but it's not fitting that my wife should be working in the sheds like a hired hand. By all means visit them now and again to see what is developing. That is different. It won't be long before the larvae begin to spin their cocoons. Until then nothing of any real consequence happens to compel your presence here."

Her eyes flashed dangerously. He was forbidding her access to the silk-sheds! "Are you condemning me to boredom?"

He kept his patience. He had been prepared for difficulties in his marriage, aware from his first meeting with her that she was quick and intelligent and independent. Yet, if anything, he was more in love with her than ever.

"You can find plenty to do. It's high time we returned some of the invitations we have accepted over the past weeks. We've had no one to the house since Jules and Hélène were here."

"I can arrange a supper party," she said stiffly. "With a hired orchestra, and there could be dancing on the lawn."

"A capital idea!" he declared with more enthusiasm than the suggestion warranted. Then he took her by the shoulders, choosing to ignore her rigid stance, and his voice softened in tone. "The time has come for you to fulfil your rightful role in life."

Her face became bleak with disappointment. Jerking away from him, she flung up her hands in exasperation. "I can't remember a time when men have not tried to thwart my interest in silk. Everything I have ever learned has been through my own efforts, and it was my dream that one day my father would relent and let me take my place with Henri in the business. If my father had only seen that I had talent to match my brother's, I could have put new life into Maison Roche."

"Did you have the same aims towards the Valmont silk farm when you decided to marry me?"

She regarded him frankly. "Surely you guessed that? You had shown me that you were an enlightened man, ready to accept that the Revolution had given women like me new freedom."

His gaze was cool. "Is that the only reason you married me?"

"No! I visualized a true partnership, my role a dual one of wife and business aide." Her expression relaxed and she came forward to rest her hands against his chest, looking up into his face. "More than that, I respected and admired you. I would never want any difference of opinion to come between us."

He cupped her chin in the palm of his hand. "Accept my ruling, my dear. It is for the best. I love you, and what I want above all else is that you should become completely mine, as I am yours."

She turned uneasily away from him. If it had been possible to wish herself into being in love with him, she would have done it, for he was a good man with much kindness in him. But so far, fondness and loyalty were all she could offer. She said in a quiet voice, "I'll go and draw up that guest list."

404

In the days that followed, she went ahead with arrangements for the party, and even began to look forward to it. The invitations went out, and she was disappointed when Hélène declined, because of her pregnancy. It mattered less when Henri and Yvonne were also unable to accept. As for her father, he had never attended any social function outside his own home. Still, the expected friends and business acquaintances numbered over a hundred.

Despite Emile's restrictions on her visits to the silk-sheds, Gabrielle snatched a few minutes now and again from her very busy schedule to see for herself when the silkworms had stopped eating and were about to spin. The delicate process began three days before the eve of the party. She watched the silk from the silkworms' spinnerets harden when it came in contact with the air, and envelop the worms in misty veils.

By the day of the party the majority of the silkworms were encased in small golden-yellow cocoons of silk, rounded and feather-light. Gabrielle's affections were lodged with the humble silk moth that would emerge from each cocoon. No longer able to survive in the wild, totally dependent upon man, it gave in its turn the means to create the queen of fabrics—beautiful, waftingly light, warm and strong. As she and Emile stood looking at them, he said, "I'm sure of a good season this year, and at the end of it you shall have a gown of Valmont silk."

She flashed him a look of delighted surprise. "I'll weave it myself on the loom I brought from home." Swiftly she planted a kiss on his mouth, and he clasped her to him.

The evening of the party was warm and mild, the velvet sky full of stars. Paper lanterns had been hung in the trees, twinkling rainbow-coloured lights between the branches. People arrived in open carriages, the women wearing jewels and pastel gowns. Gabrielle's own gown was cream lace over peach silk, and it wafted gently against her body. Emile had picked her a perfect cream rose, and she wore it fastened by a pearl brooch amid the lace.

They stood side by side in the hallway to receive their guests. When the dancing began, some chose the wide terrace, to be near the orchestra, while the rest spread out across the lawn in the glow of the little lanterns. After partnering each other in the first quadrille, Emile and Gabrielle separated to dance with their guests. Shortly before supper he reclaimed her attention as she stood talking to several young people from Lyons. "Gabrielle, my dear, I should like to present a guest who was delayed in getting here. Here he is . . . Monsieur Devaux."

For a second or two she did not move. Then abruptly, she turned her head and looked fully at Nicolas. The sight of him brought delicious shock waves to her heart, and she saw a muscle clench involuntarily in his jaw, as if seeing her again had been the same for him.

"We have already met, have we not, Monsieur Devaux?" She felt weak, engulfed by pleasure. And dread. Out of the corner of her eye she caught Emile's glance of surprise.

"You know each other?"

"It was the briefest of meetings," Nicolas said, bowing.

A chord of warning struck in Gabrielle, and she adopted a bland tone, saying, "I know I echo Emile's wishes in hoping you have a pleasant evening at our home."

"I thank you. You are most kind."

Emile took charge of him again, presenting him to the others in the group. As soon as possible, Gabrielle slipped away and went into the house, needing to adjust to the impact of this unexpected reunion. In her bedchamber, she sank down onto a chair and reviewed the situation.

What she was feeling in her heart she had known when she was seventeen. Now it had returned a thousandfold, stirring her mind and her body towards a path that was full of danger. It would take every bit of her strength of character to withstand the attraction of a man who was, to all intents and purposes, an enemy of hers and her family's.

She braced herself to face the rest of the evening, and returned downstairs. Emile met her when she came out onto the terrace. "I've been looking for you. Is anything the matter?"

She assumed a bright expression. "Nothing that can't be mended. We'll talk later. I think it's time for supper now."

There was a rising buzz of chatter as people strolled into the long salon, where the buffet awaited them. Warily she watched for Nicolas, and she soon saw that he was with a group of her friends and being well entertained.

Resolutely smiling and gracious, she moved among her guests, ensuring that plates were full and glasses replenished. She deliberately avoided the corner where Nicolas and her friends had seated themselves and eventually found herself next to Emile. She realized she had instinctively come to him for protection.

By the time the dancing was once again in full swing, the weather had changed and a storm threatened. A curiously warm wind had come up to send clouds scudding across the sky, and it was having an exhilarating effect on the women, swirling their skirts and buffeting them into closer contact with their partners. The orchestra, caught up in the same spell, had switched to a lively *contredanse*. Everybody joined in, Gabrielle among them. Linking hands, the dancers formed a large circle, which changed shape as they made their way across the lawn, winding in and out of the trees of the copse, where the shadows were dark and secret. The chain broke at every twelfth step so that people could catch hands with new partners.

Then, just as thunder rumbled and clouds gathered still closer, Gabrielle whirled forward to find herself facing Nicolas. His face was

highlighted, as was hers, by the swinging lanterns overhead, and he saw her sparkling expression as his outstretched hands seized hers. He laughed under his breath, totally triumphant. "I've been waiting all evening for this moment!"

She laughed with him, feeling completely reckless as he swept her into the steps of the dance. The thunder had caused several couples to look skywards uncertainly, and in breaking the chain they had left Gabrielle free to dance on with him. "I must confess that you were quite the last person I had expected to see this evening," she said quietly.

He was thoroughly amused. "You must have known that sooner or later we would meet again."

She looked down and away from him, sensing danger. It was a long time since she had felt so buoyant and light-hearted. "I didn't expect it to be in my own home out in the country," she said.

"Should I not have come?" he asked.

"Oh yes. Why not?" She tilted her head back challengingly, her eyes full of mischief, her windblown skirt whirling about.

He had slowed the pace of their dancing to a leisurely drifting in and out of the trees. Inevitably, they came to a standstill, she to lean back against a tree, he to stand facing her, resting one hand on the bark beside her. The rumbling of the thunder was nearer.

"Have you been living in Lyons since the day we met?" she asked him.

"No. I returned to Paris the following morning. That's where I have my silk looms. I'm back in Lyons now for a few days' visit to see about the repair of the family house in the Croix-Rousse. It's going to take months to put it in order again."

"Why is that?"

He could see that she did not have the least idea what damage had been perpetrated at her father's instigation. "Damp and dust are hard on silk. There's some other damage, too."

Around them, other couples had spread out to linger by themselves. For Gabrielle the erotic atmosphere created by the approaching storm was spiced by an awareness of stolen kisses and embraces out in the heavy darkness. Suddenly she felt she had to keep talking.

"Do you plan to return to Lyons when your house is habitable?"

"That is my intention. More than that, I hope to settle here. Nobody born in Lyons ever feels really at home anywhere else."

That completed her feeling of being in full harmony with him. "Would you like to know my most favourite part of Lyons?"

He could not take his eyes from her. "Tell me," he urged.

"It's on the slopes of Fourvière. I should like to build a house there. It would be away from all the houses, streets and mills of the city, and yet the view would make it more a part of Lyons than my childhood home on the Rue Clémont."

408

"Have you picked the exact site?"

She smiled. "Once. Long ago. My brother Jules and I were children and went on a picnic there. We found some Roman pottery. I marked a special spot with one of the shards."

"I should like to see it." He was serious. The mood between them had changed to a deeper, more intimate level. She realized too late what had happened, and attempted a teasing note.

"Then you must search for it yourself. It is my secret."

It did not work. His gaze remained steadily fixed on her. "Do you feel cut off from Lyons out here in the country?"

"I miss being at the centre of everything in the silk trade."

He smiled. "Not many women would have given such a reason. They would have said they missed the social life, the gossip, the dressmakers. But then you are not like any other woman I have ever met, Gabrielle."

At his first use of her Christian name she rolled her head slightly away from him, looking back towards the distant lights of the house. "Am I not?" Her voice was barely audible.

"If time could be turned back to the day we met, I wouldn't stand aside and let you go."

She turned her head to look at him again. The rich pleasure she was experiencing in being with him must be strictly confined to the time left to them tonight, never to be repeated. "I'm happy that we met this evening," she confessed gently, "even though I shall try to ensure that our paths don't cross in the future."

He moved closer, looking down into her eyes. "I came here this evening only to see you. You know that."

"Then let us both be content with having had the chance to stop wondering about what can never be."

A great streak of forked lightning suddenly split the sky. In the fleeting bluish glow each saw the other's face nakedly revealed, and any last doubts about the magnetism that had first drawn them together were swept aside. He wrapped her in his arms and kissed her with such passion that she could only cling to him in frenzied response. She knew then that she had been made for this man alone.

Then came the rain, in great heavy drops. Nicolas and Gabrielle defied the downpour. It was only when someone charged past quite near them that they finally broke apart.

"Come away with me!" he urged. The lightning showed the wrenched passion of his face. "Now! This minute!"

"No! You must be mad!" she shrieked, making herself heard as the thunder boomed like a cannonade.

"It's a second chance! Don't you see? We belong together!"

"Never! I'm not yours! I never will be!" She was almost beside herself with panic. "Go away! Go out of my life!"

She swung about and ran from him. He shouted, "Keep away from those tall trees! They're dangerous in this storm."

She stumbled to a halt. "The orangery is close by," she called out. "I'll lead the way."

He nodded to show he had heard. As the people clustering under the trees crowded after her, lightning showed the way. When she opened the door of the orangery, an aromatic scent drifted out to those following her. Inside, the women began shivering in their damp gowns, for the temperature had dropped sharply with the coming of the rain.

Eventually Emile arrived with servants, who were holding up tarpaulins under which guests were hurried towards the house.

Once everyone was indoors, the party drew automatically to a close. Gabrielle, upstairs with some of the women at the time, did not see Nicolas leave.

When the last carriage had gone, Emile went to pour himself a large cognac. He was chilled and shivering. "I think we can congratulate ourselves on a successful party," he said to Gabrielle, who had put a silk stole about her shoulders for warmth, "even though it did end in such inclement weather."

"I agree. But there's just one thing." Her throat tightened. "Monsieur Devaux must never be asked to this house again."

"Why not?"

Her answer came readily. "I should have thought it unnecessary for you to ask. He is a Devaux. Surely you have heard of the old enmity between his family and mine?"

Emile was unperturbed as he swallowed a gulp of cognac. "You should let bygones be bygones. No good comes of keeping up old hatreds. Dominique is a man who harbours totally unbalanced grudges. Maybe he let a grudge run away with him in those revolutionary days when he denounced his enemies."

"You're turning this talk away from my simple request."

"I'm trying to remove the reason for it." He weighed his words carefully. "Devaux strikes me as a man who will do much for the silk industry. I intend to do business with him."

"No!"

"We discussed the amount of raw silk he requires for his Paris looms, and when he places an order I shall fill it."

She took several paces towards him, her hands clasped in agitation. "I think it best there should be no further contact, in order to avoid any possible trouble in the future."

Wearily Emile loosened his rain-dampened cravat and ran a finger round his high collar. "Be logical, my dear. I can't turn aside good trade. When this man reopens the Devaux mill in Lyons, he is going to be in the market for still more raw silk."

410

It was as if there were nothing to stop her hurtling towards Nicolas, no matter how hard she fought against it. She made a final, desperate appeal. "Do business with him if you must, but I beg you to excuse me from meeting him socially."

"Very well," he conceded. Something he saw in her eyes disturbed him, for it revealed an inner torment that was totally out of proportion to the situation. Intending to reassure her, he touched her face with his fingertips, but involuntarily she recoiled from his ice-cold hand, then caught it within her own.

"You're frozen through!" she said. "I had no idea! Get out of those wet clothes at once." He went without protest.

In the morning the good weather returned as if the storm had never been. Keeping tiredness and a headache to himself, Emile announced to Gabrielle that he had suffered no ill effects from the storm of the night before. As she poured his coffee she was unsure. His complexion looked patchy and his eyes red-rimmed.

By midday her worst fears were confirmed. Emile returned to the house from his office in a state of high fever. His doctor was summoned at once, and Gabrielle helped him to bed, where he collapsed thankfully.

It did not take Dr. Jaunet long to arrive. A cheerful, rotund man of middle age, he leaned forward to put an ear to Emile's chest and then his back. His face gave nothing away, but outside the door he spoke seriously to Gabrielle.

"Nurse your husband with great care, Madame Valmont. The danger of a fever like this is that it can cause permanent damage to the lungs, resulting in consumption. It will be a hard fight."

"I'll do everything I can."

It proved to be a fight for Emile's life, and it lasted many days. Hélène, hearing how ill he was, earned Dominique's displeasure by leaving him and going to help Gabrielle care for her husband. Hélène was showing her pregnancy now, her health radiant. It was a challenge to her that she should help get Emile well again, although she did accept Gabrielle's decree that for the sake of her baby she must refrain from night duty and from lifting the patient.

With Emile indisposed, it was inevitable that those working in the silksheds should request his wife's decision on certain matters. He was still in a state of crisis when the *maître ouvrier* consulted Gabrielle over the most important issue to date.

"I regret having to trouble you, madame. Could you tell me the approximate number of cocoons that Monsieur Valmont intended to set aside this year for breeding purposes?"

Emile had never mentioned it. "I don't know, and my husband is too ill to be asked. At the first opportunity I shall find out."

For another few days she did not think of the cocoons. Emile was delirious, and there was nothing she could do but sponge him with cool water. When the fever finally broke and he slipped into a peaceful sleep, Gabrielle gave way to helpless sobbing. Hélène put an arm round her and led her away.

The next day, refreshed by a sound sleep, Gabrielle returned to the sickroom to hear that Emile had woken, taken a few sips of egg wine and slept again. She decided to go now to Emile's office in the hope of finding the information that the *maître ouvrier* needed. Leaving Hélène in charge, she left the house. It seemed like months since she had felt sunshine on her face.

In the small outer office, the clerk greeted her. "I heard the good news that Monsieur Valmont is better. How soon can he get back to work?"

"That will be a long time yet, I'm afraid."

"I have letters I can't send without his authorization," he said.

"Let me have them."

At Emile's desk she unlocked a drawer with his key. There was a purse of gold coins, a number of official-looking documents and some private letters, as well as an almanac. She glanced through its pages, and there, entered only a few days before his illness, was the information about the cocoons to be set aside. The *maître ouvrier* would be relieved to be able to go ahead. She began to go through the correspondence the clerk had given her. There was nothing so complicated as to necessitate her putting it aside for Emile. Then she came to a letter sent from Paris. She felt her heart stop. It was from Nicolas—a confirmation in writing of the amount of raw silk he would require.

This letter called for a penned reply. She wrote that the Valmont silk farm would not be able to supply the Devaux mill with raw silk, now or at any time in the future. She signed the letter, folded it and sealed it with red wax. There would be serious trouble when Emile found out about it, but that was a risk she had to take. All that mattered was that by this letter she had eliminated almost any chance of meeting Nicolas again.

She went through the rest of the correspondence, certain that she could keep the business running smoothly until Emile was well enough to take over. By then she would have established proof that she was able to combine the roles of wife, housekeeper and manager. She felt herself to be a whole person again, independent in her own right once more.

CHAPTER THREE

Emile's recovery was slow. When he was able, he asked about the business. Hélène, who happened to be alone with him at the time, told him soothingly that he had nothing to worry about. "Gabrielle is looking after everything," she said, with the best of intentions.

To her surprise he uttered a tortured groan. Gabrielle, forewarned by Hélène of this reaction, sent the *maître ouvrier* and the office clerk to his bedside as soon as the doctor permitted it, to tell him of the work in hand. They kept their reports brief and reassuring. Emile was left with the impression that his wife was only a temporary figurehead, while the business continued to run according to his rules.

One month from the day of the party the cocoons put aside for breeding purposes began to show signs of life. Gabrielle and Hélène were in the sheds to see the first of the silk moths emerge. Dark and damp, they would soon be creamy white, with wings that would flutter ceaselessly.

"Won't they fly away then?" Hélène asked uncertainly.

Gabrielle shook her head. "Centuries of domesticity have deprived these little silk moths of the power of flight." Then she added wryly, almost to herself, "Like women given in marriage."

The clerk from the office had entered the sheds. "You have a gentleman waiting to see you, madame."

"Who is it?" she asked, already on her way to the door.

"I think he's a new customer. A Monsieur Devaux."

She blanched upon hearing the name. She felt such a powerful love-attraction for Nicolas that she doubted her strength of will if she should be alone with him again. Nevertheless, she left Hélène, hurried down the path that led to the office and entered by the side door, taking her place at Emile's desk.

She rang the handbell, and the clerk showed Nicolas in. She saw at once that it was going to be a difficult interview. His expression and his whole stance boded trouble.

"Good day, Gabrielle. So you are in charge for the time being?"

"I am," she replied evenly. "Please be seated."

He put his hat and cane aside before taking the chair in front of her desk. "I hope Monsieur Valmont is well on the way to recovery," he said genuinely enough. "Your letter was a puzzle to me."

"Emile is making good progress, I'm thankful to say." Her voice tightened defensively. "Why should my letter have puzzled you? It was perfectly clear."

"Not to me. Your husband agreed to sell me raw silk, and I can't believe he would have changed his mind unless—"

She gave an abrupt shake of her head. "No, I didn't tell him of what passed between us. I can't understand why you should even want to buy from the Valmont silk farm. I think it is in questionable taste to want both a man's wares *and* his wife."

He became rigid with anger. "It would be, if the incident between us had not ended as it did. I will remind you that I am honour-bound to keep my agreement with Monsieur Valmont."

413

"I rescind whatever agreement existed on his behalf and take full responsibility for it. You are a Devaux and I am a Roche. Our families have never done business together."

"You *were* a Roche," he emphasized crisply. "As a Valmont you are in another category altogether."

"I'm still a Roche at heart."

Unexpectedly, he leaped up out of the chair to slam both hands flat on the desk in front of her. "I have to overcome old prejudices against my family in Lyons if I am to reenter the *Grande Fabrique*, and I won't have the ground cut from under me by having it known that I wasn't considered a reliable customer by the Valmont silk farm!"

She stared at him unflinchingly. "The matter is closed."

He grabbed her by the wrists, pulling her to her feet on the opposite side of the desk. "Raw-silk buying has nothing to do with what is between us! You can't change that!"

She wrenched herself away from him. "There is nothing between us! And your order is cancelled!"

In the heat of the moment, neither heard the handle of the door turn. Emile spoke from the doorway. "I must ask you to leave, Monsieur Devaux. I uphold my wife's decision."

They both swung round towards him, equally startled. Emile stood leaning for support against the doorjamb, his face ashen, Hélène holding him by one arm. Gabrielle gave a cry of concern. "You should never have come this far! It's too soon."

He ignored her, continuing to address Nicolas. "You heard me. And you have my word that this will remain a private matter."

"Then I'll not dispute your decision." Nicolas's face was still dark with anger. He picked up his hat and cane. "I'll take no more of Madame Valmont's time, or yours." He bowed and left the office at a stride.

Emile sagged weakly, and both women helped him to a chair. Gabrielle snatched a shawl to put round his shoulders, terrified he might suffer a complete relapse. "What made you come here?"

Hélène answered. "It was my fault. I told Emile that someone called Devaux had arrived."

Gabrielle crouched down to look into his exhausted face. "How did you know I had refused Monsieur Devaux's order?"

He answered haltingly, breathless with exertion. "I didn't know until I heard what you were saying as I opened the door."

"Are you angry with me?"

"Turning away a new customer and new orders is hardly likely to aid my peace of mind, or my pocket. Hélène, leave us, please."

As Hélène closed the door Gabrielle did not move from where she was. "I know I went against your wishes, and yet I can't pretend that I didn't enjoy being in charge."

414

He liked her frankness and candour. "I suppose I can't blame you for trying to get rid of Devaux," he conceded.

She saw his eyes had softened. "You are very understanding."

"If Devaux had been Bonaparte himself, I would never stand with another against my wife."

Impulsively she pressed her cheek fondly against the back of his hand. He had shown her the same loyalty that all along she had vowed to show him. Why, then, was the misery of Nicolas's departure making her scream inside as if she were dying?

EMILE'S EFFORT IN REACHING THE OFFICE proved to be a turning point in his convalescence. Hélène felt free to·go home to Lyons, and every day Gabrielle spent a few hours with Emile, going over the work she had done during his illness. Apart from some minor criticism, which was more to enlighten her than to find fault, he approved everything.

Then, one morning at breakfast, he said what she had been half expecting to hear for over a week. "There is no need for you to go to the office today. I'm sure you have plenty to do here, and it's time you made some social calls again."

As if to reward her brave nod of acceptance, he brought her a long-promised gift, later that day. Some raw silk had come back from the workers, and he had filled a muslin-lined wicker basket with hanks that were white and lustrous, almost weightless.

"Here's the Valmont silk for your gown, my dear. Choose a colour that you like, and the dyers shall dye it for you."

Her radiant expression was balm to him, for he wanted nothing to destroy the new harmony between them. In Gabrielle he had entirely the woman he wanted, and he was determined never to lose her.

She chose a soft apricot shade for the silk. On the day it was dispatched to the dyers, she spotted a notice in the newssheet which she brought to Emile's attention. "It says here that Joseph Jacquard is to demonstrate his new loom in Lyons." Jacquard was a weaver's son who had gone successfully into hat-making, and then loom-making. "I should like to see the demonstration. Do let's go."

"I can't leave the business just now, my dear." He smiled at her. "Why don't you go? You could spend a few days at your father's house. It would do you good to visit Lyons again."

She left for the city two days later. The coach made good progress and the journey took less than the usual hour. They entered Lyons by way of the hilly Fourvière quarter, and she told the coachman to halt for a few minutes at a certain point. Shimmering mistily in the heat, Lyons lay spread out below, and up the hillside beyond, the Rhône and the Saône rivers threaded through the city like satin ribbons. She thought it wonderful to be returning to the city's throbbing life once more.

At her Father's house, Hélène met her at the door and they embraced affectionately. Gabrielle noticed at once that there were shadows under her sister-in-law's eyes. "Has helping me with Emile's convalescence taken its toll of you?" she asked.

Hélène shook her head. "No, no. I did so little; and his convalescence was as much a rest for me as it was for him."

"Is it Father, then? Is he showing you no consideration?"

Hélène waved the query aside. "Don't look so worried. I've been suffering from the heat since my return home."

Gabrielle settled into her old room, and later Dominique received her in his office. He sat at his desk and greeted her stonily as she took a seat. "So Emile's silk crop is good this year?"

"Yes, it is."

"It's rumoured that the Devaux silk mill may be opened up again." He leaned forward in his chair, his expression one of malicious satisfaction. "Hélène told me how you refused the Devaux order and sent the fellow packing. Give me the details."

She had no intention of discussing it with him. "I did what had to be done. The authority was mine and I used it."

He rubbed his chin thoughtfully. He was beginning to see there was much of himself in Gabrielle. By her action over the Devaux matter she had shown that she was a Roche through and through, ruthless when the need arose. In addition, she seemed to be applying herself well to the responsibility of her husband's business at a time of emergency. "What brings you to Lyons now?" he asked.

"I want to see the Jacquard loom demonstrated. It may be that Maison Roche could benefit from changing to that loom if it should prove to be all that is claimed for it."

Dominique raised his bushy eyebrows cynically. "I remember Joseph Jacquard. He was, like the Devaux family, a traitor. All he wants is to line his pockets. There'll be no change of looms for Roche silk unless Henri brings me an extremely convincing report."

She was affronted by his remark. "Henri has never sought change in his life."

"I suppose you would consider your opinion superior to his."

"I've always been ready to listen to new ideas and to judge for myself. I'll go to the demonstration with Henri and give you my own report." At that she left his office.

On the day of the demonstration it seemed as if the whole of Lyons was converging on the Place Sathonay. Weavers had left their looms to see the new invention for themselves, and the silk merchants and negotiators had filled the section reserved for them at one side of the platform on which the loom had been erected. It was with difficulty that Henri and Gabrielle pushed a way through to the enclosure.

At first sight there did not appear to be much difference in the loom, except for a curious rectangular contraption supporting a circle of perforated cards, laced together and mounted on the top. Gabrielle saw immediately that many of the low-ceilinged workshops and loom rooms would not accommodate this extra height.

Henri, conscious of his own importance in silk circles, made sure that he and his sister were right at the front, where they could view the loom at close quarters. A civic dignitary mounted the steps to the platform. In his wake came Joseph Jacquard, a middle-aged man with mild eyes and thinning grey hair that fell straight on either side of his face.

The dignitary cleared his throat. "Citizens of Lyons! A man of our city comes before you today after an absence of some years, during which he received a place personally recommended by General Bonaparte in the *Conservatoire des Arts et Métiers* in Paris. Citizen Joseph-Marie Jacquard has captured a combination of all the principles of weaving in his machine. I will now ask him to clarify the workings of this new loom."

The dignitary left the platform. Jacquard bowed before he addressed the crowd. His voice was thin, but it carried well in the attentive silence that had fallen.

"Fellow Lyonnais! It is my earnest hope that my machine will bring a new prosperity to our city. It converts into a speedy process the making of the most complicated of figured silks." He spoke in some detail, then went to the loom and began to weave.

Gabrielle watched carefully. The pressing down of the treadle operated the harness and transformed the information on each punched card into the selection of the correct pattern of warp thread. When the treadle was released, the needles sprang back into position in readiness for the next card. The pattern was repeated swiftly along the length of fabric every time the card completed a full circle. She was deeply impressed. If this mechanism was generally adopted, it would increase the production of Lyons silk a thousandfold. And it would abolish for ever the need for little children to crouch hour after hour under the looms to retie the threads as they broke.

"What do you think of it?" she asked Henri eagerly.

He shrugged noncommittally. "Silk would lose by it. There's no substitute for handwork."

"The loom produces the end product in any case," she said. "This would merely speed the process and help to bring down the cost of production. More people would be able to afford silk."

"Silk has never belonged to the hoi polloi. It never will, either, if I have anything to do with it."

She fell silent. Reaction among the other merchants seemed mixed; some were in favour of the new loom, some vehemently against it, for the same reasons as Henri. The rumble of their voices grew, but it was being outweighed by loud and undisciplined dissent from the weavers in the other part of the crowd.

"Your loom would bring starvation to us, Jacquard!" "What of work for our children?" "You're a traitor!" It was a mood of fear that gripped them, for they saw their numbers being diminished by this mechanized loom. Their would-be benefactor tried to calm them.

"My friends, you are mistaken! My mechanism would not decrease your work. It would increase it beyond your wildest dreams. And your children can grow tall and straight without their present labour that deforms their limbs! With my loom your income will rise steadily, as more people find they are able to afford the lower prices of silk!"

The tumult of shouting was fast turning the weavers' crowd into a furious mob. The mention of lower prices was the last straw. A single cry was taken up. "Down with him! Throw him into the Rhône!"

Jacquard went pale and backed a pace towards his loom as the first of the mob began to clamber up onto the platform. Henri tried to hustle Gabrielle away, but their path was blocked by fellow merchants. Gabrielle, buffeted and crushed, glimpsed Nicolas as he swung up onto the platform to charge against the hostile attackers, hurling them back.

Bedlam erupted. Men swarmed onto the platform from all sides, howling for Jacquard's blood. Gabrielle turned cold with horror as Nicolas and the hapless inventor became caught in the midst of them.

"Help those two men!" she cried in appeal to the merchants, but Henri was trying to pull her away with him.

"Have you gone mad?" he shouted. "We'll be drawn into this!"

As he spoke, Nicolas and Jacquard reappeared out of the melee, their clothes torn, to leap down onto the cobbles within a few feet of her. The inventor stumbled, but Nicolas hauled him upright and pushed the exhausted man forward. Pursuers came after them. Gabrielle stuck out her foot, and the leader tripped and fell headlong, causing others to collide behind him. This brought about a brief delay, and Henri, fearing the mob's wrath, was able to bear Gabrielle away. She looked back over her shoulder and saw that Jacquard's loom was being knocked to pieces with axes and mallets by those who had come prepared to destroy what they saw as a threat to their livelihood.

She heard later that Jacquard had escaped and left Lyons in haste, fleeing his fellow townspeople for the second time in his life. Whether Nicolas had gone with him, nobody seemed to know. From the general gossip she learned that the Devaux and Jacquard families had been long acquainted; privately, Gabrielle commended Nicolas for going to the rescue of Joseph Jacquard.

Dominique taunted her with the fiasco of the Jacquard demonstration. "A fine waste of time that was. Jacquard won't dare show his face in Lyons again for many a year, I can tell you that."

She feared he was right, and was saddened by it. By way of consoling herself she remembered that during the time she had managed the Valmont silk farm, she had had dealings with a Madame Hoinville, a stouthearted widow who owned several looms in Lyons. When Madame Hoinville had negotiated with her for raw silk, she had made it known that she appreciated Jacquard's innovations.

Gabrielle went to inspect the widow's small mill in the weaving district. Within her ancient house Madame Hoinville had two workshops with two looms in each. From street level a couple of stone steps led down to a floor that had been lowered in the distant past to accommodate the height of the looms, although not even these rooms would be able to take the extra height of the Jacquard mechanism.

The talk between the widow and Gabrielle turned inevitably to the Jacquard demonstration. "It was a pity that the loom was destroyed before I could get a closer look at it," Madame Hoinville said. "I should like to see my weavers' burdens lightened. Even the strongest of the women tire quickly at these looms, and their poor backs pay the price." She put a hand to her own spine. "Since I take my turn working with them, I know what a benefit Monsieur Jacquard's invention would be."

"I agree completely," said Gabrielle.

The work that the Hoinville looms produced was selective and exquisite. Gabrielle thought it no wonder that the enterprising widow had created her own niche in such a competitive market.

When she left the premises Gabrielle turned homewards in a direction that would take her past the Devaux property. As she came level with it, she saw that the house was closed and shuttered.

HÉLÈNE'S BABY WAS BORN in December of that year of 1804, the same month in which Napoleon Bonaparte became Emperor of France. Dominique did not hide his disgust that his daughter-in-law had given birth to a girl. A grandson would have been a hope for the future of the business, but a granddaughter was useless.

Dominique developed a senile jealousy of healthy, bonny little Juliette, who deprived him of Hélène's undivided attention. The truth was that he felt himself abandoned in the midst of his own family. He thought it a bitter trick of fate that Jules, the only child who was dear to him, should always be far away. He knew that his older son, Henri, was in for a fine shock when his will was read, a joke Dominique would be enjoying from his grave. Jules was the one who would receive the full inheritance of Maison Roche and carry on its tradition. Surely by that time Hélène should have borne him a son or two.

With this in mind Dominique made no objection when Hélène told him that she intended to visit Jules, who had been posted to the Channel coast in preparation for the emperor's planned invasion of England.

Gabrielle accompanied Hélène and the baby on their journey to Boulogne. They travelled in a Roche carriage, attended by a coachman and two maids. The journey went well.

As they neared the seaport they could see the camp followers' tents clustered untidily at the edge of the large army encampments.

Jules had posted a lookout, and before the carriage reached the gates of Boulogne he came riding at a gallop to meet them. As soon as the women got out, he joyously embraced his wife. When Juliette was put into his arms, she rewarded him with a smile, and he was filled with pride. As the journey continued he rode alongside the carriage, talking to Hélène and Gabrielle through the open window.

"I'm afraid the accommodation I found for you is far from luxurious; yet I was lucky to get it. Every room is in demand."

He had not exaggerated the congestion in the town. Boulogne had become one vast army camp, teeming with soldiers, cannon, wagons and other equipment. *La Grande Armée* had gathered its strength into two hundred thousand men for the onslaught across the Channel. Only one barrier was delaying them. England's Royal Navy still had mastery of the seas, and there was no point in putting barges of troops out into the Channel for them to be sunk halfway across.

The accommodation Jules had found was in a small inn, and Gabrielle had to share a room with Hélène and the baby. It was only when Gabrielle went out that husband and wife were able to be alone together. As a result, Gabrielle came to know Boulogne well. She spent hours strolling by the seawalls, exploring the winding streets and the markets. In one shop in a narrow side street she found a rare silk moth in a carved box and bought it for Emile to add to his collection.

The time passed quickly, and the end of June came with no sign of any movement being launched across the Channel. Rumour had it that Jules's regiment might soon be moving out in an easterly direction, since Austria and Russia were massing forces in readiness for an attack. Soon an order came through that the hussars were to leave Boulogne for another destination. Hélène courageously accepted the imminence of Jules's departure.

Two days later she and Gabrielle watched Jules ride out of Boulogne with his regiment. With the standard flying and the pipers and drummers of the band leading the way, the hussars were a spectacular sight in their red-plumed helmets, fur-lined cloaks and crimson boots. Hélène held Juliette high in her arms, and Jules saluted them both proudly. When she could no longer see him, Hélène broke down. Gabrielle took the baby from her and helped her into the waiting carriage.

It was not long after their return home that the emperor abandoned his plans to invade England, and the bulk of the *Grande Armée* left Boulogne to meet the growing threat of attack in southern Germany.

Then, in October, the British fleet scored a tremendous victory at Trafalgar; many French and Spanish vessels were sunk. All chance of a French invasion of England in the foreseeable future had been effectively destroyed.

As autumn turned to winter, the newssheets reported with triumph the victories of the *Grande Armée* at Ulm and Austerlitz. Never had France had such a brilliant leader. By mid-December the Austrians had surrendered unconditionally, and the tsar's forces had retreated into their own country.

Meanwhile, Gabrielle occupied herself with the business of selecting dyes for the new silk crop, and visiting the dyers. Emile was busy all the time and happy with her, and so she was content.

EARLY IN THE NEW YEAR of 1806 Gabrielle came out of the house one morning to find Emile waiting for her at the foot of the steps. "Have you left work to come for a walk with me?" she asked light-heartedly, drawing on her gloves. Then she saw the expression on his face. A sense of foreboding overcame her.

Her question came shakily. "What is it?"

"I have bad news, I'm afraid," he said sadly. "A messenger from your father's house came to the office a few minutes ago. Word has been received in Lyons that Jules died twelve days ago of wounds received on the battlefield at Austerlitz."

Every vestige of colour drained from her face. Emile darted up the steps to her, and she threw herself into his comforting arms.

CHAPTER FOUR

It was due to the determination of a hussar sergeant that Jules's body was brought home for burial. Officers, unless of exceptionally high rank, were usually buried near the battlefield, but Jules had once said he would like his final resting place to be in Lyons. Sergeant Gaston Garcin had heard him and remembered.

Gaston had been through every campaign with Jules since he had joined the regiment. And Gaston was wounded in the leg at the same time as Jules suffered his fatal wounds. As a result, he found himself invalided out of the army. With his left leg still bandaged, he began the long journey with the coffin-wagon, out of Austria and across France.

In his mid-thirties, he was a broadly built, hefty man with unruly tow-coloured hair, a rough-hewn face and eyes like onyx. He had been a good soldier, clear-headed in a crisis, and had been proud to serve his country as a cavalryman. He had enjoyed the excitement of the campaigns and knew that he would feel lost without them, and would miss the horses as much as he would miss his comrades.

During the journey, people in towns, villages and hamlets stood in respect as he drove past with the flag-wrapped coffin. On the outskirts of Lyons he unfolded a fresh Tricolour and spread it over the coffin to complete Jules's last homecoming in full splendour.

Gaston was sighted as soon as he turned into the Rue Clémont. When he drew up in front of the house, the family, alerted to his imminent arrival in a letter from his commanding officer, had gathered on the steps. Hélène came towards him. He clambered down awkwardly from the driving seat, his leg cramped with pain, and she spoke to him gently. "Thank you for bringing my husband home to me, Sergeant Garcin." The servants then came to shoulder the coffin and bear it inside.

After the funeral Hélène received Gaston on her own in her salon. For over an hour they were closeted together while he told her of Jules's last days, and recounted anything he could remember of happier times. When she gave way to tears, he sat patiently until she dried her eyes and was ready to talk again. "What are your plans now?" she asked him. He had already told her that he had no family.

"To find work, madame. I'm strong, and good with my hands. My game leg is not going to stop me from getting around."

"I think I can help you. I shall speak to my brother-in-law. I'm sure he will be able to provide employment for you."

Gaston was appreciative. Unemployment was high in these times, for war had brought its own financial difficulties to commercial interests.

Henri, having no need of an extra hand himself, sent Gaston with a letter to a civic official of his acquaintance. As a result, he found himself employed, but in the city's foulest and lowest-paid work, clearing household cesspits during the night. Hélène, however, was told by Henri only that Gaston was working for the city, and thus pictured him secure in a post of responsibility.

SEVEN MONTHS LATER the Roche family gathered for another funeral. Dominique had been grief-stricken by the death of his favourite son and had never recovered. For three days he had allowed no one in the family to come near him. Then, on the evening of the third day, he had suffered a massive stroke that left him paralysed.

Hélène was with Dominique constantly. When he died, the family were all at his bedside, but it was she who held his hand. Gabrielle's grief was tearless, and the more harrowing for it. She was filled with sorrow for what had never been between her father and herself. She would not have attended the reading of Dominique's will if the lawyer had not insisted that every member of the family be present.

There were some small bequests, which included an income for Hélène until such a time as she should marry again. Then came the moment for which Henri and Yvonne had been waiting. The lawyer cleared his throat. "'The rest of my estate, my house and its contents, together with Maison Roche,'" he read, "'I bequeath to my daughter, Gabrielle Valmont, to be held in trust for any son, or grandson, of hers. In the event of her failing to have such issue, the estate shall pass to my granddaughter, Juliette Roche, and in turn be held in trust for her son. It is my earnest wish and belief that Gabrielle will bring to the business the initiative and imagination that once were mine.'" There was a stunned silence as the lawyer looked up from the document. "That is all, mesdames and messieurs."

Gabrielle sat dazed. Maison Roche was hers! Her dream had come true.

Henri leaped from his chair with a great roar. "Damn him! Damn him to hell! Maison Roche is my birthright! I'll contest the will. I'll prove he was senile when he signed it."

The lawyer shook his head. "I drew it up two days after he had heard of Jules's death, and Dominique requested that a doctor be present so that he be judged of sane mind."

"He changed it *after* Jules's death?" Henri glared, jowls shaking as comprehension dawned. "The old devil never meant me to have the business, did he? He left it to his golden boy until an enemy cannon put an end to that dream, then bequeathed it to Gabrielle. A woman! Untrained and useless. The daughter he hated from the day of her birth!"

Emile rose abruptly from the sofa, where he had been sitting beside his wife. "I will hear no more of these insults, Henri. Gabrielle has come into this inheritance through her own determination to learn the silk trade as well as any man. She deserves the full support of her family."

Gabrielle looked up at him gratefully.

Henri now rounded in exasperation on his wife, who was sobbing noisily. "Be silent, woman! Haven't I enough to endure without your caterwauling? Maybe if I'd taken my father's sound advice to divorce you for your spendthrift ways, I wouldn't have found myself in this ignominious position!"

Yvonne was furious, her face flushed high. "Don't try to shift the blame onto me! You shouldn't have quarrelled with him so much. But that's like you, always thinking you're right!"

With an exclamation of wrath he seized her by the arm, wrenching her to her feet, and thrust her out of the room before him. Their quarrelling faded out of earshot.

Hélène, who still sat on one of the scroll-ended sofas, watched the lawyer bow over Gabrielle's hand, offering to be of assistance at any time. Of all those who had listened to the will, Hélène had been the least surprised by its contents, recalling how highly Dominique had come to regard Gabrielle after her handling of the silk farm during Emile's illness. Getting up from her seat, she went across to her sister-in-law to embrace her in her good fortune.

DURING THE NIGHT Emile woke to find that Gabrielle was not there. For a while he did not stir, thinking over the change that had come about in their lives. She had made clear to him her determination to run Maison Roche, in the discussion they had had after coming to bed. He had thought it prudent to say nothing of the private talk he had had with Henri in the library. His brother-in-law had calmed down by that time, and it was agreed that Gabrielle should be given the reins for a few weeks, long enough for her to believe she had everything running her way. Then Henri and Emile himself would both exert pressure to get her to relinquish her responsibilities and become head of Maison Roche in name only.

His brow creased in a thoughtful frown. He had heard in business circles that Devaux had put to rights the damage done to his property in Lyons and had made the old looms serviceable again. Emile recalled the unease he had felt when he saw his wife and Devaux alone in his office. Yet his wife was not one to be led astray by any would-be seducer. No, it was not Devaux he need fear as far as Gabrielle was concerned, for it was not another man that would drive a wedge between them. It was her own good fortune in receiving a rich inheritance.

"Damnation to it all!" Thoroughly disgruntled, he flung back the bedclothes and put his feet to the floor. He slipped his dressing gown over his nightshirt as he went from the room and down the stairs. As he had expected, a chink of light showed under the door of his late father-in-law's office, which Gabrielle had already decided to make her own. He pushed the door open.

She looked up from a pile of documents that she was leafing through at her father's desk, her feet showing bare beneath the hem of her nightgown.

"This is madness!" he pronounced angrily. "There's no need for you to be working at this hour."

She sat back calmly in the chair. "I couldn't sleep, and there's so much to be done. I can't discuss anything with Henri until I'm up to date with every fact and figure."

"Come to bed!"

"I think not. I'll read for a while longer."

His temper snapped. All he could think of was the threat that Roche silk would take her away from him. He had never laid hands on her roughly before, but now he seized her, dragging her to her feet. She struggled against him, resisting the urge to cry out for fear of waking the household. He overpowered her and carried her back through the hall, upstairs and into their room, where he threw her down on the bed.

She had endured it all without a sound. Now she rolled her head away from him, resisting his attempts to turn her face towards him. Then suddenly, he flung himself down beside her and began to sob—heavy, wrenching sobs that shook the bed. Half raising herself, she looked at him. He was lying flat on his stomach, face in the pillows, his arms outflung, his hands clenched in despair. A tender, considerate man, he had succumbed to ungovernable rage because he could not bear to share her, not even with Maison Roche.

Unable to withstand such grief in another human being, she put out her hand to stroke his hair. At her touch he raised his tortured face to look at her. Reading compassion in her eyes, he hesitated only briefly before putting an arm round her to draw her close to him. She cradled him, and eventually he slept.

Then her own tears flowed. She yearned to be able to turn the clock back to her wedding day. Fate had given her a last-minute chance to change the course of her life and direct it towards another man. For Emile's sake as well as her own she should have seized it.

HÉLÈNE LISTENED ATTENTIVELY when Gabrielle told her of Jules's wish that his wife should not remain in the house after Dominique's death. It had been settled that Henri and Yvonne should continue to live there. "But Jules did not know you would be mistress of the family house," Hélène replied. "You will need someone to be in charge of your housekeeping arrangements."

"I'll appoint a housekeeper. You must be free now to make your own home with Juliette. That's what Jules wanted."

"But I like living here." Hélène glanced about her at the small salon that was hers. Circular in shape, its walls were covered in a fruit-and-flower-patterned damask. "It was in this house that Jules was born and grew up. I feel close to him here." Her eyes were full of appeal. "Don't make me leave yet. I will in time. When I'm ready."

Gabrielle knew she must respect her sister-in-law's wishes, but she immediately appointed a capable housekeeper. Hélène was thereby able to devote time at last to Juliette, and find consolation in being with her.

Next Gabrielle interviewed several designers, looking for artists with clever new ideas. Eventually she engaged a young man named Marcel Donnet, who had recently come to Lyons from Paris. His work was brilliant. She asked him if he had seen the Jacquard loom.

"Yes, madame." His face sharpened with interest. "Have you considered introducing this mechanism?"

She set her elbows on the desk. "I'm keeping an open mind. I must try weaving on one of them myself before I make a decision. Do you think the finished product loses by this loom?"

"Not at all. On the contrary. Many human errors are eradicated."

After he had left, Gabrielle found herself heartened, and she needed heartening at the present time. Her relationship with Emile was considerably strained by her devotion to Maison Roche, for she was spending more and more time away from him in order to be in Lyons. As for Henri, she had the feeling he was watching her like a hawk. When she explained this to Emile, he merely shrugged and said it would be much better for her if she allowed Henri to be her manager.

Late one Friday afternoon she decided to do no more work that day. She had promised Emile she would leave Lyons and go home to the silk farm to be with him until Monday. It was a bitter cold December. She was warmly dressed, and in the carriage she had a muff for her hands. She had been thinking of investing in some younger, faster horses and buying one of the new speedy *calèches* that would be able to make the journey between Lyons and the silk farm in less time.

As she rode, her attention was drawn suddenly to a beggar who was slumped against a wall as if he no longer had the strength to stand alone. It was the military colour of his ragged coat that caught her eye. The man was thin as a skeleton, his unshaven face stamped by hunger. She recognized him.

"Stop!" she ordered the coachman. Alighting quickly, she ran to the beggar. "Gaston Garcin! What has happened to you?"

"Madame Valmont." He was filled with shame and tried to stand up straight. "I've had a spell of misfortune. It will pass."

"But I heard you were employed by the city."

"I fell ill, madame. A contagion contracted through my work. Since my recovery I have been unable to get anything else."

"Your recovery! You still look far from well to me." She remembered how fine his military bearing had been at Jules's funeral, in spite of his wounded leg. "You're coming home with me," she said to him. "I'm going to see that you get well and strong again."

He passed a hand across his eyes, embarrassed by the tears that were rolling down his face. "You have saved my life, madame."

At the silk farm, Gabrielle discussed Gaston's future with Emile. He was in full agreement that employment should be given to the man, but he disagreed strongly with the situation Gabrielle wanted to offer him.

"A new *calèche* is an unwarranted extravagance, and so is making Gaston your coachman. He can work on the silk farm."

"I've made up my mind," she replied firmly. "I've seen a *calèche* at a coachbuilder's in the Place des Célestins and it's exactly what I want. If you would help me purchase the horses, I should be grateful."

"Are my wishes no longer important?" he asked bitterly.

"You know they are," she protested. "This whole idea came about because I want to get home to you as quickly as possible."

He was unimpressed, and retreated into one of his quiet, withdrawn moods. Yet, when the time came for her to buy new horses, he went with her, to ensure that she had the best available. Gaston was fitted out with new clothes and drove the *calèche* in a dark blue caped greatcoat while the cold weather lasted; with the coming of spring he was able to display his black-and-white-striped waistcoat and his lightweight blue coat with brass buttons. A wide-brimmed black hat turned up in the front with a military cockade from his old regiment, gave him a dashing appearance.

Almost from the first day she had taken over Maison Roche, Gabrielle had felt that too much bread-and-butter work had been done in recent years. This was silk in traditional designs, made for retail sale shops as well as for dressmaking and upholstery workshops. She did not belittle the importance of such work, for it kept the looms going, but with her new designer, Marcel Donnet, she was aiming for the attention of *Le Mobilier Impérial*. This was the Paris-based committee that had the authority to restore the great palaces of France and to commission beautiful furnishings for them. Gabrielle was certain that Marcel's marvellous designs were worthy of a commission from the *Mobilier Impérial*, and she was having samples woven for presentation. When they were ready, Henri would leave for Paris with them.

She and Henri were examining some of the completed samples when he gave her the news she had long awaited. "Devaux is back in Lyons. To stay this time, I hear. He's taking on weavers for his mill in the Croix-Rousse."

Her heart leaped. How was it possible for her to have this reaction to hearing Nicolas's name spoken after such a long time?

"I thought his silk interests were in Paris," she said levelly.

"He has sold them. Held out for a high price, I was told." Henri indicated the samples on the table before him. "If he's thinking of competing with us, he's in for a surprise. In all my years in silk I've rarely seen anything better than what we have here."

When all of the samples for the *Mobilier Impérial* were ready, Gabrielle supervised the packing of them herself. On the morning that Henri departed for Paris, she went into the design room to tell Marcel that his work was on its way. He put the brush he was using back in its jar before getting up and bringing over another high stool for her to sit on.

"Let's hope Monsieur Roche secures the commissions we're looking for," he said, reseating himself.

"It would be a turning point for Maison Roche. Of course, we stand a good chance with your designs."

He leaned an arm on the sloping surface of his drawing desk. "Speaking of turning points, there's something I've heard about the Devaux mill."

"Yes?" She was immediately alert.

427

"I was told that the new Jacquard looms have been installed throughout by Monsieur Devaux."

She felt an odd burst of excitement. She welcomed the chance to compete with Nicolas in the manufacture of Lyons silks, to match her designs against his, to become his rival in the race to secure commissions. She truly believed that rivalry was the only way to dispel the yearning that had no place in her life.

"Isn't he expecting labour troubles after what happened at Joseph Jacquard's demonstration?" she wanted to know.

"Ah, it's a few years since that demonstration took place, and last year was the hardest the industry has experienced for a long time. Men who are desperate for work are not going to turn down this chance. There may be demonstrations, but if Monsieur Devaux has the workers he wants, it is not going to trouble him."

"How I should like to see inside that mill."

"Monsieur Devaux probably has design secrets that he'll be guarding closely. It's my guess he won't let strangers in."

She smiled to herself. Marcel had no way of guessing that she did not consider herself to be a stranger to Nicolas, but business was business and they were competitors now.

She proved to be right in her belief that Nicolas would meet strong opposition to his Jacquard looms. She heard a few days later that weavers had advanced on Maison Devaux with bludgeons, homemade pikes and rocks to throw. It had taken a strong force of police to disperse them, and many arrests had been made.

Gabrielle's desire to see the interior of his mill persisted. Late one evening she asked the housekeeper to bring Gaston to her. As soon as he appeared she outlined a plan she had made.

He looked at her steadily for a long, unblinking moment. "What you ask can be done," he said at last. "Leave everything to me."

"Thank you, Gaston," she said, with feeling. "I was certain I could rely on you."

Henri returned from Paris a week later. He was cautiously optimistic. The *Mobilier Impérial* had informed him that he would be notified of their decision in the near future.

During the days that followed, Gabrielle had to learn patience. Gaston made no comment on whatever he was doing to further her secret plan, but one morning when he came to see her in her office she knew that he had finally made the necessary arrangements. "You want some money for the bribes now?" she asked.

"The sum to be paid is almost negligible, madame." Amused self-satisfaction passed across his face. "I made it my business to strike up an acquaintance with a young woman named Hortense, who winds thread for the Devaux mill. When I asked a favour of her, she did not refuse me."

"Indeed?" Gabrielle observed.

He gave an oddly crooked grin. "The only money needed is for Hortense's sister, a fellow worker. You will take her place for a day. All the girl wants is compensation for her loss of pay."

"And how much is required?" Gabrielle took out her purse.

He told her. It was a modest amount, and she added extra.

The day came for Gabrielle to take the girl's place. Suitably attired in a cotton cap, plain print dress and sturdy shoes, she left the house with Gaston just before dawn. It was quite a long walk to their destination, but a Roche carriage or her own *calèche* would be noticed in the early morning streets near the Devaux mill.

As the sky filled with rising gold, Gaston led her down a dank alleyway, where he knocked on a door. It opened, and Gaston's acquaintance, Hortense, admitted them. She was a strong-looking girl, with fine dark eyes. She addressed Gabrielle.

"*Bonjour*, citizeness. My sister and I are doing this as a favour to Gaston. If you're nabbed, say you're just an outworker who heard that my sister was sick and asked to take her place. Do you have a noon piece?"

Gabrielle patted her apron pocket, where she carried a packet of bread and cheese. "Yes, I have."

"Come along, then."

When the three of them reached the end of the alleyway, Hortense blew Gaston a kiss from her fingertips and turned up the street with Gabrielle.

"How do you like working at the Devaux mill?" Gabrielle asked her as they hurried along.

"It was frightening at first, when the mob gathered outside, but now Monsieur Devaux has his own force of law keepers."

"What about the working conditons for you and the others?"

"Good. Wages are fair, and we can earn bonuses. The hours are long, but that's the same as everywhere else. Did you know Monsieur Devaux was born in Lyons?" Hortense did not wait for a reply, but chattered on. "He's a handsome man, no doubt about it. There's a woman from Paris, a Madame Marache, staying at his house now. She's quite a beauty." She drew breath. "Here we are. Keep your head down and follow me."

Male and female workers entered by the same side entrance. In the hallway there was chatter among them as hats and coats were hung on pegs. Some were already in the workshops and had set their looms going. To Gabrielle the looms had a new and unfamiliar sound. Gone was the *thwack, thwack* of the old handloom. This loom had a voice of its own— *bistonclaque, bistonclaque*.

At Hortense's side, she went into the loom room that opened out of the hall, careful not to draw the attention of the *maître ouvrier*. And with

Hortense she fetched the rich yellow hanks she needed for winding. Sitting down at her wheel, she began the work of winding the continuous fine, glossy thread of the hank onto a bobbin. It was quite a few years since she had learned to wind, but the old skill soon came back to her. As she worked she began to take note of her surroundings.

She saw that this loom room had been of normal height, but the whole of the floor above it had been removed, leaving plenty of space for the mechanism at the top of the Jacquard looms. Beyond the first loom room was another. Gabrielle estimated there were at least seventy looms in operation.

"Watch what you're doing!" Hortense hissed, leaning over from the neighbouring winder. "You're overwinding."

With dismay Gabrielle saw she had put too much silk onto the bobbin, and had to rewind it. Later, when she had done several, these bobbins would be collected by one of the few children now employed at the Devaux mill for such tasks.

Gabrielle's confidence grew, her speed on the winding wheel increased, and by the noon break she had become quite proficient.

In midafternoon some trouble developed on one of the looms in the other workroom. She could see the *maître ouvrier* on a ladder beside a repairer, investigating the trouble. It gave her the chance she was waiting for. She had seen that the designer's workshop was adjacent to the storeroom where the hanks were kept. On the pretext of fetching another hank, she paused by his door, tapped on it and entered quickly, closing it behind her. The designer, a young man, sat on a stool before his sloping desk. He paused in his work to look over his shoulder. "Yes, mam'selle?"

"I'm sorry to interrupt you, but I'm new here and I want to learn everything. Could you tell me exactly what you are doing?"

He was struck by her well-spoken voice and lovely face. "Come and take a look," he invited good-naturedly. He explained how he was transferring the sketch, which was of a new pattern shortly to go into production. It was of bees woven in gold on a rich blue background. "A card cutter will use my draft to punch holes in the cards, which will then be laced together as you see over there." He indicated some cards already laced and hanging on a frame. "The holes will convey the pattern on the loom. Every time the circle of these punched cards goes round, the pattern is repeated along the length of the fabric."

She asked him a few more questions, then thanked him and left. Of the work being done on the Jacquard looms, she had now seen more than enough to know that herein lay the whole future of Lyons silk: the work being turned out was perfection. The pattern of the golden bees on the designer's desk told her that Nicolas had a commission from the *Mobilier Impérial*, for Bonaparte had taken the bee as his imperial emblem.

Nobody could weave the bee except by the emperor's express demand. Nicolas was much further ahead of her than she had expected.

It was near the end of the working day when events took an unexpected turn. "Monsieur Devaux has just come in," Hortense said, giving her a prod. "He's looking at that faulty loom."

Overcome by curiosity, Gabrielle rose from her seat to get a better view and saw that Nicolas stood beside the repairer. Then she caught sight of a fashionable woman, tallish and with feline looks, wandering along and glancing at the looms. This must be his guest and present companion, Madame Marache.

Gabrielle sat down again and bent her head industriously over her work. Out of the corner of her eye she saw the woman approach; her long-sleeved gown of carnation velvet was worn with satin shoes to match. At the sight of the winders Madame Marache raised her eyebrows. "What is going on here?" Her voice was attractive, her tone half amused. Hortense answered her, explaining the task in hand and its purpose. A ringed forefinger tapped Gabrielle patronizingly on the shoulder. "Let me take your seat, girl. I should like to try this bobbin winding with your tulip-yellow thread."

Dismayed, Gabrielle gave up her seat. The last thing she wanted was to be standing up conspicuously if Nicolas should come this way. Fortunately, Hortense rose to instruct Madame Marache, and Gabrielle took Hortense's place.

The woman proved to be surprisingly deft, but what was a game to her was a loss of earnings to Hortense, who glowered. Gabrielle, glancing across the room, was alarmed to see Nicolas approaching the winders' section. Her heart began to hammer against her ribs, and she bent her head still further over her work to avoid any chance of his recognizing her. Worst of all was the bittersweetness of being near him again.

"Is this where you are, Suzanne?" he exclaimed with a chuckle, sighting Madame Marache at the winding wheel.

"Come and look, Nicolas. I'm doing well, am I not?"

Gabrielle did not dare to look up, and so she was only able to see as far as the middle buttons on his cream silk waistcoat. He moved round to stand behind Madame Marache, taking both her shoulders into the curved palms of his hands. "Splendid! Who would have thought that I'd gain a new winder in my mill today?"

"Have you mended the faulty loom?" she asked.

"It was nothing more than a simple adjustment. Shall we go?"

She stood up then, sliding a hand into the crook of his arm, heedless of the disruption to work she had caused. It was he who thanked Hortense for showing Madame Marache how to use the winding wheel. As the two of them strolled back along the aisle, Hortense swore savagely over her loss of time and money. Gabrielle, changing places to sit at her own wheel again, stood briefly to watch Nicolas and the woman in his life. She saw him pause to have a word with the *maître ouvrier*, Suzanne Marache going ahead of him through a doorway. The *maître ouvrier* glanced back at the winding section, and Gabrielle took her seat quickly, out of sight.

When a handbell rang at six o'clock, the winders sighed with relief, halting their wheels. The looms fell silent and the weavers took brooms to sweep up their scraps of silk and thread. Gabrielle took her shawl, and wrapped it round her. She was leaving with Hortense, but not going back home with her. Gaston would be waiting a short distance away.

There was quite a crush of people in the doorway. As Gabrielle reached the threshold and felt the cool evening air on her face, a heavy hand fell on her shoulder and gripped her hard.

"Not you! You're not leaving yet."

It was the *maître ouvrier*. At the last minute he had noticed she was a stranger. She reacted swiftly, wrenching around to loosen his grip, but it was in vain. The man seized her with powerful hands then, holding her in the hallway. When the last workers had hustled out, he said to Gabrielle, "What are you doing here?"

"It's simple," she answered. "I needed work, and one of the winders was sick. I took her place."

"I'll do my investigations among the workers tomorrow. For the moment the matter is out of my hands. Monsieur Devaux wants to see you in his study. I'm to take you there."

When she made no attempt to follow him, her face drained of colour, he beckoned impatiently. "It's no good thinking you can persuade me to let you go. Now, come along."

He led the way through both loom rooms to a small inner courtyard dividing the mill from the house. As she crossed the threshold into Nicolas's home, he himself stood by an open doorway leading off the hall. "This way, Gabrielle," he said in a hard voice. She lifted her chin, summoning her courage. With even steps she walked past him into his study and went to stand by the fire. He closed the door, and they were alone together.

CHAPTER FIVE

"Why?" Nicolas demanded harshly. "Of all people, why should you become what I can only term a spy?"

She swung round to face him. He was only a few feet from her, and he had so much anger in his eyes that she almost flinched. "I didn't think of it as spying. All I wanted was to see how you had adapted your building to take the height of the Jacquard looms."

"You could've asked me to show you."

432

"I was in no position to ask favours. We are now rivals in business. I admit I was in the wrong by coming here today, but in some ways it was an irresistible adventure."

"Adventure is not the word I would have chosen for tricking my designer into showing you our most secret pattern. It never occurred to him that an ordinary mill girl would understand the significance of the imperial bee. But you did!" He gave a sigh and rested his weight on the edge of his desk. "And now that you know how I've fitted in the Jacquard looms, do you intend to do the same?"

"Yes, if I'm not sent to prison."

"I'll not press charges." He still sounded grim. "I'm just thoroughly out of temper with you."

She moved with relief to take a chair. "If you mean what you say, I'm thankful for it."

"I mean it. As a matter of fact, I welcome you as a rival in the silk trade." He studied her from where he sat. "I hear you have been through the affairs of Maison Roche like the proverbial new broom and have changed almost everything."

She stiffened warily. "How could you know about that?"

"I've heard all I need to know from general talk. Your name is on everyone's lips as a new force to contend with in Lyons."

She sensed that the atmosphere was changing swiftly between them. Until now a degree of hostility had kept all else at bay, but their yearning for each other was coming to the fore again. He had moved his hands to grip the edges of the desk, almost as though he thought they might reach for her of their own volition, and she felt her insides melt at the thought of being held by him. It was time to leave. "I must go now."

He led her through the house to the front door. He opened it for her, then barred her way with his arm. "We're two of a kind," he said intently. "I look forward to competing with you for commissions from the *Mobilier Impérial* in the future."

"I shall welcome the competition." Then she was unable to resist asking him a question. "How did you know it was I in the winders' section this afternoon?"

He brought his face nearer hers. "I would know you anywhere."

She saw he was going to kiss her, and she was powerless to move, exulting in the prospect, her lids lowering as his mouth came closer. Then a step on the stairs shattered the moment, and Suzanne Marache's voice cut through to them.

"*La*! There you are, Nicolas. Our food is getting cold."

His arm fell away from the door, and Gabrielle darted through it, escaping into the evening air, the return of sanity like a physical shock. But that night she lay awake, unable to stop wondering how it would have been between them.

In the morning she was back in her office, working with renewed energy, taking the only course of escape from hopeless dreams that was open to her. When she heard not long afterwards that Suzanne Marache had returned to Paris, she told herself that it was of no significance. Nicolas would soon take somebody else into his life. Even if he did, he could be no further from her than he was already, for Emile would always stand between them.

HENRI RECEIVED WITH DISMAY and disbelief the news that his sister intended to install Jacquard looms for the weaving of Roche silk. "You're out of your mind! The weavers would never tolerate them. You saw that for yourself. In any case, their houses aren't built to accommodate the height of those looms."

"I've considered every point you could possibly raise and I'm going ahead," she said. "There's an old convent that was abandoned when the Revolutionary Convention outlawed Christianity. I've offered a fair price and believe it will be mine."

"You would turn it into a mill?" Henri could scarcely believe what he had heard. He glared at her belligerently. "I'll not let you do this. I'll query it with the lawyers."

"Calm yourself," she advised. "The lawyers are on my side, and the looms have already been ordered."

"This will ruin the business. I'll oppose you all the way!"

Her face grew stern. "Then you will be the loser, Henri. I will have co-operation from you, or you will not remain on the board. Are you with me or against me? Make your choice."

After spluttering in exasperation, he gave a reluctant nod. "I can see I must stay with you for your own good."

When she was alone, she thought how her life had become a series of battles. She had to contend with Henri every day in Lyons, and whenever she was at home in the country Emile tried to persuade her not to go into Lyons more than once a week.

"I'm not being unreasonable," he said patiently, during her very next visit. "I miss you, my dear. It's lonely in the house when you're not here."

She had given up arguing that if she spent only one day in Lyons she would be reduced to a figurehead, with Henri in charge, because she had soon grasped that this was exactly what Emile wanted. Instead, she implored, "Please don't feel neglected." He had taken her onto his knee where he sat in his chair, and she had her hands linked behind his neck. Always when she was at home she demonstrated affection for him.

"I love you, Gabrielle," he said gently. "If I did not, it would be a different matter. Why—"

She interrupted him. "Why is it I am not like other wives?"

He gave a laugh. "I wouldn't have you any different, even if you do have a brain more suited to a man than a woman." His gaze softened. "I was about to say, why is it, I wonder, that you have not yet given me a child?"

She turned her head away. Certainly she wanted a son to inherit Maison Roche. "The time will come," she said huskily.

"I believe the same. Your body is too perfect for there to be the flaw of barrenness in you."

Later, lying in his arms, she pondered her failure to conceive. Always after their lovemaking she felt that something indefinable had eluded her, some spark left unignited. Maybe if her fondness for Emile could develop a little more, just to tip the scales to love, conception would follow. Then reason took over, causing her anguish. How could she ever hope to love Emile when another man kept her heart from him?

WHEN GABRIELLE APPROACHED her weavers about coming to work the new looms she had ordered, they were suspicious and dubious; she even received threats and warnings. But by the time the final papers were signed and the convent became hers, she had hired almost a full complement of weavers for the number of looms about to be installed.

She supervised the positioning of the looms herself, having worked out exactly where they should be erected for maximum space and ease of access. And after the work started, a police watch was kept on the building in case there should be disturbances. When nothing occurred to disrupt the peace, the police were withdrawn to other duties.

It was the Saturday afternoon at the end of the first full working week and Gabrielle was finishing off some work before Gaston arrived to drive her home to Emile. Nobody else was in the building except the caretaker. Concentrating on her work, Gabrielle did not notice a rumble somewhere in the distance until suddenly her office door was flung open and the caretaker stood there shaking with alarm and shouting, "Rioters, madame! On their way here! Flee while there is time!"

He sped away. Hastening round her desk, Gabrielle went out to the entrance doors, which had been left open by the caretaker. She stood at the threshold and looked up and down the street; then she felt herself quail. The rioters were advancing from both directions, armed with spikes and staves and carrying banners that read DOWN WITH JACQUARD! SAVE OUR LIVELIHOOD! PRESERVE OUR LOOMS!

She was not going to see everything she had worked for destroyed by a mindless mob. Darting back inside, she slammed the heavy doors and shot the bolts home. Then she ran into the first of the loom rooms and closed the shutters. The roar of voices in the street was now reaching a new dimension. Fearful of being attacked at the rear of the building, she raced to check that the doors were barred, and found all secure except the one leading out into what had been a herb garden. She was just in time. As she bolted the door she saw through the grille that the garden gate was giving way under the pressure of the men behind it.

Breathless, she paused to think if there was anything she had overlooked. She started violently as a rock thudded against one of the high shutters, smashing the glass outside. Next came a positive barrage as window after window disintegrated. An even more ominous sound followed. The rhythmic thudding of a battering ram against the entrance doors. Each thud seemed to shake the building, and she doubted that the ancient timbers of the convent could take the strain much longer.

She made a lightning decision. In her office there was a silk sample freshly made up from one of Marcel's latest designs, a spectacular blaze of sunflowers on cream satin. She ran to get it and draped it round herself like a giant stole. Then she returned to the archway of the first loom room and summoned up her courage as she waited in readiness.

With a resounding crash the entrance doors gave at last, and the rioters with the battering ram spilled into the hall, some falling in the melee. It gave her the chance she'd been hoping for. She stood in the archway in a silken dazzle of orange, yellow and gold. The brilliant effect was further enhanced by the sun slanting in through the smashed doors to touch her from head to foot. Her chestnut hair was bright as flame.

"Weavers!" she cried in a tone of authority. "Stay where you are! Most of you know that I learned to weave in some of your homes and loom rooms. Would I betray my own apprenticeship? Trust me as you used to trust me! Let me show some of you the new life that the Jacquard loom has brought to Lyons!"

Those already inside the building were gaping at her. The suddenness of her appearance, the splendour of her silk drapery and her courage in standing up to them caused each man to stay where he was. "Give me a chance to save what I have achieved here," she added. "I even have work for those who want it."

She would have succeeded if it had been left to the ringleaders in the forefront. But there came a great surge of movement from the crowd outside, and those on the threshold were helplessly thrust forward. Nobody knew who threw the stone. It could have been aimed deliberately, or perhaps it ricocheted off the doorway. But it struck Gabrielle on the side of her head, and she reeled back, stunned by the pain. As she collapsed in a tangle of the satin stole, blood staining it, she felt herself thrust to one side by someone coming from the loom room behind. The mob swarmed in from the street, shouting and yelling. She heard a pistol shot; then Nicolas's voice roared forth.

"Get out! All of you! That was only a warning. I'll shoot the first man who takes another step forward!"

Gasping, she managed to look up. Nicolas stood with feet apart under the archway, a pistol in each hand. She let her head sink back again.

436

There was a click as he cocked the second pistol, and it was enough to cause an immediate withdrawal of the intruders.

She could no longer concentrate. There was more shouting, the banging of a door somewhere, Gaston's exuberant laugh, and then Nicolas was lifting her up and carrying her to the sofa in the office.

"Is she badly hurt?" asked Gaston, serious and concerned.

"Just stunned. But it's quite a deep cut." Nicolas was stemming the flow of blood with a linen handkerchief. He drew away to remove his coat, then draped it over her. "Is the street cleared yet?"

Gaston went across to the window. "Yes, your men and the police have done their work."

"Then bring the carriage to the door from wherever you left it. We must get Madame Valmont home to her sister-in-law."

Gabrielle wanted to thank him for all his help, but she could only lie there, dizzy with pain. Suddenly Nicolas was carrying her again. Her head was against his shoulder, and he continued to hold her cradled to him as Gaston drove them to the Rue Clémont.

At the house, a manservant opened the door and Hélène's startled cry came from the hall. An explanation from Nicolas followed as Hélène led the way upstairs. They had reached the landing when Henri appeared.

"You!" he bellowed, spotting Nicolas. "How dare you enter this house! What have you done to my sister? Give her to me!"

Gabrielle felt Nicolas's arms tighten about her. Now it was Hélène who took command. "Out of our way, Henri! This is no time for quarrelling. You should be thanking Monsieur Devaux instead of shouting your head off at him." She thrust him aside, sweeping forward to open wide a bedchamber door, and Nicolas carried Gabrielle through.

Hélène folded the bedclothes back, and Gabrielle felt herself being lowered onto the bed. She moaned a soft protest as Hélène slipped Nicolas's coat off her and returned it to him. This was the only way Gabrielle was able to convey that she wanted him to stay. Somehow he must have understood that. He took her hand in his and pressed it lovingly. "I must go," he said quietly. Then he went from the room.

Gabrielle learned the missing details from Hélène. Gaston had been on the alert for trouble. He had decided that, in the event of an emergency, a small loft window of the Roche mill could be entered from a neighbouring roof. It was by this route that he and Nicolas—who had heard of the uprising from a guard—had got into the building, he to face the mob in the herb garden and Nicolas to take the main entrance.

As soon as she was able to travel, Gabrielle was taken back to the silk farm. The doctor, who had put four stitches in her wound, had advised complete rest for three weeks, a period that Emile was determined to extend. All his suspicions about Devaux, which had been dormant for a long time, had erupted again.

IT WAS AT AN EXHIBITION of silks in 1808 that Gabrielle was to see Nicolas again. Her mill was thriving and she leaped at the chance to show that her silks were among the best.

In the exhibition hall a space was allotted to each member of the *Grande Fabrique*. Although Maison Roche, as a prestigious member, had received a place in the coveted main hall, it was in a far corner, away from the doorway.

When she had exclaimed in indignation that Maison Roche did not have a prominent stand, Henri shrugged. "What can you expect?" he said. "Roche silk is in a woman's hands now. Think yourself lucky you have a place at all in the exposition."

Her face had flashed her defiance of both him and the organizers. "I'll see that our silk is not overlooked, I promise you."

Henri took an enamelled snuffbox from his pocket, inhaled a pinch of the contents and blew his nose ferociously. "What designs have you finally decided to show?"

When she told him, he glared at her in disbelief. "You can't show those. I forbid it. Keep to flowers, vine branches and rosettes. That's what buyers will be looking for. I know."

She answered him with firmness. "The day when anyone had the power to forbid me to do anything has passed, Henri. Marcel did the designs months ago, and all the fabrics are ready. That I was given such a poor position in the hall makes me even more determined to ensure that Roche silk never gets relegated to inferior status again."

The day before the exposition she arrived at the hall with Marcel and Henri. Emile was also with her but he went off to a room set aside for raw silk dealers. She paused to look at the board showing the plan of the exposition and saw that Devaux silk was to occupy the very place she would have chosen for herself. It gave Nicolas a definite advantage, and that in itself she found stimulating. Now, any small victory she gained would count all the more. Even as she smiled to herself over this thought she saw him, and her heart lurched.

She felt weak. How was this possible? She was nearly twenty-five, with four years of marriage behind her—no longer a girl, to be tossed from one emotional crisis to another. In a perverse way she resented loving Nicolas, while at the same time she welcomed the feeling of coming alive.

She and Marcel were able to assemble the Roche display without gathering much attention, and then it was covered with soft cambric dust-sheets to protect it and keep it from view. There was a tacit understanding between exhibitors not to see rival stands until the day of the exposition, part of an old tradition of secrecy in the silk trade.

In the morning Yvonne was up early, ready to accompany Henri, Gabrielle and Emile to the exposition, instead of waiting to come later with Hélène. All three women had new outfits in the finest Roche silk.

Gabrielle had chosen a jade colour, and her dashing hat, in the latest military-influenced style, had a small rolled brim and a high crown trimmed with a plume placed upright in the front. Yvonne's velvet coat echoed the same influence in its braiding, and she preened a little in front of the looking glass in the hall before going out to the carriage in which she and Gabrielle and their husbands were to be driven to the exposition.

"Here we are," Emile said, leaning towards the window as the exhibition hall came into sight. In the busy entrance they were met by Marcel, who joined Gabrielle and Henri to go to the Roche stand, while Emile went to his own allotted place in the raw silk room. Yvonne began to saunter through the main hall, slowly studying everything that had already been unveiled from the lightweight dustsheets.

At the table adjacent to the Roche display, where orders would be taken, Henri arranged his inkpot, pens and order books. Gabrielle went to tour the main hall. Now that the displays were unveiled, the whole place was transformed, with fabrics of every texture and hue. Jewel colours blended with the metallic glint of lamé, and there was a whole range of pastels, all marvellously patterned in damask, velvet ciselé, chenille, satin, moiré and the output of many other special silk-weaving techniques.

When Gabrielle came to the Devaux display she wanted to applaud, to laugh with praise, to exclaim her admiration. Almost as if there had been connivance between them, Nicolas was the only exhibitor other than herself to take a single colour and show it in every variation. And dominating his stand was a spectacular swirl of sapphire damask on a satin ground, woven with the design of golden bees. It was a masterpiece, showing what could be achieved on a Jacquard loom.

Nicolas was writing at his table. Had he taken an order already? Then he turned his head abruptly and looked straight at her.

"It's good to see you, Gabrielle," he said, his eyes full of smiles. "How are you? Busy, of course."

"All the time. My congratulations on the Devaux display. It will be the sensation of the exposition."

He gave a shrug. "Do you realize that you and I are going to face severe criticism of our work? We are the only manufacturers here exhibiting work woven on the Jacquard loom."

"Maybe our work will persuade others to make the change."

"That's what I'm hoping. Monsieur Jacquard is going to put in an appearance today. Do you want to meet him?"

Her face shone. "Yes, I do. What a pleasure! I saw him demonstrate his loom."

"You were there, were you?"

"Yes, and I admired your rescue of Monsieur Jacquard."

He dismissed her praise with a sweep of his hand. "He is an old friend of my father's, and I served in the *chasseurs à cheval* with his son, Charles. Because of false accusations, the Jacquards had to flee Lyons during the siege, as we did. I'll bring him to you when he arrives. Incidentally, I haven't seen your display yet."

He went with her to a good vantagepoint. According to her instructions, Marcel had waited until a minute before the public was to be admitted and had just removed the last dustsheet from the stand. Fellow exhibitors in the vicinity were already glancing towards it with surprise. Gabrielle watched Nicolas's reaction to her silks. His eyes deepened into a twinkle that told her she had won his full approval.

She had chosen *gris-de-lin*, a rich shade of violet, patterned with gold eagles in flight, to hang as though in a throne room. To the forefront, carefully arranged, was a profusion of silks from deepest pansy to heliotrope and lilac, as if the eagles were flying above a turbulent sea flecked with silver and gold. The effect was handsome and dramatic.

He turned to her. "It's my turn to congratulate you." The amusement was still in his face, and she chuckled. The joke was their own. They saw the strange coincidence of their stands being the only two steeped in a dominant colour as an affinity of thought. Neither knew that they were being observed by Emile, who had come across the hall with the intention of wishing his wife good luck. He watched them suspiciously. Knowing Gabrielle as he did, it seemed to him that her every little gesture proclaimed an exceptional interest in Devaux. Something the man said to her caused them to laugh together, and this increased Emile's resentment. As a handbell was rung to announce that the exposition was about to open, he saw his wife and Devaux part company, still smiling at each other, Gabrielle's face full of secrets. Emile turned away to return to his own trade site.

Gabrielle remained looking towards her display as Henri approached. "Well? What do you think of the opposition?"

"I think our most serious rival on the floor is Devaux."

Henri snorted. "You've only yourself to blame if Devaux takes orders away from us. You should have listened to me." He cast a contemptuous glance at the Roche display. Eagles! Customers wanted doves, or birds of paradise. The imperial eagle had no place in the average well-to-do man's home.

Contrary to Henri's gloomy expectations, the day proved to be an exceptionally good one. Both the Roche and Devaux stands drew immediate interest because their silks had been woven on the Jacquard loom. The dais by which he sat was surrounded by the first arrivals, a crush that continued without respite. By choosing the imperial eagle, Gabrielle had caught the current pro-Bonaparte mood of the *Grande Fabrique*. Since Bonaparte now ruled half of Europe, many old political symbols were being replaced by tributes to the emperor. On both the

Devaux and the Roche stands were some marvellous examples of what could be hung in refurbished rooms of state.

Hélène came to see the Roche display in the afternoon. She was full of praise.

"From what I can see, you and Monsieur Devaux have taken the world of the *Grande Fabrique* by storm," she said to Gabrielle. "I spoke to him on the way here. He presented Monsieur Jacquard to me. They're coming over to you shortly." Her attention was attracted by a movement in the crowd. "I think they're on their way now."

Nobody knew who started the clapping, but it was taken up on all sides, people moving to make a path for this man whose name had been passed from one person to another since his arrival. Joseph Jacquard looked startled and shy, but as more and more people joined in the applause around him, he began to smile, nodding his appreciation. His birthplace of Lyons, which had so strenuously rejected him, had taken him back into the fold at last.

DURING THE DAYS THAT FOLLOWED, until the exposition closed, Gabrielle saw Nicolas many times, mostly at a distance. Whenever they did get a chance to speak, their words bore no relationship to the silent communication between them. She knew he was waiting for her, certain that the day would come when she would forget the bonds that held her. It gave danger and excitement to these encounters, but the aftermath was always sadness and a struggle to face again the reality of life.

One morning when the first orders were being put into production, Gabrielle took time off to buy theatre tickets. She was crossing the Place des Célestins on foot, the day being fine and dry, when unexpectedly someone held a bunch of crimson roses in front of her. She halted in surprise and laughed when Nicolas appeared in front of her. "Accept my tribute for brightening my day beyond measure."

She laughed again, taking the roses from him. "These are lovely. How kind and how gallant. You really surprised me."

"I could see you were deep in thought. I probably have the same expression when I'm wondering if all is going well at my mill. Where were you going just now?"

"To the Théâtre des Célestins." She indicated a building a few yards from where they stood. "I'm going to pick up tickets for tonight's performance. It's a play that Hélène wants to see, and I encourage her to go out as much as possible."

"Have you time to take coffee with me first?"

She hesitated only briefly, through the habit of always being wary in his presence. "I think so. That would be welcome."

They chose a cafe and sat at a table under a bower of foliage, dappled by sunlight and shade. A young girl sat by an upstairs window playing a

442

flute, and the notes were clear and sweet as a bird's song. They ordered coffee and it came almost at once. Since there was only one other customer, well out of earshot, they were able to talk freely.

"Will you and your sister-in-law be going unescorted to the play this evening?" Nicholas asked. "I could come with you."

She lowered her glance to the coffee steaming in the cup in front of her. "I'm afraid not. Henri and Yvonne will be with us."

"Ah." He sighed expressively. "Another time, perhaps."

"Perhaps," she said uncertainly.

"Gabrielle." His tone was soft. "Look at me."

Slowly she raised her head and met his loving gaze.

"You are the most beautiful woman I have ever known. All I want is to see you, to be with you." He leaned towards her as he spoke, reaching out his hand to take possession of hers and enfold it within his own. "I love you."

"That should never have been said," she protested shakily. Her heart was palpitating wildly.

"Do you love Emile Valmont?"

Her lustrous eyes were large with pain. "He loves me."

He increased his clasp on her fingers. "I repeat my question."

"I've given you my answer. It covers everything."

"Even divorce?"

It came as a shock to hear the word spoken aloud. Somehow she found the voice to reply to him. "Even divorce."

He caressed her hand then, the loving look in his eyes unshaken. "I want you for ever, Gabrielle." Drawing her fingers up to his lips, he pressed a kiss against them. She was never to know if she might have spoken then of her love for him. A couple had been shown to a nearby table, and the moment was gone.

She picked up the roses, and he went with her to the entrance of the theatre. There she selected one of her flowers and held it out to him. The simple, eloquent gesture said all she was unable to voice. They shared a smile as he took it and broke off the stem to slide it into a buttonhole in the lapel of his coat. Then she entered the foyer of the theatre.

CHAPTER SIX

Gabrielle suffered an unexpected setback. The order for imperial hangings, which she had hoped to gain from the *Mobilier Impérial* after her display at the exposition, went to the Devaux mill instead. She accepted the news in silence, while Henri ranted and raved over it until she could endure his tirade no longer.

"Be quiet, for mercy's sake, Henri!" she exclaimed fiercely. She was sitting at her desk, her hands clenched together in front of her. "There are other chances. We've yet to hear who is to make the campaign tent for the emperor."

Bonaparte wanted a tent lined with Lyons silk to use in the field that year of 1809, and in many ways this was the most coveted commission, since it was of a personal nature. All the major Lyons manufacturers had submitted designs. Marcel's incorporated a lion and a lamb, which surely symbolized the emperor's aim for the future, a peaceful Europe under the French flag.

"We have a good design," Henri answered, "but so long as you are sitting in that chair, we shall go on losing top commissions. You must accept that, as a woman, you're a hindrance to the business."

She jerked up her head. "I won't give in to prejudice."

Henri's face was thunderous. "If we get the commission for the tent, I'll continue to back you. But if we lose it, I'll demand your resignation. I warn you that I'm not prepared to see Devaux skim away the cream from us for the rest of our days!" He turned away and left the room.

She was aware that she was trembling. There was nothing Henri could do to dislodge her, but there were other issues at stake. She saw every victory that Nicolas achieved as an undermining of her own emotional security. Unless she could be his equal in the silk world, how could she find the strength to master her love for him? She came close to a sense of panic, as if at last she had reached the quicksands. Packing up her work for the day, she left early to go home to Emile.

All the way from Lyons to the silk farm she made a silent plea to her husband. Help me, Emile. Please realize the danger our marriage is facing and help me. Nicolas is drawing me to him. I don't know how long I can fight my love for him.

Emile was not at home; she learned that he had gone unexpectedly on business to Avignon. All too often now their individual interests separated them. She spent the next morning in the flower garden gathering fresh flowers for the rooms, and then strolled through the woods, as if to gather the tranquillity of the surroundings into herself.

A FEW WEEKS LATER Henri Roche was preparing to go out for the evening with Yvonne when a servant came to tell him that a prowler in the stable yard had been overcome by a couple of grooms. "Has he stolen anything?" Henri asked.

"No, sir. He swears he came to keep an assignation with a maidservant, and mistook the address. He's in the scullery under guard now."

"Well, I'll take a look at this rogue."

It was rare for Henri to go below stairs. Kitchen staff, whom he could not remember ever seeing before, stood amid scrubbed tables and gleaming copper pans to watch him go through to the scullery. There, the intruder, a middle-aged ferret-faced fellow, was seated in a chair, his arms bound at the wrists.

"Well, well. So it's Monsieur Brouchier," Henri remarked, recognizing the intruder. "This is a surprise." He addressed the servant who had led him there. "Release him and bring him to my study. This is a matter I want to investigate myself."

In Henri's study, Brouchier accepted his invitation to be seated, thanking him for his release. "It was a nasty moment for me," he confessed. "I pride myself on never being nabbed."

Henri poured himself a glass of wine and sat down. "Ah, you're not out of the woods yet; I want to know what tricks you are up to. Is my wife having me followed?" Years ago he had employed Brouchier himself to keep watch on a mistress of his.

Brouchier gave a rusty laugh, shaking his head. "Monsieur, I am a man of honour and can't betray my clients' names."

Henri pointed a finger at him from the hand that cupped the wineglass. "I can have you taken in for trespassing with intent to rob. You'll tell me everything. Speak!"

Brouchier shifted uncomfortably in his chair. "Emile Valmont, your brother-in-law, has engaged me to keep watch on his wife."

"What?" Henri sat forward, astonished. "Who's the man?"

The answer to his own question came to him even as Brouchier replied, "Nicolas Devaux."

"What evidence have you gathered?" he demanded hoarsely.

"Nothing of significance so far. They met some weeks back in the Place des Célestins. Since then there have been no meetings that I've discovered. As it happens, Devaux is among the guests at the dinner party the Valmonts and your sister-in-law are attending this evening. I was just about to follow their carriage."

Henri took a swig of wine and regarded his visitor grimly. "I'll not detain you any longer, but on one condition: anything you tell Monsieur Valmont you must also tell me."

Brouchier stood up. "I daresay that can be arranged, seeing that you're a former client, and one who was generous to me."

Henri took the hint. "You'll be rewarded." He swung his wineglass dismissively. "Now, get out of here."

For a while Henri sat on alone in the room, thinking. It seemed he had an ally in Emile against Devaux, and he felt that they were gathering their forces for attack.

GABRIELLE HAD NOT KNOWN that Nicolas would be at the dinner party. She had barely been received by her host and hostess when she saw him coming across the room towards her. Her luxuriant hair caught bright tints from the candles' glow, framing her lovely face to perfection. She

445

was in a white silk gown with a décolletage bordered with gold embroidery, and she outshone every other woman present. When Nicolas reached her, he pressed the fingers of her hand lovingly.

"The gods are being good to me this evening."

She sighed in soft wonderment, completely captivated by his presence. "Who would have expected anyone in Lyons to invite a Devaux and a Roche to the same table?"

"It's only because our hostess knows nothing of local disputes."

"How fortunate for us," she whispered, thoroughly amused. Sharing their private joke, he led her in to the gathering.

There were writers, artists and musicians present, as well as the prefect of the city. The conversation was mostly intellectual, but one disturbing piece of news from Paris was reported—that the emperor was considering a divorce from Josephine. He wanted a son and heir, something she had been unable to give him.

At dinner Nicolas and Gabrielle were not seated together. He was on the opposite side of the table from her, distanced by candelabra and carnations in silver bowls, but the angle at which they were placed enabled him to view her without hindrance. Every time she glanced in his direction he met her gaze instantly, sending her silent messages that made his eyes glow as darkly as wine. His constant attention had its effect on her: she was assailed afresh by love and desire. Hélène, who was more of an observer than a conversationalist, hoped she was the only one noticing the interchange between them. Emile, at the far end of the table, did not seem to be.

During coffee, served in a salon panelled with ice-green silk, everybody was asked to take seats for the musical interlude. Nicolas reached Gabrielle in time to sit beside her. The music heightened her awareness of Nicolas's nearness, as if she were conscious of every breath he drew. When they rose to applaud, they did not disperse but remained facing each other.

"Meet me tomorrow," he implored quietly. "At the cafe in the Place des Célestins. There's so much more to be said."

She could not have refused him. They had to see each other again soon. "I will be there," she promised.

IN THE MORNING the news broke throughout Lyons that the Devaux mill had received the emperor's personal commission for the new campaign tent. For Gabrielle it was a shock on two counts. Once again Nicolas had gained on her through his own well-deserved success, and at the same time nothing symbolized the advance he had made on her emotionally more than his capturing this sought-after commission.

At the arranged time she arrived for their meeting at the Place des Célestins in a barouche driven by Gaston. Nicolas was already at a table, and he stood up to meet her, able to see by her face that once again a gulf had come between them.

"I can't stay," she said. "I just came to give you my warmest congratulations on your latest commission."

"Thank you. Please sit down for a few minutes."

If she sat there, she would be lost again. There was too much love in his eyes. "No, I must go. But there's one thing I want to ask you. Did you know last night that you had the commission?"

"I knew a week ago."

"Why didn't you tell me when you had the chance?"

"I love you, Gabrielle. I don't want to lose you, and yesterday evening we came so close that I wanted nothing to come between us. For myself I consider it a sad day for France that the emperor should need a campaign tent at the present time." He was referring to Austria's new declaration of war against France and to England's landing in Portugal to aid Spain in driving the French out of Portuguese territory. "I should have preferred to weave silken banners to celebrate peace throughout the empire."

"Perhaps your tent will play a part in securing that peace. *Adieu*, Nicolas. I hope to see the tent when it is finished. I'm sure it will be a handsome sight." She hurried back to the barouche, pale with distress.

All day Gabrielle expected Henri to arrive at the mill in a raging temper over the lost commission, but he failed to appear. Instead, he met her in the hall when she arrived home at the Rue Clémont. He appeared calm and in charge of himself, although there was a truculent set to his features. "You've heard, of course," he said to her.

She nodded. "It just shows me that Devaux silk still has the edge on Roche products. I intend to counteract that."

"Indeed? Come into the salon. Emile's here."

She was not unduly surprised. Over recent weeks Emile had taken to coming without notice to Lyons, sometimes to spend time with her, at others to accompany her home to the silk farm when it was the close of a working week. He turned from the window when she entered the salon. To him she always brought the sun into a room with her, but today he kissed her on the cheek with little warmth.

"Henri sent for me," Emile said. "The news of the lost commission this morning must have been a great disappointment to you."

"Henri sent for you?" She flashed a wary look from him to her brother's belligerent face. "In the world of business I have to take setbacks from time to time, as do many others."

"But don't you think those setbacks are happening all too frequently now, Gabrielle?" he asked. "The time has come for you to ask yourself if you are fulfilling your late father's wishes. The world of the *Grande Fabrique* has set its face against you, and the dreams you cherish will never be fulfilled."

She was incredulous that her husband, who had suppressed his own wishes in order to give her his full support after the reading of her father's will, had chosen to desert her now. "Do you believe what you are saying, Emile?" she challenged fiercely.

"I do, my dear. I would not support your brother if I didn't think he was right. Dominique would never have wanted a Devaux to gain superiority over a Roche, and that is what has happened and will continue to happen unless you make Henri your deputy and retire from the public scene."

"I don't accept that I have failed. It's early yet—"

"Three years," Henri interrupted. "You've had three years."

She rounded on him. "That's nothing! I have a lifetime of silk still before me. I won't give up, for you or anybody else."

Emile spoke quietly. "You may have no choice in a few months' time. It might be better to start the changeover now."

She was puzzled. "I don't understand."

Emile indicated with a brief lift of his head that Henri would clarify the remark. She saw the malevolent satisfaction stamped on her brother's face. "Yvonne is *enceinte*," he rasped. "If it is a boy, I shall have the legal right to contest our father's will and establish my own claim to the trust."

Gabrielle released a long sigh. "So that's it. I wish you a strong and healthy child, Henri, whether it be a boy or girl. As for the trust, father willed it to me in faith and I'm going to prove I'm worthy of that faith. In the meantime, everything is as it was before we had this discussion." She glanced in turn at both of them. "Now I'm going to change for dinner."

She went from the room with her head held high. It was not until she was out of sight that her whole body drooped as if all the strength had drained from her.

WHEN THE DEVAUX TENT for the emperor was finished, it would be shown at the *hôtel de ville*. Gabrielle received an invitation to the first viewing for the elite of the *Grande Fabrique*, and made a point of mentioning it to Emile.

"I'm most interested to see this tent," she said to him over breakfast one Sunday morning. "I want to see why the Devaux design won."

He put down the cup of coffee he had been drinking and regarded her fondly. They had had a fine weekend together, and last night they had been together as husband and wife should. Let her see the tent and Devaux in the midst of a crowd of silk merchants, he thought. There was no danger in that. Brouchier had not come up with a single scrap of further evidence against her, and in his own mind he considered that the little flutter she had experienced was well and truly past.

"Would you like me to go with you?"

"Yes, if you would like to come," she answered readily.

That pleased him. No hesitation there. "To be honest, I have other commitments here that day. You can tell me about it afterwards."

As the days dwindled down to the time of the viewing, the dispassionate air she had tried to maintain towards the event was dissolved without warning into a raging torrent of wanting to see Nicolas again. So much had happened since she had last seen him! Not long before Christmas the emperor had divorced Josephine, and rumours about the new bride were rife. As for the *Grande Armée*, that had been divided into two sections—one to defeat the Austrian threat once and for all and the other to surge forward in Spain, in a bloody conflict with the British, Spanish and Portuguese. Bad weather in Spain that year was adding to the misery of the troops on both sides.

It was a bitterly cold evening when Gaston drove Gabrielle to the *hôtel de ville*. Both were surprised to find no crush of carriages outside the building. "Are we early?" she asked him.

"No, madame. Right on time, as you wished."

It was a relief to get into the warm building. An attendant led her along a corridor into a domed hall, leaving her there. She found herself to be the sole spectator of the campaign tent.

Pegged out on a green carpet, as if it stood on grass, the tent was a large, pleasing oval. Woven in stripes of blue and white cloth, the roof was embellished with scarlet embroidery and braided with black. Gabrielle slipped off her cloak and put it with her muff on a chair by the wall, before approaching the tasselled ropes that formed a cordon round the tent. As she circled it she came to a gap where the entrance flaps of the tent were fastened back for access, and she went inside.

Lit by lanterns suspended from poles supporting the canopied ceiling, the interior was spacious and well proportioned. It housed an easily transportable camp bed, and chairs and tables, all foldable. One of two campaign chests, lined with red and white cloth, was open. It held maps to demonstrate one of its uses. She was enthralled by the splendour of the silk hangings that lined the whole interior. The pattern of red and blue bouquets was simple and stylized against a pale grey ground, the effect as light and airy as a new morning.

Outside in the hall the door opened and closed again as someone entered. Footsteps crossed the floor to become swallowed up on the green carpet. Her back was to the tent's entrance and she did not turn. Nicolas's voice addressed her. "What do you think of it?"

She closed her eyes briefly at the almost unbearable joy of being near him again. "It's splendid. Just as I knew it would be."

A lantern threw his shadow in front of hers as he came to stand by her side. "I've missed you, Gabrielle."

Unexpected tears filled her eyes and choked her throat. "I've missed you, too," she admitted huskily.

He took her gently by the shoulders and turned her slowly to face him. Speech deserted them both at what they saw in each other's eyes. As his arms went about her ardently, she strained forward swiftly against him, savouring the moment, kissing him from the depths of her heart.

When finally they drew breath, she felt a century had gone by. As if in a dream, she let her head sink onto his shoulder.

"My darling," he whispered. "I can hardly believe you are in my arms."

Her voice was soft and barely audible. "I hadn't expected to find there would be no other visitors at this hour."

"I had to see you alone. It was a chance not to be missed." He took her hands. "Let's talk of the future and how it would be to make a fresh start together, both of us to make amends for having let the other go."

"That was nearly six years ago," she said brokenly.

"Yet nothing has changed between us."

She knew it to be the truth. The love they shared had proved itself to be of unassailable strength. How could she go on resisting this man who held her whole heart? She drew up Nicolas's hands with her own and covered them with little kisses. "I love you," she whispered. "I belong to you. I've fought against my feelings until I can't fight any longer."

"My darling, beautiful, wonderful Gabrielle," he whispered in return. "Now there are no more barriers between us."

Her face was full of longing. "I wish it were true. I'm not free to come to you of my own accord."

"When will you be?" He was impatient, desperate. "So much time has been lost. We need each other. I shall go to Emile—"

"No! You must not go to him!" She was adamant.

"Then how is this dilemma to be solved?"

"I don't know. All I ask is that you allow me a little time. Then I'll come to you. Somehow I'll come to you."

He did not doubt her. The hope in her was infectious, and they smiled as if they were already free to be together. With his arm about her waist they left the tent together and went into the corridor. He helped her on with her fur cape, and they faced each other in parting. "When am I going to see you again?" he asked her.

"I can't say when. Don't come with me now and don't try to see me. That would only complicate matters. I must find my own way out of the maze to reach you. Goodnight, my darling."

Holding her cloak about her, she went from him to her carriage.

A LETTER FROM BROUCHIER was delivered to Henri at breakfast in his office. As he broke the seal he had little hope of anything of interest. Then, as he read that Gabrielle and Devaux had been alone behind a closed door at the *hôtel de ville*, he saw that the situation was beginning to move at last. This information was something to hold on to until his son

450

was born. Then he could present a strong appeal to the courts. He locked the letter safely away in the desk that had been his father's.

To Emile, however, Brouchier went in person to deliver his report, riding out of Lyons at an early hour. When he arrived, he asked for Monsieur Valmont and was told he was at the silk-sheds. Following directions, he took a path through the trees and happened to spot his client coming out of one of the buildings.

Emile stiffened when he saw Brouchier. "You have something for me?" he asked.

"Yes, monsieur, what you've been waiting for." Brouchier took a sealed paper from his pocket and gave it to his client.

"Stay here." Emile took the report into his office and read it through. Then he unlocked a drawer where he kept money, slipped a certain amount into a moneybag and took it out to where the spy waited. He tossed the moneybag to him. "There you are. Your task is at an end. Get out. Never let me see you again."

Emile passed a shaking hand across his brow. He had planned what he would do if ever full confirmation of his fears came into his hands. Now he must put that plan into action.

WHEN GABRIELLE CAME HOME at the week's end, Emile was in Paris. She had been fully prepared to put the whole matter of Nicolas before him, hoping he would show compassion towards her request for freedom. He had still not come home when she returned to Lyons, and it was to be another two weeks before she saw him again, for the following Friday Yvonne went into labour. Thirty-six hours later she gave birth to a daughter. The infant was weak, and lived only a few hours.

Henri did not go near Yvonne for two days. For him their loss meant that he must find some other means by which he could gain control of Roche silk. He refused to admit defeat. Brouchier should be retained, because there was always a possibility that, through Devaux, Gabrielle would fall. He sighed impatiently.

When Gabrielle, in Lyons, received a letter from Emile saying that he was home at the silk farm again, she felt completely weighed down. The tone of his letter was affectionate, expressing regret at having missed her. She had to talk to Nicolas before Emile arrived in Lyons. She was in the process of writing him a note at her desk at the mill when the door opened without warning and he was there. The joy she always felt at the sight of him was immediately tempered by the anxiety in his face. "What's happened?" she asked with trepidation.

Without reply he closed the door and came towards her, pulling her into his arms for several moments of wordless embrace. Then he looked down into her face as he broke the news.

"I have to go away, Gabrielle. I have to leave Lyons."

"Tell me why!"

"Something has happened that I never expected. I've had orders to rejoin my old regiment of the *chasseurs à cheval*."

"Oh, no!" She was aghast. Her arms tightened about his neck. "When did you hear? Perhaps there's been a mistake."

"There's no mistake. Less than an hour ago I received my papers telling me to report for duty. I depart tomorrow morning for the campaign in the Iberian peninsula. That's why I had to see you. Good can come out of this posting to Spain, if you agree to go with me."

"Go with you?" she repeated uncertainly.

"It is only a matter of time before you will be my wife. Don't you see? Emile would never try to hold you once you had left with me." He kissed her tragic face and tried to cheer her with an encouraging smile. "We can be married in Spain as soon as you are free. When the war is won, we shall return to Lyons together."

She thrust herself from him. There was not a vestige of colour in her face. "It's too late, my love—my only love. I have to stay here and remain wife to Emile." Her voice faltered. She dreaded what she had to say next. Only recently had her private suspicions been confirmed. "I'm going to have his child."

He stepped back and stared at her, stunned. "Are you sure?"

She nodded helplessly. "There have been signs."

He drew her to him again. "You can still come with me to Spain," he insisted. "Nothing can come between you and me. I love you, and I'll love any child that is part of you."

Her heart was breaking in its own terrible anguish. "I would follow you anywhere if I were free," she said, "but in my present state I couldn't undertake such an expedition."

He took her chin in his hand. "Then after the baby is born—"

"No!" She jerked herself from him. "Don't you see? Can't you understand? Whatever chance we had to be together has gone!"

His anger flashed now, for this was a total rejection of all hope. "I want a promise from you that at some time you will at least visit me in Spain or wherever I might be sent afterwards. I've desired you for too long to be denied some part of your life."

"You'd try to make me stay." Her voice deepened in despair.

"You have always withheld yourself from me!" he accused.

"Not through my own wish! When Emile held me in his arms, do you suppose I didn't yearn for you? I told you in the emperor's tent that I would come to you when I was free. That still holds, except that I'm no longer able to see how or when, or if ever, it might be."

"'Never' appears to be the appropriate word!" The hurt in his eyes was as stark as if he had been ripped apart inside. "It would have been better for both of us if we had never met. Farewell now, Gabrielle."

Turning, he opened the office door and went out. She stood as if all power to move had left her, hearing and seeing nothing, only remembering the last words spoken to her by the man she would love until the end of her days.

CHAPTER SEVEN

Emile arrived in Lyons earlier than expected. Henri went to meet him in the hall. "Gabrielle is not home from the mill yet, Emile. Let me offer you some refreshment. A glass of wine?"

Emile declined with a dignified gesture. "Thank you, but no. I'll wait until Gabrielle is here. How is Yvonne?"

"She appreciated your letter of condolence. It was a great disappointment to us both that the infant did not survive. But come. There is no need for us to converse in the hall."

The two men strolled into the gold salon, one of the smaller rooms in the house. "What has been happening in Lyons?" Emile asked. "It's four weeks since I've seen Gabrielle, and longer since I was here."

Henri's eyes gleamed with satisfaction. "Devaux has gone, for a start. Recalled to the colours. What do you think of that, eh?"

It seemed to Emile that his brother-in-law's tone bordered on the conspiratorial. "Indeed? Then the Devaux mill has closed?"

"Far from it. He left a manager in charge, a Parisian by the name of Michel Piat. A capable man, I've heard."

"Where has Devaux been posted? Do you know?"

"To the Iberian peninsula. From all reports it's a difficult campaign. The Portuguese refused to obey the emperor's command to close their ports to British trade. We had to move in to take Lisbon and settle the matter. Our soldiers would have dealt with the Portuguese long ago if the British hadn't interfered."

"But Portugal was neutral," Emile said. "It had a right to decide what it wanted to do. The British will not be driven out easily."

Henri's expression changed slyly. "That suits you, doesn't it? You have your reasons, just as I have mine, for wanting Devaux in the emperor's army and out of the way."

Emile answered him with icy civility. "Why should I? The feud belongs to your family and is nothing to me. Devaux never purchased my raw silk, so I'll not miss his business."

"It was not his business I was referring to. I'm talking about Devaux's interest in Gabrielle—your wife and my sister."

"You have me at a loss," Emile bluffed coldly.

Henri's grin was malevolent. "Then why did you set Brouchier on to her comings and goings?"

Emile regarded his brother-in-law grimly. "He reported nothing incriminating. I dispensed with his services a while ago."

"So he told me. Brouchier is accurate and reliable; I retained him mainly to keep an eye on Devaux. That's how I know that Devaux went to the mill to say farewell to Gabrielle a couple of days ago. It was a brief meeting. You need not worry. They won't be seeing each other again."

Emile's carapace of calm was shattered completely. An ungovernable rage possessed him and he lunged a blow at Henri's face and saw his brother-in-law collapse heavily on the floor. After a moment Henri propped himself up on an elbow to feel his jaw.

"You could have knocked my teeth out," he growled. Wincing, he checked his mouth with a finger. "I believe you've shaken the roots!"

Emile, dazed by his own action, went forward to assist him to his feet. Henri furiously warded off his helping hand and got up by himself.

"Gabrielle is the one who deserves a beating. Your wife—"

"Get out!" Emile's temper had flared again, his hands balling into fists at his sides. Henri did not delay.

WHEN GABRIELLE ARRIVED HOME, a servant informed her that her husband awaited her in the gold salon. She found him gazing into the fire. At the sound of her entrance he glanced up and met her eyes piercingly in the large looking glass above the mantel. She thought he appeared strained.

"So you're home, then, my dear," he greeted her reflection. "I was impatient for your coming."

"How have you been since you returned from Paris?" she asked, coming to a standstill some distance from him.

He turned to face her. "I've been well. What of you?"

"I haven't been sleeping very well." She felt his sharp gaze following her every movement as she went to sit on a sofa. "Please sit down with me. I've something to tell you."

He studied her warily for a moment before he took the seat beside her. She was looking down at her wedding ring, which she was twisting round her finger. Slowly she raised her head again, her gaze straightforward and direct. "We are going to have a child, Emile."

He stared at her, stunned by what she had said. His whole expression crumpled into jubilation. "My dearest wife!" Choked by emotion, he leaned over to kiss her. He had no doubt that he had fathered the child within her, for the truth shone out of her. "When is it to be?"

"I've nearly six more months to go."

"We must get you home without delay." He was enthusiastic.

"No, Emile. The doctor insists I take no journeys of any kind."

"Do you imagine I would leave you here in Lyons, away from me, for the next six months?"

"It has to be."

His immediate pleasure over the forthcoming baby was spoiled. "I suppose the same old reason is behind your determination to stay in Lyons. Roche silk again, correct? You won't leave it?"

She noted that whenever he was out of humour he became tighter and neater, straighter and colder. She longed for the gentleness he could show towards her when so inclined.

"I liked going daily to the mill, but that will stop now. The office here has always been the main one."

"So the business is still to come before me! If you think I'll allow it to dominate our offspring, you're mistaken. After the birth you may stay in Lyons if you wish. The child shall be with me."

"Nothing shall take precedence over the baby as far as I'm concerned," she informed him strongly. "I've made arrangements. I'm sure you will recall Madame Hoinville, a customer of yours. I dealt with her during your illness. I recently offered her a post as my deputy at the mill."

"Did she accept?"

"Gladly. In fact she is already installed, and has begun to shoulder much of the work for me, and will continue to do so. I'm extremely pleased with her. I want our child to grow up with the devotion of both of us, and for that reason I shall come home to you in the country as soon as I have recovered from the birth. Once the baby is weaned, I'm hoping I need travel only twice a week to Lyons."

He was greatly mollified by her assurance. Relaxing, he raised another point. "It won't be easy for me to get to Lyons as your time advances. You know how busy I am from May onwards, when the mulberry harvest is due and the silkworms are hatching."

"I realize that. I shall write to you and keep you informed about everything. What is the forecast for the harvest this year?"

"I haven't heard yet. My trees are in splendid condition."

"Good. I would have tried to get home earlier this evening if I had known you would be here. I was looking over patterns we'll exhibit at the Leipzig trade fair at Easter. Henri and Marcel are to represent me."

Behind his back Emile flexed the hand that had struck her brother. "The more I see of Henri, the less I like him. Maybe you were right after all to hold on to Maison Roche as you have done."

She was astounded by his words of support. "I can't tell you how much it means to me to hear you say so."

He rose from the sofa and drew her to her feet. "My dear, you have made me the happiest man in the world today." His arms encircled her. "If you need to remain in Lyons for the rest of your pregnancy, so be it. All I want is for you to be safely delivered of a healthy baby. You are everything to me, my dear. You and the baby that is to come. I pray we shall have a son."

She was touched by this show of tenderness. She was glad he had remained in ignorance of her love for Nicolas and that she had caused him no suffering. It was her only comfort. Tears were never far from her since she and Nicolas had parted; they threatened to overwhelm her at the most unlikely moments.

Briefly she rested a hand on Emile's arm. "That is my hope too," she said to him.

IN APRIL OF THAT YEAR there was a royal wedding. The emperor married Archduchess Marie-Louise of Austria. With the marriage the imperial seal was set firmly upon that country, which was settling down at last after its final defeat at the battle of Wagram. It was in France that unrest was brewing. The emperor had his enemies among his own countrymen, and the political undercurrents were having an increasingly bad effect on the financial state of the nation. Every aspect of business was being affected, and Gabrielle and other silk merchants in Lyons began to fear for their markets.

Emile came to the house in the Rue Clémont for Easter. The weather was unusually warm and sunny, the sky clear and blue. He arranged a boat trip on the river and a picnic for Gabrielle, Hélène and her daughter, Juliette. The outing helped Gabrielle to stop wondering how Henri and Marcel were progressing at the trade fair in Leipzig, and it was a carefree day. Juliette's excitement over the whole event was infectious.

"Play hide-and-seek with me," she implored Emile after the picnic.

"Very well," he agreed. "You and your *maman* shall hide first, and I will count to ten. We'll leave Aunt Gabrielle to rest by the trees."

Hélène did not join the game for long, finding it somewhat hectic. As she returned across the grass, Gabrielle thought how young and pretty she looked with her cheeks flushed from exertion and strands of hair awry. She wished her sister-in-law would dispense with her mourning black and let Jules rest. It was time for Hélène to let her heart heal.

"Ah, that's better," Hélène said thankfully, sinking down onto a corner of Gabrielle's rug. "Who would have thought it could be so warm at this time of year?"

After they had talked for a while, watching the glittering river flow past, Gabrielle tactfully broached the subject of Hélène's mourning. Hélène heard her out, looking down at a small wild flower she had plucked from the grass. "When I feel the time is right, I shall put aside my black garments," she said finally.

Gabrielle understood. Hélène's mourning was her own private link with the man she still loved. It brought home to Gabrielle that she herself had no link at all with the living, breathing man who had gone from her own life.

When Henri returned from Leipzig his conceit was enormous.

Contrary to earlier fears, German customers had failed to be deterred by a tariff that had been imposed on imported goods, and had vied with each other in placing their orders. Gabrielle was highly relieved. Although Henri claimed all the credit, Marcel informed her that her beautiful silks had virtually sold themselves.

Then, like a warning knell, at the beginning of May there was news from Naples. A freak frost had killed the silkworms there and damaged nearly all the mulberry trees. At the same time it began to rain throughout the whole of central and southern France.

In Lyons the gutters of the streets ran like rivers during the continuing downpour. Torrential rains kept the mulberry trees soaked and made harvesting impossible. Silkworms were hatching, and there was little to meet their voracious appetites. Before long the Rhône valley was flooded, and still it rained.

The clatter of a carriage arriving in haste took Gabrielle to her window one morning in time to see Emile leap out and run up the steps into the house. She hurried to meet him. One look at his haggard face as he removed his rain-spattered coat in the hall prepared her for bad tidings.

"The harvest is a total loss!" he exclaimed, as soon as the door to the salon was closed after him. "The mulberry trees have been attacked by a blight."

"Oh, no!" she breathed in dismay. Blight was a catastrophe dreaded by every silk farmer. The exceptionally bad weather must have created the right conditions for it to take hold. "What will you do? Could you ship in leaves from elsewhere?"

"You don't understand. The blight is developing everywhere."

She sank onto a chair, stunned. "Are you sure?"

He nodded despairingly. "I saw the first warning signs yesterday. It's only a matter of a day or two before the news breaks that there'll be no mulberry harvest in France this year. I came to warn you. You must buy whatever raw silk you can lay your hands on."

Her mind was racing. Dominique's trust would release the money she needed. She must summon her lawyers and a representative of her bank, disperse agents to buy on her behalf and, not least, send Hélène across the city on a special mission. "I'll act at once!"

Springing to her feet, she swayed and almost fell. Emile darted forward to catch her. "Not so fast! Remember your condition."

She took a deep breath. "I am remembering it. I'm also thinking of my weavers, their families and their unborn babies. You and I will not go hungry, but if I fail to secure the raw silk needed for weaving, they may starve."

The prospect haunted her as she began dispatching servants from her office with written messages, aided by Henri, who was moving more quickly under this threat of financial loss to Maison Roche than he had

457

for a long time. The repercussions from the failure of the "Tree of Gold" would be devastating to the entire weaving community in Lyons. Although Maison Roche was in a position to weather the storm, not all the silk merchants would be so fortunate, and bankruptcies were inevitable. It was as if the lifeblood of Lyons were in danger of drying up.

At the first chance Gabrielle left her office to go in search of Hélène. She found her in the kitchen, supervising the arrangements for dinner. By the pantry door, out of earshot of anyone else, Gabrielle told her what had happened and explained what she wanted her to do.

Hélène nodded briskly. "I'll leave now, on foot. In that way I'll draw less notice to myself than I would by arriving in a Roche carriage."

"I thank you." Gabrielle embraced her. "You're the only one I could ask to do this for me. Now I must get back to my desk."

She returned to her office only minutes before the lawyers and a representative of her bank were announced. They arranged everything to her satisfaction. Letters of credit were drawn up for her agents, who would be going out of Lyons as soon as the papers were in their hands. Henri also received the necessary authority to buy raw silk. As the lawyers and the bank representative departed, he came downstairs ready to leave for Genoa.

"Good luck, Henri," Gabrielle said.

"Leave it to me," he replied complacently. "Father and I used to buy from this particular grower. He won't have forgotten I was once a good customer." He was driven away from the house, and in a short time Hélène was overtaken by his carriage. She thought it unlikely that her brother-in-law, sitting back in comfort, would have seen her. It was a strange task on which she had been sent, and she could not deny she felt timorous about it. If she had needed proof of Gabrielle's feelings for Nicholas Devaux, she had it now.

The clacking of the looms as she drew near the Devaux mill, to which she was bound, told her that Nicolas's absence had made no difference to the pace of work going on there. At the street door of the house she banged the heavy knocker. A maidservant answered.

"I want to see Monsieur Devaux's business manager, Monsieur Piat, at once. Please tell him it's an urgent matter."

"Yes, madame. Your name, please?"

"I will give it only to Monsieur Piat."

She had only a few minutes to wait until the man came through a door from a small courtyard. He was tallish, with light brown hair, his face thin and severe but not unkindly. His whole bearing was authoritative and purposeful. Hélène judged him to be about forty years old. As he approached her, she spoke firmly.

"I'm Hélène Roche, sister-in-law to Madame Gabrielle Valmont. I have to speak to you in complete confidence."

"This way, madame." He led her into a study and held a chair for her before seating himself. "What did you wish to speak to me about?"

"First of all, I want your word that no one will ever know that I was here today at my sister-in-law's request."

"My employer is now Captain Devaux of the *chasseurs à cheval*. Since I am entirely responsible for his interests while he is away, I can't give any such assurance until I know what it is you have to tell me."

She began nervously. "I came entirely with my sister-in-law's goodwill. She wanted me to give you warning that there will be little or no mulberry harvest this year. A terrible blight has taken hold everywhere. Madame Valmont doesn't want you to lose the chance of buying raw silk on Monsieur—er—Captain Devaux's behalf, while there is still time. Please believe me and act now!"

He looked surprised at her words. "I don't disbelieve you. Fortunately, my employer was farsighted enough to cover any contingency during his indefinite absence. He bought all the raw silk he could before he left Lyons. I have a year's supply in hand."

Her sweet smile broke through. "I'm so glad to hear that."

He smiled too. "Please thank Madame Valmont for her concern."

Now Hélène leaned forward in appeal. "There's no reason for you to mention anything of this visit to Captain Devaux, is there? My sister-in-law was most insistent."

Michel Piat answered at once. "I'll say nothing."

Hélène was thankful that she had secured the promise Gabrielle wanted. She stood up. "I mustn't take up any more of your time."

"It's been a pleasure to make your acquaintance." He moved to the door with her and reached forward to open it. "I've never met your husband, although I saw him at the Leipzig trade fair."

Her eyes went cold. "That must have been my brother-in-law you saw—Henri Roche. My husband died at Austerlitz."

It was then he realized that beneath the black cape, her dress, shoes and gloves were all in black for bereavement. "My condolences, madame," he said, regarding her in a new and compassionate light. "I lost my beloved wife, Elyanne, not long before I came to Lyons. I'm afraid that I have unwittingly caused you some distress."

She felt a sudden empathy with this man who had been through the same heart-tearing loss. "Please think no more about it. Do you have children, Monsieur Piat?"

"No, I haven't. Are you more fortunate?"

"I have a daughter, Juliette. She is five years old."

"A delightful age. She must be a great comfort to you."

"She is indeed. We have such fun together." She wanted to hear that his life was mending. "Have you settled down here? Do you like living in Lyons?"

"Very much. I'm still exploring it. Do sit down again if you can spare the time. Are you a Lyonnaise by birth?"

She told him about herself, and he in turn told her about his life in Paris and how he had worked there for Nicolas Devaux. This led to talk of his home and inevitably to his wife again. He spoke of how courageous she had been through her illness.

"Elyanne insisted I should never wear mourning for her. She wanted me to look to the future, not cling to the past. I need hardly say that doesn't mean I remember her less."

Hélène's brows drew together in a thoughtful little frown. "I don't suppose Jules would have wanted me to wear mourning for a long time. Yet it is a comfort to me."

"A shield perhaps?"

He had startled her, and he saw it. It was something she had thought about herself, but this was the first time anyone had brought her face to face with the truth. In a cocoon of mourning she was isolated in her past love, safe from any fresh hurt. She spoke wonderingly. "Isn't it strange? I came here to help you, and instead, I believe you have helped me."

"I prefer to think that we have helped each other."

The long look they exchanged seemed to come to both of them from far away. Once more she rose to leave, and she gave her hand in farewell, still bewildered that this meeting should have taken such an unexpected turn. "*Adieu*, Monsieur Piat. I wish you well."

"*Adieu*, Madame Roche. I hope we shall meet again soon."

As she turned homewards Hélène thought deeply over all that had been said. Back at the Rue Clémont, she gave Gabrielle the details of her trip to the Devaux mill, noticing how her eyelids lowered when she learned that Nicolas had a year's supply of raw silk. It was obviously a tremendous relief to her.

Later, resting on her bed, Gabrielle marvelled that Nicolas should have shown such foresight in stocking his storerooms to cover any emergency. The financial outlay would have been tremendous. He must have been certain of Monsieur Piat's ability to manage the business. She would like to meet the man. Hélène had spoken well of him.

IN THE MORNING the news broke. Only the Roche and Devaux houses remained detached from the turmoil throughout the city. Silk merchants bid against each other at a cutthroat level for whatever raw silk was still available. Many mill owners foresaw closure and bankruptcy. The twenty-three days of rain without respite had brought as great a disaster to the Lyons silk industry as had the Revolution some seventeen years before. There was further consternation when a quantity of Italian raw silk disappeared without trace before leaving its country of origin. There seemed to be no end to the chain of calamities for Lyons.

Henri, however, returned from Genoa with three wagonloads of good raw silk for the Roche mill. He also returned full of smug satisfaction. He could have told his fellow Lyonnais where the missing silk had gone. With the cooperation of his contacts in Genoa, it had been smuggled out, and the transaction had secretly lined his own pockets very generously.

As for Gabrielle, in addition to what Henri and her agents had managed to purchase, she had a good deal of surplus silk from Emile. She was grateful to him for letting her have it, when he could have sold it at exorbitant prices elsewhere. In all, she was confident of keeping her weavers at work throughout the difficult times ahead and of fulfilling her orders from the Leipzig trade fair.

NEWS OF ALL THAT HAD BEEN HAPPENING in Lyons did not reach Nicolas until late summer. Very little mail from France reached the Iberian peninsula, and he considered himself lucky that a letter from Michel Piat had finally come into his hands.

In blistering sun, his uniform jacket open and his neckcloth and shirt drenched with sweat, Nicolas sat beneath an orange tree. Eagerly he broke the seal and began to read the letter. It was the first communication he had received from his manager.

As he read on, the tribulations of the *Grande Fabrique* seemed unimportant beside the horror of the war in which he was steeped. Only one line stood out from Piat's letter. "Madame Valmont has secured sufficient raw silk to see her looms through the dearth."

He folded the letter slowly. At times he dreamed of Gabrielle. He loved her. That was the beginning and the end of it, and the cruel fact was that he would probably never see her again.

"Captain Devaux! Your new mount is ready."

He looked up. Lost in thought, he had paid no attention to the sound of a horse being led towards him. Now he saw at once that the horse was a fine animal with an arched neck, an intelligent head and strong flanks. It was ready with his own saddle and saddlecloth, and Nicolas grinned as he pushed the letter inside his jacket and fastened the silver buttons.

He rose to his feet. This new horse was to bear the name Warrior, the same as that of his former mount, which had been shot from under him. He clapped Warrior's well-groomed neck.

"Well done, sergeant," he said with satisfaction. He swung himself into the saddle and turned the horse into the main dirt track through the village where the brigade had bivouacked for the last couple of days. It was a poor place, as were most of the peasant villages, and not one of the hovels had escaped damage. The inhabitants had long since fled.

Nicolas glanced about him as he rode along at a leisurely pace. Smoke rose from army campfires where scavenged fowl, wild birds and hunks of maggoty meat turned on spits over the flames. A strong smell of soap

461

drifted from the laundry area, where soldiers' wives were washing clothes. The army depended on the cooperation of a brave collection of women to nurse the sick and wounded, and Nicolas held them in high regard. Their lot was entirely different from that of the officers' wives, who were kept far from danger zones and who enjoyed a pleasant social life in Madrid and Seville and other cities considered safe.

Nicolas found it a relief to come into the shade of some fragrant orange trees towards the outskirts of the village. Everything was still and quiet away from the hubbub of the bivouac. The whole peninsula was a place where beauty and terror existed side by side. The magnificence of the brilliant landscapes never failed to please his eye, but in contrast to these vistas were the shell-wrecked cities and villages and the carnage of battlefields. The stench of death was commonplace; it was rare to breathe the pure scent of flowers without that pervading taint.

At times Nicolas found it difficult to believe he had ever been the young hothead who had joined Bonaparte's army after he and his parents had fled from Lyons. Then, he had had a reckless, dashing attitude to soldiering, following a leader who exuded the promise of a great and glorious France. Now, his love for his country was as powerful as it had ever been, but this war had changed him in many ways. It was not a fight between soldiers. In this conflict innocent civilians were caught in the direct firing line, simply because the whole Spanish nation had risen up against those whom they regarded as foreign oppressors.

Bonaparte's claim that it had been necessary to invade Portugal to close the last European ports open to British trade no longer impressed Nicolas. He had come to see that it was a ploy by which the emperor intended to annex Spain. Although he accepted that Bonaparte's masterly government had restored France to greatness, he saw him now intoxicated by power, ready to override the wishes of whole nations to further his empire. The principles of liberty and equality were being dragged through the mire by the very man who had once upheld them.

Nicolas kept his views to himself. To have voiced them would have brought his loyalty to the tricolour into doubt, and that was unchanged. He would do whatever he had to do for his country in this campaign. If it brought about his death, so be it. Disillusioned, he rode back through the ruins of the village.

CHAPTER EIGHT

In Lyons, Gabrielle had developed backache that morning. By midafternoon Emile was notified via messenger that she had gone into labour. He set off at once for the city, full of trepidation now that her time had come, and certain he should be nearby during her ordeal.

He was not prepared for what the sight of her pain-filled eyes and her attempts at a smile did to him when he reached her bedside. Immediately he was overwhelmed by a sense of helplessness and inadequacy. There was nothing he could do to ease his wife's suffering. Somehow he managed a few encouraging words, then Hélène tapped him on the arm.

"I think you'd better leave now," she said tactfully.

He was relieved, although he was at a loss as to how to spend the time. For a while he wandered aimlessly about the house, shuddering at Gabrielle's cries. Then he went for a walk. He stopped for wine at a cafe, and then dined at a restaurant. When he arrived back in the house, it was almost midnight. As he stepped into the hall a long, agonized moan came from the direction of Gabrielle's room.

"Dear God!" He was ashen. "It's not over yet?"

"No, monsieur." The manservant took his hat and cane from him. "The doctor came two hours ago."

Cold with dread, Emile went into the blue salon to sit and wait. It was the longest night he had ever known. The sounds of Gabrielle's torment made him weep. Yet, to his shame, he did sleep.

A hand shook him. It was Hélène. "Emile! Wake up!"

He opened his eyes to see the room flooded with morning sunshine. He leaped to his feet in panic. "What has happened?"

Hélène, heavy-eyed with tiredness, was smiling at him. "You have a son. A beautiful boy with strong lungs. Gabrielle is exhausted, but she is going to recover quickly."

Emile was beyond words in his joy. Hélène laughed as he embraced her, lifting her off the ground in his exuberance. He set her back on her feet and hurried to Gabrielle, taking the stairs two at a time. He reached the open doorway. Gabrielle lay white and drawn with her eyes closed in the freshly made bed, her hair brushed and shining. As Emile came into the room she turned her head and saw him. His expression was so joyous that she smiled, lifting a hand to hold it out to him. He rushed to the bedside to take it in both his own and press it to his lips.

"My dearest wife." His voice was choked, and there were tears on his cheeks. "If I had lost you—"

"Hush." She smoothed away his tears with her fingertips. "I'm here. I will always be here. Why not take a look at your son?"

He gazed into the cradle at the scarlet-faced infant. "My cup of happiness is overflowing, my son," he said quietly.

Gabrielle, watching him, was thankful she had been instrumental in bringing him that happiness. Never had she been more grateful for the fact that he did not have the slightest suspicion that the love he yearned for had gone to another man. Through their newborn child, she had found a way in which to make up to Emile for her inability to give him her whole heart.

THEIR SON WAS DULY NAMED ANDRÉ, after Emile's father. Hélène was a natural choice for godmother. On the day of the baptism she surprised everyone by appearing out of deep black for the first time, in a half-mourning shade of grey. Gabrielle, placing her son into her sister-in-law's arms, smiled in admiration.

"You look marvellous."

"It's in honour of your son. This is a time of new beginnings."

Gabrielle and Emile kissed her, then took Juliette by the hand to lead her out with them to the waiting carriages. Hélène and the rest of the christening party followed. Juliette kept looking back over her shoulder, enchanted by her mother's new appearance. It was as if the touch of a magic wand had transformed her.

True to her word, Gabrielle left the Rue Clémont for the country as soon as her doctor pronounced her fit to travel. The silk farm was not entirely at a standstill, because of the recovery of a cluster of mulberry trees that had escaped the worst of the blight. Second harvests did occur elsewhere, mostly in Italy, but hardly any of them came up for sale. Rumours were rife of their being shipped out to England, to the silk-weaving mills of Macclesfield. It was feared that the British might now take markets that would be difficult for the Lyonnais to recapture.

As if Lyons had not suffered enough ill luck, another blow fell. The tsar had decreed that luxury items of any kind were not to be imported into Russia, due to an urgent need to preserve currency. All over the city, silk merchants, including Gabrielle at her country retreat, received cancellation of the Russian orders that had been taken at Leipzig. Those who had risked everything to buy raw silk to fulfil these orders found themselves in deeper trouble.

By now Madame Hoinville had proved her excellence as a deputy. She made the journey twice a week to see Gabrielle and lay business matters before her, including new designs by Marcel for her approval. Altogether, Gabrielle was able to keep abreast of everything. She would have liked, however, to keep a closer eye on Henri, who merely corresponded with her.

Emile had never been more contented. His son was thriving, a healthy, bonny baby, and he had Gabrielle settled under his roof, with nothing to threaten their lives together any more. As a surprise, he had equipped an office for her next to his, and she had been delighted with it.

On the occasional visit Gabrielle made to Lyons in the first two months of the new year of 1811, she saw the misery and suffering of those without work. It was many years since there had been so many beggars in the streets. Everywhere mills were closed and loom rooms stood silent. Her own mill and the few others still in operation were besieged daily by unemployed workers.

Throughout the whole period Hélène distributed food, paid for out of her own pocket, to those with young children whom she knew to be in dire distress. Once, when the early spring weather was easing the cold away, Michel Piat caught up with her just as she left a house in the Croix-Rousse, not far from the Devaux mill.

"Madame Roche! What an unexpected pleasure. How are you?"

She turned her head, eyebrows raised in surprise. "Monsieur Piat! I'm very well, and extremely thankful that this dreadful winter is at an end. Pray God we never see such suffering again."

"I agree. At least there are signs that the mulberry has everywhere recovered sufficiently to give a reasonable harvest."

"Yes, isn't it splendid. Are you still busy at the mill?"

"Yes, we had many German orders, and far fewer from Russia; we felt the tsar's decree less than most mills. How did your sister-in-law fare?"

"She lost a large number of Russian orders, but all her looms are operating at full pace."

"I'm glad to hear it." He paused. "I wonder if you would care to see the Devaux mill, now that you are so near?"

Hélène had made her last call of the day. "I'd be delighted."

He gave her a complete tour, for she had a natural feminine interest in the beauty of silk that made it close to her heart. She stopped by one loom where a particularly delicate design of wild roses was being woven—misty pink and green against a pale cream background.

"That is quite the loveliest fabric I have seen for a long time," she enthused. "You have a talented designer here."

"We think so."

After the tour they had coffee together in a charming salon with panels of green and white damask in a pattern of acanthus leaves. Michel told Hélène how Nicolas had restored the house upon his return to Lyons with some of the first silks to come from his Jacquard looms. Then he paused. He would have shielded any other woman from the ugly facts of war, but to Hélène he said, "I received a letter from Captain Devaux last week. At the time he wrote he was still in the winter cantonments. Now, we have heard recently, the desperate fighting has resumed once more."

Her cheeks hollowed. "War is obscene, Monsieur Piat. I have never seen any glory in it. I understood my dear husband's passion for the army, his deep need to serve, and I shared totally his consuming love for France, just as I do today, but every time I watched him ride away, I knew that, even if I were lucky enough to have him home again, there would be many women less fortunate. My prayers are always for peace." She looked down quickly at the empty cup and saucer she held on her lap. "I'm talking too much. May I have some more coffee, do you think?"

He was even more impressed by her than he had been when she first came to warn him about the mulberry blight. He turned the conversation along other lines.

465

Two weeks later he sent her an invitation to dine. She accepted, and enjoyed the evening, for Michel was an excellent host. Then, on the first day of spring sunshine, Hélène finally discarded her half mourning. A miniature of Jules remained by her bed, where it was the first thing she looked at every morning, but the rawness of grief had finally healed.

Her dressmaker had delivered a dozen new gowns, including three of Roche silk—one in Pompeian red, one in deep gold, and one in sapphire. She planned to wear the gold one when she attended a ball to be held to celebrate the birth of a son to Napoleon and his empress. The widespread national rejoicing had been marred somewhat by the recent news that Masséna, Napoleon's marshal, had been driven back out of Portugal. But the general feeling was that the tide would soon turn again, and that nothing should be allowed to spoil the Lyons ball, which was an expression of loyalty to the emperor.

Emile and Gabrielle were coming to Lyons especially for the event, leaving their bouncing nine-month-old son in the care of a devoted nursemaid. Henri was making his own plans for the evening, which he would be attending with Yvonne. By arrangement, he had recently met Brouchier in a back-street cafe and given him instructions in low tones. A purse of gold was pushed surreptitiously across the table at which they sat, and there would be more when the spy's task was completed.

Nicolas Devaux's departure for the peninsula had not lessened Henri's resolve to wipe Devaux silk from the face of Lyons. What he had not expected was that the birth of an imperial heir would be instrumental in the timing of this final act of revenge. It was almost as if he and the emperor had both been waiting to achieve a special aim.

The evening of the ball was mild, fragrant with the scent of lilacs. Gabrielle, in a dress of copper silk, and Hélène in her gown of gold, were visions of beauty and elegance as they entered the ballroom with Emile, their white-gloved escort. As the dancing began, Michel Piat came to bow to Hélène. "My dance, I believe, Hélène."

She had promised him the first dance at their last meeting, when they had begun using each other's Christian names. There was firm guidance in Michel's capable hand as he took her fingers to lead her into the steps of the dance. Her feet felt curiously light. Suddenly it was almost as if she were waltzing on air.

For Gabrielle the highlight of the evening was meeting Nicolas's manager. The introductions took place when her sister-in-law and Michel Piat came in from the terrace. As it happened, Gabrielle's polonaise partner and Hélène were promised for the next dance together, and as they swept into a gavotte Gabrielle and Michel found themselves able to talk on their own. Inevitably, the topic was silk and the difficulties of the past winter. It brought Gabrielle to what she had wanted to ask from the first moment.

"I trust Captain Devaux has suffered no harm on campaign?" She was conscious of holding her breath, of being on guard against giving herself away by crying out if she should hear he had been wounded.

"No harm that I know of," was the reply he gave her. He went on to tell her of the one communication he had received, although not in the detail he had given Hélène.

On the ballroom floor the gavotte had ended. When Gabrielle was claimed by a new partner, Michel stood by one of the balcony pillars and watched Hélène amid the twirling throng of dancers. He was content to wait until the supper dance, when he could take her hand again. On the terrace he had made his feelings known to her and told her of his prospects for the future. It had not been his intention to speak yet, but this evening there had been a special rapport between them. He had never thought he would find another woman he could truly love.

At the close of the evening, when everyone streamed out onto the terraces to view the fireworks over the river, Michel was with the Valmont party. The only person who made him feel unwelcome was Emile Valmont. The man was thoroughly distant.

"Ooooh . . . ahhh!" The sounds rose from the crowd as the fireworks soared into the air to burst into multicoloured stars, lighting up the buildings and the upturned faces far below. Applause rippled out at the spectacular displays. The sky was full of silver stars fading away when another kind of glow was seen in the direction of the Croix-Rousse.

"Fire! Look, there's a fire!"

Michel was immediately uneasy. He turned to Gabrielle.

"Madame, might I have the loan of your carriage to get me to the fire? It may be nowhere near our mill, but I have to be sure."

"Of course. I'll take you to my servant Gaston. He will get you there in no time at all." She edged her way through the crowd, Michel and Hélène following her. The three of them hurried from the terrace and ran along the path that led to the courtyard.

"Gaston! Gaston!" Gabrielle called twice to make herself heard above the buzz of voices and the explosion of fireworks.

He heard her and broke away from the group with whom he had been watching the flames rising into the night. "Madame?"

"Take Monsieur Piat to the Devaux mill as fast as you can."

"Yes, madame. It's been confirmed, has it?"

"What do you mean?"

"Somebody came riding by just now and said it looked as though it was the Devaux mill that was afire."

She was never sure why she got into the carriage with Michel. It was not a conscious decision, simply an instinct to try to do whatever she could for Nicolas's property. Hélène scrambled into the carriage with her, and they were tossed about as Gaston, his servant's uniform etched

467

against the night, drove the horses at a gallop through the dark streets.

They had to alight at the head of the street, for a crowd had gathered. Michel groaned aloud at the sight that met them. The whole Devaux mill was ablaze, black smoke billowing over the rooftops. He plunged into the spectators to shoulder his way through. Like a bear, Gaston spread his arms out to envelop Gabrielle and Hélène, and they followed, half falling into the clearing.

An attempt was being made to save the Devaux residence, as well as the tall houses at the far end of the mill. Several chains of buckets were being passed from both ends of the street to the nearest public water ducts. Gabrielle rushed forward to take a place in a chain reaching into Nicolas's house, which was already on fire, the upper floors having been ignited by sparks from the mill roof. Gaston gave a hand to those salvaging furniture, and Hélène helped drag to safety some of the lighter pieces. Michel had dashed through the house to try to get upstairs to save some of his own possessions, but the smoke wrenched at his lungs and he fell back, choking. People were shouting to him to come out. He reached the hall in time to see through the open doors the beginning of the destruction of the green and white salon, as flames crept up from the floorboards and down from the ceiling.

He had just enough time to snatch up a package he had left behind earlier that day, before Gaston's big hand descended on his shoulder and thrust him, dazed and coughing, through falling sparks and burning splinters into the street. There was a crackling in his hair, and Hélène hurled herself at him to smother the flames with her hands. He could hardly see her for the swelling of his red-rimmed eyes, but he threw his arms about her in the certain knowledge that she was his for the rest of his days.

Emile had not seen Gabrielle leave the terrace with Hélène and Michel and, unperturbed, continued to watch the fireworks. It was only when they ended that he learned of Gabrielle and Hélène's hasty departure with Piat, and the reason for it. Something seemed to snap in his head, releasing all the blackness of mind and soul that he had begun to believe might have left him for ever. With it came fury with Gabrielle. How had she dared to go running off to Devaux's mill, deserting him?

He was shaking with temper as he hastened across the forecourt in search of a hackney. One came driving up quickly.

"Hurry!" he instructed the driver. "There's a fire in the Croix-Rousse. Go as fast as you can."

He sat back in the stale-smelling interior and tried to drive away the thundering despair that had come upon him. All these months he had been harbouring the illusion that he had at last won Gabrielle's love. His own happiness had prevented him from seeing that what he wanted most from her belonged to another man.

468

Lunging forward, he thumped a fist against the carriage wall behind the driver. "Faster! Do you hear me? Faster, I say!"

The hackney took him as far as possible. He leaped out, tossed the fare at the driver and ran forward to reach the crowd. He was at the south end of the fire, close to tall houses that had been ignited by the mill, which was clearly destined to be a total loss. He could see that Devaux's house was also completely ablaze. Suddenly, he saw Gabrielle.

She looked exhausted, standing beside Gaston at the front of the crowd, gazing sadly up at Devaux's house as the fire consumed it. Her gown was torn and her face streaked with smoke and grime, the gleam of her gold necklace an incongruous touch. He began to push through to the police line, shoving angrily at anyone who blocked his way.

"Not so fast, monsieur. You can't go in front of those buildings."

Emile glared at the policeman. "Let me pass! My wife is over there!" He pointed across to Gabrielle, who caught the disturbance out of the corner of her eye. "She's waiting for me. Can't you see?" With that, he thrust himself forward, full of jealous rage.

Seeing him approach across the water-sloshed cobbles, a dark figure illumined by the glow of the flames, Gabrielle took a step forward. He saw, almost to his disbelief, that she looked relieved and happy to see him. She smiled, giving a little wave in order that he should not miss her whereabouts in the confusion.

Her smile went right to his heart, and his anger ebbed. Maybe he had made a mistake. Maybe it was not as he had feared. Then, abruptly, her expression changed, a look of terror stamping her face. She made a sharp move, as if to run to him, arms outstretched, but her coachman grabbed her back. Instinct told him what was happening. The fire fighters were scattering, running in total panic. There were screams and warning shouts mingled with a deafening roar and a rushing sound as the whole side of the mill began to bend and disintegrate into white-hot bricks and flaring wood and searing ashes. The cascading sparks were brighter than any firework display.

Gabrielle screamed as if she herself were dying. Gaston pressed her face into his shoulder and spared her the sight of Emile's instant but terrible death.

GABRIELLE BORE HER BEREAVEMENT with dignity. The funeral took place in the village near the silk farm, where Emile was laid to rest in the little churchyard. Special prayers were included in the service for two other victims of the fire. Afterwards, family and friends went to the Valmont house for refreshments.

When everyone had gone, Gabrielle went to sit for a long while by her son, who was sleeping in his cradle in the softly lit nursery. Her thoughts were full of Emile.

As for Henri, he did not appear to take long to throw off his sorrow and behave in his normal fashion again. Things were finally as he had always wanted them to be. After the fire there was no longer a Devaux loom left in Lyons.

Henri also had cause for relief in that Brouchier had not approached him for the rest of the fee for a job well done, but had prudently decided to leave Lyons until all official inquiries about the fire were at an end.

The situation between Michel and Hélène had reached a distressing stalemate because of the fire. His prospects, which he had mapped out to her on the terrace during the ball, had vanished in the flames. Until he could be certain of his future once more, he felt himself to be in no position to propose marriage formally. She suffered her disappointment privately.

Michel seemed to be the only one unconvinced that the fireworks had ignited the mill. In the morning he had walked through the still smoking ruins. He saw that there had been some fire on the top floor, but that the flames had swept through the loom rooms in seconds. He remained suspicious, even though a burned-out rocket had been found on the cobbles in a neighbouring street. Michel wrote a letter to Nicolas informing him of the fire, and the prefect of Lyons agreed to use his influence to get it sent with military dispatches to ensure its arrival.

Since Gabrielle no longer came to Lyons, Madame Hoinville resumed her visits to the country. Gabrielle seemed to have become thinner and paler every time they met, and Madame Hoinville found her inattentive to anything but the silk farm.

Gabrielle had taken on Michel to assist her, and she found him invaluable. The mulberry harvest was all that could be expected in view of the setback of the previous year, and there was no disease among the silkworms from the replacement cocoons that Emile had purchased at great cost. His finances had been left in a sorry state, and she could guess at the worries he had endured.

Hélène was becoming increasingly concerned about Gabrielle. It was as if, with Emile's death, she had succumbed to his domination as she had never done in his lifetime. The cause lay in the confession that had slipped out of her in the midst of her wild grief on the night of the fire. Hélène, holding her in comforting arms, had heard what she had already guessed.

"He was there because of me!" The tears had gushed from her beautiful eyes. "I saw his expression in those last seconds before he realized what was happening. There was only gladness in his face at the sight of me." Sobs overtook her again.

"Remember that," Hélène urged gently, rocking her as she would have rocked a child in distress. "Be comforted by it. Emile would never have blamed you for what happened."

470

It seemed that her advice was heeded. It was only when Gabrielle was with André, cradling him in her arms, caring for him and sometimes singing him a lullaby in a low, sweet voice, that she relaxed, letting the tautness of spirit go from her. Two months to the day after Emile died, she collapsed. She was in a silk-shed when she crumpled onto the stone floor without a sound. Michel was the first to reach her, and he gathered her up to carry her along the path into the house. Hélène was sent for, and by the time she arrived, Dr. Jaunet had been called.

"Why hasn't Madame Valmont been eating?" he demanded.

"I knew she had little appetite these days, but I thought it would right itself in time."

"In time! Good heavens, madame, malnutrition is more than a decline in appetite. You must get nourishment into her now, even if you have to spoon-feed her like a baby."

Hélène, experienced in nursing the sick, carried out her assignment efficiently, and soon Gabrielle was on the road to recovery. But contrary to Hélène's hopes, when Gabrielle did begin work on a full scale, it was again the silk farm that came first with her. Not once did she drive into Lyons to visit the mill or the design room.

Gradually various commitments made it necessary for Hélène to return to the Rue Clémont. "Why not come back to Lyons with me for a few days?" she suggested to Gabrielle. "You could catch up on business." They were sitting on the terrace in the balmy evening air, both André and Juliette asleep in bed.

Gabrielle brushed a tendril of hair away from her brow with a relaxed hand. "I should like to, but I'm too busy here."

"Have you considered selling the silk farm?"

There was a slight intake of breath from Gabrielle. "At the present time there are no buyers for struggling silk farms."

Hélène saw through her. "Am I to believe that it may be years before you return to the work you have always liked best?"

Gabrielle maintained her casual air. "Yes, that is how it is." Then, suddenly, her reserve broke and she sprang to her feet and went with a few swift steps to the edge of the terrace, standing looking out over the dark garden. "Why should I pretend with you? You are closer than any sister could have been. I hate it here."

Hélène was amazed. "Then why stay?"

"I must." Gabrielle continued to look away, clenching her hands together in front of her. "What you haven't realized is the effect that rejecting Nicolas's love has had on me. It was like a denial of life itself. To go back to Lyons would be to revive every association with the times he and I had together. Here, I am Emile's widow and Nicolas is far from me in the peninsula." Her voice broke. "In Lyons he would be back in my heart." She bowed her head, covering her face with her hands.

Hélène hurried to her. "Forgive me. I didn't mean to probe. I have been thoughtless and unkind."

Gabrielle raised her head and took Hélène by the arms. "Never say that. You are incapable of unkindness. You had to know why I can't face seeing Lyons again. I'm thankful I've told you."

On the morning Hélène left with Juliette they were accompanied by Michel, who had business in the city. As Hélène settled her daughter onto the seat of the carriage she glanced across at him.

"In the letter you sent to Nicolas notifying him of the fire, did you mention that Emile Valmont had died?"

"No, I said there were three fatalities, but the whole of the letter was taken up with matters of insurance and so forth. I listed the casualties in a letter I sent later."

"Pray God he receives it," Hélène said, almost to herself.

When Hélène arrived home at the Rue Clémont, she found that Henri and Yvonne had had their quarters in the house extravagantly refurbished; in addition they had annexed the Grand Salon, where important customers were received. Its walls had been redecorated with gleaming orange-red brocade woven with sunflowers.

"What do you think of it?" Henri asked with an expansive sweep of his arm as he led her into it.

Tired and dusty from the journey, Hélène frowned questioningly. "I thought Gabrielle had halted this kind of expense until the trade situation was better again."

"I'm in charge now. I make all the decisions now that my sister has chosen to bury herself in the country." Then he added, seeing that Hélène was about to stalk away, "Oh, there's something I have to say to you. In the future, would you keep your daughter from running all over the house? It disturbs Yvonne."

Hélène halted to stare at him in astonishment. "Juliette has never invaded the privacy of your apartments."

"No, but I'd be obliged if you would keep her in your own rooms whenever she is at home. You'll notice that a few changes have been made in your absence. It seemed foolish for Yvonne and me not to use the whole house when it's beginning to appear unlikely that Gabrielle will ever return here on a permanent basis. Yvonne has hired a new housekeeper and will settle the menus with her daily, so there's no longer any need for you to feel obliged to take part in running the household."

"I never thought of it as an obligation. I looked upon this house as my home from the day I came here as a bride."

"That may be, but you'll find things have changed."

Hélène angrily entered her own apartments to find that Yvonne had had several family pieces of furniture taken away. Closing the door behind her, Hélène was pensive. She had said long ago to Gabrielle that she would leave the Rue Clémont when she felt the right time had come, and Henri and Yvonne had now shown her they no longer wanted her under the same roof.

Unfortunately, it was not now convenient to leave. Michel's plans were still uncertain. He was applying for posts better suited to his abilities than the silk farm. When he was relocated, she would marry him, and they would have their own home. In the meantime, she must put up with the situation.

THE COOLER DAYS of autumn had come when Hélène received a message that Madame Hoinville wished to see her at the Roche mill. When she arrived, one of the spinners took charge of Juliette, leaving Hélène free to go into Madame Hoinville's office.

"Thank you for coming, Madame Roche," the woman greeted Hélène. "It was most urgent that I see you."

"You realize I have no connection with the business?"

"Of course. But you are close to Madame Valmont. I must ask that you do everything in your power to persuade her to return to Lyons. I believe she is being swindled in her absence."

Hélène was startled. "Please explain."

"Valuable orders, which should be coming into this mill, are being siphoned off by someone who is producing illegal copies of Roche designs."

"How can you be sure?"

"Some faulty brocade was returned to this mill directly from a foreign customer. There was only a minuscule flaw, but it was consistent throughout a very expensive piece. I went to compare it with a pattern that had been made up with the same dyed yarns and supposedly on the same looms. I was able to see at once that it had not come from here, and yet it was a design exclusive to Maison Roche."

"Why don't you tell all this to Madame Valmont? You have only to show her the piece and the pattern. There is your proof."

Madame Hoinville sighed. "I'm unable to do that. The faulty piece was removed from its shelf without my knowledge."

"Do you know who took it?"

"I was told. There was no secrecy about the removal. Rejects are frequently sold off. However, if an inquiry should be made, I would expect to hear that the purchaser was a stranger who passed through Lyons and is now gone without a trace."

"This is an extremely grave matter. I must insist that you tell my sister-in-law everything you have told me."

"Madame, I cannot!" Madame Hoinville took a deep breath. "It is not for me to point a finger at her brother without positive proof. Yes, it was Monsieur Roche who removed the brocade."

474

Hélène drove out of Lyons to see Gabrielle the next day. Upon arrival she told her everything that Madame Hoinville had said. Although Gabrielle sat listening, her hands quiet in her lap, her gaze was directed sadly out of the window. Afterwards she turned her head to look at Hélène.

"How impossible it is to escape destiny. It seems I have to return to Lyons after all. I'll not have my son's birthright eroded by Henri's pilfering. I'll be ready to leave this evening."

Hélène helped her to pack. It was noticeable that Gabrielle was taking no mourning garments with her. By evening, dustsheets covered all the furniture, valuables had been packed for transfer to the Rue Clémont and shutters were closed. An agent had been called in to arrange the sale of the silk farm, which Michel was to manage until it changed hands.

At the moment of departure Gabrielle was the last to leave the house to which she had come as a bride. She stood alone in the silent hall. "Farewell, dear Emile," she said softly. Then she turned and went out of the house, locking the door behind her.

When she arrived at the Rue Clémont with Hélène and André, it was to find that Henri and Yvonne were holding a musical soirée.

"Don't interrupt the festivities," she said to the servant who had admitted them. "Just make sure that all the baggage is unloaded quickly, and inform the housekeeper of our arrival. You may bring a supper tray to my office. I shall be working there."

"Er—one moment, madame. Monsieur Roche moved from his office into yours several weeks ago."

"Indeed?" Gabrielle raised her eyebrows. "No matter. It is mine again now, and that is where you will find me."

A glance into Henri's old office showed that her possessions were stacked there as if in readiness for storage. As she opened the door into her own domain she saw that he had ensconced himself in a masterly fashion, with his large desk, which had once been their father's, his ornate silver inkstand with its inset sand shaker, and his leather chair. He had also had every one of his cupboard files brought in.

She set to work on the files at once, estimating that she had two hours before Henri learned she had returned. A supper tray was brought in. She nibbled at some of the food, hardly aware of what she was eating. Again and again the files revealed nothing in the least incriminating. Everything was in perfect order.

It was midnight when the company departed. Then, as she had expected, heavy footsteps came hurrying in the direction of the office, and Henri burst into the room. "What are you doing here?"

She gave him a direct look. "I'm back to stay, Henri."

"What about the silk farm?"

"That's to be sold. Whatever it brings will be most welcome at the present time. The coffers of Maison Roche are low."

He glared about the room. "All these files were locked. You had no right to go through any papers without asking me."

"Then it was careless of you to have left the keys in my office. You need have no fear that I looked at anything that did not deal with Roche silk, and for that I don't have to ask permission."

"Are you satisfied with what you've seen?" His whole stance was belligerent, and he looked as if he might strike her should she give anything but an affirmative answer.

She gestured at what she had been reading. "Nobody could fault these ledgers. Everything is recorded meticulously."

"Since you are determined to work here," he said, "I'd like to get my desk and other possessions back into my old office right away. The file cupboards can stay here."

She collected up the papers in front of her. "I think I will go to bed. The changeover of the furniture can wait until morning."

"No, it shall not." He jerked a chair aside, as if prepared to pull the desk out of the room unaided if need be. "Tomorrow I want to be able to begin work without hindrance."

As she left him he summoned servants to effect the move.

That night, while preparing for bed, Gabrielle thought about Henri. She had always thought it impossible that he might be capable of doing her or anybody else serious physical harm. But tonight something had made him desperate. His near panic at finding her there in the office was an indication that under this roof was evidence that would incriminate him.

Then something stirred in her memory. She pictured her father sitting at the desk that was now Henri's. Once in her childhood she had entered the office when her father was searching for a paper he had misplaced. He had not seen her enter. He had been annoyed when he looked up and saw her standing there, and had jumped up from his desk to hustle her out of the room and close the door again. Now she had a clue at last to the whereabouts of what she was seeking.

She ran to Henri's office. The door was unlocked. Putting the lamp on the desk, she sat down in the chair and removed the small middle drawer. Then she reached into the aperture. After a few minutes of fumbling, she found the catch of a secret drawer and released it. The drawer slid forward into the lamplight, packed tight with papers.

She began to go through them with trembling hands. It did not take her long to discover that Henri had his own mill of the same name just outside Lyons, established not long after Maison Roche became hers. Ever since that day he had stolen orders, or sections of orders, from her, recording them in his files but not in the Maison Roche ledgers. It was impossible to estimate even roughly how many thousands of francs had been diverted from Maison Roche by her own brother.

Suddenly the door was flung open. Henri stood there in a dressing robe, his face congested with violent rage. "You prying wretch!"

He lunged for her as she sprang up, seizing her by the throat and shaking her, the pressure of his hands choking her protests into gurgling sounds. He was enraged beyond control. Her arms flailed and her fingers touched the heavy silver inkstand. She managed to grab it and swing it upwards, sand and ink pouring from it down her arm and splashing over him until it crashed to the floor.

"Henri!" Yvonne's shriek of outrage came from the doorway.

He released Gabrielle, and she collapsed to the floor. Then he slumped down in a chair and began to sob. Gabrielle was aware of Yvonne propping her forward to help her get her breath back. Then Hélène, who had been aroused by Henri's bellowing, rushed to the office to kneel by Gabrielle. Supporting her with an arm, she wiped her face with a handkerchief. Then she poured a small cognac from a decanter and held it to Gabrielle's lips. "Give a large measure to Henri," she instructed Yvonne.

Henri, still sobbing, emptied his glass at a gulp.

"What's all this about?" Yvonne now demanded shrilly.

He glanced at her with a hangdog air and looked away again. "Gabrielle has discovered I have a little sideline."

"You fool! You could have broken away from Maison Roche and started your own fabric house if you had wanted to do it."

He jerked himself out of the chair. "With your extravagant ways what other chance did I ever have?" he roared back. "Your debts have been a millstone round my neck for years!"

"So I'm to blame?" She wagged her head in mockery of him. "What of your gambling? You never were a winner! That's why your father never left you Maison Roche in the first place!"

He hit her with his fist. Then he went on hitting her, as if a second bout of madness had overtaken him. Yvonne screamed as he beat her down to the floor. Hélène left Gabrielle to try to intervene, but Henri thrust her from him, shouting, "Keep out of this!"

Then Gabrielle swayed to her feet to try to reach the bellpull to summon help, but before she could stretch out her hand to it, Henri stopped his onslaught as abruptly as he had begun. He stood over Yvonne, who lay whimpering on the floor.

"I've finished with you!" he bellowed. "You'll get out of my sight and out of this house tonight!"

He turned and charged for the door. Gabrielle stepped in front of him and rested a hand on either side of the doorjamb to bar his way.

"It's you who must leave tonight, Henri. I always knew you were a bully and a coward, but I never thought you would go to the lengths I've just witnessed."

"You can't turn me out of my home," he blustered. "I was born here."

"It *was* your home, and would have been to the end of your days if you hadn't chosen to do what you did. This is André's house now. I only hold it in trust for him, as I do Maison Roche, and nobody in the world is going to harm his interests, not even my own brother." She was sickened by him. "Now go, Henri. Both of you go, and never come back to the Rue Clémont." Her arms dropped to her sides, and she leaned back against the wall to let him pass.

He stared at her, his lips drawing back in a grimace of vengeance. "Damn you and your high-and-mighty ways. I always pitied Emile for having you for his wife. During the time when you and Devaux were meeting secretly, there was always a spy trailing you. It's my guess Emile went to his grave not knowing whether or not he had fathered your son!"

Gabrielle, already ashen from her ordeal at his hands, pressed herself against the wall as if to stay herself from falling. "Go, Henri," she repeated with colourless lips. "Go!"

With a self-congratulatory snort at what he had done to her, he strode from the office. Gabrielle looked wordlessly at Hélène, who had risen from attending to Yvonne to stand statuelike, struck into horrified immobility by the cruelty of the words Henri had directed towards his own sister. Gabrielle opened her mouth twice in an attempt to speak, but her voice seemed to have gone in the shock of what had been disclosed.

CHAPTER NINE

Gabrielle, elegant in her gown of tangerine silk, a gold brooch at her throat, was receiving an important visitor in the Grand Salon. Monsieur Morard of the *Mobilier Impérial*, a distinguished-looking man with grey hair, came across the room to bow over her hand.

When the preliminaries were over, he explained the nature of his visit. "The emperor has decided that the Palace of Versailles, which has been little used since the Revolution, when its fine rooms were destroyed, is to be completely refurbished. We of the *Mobilier Impérial* are interested in commissioning silks from you for several of the salons."

Gabrielle flushed with excitement at what was happening at last. Then, suddenly, her pleasure dimmed. "Am I to receive this commission because Maison Devaux is no longer in operation?"

"Not at all," the man hastened to assure her. "As there are many rooms in Versailles, we are also commissioning from other leading silk houses in Lyons. If the Maison Devaux had not been burned down, it would have received its share of orders. The emperor wants to make this palace the most magnificent the world has ever seen."

"I shall be proud to take part in such an enterprise."

She then showed him a wide selection of exquisite designs, several incorporating the imperial bee. He picked out a number to put before the committee for a final selection.

"You should not have long to wait," he said as he was leaving.

As Monsieur Morard's carriage took him away, Gabrielle gave a laugh of sheer exuberance and went in search of Hélène. The good news was in keeping with the whole atmosphere of the house now that Henri and Yvonne had gone.

Henri had left in the early hours of the morning after that terrible night. Yvonne was permitted to stay until her injuries were healed, but when a letter from Henri was delivered ten days later, she rose from her bed, packed her belongings, ordered a carriage and left the house.

Now, once again, Juliette played wherever she wished, and André toddled about after her whenever he could. She was like a sister to him, and Hélène was a second mother, always in charge until Gabrielle came home. It was Hélène who had made life bearable for Gabrielle after Henri's terrible disclosure.

"Never let your brother's evil words taint your memories of Emile," she had said the next day. "I remember Emile when André was born. I have never seen a man so happy. There was not the least doubt in his mind as to whether André was his child. He said to me more than once, 'I can see my father in my son.' "

Gabrielle felt very grateful for Hélène's reassurance. Now she opened the door into Hélène's salon with a flourish and found her writing at her escritoire. "Tra-la-la! It's happened! Roche silk is to hang at Versailles!"

Hélène put down her pen to clap her hands. "Congratulations! How wonderful!"

Gabrielle swept herself onto a sofa. She related all the details to Hélène and then said that her fears about gaining at Nicolas's expense had proved groundless. "That mattered to me more than anything," she confessed soberly. She let her head drop onto the back of the sofa, her gaze far away. "I live for his return, Hélène. Being back in Lyons has done everything to me that I knew it would. Although the past is still with me, and always will be, I'm looking to the future, not only my own, with my longing for Nicolas, but my son's and that of Maison Roche."

"Have you written to Nicolas yet?"

"No. I do not dare. If I wrote, and received no reply, I would have no way of knowing if he had written to me or not. That would be more torment for me. When we see each other again, all will be well, I'm sure of it." Her face was suffused with hope. "I know Nicolas is going to come through the Peninsular War. I feel it in the marrow of my bones."

"I pray he does," Hélène said sincerely.

That same week the silk farm was sold, at a higher price than Gabrielle had hoped to get. It seemed that she was on a crest that nothing could spoil. Michel returned to Lyons, and she offered him the post of manager of Maison Roche in Henri's place.

"I'm honoured," he said enthusiastically. "I have served one great silk house in Lyons, and now I am to serve another."

He went without delay to tell Hélène of his new appointment. She rose excitedly to give both hands into his outstretched clasp.

"That's splendid news!" she exclaimed.

"It means we can look to the future now." He kissed her gently. "We can set a marriage date as soon as we find a house."

"Let us live here in this house for a while before we get our own home," she said. "It is a help to Gabrielle to know that André is in my charge when she is busy, and when the orders come in from the *Mobilier Impérial* you and she will not have a minute to spare." Smiling lovingly at him, she linked her fingers behind his neck. "In any case, I don't want to wait for house buying before we marry. Let it be soon."

"Tomorrow?" he teased.

"The day after," she said, not teasing.

There was a civil ceremony, followed by a religious marriage at the Church of St. Nizier. Only a few close friends were present, and the bride wore a gown of Devaux silk. Michel had rescued the length from a package in the midst of the fire. It was the cream silk with the pale pink roses that she had admired on her visit to the Devaux looms, and he had had a piece put aside for her. To Gabrielle the beautiful, shimmering gown was like a banner being flown for a silk house that would rise again.

The bride and groom left for a honeymoon in the fishing village of Antibes, on the Mediterranean coast. During their absence Gabrielle heard from the *Mobilier Impérial*. She was commissioned to produce the fabrics for eight rooms at Versailles, including a study for the emperor himself. This marvellous commission encompassed wall hangings, draperies and upholstery fabrics. Alone in her office, Gabrielle twirled around with the letter like a young girl. Her looms would gleam with woofs and warps of imperial colours, and glitter with silver and gold *filé* and *frisé*, to bring Maison Roche to the notice of the world.

By the time Michel and Hélène returned, she was already getting samples of dyes together. Michel took up his work as if he had been with Maison Roche for years. One morning at the mill, a letter was brought to him. After reading it, he returned to the Rue Clémont, where he went in search of his wife. When she had read the letter, he said, "I thought it best that you be the one to break the news to Gabrielle."

She nodded sadly. "I'll do it now."

Hélène went to the design room, where Gabrielle sat perched on a high stool beside Marcel. She waited until Gabrielle, catching sight of the letter in her hand, came towards her, able to tell by her expression that it was a serious matter. "Let's go to the blue salon," Hélène said, turning.

"Wait!" Gabrielle put out a restraining hand, her voice low and hoarse with dread. "Is Nicolas dead?"

Hélène was dismayed by the query. "No! Nor is he wounded." She put an arm about Gabrielle's waist.

"It's still bad news, isn't it?"

"I'm afraid so. Michel heard from Nicolas today. One thing is certain. Although Michel's letter about the fire got through, the later one, telling of your widowhood, never reached him."

"How do you know that?"

"Two reasons. The first is that in the last paragraph Nicolas sends his compliments to Monsieur and Madame Valmont."

Gabrielle's face did not change. "And the second reason?"

"He has put the site of Maison Devaux up for sale, and written that he never intends to return to Lyons."

"That's impossible!" Gabrielle put her fingertips to her temples. "If peace should be restored tomorrow, there would be nothing to stop him from going anywhere in the world, and I might never find him."

Hélène briskly dismissed this statement. "The campaign in the peninsula is far from over, which gives us the time we need. Somehow we must find a way to get a message through to him."

"The time for letters and messages is over. Would you look after André for me if I go away? I could never leave him with anyone else."

"You don't have to ask me. I love taking care of him. You know that." Hélène's brows drew together. "But where are you going?"

There was an eager determination in Gabrielle's expression. "To Nicolas! I promised him once that if ever I was free, I would go to him. That time has come."

"You can't! No woman can travel alone into a field of war."

"I'll not be alone. Gaston will come with me, I know. He's an old war-horse himself, and I'm sure he'll leap at the chance." She began to outline a plan. "I should be able to get to Ciudad Rodrigo by Christmas. There'll be no fighting at that time. The troops on both sides will be in their winter cantonments. I should be able to have at least a week or two with Nicolas before turning homewards again." There were tears in her eyes that she could not keep back. "The hardest thing for me to bear will be my separation from André. He will miss me, as I shall miss him."

"Then please don't go." Hélène's voice shook. "I beg you."

"I have to. I realize now that this is why destiny brought me back to Lyons. I'm being given a last chance to share my life with Nicolas."

Hélène could not say anything more to dissuade her.

As GABRIELLE HAD EXPECTED, Gaston did not hesitate when she put her request to him. Without asking why, he simply wanted to know how soon she wished to start.

"As soon as possible," she replied.

"Allow me two days, madame, to select horses and put together supplies."

His first step was to make inquiries about any departure of reinforcements from the local barracks. He learned that a baggage train would be moving out under military escort at dawn the next morning. It was bound for Salamanca, which was on the same route as Ciudad Rodrigo. They would not have many miles to go after that, and all within range of French protection.

After notifying Gabrielle to be ready sooner than expected, Gaston worked the rest of the day and into the night. She had given him the money to pay for everything. Swiftly he ticked off the items: spyglass, canteens for water, horseshoes, hammer and nails, kettle, cooking pot, tinderbox, knife and hatchet, storable food. There was also feed for the horses, his musket, a bludgeon, pistols and ammunition, as well as blankets and extra clothing.

Shortly before dawn he and Gabrielle rode away down the Rue Clémont, a packhorse in their wake. Her last action before embracing her sister-in-law had been to kiss her sleeping son.

Gabrielle had chosen to travel in a warm, comfortable and thoroughly unfashionable riding habit cut straight round the hem, with leggings beneath. Her black hat was flat and brimmed, and over her shoulders hung a cape that was virtually rainproof. Gaston, also practically clad, wore a goatskin jacket, thick breeches, a cloak, and a well-worn rust-red felt hat. They could easily have been mistaken for a farming couple.

At the barracks, Gaston reined in to wait, and Gabrielle followed suit. Soon officers on horseback, soldiers on foot, and wagons loaded with ammunition and other supplies emerged from the archway with a clatter of hooves and a rumble of wheels over the cobbles. Gabrielle and Gaston fell in with the wives and other camp followers, behind the rear guard. As the sky lightened, the whole convoy passed across the wide and spacious Place Bellecour. On the slopes of the city rising beyond, the first rays of the wintry sun touched the tips of the tallest spires.

Contrary to Gabrielle's hopes, she was not to be in Ciudad Rodrigo by Christmas. As the days passed she wondered if she had ever lived any existence other than jogging along in the saddle behind creaking wheels and thudding feet. The suburbs of Salamanca were reached in the first week of the new year of 1812. While the baggage train turned towards the centre of the city, she and Gaston continued alone.

They came within sight of Ciudad Rodrigo on the evening of January 12. Gabrielle wished to ride on then and there to reach the fortress city, but darkness was falling and Gaston did not want to risk the dangers of travelling on an unknown road.

In the middle of the night Gabrielle heard a clink of metal. Gaston had heard it too. Throwing off his blanket, he knelt on one knee, listening intently. Then he heard it again. Weaponry. He thrust one of the pistols he always kept by him into Gabrielle's hands.

"I'm going to scout around to find out what is happening."

He slipped between the trees. It was a moonless but starry night. Coming to a place where the land sloped down, he saw a whole sea of men making their way towards a hill where a few lights twinkled at the top. He guessed the lights came from a redoubt, part of the defences of Ciudad Rodrigo, and these were not guerillas he was observing, these were British soldiers! They were going against all the traditions of warfare, breaking out of winter cantonments early in January to make a surprise attack on his unsuspecting countrymen. There was nothing he could do to warn the redoubt, but he had to find a way to get Gabrielle away from here and out of danger.

When he came back to her, she refused to consider going home. "I haven't come all this way to turn back now! Ciudad Rodrigo is only a few miles from here. I don't care about Wellington or the rest of the British. I'm getting to Nicolas, whatever happens."

"That's what I thought you'd say," he commented phlegmatically. "Now you'd better get to sleep. The enemy won't stray in this direction. They've something else to do."

He slept as soundly as she did, both of them finally overcome by the exertions of their journeying. They awoke at dawn and were starting their day when the attack on the redoubt began. Gabrielle paused as the staccato gunfire sounded in the distance.

"Let's hope the redoubt holds," she said fervently.

It was approximately twenty minutes later when silence descended again. By then they were riding through the trees to where they could look through Gaston's spyglass towards the hill, in the strengthening daylight. The surprise attack had been successful. Scarlet jackets were streaming like ants through a gateway.

"The next target will be Ciudad Rodrigo," Gaston stated grimly. "All my experience tells me to keep you away from there."

"Just try!" She flicked her whip against her horse's rump and went galloping off down the slope, her cape billowing. He followed, leading the packhorse. Everything depended on whether he and Gabrielle could reach the city before the British.

Keeping a safe distance from the enemy, they rode on and skirted the gates of the fortress city. It was virtually surrounded by a seething swarm of men and horses, but there were gaps and one of these was where the River Agueda formed a natural barrier. Through his spyglass Gaston could see there was a French outpost placed to defend a bridge that he and Gabrielle should be able to reach. Borrowing a white kerchief from her, he tied it to his musket and held it high as they rode forward, urging their tired horses to a canter to cover the ground as quickly as possible. When they were within hailing distance, they were ordered to halt and declare themselves.

"Gaston Garcin and Madame Valmont on an important mission to Captain Devaux of the *chasseurs à cheval.*"

"Pass, friends."

Gaston gave Gabrielle a wink as they rode across the bridge into the outskirts of the city. French defences were set up everywhere, the cannon muzzles gleaming above empty pig-pens and by closed wine-shops. They had ridden only a short way when the British assault broke forth in a tumultuous burst of artillery fire. The French cannons leaped in reply. Gaston urged his horse into a gallop, and Gabrielle followed closely behind.

When they were near the wide-open city gates, a sentry shouted to them, "Stand clear! The cavalry is coming."

Gaston reached over and seizing the bridle of Gabrielle's mount, hauled the horse onto the verge of the road. In a burst of colour and a jingling of harness a squadron of the *chasseurs à cheval*, two hundred and fifty strong, came out of the gates at a gallop, sabres drawn. They wore their hussar-style fur hats, green and red plumes swaying back and forth, and their fur-lined pelisses hung from their left shoulders and flew out behind them. Gabrielle, who had been staring wide-eyed from the second they appeared, sighted Nicolas and screamed out his name.

"Nicolas! I'm here!"

He neither saw her nor heard her cry, and galloped by within a few feet of her. Seeing him again, it was as if her whole soul had flown to him. When the last horseman had gone past, she turned her mount to follow him, but again Gaston seized her bridle.

"No, you don't. That's no place for you."

Her face was pale and strained. "Then I'll wait for him here."

"You'll not do that either. We'll go into the city, where you can eat and rest and be refreshed for his return. He'll be back." When she remained as she was, still staring down the road at the disappearing *chasseurs*, he leaned over to tug at her sleeve. "Remember what you once told me? You said you were sure Captain Devaux would come through this campaign."

She turned her staring eyes on him, her mouth tremulous. "Then why do I feel so afraid for him now? Everything seems to be slipping out of control."

"It's only because you've seen a battlefield for the first time, and that has unnerved you. Nothing else has changed. You and he are the same as before. Come along now." She obeyed him finally.

They rode to a nearby hostelry, where Gaston secured a room and stabled the horses. The room was small, with dirty straw on the bed and no bed linen. He removed the dirty straw, washed the bedstead and let it dry for the blanket he would spread on it.

"You'll be better off on this, even if the wooden slats are hard."

She turned from the window where she had been looking out. "It's getting dark," she said, her thoughts far away from the room.

"The maid I summoned will be bringing up a jug of hot water for the bowl any minute. I'm afraid that was the best I could do."

Wrenching her thoughts back to him, she came forward to give him a smile of gratitude. "Forgive me for being distracted. I appreciate everything you've done to bring me here safely." Her voice faltered. "Shouldn't Nicolas be back by now?"

"I'll go to the gates and make inquiries."

Once in the street, he made his way to the gates. The bombardment was still in force, which was a cause for concern.

"No news yet," was the answer, which did not surprise him. While waiting, he went into a shop and bought a pair of men's breeches that he judged would fit Gabrielle should an emergency arise. With his spare coat on her and her hat pulled down, she would pass for a boy well enough. He had just paid when a shout came from the gates. He hurried out with his purchase.

Soldiers were clearing the street, shoving people back with brutal haste. "Make room! The army is coming in! The whole defence line is falling back! Get back there!"

Gaston drew into the shelter of a doorway to watch the mass exodus from the battlefield. Through the gateway came a torrent of men, horses and gun carriages. A number of *chasseurs* rode in, some wounded but still in their saddles. As far as Gaston could see, Devaux was not among them. He set off to find out what he could.

For Gabrielle the hours of waiting were endless. Each time there was a step on the stairs, she looked out and was disappointed. Finally, it was Gaston coming up the stairs.

"Is Nicolas back?" she cried.

He paused to look up at her. She looked as fresh and beautiful as a spring morning, her hair newly washed and entwined with a narrow pink ribbon. She had prepared herself for her lover, and Gaston had to shatter her hopes. He cleared his throat.

"Captain Devaux has been taken prisoner. He will be shipped to England and kept there until the emperor makes a truce with King George the Third's government. The war is over for him."

Gabrielle cried out, overwhelmed with despair.

FOR TWO DAYS the fortress artillery kept up a roaring barrage against the British, the acrid smoke from the guns drifting down over the city. But by the third morning the British had entrenched themselves dangerously

near, and their artillery began to have greater effect. Buildings were badly damaged by shells and roundshot; fires broke out.

On the fourth day of the siege the enemy blasted two breaches in the fortress walls. The next evening hundreds of British burst through, shouting their vengeance, fighting like madmen and impossible to stop. Stabbing with bayonets, firing muskets point-blank and lobbing grenades into buildings as they came, the redcoats began to sweep through the streets like a scarlet river.

It took them two hours to take the city, and even then the killing went on, the frenzied victors striking down anyone in their path. Gaston, who had left Gabrielle from time to time to fire his musket at a defence post, was on his way back to her now. He hastened through dark passageways that threaded between and behind buildings, and relieved two dead French soldiers of their coats and waistcoats.

He found Gabrielle pressed against the wall of her room, watching the carousing in the streets through the window. At the sight of him she sprang forward, her features gaunt with fear.

"You're back! I was so afraid. They've been dragging out the women! Even old women and young girls." She pressed the back of her hand to her quivering mouth. He did not pause to answer her but threw the military clothes to her.

"Put these on!" He darted to his saddlebag and pulled out the breeches he had bought for her. "These too! And hurry!" Turning his back, he yanked off his goatskin jacket and thrust an arm into the sleeve of the other uniform. It felt soggy. Swinging round, he saw that Gabrielle was holding the clothing and staring at her left palm, seeing it was wet with blood. He had to break through her shock, and he bellowed at her, "Put it on! If you don't, it'll be your blood and mine next. The redcoats are on the rampage. There's a bloodbath taking place in this city tonight!"

She pulled herself together and nodded. "I'll put it on."

"Our only chance of getting out of this mess alive is to be in uniform. It will take the British officers time to restore order. In the meantime, they'll be doing their best to save lives by taking prisoners and herding them into a place where they can ensure protection. My guess is that it will be the main barracks. Are you ready?"

"Yes."

Gaston looked at her. She had buttoned the breeches at the knees and tucked them into her boots. The waistcoat was loose enough to disguise her figure, and the blue cutaway coat would pass on her, although blood darkened it all down the right side.

"Get that hat on," he ordered. "Whatever happens, leave everything to me. If a British officer should question you, be too dazed to reply. That's normal with the drummerboys, and you look young enough in those clothes to be one of them. Now, let's go."

They crept from the building. Sometimes, Gabrielle had to hold on to his coat tails where the passage became a tunnel and everything was pitch-black. Every time there was an opening into the street, she glimpsed bodies slumped and sprawled in death. Women's screams echoed and reechoed against the stone walls. Gaston brought her to the east wall of the barracks and left her there while he scouted ahead. In minutes he was back.

"The barracks yard is full of captured French soldiers. We'll wait until another batch is being brought in, and then we'll fall in with them. You'll not let the British officers know you're a woman until discipline is restored, and then it will be safe for us to leave the city and start for home. I've only to show them my game leg to prove that I'm no longer a regular soldier, so they won't keep me a prisoner."

In that second Gabrielle made her resolve. She would remain a prisoner of war and be shipped to England. Then she would reveal her identity and be set free to find Nicolas. Suddenly hope was high in her again. A new phase of her life was about to begin.

CHAPTER TEN

It had not been Gabrielle's intention that Gaston should accompany her into captivity. When he failed to sway her from going ahead with her plan, he stated he would come with her. She was aghast.

"No! I beg you. Don't come with me. You must get the horses and go back to France. I would not have a minute's peace if you should risk permanent incarceration because of me."

"I made a promise that I'd see you safely back to Lyons," Gaston said. "You can't ask me to go against that vow. I may not be a gentleman born, but I have a soldier's pride in keeping my word."

They were marched out of the city that afternoon, a long column of blue-coated Frenchmen and one disguised Frenchwoman, with a redcoat escort. Before long they were out in the countryside with the whole of the battle area left behind. Gaston's game leg had been troubling him before the march, and by the time they reached Oporto, the port of embarkation, he could barely hobble along, and was forced to lean heavily on Gabrielle for support.

On board ship the men were packed together, with no room to lie down, and as they were below water level the only light came from lanterns swinging and flickering overhead. For Gaston it was particularly difficult, because he had to sit with his leg stretched out before him, and it was frequently knocked or kicked accidentally.

Gabrielle had decided she must wait twenty-four hours before revealing the truth to the authorities, for she would not risk being set ashore if the ship put back into port for any reason. After a night filled with sounds of groaning and retching and snoring, sailors appeared with bread and cheese and drinking water. At eleven o'clock the ship's surgeon, Dr. Rogers, a hawkish-looking man immaculately dressed in blue and white naval uniform, came to attend the ill and the wounded.

"Now's your chance," Gaston muttered to her. "Good luck."

They exchanged an encouraging clasp of hands before she left her place to wait by the companionway. As the surgeon came to remount the steps she spoke to him.

"Doctor! I am a woman and should not be here."

He narrowed his eyes at her. "Follow me," he said in French.

In his cabin, she gave him her name as she took off the hat she had worn night and day. He invitied her to sit down and asked whether she was a soldier's wife.

"No. Nor am I a camp follower."

"I did not think you were, Madame Valmont. I have spent some time in France, and your voice tells me you're a woman of some standing. My guess is that you are following a lover. Am I right?"

"You are," she admitted.

"What is the name of the prisoner of war you are following?"

"Captain Nicolas Devaux of the *chasseurs à cheval*. Might he be on this ship? He was taken into captivity before me."

"There are none of that regiment on this ship. I did hear that a number of *chasseurs* boarded the warship in the harbour a few days ago, bound for Portsmouth. How far have you come?"

"From Lyons." She told him the whole story of the journey, leaving out only the personal details that had caused her to set out in the first place. Lastly she mentioned Gaston's game leg.

"If your companion is in such pain," the doctor asked, "why was I not informed as soon as he came aboard?"

"He wouldn't allow it. He said it would only lead to questions as to why he, a soldier invalided out of the army, should be here. It was for my sake that he did not take the risk."

The doctor sat back in his chair, putting the fingertips of both hands together, and looked grave. "Your friend is in an exceptionally awkward position. He has marched with the French army, wearing a uniform, and is a prisoner of war. He could face the charge of being a spy and thus suffer the death penalty."

"Gaston is no spy!" She reeled as she stood up. "Let me go down to his deck again to tell him what is happening."

The surgeon was fierce. "You seem to forget you are an enemy noncombatant and will come under the rules that apply to one in your position. I shall arrange for some hot water to be brought here, and you will wash yourself from head to toe, because there must be no risk of infection being brought to the upper decks. There are two officers' wives on board, one English and the other Portuguese, and I am sure they will be charitable enough to find some suitable garments for you. Discard your uniform, such as it is, and when you are ready, you will report for registration to the officer in command."

With that he left. Alone in the cabin, Gabrielle was desperate that Gaston should be facing either years of imprisonment or charges of spying. If only she could warn him.

Two sailors brought the hot water, and she bathed herself thoroughly to ensure that the last traces of travel and imprisonment had gone from her body. Then she put on the clothes provided. The donors had been generous. Fine undergarments and a green woollen gown were accompanied by a thick woollen shawl.

Registration was completed quickly, and after it was over, she was escorted to a tiny cabin, where the two wives lay on narrow bunks, one above the other, both recovering from seasickness. A sailor showed her how to set up a hammock almost at floor level, and then Gabrielle introduced herself and thanked the women for the clothes.

The Englishwoman glared at her. "I do not speak French!" she said in English, turning her back rudely. There was a different reception from the very young Portuguese woman on the top bunk, who propped herself on one elbow and regarded Gabrielle with magnificent long-lashed eyes. She had rich black hair that tumbled down about her shoulders, and she seemed no more than sixteen years of age.

"I'm Isabella Harding, and it's Mrs. Moncrieffe in the bunk below. I sent you the clothes." She spoke in fluent French, and reached out a hand to Gabrielle. "Please help me down the ladder. I'm nervous about falling and"—her voice dropped to a whisper—"that creature will do nothing to help me. You see, her husband is a colonel and mine is only a lieutenant. She thinks she should have the cabin to herself."

Once on the floor, the young woman sat on a wooden travelling chest set against the wall. Gabrielle saw she was pregnant.

"What made you decide to have your baby in England?" she asked as she took a seat beside her on the chest.

"My dear Edward is on his way with the Duke of Wellington to Badajoz, and he wanted me to have our baby at his home in the county of Berkshire. My own home was destroyed, and all my family killed, during the French invasion of Portugal. I escaped only because I was visiting friends in Lisbon, where I met my English husband."

Gabrielle gave a little shake of her head, moved by what she had heard. "You have suffered much through the actions of my country, and yet you sent me the clothes."

"It is men that make wars. Never women. We are innocent of their

490

crimes." Without warning, a sob choked her, and the tears spilled down her face. She fumbled for a handkerchief. "Forgive me. My grief still overcomes me at times. I miss my mother more than ever now."

"I'm sure your husband's family will receive you kindly."

"Will they? I wish I could be sure." Isabella blinked away her tears. "How do you expect to fare in England?"

"I don't know. It never occurred to me that I would be treated as a noncombatant taken in battle." She told Isabella about her search for Nicolas and how close she had come to a reunion, only to lose him again. Isabella listened to it all eagerly.

That night the ship hit a great storm in the Bay of Biscay. In her hammock, Gabrielle fared better than the two women in the bunks, for they constantly slithered from side to side, Isabella frequently crying out in fear. Gabrielle, who had folded blankets on either side of Isabella's bunk as padding to prevent her from knocking herself against the wooden guardrail, occasionally left her hammock to hold the girl's hand and comfort her. In the morning Dr. Rogers came to see how Isabella was. He beckoned Gabrielle to follow him out of the cabin afterwards.

"She is more advanced than she thought, and may go into labour at any time. Would you know how to help with a delivery?"

"I attended the births of both my sister-in-law's babies, and I have a son of my own."

"Then I shall count on you when the hour comes."

"Yes, of course. What of Gaston?" she inquired anxiously.

"I've seen him. My diagnosis is that it is an old wound aggravated by recent active service. He is a prisoner of war."

She stared after him as he walked away. He had believed her account and thus had chosen to spare Gaston the charge of spying. It was a merciful act; yet it condemned Gaston to a terrible future. Somehow she would have to work for his release and her own.

The storm lasted another two days. As the wind began to ease, Isabella gave a cry that was different from her cry of fear. Gabrielle went at once to the surgeon's cabin to notify him that the labour had begun. Isabella was carried to his cabin on a litter by two sailors and placed in his bunk. He gave Gabrielle one of his aprons, and she tied it about her before rolling up her sleeves.

"It will be several hours yet," the doctor said to her. "Do what you can to comfort Mrs. Harding. She's frightened and nervous. I shall look in now and again until it is nearer the time."

Gabrielle sat by the bunk and did all she could to help Isabella through the labour, bathing her forehead and talking soothingly to her.

At dawn, when the sea lapped yellow and gold, Isabella gave birth to a daughter, and when the infant was placed in her arms, she sighed with happiness. "I shall name her Luisa, after my mother." It was both pain and pleasure for Gabrielle to hold and bathe the baby, for memories of André tugged relentlessly at her.

It was not until the ship was sailing up the Thames that Isabella began to worry again about the meeting with her husband's parents. By the time the ship docked in London, she was panic-stricken. A knock came on the door then, and a sailor stood there. "Mrs. Harding, a lady and gentleman are waiting for you. Shall I take your baggage now?"

Isabella threw her arms about Gabrielle. "I'll never forget your kindness to me."

"Now don't worry. Everyone will love you and Luisa."

"And you'll find your Nicolas. I know you will."

Gabrielle carried the baby as far as she was allowed to go. When a guard moved his hand in warning, Isabella, white-lipped with anxiety, took Luisa in her arms. Then she disappeared out onto the deck.

As Gabrielle returned to the cabin Mrs. Moncrieffe came out and swept past her without a word of farewell.

A customs officer now came to take charge of Gabrielle. He told her his name was Woodbury and that he and his wife were to be her custodians until such time as she should be granted parole. She collected her bundle, which contained two more dresses that Isabella had given her, and followed the man to the deck. The fresh air and the bright daylight dazzled her after the gloom of the cabin. The Thames was busy with ships, and there was a forest of masts at the dockside for as far as the eye could see. She had hoped she might catch a glimpse of Gaston, but the customs officer shepherded her away before the disembarkation of the prisoners began.

Further on she saw a line of warships that housed many thousands of prisoners of war. The sight struck a chill into her, sharper than the crisp February day. Everything, from the rigging to the figureheads, had been stripped away from the vessels, which had been tarred a dismal black. Each had a gallery built round it for patrolling guards.

The Woodburys' home was near the customs house. It was small, neat and clean. Mrs. Woodbury, a plain, well-meaning little woman, appeared nervous at having a Frenchwoman of some style under her roof. But when Gabrielle smiled and greeted her in English, as she had been taught by Isabella, the ice was broken. Even Mr. Woodbury's strict countenance showed satisfaction when Gabrielle produced a gold piece for her keep; she guessed they had been expecting to give her bed and board on a meagre allowance paid to them by the authorities.

Every evening a young warehouse apprentice, Oliver Burns, gave Gabrielle English lessons, as she had requested. During the day she studied. She was not allowed to go beyond the garden gate, but would lean over it to gaze down the cobbled street towards the river. Through Oliver she learned that the prisoners from her ship were lodged in the hulks along these wharves. She asked him if he would try to find out where Gaston was.

Her letters requesting parole went unacknowledged. As March warmed into spring, and April daffodils gave way to lilac, she developed a growing command of the English language. By now she knew which hulk Gaston was housed in, and Oliver had managed to get a note to him. The reply came back, "Am well, but troubled by my leg. We will meet at the prisoners' market when you get your parole. Gaston."

One afternoon at the end of June a government agent came to see Gabrielle. He had the news she had long awaited. "You have been considered for parole, Mrs. Valmont."

"At last!" She breathed with relief. "I wrote many letters of appeal."

"Perhaps they went to the wrong department. Your name only came to my notice after a gentleman asked about you."

She was puzzled. "What was his name?"

"I can't recall. It was some weeks ago. As far as I knew you were not in my district, or I should have given him your address."

"Did he leave an address?"

"No, he did not. Now, let us get down to business. I shall first read you the conditions of your parole."

She listened, nodded and duly signed the declaration that she would abide by all that was set down there. He then paid her the first allowance due to her, explaining that noncombatants in British hands were paid on the same scale as army and navy lieutenants. She was glad of the money, for the funds she had brought from Lyons were very low now.

"I should like to apply for a change of address," she said. "I want to go to Portsmouth. I have reason to believe that someone I know was bound for that port. I'd like to meet him again."

The agent gave a nod. "I've no objection. I'll give you a written permit, but be sure to report with it and your new address to the government agent in Portsmouth on the day you arrive. Now I'll bid you good day." On his way out of the house he paused and looked back at her. "I believe I recall the gentleman's name that eluded me. Harding. Yes, that was it."

As she closed the door after him, she smiled to herself. It must have been Isabella's father-in-law. Dear Isabella. It was a comfort to Gabrielle to know that she had a friend in England. And an even greater comfort was the knowledge that reunion with Nicolas had come one step nearer.

HAVING BADE A TEARFUL GOODBYE to Gaston when they finally met, as arranged, at the prisoners' market, Gabrielle took the stage to Portsmouth. She began a search of the city that went on for weeks, and then months. In December she was no nearer finding Nicolas than she had been when she first landed. She could not think what else to do. Her longing for her son, which never left her, added to her deep despair.

It was close to Christmas when she returned late one afternoon to the Dolphin Tavern, her present address. A visitor was waiting to see her. He was a distinguished-looking man, with wavy brown hair greying at the temples and a clever, sharply honed face with keen and alert blue eyes; his mouth, severe in repose, was charming in a smile. He addressed her in the hallway.

"Good day to you, Madame Valmont. I know you from Isabella's description. I am Andrew Harding, at your service."

"Mr. Harding!" The sadness that had been lodged in her eyes was lifted at this surprise appearance of her friend's father-in-law. "How is Isabella? And Luisa? Oh, there's so much I want to ask."

"I've ordered dinner and wine to be served to us in the private dining room, where we can talk undisturbed."

At the table, he told her that Isabella had become increasingly worried about not hearing from her, convinced that some calamity had occurred. Whereas the girl might have settled down happily enough, for she had been warmly welcomed by the Hardings, her anxiety about Gabrielle had added to her homesickness. "I was certain that sooner or later you would come to light," Mr. Harding said, "and when I investigated again, more recently, I was given your address here in Portsmouth."

"You speak as if you have access to government records."

"I do. I am the Member of Parliament for the Berkshire borough of Twyford."

"I had no idea. But then," Gabrielle added, sharing a smile with him, "Isabella talked of little but her baby for most of the voyage."

"That brings me to the other reason I wanted to find you. My wife and I would like to do something for you in return for your part in bringing our grandchild safely into the world. I must tell you that I know your whole story, related to me by Isabella. I can only suppose by my finding you here on your own that you have failed to trace Captain Devaux?"

"That is correct." Her breath was suddenly tight in her chest.

"I shall find him for you," he said with assurance. He could see she was momentarily beyond speech. She hid her face in her hands until she had recovered, then raised her head again.

"I can never thank you enough, Mr. Harding."

"There is no need for thanks. I regret having to ask you to exercise patience for a little longer after all you have been through, but the list of captives is immense, close to one hundred and twenty thousand."

"You said you had heard my story from Isabella. Then you will also know of the part that my servant, Gaston, played in it, surrendering his freedom to protect me. He is in one of those hulks on the Thames. Is there any chance of his being moved to a better place? More important, is parole ever granted to the men, in exceptional cases?"

"Men have been repatriated for special reasons. His case interests me.

494

My solution rests with an invitation that my wife and I hope you will accept, which is to stay with us at our home in Twyford until I can send you in one of my own carriages to Captain Devaux. It will give Isabella the greatest happiness to have your company again, and we want to do all we can for you. As for your servant, I can get him released if you will guarantee he is to be trusted and will not attempt to escape."

Gabrielle was overjoyed. "I can guarantee that."

"Then I'll arrange everything. We'll leave for London in the morning." He took up his wineglass. "Now a toast. To reunions!"

"To reunions," she echoed, her face radiant.

THE JOURNEY TO LONDON took them to the Houses of Parliament, where Mr. Harding's clerks secured the papers for Gaston and for her. Then, on the wharf, he told her to wait in the carriage while he went aboard one of the hulks. She watched in suspense for Gaston to appear. Finally she saw to her dismay that Gaston was being carried off the hulk on a canvas litter borne by two soldiers, Mr. Harding following behind. She leaped from the carriage and rushed across to the gangway. Gaston's face broke into a smile at the sight of her, but she was staring horrified at bloody bandages about a stump. His game leg had been cut off above the knee.

"What have they done to you?" she exclaimed frantically.

"All the life was going from my toes, and the condition would have spread. Have you found Captain Devaux yet?"

"Not yet, but very soon, Mr. Harding says."

"Good. We're having a bit of luck at last, aren't we?" He smiled again. "I'm going to be nimble and without pain once I get the peg leg that the gentleman has promised me."

"Oh, Gaston." She was between laughter and tears. "You are indestructible."

He was carried to the home of the Woodburys, Gabrielle's former custodians. Between them, Gabrielle and Mrs. Woodbury bathed him clean of all traces of his prison life, put him in one of Mr. Woodbury's nightshirts and made him comfortable against some pillows. Mr. Harding arranged payment with Mrs. Woodbury for care of the patient, and left a purse of money for new clothes with Gaston. When Gabrielle kissed him on the cheek in farewell, he held her by the arm.

"Getting out of that hulk has made this the best day of my life so far. Yours is soon to come."

THE HARDINGS' COUNTRY HOME was of ivy-laced plum-coloured brick, and the graceful windows were enhanced by dressings of cream stone. Isabella's face appeared at one of them as Mrs. Harding came out to welcome Gabrielle. Moments later Isabella raced down the staircase with a shriek of delight and hugged Gabrielle with such exuberance that she was almost swept off her feet. Still in the same whirl, Isabella flung her arms about Mr. Harding.

"Thank you for finding her, dear father-in-law!"

It amused Gabrielle that this rather staid English couple should regard their flyaway daughter-in-law with such enchantment. Since Edward was their only son, she could guess how Isabella and the baby were filling a gap in their lives until he returned. Luisa, now ten months old, was a bonny, fair infant with big long-lashed eyes like her mother's.

Christmas was the happiest that Gabrielle had known for years. There were carols to sing and hot punch to drink, and she tasted mince pies and plum pudding for the first time. She was able to relax completely and enjoy herself, all the while carried along by the knowledge that Nicolas was only just beyond her reach.

Two days after the holiday festivities were over, Mr. Harding opened a letter at the breakfast table, read it through and then smiled at Gabrielle. "We have what we have been waiting for. Captain Devaux is lodging at Holly House, Paradise Lane, in Macclesfield, and is employed as manager at the Barnett silk mill there."

It was Isabella who gave a jubilant cry. Gabrielle sat silent and thankful. She was on the brink of her great day.

In a Harding carriage she journeyed to Macclesfield, staying overnight on the way. In the early afternoon of the next day the carriage drew up in the forecourt of Holly House. She rang the shiny brass bellpull, and a maidservant came to the door.

"Is Captain Devaux at home?" she inquired.

"No, ma'am. He's always at the mill at this hour."

"Thank you. I shall go there."

The maidservant closed the door and turned back in the direction of the kitchen. As she did so a fragile young woman came down the stairs. She looked over the banister at the maid as she passed below. "Who was that at the door?"

"A foreign lady asking for Mr. Devaux," the maid answered. "I told her he was at the mill." The green baize door to the kitchen swung shut behind her. On the stairs the young woman stood with a hand pressed to her chest, as if trying to still the frightened drumming of her heart.

Gabrielle soon arrived at the mill. It was as if her feet were not touching the ground in her excitement. The clatter of the looms made everything seem warm and familiar. It was as though there had been no time between this day and the last time she had seen Nicolas. She reached the door that had his name on it. Lifting the hood of her cape from her head, she opened the door swiftly and just as swiftly closed it behind her, leaning against it. Nicolas was sitting at a large desk going through some designs and did not look up, although he held out a hand in her direction as if he was expecting her to be a clerk, with papers for him.

"You did those quickly, Briggs," he commented.

She was glad of those few seconds in which to gaze at him in profile, to absorb the sight of him into herself. He, mystified at getting no response, glanced up and saw her there. Never would she have believed that love could show itself so instantly in a man's face, filling his wondering eyes and his whole being.

"Gabrielle!" He was out of his chair and had her in his arms before she could take another breath. They kissed, wildly embracing, starved for each other. "What are you doing in England?" he gasped exultantly, and then kissed her again before she could answer him. Lips and caressing hands blended together in the mutual expression of their love and long-denied passion. But then the door opened, and they drew apart as a horrified hiss cut through the air like the swish of a sword's blade.

"There is someone here you must meet, Gabrielle," Nicolas said in a low, sad voice.

She gazed questioningly at him, then turned within the circle of his arms. She saw a pale young woman, with soft fair hair thoroughly windblown, leaning as if for support against the jamb of the open door. Gabrielle glanced back at Nicolas. "Yes?"

His embrace tightened still more about her. "This is Jessica. She is my wife. We were married on Christmas Eve."

Gabrielle stared for a long moment at this woman, as she screamed inwardly in an anguish too profound to be borne. She fell forward in a dead faint, but Nicolas swept her up in his arms before she could fall. Jessica straightened herself in the doorway, shuddering from shock.

"Send her back wherever she came from," she beseeched Nicolas in a highpitched voice. Then she sped back in the direction of her home. Her lungs tore on every gasping breath in an effort that had been forbidden her since a childhood illness, but she did not stop until she could lose herself in tears in the privacy beyond her bedroom door.

At the mill, Gabrielle soon returned to consciousness. Nicolas sat massaging her wrists as she lay on the bench in his office.

"How do you feel?" He peered anxiously into her face.

She avoided his eyes. "I'll be all right in a moment or two."

"How did you manage to get across the Channel?"

"It's too long a tale to tell. I came because I promised you once that if ever I was free, I would come to you."

"Are you saying Emile is dead?" he demanded incredulously.

"When Maison Devaux burned down, he was one of the victims."

"So long ago! I never knew . . ."

She met his tormented gaze. "I realize that now."

"Oh, Gabrielle." He caught up her hand and pressed the palm to his lips. "I've never stopped loving you."

She was glad he made no excuses about his marriage. He told her he had made Jessica his wife simply because he had never expected to see her—Gabrielle—again. It was all she could do not to caress his face once more, to touch his lips.

"I must go." She stood up, and found that her head had cleared. Mercifully, her heart was still numb. "We have come to the end of all that has been between us. I wish you well with my whole heart, as I have always done. This meeting mustn't be prolonged, for your sake and for mine. Farewell, Nicolas!"

He seized her wrist as she reached the door, bringing her to a standstill. She did not look back at him, her whole straightbacked stance a rejection of any last attempt at persuasion, and he released his hold. His final words followed her. "You are my life, and always will be."

THE NUMBNESS STAYED with Gabrielle all the way back to Twyford. Once there, she concluded that she should return to France and take up her life again. But despite this decision, war conditions forced her to accept the Hardings' compassionate hospitality for an extended period. As soon as Gaston was well enough, he too was invited to stay in their household, and was in his element when allowed to care for the thoroughbred horses in the stables.

Finally, developments on the other side of the Channel began to make Gabrielle's plans a possibility again. Bonaparte's empire was beginning to disintegrate. The tsar had now allied his country with Britain, Prussia, Sweden and Austria. As a result, the remnants of the *Grande Armée* had not only been forced to retreat from Russia but were being driven across Europe. In the west Wellington was advancing towards the Pyrenees, the last barrier before reaching French soil.

In October 1813 Napoleon was soundly beaten by the allied forces in the Battle of the Nations, near Leipzig. A few weeks later Mr. Harding arranged for Gabrielle, Gaston and seven other noncombatants to be escorted under armed guard down to Dover, where they were put on a fishing smack. The sails flapped and filled in the fresh wind. Gabrielle, looking back at the white cliffs, was saying farewell to Nicolas and to love itself. There would never be anyone else for her. When the cliffs finally melted into the sea, she turned towards France, the wind tugging at her hair. She was going home. Home to Lyons and her son. Home to Maison Roche and her looms.

CHAPTER ELEVEN

Gabrielle took down the silk portrait of Napoleon from the wall of her office in the Rue Clémont and regarded it with mixed feelings. It should have come down at the time of his abdication the previous April, or when he had gone into exile on the island of Elba. Yet, somehow, all the main events of her life had been bound up with the actions of this extraordinary man. Through his attack on Austria she had lost a brother, and Gaston had come to Lyons. The imperial invasion of Portugal and Spain had taken Nicolas away from her for ever.

But the emperor had done what he believed right for France, and had given it laws and reforms that would endure. Moreover, he had helped Lyons to become once again the greatest silk centre the world had ever known, although, sadly, her marvellous Roche silks, commissioned for Versailles, had gone into storage and might never be hung in that great palace. An imperial era had passed, and with it all its splendour.

Sadly, she placed the silk portrait in tissue paper and put it in a drawer with other rare samples that belonged to the history of Maison Roche. Her decision to remove it today had come with the news that five days ago, on March 1, 1815, the emperor, having escaped from Elba, had landed in the south of France. He was raising a new army to advance on Paris and drive King Louis XVIII from his throne.

Having seen war for herself on the peninsula, Gabrielle wanted no more of it for France. Good relations had been restored with Britain and the rest of Europe. Even Wellington had said that France had no enemies—it was only that Bonaparte had to be deposed. Her country needed peace now, not more bloodshed. Because she could not condone the emperor's return, she was shutting the drawer on a visage that belonged only to the past.

"*Maman!*"

She turned as André came running through the office door towards her. A boisterous five-year-old, he had just come home from a walk with his nursemaid and, as always, had sought her out immediately. Laughing and stooping to sweep him up in her arms, she swung him round before hugging him to her, his rosy cheek cool against hers from the March wind.

"Have you had a splendid time? Did you meet Aunt Hélène? She bought you a candy stick? *La!* What a lucky boy you are!"

Gabrielle let him spend as much time as she could with Hélène and Michel in the home they had bought just before the birth of their twins, a son and a daughter. His initial shyness after her return home to Lyons had been painful to bear, but gradually a normal relationship was restored between them. If she had to be away on business, he was content to stay with the Piats. A trip was in the offing now. Gabrielle was to visit a large country estate where Roche silks were being hung. Maison Roche was fast becoming the silk house that people consulted when they wanted an entire residence refurbished, and Gabrielle always viewed the finishing stages to make sure every detail was perfect.

Some of André's happiest moments were spent at the mill with his *maman*. He loved the colours and the patterns of the silks, and the smell of the place. "When can I come with you to see the silks hung?" It was his usual question.

"When you're older," she promised, as she had before. "You will be in charge of everything when you're grown up."

While she was preparing for her journey, news and further details of Bonaparte's swift approach swept in. All along his route veterans of the *Grande Armée* were rallying to him with shouts and cheers of welcome. The old magic was still there, undiminished by months of exile, and he was rekindling France once more.

The day before Gabrielle was due to leave, she took André to the Piats' house. On the way their barouche was brought to a halt by a surging crowd. Bonaparte was entering Lyons, and the Lyonnais were going wild. André, excited by the noisy cheering, the waving of the tricolour and the lusty singing of the *Marseillaise*, bounced up and down on the seat. Gabrielle opened the window and held him to it as Bonaparte came into sight above the heads of the crowd. He rode proudly, clad in his grey campaign coat and black bicorne hat. Gabrielle felt herself gripped again by his mesmerizing personality.

"Now you have seen the emperor," she said to André. "Whatever else he's done, remember he did more for Lyons—and for France—than any other Frenchman who has ever lived."

Celebrations were still going on when she left the city the next day. She missed Gaston's presence whenever she was in her coach. He had left her household and gone south to the coast. "Every old warhorse dreams of peaceful pastures," he had said. "That time has come for me, madame."

She did not let him go empty-handed. He had a good horse, a new suit of clothes and a banker's draft to give him a moderate income until the end of his days. It was a long time before she heard from him. Then it was to let her know that he had settled in the peaceful little village of Cannes, where he was looking after the horses of a retired colonel. She hoped he had found contentment.

The great country mansion in which her silks had been installed was only a few miles from Limoges. She stayed for over four weeks, until the very last of the upholstered pieces had been delivered, making sure that all her silks had been used to perfection. While there, she heard that the emperor had received a tumultuous welcome in Paris after King Louis' hasty departure for Belgium. Throughout the Tuileries the white lily of the Bourbons had been stripped away from hangings and carpets to reveal the imperial bee once more. It seemed as if her silks for Versailles would soon be taken out of storage after all, but what was the cost in lives going to be this time? Already newssheets were proclaiming that the emperor had three hundred thousand loyal Frenchmen under arms, and hundreds more were volunteering.

The news was bad when Gabrielle arrived back in Lyons. British and Prussian troops were massing in Belgium, and the armies of the Austrians and the tsar were gathering in force further to the east. France was again surrounded by enemies.

It was too late in the evening to fetch André home. She would collect him in the morning. After she had bathed and changed, her maid brought a letter to the blue salon, where she was about to have a light supper. "I think you should see this immediately, madame. A gentleman came six or seven times in as many days, in the hope of your having returned. Yesterday he left this letter with the request that it should be given to you as soon as you arrived home."

The handwriting almost made her heart stop. It was from Nicolas. She drew in a deep breath before ripping it open.

> Jessica died of consumption six weeks ago. Her courage, as well as her devotion to me, will remain in my memory always. I have returned to France to find you again in the hope that there may be some time left for us to spend together.

"Oh, my love!" Gabrielle breathed, reading on.

> I never thought I should come back to the land of my birth. But the end of hostilities between France and Britain released me from the code of honour which had kept me to British shores, and I have come back to Lyons and rejoined my regiment. I have a heartfelt belief that every Frenchman is needed at this time. I will not see France defeated as the world intends now. If you have any love left for me, allow me to see you once more before I leave Lyons.

She ran from the room, calling to her maid as she went. "My cloak! Quick! At once!" It came, and she threw it about her shoulders, rushing from the house and across the square. She knew the address on the letter. Her shadow flew in and out of circles of light cast by the overhanging streetlamps. A few minutes later she arrived breathless at the door of the house and hammered on the knocker. The door was opened by an army servant.

"Is Captain Devaux here? I'm Madame Valmont," she said.

"He's out, madame, but I had orders to fetch him immediately if you should call, at any time of the day or night."

He showed her into Nicolas's apartments on an upper floor and left her there. Regaining her breath, she loosened her cloak and let it drop across a chair. She went to the window, where she watched until a hired *calèche* approached at a gallop, and she saw Nicolas fling himself out of it and into the house. He came bounding up the stairs. The door was thrown wide and there he was, as if their separation had never been.

Once again they were looking at each other as they had done long ago, when a wedding carriage and a funeral-cortege coach had clashed wheels and first brought them into each other's lives. This time they were alone. This time the hour was theirs at last.

"Nicolas," she breathed, holding out her arms and swaying towards him. "Show me this is no dream."

"My own Gabrielle!" He rushed to her and held her to him, kissing her. Tears of happiness trickled from under her closed lids, and she buried her fingers in his hair, as if she might die should he lift his head and take his lips from hers.

Lifting her up in his arms, he kicked open the door that led into the bedchamber and carried her through. The bed, large and wide and downy with pillows, awaited them. It was loving such as she had never experienced. As he lay beside her, she slowly trailed her fingers down the back of his neck and kissed his forehead lovingly.

"I love you," he murmured, as if he had not said the same words already, more times than either of them could remember. "Marry me. In the morning. Before noon."

Abruptly the truth dawned on her. "You're going away soon?"

"Tomorrow. Before evening."

"Where are you going? Do you know?"

He propped himself up on his elbows. "The emperor has already led an advance across the border into Belgium. The Prussians have massed at Ligny, and it is said that Wellington is moving troops to a place called Quatre Bras. When these armies are defeated, we march into Brussels." His face relaxed into a smile. "Will you meet me there, my love?"

"I'll do more than that," she replied fervently. "I'll travel with you. This time I'll be with the officers' wives. I'm not going to lose sight of you as I did at Ciudad Rodrigo." Then she told him the whole story. He resolved that somehow he would live through whatever lay ahead and make up to her, in the years to come, for all she had been through.

EARLY THE NEXT MORNING they went together to see the priest at a little church nearby. It was arranged that the marriage should take place at eleven thirty, after a short civil ceremony at the *hôtel de ville*. While Nicolas went to check on the final orders for departure at the barracks, Gabrielle went home to pack and write notes to Hélène and André, with explanations to cover her hasty departure. She flew into the house and was halfway up the stairs when she heard the well-remembered thump of a wooden leg coming from the direction of the kitchen. She spun round to race down again. "Gaston! Of all people!"

He looked extremely spruce, with a stout cane, a green brass-buttoned coat, and a gold pin in his cravat. There was no mistaking his joy at seeing her. "Madame! I've been trying to find out where you were."

"About to be married! I've found Nicolas again. At last we are to be together. Wish me joy, Gaston! Come and be a witness at our wedding. Nobody belongs there more than you."

He gave her a shrewd look, with something close to a twinkle in it. "I'm wed myself now. My Jeanne is a lively creature, full of spirit, and we've a child on the way."

"I'm so glad to hear that. Have you brought her with you?"

"No. I left her safely in Cannes. She is linen-maid in the colonel's house where we both reside, and soon we're to have a cottage to ourselves."

"That's marvellous news. Why are you here, then? Don't tell me you followed the emperor from Cannes?"

"I did indeed. All the way to Paris." Gaston had witnessed touching demonstrations of loyalty en route and cheered with the rest when whole battalions, with their officers, had joined the swift march towards Paris. Then, once the capital had been reached and the emperor again installed in the Tuileries, Gaston had begun the journey homewards. And that was how he had arrived at the house in the Rue Clémont.

"Come with me to the *hôtel de ville* and then to the church," Gabrielle urged him. "I have no time to spare. Today Nicolas leaves for Belgium, and this time I'm going too. I'll never be parted from him again."

Gaston gave one of his deep chuckles. "Then it seems I couldn't have arrived at a better time. What hour do we depart?"

She raised her eyebrows at him in astonishment. "You would accompany me to war again?"

"It will be like old times, and I've a mind to see the emperor win a great victory once more. What do you say?"

"I shall be glad, my good friend. So very glad."

In the church, with its shining altar, the bride and groom exchanged wedding vows. When the ceremony was over and the priest's blessing received, Nicolas and Gabrielle had to part on the church steps. He held her lovingly and kissed her. Then he clapped a hand on Gaston's shoulder. "Look after my wife for me, as you guarded her once before."

"I shall do that, captain. You may depend on it." It was an easy promise for Gaston to make. Now that he was with Gabrielle again, his own wife was all but forgotten—not out of heartlessness, for he loved Jeanne, but because his protective loyalty towards Gabrielle had been rekindled and was as strong as ever.

The squadron left the city two hours later, preceded by the regimental band playing a stirring tune. Behind the *chasseurs* came the wagons, the spare horses and the usual collection of women and children. Gabrielle and Gaston brought up the rear. During the ride from Lyons to the Belgian border, the squadron bivouacked at nightfall outside villages. Gabrielle would take lodgings in an inn or farmhouse, and Nicolas came to her there. They lived for the hours they shared.

On the seventeenth of June, on Belgian soil, Gabrielle saw Nicolas's squadron join forces with the emperor. Napoleon's successful army had captured Charleroi and won a battle at Ligny, putting the Prussians to flight and forcing the British to retreat. Torrential rain descended, but nothing could dampen the high spirits of the troops. Tomorrow would come a great battle with the British, near the village of Waterloo.

That night the accommodation that Gabrielle secured was in a peasant family's cottage. Overhead the unrelenting rain continued to drum on the roof, but she and Nicolas were aware only of each other in the deep warmth of the feather bed.

"Since I found you again I have known the happiest hours of my life," Nicolas said to her as she lay against his shoulder, within the circle of his arm. "If I should not come back—"

"Don't!" She pressed her fingertips against his lips.

Gently he took her wrist and drew her fingers away. "I only want to say it is my hope that we shall have a child from these hours of loving, because then I shall live on for you, no matter what the outcome may be in the field tomorrow."

He left her at daybreak. She was sleeping and did not feel him go from their bed. Closing the door quietly behind him, he went down the stairs and out into the dawn light. It had stopped raining on this Sunday morning, and the air was sweet and balmy. His army servant was waiting with his mount, and he swung himself into the saddle. As he turned his horse he saw that Gaston was waiting by the gate. The fellow saluted him as he rode through.

"Good luck, captain."

Acknowledging the salute, Nicolas cantered away.

GABRIELLE WOKE TO THE SOUNDS of a commotion in the yard outside. She had been alone for more than an hour. Slipping on a robe, she went to the window and looked out. The family of the cottage were departing, their possessions bundled up in the back of a donkey cart. Others were also on the move, getting out of range while there was still time. Meeting them from the opposite direction were all kinds of military traffic, from ammunition wagons to riders on army business.

Gabrielle watched the passing cavalcade as she washed and dressed. When she came downstairs, she found Gaston making coffee in the fire-blackened camp kettle he had brought along.

"I can hear the *Marseillaise*," she said, listening intently.

"The emperor will be reviewing the troops. It's customary."

She went to sit down at a rough table, where he had set out breakfast for her. She had little appetite but she ate doggedly, needing to take nourishment to sustain her through the hours ahead. "What time do you think the fighting will begin?" she asked, tapping an egg with a spoon to crack it open.

"My guess is, not for two or three hours yet." Gaston had seated himself opposite her. "It's no use trying to do battle until the ground has had a chance to dry out. In its present state horses and men would slither about in the mud, while the guns would be completely bogged down. The emperor will strike when the time is right, never fear."

"I'm not sitting around here for hours twiddling my thumbs," she stated. "I'm going to one of the field hospitals to offer my assistance."

"You'll need a strong stomach," Gaston warned.

But her face was set grimly, and he could not argue with her.

They covered the distance on foot to where the field hospitals had been set up, the traditional black flag flying above them to denote the site to friend and foe alike. The tents had been erected at the edge of woods, with reasonable access to the battlefield.

The surgeons were passing the time until they should be needed, sitting about in camp chairs, talking together, reading and dozing. Within the tents, operating tables had been set up, the surgical instruments glinting on side tables. Outside, there were barrels of wine ranged on trestles, the opiate and strengthener for those about to face surgery. The orderlies were organizing some of the women accompanying the army to open bundles of clean linen for the binding up of wounds.

Gabrielle looked towards the valley where the battle would be fought. It lay framed by the foliage of trees on either side of a gap in the woods. Away to her left she could see her countrymen waiting.

Another two hours of steadily mounting tension went by before the drums began to roll, sounding the call to arms. The surgeons began to move, discarding their jackets and donning leather aprons. Orderlies snapped shut the camp chairs and took them out of the way. One gave Gabrielle a thick canvas apron, such as the other women were wearing, and she tied it on. Gaston had the task of helping with the wounded as they arrived, making sure that the most seriously injured had priority.

At exactly half an hour before noon the French cannons opened fire with a barrage of earthshaking force. Gabrielle wondered how the British would withstand such a terrible bombardment. Thick clouds of smoke drifted across the treetops and over the black flag.

The first casualties to come through the gap in the woods were soldiers hit by stray roundshot from enemy guns. Distressed, Gabrielle watched them being carried into the tents. Then one of the surgeons hailed her. "Madame Devaux! Prepare for bandaging!"

"I'm coming, Major Arnoul!"

She grabbed a basket of clean linen and took her place at an operating table. It was her initiation. She saw it all—the orderlies tipping wine into the mouths of the groaning men on the tables, the flowing blood, the holding down of patients as the saws rasped through bones that could never be made whole again. When the time came for her to pad and bandage her first patient, she and a young orderly worked together.

The French cannonade stopped as abruptly as it had begun, giving way to the drumming of the soldiers' charge. On her way to replenish her linen basket, Gabrielle paused to look down towards the valley. Wide columns of French infantry were advancing shoulder to shoulder, with at least one hundred and fifty men in each straight rank, flanked by cavalry. From the distance they looked like toy soldiers set in formation, as if on a parade ground. She hurried on to carry out her task.

When the opposing forces met, the noise of the battle resounded in musket and rifle fire, shouts and yells, the booming of British cannon and the screams of men and horses alike, as the killing went on. The river of wounded began to flow in. Gabrielle, sighting a *chasseur* with a slashed arm, hurried across to ask him if he knew Nicolas and if he had seen him. He nodded, holding his arm to ease the pain, his face chalk-white.

"He had three horses shot from under him. Each time, he grabbed a riderless one in the field and remounted. Don't worry, madame. He was very much alive when I saw him last."

As the day went on, a picture of the battle emerged. The British had suffered heavy losses and were pressed back into a defensive position; the French were at a strong advantage. By late afternoon Gabrielle had lost all sense of time. She was soaked in blood. One of the women told her that a massive French cavalry charge had thundered down the valley and over the British ridge. The battle was almost won. She uttered a silent prayer for Nicolas as she continued to bind a bayonet wound.

More good news came. The defences of the British had been diminished. Wellington's hours were numbered. Everyone was waiting for the emperor to deliver the final blow.

The sun was beginning to set. Gabrielle looked up once after that as an orderly appeared in the entrance of the tent and shouted, "The emperor has sent in the *Garde Impérial*!"

The cream of the whole army! The emperor's chosen men! Now they would wipe out everything in their path.

Lanterns were lit in the tent to aid the fading daylight. Outside, the wounded waiting for treatment covered almost every inch of ground. The torrent of casualties was increasing all the time. Cries for water were constant, and Gaston had joined the women as they went from man to man putting cups to parched lips.

All these wounded could count themselves fortunate, for lying in the valley were thousands of their comrades, similarly wounded, who could not be reached in the fighting. Some struggled weakly to find a place out of the fray. Nicolas was among them.

He had no clear recollection of being wounded. Vague images came into his mind between bouts of unconsciousness. Everything was muddled and confused. His lifeblood was flowing out of his wounds and his strength was ebbing as he lay face down amid the muddy carnage of men and horses. Beneath him the earth began to tremble again, coinciding with one of the brief lucid spells that still came periodically. Another cavalry charge was on the way. Was it two or three times he had been ridden over where he lay? To add to his wounds, the thundering hooves had crushed his right hand and snapped his arm like a twig. Now the cavalry were coming again.

With an effort he opened his eyes. The sky had become the rich orange of sunset. In its splendid light the horsemen were coming at full pelt, and in their wake thousands of running foot soldiers, the brass cap plates on their bearskins flashing the sun's late brilliance as they came. Recognition dawned. It was the *Garde Impérial*, finally thrown in to smash those seemingly impenetrable British lines and take the glory of the day. Yet what was amiss that his pain-wearied brain was unable to define?

The charge swept over him with crashing hooves and pounding boots before he slipped into oblivion once more. When his mind cleared, he realized that it had not been an advance that had passed over him but a retreat. An ignominious rout. The *Garde Impérial* had broken and fled before some final strategic attack of Wellington's that, in spite of all odds, had won the day. Cheering echoed from the British ridge.

A great yell of rage and disappoinment welled up in his throat, giving him the superhuman strength to rise up with it, a swaying half-broken figure in the sunset's blood-red glow.

"No!" he bellowed, crazed beyond reason. "*Vive la France!*"

He staggered forward, then fell motionless.

THE EVENING DARKENED and the stars came out. Nicolas opened his eyes and saw garlands of red and blue flowers glowing about him in the pale moonlight, under and around him like a rich tumbled carpet. It was the silk his looms had woven for the emperor's tent, which now lay on the ground, knocked over and trampled into the mud by a fleeing army. He and Gabrielle had declared their love in the midst of these garlands. Now this Devaux silk was to be his shroud.

He closed his eyes slowly, feeling his strength go. He thought he heard her voice and spoke her name. "Gabrielle."

In the surgeons' tent the work went on. The lights were attracting moths, which caused fluttering shadows to dance here and there. Gabrielle, finished with one patient, turned for the next and saw Gaston standing in the tent's entrance. The expression on his drawn face confirmed her fears.

Wordlessly she removed her apron and went towards him.

"I have had reports from five different sources," he told her huskily. "Captain Devaux is dead. In the midst of one of the great cavalry charges he was badly wounded protecting the standard, and although he handed it over and went on towards the British lines, he fell almost at once from the musket fire."

She nodded starkly to show she had grasped all she had heard.

She turned over her duties to another and with Gaston she left the tent and walked down along the paths between the wounded, into the woods and to the peasant's cottage. He sat her down in a kitchen chair and fetched a bowl of water. Then he washed the smudges of dried blood from her face and bathed her hands.

"Now," he said, raising her up from the chair, "go and change while I get a fire going. The evening is turning chill."

She paused at the foot of the stairs. "I want to find his body and take him home to Lyons. He shall not be buried in foreign soil."

Experience had taught him to know when her mind was made up. While she changed her garments upstairs, he checked the pair of pistols in his belt and made sure he had plenty of ammunition. He knew what a battlefield was like when darkness fell and looters from the local peasantry moved in.

When she came downstairs, she was simply and warmly dressed, a shawl about her shoulders. He had found a couple of lanterns and lit them. She took one from him, and together they went out into the darkness. They harnessed one of their horses to a light farm cart from the peasants' barn and drove to the place where earlier that day the vast spread of men had been waiting to move into their battle lines. It was deserted now, the earth churned up by thousands of feet. Their horse became alarmed as they went on, scenting death. By some trees Gaston brought the horse to a halt and fastened it securely, before he and Gabrielle set off on foot with the lanterns on their search.

The dead of both sides lay everywhere, and the lanterns' glow passed over many awful sights. Most heartrending to Gabrielle were the pleas of the wounded for water. Gaston had had the foresight to bring four full canteens with him, and he and Gabrielle paused to give drinks to French and British alike. Some of the wounded clutched at her skirts, begging, for fear of looters, not to be left. Whenever possible Gaston salvaged a pistol from a dead soldier nearby to leave the wounded some protection.

The search for Nicolas went on for hours. The canteens were empty, and there was nothing left to give as they went on shining their lanterns, hoping for the sight of a *chasseur*'s green jacket. It was dawn when the rising sun picked out a gleam of flowered grey silk with a familiar figure in dark green sprawled across it. A cry burst from Gabrielle's throat.

"There!"

She ran to Nicolas, stumbling and dodging and leaping over obstacles. Flinging herself down on her knees beside him, her tears coming at last, she drew his head gently into her lap and bent over him, rocking in her grief. "My darling. My love. My life." Then, under her fingertips she felt a faint pulse beating in his neck. "Merciful God!" she breathed incredulously. "He is alive!"

Gaston thumped down on the knee of his good leg and reached inside Nicolas's jacket to feel his heartbeat. "Only just," he said heavily, forewarning her.

She thrust her face forward. "I'm going to keep him alive!"

"Let's make a litter of this silk, then, and carry him to the cart."

With his knife he cut the amount needed. Since Nicolas was already on the roughly shaped rectangle, they had only to turn him gently onto his back to ensure that he would be as comfortable as possible. Then began the arduous task of hauling him to the cart. They struggled and stumbled along. Getting him into the cart was eased by Gaston's rounding up of two looters at pistol point to help with the lifting, and he made them run ahead to be at hand at the cottage to bear the wounded man upstairs.

When that was done, he booted them off the premises and returned to the upper room where Nicolas lay, with eyes closed, on the bed. Gabrielle was cutting away his uniform. "I'll fetch one of the surgeons from the field hospital," Gaston said.

"No! In the circumstances we can do better here. Get me some wine and hot water, and bring me my saddlebag. I've some clean linen in it. After that, build up the fire. He must be kept warm."

He obeyed her without question. Then, together, they set the patient's broken arm and fingers with splints. She gouged grapeshot out of his flesh and stitched the lips of a sabre slash together. When she had done all she could, she dripped warm wine over the wounds, a process that was to continue for days. Nicolas was highly feverish, his thirst insatiable, and his delirious mumblings were frequently broken by screams of pain. Gabrielle never slumped or showed a sign of fatigue, sleeping and eating only when it was Gaston's turn to keep vigil.

Downstairs, the peasants had returned home and were resentful at finding one of the defeated French still under their roof—until Gabrielle changed their attitude with a handsome payment.

Gradually Nicolas's fever began to subside. The day came when recognition dawned in his sunken eyes and he knew the face of the woman by his bed.

"I thought you were here," he whispered.

"Yes, my darling." She kissed his forehead, choked with emotion. "It won't be long now before we'll be able to go home."

It still took a number of weeks. As soon as it was safe to move him, they travelled as far as a small town just inside the French border, where Gaston had found comfortable accommodation for them. After a further period of convalescence, Nicolas was able to walk again and it was decided that they could now cover the last lap. It was then that Gaston said goodbye, first to Nicolas and then to Gabrielle on her own.

"You have Captain Devaux now," he said to her. "I don't suppose you'll ever need me to escort you anywhere again, but remember, if you do, I'll come at once."

"I'll never forget you, my friend. May God go with you."

He mounted his horse and waved to her as he rode away.

NOT LONG AFTER Gaston's departure Gabrielle and Nicolas came back to Lyons by way of Fourvière. It had been her suggestion that they should see the city again from her favourite place. Even though she was joyfully impatient to see her little son once more, she stopped the carriage at the spot she had always liked best, alighting first to run forward and look out eagerly at the view.

"Look! How clear everything is today. See those ripples in the wake of that boat down there on the Saône."

Nicolas had followed more slowly to reach her side. Pain was still with him, and would be for months to come. But he had survived and could look forward to the years ahead with the woman he loved. She was going to continue to produce Maison Roche silk until André was of an age to take over, while he would build up Maison Devaux from scratch. They would be business rivals, lovers, and partners. Their marriage would never be dull, and if recent signs proved to be right, it would be fruitful.

"It's a fine sight," he agreed, putting his arm round her. Pointing with his cane across the river, he indicated a large plot of land that was up for sale. "That would make a good site for Maison Devaux, down there on the quayside."

"I agree. But there's still the question of where our new home should be." They had decided between them that the Rue Clémont house should be closed up until André was of age. They themselves would build a new residence.

He smiled broadly, turning her to him. "I think that was settled a long time ago, when you told me of marking out a place here on these slopes with a piece of Roman pottery."

"So you have remembered that." She was deeply moved, putting her hand lovingly against his face, and he covered it with his own.

Then together they looked out again towards the mellow vista of roofs and glinting spires and lush treetops and gleaming water that would be theirs for the rest of their lives. She drew it into herself as though it were the air she breathed. Lyons. Her beloved city.

ROSALIND LAKER

The inspiration for *Tree of Gold* came to historical novelist Rosalind Laker during a visit to New York several years ago. One of Napoleon Bonaparte's campaign tents was on show with other early nineteenth century silks from Lyons. "The tent was lined with exquisite silk, patterned with red and blue garlands," says Miss Laker, "and immediately I thought of the rivalry for the commission to weave that silk. From that single idea this book developed."

Relentlessly curious, the author researched her story by travelling to Lyons, where a number of silk mills still operate. "I saw marvellous examples of Lyons silk there. Next I visited Fontainebleau to see the Empress Josephine's own choice of silk hangings for her salons, and then I went to Versailles and other palaces." Miss Laker also watched the weavers at work in the Paradise Mill Working Silk Museum in Macclesfield, and made a trip to the Lullingstone silk farm in Kent, where the silk was spun for Princess Diana's wedding dress.

Perhaps one of the most interesting aspects of the story of Lyons silk is the evolution of the Jacquard loom. "The whole mechanism was most extraordinary," Miss Laker explains, "because its possibilities didn't end with silk. The punched cards that chose the individual threads for weaving led to the punched cards used in computer systems. An American named Herman Hollerith utilized Jacquard's principle for his tabulating machine, and the company he founded in 1896 later expanded and became known as IBM."

Rosalind Laker lives with her Norwegian husband, Inge, on the Sussex coast, and they have two grown-up children. With over twenty novels to her credit, this popular author has much to be proud of already. Just recently, she was thrilled to discover that *Tree of Gold* has been shortlisted for The Romantic Novelist of the Year Award.

PICTURE CREDITS: Page 383: Mike Phillips; page 511: Chris Grout-Smith.